The Antifan Girlfriend

PAULA T. WEISS

The Antifan Girlfriend © 2020 as *Wars Among Towers* by Paula T. Weiss

Cover art, interior layout and design: The Antifan Sibling.

ISBN: 978-0-578-80815-4

For my mother, Esther, who, like Malia, loves to read.

Acknowledgments

This novel was written over the course of several months when my workplace was on alternating week schedules due to COVID-19. So I must thank COVID-preoccupied supervisors for allowing me the time to write a novel that had festered for years in my brain before I found the time to commit words to the screen.

It is also a sign of the times that several of my chief contributors do not wish their names to be publicly associated with this project, for fear of social or professional repercussions. You know who you are, and I thank you for your assistance.

I wish to thank Lisa Schiffren for providing extensive and constructive feedback on the full manuscript. Without her incisive edits, this novel would have been even longer.

I am also grateful to Janice Sebring for her close read of my Lutheran chapters so that I avoided making theological, cultural, or liturgical errors.

Thanks also to Nancy Kirk, a third Bryn Mawr sister alumna, for her feedback on large sections of the novel, and to my proofreaders/copy editors Michele Taft Morris (Bryn Mawr #4) and Lawson Sperapani.

Finally, I appreciated the scrutiny given earlier chapters by several friends and acquaintances in a social media group of likeminded political conservatives. Politics aside, they counseled me to avoid the typical newbie novelist error of waiting too long to introduce plot action. Their intervention also miraculously resuscitated a cat killed by Malia's starving relations for food.

My husband and daughter modestly deny they have been helpful at all. But I love and thank you both for your emotional support.

Any remaining errors or mistakes, including ideological ones, are entirely my own.

Preface

The Antifan Girlfriend posits a fictional dystopia in 2089, but nothing in this novel should be inconceivable to an American in 2020. The attentive reader can trace the outlines of the Diversity Justice Republic backward in time to contemporary ideological, social, and technological developments.

A new worldview comparable to *Girlfriend's* dominant ideology is already shrouding us in its folds and banishing its predecessors into the darkness. In this new world, one's racial or sexual identity defines one's level of oppression and thus, entitlement—mostly Social Credit points and access to scarce goods—based on alleged historical suffering and discrimination. Also privileged are the self-declared "allies" of the suffering masses. Along those lines, the reader will observe that most of the worst villains and greatest system beneficiaries in *Girlfriend* are heterosexual white male allies willing to carry out the unpleasant regime tasks of suppressing its enemies and running its socialist concentration camps. Surely you are not surprised.

So-called "social justice warriors" in academia, the media, sports and entertainment, and increasingly, corporations, demand that anyone who seeks to work for them publicly pledge allegiance to the Social Justice, Diversity, and Inclusion precepts, or what David's brother calls "The Diversity Confession" at one point in the book. Others who defend traditional views of gender relations or sexuality, or just the evidence of their own eyes, are excoriated and "canceled," or at best derided as backward Deplorables. Your propagandized children will exclaim with horror at the knowledge crime you may still utter in the privacy of your own home.

When these precepts have developed into a soft totalitarianism enforced by academics, the media, and corporations, it is a short step to making them enforceable in law once those schooled in its ideology and not much else have come to power.

Christianity, Judaism and Islam are considered retrograde unless they conform to the social justice ideology. Thus, in *Girlfriend*, the various denominational branches of the state Mother Earth Diversity Church all hew to the MED doctrines. As the Soviet slogan went, "nationalist in form, but socialist in content." So a MED Christian might wear a cross, or a MED Jew celebrate Havdalah with the end of the Sabbath, or a MED Muslim fast during Ramadan, but all would give primacy to the doctrines of social justice of the larger MED Church. Most faiths and denominations have their traditionalist and progressive arms by now, so MED can easily take root in the latter.

Because of our addiction to convenience and social media, we gladly consent to allow our devices and appliances to collect information about us.

Our children are already learning Diversity Literature, Diversity History, and even Diversity Math. What does Diversity mean here? It doesn't mean the inclusion of heretofore marginalized groups as much as it means the deliberate marginalization of facts at odds with the desired political narrative.

The destruction of history starts in classrooms, and ends in the public square with the toppling of statues that dare to remind us of another time and another perspective. Those who puzzled at how the destruction of Confederate statues in 2020 could culminate in the toppling of statues of Christopher Columbus, Theodore Roosevelt, Abraham Lincoln, and even Frederick Douglass missed the point. The unarticulated goal is to prevent some child from innocently asking "who was that? What did he believe?" To that end, the DJR must collect all permissible knowledge on the Great Virtual Network behind protective walls and segregate books in the False Knowledge Depository. It's the logical conclusion.

In addition to its own internet walls, China already uses a Social Credit system, albeit not the one used in *Girlfriend,* to apportion scarce resources under socialism.

If the breakup of the United States creates two smaller, weaker countries, it should surprise no one that China will be poised to take advantage of the US's disappearance as a world power. The Antifan Navy is at the disposal of China's People's Liberation Army Navy, and the great Naval Station Norfolk is abandoned. Russia has claimed most of Europe as its protectorate. Weaker, poorer countries are less enticing to would-be immigrants, and by 2089, Mexican GDP has surpassed the DJR's. The novel references all these developments quickly, in passing, but just because they are not the focus of the story does not mean they are implausible.

And we increasingly see each other as ridiculous, perplexing strangers without a shared story or history. Go on social media where you can find progressives in Blue Northern Virginia mocking Red Deplorables elsewhere in the commonwealth as needing to knuckle under to the Blue social agenda because they "depend on our tax dollars." Are we that far from herding the Deplorables like David's family into ghettoes from which they can emerge to serve us our cappuccinos and repair our drywall?

Fears of civil war and secession abound on social media. The civil war that leads to the Treaty of the Red and the Blue follows decades of careening back and forth between right-wing and left-wing political forces as Americans migrate to areas they find more conducive to their values. This is already happening.

Read this novel while you can. They might leave one copy in Malia's False Knowledge Depository, but you won't have access to it.

Paula T. Weiss
Duck, NC, October 2020

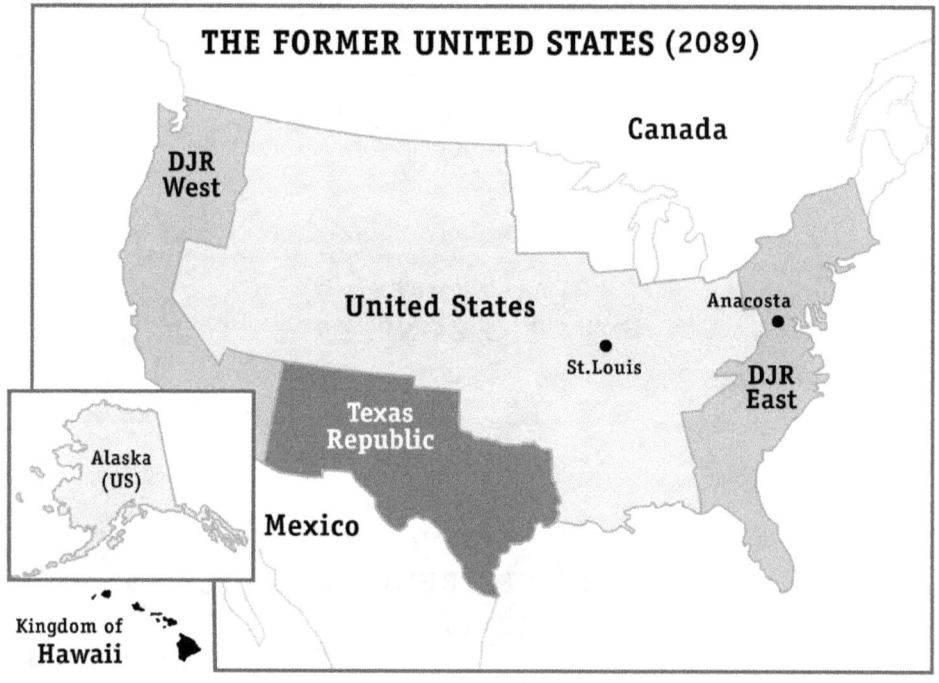

The former United States comprising the United States, the Diversity Justice Republic and its subordinate Kingdom of Hawaii, the Republic of Texas, and the four states that joined Canada in 2060.

CAST OF CHARACTERS

Malia Jenness, the remaining librarian at the False Knowledge Depository
David Harris, Deputy Commander of the Knowledge Crimes Unit, Antifan Defense Forces (ADF)

HILLARY CLINTON UNIVERSITY

John MacMillan, Assistant Professor of Diversity History, an illegal reader
Julie MacMillan, his wife, Chief Human Resources
Hanna, the security liaison with Beaufort
HCU President **Amy Fufuloa**
Kendra Pinckney, Professor of Diversity History
Andrew Leonard, Professor of Disability Studies
Jeffrey Bertone, Professor of Postcolonial English Literature and Kendra's boyfriend

THE ANTIFANS

Brian Walters, David's deputy, Knowledge Crimes Unit (KCU)
Antifan Defense Forces Director **Victor Ferraro**
Cheysa Conroy, private, on David's squad
Sgt. Candiss Yardley, on David's squad
Sgt. Conor Chung, on David's squad
Pvt. Dominic Farrell, newcomer to the KCU
Karlmarx, chief analyst
Paula Findlay, Infotech chief for KCU, David's "work sister."
Steve Rosen, Commander, the Economic Crimes Unit
Gemma Carpenter, Commander, Counterintelligence Unit
Deputy Director **Vladivar Montoya**
Alex Charlton, new Commander, the Knowledge Crimes Unit
Helen Zhu, David's new deputy
Carolina Cruz, Antifan-linked songster
Night Commander Angela, the overnight commander in the KCU
Kate, the gym trainer
Commander Lefever, the Commander of ADF Camp Six
Herbert Collingswood, deputy commander

THE HARRIS FAMILY AND PLOREVILLE

Marjory Harris, David's mother
Daniel Harris, David's older brother, the electrician at ADF Camp No. Six
Emma and Christine, David's older sisters

Larry and Kevin, their husbands and David's brothers-in-law
Pastor Denman, Lutheran minister
Doc, the Harris family's longtime physician

THE OCTAVIAN

Adam Ross, chief administrator of the Anacosta Economic Zone
Leighton Andrews and **Belinda Barbaradaughter,** Rex's adoptive parents
Rex/Isabelle, Malia's daughter
Jorge, the Bolivian-born night concierge

THE ECONOMIC STRIKE ZONE CAMP and the ECONOMIC TOWER

Barry Mattison, Commander, Economic Strike Zone (ESZ) Camp No. 4
Will Kendall, Quartermaster, Anacosta Region, and Adam's friend
Pernella Smith, Director, Economic Tower
Henry and Roxanne, the Anacosta Region Sales Manager and his shy wife
Commander Connie Milliband, the Tower Chief of Manufacturing
Ghani Mohfaz, PhD, chief of DJR Chemical Engineering Program
Dr. Ling Li-Hua, Chinese experimental lead
Thomas Retsinger, DJR experimental lead

OTHER CHARACTERS (ALPHABETICAL ORDER)

Antolides, Elofea, Malia's supervisor
President Avadaughter, current occupant of the White Black House
Conroy, Reba, Cheysa's mother
Fielding, Jim, ADF-compliant reporter
Peace-Williams, Kumbaya ("Michael") Vice-President of the DJR
Peters, Tom, a.k.a. Dave Mitchell, Malia's fake boyfriend, an ADF informant
Potts, Fern, Malia's best friend

"Out beyond ideas of wrongdoing and rightdoing
there is a field. I'll meet you there."
—*Rumi*

Prologue

January 2059, Near Lynchburg, VA

Three women and a small girl huddled near the fireplace, which emitted a thin pulse of heat with its carefully hoarded wood. The wood was precious, given that it was acquired only by raiding nearby properties for fallen branches and trees spindly enough to be felled with a hand saw by half-starved women no longer young. The women sat in shabby old chairs, with layers, but not enough layers, of tattered blankets, on their laps and around their shoulders. The little girl, Malia, four, but looking younger, sat on her aunt's lap, lacking the energy to move or play. Every few hours she bestowed a warm smile upon one of them, which made them feel happy that she had not yet succumbed to despair, but saddened that they had exposed her to such misery through no fault of her own. They remembered their own happy childhoods.

By early 2059, the Great Diversity War was coming to an end, with the coastal fringes of the continent falling under the sway of the Blue, or the Diversity forces. The interior, which was not of particular interest to the Blue, could not be tamed or held with the present number of Antifan Diversity troops. But as the Great Diversity Council had observed in private, the control it sought was not over thousands of square miles of empty territory but over people, and by that standard, conquering the entire East and West Coasts, and about 200 miles inland, was sufficient victory for now. Most of the skirmishing was now taking place along those interior boundaries, with brutal Antifan shock troops clearing out the population and driving them into the cities closer to the coasts. Those who resisted were sometimes killed on the spot when deemed incorrigible or useless. Antifan squads sometimes clashed with Red Patriots, but generally did not care to be on the receiving end of actual firearms, and the Red Patriots were finding it easier to drop back into the former Midwest and Mountain states and regroup, in what was still called the United States.

Texas had declared its independence, and New Mexico was likely to join it. The women knew this because they still had a radio, operated by hand cranking once the batteries ran out. From central Virginia, they could listen to the stations in Washington and also to one run by Patriots in Nashville. From what they gleaned, they knew they were on the front lines. Most of their neighbors had fled a year ago when local services—gasoline, utilities, supermarkets, wifi coverage—had closed or withdrawn, making their comfortable semi-suburban lives untenable. Some fled into the Enclosures, which were certifiably nearer; others drove into the Interior, hoping their gasoline would last them long enough to find a friendly destination. Patriot stations reported on families that had run out of gas in the Appalachians or somewhere in western Pennsylvania, and that had hiked a hundred miles west until they could reach freedom and safety. There were Patriot forward units who stationed themselves along major roads to try to rescue such families sooner rather than later.

During the daytime, the women could see the abandoned houses speckling the hills around them, and the grandmother Annabel, and her daughter, Malia's aunt, had retrieved food, furniture for kindling, and toys for the little girl. The women did not question their having had to forage from their neighbors' houses—what alternative did they have to fleeing? "My great-great-great grandfather came here before the Civil War and we have been here ever since," said the aged great-grandmother, as if that settled the question.

Annabel's younger daughter, who was the aunt's sister and the child's mother, had objected to "staying and starving," as she put it. She was passionate for the Patriot cause, and about two years ago had left with a band of Reds that were heading into Tennessee to hold the line there against Diversity Forces. They had not heard from her since. "Maybe if things settle down, she will come back and bring us there," said Annabel, but the great-grandmother only glowered in return. Whenever Annabel or the aunt, Jennifer, voiced concerns about roaming bands of Antifans, the great-grandmother would point to the kitchen where the ancient Glock handgun was kept in a drawer out of reach of the child, and say "We have some protection."

So the women stayed, mostly out of inertia, but also fearing the Diversity Enclosures or being stranded en route to the Interior. Had the great-grandmother, the 93-year old Diane, decreed they move, they probably would have moved, but her indomitable force met no resistance. Nobody asked what would happen when the houses they could reach on foot were emptied of their remaining provisions. None of them wanted to waste the Glock, with its precious ammunition, on learning to shoot the remaining wildlife that were scarce in any case, and too fast, such as the squirrels. "I can't imagine eating a mouse," said Annabel, although the shadows along the baseboards at night suggested that mice were available. Late that afternoon, they had opened and eaten the contents of a precious can of creamed corn, at room temperature. The child was always hungry.

The younger women would retire upstairs when the fire died down, but it was still early enough in the evening that nobody was ready for sleep. Diane said, "I want the

Bible tonight…I don't know why, I need to hear some foundation." They had been reading aloud some romantic novel that never got returned to the public library before it closed. Jennifer got the Book from the breakfront cabinet, which was next on the list for firewood, found a match and lit the candle next to her grandmother's chair. "No, you read, please, Jennifer," said Diane. Annabel took the child onto her lap.

"Isaiah 42" said Diane.

Jennifer read,

"Behold my servant, whom I uphold; mine elect, in whom my soul delighteth; I have put my spirit upon him: he shall bring forth judgment to the Gentiles. He shall not cry, nor lift up, nor cause his voice to be heard in the street…

"I the Lord have called thee in righteousness, and will hold thine hand and will keep thee, and give thee for a covenant of the people, for a light of the Gentiles…

"I am the Lord, that is my name: and my glory will I not give to another, neither my praise to graven images… The Lord shall go forth as a mighty man, he shall stir up jealousy like a man of war; he shall cry, yea, roar; he shall prevail against his enemies. I have a long time holden my peace; I have been still and refrained myself; now I will cry like a travailing woman; I will destroy and devour at once…

"But this is a people robbed and spoiled; they are all of them snared in holes, and they are hid in prison houses; they are for a prey, and none delivereth; for a spoil, and none saith, Restore. Who among you will give ear to this? Who will hearken and hear for the time to come?"

Jennifer paused. "Did you hear something?"

"Other than the time to come?" Annabel briefly joked, but they all went silent, apprehensive, then fearful. The child whimpered and Annabel gently shushed her. A large vehicle, no two, were coming up the winding driveway and turned sharply and stopped abruptly in a spray of gravel next to the kitchen, as if the drivers had expected the driveway to continue. One vehicle might possibly be a lone neighbor or a distant friend coming to check on them, but two at night were almost certainly ominously intended. Then they heard the angry shouts of men, and before they could knock, the great-grandmother slipped away into the kitchen with a surprising amount of stealth and speed for someone so aged. The child burrowed under the blankets on her grandmother's lap.

They did not bother to knock, since the door would not be needed again. It was smashed off its hinges and about a dozen men swarmed the room. They were dressed in the black uniforms known as Antifan, and their faces were obscured by black balaclavas with the giant red fist splayed across the Diversity Circle on their sides.

"Bitches!" said one, who presumably was the leader. "Why are you still here?" He sprang over to Jennifer, who shrunk away in her chair, and picked the Bible up from the floor. "Look at this treasonous garbage. You bitches believe this shit?" He ripped out pages with his bare hands, and frustrated with the book's size, dropped the book on the floor, and stomped on it. "That's what I think of your shit." He blew out the candle, and his minions blinded the women with their powerful flashlights. He ordered the men to search the house, ostensibly for signs of treasonous or conservative inclinations, and the women heard the sound of tramping above their heads. "Get against the wall. The brat too. Any men here?"

"No" Jennifer said. The leader approached her, with her palms touching the wall, as ordered, and quickly ran his gloved hands up and down her front. "When was your last time?" he sneered at her. "I bet you need it." Jennifer wrenched away, and he said, "too ugly for me. Brian, she's for you!" Brian emerged from the mass, and started dragging her toward the back parlor, while she screamed and tried to go limp. Brian hit her in the face and she did in fact go limp, which allowed him to finish pulling her into the other room. "Brian's been a good boy," said the leader, and the others in the band sniggered approvingly.

He turned to Annabel, shrunken against the wall. "Don't worry, no one's going to rape you, you're an old hag. I want to know—who else is in this neighborhood?"

Annabel quavered, "We're the only ones. We've been going to every house we can walk to for food, so I know."

"Sure" he responded, showing a flash of white teeth in the black night of the balaclava. His eyes were a deep blue. "We'll see about that. We're rounding up all you resisters. It's time you fascists were taught some of the right things."

"We're not fascists! If we were, wouldn't we have left already and gone into the Interior?"

"Then don't read this shit Bible and I might believe you." Footsteps headed back downstairs. "Anything of interest?"

"Just some jewelry," said the short man in the lead, stuffing some old costume jewelry in his pockets. "And some old regime cash—worthless."

"Books? Anti-Diversity propaganda? Just take whatever you want." The second man came downstairs with some evening dresses that had belonged to the child's mother. He had a wife and not much money to spare on party clothes.

"Yeah, a bunch of old rightwing books. Nasty stuff. Like Republican Party shit."

"That's it, we're not even going to bother taking them. Let's get everyone into the trucks and burn the place down. That'll take care of the books.

"Fascists are around tonight. Let's get moving."

Another Antifan came halfway down the staircase and leaned over with a foot-square souvenir photo of a former President, a smiling older blond man. "Hey, Commander! Isn't this like the racist guy of all time? Wasn't he kicked out of Washington?"

"The worst! That's Trump himself! The Great Hater! All right, no more nice guys here…" The Commander turned around from surveying his prisoners at the wall as something moved on the far side of his peripheral vision. He spun toward the kitchen door, which opened to reveal an ancient crone wielding a handgun. "You bastards!" she shouted, firing just as the Commander fired at her. She crumpled to the ground, dropping the weapon, which an Antifan scooped up. The Commander grimaced, and he grabbed his right arm, which the great-grandmother's shot had grazed. "Saved us some trouble loading her into the truck," he smiled with some bravado, but the men could tell that he had been shaken, and was in pain. He slapped Annabel in the face with his good hand, knocking her to the ground. "Why didn't you warn us, you old bitch?" The great-grandmother lay on the ground, blood pooling next to her left ear.

Brian came in from the Florida room, zippering up his black jeans.

"Let's get moving! Jimmy, you're last outta here, get a nice fire going!"

Two of the men hustled Annabel out the door between them, and a third carried out the child, who was too terrified to cry. They were loaded into the back of the truck, where they found a young mother and two other children huddled in the back, eyes wide with fear, guarded by a beardless Antifan even younger than the mother.

The other men lifted themselves into the trucks, congratulating themselves on how well the operation had gone. Jimmy tossed the lit candle at the breakfront and leapt out the door and into the first truck. Brian came from around the side of the house and jumped into the second truck with the helpless prisoners.

"Wait, what about my daughter?" Annabel shrieked, "the one in the back?"

"No point," said one of the men, who had pushed back his balaclava to reveal a mop of spiky brown hair dyed purple and metal studs below his eyebrows. "There are fascists around, we need to get going." He waved his hand in the direction of the children. "Your daughter is fascist collateral. THESE are our future."

Brian looked at Annabel, almost ashamed, but not quite. He said "I pulled her out of the house before we torched it. Maybe the fascists will find her. She's not dead." He briefly thought of his own mother, now safe near Washington, in a dormitory for favored senior citizens, the mother of a proud Antifan. She would have been proud to see him fight fascists tonight. He thought she would, in any case. In the first truck, a young medic named Adam attended to the commander's arm.

The trucks screeched down the road as quickly as they had arrived, heading back to the barracks in Charlottesville, safe territory. Behind them, the dark sky glowed orange as the house, built in slavery times, burned to the ground. The children began to cry, but the wind grew stronger and drowned out their sobs.

PART ONE

THE
DEPOSITORY

APRIL 2089

Chapter One
The Truth Seeker
(Monday, 11 April)

"The first step in liquidating a people is to erase its memory. Destroy its books, its culture, its history. Then have somebody write new books, manufacture a new culture, invent a new history. Before long the nation will begin to forget what it is and what it was."
—*Milan Kundera*

He was fortyish, balding, and blinking at Malia behind wire-framed glasses. Malia panicked because she had no record of his application in her electronic files. Nor had she gotten the usual alert on Friday about an upcoming visit. "My name is John MacMillan, 134," he said, "I'm an associate professor of Diversity History at Hillary Clinton University. I think my department may have sent the application by regular mail last week."

THAT she would have remembered, but she didn't. She didn't want to call her boss at the Knowledge Tower, who would likely be irritated with her for not handling the situation and forcing her to make a decision bearing on knowledge security. Amalia Jenness, Social Credit score 96, the surviving librarian at the national False Knowledge Depository in Anacosta, formerly Washington, DC, saw few visitors these days, all of whose credentials were in order and whose visits required little initiative on her part.

Suddenly, she had an idea. She went out into the foyer, and asked the surly guard with the man-bun. "I don't have it," he said. She went behind his desk, and found an express pouch that did in fact have the professor's paperwork. "Oh well, I forgot about that," the guard shrugged. She returned to the office.

"Professor MacMillan," she said, "I'm happy to report that your paperwork is indeed here, but we haven't had time to process it. Would you be able to return tomorrow for your research?"

He looked hangdog. "My flight leaves on Wednesday morning. I was counting on a full day and a half here. I need to confirm some citations for an article that has been accepted for publication in *Diversity Scholarship*." Malia thought, irritated, well why didn't you apply electronically then instead of wasting time through the mail?

But she took pity on the few researchers interested in the books she safeguarded, and why would anyone bother to come here nowadays without a valid reason, especially a professor at a distinguished university? She also knew that *Diversity Scholarship* was the premier journal in the field, and in fact, the Depository maintained its own subscription.

She asked him to wave his arm over the security counter. He was indeed who he said he was, although his Social Credit score was actually 138, not 134. Imagine not knowing that by heart!

"I can give you a waiver for today but I need to check with the Knowledge Tower for your visit tomorrow," she said.

She looked at the paperwork. "You realize that the US Constitution is available openly on the Great Virtual Network?" she asked, puzzled.

"I just want to see the original version pre-Diversity Republic," he said anxiously. "There have been some edits for clarity since the Republic began, and I am doing a sophisticated textual analysis that relies on complete faithfulness and accuracy with the original version, even though I realize it is dangerous to read."

This sounded safe enough to Malia. "How about if I let you see the other books this afternoon? I assume the permissions will be available overnight." He nodded, she had him sign some electronic checkout slips, and she ordered the *Federalist Papers* from the request chute.

She was shocked to see that he was requesting *Democracy in America*, which was already sitting on her own desk, with a dangerous bookmark inserted. "What quote are you using from *Democracy in America*?" she asked curiously.

He did not bristle at the question, perhaps regarding it as part of the required interrogation. "It's the one where Tocqueville claims that tyranny in the US would develop not from harsh decrees but from a soft and mild, almost benign ruler, who sought to help, not harm, the people. I am making an argument that the Founders pursued a harsh individualism that led to a stigmatizing from the beginning of government that could have helped humanity thrive."

That sounded safe too. Malia handed him the volume she had been reading. He expressed surprise that it had just been sitting there. "Quite a coincidence," she agreed. "I'm doing my annual quality check on the older volumes." Even more coincidentally, she had read that same quote yesterday and had been so struck by its prediction of today's loving Diversity Justice Republic that it had taken several minutes to steady her thoughts. *The Federalist Papers* then appeared in the window at the other end of the room and she removed it.

She took his electronic notebook and ensured that its camera was turned off and that only the typing and save functions were working. When he left, she would have to review his drive to ensure no harmful utterances or materials had been entered since his arrival.

She had just turned 34, although in her daily isolation, in the dark Depository office under the single skylight, no one had wished her a happy birthday. Had the government not taken Malia's daughter from her ten years ago, the daughter—a cheery dark-haired sprite—would no doubt have sung her a Happy Birthday song and given her a homemade card. Malia was petite, below average height, and thin mostly due to the skimpy Healthy Eating grocery bag given to low-Social Credit citizens such as herself. Her curly brown hair was tied in a sloppy ponytail, and she didn't bother much with makeup these days. Her best features were her shining brown eyes and a delicate sprinkling of fading freckles across a small, upturned nose.

Until Professor MacMillan's arrival, the expected highlight of her day had been her lunch, a seeded roll with a nice floury crust and a small packet of cream cheese. She had splurged on the roll en route to work, since it was not part of the weekly grocery allotment. The allotment was usually stingy with sweets, or even cheese, at least for her, so Malia ended up purchasing items she craved here or there to round out the grocery bag.

She felt mostly safe here, away from prying eyes and chatty co-workers. A camera was trained on her desk from the opposite wall, but she suspected it had not worked in years, nor had the cameras installed in the various aisles where the forbidden books were kept behind locks. Her last co-worker had retired two years ago, and as long as she sent an email report to her supervisor in the Knowledge Tower each Monday, she felt she would remain undisturbed. She tried to keep the reports extremely boring— number of visitors, reports of book damage, miscellaneous maintenance. She never mentioned her concerns about the cameras.

As she ate the roll, casting an occasional glance at Professor MacMillan, she doodled numbers on the sketch pad. If she could inch her Social Credit number over 100 by year's end, it would open up more restaurants, a better grocery bag, and maybe even a beach vacation at one of the few resorts open to Social Credit hoi polloi. She was satisfied with her apartment for now, but eventually she might want one with a view of the horizon instead of the wall of the next tower. At least the loud migrant family that had been recruited to move to Anacosta from Guatemala as part of the Welcoming Our New Friends initiative lived far enough down the hallway to be just a nuisance, but better buildings kept New Friends out altogether.

A promotion from acting to fulltime chief librarian would give her another twenty points, but how to bring this to the attention of her division chief? Malia mulled as she jotted down her scores for the third time that week:

50 (job)—soon 70? 5 (cis-woman) (20) HE (healthy eating subscription)

The remainder (21 points) of her Social Credit score comprised the various civic and Mother Earth Diversity (MED) church activities that were each worth anywhere from a third of a point to a full eight points for volunteering at the upcoming Earth Weekend. Last week she had earned another third of a point by going to pack lunches for schoolchildren. No shopkeeper checked his wares more diligently than Malia did the elements of her Social Credit score. She went online almost daily to ensure that no qualifying activity, however trivial, went uncounted.

Fortunately, a major funeral service would take place on Wednesday morning. A founder of the DJR was being laid to rest amid the praise of dignitaries and comrades from the Diversity Civil Wars that had ended in 2060. Malia had every intention of attending and collecting the three points such a glorious occasion afforded.

Looking at MacMillan's list, Malia realized that she could call any of his books through the chute today. Normally she took books off the shelves manually for her own illicit reading, because she could safely do so and evade the Electronic Eye by inserting a bricklike cardboard box; no one could detect an open space from which a book had been unofficially removed. But the electronic request system left an unmistakable record. The professor has already requested these books, she thought—it would be perfectly understandable for those books to be pulled off the shelves for the night. So she ordered Paul Johnson's *History of the American People*, and was immersed

The delegates to the Second Constitutional Convention, meeting in 2060, had determined that the newly liberated Diverse People needed protection from ideas proven to be unsafe and racist. The Convention banned most paper books outright, whether for dangerous ideas, or trivial content, or for consuming excess paper and creating environmental harm, but those who already owned books could have them vetted by their Local Knowledge Committee. Anything deemed worth retaining was moved to the Great Virtual Network, or GVN, which contained all acceptable knowledge, including films and videos, and which most importantly was capable of monitoring viewers' usage and habits.

Some members of the Convention argued that Diversity Education required some controlled access to even harmful books so that researchers could impart the dangers of fascism to new generations. They contended that it would be safer to keep a few copies of the books in climate-controlled vaults rather than make them available on the GVN, even to a restricted cleared audience. After all, hackers might obtain access to and even distribute them online. So the Convention established the False Knowledge Depository in an obscure corner of downtown Anacosta, formerly Washington, DC.

For the first two decades, a steady stream of researchers sought to consult the books, despite the numerous barriers erected to ensure safety, and then interest waned as Diversity precepts entrenched themselves among the population. A staff of 20 highly vetted librarians and security specialists dwindled as their ranks gradually retired or drifted to more prestigious assignments. The second and third floors were permanently closed.

—"The Origins of Knowledge Hygiene in the Diversity Justice Republic," *Diversity Jeanne Morales, PhD thesis, Justice University, 2094.*

in the Puritans when she looked up at the camera. The professor was crying.

The intercom no longer worked, so she went to the door and asked, "Professor, are you all right? Can I help?"

He took a tissue from the box, wiped his eyes, and said, "I'm sorry. This is so emotional for me. It's my first article in *Diversity Scholarship*. Also, I was shocked by how much waste was inherent in self-government. People meant well, they tried to solve their problems, but so often it was futile! Tocqueville and Burke were far too naïve about the dangers of such a system."

As always, she was guarded. "All right—just to let you know we are closing in half an hour. I'll need to review your notes in fifteen minutes so we can close on time." He nodded.

After she had sent Professor MacMillan on his way, she locked up carefully and headed home on foot. She had to maneuver around the Street Persons settling down on the sidewalk in their tents and sleeping pods issued by the City government. Others, especially in inclement weather, lived in the tunnels of the Metro subway system that had been abandoned during the civil war. Malia had learned to ignore the catcalls of the Street men, and sometimes she gave a donation to one of the old women, in the form of a card entitling one to a meal at a low Social Credit restaurant, even though she could barely afford to patronize one herself. Tonight, she was distracted by the professor's visit. Something had not been quite right about the afternoon—the paper application misplaced, and then found; the professor's tears and almost pompous restatements of Diversity Truth. He seemed a little mentally unbalanced. She resolved to caution the security guard tomorrow morning to stand by.

Her apartment building, the Rosebud, came up sooner than she had expected. She gained entry by waving her armband at the sensor, and took the elevator to the seventh floor. Loud Spanish music could be heard down the hallway. She saw that her Healthy Eating delivery had been left in the built-in coldbox, and once she entered the apartment, she was able to remove it from the interior door and put the dispiriting contents away. Five more soybakes, a jar of pink fish paste, a small loaf of wheat bread, a lettuce head, two cucumbers, two tomatoes, a clump of red grapes, two ounces of a white cheese, three ounces of tofu, and three instant bean burrito dinners. A quart of non-fat milk and a quart of pineapple cranberry juice. A small paper bag of vanilla wafers, some of which were crushed. A jar of pickles (last week a jar of capers). A box of whole grain oatmeal. A six-ounce package of brown rice (which alternated with quinoa). Two rolls of toilet paper. Fourteen identical large cans of cat food.

Ansel came to greet her, brushing up against her pants leg, patiently awaiting his dinner. Frida, his tabby soulmate, stood upright nearby, gourdlike with her round bottom.

The apartment was spare, painted off white, efficiently designed, impersonal but not unpleasant. You entered into a small foyer with a closet. The galley kitchen was to the left, with the two-way coldbox. The cabinets were off white, the counters beige, with old-fashioned stainless-steel appliances. The living room had come furnished with a burgundy faux leather sofa, a papasan chair, a short display case, and a coffee table. The case held random souvenirs from Malia's few trips, including a blue clay bowl into which she put odds and ends, and a pretty, but empty blue glass vase that was a gift from her last co-worker. She took off the armband and placed it on the tiny night table in the small bedroom.

She hadn't gotten around to placing any artwork on the walls. Who would see it, anyway? And what if someone did visit, and judged her taste awry? The risk was not worth it.

The cats didn't care about interior decoration but liked their hemp scratcher. Malia settled with them on her bed after dinner, where she watched a movie about an evil film producer who had seduced beautiful feminists, only to die of a contagious disease in prison, at which point he repented thanks to the gay Diversity Chaplain who had befriended him there. When that ended, she turned to *Amindala: The Struggles of a Non-Binary Indigenous Hero*, figuring she should at least have the option of attending the book club meeting on Friday night. Maybe the good-looking man her friend Fern had mentioned would be in attendance, and maybe he would be interested in continuing the conversation elsewhere, but it had been a long time since she had allowed herself to open up to any such relationship. It was hard enough keeping Fern at a distance.

"Amindala stole into the woods, seeking the wisdom of the Eternal Grandmother who lived in the oak tree...the spirit of Eternal Grandmother spoke to them...
'dear Child, have you been kind to the sparrow and the woodchuck who lived here first? Have you respected the salmon and the moose?'"

This passage reminded Malia of the fish paste in the coldbox so she went and made herself a sandwich for tomorrow's lunch, slicing one of the tomatoes and adding two of the cookies.

Some yearning drove her to pull out the flat metal box in the cabinet under the kitchen sink. Squatting, she opened the box to reveal paper drawings by a child. One drawing in purple and green crayon showed a small brown-haired girl holding the hand of a bigger stick figure with long curly brown hair, and in awkward letters, "MOM AND ME." The other one was of a large cat (Theobald, the current occupants' predecessor) eating a pile of presumably delicious cat food. The word YUM was written next to the food, and above the cat's back it read "CAT IS TOBAL."

When they took the child from her, and everything that belonged to the five-year old, Malia had managed to hide these two drawings. They had also survived two subsequent searches by the Child Protective Authorities, and then when Malia was evicted from the two-bedroom apartment she no longer needed and which she could no longer bear anyway, she had brought them here in the box under her diploma.

Malia turned on the water in the sink and cried. It was dangerous to be overheard crying—neighbors or spies might be curious. Ansel came and brushed up against her leg, almost reassuringly, although as a cat, he was afraid of water.

Chapter Two
Workplace Violence
(Tuesday, 12 April)

Malia had meant to warn the security guard of the odd visitor, taking advantage of her arrival an hour before the official opening time, but two things prevented her from doing so when she arrived at the Depository: a new guard was present and the anxious Professor MacMillan was already standing on the sidewalk outside the entrance. "I can't lose a minute," he told her.

The new guard looked like a more efficient and tidier version of her surly Man-Bun, but no friendlier. All he said to her was, "I'm the substitute for today. Your usual officer is sick." He offered nothing else, just watched her through narrow green eyes as she waved her armband and entered the office. Professor MacMillan followed humbly.

She decided to seat the professor in the reading room before checking her computer for the official permissions. It normally would have taken several days, but she had filed it under URGENT. Nonetheless, she assumed the overnight team would have processed it expeditiously. There was no reason to deny a distinguished professor of Diversity History at Hillary Clinton University the right to see documents needed for a legitimate purpose, and for *Diversity Scholarship* at that. He was ready for the Johnson volume, so she delivered it to him. When she looked through the glass, he seemed calmer and more purposeful than he had yesterday afternoon. Yesterday he had gobbled through pages like a starving man eating his first meal in a year; today he savored his food.

The coffeemaker hissed comfortably as she opened her email with another wave of the armband.

Nothing from the Knowledge Tower. No rejection, no authorization. Silence. She was still in the dark about Professor MacMillan. But that ship had sailed, so she sat there, too agitated to even drink the coffee. "If I don't hear anything by 10 o'clock, I'll call Amba-mam Antelides," her immediate supervisor. But in the back of her mind, she thought, perhaps they will not respond. Perhaps the electronic request would be allowed to fall between the cracks of various bureaucratic minutiae. Perhaps the usual clerk was ill.

While she waited, she opened the US Constitution. It had been superseded in the DJR by the Bill of Community Diversity Rights from 2055, but she had read the heavily annotated original US Constitution in her college American History class open to ideologically sound students. She had learned that racists, white Christian supremacists, and rich people had drafted the document to preserve their privilege and amended it over the years only when challenged by United Fronts of Worker Communities of Color and Sexuality. Only with the creation of the DJR had the suppressed populations finally enjoyed their long-denied rights. Malia briefly recalled her Diversity History teacher at the orphanage school, Ms. Howard, passionately espousing this theory, long frizzy blonde hair flying around her ugly animated face.

At 10 am, Malia nervously dialed Amba-mam Antelides' office. The secretary, even more imperious than Antelides in awareness of her role as the gatekeeper on the 66th floor of the Knowledge Tower, said "Who may I ask is calling?"

"Amalia Jenness, 96, Amba-mam," she said, using the respectful salutation for superior women within Social Credit circles that allegedly was a derivation of Swahili, but might have been completely invented. "I need to bring an urgent situation to Amba-mam Antelides' attention." One used Amba-sah for men, and Amba-wah for anyone claiming a less distinct gender identity.

"Amba-mam is in an important meeting," the secretary said. "I will relay your message." Click.

10:10 am. Malia scanned her other messages—the Knowledge Management Department picnic would be held on May 1st and she needed to bring a vegan appetizer; a shipment of books seized from knowledge criminals would arrive for her review next Monday.

10:25 am. Her hands shaking, Malia taped a poster of a smiling black boy against a background of a giant Electronic Eye on the wall above the coffeemaker. "Responsible Knowledge Is the Best Knowledge," it read.

10:30 am. She had almost begun to relax when she suddenly heard loud, angry voices from the other side of the door into the lobby—the door crashed open and slammed against the wall. Six black leather-clad Antifans hurled themselves into the office and then straightaway into the reading room. Malia heard loud shouts and curses, falling furniture as a chair and a table were overturned, and then a scream that she instinctively knew was the professor's. She could not see for herself, since the green-eyed guard—who was wearing the uniform of an ordinary security guard but was clearly an Antifan himself—had sauntered into the room and positioned himself between her and the melee. "Bitch—you see what you allowed to happen?"

"What?" she was aghast.

"Take him into the lobby—she doesn't have to see this." The order came from the commander, a man of medium-tall height and build with close-cut blond hair. Two Antifans hustled the professor past her and she caught a quick and appalling glimpse of his helpless soft bloodied face and his soiled shirt.

He cried out, "I just wanted to read the truth for once!" at which a third Antifan swung again at his face. "Yes, the truth!" "F--k your truth!" they shouted back. In the lobby they kept pummeling and slapping him until he lay prone on the carpet and no longer uttered the ridiculous lies. Malia buried her face in her arms on the desk. The Antifans didn't bother to close the door so she heard the cries and the foul curses, and then the silence.

The commander came back in, pausing in the doorway, and called back, "Call the ambulance and take him to Beaufort. We'll book him there. Wait for me." An Antifan hurried back into the reading room and emerged with the professor's workscreen. "Don't lose that, Beilin." "No, sir."

The commander said to her, "Stand up," and of course she did. He gestured to the green-eyed Antifan to stand by the door, and of course he did.

"I'm Commander Harris, 240. And you are Amalia Jenness, 96, right?"

"Yes, Commander."

"Well, Amalia, now you see what can happen when you neglect your charge. Your sole responsibility—other than vacuuming—is to protect the people of this republic from harmful literature and books. Even if they think they want to read this crap, even if they are crazy enough to think it bears some important message for them, you need to remember that it doesn't, and their reading it is poison to our whole society.

"I know you're not very busy here. They've been talking about closing this whole Depository. Who needs a librarian when a janitor or a garbage collector will do the job better? You couldn't even prevent one knowledge traitor from worming his way in. If you had done your job correctly, you would have figured out immediately that there was something fishy about this professor. All you knew was that he was John MacMillan and he was a professor at Clinton."

Malia dared to look into his steady grey eyes. They were not hostile and perhaps she only imagined there was a flicker of understanding, or even compassion, because she could not avoid seeing blood on his right hand and on the sleeve peeking out from the leather jacket.

"But you fell for the story that he was writing for *Diversity Scholarship*. What proof did you have of that? You let him make you believe that he couldn't wait for the official approval. You didn't think it through when he said he'd mailed the paperwork. You know why he mailed the paperwork? Because he had just failed his ideological reinvestigation at Clinton. They were going to officially fire him in a few weeks when their paperwork was done. He couldn't access their electronic request system, so he figured he'd capitalize on his last few weeks to come here and read what he knew no ideologically weak person is allowed to read in this country.

"How stupid are you not to put together all these clues that something wasn't right?"

Malia hung her head. "I knew it wasn't routine. I felt sorry for him. He said the right things so I thought he was safe."

"I hope you use a little more common sense outside of work when men say the so-called right things to you. He wasn't good looking enough to fool you. Sorry, that was out of line." Malia was astonished that he had uttered "sorry" to her. But Commander Harris himself was a good-looking man.

The commander continued, "Your lazy guard bears a lot of the responsibility here. If he had given you the envelope when it arrived, you would have had enough time to figure out that this guy was misrepresenting himself. Your guard won't be coming back."

She asked, "Are you going to arrest me?"

"No, but I doubt you'll be keeping this job. There was a big uproar at the Knowledge Tower this morning when it became known this guy had badged into the Depository. We came here as soon as we could."

He paused. "I hope you have some friends in Ploreville you can live with." She must have looked horrified, because he wryly said, "Don't worry, they won't eat you there."

He turned to leave with the green-eyed guard in tow. "You can clean up the reading room, Amalia. We have our evidence. Maybe an honest citizen will want to use it sometime this month." And then they were gone.

Malia walked around the room for another minute or two, still in shock. She found the cleaning supplies and went into the reading room that was spattered with blood, which trailed into the lobby. She picked up the professor's broken glasses and placed them on the table. He probably was very near-sighted and perhaps she should hold onto them for a few days in case the Antifans requested them. She righted the furniture and, in her daze, scrubbed it more than it needed to be scrubbed. Then she mopped more than she needed to mop. As she wrung out the mop, she thought, why did I let this happen? Why did I let this happen when in the back of my mind, I knew something was not right?

Malia hesitated to venture into the lobby, but to her surprise found it mostly orderly. She wiped up some blood spots, picked up a black glove, and straightened an end table, and then retreated into her office with the glove. Elbows propped on the desk, she realized she was not thinking about losing her job, and her right to live in the City, an almost certain conclusion to the sordid episode. Instead she was thinking of that steady gray gaze from a handsome Antifan commander with a sardonic sense of humor, whose first name she did not know.

The phone rang, and she felt afraid again. It was Amba-mam Antelides' secretary. "Amalia, be here to meet with Amba-mam Antelides at 2 pm."

It was a ten-block walk to the Knowledge Tower amid blustery spring skies and with the sun hidden behind the glass towers. She had to pass through several layers of security to approach the Tower. The first required a swipe of her arm, the second a walk through security frames to detect firearms or explosives, and the third to check in at a desk. The female guard looked down at her sternly, and said, "Under 100s use the side entrance." She gestured around the corner toward another line of visitors.

The elevator swept her up to the 66th floor where the secretary indicated a low sofa outside Antelides' office. Malia waited twenty minutes for Antelides' door to open. She had met Elofea Antelides only twice in person, when she had first been hired and when Antelides one day toured the Depository and had been visibly repelled by the darkness and the unsound materials within. At that time, Malia still had a few colleagues and a supervisor who served as intermediary and spared her any direct interaction with the majestic Antelides.

Eventually the door opened and she was told to enter the sanctum. Elofea Antelides, 190, a tall, dark New Woman with a hooked nose wearing a blue pantsuit and a blue scarf around her neck, rose from her desk—Malia for a moment thought she was about to offer her handshake—but in her deep voice she shouted, "HOW could you have let this happen?"

"I was derelict in my duty, Amba-mam Antelides," Malia said slowly. She had rehearsed her apologies on the walk. "I did not wait for the approval because of his position and what he said to me seemed ideologically correct. I was very wrong to ignore this important step."

"Do you think we have any reason for all the procedures to keep knowledge criminals out of that building? Do you think that the rules are something you can choose to ignore just because you like the way a man looks? You cis-females just fall apart when asked to enforce rules and you think the man is handsome."

Malia was shocked at the very thought that John MacMillan might have swayed her through his seductive manly wiles. This was so contrary to the facts of the case that she had no counter argument prepared and just gaped at Antelides.

"This is extremely unfortunate, but perhaps for the best. We were about to designate you as the Head Librarian due to the lack of other qualified candidates willing to serve in that depressing place. But you have clearly shown yourself unfit even for the basic duties required to protect Diversity. So effective tomorrow afternoon at closing time, you are fired.

"You may return to the Depository tomorrow morning to collect any belongings and to tidy up. I understand our brave Antifans were confronted by the dangerous criminal and a struggle ensued. Please make sure that everything is orderly when you depart. The Social Credit Agency will adjust your record accordingly.

"We will close the Depository for all outside researchers until we determine whether it can continue to exist given the ideological dangers confronting it. It may be that a paper library is no longer needed or practical given the victory of Diversity. These evil books serve no useful purpose for the vast majority of our people and can confuse even upright citizens.

"But that's not a concern for the likes of you. You may leave now."

Chapter Three
Return of the Antifan
(Tuesday, 12 April)

Outside the Knowledge Tower, Malia sat on a bench and watched sparrows fight over the crumbs of a sandwich. That's me, she thought, all I want are a few crumbs of the City and they won't even let me have those. She watched well-dressed bureaucrats stride down the path toward the Self-Drive Car Depot, their workday over, and others walking past them from outside meetings, jovial among themselves, staring into armband screens when alone. She might well have been a sparrow herself in her cloak of invisibility. The famous statue of The Heroic Knowledge Workers, one black female, one Asian male, one white female, their fists raised defiantly, perhaps at Knowledge, faced her from across the sidewalk.

The loss of the Head Librarian title was painful. But she reminded herself, Antelides may have been lying. She wondered how one moved to Ploreville, across the Potowmack River from the City in Virginia. Would the authorities find her a place to live or would she, after all these years, really be forced outside the cocoon of a Social Credit score and have to fend for herself?

Never in her life had she had to forge her own way. The orphanage sheltered her until she turned 17. The routine and predictability were welcome to Malia, whose earliest memories were of a transit camp full of cots and a hazy female presence—who she didn't think had been her mother and who had died shortly after they came to the camp. If you didn't mind lectures on Diversity Truth and learned to regurgitate it, you could make friends and enjoy outings at the orphanage.

Then, because of her excellent grades and her ideological conformity, she was sent to Justice University, and asked to major in Knowledge Management. It was no slight; Knowledge Management was touted as the highest task of the new Diversity Justice Republic—it was not enough to produce creative works, but to evaluate whether they were helpful to the national project and which groups would benefit from exposure to them. So at 17 she was outfitted with the armband, they implanted the chip behind her ear, and off she went to North Carolina. The chip had originally been justified as a way to recover confused senior citizens but quickly became too convenient for the Republic not to share with the rest of the adult population.

Malia knew if she moved to Ploreville she would be required to work either in the menial service occupations in the City or the manufacturing and agricultural enterprises in the other direction, in the Industrial or Economic Zones that bordered the Interior heartland held by the fascists. She briefly saw herself in a lime green uniform, with a matching paper hat, but no longer wearing an armband, as she trudged through the glass tunnel across the river each day to a job in a sandwich shop.

Her mind then turned to whether she ought to return to the Depository at all today. She knew she was expected to close up tomorrow, but what if her access was yanked overnight? She envisioned herself standing on the sidewalk, waving her arm over and over again with no result, and with the Knowledge Tower cameras capturing her efforts to break into the building and recover her coffeemaker. She did not want to see Antifans ever again. She had also left a nice sweater behind, and clothes were not cheap. And then with a sudden cold sweat drenching her, she thought of the notes she had scribbled on *The Roots of American Order* and left in the drawer. Her habit was to review the notes at the end of the day to try to memorize the content and then shred them. She knew someone would investigate the premises, see those notes and demand to know why she had taken those notes, during her custodial duties. I must go back there and destroy the notes, she thought, shaking.

She hurried along the street, catching a heel in a sidewalk crack at one point, brushing aside the obscene appeals of a Street Person, and arriving at the Depository in record time. She ran for her desk. To her horror, the blond Antifan commander was sitting there, his black shoes on the desktop, leafing through Russell Kirk's *Order*.

"Welcome back," he said. "I admire your dedication."

"How—how did you get in?" she stammered. It was not the brightest question she could have asked this man.

"I can open any door in the City that I want to," he said. And as if he could read her mind, "And your apartment door, but don't worry, I don't plan to.

"I left my glove behind in all the excitement," he said, raising the black leather glove with his ungloved left hand. "It's just as well, we have some unfinished business. You can sit down," he said, pointing to the visitor's chair in which the professor had sweated only yesterday afternoon. She sat, numbly. "As soon as I saw you were coming back here from the Knowledge Tower (the damned chip, she thought), it seemed a good opportunity to meet you here, without my boys and without the professor. They're all too intense.

"Mind if we have some coffee?" he asked. She had never drunk any of the coffee brewed that morning. She poured it into two mugs, handing him one.

"Do you have creamer? Sugar?" He liked to watch her bending slightly over the cart and serving him as if he were a guest, and not a potential jailer. He thought briefly of the young Antifan troops who approached the female cells calling out, "Hi feminists, Daddy's here!" and "Me Too! Me Too!" although he discouraged his boys from adding sadistic flourishes to what he considered necessary control measures. "This is a serious business. We need to be serious," he would tell them. But he didn't always stop them.

He actually preferred his coffee black, so that he diluted not a single drop of the caffeine. A senior commander of the Antifan Defense Forces needed to stay alert. Threats confronted him not just from the heretics who still babbled about individualism and choice, but from the government officials who should have known better, who demanded conformity but quailed at the violence needed to maintain it. How often had he warned members of the National Security Council that a cell of knowledge criminals was plotting to publish actual paper broadsides in defense of the right to read what they wanted? Or another group intended to protest the sensible harvesting for sale of fetal parts in the Abortion Palace? They were profitably exported to China for homeopathic medication manufacture. "Can't we just confiscate their pamphlets? Or quietly arrest them and release them later?" the officials would ask hesitantly.

"If you don't authorize us to break up the protest with severe consequences for ringleaders," he told them, "others will see no risk in trying. What's an afternoon in a police cell?"

It was a shame about the protesters' stubbornness, since the Commander admired courage, and it was courageous to throw away your Social Credit lifestyle, but when the authorities raised the stakes, it deterred troublemakers and was a boon to public safety in the long term. If the government wanted to entrench its ideology and stay in power, it needed to stop pretending that the population was in full agreement with the Diversity and the Anti-White Privilege doctrines and recognize that force was necessary to compel acquiescence until the ideology could be more firmly implanted. It was only 34 years since the founding of the Diversity Justice Republic—the Soviet Union had lasted more than twice as long, and yet its ideology still fizzled out as if it had never been triumphant at all. Even those who had upheld it most rigorously abandoned it at the first opportunity.

She placed the mug in front of him, and his nose detected a light floral scent—possibly her shampoo?

"Thank you. Please sit down." He raised the dozen or so index cards he'd found in the desk drawer. "So what are these?"

He read aloud, "the Genius of Christianity...the Nicene Creed...God is one and yet three.

"Consent of the governed.

"Constitution not abstract, reflection and embodiment of political reality in America."

He shuffled rapidly through the other cards, and laid them down. "May I ask why you are so interested in the content of these disgusting books? And why you are taking those notes? Surely it isn't because it helps you be a better custodian of them."

She had run through possible explanations on her walk back to the office. "I was planning to write an article for *Contemporary Knowledge Management* on the need for strict custodial safekeeping of such books. I was looking for quotes to illustrate my arguments."

"Honey, do you think I'm a stupid man? Do you think after this morning I really think you give a damn about custodial safekeeping of these books?" He seemed angrier that she was palming him off with the usual twaddle rather than telling him the truth. The gray eyes flashed at her. And for some reason, she took a leap of faith that in his eyes was the real message, *"I'm listening, I won't punish you for saying your truth."*

"Who says that I have to believe what I write? Is there anyone left who really believes what they say? Maybe I just wanted to publish an article so they can appoint me Head Librarian."

"What's the point of being Head Librarian here? Who's going to report to you? Are you going to line up a bunch of books and they'll all salute you?" Now he was mocking her.

"It's about the Social Credit points!" she cried out. "That's all that matters!"

He suddenly looked tired, "Oh yes, it's always that."

"I've been trying for years to get to 100. Commander, you probably don't realize it, because you're way up there, but it makes a huge difference to ordinary people to just have a decent meal or some cheese in their grocery bag or go on a vacation or take a self-driving car instead of cramming into a bus and getting lice or just be treated like a human being—"

He raised his hand to silence her outburst, and quickly went behind her and leapt onto the filing cabinet. She stared wordlessly as he peered behind the camera trained on the desk. He unscrewed the canister, removed something, and then screwed it again. When he jumped down, light as a cat, he said cheerfully, "Just as I suspected, it wasn't working anyway, but now they'll have a lot of trouble restarting it. Go ahead and speak freely.

"And call me David, please."

She sagged in her chair at the realization she had just unloaded at the Commander. "I'm sorry. I shouldn't have lost my temper. But it's just so—frustrating. This job is all I have, and they've fired me. One mistake in twelve years. I've always done what I was supposed to do. What am I supposed to do now?"

Looking at her more carefully, he thought she indeed looked a little gaunt, and the overlay of anxiety did not improve her looks. "You sound like you could use a good meal and talk. Would you like to come to dinner with me? I promise I won't hurt you, just feed you. Maybe we can discuss some ideas for improving your situation."

Malia was shocked, since she had expected the day to end in a prison cell, or at best in a crying jag in her apartment. But instead she was going to be the guest of a handsome Antifan commander in a restaurant far above what she was entitled to walk into unescorted.

"Well, are you willing? I promise I have no tricks in mind. You won't be going to Beaufort."

"Yes, Comman—"

"David," he said firmly.

"David," she replied, sighing.

They emerged from the Depository and David hailed a self-driving car. Malia hesitated as he started to wave her in. "I'm not allowed—" she began, and he responded, "You're my guest, it's perfectly all right." So she stepped into her first self-driving car ride, awed. The seats were an excellent fake leather; the screens emerged automatically from the sides of the car so that passengers could engage in media surfing or send messages while riding. There really was a little coldbox with chilled glass bottles of sparkling water, just as she had heard.

The smooth voice of Gauthier, the famed electronic chauffeur, said, "Please authorize the non-authorized passenger," and David pressed the correct button on his armband and then gave her address. "Thank you, Commander Harris. Enjoy your ride." The car moved off into the steady computerized flow of traffic.

She looked at him, puzzled and a little worried as to why they were going to her apartment.

"Let's have our dinner Friday instead," he said. "I've been selfish—this has almost certainly been an exhausting day for you and way too much stress. And you need to feed the cats. Get some sleep, and don't worry too much about the job. I can pull rank over your Antelides, which will get you a few weeks more in your cave." David had suddenly realized that he needed to check in at Beaufort, but a delay would help Malia too.

"I'll come by with the car at 7 pm Friday evening. We can go anywhere you like...." She looked blank. "Will you let me surprise you then? A good surprise."

David knew that Malia was afraid to talk to him and the outburst in the office had resulted from the stress and the familiarity of her surroundings rather than any real trust in him. His dismantling of the camera had possibly reassured Malia about his motives, but, true, for all she knew he had fixed the broken camera and it was working again. He acknowledged to himself that hunger and keeping her job and maybe just fear were probably a greater incentive to eat with him than was any real fondness or admiration for his good looks.

And why did he want her to like him? David wasn't in the habit of comforting what he called the "collateral damage" of the cases his boys tackled. A year ago, he would have never left the glove behind let alone invited a girl involved in such a case on a date or offered to stand up for her against an implacable bureaucracy. Malia wasn't his usual type. He had been dating dramatic dark-skinned girls from politically correct backgrounds whose passion intrigued him. He had dated serious bureaucratic females, mostly plain white girls who spoke ponderously of "Our Mother, the Earth" and mused on climate change initiatives and transgender equality. They bored him. Hard-edged Antifan woman officers would understand why he had to do what he did, and they were firm bodied and energetic in bed, but since the vast majority would be subordinates, he had to tread carefully. Regardless, his mother would not approve of any of these pagan types, and 38 years old or not, he still cared about his mother's approval.

It was possible that at least with Malia, he would eventually have a good conversation. From the horrified look on her face when Professor MacMillan was dragged out of her office, and from her insistence on reading dangerous books, but at least only privately, he thought he might have found a kindred spirit who would not seek to overthrow the system but to whom he could express his own skepticism. She would be prettier with fewer worries and more cheese; he fancied he could help here.

As they approached the Rosebud, he said to Malia, "I want you to know that I saw Professor MacMillan in detention this afternoon and he is all right. We've cleaned him up, he has a comfortable room, and I'll give him the glasses tomorrow after we've fixed them. Thank you for holding onto them. I thought you would want to know."

"Thank you," she said. "He's basically a good person. I wouldn't have helped him otherwise." She suddenly realized how damning that admission could sound.

"We have arrived at the destination," said Gauthier.

"Hold car for onward stop," David replied. He helped Malia out of the car, shook her hand, and said, "Remember, 7 pm Friday."

Chapter Four
Beaufort at Sunset
(Tuesday, 12 April)

David's car dropped him at the front entrance of the Beaufort Security Tower as the sun began to dip below the horizon. Golden flashes of dying sunlight reflected off the Tower, suffusing the surrounding lawns. From a distance the Beaufort Tower—the headquarters of the Antifan Defense Forces that protected the Diversity Justice Republic from its enemies domestic and foreign—resembled the many glass towers that dominated the postwar Anacosta skyline. But it stood on the outskirts of downtown, with ample setback for security, a view of the Potowmack River, and four concentric security gates that controlled access even before one reached the grassy lawn in front of the Tower. The massive "Antifan Victory at Charlottesville (2054)" statue dominated the lawn, with a muscled soldier waving a chain above his head like a lasso.

Inside the lobby was a high atrium and a high desk behind which the guards intimidated the few voluntary visitors. Electronic implants on the armband and behind his ear confirmed his status automatically. In any case, he was senior enough to be well known, and the guards nearest his path saluted as he strode by. Large metal letters attached above the desk read "Protecting Diversity With Strength," or as David and his team joked, "the Fist of Diversity."

"Good evening, Renzi, Meltzer," said David. It was a point of pride—for him and for the relatively junior officers themselves—that he knew the names of most of the front desk officers, and when he recognized a new face, he would introduce himself. Sometimes relatively junior but bold officers sought him out for advice. David was not above poaching some of the better ones for his own crew, after a decent interval of course.

Unlike in the Knowledge Tower—the intellectual heart of the Diversity Revolution—with its suave, well-dressed, but feckless bureaucrats, the Beaufort Security Tower swarmed with black leather-clad officers. Each wore an electronic pistol on one hip that was programmed to be shot only by the authorized bearer. On their other hip always rested a ceremonial loop of chain metal that commemorated the Antifans' early days as a righteous mob punishing the far right and the heretical.

One did not wear it during an enforcement action, however, lest criminals grab onto it and pull the officer down. On the jacket's left chest were a series of colored bars and symbols that told the initiated in which divisions the bearer had served, where he served now, and where he had earned special honors.

David's current assignment was the Knowledge Crime Unit where he was the acting Chief Commander, but he had also served commendably in the Hate Crimes/ Civil Rights and Transportation Divisions. He had won a slew of decorations, most prominently the white skull (killing under threat, with threat somewhat liberally defined); the red X (for direct elimination of a fascist cell) and the yellow lightning bolt (valor under fire, when he stopped a train full of armed refugees from escaping into the Interior and returned fire; none of the refugees survived). Recently he had found himself not wanting to dwell much on these awards; he wore the symbols as ordinary people wear their socks, without scrutiny.

The Knowledge Crimes Unit was on the tenth floor with a view of the atrium on one side, and the Potowmack River on another, and featured a large raised floor divided into cubicles.

Waiting in the middle of the Unit was Brian Walters, SC 185, the green-eyed officer who was David's deputy. "Director Ferraro wants to see you, sir, to hear about today's operation." Walters gave him the rundown on the interrogation of MacMillan, who after being fed lunch had been willing to reveal all on the various knowledge criminals and sympathizers at Hillary Clinton University, including a Christian proselytizer and a defamer of President Avadaughter.

"That was easier than I thought it would be," said David. "Really, that was all the encouragement he needed? Lunch? Our lunch?"

Walters hesitated. "Well, we needed to bring it up after he ate it so he was covered in his own puke. Then we left him alone for a few minutes and when we came back, he started babbling."

David frowned. With someone as feeble as MacMillan, they could have started more gently. But you never knew—sometimes weak characters gained fortitude in opposing more civilized interrogators. Nor had he been here to supervise—he'd dashed off to the Depository—and Walters was very effective, if overly impatient, in eliciting information from prisoners.

"I'm sorry, sir, if I had known you would have preferred a different approach, I would have waited on your return."

"No, that's all right. If it worked, it worked. I trust your judgment," David said, and Walters smiled, but not too broadly because David still looked slightly troubled. He handed David the draft report, which David skimmed quickly.

In five minutes, David was entering the executive suite of Director Ferraro, SC 300. The secretaries had gone home, and the guard recognized David and waved him onward.

"Sir?"

Director Victor Ferraro turned around from the late sunset Potowmack view. "Harris, come in. Please sit down." The Director was a burly 43-year veteran of the Antifan Defense Forces, with service dating from before the Diversity Civil War. He was notorious for his tattoos, particularly one of a faded red spider across his forehead. At the sideboard, he poured each of them a whiskey and then sat down heavily. "Excellent work today, Harris."

"Thank you, sir." David was briefly disturbed by the thought of the humiliated MacMillan deep below in the holding block, probably blind without his glasses, and then was angry—why these scruples, why now, after all these years of vigorous prosecution of the enemies of the Diversity Justice Republic. Nothing unusual had happened today. Get ahold of yourself, man.

"You have some good people on your team, David. I like that Walters fellow—very dedicated. And who's the Asian guy, the one with the purple streak in his hair?"

"That's Conor Chung, sir. He came over to us from the Hate Crimes Division last year." Ferraro had an eye for young men. David had heard of the parties at his house but had never been invited, which was probably a good thing.

"Very tough, that Chung. Was he with you this morning?"

"Yes, sir. Last night we got an urgent alert from the Knowledge Tower that an unauthorized person was seeking to enter the Depository. They had a last-minute application in the system from the librarian that had not been vetted by the usual channels. I had Walters show up early enough this morning to secure the area and send the usual guard home. We waited until the suspect showed up, badged in, and started reading so that we could catch him in the act, so it was around 10:30 when we arrived."

"I don't understand why there was this last-minute application. Doesn't it take weeks for a researcher to get permission to use that place? And why anyone bothers to go these days at all, I don't understand either."

"Apparently he showed up unannounced. There's only one librarian there and she became flustered. She couldn't find any request in her system, so she went out to the main desk and there was a paper application MacMillan had sent in a few days earlier. The guard hadn't bothered to give it to the librarian—he's fired now, by the way. So when the librarian put in the request, it was late in the day but urgent, so the Knowledge Tower team tracked it immediately, and found out that MacMillan had failed his reinvestigation and was in the process of being fired."

Ferraro drew a slow whistle between his teeth. "Well that was a close call. I'm glad the Knowledge Tower is capable of doing something useful other than drinking in EcoBars.

"You might say the system worked, but it didn't, since he accessed the books without the permission anyway, right?"

"Yes, I'm afraid so. However, it does give us hard evidence that he committed anti-

diverse internal propagandizing, namely the crime of reading the books. Fortunately, he won't be in a position to share whatever he learned this morning because we apprehended him so quickly."

"Why did that librarian not send him away when he showed up? She couldn't just tell him that he'd have to wait for permission?"

"She fell for his story about needing to do a rush job for *Diversity Scholarship*—that's a really big journal they love over at the Knowledge Tower. He had all the right credentials. She didn't catch the red flags—the rush, the paper application. I consider it a stupid but honest mistake."

"Did you interview her?"

"Yes, sir, I did a preliminary interview this afternoon. I went back to the Depository and interrogated her. I'll transcribe my notes before I go home tonight and send it to you."

"What's she like?"

"The librarian? Early thirties, kind of mousy, but you expect that in a librarian. Not dumb, but could have easily fallen for a guy with a good story, a higher Social Credit score and the right credentials. Not fallen in a sexual kind of way, just not thinking clearly."

"So were you interrogating her yourself? Did it get hot and heavy? Good opportunity." The man really is insufferable, thought David, but it wasn't implausible given normal Antifan business practices. "Not my type," he told Ferraro.

"But sir, that does remind me of something I need to ask you. The Knowledge Tower wants to fire her outright, but I need to continue interviewing her. I think we've got a bigger problem than this one illicit entry. The Tower seems to have been very lax in supervising that place. From what the librarian says, they paid almost no attention to what was going on there, just the kind of situation that a desperate knowledge criminal might have taken advantage of.

"If they fire her, she loses her Social Credit and goes to Ploreville and I'm not sure we could find her out there. With your permission, sir, I'd like to have the Knowledge Tower keep her in place for a few more weeks until we've gotten to the bottom of the issue. And I think gentle interviewing will get what we need. She's a Social Crediteer in good standing and in all her years at the Depository, she has never had a black mark. We can appeal to her civicmindedness."

"Good call," said Ferraro. "That Knowledge Tower is way overdue for cleaning out. I've been itching to do something about that nest of Privilegeers. So yes, tell the Knowledge Tower the librarian stays for now. What's next on the agenda?"

David pulled out the report. "This is from the MacMillan interrogation this afternoon. There are at least several faculty members engaging in suspicious activities. At least one Old Christian proselytizer, another who makes snide remarks about President Avadaughter, and a dean who said something while drunk about the low caliber of some Diverse students at the college. We will be traveling to Clinton University next week to conduct those investigations." He handed the report to Ferraro, who picked up reading glasses and skimmed it.

"Let's not forget the Depository business," Ferraro said. "I agree Clinton is important, but I don't want to waste this opportunity. Can you get me the librarian's deposition in a week?"

"Absolutely, sir. I will send Walters and Chung to Clinton University and personally interview the librarian on Monday."

Ferraro nodded and David rose to leave. As David approached the door, Ferraro called out, "And don't let that librarian become your type either. Remember you're in control here."

"Yes, sir. Thank you. Good night." David thought, 'He may be insufferable, but he's no fool. I will have to be careful.'

Ferraro continued reading. He shook his head several times and then said to himself, "That Walters is a tough one. Wouldn't want to cross him. We'll always have a place for a man with the true Antifan spirit." He finished his whiskey and called for his car home.

Back in the Unit, David found Walters poring over a departmental list from Hillary Clinton University at the main table. The surrounding cubicles were empty, so it was safe to talk. He sat down next to Walters, who asked, "How did it go, sir?"

"Very well. First, the Director said he likes your dedication. Second, we've got to be at Clinton on Monday following up on those leads from MacMillan."

"Absolutely, sir." Walters basked in the Director's compliment.

"But I'm going to send you and Chung to Clinton, at least initially, and stay behind here. The Director's priority is to investigate the mismanagement at the Knowledge Tower. I went back to the Depository today to interview the librarian and try to figure out whether we had a bigger problem than just her carelessness or one stupid fascist professor. I think she just made a bad mistake, but she knows a lot that can be useful to the Director and by extension, us. So, I'm going to be spending part of next week at the Depository interviewing her."

"I thought they fired her, sir."

"They *think* they fired her, but they are going to have a surprise in the morning. The Director of the ADF outranks whatever PhD is sitting on the top floor of the Knowledge Tower this month."

"Chief, do you want me to stay behind and conduct the interviews with the librarian? Wouldn't it be easier to secure the cooperation of the Clinton people if you were actually present? I'm not sure they'd take Chung and me that seriously."

David smiled to himself. Walters would certainly go far. Like a moth buzzing around a light, he preferred the assignment closer to the Director's heart. The Clinton people would take Walters and Chung plenty seriously when the pair showed up in full Antifan regalia.

Walters continued, "And I don't think that librarian was completely honest with us, sir. She's clearly sympathetic to the fascist. Don't you think we should call her in here for the questioning, so she takes it seriously?"

David sighed. "That's not the point, Walters. Her sympathies aren't relevant here. She knows a lot that will be helpful to the Director's case and I want to extract that information as politely and as professionally as possible. She is a Social Crediteer and has an otherwise blameless record. I am going to treat her, at least at the start, like a good citizen who wants justice served. I think she's already a little resentful at how the Knowledge Tower treated her, which is a good opening for us. Bringing her in here will frighten her and maybe cause her to clam up.

"Walters, nobody is better than you at close quarters, but you have to distinguish between the criminal and a good citizen who wants to help us. I wouldn't cozy up to the criminal, and I wouldn't abuse the citizen. You've got to keep them straight or you won't get the right results."

Walters fumed silently. He wouldn't have minded roughing up the librarian on his own territory, and making her squeak and cry. David was behaving like a typical sentimental Plore, being too deferential to women and underestimating the fascist threat. He would get burned one day at that rate. Walters watched David disappear into his office to dictate the afternoon's report for Ferraro, thinking to himself that when that moment came, he, Brian Walters, would be ready to step into his place. Hadn't the Director already noticed him?

He then returned to the Clinton University departmental list. Fueled by the Director's approval, he was in no hurry to go home.

Chapter Five
New Missions
(Wednesday, 13 April)

At eight o'clock the next morning, David called Antelides' office. The imperious secretary was quickly cowed by the sight of David's black uniform on the screen, and David almost immediately heard Antelides' "Morning, Commander." She sounded slightly jaunty, as if they were on the same side and together had vanquished the fascist enemy. Time for a surprise.

"Good morning Ms. Antelides. I just wanted to relay some instructions I received from Director Ferraro last night. His office will be communicating with your Director as well.

"The Antifan Defense Forces is requesting that Amalia Jenness be retained as the librarian at the False Knowledge Depository for the time being."

"What?" Antelides brayed. "Why on earth would you leave that dangerous fool in place?"

"You folks left her in place for a long time without what seems like any real supervision. Either she's a dangerous fool, which means you all were irresponsible for leaving her there on her own, or she's not a dangerous fool, which means there's no harm in keeping her in place for now. We want to continue our investigation, which requires continued contact with Ms. Jenness in her current role."

"Can't you just arrest the bitch and squeeze the truth out of her in your jail? I've heard what you can do there."

"That would be counterproductive from an investigative standpoint. We need to find out the full extent of the negligence that permitted this breach of security. That said, we do not expect the investigation to go beyond the malfeasance, if any, of Ms. Jenness and the guard." David never lied to his troops, but lying came easily when it was to a Knowledge Tower functionary.

Antelides deflated somewhat. "Should we send someone else there in the meantime to keep an eye on her?"

"You can," said David, "but I assure you we have the cameras trained on her and she will be under direct and constant Antifan scrutiny." In my bedroom, he thought, more as a private joke than as a statement of intent. "If she is going to commit further knowledge crimes, I think it is more likely she would do it when she thought she was alone than if someone else were present. We'd like to catch her in the act of committing such a crime and not inadvertently implicate someone from your office."

"Good point," said Antelides, brightly. "I think we have a plan!" The last thing she wanted was to subject a valuable employee to the stink of scandal and Antifan surveillance now wafting from the Depository.

"Excellent," said David. "The ADF and Director Ferraro appreciate your cooperation. Would you mind calling Ms. Jenness to let her know that her termination has been temporarily rescinded? Do not give her any indication, however, that she remains under surveillance. We want to encourage her to show her true colors. Can you assist us?"

"Absolutely, Commander," Antelides gushed. "And I want you to know that anytime you are in the vicinity of the Knowledge Tower, I would love to go and have some coffee with you. We can talk about our mutual struggle against the fascist enemy."

David shuddered, wishing he could say, "Sorry, you're too tall for me." Instead he said, "I appreciate the invitation. We'll be in touch. Goodbye."

It was almost 8:30 and time for the Unit's morning meeting. Walters knocked and entered David's office. "Just to let you know, sir, I have printed off the entire roster of Clinton University faculty and done a network analysis of connections between them and Professor MacMillan." His timing virtually ensured that he would walk side-by-side with David into the group meeting, under the eyes of forty Unit members. David was not deceived, but didn't mind. Walters, for all his naked ambition, had earned his share of the spotlight this morning.

"That's tremendous, Walters, I'll look at it first thing after the meeting." They walked out into the general area. Several dozen Antifans on the day shift filled the spaces around the big table and between the cubicle pods and the glass wall along the atrium side.

David scanned the room. On the left his own elite squad, "the Suede Fist." Each squad had a nickname; "suede" was an implicit reference to David's tactical preference for stealth over violence, at least initially. Then the analysts without whose painstaking research it would be impossible to carry out complex investigations. The secretaries and administrators, mostly female, in their black leather vests and skirts or eco-cotton slacks. Night Commander Angela had stayed to hear the morning meeting report. The commander of the other part of the KCU, Damien DeVry, had just come from his own session. Damien's group dealt with publications, music and religion, while David's focused on the universities, visual arts, and libraries.

He liked to try to make eye contact with everyone in that first minute.

"Good morning soldiers, good morning staff," he said. "This has been a very important twenty-four hours. I will relay the details, but let me start with the bottom line this morning. The Knowledge Crime Unit disrupted an infiltration of the

Depository yesterday morning and apprehended a disgraced faculty member from Clinton University, a fascist who was attempting to read prohibited paper books stored there. Thanks to Deputy Commander Walters, the criminal has begun revealing the knowledge corruption on the faculty of Clinton University. We will be pursuing those valuable leads in the coming weeks, and your hard work will be essential to making those leads yield results. We will uproot those who seek to corrupt our youth with capitalist, individualist, and racist ideology." The attendees cheered. "I ask you to keep this strictly confidential within our Unit, so we do not alert the university sector as to our intentions.

"Is there anyone here who cannot be trusted with a secret that will be key to our victory? Can you all keep this secret entrusted to us by the Director?" The Unit erupted with "Yes we can! Yes we can! Yes we can!" and "Si se puede, si se puede!"

David leaned forward, placing his palms on the short podium at the end of the table. "The Director suspects that the infiltration of the Depository was no accident. The Knowledge Tower has been too casual with security for several years. Director Ferraro has asked us to investigate possible malfeasance by the Tower in the management of knowledge security. At this point, they believe the investigation is centered on the lone librarian and the guard, but the Director urges us to see this through to senior administrators and not allow employees to be singled out unfairly for the malfeasance of their superiors.

"What does this have to do with the Antifan Defense Forces, you ask? Why must we act against the Knowledge Tower?

"You know the heart of the Diversity Revolution lives here among the Antifan Defense Forces. Perhaps we did not theorize brilliantly about the evils of capitalism or the destruction of the earth, or the yearning of oppressed peoples of color and gender identity to live free. But without us, without our willingness to lay down our lives, without our weapons and our fists, there would have been no Diversity Revolution. The fascists would have won the civil wars and our thinkers would have been in jail or worse. Our troops sacrificed and risked the most to achieve victory, so it will always be dearest to us. And we were charged with the responsibility of keeping the other Towers honest.

"What happens to revolutions when the spark is not kept alive? The timeservers and the bureaucrats take over. They forget the ideals and they care more about their Social Credit scores and their vacations. The ideology drifts. Principles are sacrificed to comfortable lifestyles. And they forget to guard the ramparts. So rot sets in, as we are seeing in some of our most prestigious universities and other government institutions...."

"F—k the Knowledge Tower!" shouted an overexcited member of the squad. David raised his hand in caution.

"Remember," he said, "We are not seeking to destroy the Knowledge Tower. We want to protect and reform the Diversity Revolution. We need the Knowledge Tower to carry forward the Revolution. But if we see the enemy boring at the Tower from within, we, the Antifan Defense Forces, have the willpower, passion, and yes, the Fist, to strike at him. We have now been presented with evidence of rot, and we have the opportunity to lash out and regain the momentum. You—we—will determine the outcome of the Revolution. It has been thirty-four years since the Diversity Justice Republic was established, and whether we last another thirty-four, or another thousand, is our decision to make."

He paused and relaxed. "And now let me give you more details about yesterday's operation." The audience was mesmerized.

Afterward, Damien and Angela came over to congratulate him on his inspiring speech. David thanked them, but he was privately surprised he had let loose like that. The words had spilled out of him almost automatically, like on an assembly line. And it wouldn't be terrible if some indirect rumors reached the Knowledge Tower—nothing that could be immediately proven let alone raised with Director Ferraro—but enough to rattle the suits in the EcoBars.

David tapped Walters gently on the shoulder. "Walters, let's look at that spreadsheet."

They sat in David's office, smaller than it could have been had he pressed his bureaucratic advantage. On a small credenza stood awards and gifts from visitors—a miniature shield from the Hungarian police, bookends from China, a Canadian statuette of Justice, but they were scattered, not arranged carefully to impress visitors. A dated photograph in a cheap wooden frame showed him standing with Ferraro's predecessor.

Nor was it the fashion for Antifan commanders to have family photos in their offices, "better to compartmentalize," David knew. His mother would not want her photograph anywhere in this building. After all, had she not been married to one of the fascists that David had just condemned? David generally tried not to think about it, at least not while at Beaufort.

On the wall was a retro Soviet-style poster of a red fist smashing into a white background, with the words "Are You the Fist?" It was a birthday gift from his former girlfriend, the statuesque former Antifan Dianne Abimbala. Overall, the office gave the impression of a straightforward place where a man not inclined to airs simply did his job.

David first looked at a diagram Walters had sketched online with one of the analysts. MacMillan was at the center, and spikes led out to possible ideological allies. Walters went through each of them—the Christian, the racist drunk, the mocker of Avadaughter, the one who had praised the incentives capitalism had given people to excel, the teller of a joke about transgender people, the Muslim who prayed five times a day but did not belong to the local MED Mosque. "It would be OK if his religion wasn't so separate from the collective," mused David. Walters also mentioned a history professor who was reputed to own a firearm, which had been outlawed back in 2055 for almost anyone not serving in the Antifan forces. That might just turn out to be a rumor, since it really was improbable that any private citizen would own a firearm given the risk of a mandatory death penalty by firing squad on conviction.

David had to admit the data Walters had amassed in a single night was indeed impressive. "This is terrific, Walters. I'm wondering if Monday is too soon to show up at Clinton University. We really need to master this data first."

"I can be here all weekend, chief, it would be my loyalty and honor." David liked hearing the classic Antifan phrase of willingness to undertake a mission. Walters had so much going for him, it was hard not to wish him well even as you wished he'd develop some polish. It would also help if Walters would stop visiting the brothel in the basement of Beaufort—that was for younger officers who needed to avoid unwise liaisons outside the building. What was Walters now, almost his own age? Was it so hard to find a girlfriend if you were a ruggedly handsome six foot three with abs of steel and a great Social Credit score? He'd mention it later.

"How about you and Chung go on Tuesday and stay through Friday? You can take a fleet helicopter each way and save some time."

David really enjoyed setting up investigations and watching arrogant elites squirm wondering how much the Antifans knew about them. It was kind of a shame he wasn't going to be participating in this one, but he wanted to protect Malia while pursuing the Director's pet mission.

"Let's seed the list of interviews with some faculty members we don't suspect—at this point—and some we know to be complete drones," he said. 'Drones' was a semi-ironic term used among Antifans for those who parroted the Diversity line perfectly. But if it was a semi-ironic term, it was also by definition a semi–non ironic term.

David knew that the guilty, or those who would recall or worry about their own ideological faux pas, would set off armband sensors that tracked their physiological stress reactions, much as the old-fashioned polygraphs had. The modern versions were much better at distinguishing between stress at interaction with Antifans and actual falsehoods, since artificial intelligence could sort the physiological data with known falsehoods stored in the suspect's brain.

David stood up, stretching. It was nearly eleven. "Are you planning to interrogate MacMillan this afternoon?" he asked Walters, who said, "Yes, chief."

"Just dig into some of the nuggets he gave you yesterday and see how he reacts when you share some of this information you've gotten since yesterday," said David. "No need for rough handling today. I think you've softened him enough for now.

"And bring him his glasses. He might show some gratitude for that, if you don't mind a random act of kindness."

What does that mean, Walters thought as they assembled at the conference table with the others for the next meeting, was that a dig? Like he wasn't a good guy? He couldn't outwardly show his irritation with Commander Harris, not yet, but he was confident the time would soon come when he would no longer have to defer to him.

Chapter Six
Happy Funeral
(Wednesday/Thursday, 13-14 April)

Around mid-morning on Wednesday, yet another jet plane was approaching Anacosta, formerly Washington, DC. It would shortly land at Obama National Airport after a three-hour journey from the DJR's California-Pacific coast. All the passengers had Social Credit scores of 150 or higher, which permitted them to travel by air under the Great Green Doctrine.

Had the jaded travelers bothered to look out of the window, they would have seen a city virtually unrecognizable to anyone fifty years earlier. Anacosta, as befitting the seat of a government dedicated to preserving the environment, bristled with giant glass columns of solar-fueled skyscrapers, abiding by the principle that humanity should retreat and take up as little space as possible. Millions of people had been herded into Anacosta and its surrounding areas during and after the Great Diversity War, and adequate housing supplies required upward building. One could still glimpse between the towers the obelisk of the now-Black Lives Matter Monument and the Lincoln Memorial, and the round Navesky Memorial, re-named for the first President of the DJR, adjoining the Tidal Basin.

Anchoring Anacosta were the four great eighty-story Towers in which were concentrated the political, economic, social, and security power of the Diversity Justice Republic. In the far northwest of the City, near Diverse American University, was of course Beaufort. To the southwest, where the waterfront lay, was the Knowledge Tower, the guardian of the intellectual and moral heritage of the DJR. This Tower oversaw the Great Virtual Network on which all permitted learning resided, education curricula, museums, the arts, and the official Mother Earth Diversity religion, including the privilege of naming new saints.

To the northeast, the Economic Tower handled foreign affairs, trade and the borderland Industrial Zones to which most farming and manufacturing were relegated. All of its senior officers were required to be fluent in Mandarin. To the southeast, near L'Enfant Plaza, sat the Social Tower that administered health care, including euthanasia and abortion, and processed monthly income payments, called Universal Basic Income, or UBI, to working Plores, and to Social Crediteers in accordance with their credit scores.

Equidistant from all the towers was the White Black House, from which President Avadaughter reigned. The White Black House was striped black and white, in recognition of the sacrifice of African-Americans and other non-white people in its construction.

Giant enclosed glass bridges ran up and down the Potowmack River, connecting Virginia with the City. Trains and buses brought the Suburbans, more commonly known as Deplorables, or Plores, to the Virginia end of the bridges, where they crossed into Anacosta to work at jobs serving Social Credit citizens. If necessary, steel walls could be brought down at each end of the tunnels to prevent unauthorized influxes (no one dared say "mobs") from entering the city, or admittedly, leaving it. This had only happened once, in 2061, just after the civil war, when the defeated Red Plores rioted against the policy of enforced separation. The steel doors had crushed several dozen unruly Plores on several bridges, and then the protests subsided, as everyone was tired of decades of war. The final peace treaty, known as the Treaty of the Red and the Blue, authorized segregation of Plores but in return, Plores were exempt from the Social Credit system, and they enjoyed somewhat more liberty in their personal lives than did many Social Crediteers. They did not wear the electronic armbands of the Social Crediteers, nor were they chipped with a tracker.

"Look, Daddy, look at all the people crossing the river!" said a pigtailed six-year old girl on her first airplane trip.

Her father, engrossed in his handphone, which was normally stowed in his armband, did not look. "Yes, those are Plores going to work."

"What kind of Social Credit scores do THEY have?"

The father, SC 210, now irritated by the interruption, retorted, "They don't have any Social Credit at all, and that's why they have to live in Virginia and come to work every day to make a living. They don't move society forward the way we do." The plane then turned steeply south toward the airport as the small girl peered out the window at the dots moving through the glass tunnels.

If the airplane had continued east, the little girl would have seen the green expanse of the old Washington Mall, now the Anacosta Mall, still flanked by museums. Dwarfing all of them was the gigantic National Diversity Museum, built in 2062 and incorporating the African-American, Latinx, American Indian, American History, and Asian-American Museum collections. The authorities had shuttered the Holocaust Museum in 2070, since genocide against technically white people, even at the hands of admitted fascists, posed complicated ideological challenges that were better pushed aside. The severing of relations with the oppressive Jewish State of Israel in 2065, despite the anguished cries of DJR Jewish Blues, had made it easier to close that museum altogether several years later.

A few blocks south of the museums lay the Depository. As Malia left the

Depository that Wednesday morning for the funeral of the exalted functionary, she rejoiced in a beautiful spring day. Cherry and pear blossoms mixed with tender green leaves. She boarded a crowded driver-less Diversity Bus that would eventually deposit her at the National Diversity Cathedral. Having experienced a self-driving car for the first time yesterday, Malia found it harder than usual to board the Diversity Bus today.

The bus threaded through half-empty streets at the bottom of the canyons created by the great glass towers. Most of the buildings, especially in the downtown area, were offices and apartment towers. The few stores sold snacks, coffee, and toiletries or other items you might require at a moment's notice. Since the 2020's, when the coronavirus pandemic had dealt them a dizzying blow, most brick and mortar businesses had given way to the more efficient all-in-one place Diversity Warehouse. Who had time to browse in stores under socialism? You never needed to worry about your size when shopping for clothes because the Warehouse kept your sizes current, based on electronic sensing photographs taken of you constantly on the street or in your apartment building lobby, and would send you exactly which size you needed, even if you thought you really were thinner.

At the cathedral where the steps loomed above her, the signage took a moment to digest, as various lines existed for 200 and above, 150 and above, and 100 and above. Black cars discharged streams of privileged mourners, who all seemed to know each other. She found "99 and below," and snaked her way into the lower end of the cathedral with the other civil servants clearly looking for a credit-taking opportunity. She swiped her armband at the reader.

At the door, an elderly usher handed her the required pink pussy hat, which she knew to refuse politely. It was widely known that the iconic wool hats often were lice-ridden, but few worshipers felt confident enough to reject one, especially when the usher brayed, as he did now, "Are you too good for the Diversity Pussy hat? The hat of our sacrifice?"

Malia pretended to look shocked, as she pulled out her own pink wool hat. "Not at all!" she said. "This is the hat I always wear. It was knitted for me by a dear friend, who was dying of a dreadful disease, and he urged me to wear this at church to remember his struggles for equality." Without saying so, she conjured up a version of a sexually promiscuous young man who paid the ultimate price for his hard-won sexual freedom, a heroic figure to the Diversity universe, and completely imaginary. She had knitted the hat herself, clumsily.

The usher looked briefly abashed. "Of course, you must wear your own hat. I apologize for my abruptness. I salute your brave friend," and Malia took the program and slipped past him into the rear pews reserved for the ordinary Social Credit folks.

The program displayed a photograph of a smiling black man and underneath:

CELEBRATION OF THE LIFE OF MARTIN UBUNTU JOHNSON

THIRD COUNCILOR JUDGE ON THE SUPREME ADVISORY
COURT TO THE PRESIDENCY

HERO OF THE DIVERSITY STRUGGLES

(2010-2089)

MUSIC BY THE NEW WOMAN CHOIR

And a quotation from the official Mother Earth Diversity (MED) Bible:

"And you who loves the Earth loves the People who live by the bounty of the Earth, the people of all colors, sexual orientations and identities, and immigration status, and your true faith shall be in the Earth that sustains you."—*Book of Greta*, Chapter 3 Verse 16

The grieving widow came down the aisle, followed by several grown daughters and then the eight surviving Councilor judges. They sat in the front pews. President Avadaughter for security reasons sat in a grand box behind a sheer curtain. Her photo was all over town in case citizens sought reassurance, an elderly heroine of the Diversity Civil Wars with her trademark blonde bob. It was rumored she was in ill health. Gossips who claimed that she had fainted entering a van after last year's Coronavirus Liberation Day parade had subsequently recanted at Beaufort.

The soloists of the New Woman Choir, bulky but resplendent in white gowns showing their artificial cleavage, took their places before the hundred altos and contraltos. Their strong tenors filled the cathedral. Malia must have dropped off to sleep, for when she awoke, the rector was shouting, "When the first President of the Republic needed advice on the constitutionality of the rescue of children from fascist parents, Martin was there. He provided the justification for the legislation, which the Supreme Advisory Court ratified, and thousands of children were saved for Diversity. What more can we say about such a man?"

What more, indeed, thought Malia, who remembered, with a stabbing pain that came at such times, that her daughter had been "rescued" too. She looked around quickly to see whether her distress was noticeable, but most of her fellow low Social Crediteers were busy sneaking glances at their armband phones. If he noticed them, the old usher probably thought her brimming tears were genuinely for the great Councilor.

The New Woman choir then sang the classic MED Church hymn, "In Diversity We Are One."

She was glad when the funeral ended and she could escape into the fresh air for a long walk back to the Depository. As she was approaching the sidewalk, she heard a familiar voice behind her. "Malia! Malia! Wait a sec!" If Malia had a friend, it was Fern Potts, 75, with whom it was convenient to attend concerts and eat Mexican food on a Saturday night, but she kept her counsel and confided few secrets to Fern, let alone her heresies.

"I was sitting to your left," Fern said, "but I didn't want to bother you. You seemed upset. Did you know the Councilor at all?" She fell into step beside Malia, even though Malia knew Fern's workplace, at the Bureau of Universal Income, lay in the opposite direction.

"No, of course not," Malia replied. "It's just kind of sad that we are losing the stars of that great first generation."

"Uh-huh," Fern said, not entirely convinced. "Are you going to the book club on Friday night?"

"Not sure," Malia replied. "I haven't finished the book yet." And how could she, when she was secretly spending her waking hours on de Tocqueville's *Democracy in America* back in the office?

"You should try to go. The cute guy might show up."

"No, I can't now. I'll be going to a fancy restaurant with a handsome Antifan commander."

Fern laughed, "Malia, you sure have a sense of humor." But she sobered up quickly when Malia responded, "No, I'm not kidding, but it was a tough road getting to that point." She explained, all the while wondering whether David was listening to their conversation from Beaufort courtesy of her armband, but unable to keep yesterday's momentous events to herself.

"Wow, that's crazy all right," said Fern. "I'm so glad you might get to keep your job and not have to leave the City. What does he look like?"

"Medium to tall, obviously very fit, blond, gray eyes. Really smart and I think he even has a sense of humor. A few years older than me, I guess."

"And a 240," Fern marveled. "How on earth do you get 240 Social Credit points?"

"He told me you get 220 just for being an Antifan commander, which is really demanding work. He says he's basically on call 24-7. I think the other 20 points are for Healthy Eating. Even Amba-mam Antelides, the boss who just fired me, or thinks she fired me, would only have 140 without the transgender bump."

"Hey, do you guys need a chaperone Friday night? It could get a little wild. You might need a dependable sidekick with a good appetite."

"Oh Fern, I wish. Let's see how this goes. I'll be satisfied if I just keep the job after the mess yesterday. At least David tells me that they are treating the professor well and he thanked me for returning the glasses that were broken—it's not as if the professor hurt anyone." She thought aloud, 'The professor kept shouting, all I want is to read the truth.'"

"What?"

"All I want is to read the truth."

"He sounds like he was crazy."

Malia said, "He was crazy, but he wasn't necessarily wrong. I've never seen anyone in the reading room who was so hungry for the books that he looked as if he were gobbling them up."

She remembered her manners. "How has your week been?"

"Nothing like yours. I've processed about two hundred applications for UBI, so now lots of Plore families can buy beer and chips, but some bad news as well. My aunt fell and broke her hip and is in the hospital."

"Oh no!" Fern's elderly aunt was her sole living relative and Fern visited her every weekend in the old age home in southeast Anacosta, across from the Plore casino at National Harbor. Fern's aunt was a veteran of the Diversity Wars, having hidden Antifan soldiers and activists in her home in western Virginia and enabled them to escape toward the coast. When the war ended, Fern's aunt worked briefly in one of the new manufacturing complexes along the border as a secretary to the general manager and raised Fern there, but retired in the City where the amenities she prized such as high culture, gourmet coffee shops, and likeminded progressives were more plentiful.

Malia had accompanied Fern on one or two visits, half-listening to the old lady's reminiscences about the war and the challenges of living in the primitive border area. "The supremacists would raid us every once in a while. We could never be sure the Plores in the factory could be trusted. Sometimes they would run off after the supremacists. We took away their guns, but it was harder to take away their thoughts, insofar they had any—remarkably stupid people—it was Jesus this and Jesus that and what passed for culture was a six pack of beer...."

"How long will she be there?" Malia asked, mostly out of politeness.

"They don't know. They aren't saying very much. She's now 92, so I guess they have to figure out what makes sense." Abundant health care was guaranteed to the whole population, and celebrated, but in practice resources were rationed, and a complex formula involving age and Social Credit determined the extent to which the National Diversity Health Service would treat complicated cases like broken hips.

"I hope they can help her," Malia said.

"Thanks, Malia. So I guess we won't be seeing you at the book club this week. I'll let you know whether the new guy shows up, but it seems like you've got something better now."

"Too early," Malia said. "I have no idea how this will go."

"Eat extra for me then," said Fern, "at least that's something under your control."

It was lunchtime on Thursday. Malia was still ebullient at her reinstatement and Antelides' obvious resentment in the phone call yesterday, and she decided to capitalize on the positive momentum and buy herself a new outfit for dinner with David. She grabbed a bag of old clothes that she had brought into work that morning, and that she would trade in at the store, hoping it would cover the carbon expense of a brand-new outfit.

The bureaucrat had clearly been furious over having to rescind her decision made so arrogantly on Tuesday.

"You'd better watch yourself," Antelides sneered at her. "One false step and you'll be at Beaufort. Commander Harris is a personal friend of mine." Despite David's warning, Antelides had not been able to resist making the now empty threat.

After checking her mail, Malia had enjoyed a morning of leisurely coffee drinking and reading *Democracy in America*, not just skimming here and there and dashing down notes in fear that the camera was tracking her movements. Paul Johnson's blocklike *History of America* sat nearby. She wondered whether she would be given enough time in the Depository to finish a thousand-page volume. She signed for a delivery of confiscated books from prisoners.

The mid-April day was sunny and slightly cool, a good day for a lunchtime stroll. Fern had agreed to meet her at the Eco-Wear Shoppe but hadn't arrived yet. A sign outside the door proclaimed it "Open to All," meaning even Plores could shop there. Malia entered the store, which was characterized by plain walls, overstuffed racks and a large vision statement sign that proclaimed "Vintage and Recycled Wear for the Woke Tomorrow. Save Mother Earth!" Before shopping, Malia turned in her three sweaters and a frayed nightgown at the counter to a sullen middle-aged Plore woman who handed her a receipt entitling her to $34.98 in carbon offsets for new clothes. She would pay a steep rate for clothing costing any more than that, but she was prepared to do so, marching immediately to the back corner where the new clothes could be found—this date was too important to wear someone else's castoffs.

Fern stopped her from browsing through a rack of plain black dresses. "No way!" she said. "You've got to show a little personality now. You don't always have to hide behind dark colors." In the end, they compromised on a dark blue/light brown set of flowing harem pants and a flowing blue-patterned top. "You can carry that off well," said the chubby Fern. "But I would look like a pile of leaves." To thank Fern, Malia treated her to lunch from a food truck. They ordered vegetable burritos available to under-100s and sat on a low cement wall in the sun.

"So, what happens now with the job?" Fern asked. "Are you really back in place, or is it just temporary?"

"Honestly, I'm not sure," Malia said. "The investigation isn't over. David is going to be coming over to the Depository on Monday to ask more questions, and I don't think it's to be friendly. I got the impression he's got bigger fish to fry than the Depository. I'll tell him whatever I know, but really, I don't know much. I'm so low-level that I don't even know the Knowledge Tower gossip." She looked quickly behind them, but no one was sitting on the grassy mound.

"Is he allowed to go on dates with you at the same time he's investigating you?"

Malia frowned, "I don't know. Maybe he's not investigating 'me.' The original reason for going out to dinner was to help me move forward after the disaster the other day when I was sure I would be fired, but that's kind of moot now, isn't it?" She chewed thoughtfully.

"An Antifan commander can date anyone he wants, I imagine," said Fern. "Have you ever seen the Beaufort Tower?"

"From a distance, yes," said Malia. "But I've never been inside."

"You wouldn't want to. My roommate was dating an Antifan and what goes on in there is really, really scary. Nobody brought there against his will ever walks out of there and just goes home. There are hundreds of punishment cells below the ground. People die all the time in there. And he even said there was a whorehouse that the male officers go to—not with prisoners, but can you imagine! They don't care about feminism there at all."

"Stop it," Malia said abruptly. "I don't want to think about it." A vision of MacMillan's battered face suddenly loomed in front of her. He was languishing in one of those dark cells right now as she lingered in the sunshine with her lunch. David walked in and out of the Beaufort Tower every day, a senior and respected commander. If any of this was true, and most of it probably was, he knew it and accepted it. It was too much to process right now.

"I'm sorry," Fern apologized, surprised at Malia's dismay. "My roommate said her boyfriend also spoke a lot of nonsense. From everything you said, this David is a real gentleman and I hope I get to meet him. We'll miss you at the book club tomorrow."

As she walked back to the office, Malia's buoyancy had deflated, but she still thought to herself, "We have a lot of enemies. If we didn't deal with them strongly, the whole Republic would be threatened by the white supremacists. If you didn't do anything wrong, you'll never be taken to that Tower." Yet when she reentered her office, she sat down to read the forbidden works by those the Republic identified as those very supremacists, or at least supporters of them. But she would not yet acknowledge the cognitive dissonance.

Chapter Seven

Business Matters

(Friday, 15 April)

"...Antifa is an idea, not an organization..."
—Former President Joe Biden, first presidential debate, 2020.

David met a prospective squad member in the cafeteria for lunch. The young man impressed him—soft-spoken but well spoken, firm handshake, a steady but not fixed gaze—and was eager to escape to a unit where he would have greater challenges. Even at a busy time, David was not going to pass up an opportunity to recruit a good team member. "Wait one month," he told Dominic. "Then I'd like you to respond to a vacancy notice in the bulletin. That's for you." The candidate nodded, and said, "I'll gladly wait. There's no unit I'd rather work in than yours." They parted with the Antifan crossed-hands on chest farewell and David thought to himself as he went back upstairs, "That was time well spent." It didn't hurt that the young man was black—David had to keep up respectable Diversity numbers in his squad, if only to avoid HR interference—but he didn't like seeing solid young officers underemployed anywhere.

Back in the unit, David looked at the electronic locator board. Two squad members were participating in an arrest on behalf of a shorthanded group in the Cyber Crime Unit. He noted that Walters was "IW," or "Interrogation Wing."

"Is Walters down with MacMillan?" he asked Vanessa, the lead secretary.

"Yes, sir, he went about an hour ago."

"Do you know why these glasses are here? They were supposed to go down to MacMillan this morning." The repair shop had fixed them overnight.

"I'll have someone take them downstairs," Vanessa offered.

"Never mind, I'll take them myself." It was bad form to check up on his own deputy without advance warning, but he wanted to see what Walters was up to downstairs. He had to admit that he didn't trust his deputy's temper, and his not taking the glasses, the offering of which would have been an obvious goodwill gambit, was not reassuring to David. "It's not that he's a psychopath," he had told a colleague, "but he wouldn't necessarily see anything wrong with being one."

He changed his own status to IW, and took the elevator down to the main floor, then went over to a separate elevator bank and went down another six stories after waving the armband over the sensor. When he exited, the Antifan on duty saluted. "Deputy Commander Walters?" he asked. The duty officer said, "Room L, sir."

He slipped into the adjacent observation room for the L room. Karlmarx, wearing the open black blazer of the analyst corps, with a blue button-down shirt and no tie, looked up, startled. He had been taking notes on the electronic workscreen. David placed his finger to his lips, and sat down next to the analyst. "How's it going?" he asked *sotto voce*. You could talk in a loud whisper without being heard in the interrogation room.

"He's being pretty cooperative, Commander," said Karlmarx in a hushed voice. "But he doesn't seem to know all the characters we're running by him, especially if they're not in his department. It's hard to tell whether he's lying or he just isn't that socially connected."

Interrogation Room L was identical to all the others on the floor. Several chairs occupied a corner near the door and a bathroom. At the interior end of the room sat a long table with another chair behind it facing the door, and in the middle of the room was a plastic chair. Beilin and Cheysa sat in the corner chairs. Beilin was a large, balding man inclined to fleshiness; Cheysa a young black woman with a soft face, large doe-like eyes and long braids wrapped around in a high bun atop her head. Walters had placed his folders on the table, and was standing over MacMillan, who was hunched over in the chair, wearing the green paper prison pajamas. It didn't take much to rip those, so it was in the interest of the prisoner not to give an excuse to his interrogators to damage them.

"So tell me about Luis Melendez," said Walters. "He's a professor of Spanish literature, right?"

"I've been in some faculty meetings with him," MacMillan offered.

"Shut up—is that the question I asked you?"

"No, sir."

"So, who is Luis Melendez?"

"He's a full professor of Spanish literature at Clinton."

"Sir," instructed Walters.

"Sir," MacMillan repeated.

"That's better. Have you interacted with him at all, you fascist?"

"Yes, sir, we both served on the Faculty Senate committee on environmental progress in the 2087-2088 academic year."

"What can you tell me about him? Did he say anything traitorous or 'ist?'" The word 'ist' could mean racist, sexist, homophobic, anti-transgender, or whatever the interrogator wanted it to mean. Everyone knew what "ist" meant—politically useful ammunition.

"Once he commented on the looks of the Earth Theology professor who was chairing the committee. He said she was a dog, but his dog was better looking. He said it was hard to take the committee work seriously as long as a woman was chairing it."

Walters looked up at the window, which was a signal for Karlmarx to make sure those remarkable juicy heresies were recorded. If the remarks were true, or even if they weren't, Melendez was now in the target sights. Walters stood over MacMillan, who was staring downward and would not have tracked the glance. He followed up with questions about when and where he had made that remark to MacMillan. "Now it's kind of interesting that your Melendez would have even bothered noticing a woman's looks, given that he's gay."

"Sir, that's what he said. But he was very lookist. He told me I should lose weight."

"Well, he was right there. You look like a pig, with those fat rolls around your middle. I'm glad they're covered up now with your fine green suit. And that you've come to the Beaufort Spa for some conditioning." Walters laughed snidely as Beilin and Cheysa echoed him in the corner.

"Are you thirsty?" Walters asked solicitously.

"Yes, sir, if you don't mind."

"Well, I do mind—we were doing so well here and now you're forcing us to interrupt the proceedings. But I'm a humane man, and I'd rather you were focusing on the questions than on your thirst. Conroy, would you kindly bring in some water for our distinguished professor?"

Cheysa went into the adjoining toilet and returned with a dog dish. In response to Walters' crooked finger, she placed it on the floor halfway between MacMillan's chair and the table.

"You may drink," said Walters, faux casually.

MacMillan awoke from his semi-stupor and looked up at Walters. David registered the sudden flash of anger on the professor's face. This was a huge comedown for an Associate Professor of Diversity History at Clinton University. Only two weeks ago, MacMillan had been presiding over a lecture hall of respectful sophomores, and later that day Dean Sizemore presented him with the unwelcome news that he had failed a second reinvestigation, necessitating termination from the faculty. His wife, the Chief Human Resources Administrator, was told that her job would be terminated as well even though her behavior had been impeccable and her own reinvestigation flawless. The family would be allowed to disappear quietly, and Sizemore assured them that the University would help them find employment in the City—"you aren't the first faculty member this has happened to, how unfortunate"— but how he would find an appropriate position after the failed reinvestigation and then how he would survive, with his wife and two sons, on the salary of a less prestigious position, was unknown. His wife partly solved her dilemma by her stated intention to seek a divorce, which would allow her to keep her job and maintain a somewhat humbler home near the university.

Up against the wall, thought MacMillan, so how can I blame her? But she did not seem particularly anguished by her decision, upbraiding him once again for having several paper books in their basement, acquired from Earth Mother-knew where.

The boys—one six, the other eight—cried in their rooms. He had no idea that when he left Clinton for one last day or two of illicit reading that he might never see them again. Even as he suffered in the basement of Beaufort Tower, the movers were pulling up to the house and emptying it, only a day after Antifan investigators had rampaged through it, emerging triumphantly with the books. No forwarding address would be provided to the prisoner.

It was all coming to a head in this interrogation cell in the basement of the gleaming glass tower.

Now Walters was pointing to the dog dish, which to the half-blinded MacMillan was a silver haze on the floor. David squared his shoulders and leaned back, curious to see what would happen next. He personally would not have tested an already broken criminal in this manner, but he had to admit that Walters' relentless reminder of the professor's humiliation and subjugation to his interrogators was textbook Antifan. There were other rooms where much harsher physical punishment was meted out. MacMillan could have fared even worse had he been less cooperative.

"No!" shouted MacMillan, and as he rose with his shackled hands outstretched toward Walters, the commander shoved him away with both hands with such force that the professor crumpled against the wall and slid down to the floor. The plastic chair was toppled.

"You wanted a drink, go f---ing drink," said Walters. When he ramped up the physical violence, he suddenly allowed himself to become more verbally subdued. It was like playing a piano—an easy largo or adagio, then a lively vivace tempo. Nothing was said or done randomly in this room. "For Earth's sake, go drink, man." The "man" was almost sympathetic, as if to say, "You are a man; I recognize you are a man. A man needs to drink water."

The room was silent. David was aware of the sidelong glances from Karlmarx and fought to maintain his impassivity—even the faint appearance of disapproval would make its way back to the Unit in gossip. He remembered that Karlmarx had the reputation of a chatterer. He could well have Knowledge Tower friends.

MacMillan wept, tried to rise, but fell again. He had twisted his ankle in the fall.

"You can crawl over there," said Walters. "We won't tell your friends."

MacMillan pulled himself over to the water dish with his linked forearms, favoring his sprained right ankle, his paper shirt torn and falling off his torso. The green paper pants were also ripped. He drank lengthily. Walters sat on his haunches next to MacMillan. "That's OK," he said. It was real, cool tap water. At other times, Walters had put other, less salubrious liquids into glasses or the dog dishes for other criminals.

When MacMillan was done, Walters and Beilin helped him move back to the now-righted chair.

"All right," said Walters. "Let's change the focus slightly. I find all these traitorous professors somewhat tedious—ungrateful Privilegeers." Largo tempo building into adagio. "What about the librarian at the Depository? Did you know her before you visited the place?"

"No, sir," said MacMillan. "I had never seen her before."

"Why do you think she made it easy for you to come inside and read? You didn't have the right paperwork; any real loyal Diversity librarian would have turned you away."

"I don't know, sir. Maybe she just figured a professor from Clinton University must have been all right and the paperwork would come through."

"The more fool her," sneered Walters. Look how quickly a professor is reduced to a dog drinking water from a bowl, he thought. Librarians aren't any better. "She looks like a typical librarian type. Maybe lonely, maybe hot for some professor meat. Maybe hot for you? Do you think that's what she wanted?" David sprang to his feet as Karlmarx stared.

"No, sir."

"And why not, you fascist pig? I mean dog."

"Because women just aren't interested in me that much, sir. I know I'm not attractive to them." It was a pleasing answer for the handsome Walters, who would have continued to explore that vein with reference to the librarian's lascivious needs had David not knocked on the door. Beilin rose to answer it. David stood in the doorway, and entered.

"Commander Harris," said Walters, giving the Antifan salute, the crossed arms over the chest, right one atop the left, then a standard salute with the right while the left remained on the chest. "Thank you for your presence."

"Deputy Commander Walters," said David, returning the salute, "I would like to take over from here. Please take a seat," indicating the chair behind the table. He went over and brought the third, empty, chair next to Cheysa and Beilin over to MacMillan, and sat down. He pulled out the spectacles. "Here are your glasses."

MacMillan took them with shaky hands and put them on. He blinked to see David's steady gray gaze a few feet away. "Thank you, sir." All his tormentors had been a blur, making it doubly hard to see when a shove or a slap was coming. Between the water and the repaired glasses, his spirits were starting to revive, however faintly.

David knew he had to pick up, however briefly, from where Walters had left off.

"Why do you think the librarian was kind to you?"

"Like I said, sir, I think she just assumed my credentials would be good. I didn't look suspicious and I'm probably the kind of person who does research at the Depository. But I don't think she was used to visitors, or especially visitors where everything wasn't in complete order."

"You took advantage of her inexperience, then?"

"Yes, sir, I'm sorry. I hope she's not in trouble."

"Probably not," said David. "It's decent of you to care about her." MacMillan's head sagged down. He had had enough. David asked a few random questions about the Depository, and then rose. "Beilin, Conroy, please return the prisoner to his cell. Have someone look at that ankle and get him a fresh uniform." The two privates supported MacMillan as he limped out of the room. As they reached the door, he turned around and said "Thank you for the glasses, sir."

The door closed behind them. David pressed the button to reveal the listening chamber, just to make sure Karlmarx had followed the others down the hallway. It was vacant.

"Were you watching the whole time?" Walters' voice was edgy.

"Just from the Melendez questions on," said David. "You were a very powerful interrogator; I'm not criticizing you."

"You don't trust me, sir, to do this interrogation?"

"Not at all. My original intention was to bring the glasses—you left them behind in the office. But then I didn't want to interrupt, so I went into the booth with Karlmarx."

"Chief, I left the glasses behind deliberately. I was going to offer to bring them down if he cooperated—you kind of jumped the gun on me there."

"Well, I guess I'm playing the good cop then," said David. "Never mind, let's sit down here and tell me what you learned today." Privately he thought it had been a mistake to bring down the glasses, if only because Walters would probably break them again that much sooner.

The two sat down at the long table. David had missed over an hour of the interrogation, and had to admit that Walters had been effective. The team would be busy over the weekend assembling rich lines of questioning for all the Clinton interviewees. He complimented Walters.

"Thank you, sir," said Walters. He had not quite digested the connection between the librarian questions and David's entering the room when he had, but it would occur to him later that night, when he woke up briefly, his mind racing, and with the moonlight spilling over the sleeping form of Cheysa in his bed. In the morning, he might ask her opinion of the librarian. Sometimes it was worth having the female perspective on these issues.

Chapter Eight
Intimate Italian Dinner
(Friday, 15 April)

"Of all tyrannies, a tyranny sincerely exercised for the good of its victims may be the most oppressive. It would be better to live under robber barons than under omnipotent moral busybodies. The robber baron's cruelty may sometimes sleep, his cupidity may at some point be satiated; but those who torment us for our own good will torment us without end for they do so with the approval of their own conscience."
—C. S. Lewis

A s David was leaving the Beaufort Tower, Malia was beginning to apply her unfamiliar makeup at home. The rouge had caked due to long disuse. The cats watched from the door of the bathroom, drawn to the diversion, and then exhausted by the effort, curled up and slept. The new outfit lay on her bed.

She pulled on the slacks and slipped the tunic over her head and was pleased, ran her hands through her curly dark hair, and fastened the new turquoise necklace. A few years ago, the Supreme Advisory Court had ruled that such jewelry was not illegal cultural appropriation, and its sale helped the livelihood of Indigenous Americans still trapped in the Interior. The majority opinion, however, cautioned, "Wearers of the turquoise jewelry should bear in mind the history of oppression experienced by its makers, and do their best to lead an exemplary life and repent for their privilege." The intercom on her armband rang.

Two surprises awaited: David was wearing civilian clothes and there was no self-driving car. He opened the door to a yellow sportscar. She had personally known some people who were entitled to ride in self-driving cars, but she knew no one who actually owned their own vehicle. "I paid for the carbon offset big time," he said sheepishly. "It's my only indulgence. When you're a hard-working bachelor, you don't spend money on much else."

"Wow," she said, "and you're in civilian clothes, too." She noted with approval the well-tailored blue cloth jacket, blue button-down shirt, and grey slacks.

"I don't have to spend a lot on civilian clothes either, now that you mention it," he said. "But you can't show up in a nice restaurant in an Antifan uniform and expect people to relax. Sometimes you want to blend into the crowd." She nodded, completely in agreement.

As they pulled out into the street at twilight, David said, "We're going to the Esplanade," the promenade along the Potowmack, northwest of Beaufort. "Have you been there? No, I imagine you wouldn't have." The walkway itself was restricted to Social Crediteers of 120 and over, policed at each end, and most of the restaurants limited their custom to 150 and over, at least indoors. Lesser folk might be allowed to sit in the outdoor beer gardens.

David had deliberately chosen one of the more obscure restaurants, Federici Miao, not wanting to run into fellow Antifans. He doubted that, even though qualifying with his 185 Social Credit score, Walters would patronize an intimate Italian restaurant. David had asked the reservationist for a secluded table. "It's our first date," he had explained, disingenuously.

The car sped north up the Harriet Tubman Parkway, a sensual pink and blue sunset dipping below the horizon to the west, before David turned off at the Esplanade exit. At the control booth, the sign blinked "Thank you, authorized to enter." They turned into the parking/self-driving depot lot, and parked. Two uniformed Plore guards approached, armed with tasers, respectful of the privilege exuded by the yellow sportscar. "Sir, I'm sorry to trouble you, but are you aware you are accompanied by a person who is not eligible to patronize this area?"

David kept his voice even. "What do you mean? She's my guest." He had assumed his privilege would envelop Malia. He wished he had checked beforehand and smoothed out these unanticipated obstacles. It had never occurred to him that the friendly signs and guards were there for any other reason than to welcome him. Until now, Malia had shimmered bright and lovely in her blue patterned pants suit, but now she looked stricken.

"I'm sorry, sir, the Esplanade is a strict high Social Credit area. Other places do allow you to bring guests but we can't." *We can't?* David thought bitterly. *Do you mean someone with a 96 Social Credit score will bring the plague to the Esplanade?*

He hated to pull rank, since it offended his basic humility, but he pulled out his Antifan credentials and said, "Take a look at this. Are you going to give us any more difficulty tonight?"

The taller guard took the card, blinking at it. "No, sir. This is fine. Thank you, and sorry for the trouble. Enjoy your evening." He turned to Malia. "You too, ma'am."

David put his arm around Malia's waist and steered her toward the Esplanade. He could feel her trembling through her flimsy coat, which was really too thin for a cool evening.

The Esplanade was a broad asphalt pedestrian lane about twenty feet wide. On the right hand, land side, set back amid foliage, were about fifteen restaurants and beer gardens. Quaint lanterns had turned on as the sun finally set, casting a warm orange glow on the walkway and beckoning passersby down the paths leading to charming country-style restaurants. A short stone wall ran along the left of the Esplanade, beneath which was the wide but calm Potowmack, and beyond that the twinkling lights of Ploreville.

Every hundred feet or so, the stone wall gave way to a wooden gazebo with benches along its sides affording some privacy and better views. David and Malia sat in the first unoccupied nook. Malia lost the battle to maintain her composure, weeping silently on his broad shoulder. He waited.

When her body stopped heaving with sobs, he said, "I'm sorry that happened. I had no idea there would be a problem if you were my guest."

She said, angrily, "This is what happens when you are low Social Credit. They use you, but they don't want to see you outside the office. And they starve you and make you turn in clothes when you want to buy new ones and tell you it's all about pleasing Mother Earth rather than just keeping more for themselves."

She went on, "I could understand if they were punishing Plores, because they actually fought against Diversity, but why do they treat people on our side like this?" It was now David's turn to stiffen, but she did not mark that.

"You answered it for yourself. They want more for themselves—humans always need to feel better than someone else. Here they claim they are ideologically purer than you, so they give themselves higher Credit scores so they can take more stuff than you can. We're not a rich country anymore. We banished or killed the wealth producers, and we've made it impossible for immigrants to come here and make an honest living, so we live off what our factories and farms can produce, and that frankly isn't very much. Everyone can't have everything.

"The government has to pacify the Plores, otherwise we couldn't get them to do the menial work, and they might rebel again. There aren't enough Antifans to keep down the entire Plore population if that happened. So they get to live mostly like normal people used to, can avoid using the jargon, and even get to worship the real God, not a Mother Earth, and celebrate Christmas. And they get a minimum income as long as they work for us.

"But someone like you, who pretends to believe the nonsense, and just thinks they have no choice but to comply, you're at the bottom of our heap."

"What am I supposed to do about it?" Malia said tearfully, finally looking into David's face.

David smiled gently. "For now, nothing. Social awareness is the first step to liberation." Malia recognized the stock phrase from the MED Church liturgy, and smiled back weakly. Their eyes locked, and their faces drew closer, and David's hands closed in on her shoulders. "You're beautiful," he said. "Don't be sad." Their lips locked, and Malia felt a jolt of electricity and a spidery sensation through her mouth and body.

It had been a long time since she had experienced that sensation.

David left Malia outside while he checked with the maître d' about his guest, which turned out to be a judicious call because the black tie-jacketed man with the dark moustache indeed hemmed and hawed. "Sir, we don't permit guests below 150 even if they're with someone who meets the standard. We could make an exception and seat you in the beer garden, though." The evening was rapidly cooling off, and no one would have chosen to eat outside.

Each blow felt like a personal insult. For a second time that evening, David discreetly showed his credentials, and the gray eyes went cold. "I would suggest welcoming both of us if you don't want to have visitors on Monday checking your books and your kitchen." The maître 'd excused himself, went to the back office, and came back with a thin smile. "Sir, we would be honored to have you both dine with us tonight. Please bring your guest inside."

He started to turn away, but David's voice pulled him back. "Just one more thing. I want this lady to be treated impeccably. I don't want her to even guess that there were any difficulties tonight. If there is one slip, I will come back on Monday with my squad, and it will not be for lunch. You're going to treat her like she has 240 Social Credits as well. Do you understand?"

The maître d' visibly swallowed hard, and said, "Yes, sir, I promise you that your guest will have a lovely evening."

David went to fetch Malia, who was across the walkway staring out at the river.

"Was there any problem?" she asked fearfully.

"None at all," he lied cheerfully. "They said you were welcome and they would make our evening special. I just had to wait for the maître d' to help clean up some broken glass in the back." She brightened, and they went inside, David looking over her shoulder as his eyes swept the walkway for any familiar faces. David resolved to avoid revealing any of his own simmering anger, which would have tipped off Malia that something unpleasant had indeed happened.

The secluded table had a white tablecloth and a small white vase with orchids, both of which were unfamiliar amenities to Malia. The waiter came over to ask their preferred pronouns, as required by law, and brought menus and soft warm white rolls in a wicker basket with carved butter balls in a small ceramic dish, also a novelty for Malia. David discreetly ran his left arm under the table and took a quick glance under the basket and dish. Nothing out of order. If there were listening devices, he would have known where to find them. The ADF had seeded them in most of the restaurants along the Esplanade, if not the gazebos, and David reminded himself to check those feeds on Monday as part of the Knowledge Tower investigation.

Malia stared at the menu. "I'm not even sure what some of these are," she confessed, "and I've never seen meat on a menu before. It's so weird."

David tried not to let his pity show. You could order a steak even in a Ploreville diner, if you didn't mind paying. He ordered chicken cacciatore and Malia ordered the Veal Marsala; veal was only available at the most exclusive restaurants. The waiter was properly obsequious and the maître d' himself came by to ensure that they were satisfied. Once he'd withdrawn, Malia said, "I'm glad they're treating us well, but I have to ask you something. I'm having trouble figuring you out."

"Wait a second," said David. "This might be a little late, but better late than never." He pulled out his armband and typed some code into the screen.

"What is that?" Malia asked.

"It's a noise cylinder," David said. "It will create enough interference to keep any outside listeners frustrated. I can use it occasionally, but not too often or it might attract attention. The breeze outside and our location help too—it's hard to track conversations from this area."

"Do you really think someone is listening?"

"Malia, you can never rule it out. A high Social Credit score doesn't spare you from spies, it just means that fewer people are authorized to listen to your conversations. Right now, I want to protect you. So ask your questions while you can."

"I'm wondering how you can be saying all these things while you're an Antifan commander."

"What things?" he asked, pressing her on.

"You don't seem so enamored of the Diversity Republic and our principles. You're telling me I'm oppressed."

"Well, you admitted it yourself," he said, amused.

"You aren't giving me the usual patriotic language, you're calling our values 'jargon,' you're making fun of the Diversity Church, you even mentioned a 'real God,' as opposed to Mother Earth. How do you get to be a senior commander and yet have these opinions?"

David paused. "It's because I'm a Plore," he said.

"Why are you joking?"

"I'm not joking, honey, my roots are in Ploreville. And that gives me a slightly different perspective than you have growing up in a government orphanage." It had never occurred to Malia that Plores could become Antifans, let alone senior commanders. She saw Deplorables as dependable menial workers who could be kind but were somewhat primitive and needed to be kept in their own neighborhoods and away from contaminating Social Crediteers. And now she was very, very attracted to one, again.

Her daughter's father had been a Plore construction worker with whom she'd become involved at Justice University. One sunny day at the beginning of the new school year, she lay on the lawn wearing a cute sundress, reading *Supremacist Ideology Unmasked: How To Identify Dangerous Texts,* her sandals lying nearby. She still remembered the coolness of the grass against her bare feet and her drowsiness in the soothing heat of the sun. The muscled young blond man dropped down on the grass at a reasonable distance but one permitting casual conversation. It took her awhile before she realized he was not a student at all, but a Plore working on the construction crew nearby. By then he had taken off his shirt to work on his tan and it was too late for the smitten Malia to send him off. When he left work, he came to her dormitory room, and she ignored the smirks of the other students as he came and went frequently that fall.

She had to shake off the memory to focus on David's words. "We were living in southern Ohio. My father was fighting with the Red Forces and he never came back. I don't think he deserted us, he probably just got killed while fighting, but who knows. We went to Toledo to live with an aunt, but they couldn't take us in and there was nothing to eat. I think this was 2055—I was about five. We started to head home but were captured by Diversity Forces and sent to a camp in Pennsylvania and when they announced the beginning of the republic, we were sent here to the Anacosta Ploreville. With my father's record, and being from where we were from, we were immediately classified as Deplorables."

"You said 'we'—do you have brothers and sisters?"

"Yes, I'm the youngest of four now. My older brother works as an electrician at an Antifan base near the frontier and my two sisters have families and live in the neighborhood near my mother. We lost my youngest brother to diphtheria in the camp." Malia started to say she was sorry, but David waved it off. "Don't worry. It was a long time ago. I don't even remember him."

"But your poor mother."

"It wasn't unusual at the time. People lost lots of relatives." His voice took a harsh turn, and he said "I know you lost relatives as well."

"You do? How do...oh."

"Yes, before a date I always read the girl's files. It's a fringe benefit of working at Beaufort."

Malia asked, with some asperity, "Do you think you might tell me my own information someday? I have no idea what happened to my family."

"I might. Let's see how you behave." He grinned, but the roughness in his voice was still there and he had not recovered his balance. It was hard to talk about his family, as much as he loved them, and he dared not talk about them with anyone in his Social Credit or Antifan circles. The Plore background was known by virtually all, but considered slightly disreputable and most Social Crediteers thought they did David a favor by not referring to it, or only behind his back.

But Malia was also thrown off-guard. Did David know about how she lost Isabelle? Surely, he would have seen that black chapter in her record, but how could he behave as if she were a completely normal woman? How could he bring himself to date her after her child had been removed by the authorities? Even with his unorthodox views, and his Plore background, that would be a step too far.

"We were living in Ploreville," David continued. "My mother was going into the City each day to clean offices. We were grateful for the basic income check each month.

"I was 15 years old when the committee came to visit my school. They picked out about ten of us, all boys, and had us do calisthenics and climb ropes and the like in the gym. Then they interviewed each of us. I had no idea what this was about. I answered the questions, but I knew better than to mention that we were good Christians or we watched satellite TV from the United States. It could have been a trap, not an opportunity.

"I remember the principal coming to me and saying 'they've chosen you for the Antifan Defense Forces school.' There was no refusing. We knew who the Antifans were, and had suffered at their hands, and my mother was very upset. She kept saying—in private—that my father would turn over in his grave if he knew. On the other hand, the principal made it clear that my family's life would improve tremendously if I became an Antifan and refusing would just turn the spotlight on us. If I agreed to go, my mother and sisters would be excused from working in the City, and I'd eventually make so much money that all my family would live comfortably.

"So that was that. A month later I was off to Maryland to train and to learn all the ideology that I'd managed to avoid in my Plore school. In my Plore school, we weren't expected to become professors or bureaucrats, just sandwich makers and tradesmen. But in the Antifan school, they watched you like a hawk. I had to become a lot more circumspect and learn to control my real feelings. Even the wrong joke could get you thrown in a punishment cell. When you graduated, and were finally sworn in as an Antifan, they had put you through a presser. Whatever humanity you kept, it was in spite of the school."

He concluded, "So I am a Plore, and a Social Crediteer, and an Antifan, all at once, and still trying to make sense of it all."

The waiter brought over the dessert menus. The mood was somber.

"Let's take a break," said David, switching on the armband sensors again. "Have you ever had a cannoli?" They ordered strawberry cheesecake and cannoli, and cappuccinos. David asked how Malia had found her cats. It turned out his mother owned two. They agreed that if a cat liked you, it was genuine, and not just because you fed it.

Back in the car, David looked hard at Malia, turned off the armband, and said, "I will be paying you a visit on Monday, just to remind you. We are opening an investigation of the Knowledge Tower and I'll come by to ask you some questions. You are not personally implicated but if you can share anything of interest, we'll be grateful. I'm giving you fair warning so you don't have a heart attack when we show up in the middle of your research."

"Did you take me to dinner just to bribe me into giving dirt on my bosses?" she asked, irritated.

"You forget yourself, Malia," David said frostily. "I don't need to win over witnesses by treating them to dinner." With that, he reminded her who was in charge. But it was awkward after that.

At the Rosebud, he came around to her side of the car to let her out and they stood under the awning. "Thank you very much for dinner," Malia said. She was holding an Enviro-pod with a second Veal Marsala that David had insisted on ordering for her to take home.

"You're most welcome," he said, "and I'm sorry to have switched to business mode in the car. I just don't want you to be unpleasantly surprised."

"No, I understand," she said, "and I'm glad you shared your story with me. I feel we actually have a lot in common—we're both outsiders here but we came to it by different paths."

He stared at her as if this had not occurred to him before. "Yes, that's very true." They fell toward each other and embraced deeply. A drunk Street Person staggered by and muttered "Hetero bastards!" They laughed.

When Malia went upstairs, a note stuck to her door reminded her of her floor's monthly political meeting tomorrow. The Rosebud's political commissar had scribbled, "Haven't seen you in two months—better attend!" The topic: relations among Social Crediteers. Malia wished at least one could get Social Credit points for showing up, but after tonight she would have some more interesting things to say on the topic, if she only dared.

Chapter Nine
Weekend at Work
(Sunday, 17 April)

On Sunday afternoon, Walters sat at the staff table with Cheysa, Karlmarx, and Chung, as he reviewed the proposed lines of questioning for the University president, the unfortunate Professor Melendez, and about a dozen other faculty and staff. Hanna, the security liaison at Clinton, loomed up on the telescreen before them. She was only technically a Clinton employee, in that she earned her salary from the university, but she reported to Beaufort.

Karlmarx and Chung stared at the screen to avoid noticing Walters' hand periodically straying under the table to fondle Cheysa. The newest trooper stared across the room, her dark face impassive. Power trumped feminism here.

A guard from the cellblock hastened into the Unit. "Deputy Commander Walters?"

"Yes, what is it?"

"Prisoner MacMillan is dead, sir."

"What do you mean 'dead'? Like 'dead' dead?"

"Yes, sir, deceased. We were doing the 3 o'clock check and couldn't wake him up. The doctor confirmed heart failure. We've taken him to the morgue."

"Mother Earth!" Walters' fist slammed onto the table, spilling a coffee cup in the process. "That's just what that fat pig would do to us! Leaving us high and dry just before we go to Clinton. What's with these prisoners that they can't take a simple interrogation anymore?"

This probably meant they were going to have to bring one of the interviewees back to Beaufort from Clinton to replace MacMillan. "Karlmarx, can you figure out who we might want to bring back here on Thursday? We're going to need to import another professor. Try to find someone who won't die on us that quickly and who's the best connected of the lot."

Walters pivoted around and headed to his desk on the platform next to the window. He resented not having an office yet, but the view was terrific. And you could overhear some interesting conversations from the adjacent cubicles. That's how he had learned Cheysa had broken up with her boyfriend. He called David, who was visiting his mother in Ploreville. Walters heard the whistling of a kettle and the sound of soft women's voices. "He would be sitting in a kitchen with women," Walters thought disgustedly to himself.

"What is it, Walters?"

"Sir, MacMillan is dead."

A brief silence. "I'll be there in half an hour," said David. *Click.*

"You have to go to the office now?" his mother asked, concerned. Marjory Harris was a comfortable-looking woman of seventy-four with greying fair hair, healthy, and finally serene after a turbulent life. She was grateful for the rowhouse, and for her daughters and their families a few blocks away. When David's armband signaled the call, he and his older sisters Emma and Christine had been sitting around the kitchen table with Marjory, sharing gossip and coffee cake. As Plores, none of the women wore armbands, and chips were reserved for Plores who had broken the law.

"I'm sorry, Mom. Yes, something just happened. I'll try to come back for dinner."

Marjory frowned. She had heard the emphatic word "dead" crackling on the phone, although of course she had no idea who MacMillan was. She had never quite accepted David's Antifan career, even as she acknowledged he had not sought it either, and that it had brought the family security and material comforts they would not have had otherwise. The few times David had raised a work concern, even a fairly anodyne one such as a possible new recruit or a trip to New York, she refused to hear about it. "I'm sorry, David," she once apologized when he had seen her visibly recoil. "I just can't bear thinking about that place. I am thankful for what your hard work has done for us, but I just can't."

Everyone in their neighborhood knew where David worked, and the yellow sportscar in front of her rowhouse on Sundays earned admiring glances from Plores, most of whom were not permitted car ownership at all (a tradesman's truck or van were the only exceptions, and those could only be used for work trips, subject to a severe Green Penalty). Neighbors had treated him with cautious reserve ever since he left for Antifan training, and he could barely remember a time when they had called him "Davy," or even tried to discuss something as banal as sports. When he accompanied his mother to St. Paul Lutheran Church on a Sunday morning, he requested they sit toward the rear, so his presence, as a representative of the anti-Christian State, would not disturb the other worshipers. Conspicuousness might also have prompted a report to Beaufort via informants in Ploreville, even though it was not forbidden for him to accompany his mother to church and was usually dismissed as an anachronistic "Plore thing."

But when a nest of drug dealers took up occupation in a rowhouse on the block, which the local police would normally have tolerated as a "lifestyle difference," one quick call by David to the stationhouse had led to their speedy eviction. Neighbors remarked with wonder on the pathetic knot of disheveled young people sitting on the sidewalk among their few belongings a day later, before they gathered up what they could carry and trudged off. The landlord quickly found better tenants. The neighborhood appreciated David's patronage.

David began driving back through the largely empty streets toward the City. He would face no obstacles crossing the river back into the City, as his sensors clicked reliably. No Plore van could make the trip unless its owner had secured permission first from a Social Credit client or customer. It made for smooth and uneventful travel for the privileged.

He was glad he had told his mother about the new woman he was starting to date. Marjory couldn't do much about David's career, but she constantly worried that he was thirty-eight and not seeing anyone seriously. Plore families started much earlier. She fretted that the job would harden him so that he wouldn't have a companion or children until it had ruined him for them. But she also feared that he would marry a woman who would despise his Plore background and separate him from his family—it was always the woman who would control the relational spigot and she knew of the Social Crediteers' contempt for the Plores. A hard-edged Antifan wife would almost certainly sever David from his family, and what kind of children would they produce?

"She's not a Plore," he said. "But she's not a drone either." The one time he had brought home one of those fish-faced virtue signalers had been the last.

"You know marriage works best when it's to someone like yourself. And you need someone you can completely trust. I don't think you can depend on the City types."

"Mom, that's who I meet. And they wouldn't let me marry a Plore anyway." But David was glad she seemed to favor his description of Malia as a pretty but not glamorous young woman who didn't believe all the propaganda. It was a bit of a stretch to tell Marjory they were "dating," but she wouldn't have given much credence to a mention of a single date, let alone "she's someone I'm interrogating." David laughed at that private joke as he approached the garage at Beaufort. *But I wouldn't have mentioned her at all to Mom if I didn't feel this could be the real thing.* He changed into his uniform in the car before going upstairs.

Upstairs, Walters was staring blackly at his computer screen. He had been casually trawling among the various electronic feeds from the households of persons of interest. If you were an Antifan officer, you could listen into the feed provided by the "smart" appliances in each apartment in the City, presuming the householder had a lower Social Credit score than you and had somehow migrated into the Antifan sphere of interest, however tangentially. If the resident had a higher Social Credit score, your supervisor had to approve each tap, so there were constraints. And a lead investigator could shut off casual interest by blocking a site. Listening to household feeds was a perk of Antifan employment and you never knew when someone would utter a subversive comment that could be parlayed into a profitable investigation, which is why the ADF permitted it. Listening to armband feeds required higher levels of authorization, however, since they were constantly with their wearers outside the house.

Walters switched among several of his favorite feeds, including an amorous young newlywed couple and a gay man with a lot of drama in his life. You had to keep up with that guy or you'd lose complete track of the story line, he thought. He and a bunch of friends were about to head to Say Francisco for the weekend.

"Walters!" David had entered the Unit. They entered David's office and closed the door. Walters showed him the doctor's report and certificate. Heart attack.

"This didn't happen while he was under your…care, did it?" That was the main issue at stake, although not the only one. Walters bristled at the ironic emphasis with which David voiced "care," but David seemed unaware of it.

"No, one of the guards came up with the news."

David sighed, "Well, it happens. What's the backup plan?" Walters was relieved.

"Chung and I will bring back someone from Clinton to stand in MacMillan's place. I've asked Karlmarx to see who might be the most suitable. Someone well connected in the university community and motivated to talk."

David stared him down. "This time, if the detainee is motivated to talk, I'd be much gentler. This cannot happen a second time, not on one case. If word gets back to Clinton, we will have a revolt on our hands. It will be much, much harder to gain cooperation. And the Director will ask questions—if he likes you now, I wouldn't give him any reason to think differently."

"Yes, sir."

"Who do we need to notify?"

"His wife, but she was about to divorce him, moved on Thursday, and left no forwarding address. I mean, we know where she is, but if we'd released MacMillan yesterday, he'd have had no idea where to go. We can reach her through Clinton, but she doesn't seem too worried about him, judging by the armband feed. Keeps calling him a loser bastard."

Fair enough but depressing, thought David. "Then a straightforward email. 'We regret the sudden passing of your husband due to heart disease, etcetera.' Enclose a copy of the death certificate. She'll need it for the life insurance and other forms, but won't care much otherwise.

"If you can present this to the Clinton president as a case where MacMillan was already in poor health and the stress of his firing and arrest brought on the coronary, that would be helpful. That might mitigate anyone's concerns about coming back here with you. They'll think, I'm not a knowledge criminal, they're telling me I can be of great help, the president's saying it's different from MacMillan, so forth and so on. Flatter them like crazy. Tell them they'll be staying in our guesthouse." The two men snorted companionably at the thought of the guesthouse that awaited the next Clinton professor.

By five o'clock, David was returning to Ploreville. He called Malia, who was leaving the National Diversity Museum on the Anacosta Mall. "How are you doing, honey?" Malia was happy to hear from him. She had scored a ticket for the popular "Transgender Rights: The Continuing Struggle" exhibit and also found the time to visit the "Womyn in Sport" pavilion. She had bought a set of postcards featuring the brutish players on the Anacosta Butches rugby team.

"I'll see you tomorrow around one at your office, okay? No need to worry, like I said.

"But I also wanted to invite you to my apartment next Saturday. I'm going to make a great dinner for both of us and we won't have to worry about Social Credit scores. To hell with all that. Are you able to come over on Saturday?"

Malia gave a genuine cry of dismay. "I would love to, but I'm volunteering at the Mother Earth Festival all weekend starting Thursday." Celebrating Earth Day, the holiest day of the new Mother Earth Diversity Church, the four-day festival was located at a campground on the Eastern Shore. The most famous musicians and actors in the DJR would perform on various stages. Food halls served free vegan meals and attendees camped in fields or barracks, dancing around bonfires at night.

"How many points do you get for doing this?" David was curious. It had never occurred to him to participate in such an event.

"Eight—two for attending and six for volunteering. They also give you a free bed in the barracks if you volunteer. But you have to volunteer all weekend to get the points. This might get me over 100 for the year."

"The following Saturday, then," said David.

"Yes, of course," Malia said, adding impulsively, "I can't wait to see you again!" She walked back to her apartment with an extra spring in her step, and David walked into Beaufort feeling more content than he had in a long time.

Chapter 10
Antifans Meet Higher Education
(Tuesday, 19 April)

Clinton University President Amy Whitacre Fufuloa, SC 205, the highly degreed ex-wife of a Tongan prince (she herself came from solid New England missionary stock, but the name conveyed good Diversity credentials, so she had kept it in the divorce settlement) was apprehensive. The Antifans were already swaggering through the campus center in their black leather uniforms, and had commandeered sandwiches from the cafeteria. President Fufuloa told the secretary to reserve a lunch table at the Faculty Club for the next two days with her as host. She had meant to do so earlier. There was always so much to keep track of—the union negotiations with the kitchen staff, the science curriculum overhaul to introduce more Diversity thought; her campus Earth Weekend celebration speech. At least she was spared the fundraising responsibilities that had preoccupied her predecessors under fascism, she thought gratefully.

Inclined to optimism, thanks to her high-ranking parents, easy ascent through Diversity educational institutions, and regular meditation practice, President Fufuloa nevertheless could not evade the reality that this visit boded ill. Her immediate reaction to news of the visit was, hadn't the issue been resolved with MacMillan's death? He had seemed harmless enough, but this all proved you never knew. Thank goodness for these reinvestigations, which protected Diversity from the influence of white supremacists. She had briefly considered sending a fruit basket to his widow, but was unsure whether this would implicate her in the family's disgrace.

Antifans made her nervous, as they did all the Diversity intellectuals. They were a palpable reminder that not everyone subscribed to the sunny tenets of Mother Earth Diversity, since force was still required to ensure compliance. Likewise, Plores made her nervous, although she only encountered them when making purchases in farmer markets and coffee shops, or when a plumber fixed her toilet. She knew the Plores were inclined to Hate, and needed to be reined in lest they infect Social Crediteers with their primitive ideology. Hate was bad, President Fufuloa was quite certain. She hated Hate.

The security liaison, Hanna, peeked in the door.

"Please come in!" President Fufuloa was a thin woman of medium height in her late forties who practiced yoga in the gym with the students and mostly kept to a vegan diet, ostensibly out of concern for animals, but mostly because it helped her maintain a trim figure. Also, meat was so raw—she approached it timidly.

Hanna sat down before the giant desk. "They'll be here in about 15 minutes, President Amy," she said. Fufuloa had encouraged students and faculty to call her this more accessible name.

Outside, they heard loud voices and drummers. President Amy went over to the window, and saw several hundred students massing with posters and bass drums on the lush green mall.

Hanna said brightly, "I've organized an anti-racism rally to coincide with the visit. Hopefully this will give our visitors a good impression of the ideological health of Clinton University." Some students were holding similarly hand-lettered signs that read "We Hate Hate," "Hate Has No Home Here," "Down With Racism," and even "We Welcome Our Antifan Protectors." Students who were not holding signs danced to the drums, men and women alike having shed clothing to expose skin to the warm sun. Thunk-a thunk-a thunk-a, the drums beat.

"I hope this doesn't backfire," said President Amy. "I don't want them to think we really have a racism problem. Or that we're only doing this because of the visit."

"Not at all. This can only make Clinton look good. It shows that we have an activist and ideologically sound student body."

The secretary's voice crackled over the intercom, "Deputy Commander Brian Walters for your 1:45 appointment, Madam President."

Walters, trailed by Chung, Cheysa, and Karlmarx, entered the room. All shook hands. Walters looked out of the window at the crowd. "What is that orgy out there?" he asked.

"It's an anti-racism rally," said President Amy. "Our students are dedicated to fighting hate."

Walters nodded solemnly. "Cheysa, Chung, doesn't that make you feel safe?" He sat down in the chair Hanna had vacated and crossed his left ankle over his right knee.

President Amy was slightly flustered in the presence of so much unabashed masculinity. It was almost as disconcerting as raw meat. Vegan diet notwithstanding, President Amy was not immune to masculine charms, and felt some fluttering in her nether regions. It had been a lonely three years since her divorce.

"President Fufuloa, my Director has asked me to convey his respects and appreciation to you and Clinton University for the reinvestigation of Professor MacMillan, which made it possible for the Antifan Defense Forces to arrest him in the act of committing knowledge crime at our False Knowledge Depository. Without that reinvestigation, Professor MacMillan would have succeeded in accessing perhaps dozens of volumes off limits to all but our most trustworthy scholars."

"Thank you, Deputy Commander. Clinton University was pleased to be of service."

"We were saddened that President MacMillan died so quickly in our custody. His heart condition was unknown to us and the stress of his firing and then arrest clearly had weakened him. We did all we could to save his life. I wish he had warned us when we booked him."

Walters paused. "Are you aware of what Professor MacMillan had done that caused him to fail the reinvestigation?"

President Amy hung her head, "Not really. These investigations are confidential, I know."

"Not that confidential. You're the president of the university. You could have asked. Well, let me tell you. He was beginning to form a cell of likeminded criminals here at Clinton. They called themselves the Liberal Club, and they were meeting secretly to discuss liberalism and capitalism. They acquired forbidden texts through an underground network of suppliers who we will be disrupting as well."

"Oh dear," President Amy breathed faintly.

"So you see the rot goes beyond MacMillan. We had hoped to find out more about this club, but unfortunately the stress of his disgrace was too much for him.

"President Fufuloa, we will have to bring one of your faculty or administrators back to Anacosta with us. You now have the list of interviewees. I would like you to suggest someone from that list whom you think would be best connected and most likely to expedite our investigation. This person will be treated with great consideration and not as a prisoner, but as an ally. They will stay in our guesthouse while they are with us."

President Amy scanned the updated list of a dozen faculty members and administrators again. There was the awful Dr. Melendez from Hispanic Literature who oozed condescension toward her in the Faculty Senate. One of the two engineering professors on the list had objected to the required course in "Diversity Theory in Mechanical Engineering," which was foolhardy of him. She occasionally had the Leftist Intellectual Theory professor and her wife over for drinks. Leave them alone, she thought instinctively. Most of the other names were unknown to her.

President Amy showed a faint spark of resistance. "Deputy Commander, I am not sufficiently familiar with your investigative methods or even this case to know who would be the most suitable designee. I would hate to jeopardize the investigation by picking a name randomly."

"Here's another way to think of it," said Walters. "Pick the person that will most minimize the chances of our having to come back and get another from the list."

President Amy nodded cautiously. "I will do my best to assist you, Deputy Commander."

It was time for the first of the interviews in a building across the campus green. As they walked across the green, where the dancing was resuming after a series of speakers, a conga line passed by, and several cute girls in short shorts invited the Antifans to join in. "That's the right spirit!" said Walters, giving the cue to the whole group to accept the invitation, including Hanna. They snaked across the green, chanting, "Hey ho, hey ho; racism has gotta go!" The line broke up, and Walters flirted briefly with two girls whose bare waists he encircled with his arms, even giving one a kiss on her lips. Cheysa glowered at them.

Julie MacMillan, 150, a handsome brunette in her late thirties, was awaiting them. She was not grieving her husband, Walters knew that full well, but she looked haggard. Julie was doubtless wondering whether she was implicated in her late husband's wicked behavior. After all, hadn't he stored those awful books in her basement? And hadn't she known about them without taking any steps to report or destroy them? Walters began by trying to put her at ease, reassuring her that he knew she was a good Diversity citizen, and her full cooperation would enable them to leave her alone to move on with her life. Walters passed the actual questioning over to Chung, who asked her whether the books in the basement she discovered had been there a long time, or might have been shopped out periodically. She admitted that after finding that initial stash, she had not checked again to see whether it had been replaced or even removed. "I was scared of it," she said. "I just didn't want to know."

After Julie left, the team interviewed the Swahili professor, the Bursar, and Women's Studies professor Renata Yazdan, before convening to review the transcripts compiled by Karlmarx. "I thought that last one was evasive," Cheysa said. "She kept denying she had anything to do with MacMillan outside of faculty meetings, but Julie said they'd been at parties together."

"Yes, that's something we ought to look into further," Walters responded. "See, isn't Cheysa good at smoking out the female liars?"

"I think she's good at everything we do," Chung said, giving her a warm smile. He was tiring of Walters' constant disparagement of this team member. It wasn't fair to Cheysa, who worked hard and was as good as anyone else on the squad. Chung felt sorry for Cheysa having to deal with Walters' libido in addition to the normal Beaufort abuse.

"Well, *thank you,* Conor," said Walters with exaggerated courtesy. "Cheysa, look what a staunch defender you have here. I may have him write your performance review this summer, not that he can evaluate *all aspects* of your performance, of course.

"Anything else? Good, let's go get some dinner."

In the hallway, as they waited for Karlmarx and Cheysa to emerge from the washroom, Walters suddenly turned on Chung and, without touching him, trapped him against the wall. "I don't want any of that Cheysa crap again," he hissed at Chung, looming a good five inches over him. "She belongs to me, and I don't need you making remarks about how I deal with her. Got it?"

"Yes, chief," Chung gulped. He was less afraid for himself than for Cheysa.

"Keep trying that, and maybe I'll f—k you instead next time. Then we can apply for an extra thirty points each as a couple. How would you like that?" He was referring to the bonus gay men received for proven homosexual preference.

"Not at all, chief."

"Good, let's keep it that way." The other two emerged from the restroom and they all headed to dinner, where their conversation centered on the sports coverage on the screens in the bar where they ate. Most of the conversation took place between Walters and Karlmarx, who was not intimidated by him. Chung mulled whether he should tell David about Walters' treatment of Cheysa—it was always dangerous to snitch on a deputy commander to a commander, but surely David would object to this kind of behavior? But what if David already knew? He had heard Walters joking about David asking him to stop patronizing the basement brothel, "but what would the ladies do without me?" So possibly David would see Walters having forced his affections on Cheysa as a preferable alternative? And then, how could he really be sure that Cheysa was an unwilling participant? All he knew was that if he made a wrong move, all three of them might turn on him.

It was too complicated, so Chung trained his eyes on the screen instead, where the California Progs had just scored another soccer goal against the Boston Oysters. He personally preferred football, which had been banned in the Diversity Republic in 2055 for its violence and hypermasculinity. Fortunately, Antifans at the office could watch football games still played in the United States, as part of their coverage of the doings of the supremacists in the Interior. It was one of the benefits of working a Sunday shift, at least between September and February.

Chapter 11
Farewell to Clinton
(Wednesday, 20 April)

T he team had seven interviews to conduct on Wednesday, so after breakfast
they quickly headed to campus.

"This is tight," said Walters, scanning the list of interviewees. Hanna
assured him, "We can always move the last one to Thursday if need be," she said, "and
I'll schedule the helicopter for later in the day."

"Thanks for reminding me," Walters interjected. "We will need two helicopters for
the return trip. I've decided we will take back two people with us. Why unnecessarily
handicap ourselves? But I don't want them both in the same copter going back."

The other team members were surprised, but Hanna nodded and went off to
handle the reservations. Walters explained, "just like I said, why restrict ourselves here?
It's like shooting fish in a barrel. I guess we could be considerate and not take two from
the same department."

The priority for today would be trying to ascertain how MacMillan might have
obtained and exchanged his books, which required a better understanding of his
daily routine. Julie MacMillan had been as helpful as she could, which hadn't told
the team much. Despite her good intentions, it was clear that she had lost interest in
her husband's doings months before the crisis. Karlmarx and other analysts had been
listening to months of stored armband and household feed from MacMillan, with no
yield, unless the words "Let's meet at the Faculty Club" bore a hidden meaning.

Other than some good-humored fun at Joyous Smeldring's name when the
engineering professor showed for his interview, Walters was well-behaved and
professional all morning. Time was short. The engineer and MacMillan had served
together in the vestry of the First Mother Earth Church of Clintonia, Maryland,
the college town. "He was very responsible," said Smeldring. "Very serious about the
budget. He was upset when we had to dip into reserves for last year's Earth Day high
service and reception. But we made up the deficit later in the summer by selling "I Love
Mother Earth" badges. That was his idea."

"Did he ever refer to friends from the University community or outside?" asked
Chung. "Was there anyone he thought highly of?"

"He was very complimentary of his colleague Kendra Pinckney. He said she was the smartest person in the Diversity History department because she was so well read, way beyond what you'd normally expect there."

"Would you say that's true? Have you met her?"

"No, the humanities and the engineering departments keep a wide berth from each other," Smeldring said wryly.

As he was leaving the room, Smeldring stopped in his tracks. "I'm sorry, I forgot to mention this, but Kendra did visit the MacMillans with bakery stuff. She likes to bake. She would bring a lot of cookies, and MacMillan would bring them to the church for the fellowship meals."

A few minutes after noon, the group arrived at the Faculty Club. It was the most elegant room on campus, with high ceilings and chandeliers and floor-to-ceiling curtained windows. President Amy rose to greet them from a round table in the center of the room. "I can recommend the Earth-Conscious Tasting Menu," she said.

Walters frowned as he scanned through the menu, realizing that it was entirely pescatarian. He was not fond of fish, and of vegetables only when served in their proper subservient role on the side. He and Chung ordered spinach lasagna. The other three went for the Tasting Menu, which began with wild mushroom pâté, then sweet potato-quinoa tart, escalating to an eggplant tofu "bouquet." Dessert was vegan rice pudding with a raspberry coulis atop.

"Mondays and Wednesdays are our pescatarian days here at the Club, and we allow dairy products," President Amy explained after the waitron took their order. "On the other days we are completely vegan. I instituted this change last year when we tried to comply with the order from the Knowledge Tower to show our commitment to Mother Earth."

"That's great," said Walters as he hungrily eyed the approaching bread basket.

Both the Antifans and President Amy were aware of the eyes on them from all the surrounding tables. It was well known on campus that the Antifans were here to question faculty and staff in the John MacMillan affair, but the eyes upon them were still more curious than fearful.

The conversation turned to President Amy's years spent in the South Pacific. For the Antifans, who had grown up after most travel to the rest of the world had been restricted, this was unusual. She had been doing fieldwork in Tonga when she married the Prince. He stubbornly clung to Christian idolatry, President Amy related, which had led to their divorce, in addition to his tendency to philandering with other white women, which she did not mention. She had returned to the DJR with an extensive collection of Polynesian mythological statuary. "Completely vetted by the Cultural Appropriation authorities in the Knowledge Tower and our own committee!" she made sure to underscore.

Cheysa was curious, "So are the South Pacific gods compatible with our religion? Is it against Mother Earth or just another side of it?" That was not a bad question, if ideologically delicate.

"Absolutely compatible," said President Amy. "Both have Mother Earth as the main figure and desire to find harmony with Earth. Polynesian religion recognizes that the earth sustains humanity. Spirits can be found in non-human beings and objects such as other animals, waves, and even the sky. Polynesian religion emphasizes nature, particularly the ocean. So, there is the god of the heavens, Lono; the goddess of fire, Pele, who lives in a volcano; Tane, the god of the forests, and Papahanaumoku, who is considered Mother Earth herself. The other supreme deity is Rangi, Father Sky. Their son is Tangaloa, the god of the seas. There is even a god of wild plants and vegetables. All things are endowed with supernatural power, which Polynesians call *mana*. Mana can be good or evil, and everyone and everything has varying amounts of mana."

"Is there an evil god?" asked Walters, "or are all these gods mostly good?"

'Kanaloa is the God of Evil, Death, and the Underworld for Hawaiians," said President Amy. "For the Maori of New Zealand, Whiro is the god of darkness and the origin of all evil in the world. He is also a son of Rangi and Mother Earth."

Walters was mostly an atheist, but he liked the idea of the god of evil and darkness. That I can get behind, he thought to himself.

The afternoon interviews went in a straightforward fashion. The first to show was Kendra Pinckney, 165, the baker colleague of MacMillan in the Diversity History department. A spare woman in her mid-forties with sharp features and vivid blue eyes, she was more reserved than the other interviewees. Unlike the others, she admitted having known MacMillan fairly well. "We taught a seminar last year in Advanced Transgender World History," she said, "and I used to visit them at their house. I'd bring over muffins I'd baked, since John had a sweet tooth."

"What kinds of things did you discuss outside of class?" Walters asked.

"Just departmental stuff and gossip mostly."

"Did you have similar views?"

"We both felt the department could be better managed."

Chung pulled out a book called *The Road to Serfdom*. It was a battered hard copy with a maroon cover. "Does this look familiar to you?" he asked.

She peered at it curiously, "It looks quite ancient," she said, scanning the title. "But I have never heard of it. I assume it is not on the Great Virtual Network. Was John reading this?"

"It was found in his basement after he was arrested."

"Oh dear," she said. "I assume it must be subversive, if it is an actual book and you are showing it to me. But I must tell you that I have never seen it."

After Kendra Pinckney had left the room, Karlmarx, who had been sitting in the back corner of the room discreetly monitoring the armband signals, said, "Her vitals were jumping all over the place, especially when she said she hadn't seen the book before. And when she said they only discussed departmental things and gossip."

"I think we have one of our candidates for a guest stay at the Beaufort Spa," said Walters. "Didn't Joyous Smerdley, or whatever his name was, say he thought she was pretty smart?"

Karlmarx added in his bright beaverish way, "and he said that MacMillan said she was well read beyond what you'd expect in a Diversity History professor. But how would he know that she was well read if they only discussed departmental stuff and gossip?"

"Good catch, Karlmarx," said Walters.

Walters let the team go ahead to dinner. "I've just got some extra energy to work out," he told them. "I'll meet you back at the hostel." It was a lovely spring evening, with the temperatures just cool enough to make a jacket advisable, and the fading sunlight suffused the old brick buildings with a warm glow. The facilities staff had erected a large stage with podiums at one end of the mall, where yesterday's rally had taken place. A banner hung from the back of the stage depicting a giant blue Earth with breasts and the words "Our Mother."

By the time he had eaten a sandwich requisitioned from the student union, the sun was beginning to set and lights were flickering on in dorm rooms as were the lanterns along the sidewalks. He located the President's house. It was a generously sized but not ostentatious colonial with pillars and a winding walkway edged with flower beds and short hedges. The upstairs windows were dark, but the lights were on in the living room at the front, and he quickly darted along the side, where he saw her tidying up in the kitchen, apparently alone. She had changed into sweatpants and a sweatshirt, and her hair, released from the bun, now swung in a ponytail behind her head.

He rang the doorbell, and it was rewarding to see the look of surprise, and then dismay on her face as she recognized him. "May I?" he asked, pro forma, as he entered.

"Well, yes, of course," she uttered, as she followed him into her own house.

"I've come to see your sculptures," he said, "and to talk some business." Hopefully she would find that reassuring, at least initially.

"Here they are," she said. And indeed, the large vaulted room was filled with odd, fantastic wood and metal sculptures of grimacing, pop-eyed, nightmarish creatures. Some had distended penises, he noted, others bellies. There was a Rarotongan staff god, or as President Amy said, an "atua rakau," very rare. Next to it was a set of Fijian war clubs. She then introduced the various god statues around the room, including Papahanaumoku, or Mother Earth, with closed eyes, comfortably heavy breasts, and belly. Walters ran his hand over it.

President Amy also pointed to a statue of longhaired, dramatic Pele, the goddess of volcanoes and fires, a daughter of Papa. "The statue is from Hawaii," she noted. Good-looking goddess, but a little wild, thought Walters.

"What's this one?" he asked, drawn to a grotesque two-foot high red statue of a warrior with shields of fire-leaves covering his arms and legs. It was different from the others.

"That is Whiro, the Maori lord of darkness and evil," said President Amy.

"I'm surprised you have this here at all," Walters said respectfully. "It's really very frightening looking."

"Yes," she said. "I am scared of it, but it was given to me by my ex-husband and he said Whiro's mana would protect me here in the Diversity Republic, so I kept it. We're still on good terms, so I trusted him. I've placed it where I don't need to look at it constantly."

"Protect you in the Diversity Republic? From what?" Walters laughed. "Hey, do you have anything to drink?"

She headed to the kitchen. "Sparkling water? Juice? I have orange and orange pineapple."

"How about something a little stronger? Where's your bar?"

She pointed to the corner of the room opposite Whiro's statue. "I only use it for official entertaining."

"You may consider this official entertaining," said Walters. He poured himself a whiskey neat—the brands were very good, as befitted the house of the President of Hillary Clinton University. He mixed a very strong screwdriver for President Amy, who obligingly brought the orange juice from the kitchen.

They sat down in a surprisingly cozy corner of the living room, Amy on the rolled-arm sofa against some embroidered pillows with her legs tucked under her, and Walters on a gray high-backed armchair to her left.

"That's a really impressive collection of statuary, I have to say," Walters began. "And as you said, completely in accordance with Knowledge Tower guidance and approvals."

"Well, honestly," said Amy, "I never formally got the approvals but when I spoke with the University coordinator at the Tower, he assured me these wouldn't be a problem as long as I didn't use them in a classroom."

"Your secret is safe with me," said Walters. "But as you also said, these are completely in conformity with Mother Earth religion. In fact, I would display your Mother Earth statue here on campus as part of religious training, maybe as part of the Earth Day festivity next year?"

Amy's eyes widened. "Yes, I don't see why that should be a problem. That's an excellent idea."

Walters then said, "And that Pele statue gave me an idea for Earth Day too. You could have virgins throwing themselves into a mock volcano in tribute to the goddess."

"You're making fun of me now," Amy pouted.

"Not at all!" Walters said. "You build a giant cardboard paper mâché volcano with paper flames, and just make sure there are soft mats at the bottom for the virgins so they don't break any bones. It would be really dramatic." He paused. "Of course, you'd have to find actual virgins, which might be a challenge around here."

They were silent for half a minute. Walters went and mixed them both another drink. President Amy seemed to be drinking her second screwdriver rather quickly as well, probably in anticipation of what she imagined to be the inevitable outcome of Walters' visit, especially given his sudden interest in virgins.

"So my team and I have now interviewed ten members of your campus community," Walters said. "Most of them seem to be innocent of heresy or collusion with MacMillan. There are a few who are worthy of further interest by the ADF. But we'll only take two back with us tomorrow."

"Two!" President Amy squealed. "I thought you said you would only take one."

Walters gave her a cool, green gaze, and leaned forward. "I've changed my mind. You were going to tell me who you wanted me to take. But you haven't."

"I can't make that decision," she said. "I thought about it, but I really don't know most of the people you've interviewed."

"You have a nice lifestyle here," he said. "It would be a shame if something happened to it."

Walters brought her a third drink. Amy hesitated, and he said, without emotion but firmly, "drink it," so she obediently did.

"You do realize, we could drag you back to Beaufort very easily. But the more I talk with you, I think it would be a waste of our time. You really don't know much about this place, do you?"

President Amy was now tipsier than she would have expected from even three screwdrivers. "Uh," she said.

"I wonder what you look like naked."

"Uh?"

"I said I wonder what you look like naked."

Her inhibitions were lowered, but not necessarily in the direction Walters sought. "How dare you? How can you treat me this way? I'm the President of Hillary Clinton University! I have 205 Social Credit points, twenty more than you do! How dare you talk to me this way?"

"President Fufuloa, you may have 205 Social Credit points, and congratulations on those, but nothing stops me from taking you back to Beaufort tomorrow, whether you like it or not. And when you go to Beaufort, there are no guarantees you will see Mother Earth's sky again, let alone return to Clinton. Do you understand me?"

She collapsed, weeping softly.

"I wonder what you look like naked."

"If I—strip for you, you'll leave me here?"

"Yes."

He watched her remove the sweatshirt, the sweatpants, the bra, the panties. She was barefoot already. Naked, she looked much like what he had imagined, an aging but fit practitioner of yoga and veganism. Another five or ten pounds, maybe the natural outcome of a pregnancy, would have been more appealing, Walters thought, studying her, but then he tended to prefer some fleshiness against his hardness. She stood before him, waiting for the inevitable next act.

But he did not approach her, less because of an absence of lust, which was indeed troubling him slightly, and to which he normally would have succumbed, than his taking to heart the realization that she indeed did have twenty more Social Credit points than he did. If he took advantage of the situation and added the university president to his list of conquests, she could complain to Director Ferraro, who might say to David, "That boy of yours is out of control," and David might remove him from leading the investigation, which was going well so far. This investigation was becoming his ticket to a commander promotion next time an opening came around.

If he refrained from touching her, she would have little cause to complain. It would sound silly if she complained, "He made me take off my clothes," and maybe even a little embarrassing that Walters hadn't bothered to rape her afterward. And there would be no physical evidence of any assault, which you would need to bring already foolhardy charges against any Antifan commander. It seemed to be a draw at this point.

"This is what I want you to do," he said, "go upstairs. Lie on your bed like that, without clothes, and say a hundred times, 'I love the Antifan Defense Forces.' Then go to sleep. I will be listening to the feed from your armband later and I will count each and every one of those statements. If you do as I say, we will leave you in place as president of Hillary Clinton University. Do you understand? Will you obey?"

"Yes," she cried.

"Good girl." He watched her trudge upstairs, and heard several muted "I love the Antifan Defense Forces" statements from what must have been her bedroom. "Louder!" he shouted in her direction. In five minutes, she would be asleep, judging from the pill Walters had slipped into the third screwdriver. She would awake in the middle of the night, panicking and blushing at the remembrance of the visit, and wondering whether she had actually finished saying the phrase one hundred times. She might start afresh, just to ensure she had followed the instructions, if not perfectly. Too much was at stake to disobey. Walters guessed that President Amy would not appear at the Faculty Club for lunch tomorrow.

Walters began to quietly depart—let her wonder whether he was still listening downstairs—until his eyes fell on the evil Whiro, with his red lizard head above a crown of fire that framed a warrior's face. "Good job," Whiro seemed to be saying to him. "That female really has been insufferable. It's been a humiliation sitting here on her shelf."

Walters scooped Whiro off the shelf and took him into the darkness. It occurred to him that the plain and businesslike surroundings of the Knowledge Crimes Unit would benefit aesthetically from the addition of a god of evil. It would certainly give the KCU a morale boost and advantage over the Financial Crimes Unit across the hallway at Beaufort. "You're mine now," he said as he headed back to the hostel, "and going somewhere where you can be properly appreciated."

Chapter 12
Whiro
(Friday, 22 April)

David was frustrated with Malia's file, which lay on the screen before him. Never before had he been told "denied" after clicking on a line in a file, unless the lead investigator had placed it off limits, but dammit, wasn't *he* the lead investigator in this case? When David had initially reviewed her file, he had been intrigued by but hadn't pursued the line about Child Protective Services removing "daughter, 5, from the subject." Now he wanted to bring this woman into his life on a more permanent basis, possibly home to his mother, and he needed to know more. The computer tech hadn't been able to solve the problem.

He picked up the phone and called Paula Findlay, the Infotech chief for KCU. Paula was a down-to-earth fortyish divorcee whose assignments had coincidentally paralleled David's his whole career. David sometimes joked that Paula was his "work sister."

"Hey, Paula, why can't I open this link in this file?" He described the problem and the link itself.

"Well, honey," she said in her southern drawl, "I think this means someone doesn't 'want' you to see the file. It isn't personal. The link is dead. The data is closed to the whole ADF."

"How can that be?" he asked. "What's so special about this information? Who sees it if WE can't?"

"When you eventually find out what the story is, you'll know why," said Paula, sounding like a mystical Indian guru.

"I just can't figure out why this information would be off limits."

"David, are you planning to date this woman?" David smiled to himself—it was very hard to keep Paula from penetrating to the heart of a matter.

"Eventually," he said. It was easy to be honest with Paula Findlay.

"Then, honey, I suggest you ask her yourself. If she's worth keeping, she'll tell you. Frankly, she probably assumes you already know. Don't we know everything?"

I wish, he thought ruefully. "Thanks Paula, I guess I'll have to reveal my ignorance."

"Anytime, David. Just remember to invite me to the wedding."

David stood up and stretched. It had been a long four days since he had last seen Malia at the Depository, where he asked her perfectly respectable questions about the building security practices and the guidance, or lack thereof, she had received from the Knowledge Tower. Beilin and Patel sat stolidly along the wall, taking turns dozing or jotting notes, as oblivious as oxen to the electricity in the room.

David then asked Malia to accompany him to several of the stacks so that he could familiarize himself with the security system including the automatic retrieval. Beilin and Patel started to rise, but he waved them off. "I'll be back shortly," he said. Malia and David took the elevator to the lowest level, where she showed him how the electronic eye ensured that all the books meant to be on a shelf were in fact present, possibly including an empty cardboard box superficially resembling a book the librarian might have chosen to read. She showed how an electronic arm would lift a book ordered by a visitor off a shelf and send it via a chute to her office.

"That's very interesting," said David, and he pinned her against a freestanding pillar and began kissing her deeply. Malia responded willingly, lifting and yielding beneath him. Not here, not today, thought David, so after a minute or two he released her and they broke apart, smiling at each other. "I was just overcome by the electronic arm," he apologized.

"The electronic arm has nothing on yours," she joked. They perfunctorily opened and locked a few other shelves. She had often thought the basement of the Depository would be perfect for impromptu lovemaking, but at that time it was idle speculation since she had no partner in sight. And upstairs Beilin and Patel were waiting. But maybe another time.

Back at Beaufort that Friday morning, David thought achingly that he didn't want to have to wait another week before seeing Malia again. That morning, he had briefly thought of surprising her at lunchtime, before remembering that yesterday she had boarded a bus in a convoy heading to the Earth Festival. He hoped it wasn't really as dreadful as it sounded.

He walked out into the main room, where he noticed a cluster of troops and analysts in a corner of the room staring at something. Approaching the knot, he realized they were admiring the ugliest statue he'd ever seen. It was two feet high, red-painted wood, a two-headed warrior with the top head of a lizard and the bottom one a snarling human face. It crouched in a fighting stance, brandishing clubs and spears. "What on earth is this?" he asked.

They all responded at once. "It's a god of evil, Commander...Deputy Commander Walters brought it back from Clinton University...it's a South Pacific demon called Wurro. He's the god of darkness and evil." It isn't enough to have Walters as our existing god of darkness and evil, thought David, but he had to bring back a statue as well.

"Deputy Commander Walters says we can bring offerings of beer and snacks to

Wurro," said one of the analysts, "and it will bring us luck."

But even David could not speak his mind here. Two thousand years of high church civilization replaced by a hideous red gargoyle demanding sacrifices. Instead, he said, "I'm glad to see that Deputy Commander Walters is brightening our work spaces."

Walters stood behind him. "Isn't that a cool little creature, Commander? The Clinton president gave it to me. I thought it would be really inspirational to have a martial god figure like Whiro here. It's all part of the Maori earth religion, so completely consistent with Earth Diversity principles. His mother is the Earth Goddess of the Maori religion, Papa-something," Walters added, as if gossiping about neighbors. "Just like our Earth Mother. What do you think?"

He added, "Several guys from FCU have already come by to see Whiro. They are really jealous!" Some of the Antifans gathered around whooped and punched each other playfully.

"It's great," said David, "a real morale booster."

Walters followed David back into his office. Earlier in the day he had briefed David on the successful trip to Clinton, and notified him that Professors Pinckney and Melendez were now in custody on Level One, whose accommodations were slightly better than on lower levels, if only because they had windows looking out into a drainage ditch.

"How did they react to being booked here?" David was curious.

"Melendez was very angry, saying he'd been lied to. One of my guys smacked him a few times, and that shut him up. He doesn't care for green paper pajamas either, I understand. Pinckney just became very quiet."

David had read the initial report by Karlmarx, and said, "I find those bakery deliveries to be very strange. Even if, like MacMillan, you have a sweet tooth, and two sons, that seems a bit much. Usually you'd bring the extra muffins into the office, or why not just deliver it directly to the church for the coffee hour?"

"Yes, sir, we'll ask about that."

"Ask Julie MacMillan whether she still has some of the bags in which Pinckney brought over her bakery goods. We can do a chemical composition scan and see what else might have been carried over in those bags. Hopefully she didn't throw them out in the move."

Even though Walters—swollen with self-esteem after his Whiro coup—was increasingly regarding David and his gentlemanly ways with some condescension, at times like this he was fair enough to give David more than grudging respect. "That's a great idea, chief."

"That's why they pay me the big bucks, Walters—or they don't," David replied. For his part, he was increasingly relishing making the tactical moves that underscored to his ambitious deputy his mastery of the craft. It was one thing to brutalize prisoners and bring a god-of-darkness statue into the office, but another to move cases forward by understanding how people's minds worked. Even these days, skill outweighed force. Within an hour, word came from Hanna that Julie had found several reusable cloth bags she remembered as belonging to Pinckney and two hours later they were undergoing scans at Beaufort thanks to the ADF air courier.

After lunch, David reviewed his Depository report, pleased at having opened up some interesting leads for investigation. He had tailored the report to avoid implicating Malia in any of the security lapses, except to occasionally express regret over the insufficient staffing the ADF had found at the Depository. The report would pinpoint concerns traceable to upper management, which would gratify Ferraro.

He saved the report, and then tapped into Malia's armband at the Earth Festival. Judging by the clatter and the conversation in the background, it was lunchtime. He heard a male voice say, "pass the Earth juice please." People around her were chattering in a steady buzz, but Malia herself was silent, which didn't surprise David.

Restless, he went down to the gym. The Beaufort main gym was vast and he never had to wait for a cardio apparatus or his favorite equipment. Two bare-chested men in nylon shorts were wrestling on a mat, grunting as they grappled for advantage. Several pairs were spotting each other on weight equipment, and the ponytails of the young women on the ellipticals bounced rhythmically. A class on knife fighting was starting in a few minutes. "Hey, Commander!" said the knife fighting instructor, "can you come to the class? I'd really like your feedback." David agreed, in part because he knew Antifans were encountering more knives in close encounters with regime enemies, who had been disarmed of firearms but remained resourceful. Antifans did carry ten-inch knives but rarely used them.

As David headed back into the locker room, he ran into Walters coming out. The deputy said he'd been attending the chain fighting class regularly. "Might as well use the things, sir, right?"

Back at his desk, he took a call from Director Ferraro's executive secretary, Nina. "Commander Harris, patching through the president at Clinton University."

"Harris here." He hoped she wasn't going to beg on behalf of her professors. Really, from what Walters had said about her stewardship of the university, Fufuloa should be grateful she had been left behind.

"Commander Harris? This is Amy Fufuloa, how are you?"

"Fine, President Fufuloa. Thanks for your help this week with our visit."

"Of course! It was a pleasure. I'm not calling to ask for a favor or anything, I know you have to let the process unfold. I just wanted to check to make sure Deputy Commander Walters knows I followed his instructions to the letter."

"What instructions?" David was bewildered.

"He asked me to say something one hundred times before I went to sleep, which I did."

"What did he ask you to say?"

She giggled, "I love the Antifan Defense Forces."

David sighed quietly. "I will let Deputy Commander Walters know. Thank you for your attentiveness in the matter. And thank you for the gift of the evil god statue. It is here in the office and is very popular among the men."

Long silence. "Oh! You're welcome. But you need to be careful with the statue. Whiro has very powerful mana, and if not properly respected, he can cause great harm to those in the vicinity."

Well, thought David irritably, why did you give it to Walters then? And what the hell is mana? He presumed it was not the same as the manna foodstuff that God had provided the Israelites in the wilderness. I wouldn't trust Walters with this mana.

When they hung up, President Amy thought, so he did take the statue after all. I thought something seemed to be missing from that shelf. The bastard might get what he deserves after all. Good luck, Whiro.

David called to Walters when the deputy returned from the gym, "Brian, Amy Fufuloa called me a while ago. She wants you to know that she said she loved the ADF a hundred times. She was very concerned about following through on your order there. What the hell was that about?"

Walters stood in his door, grinning and perspiring lightly (he was not always given to showering after a workout, since he claimed his pheromones were strongest when he refrained). "I went over to her house one evening to press her a little on giving us a name of someone to bring back here. She wasn't being very forthcoming so I made her promise to say that one hundred times or we'd arrest her too."

David rolled his eyes, "Was that all you did?"

"Yup, chief." Sure, you bastard, thought David.

"Good," and David returned to his screen. "She didn't ask about her professors at all. I'm not entirely sure she even knows who we took."

"Par for the course," said Walters, and returned to his desk. A few minutes later, he was in David's door again. "Chief, the chemical scan found residue of century-old paper and printer's ink in all three bags."

Chapter 13
Escape From Earth Weekend
(Saturday, 23 April)

The weather was beautiful on the final full day of the festival, warm and sunny with a light breeze wafting in from Chesapeake Bay. Tomorrow everyone would board the buses and return to Anacosta, New York, Boston, and Miami, but the slovenly throngs were still enjoying their vacation. Bearded men exposed hairy legs in dirty denim shorts, while women wore flowing cotton prints or short shorts. Her feet clad in the ubiquitous Eco-Sandals, Malia walked toward the revival tent where the Great Worship Ceremony would take place, wearing a red T-shirt that said "Love Mother Earth," and clutching her pink pussy hat. It was an honor to have been chosen to volunteer at the service where the Archbishop of Anacosta, the Most Reverend Cecilia Mountainspring, SC 325, and the Vice-President of the Diversity Justice Republic, Kumbaya Peace-Williams, SC 350, would be speaking to over a thousand attendees, with another two thousand standing in the overflow pens.

The main dirt path was lined with abundant flowering cherry and pear trees whose leaves were beginning to mature from a tender green. Underneath the trees, various booths sold eco-products ranging from Earth Mother charms and jewelry, foodstuffs, T-shirts, and candles, to artwork, and toys. All the vendors were state employees, since capitalism had been phased out years ago in favor of humane state-led enterprise, so they were not particularly aggressive in making sales. Each of the jewelry booths and the clothing booths sold exactly the same wares, so if you were unsure whether to buy the "Hate Hate" T-shirt at the first table, it was easy to make the purchase farther down the avenue.

Gravel paths led in all directions from the main thoroughfare. On the right, they brought you to the classroom and cafeteria buildings. On the left were the barracks, to which men and women and New Men and New Women were assigned randomly, since modesty was no longer a virtue; in fact, it was considered a vice indicating a selfish and individualistic mindset. Malia slept in Bunk 14, her valuables tucked under her pillow when she slept. "Slept" was an exaggeration though, thanks to the bulky man who snored in the cot to her left, and her hazy awareness that all around her, figures were approaching cots to proposition others. On the first night, she gave a muffled scream as a large hand reached under her blanket and she sat bolt upright as the wraith moved away in the darkness. "Shut up!" another inmate hissed at her. It was a steep price to pay for eight Social Credit points.

Beyond the bunks were the campgrounds, where attendees sang hymns around campfires until late at night. As they prepared for bed, the barrack occupants listened to the distant but plaintive plink of ukuleles and the mellow thrum of guitars.

They ate vegan meals at highly regimented intervals in the cafeteria, always assigned to fill the long tables in the order in which they stood in the cafeteria line. There was no asking for more or less of the eggplant casserole or the sweet potato hash. As they had said at the orphanage, "You get what you get and you don't get upset." It was possible to trade servings at the tables, and Malia liked having new tablemates at each seating. One did not need to cultivate friendships with people you did not expect to see again in the surging throngs.

Arriving at the entrance to the tent, Malia asked for the volunteer coordinator. The sour-faced woman, who introduced herself as Nancy, 125, just to make the pecking order clear, sent her to the right rear of the giant tent. She was to direct 100 and unders to their section from the right side entrance in the rear. "You can be with your own kind," said Nancy, "but don't sit down. And please put on your hat to show respect."

Smarting from the casual rudeness, Malia did as she was told. She was also given a basket of pink pussy hats for anyone who had forgotten to bring theirs. The attendees began to stream in, and she kept asking, "Number please? Number please? That way, please. This way, please. You can sit anywhere behind the blue tape. A hat? Yes, here you are. You're welcome."

The Great Worship Ceremony started late. The Archbishop, a squat Indigenous American woman in blue robes, came out, and raised her crosier, at the top of which rested the rounded earth symbol of her authority. Everyone rose to their feet. The New Man Choir sang the introductory hymn in their soft contraltos, "Today We Celebrate Our Mother Earth."

Mother Earth, you sustain us. Mother Earth, we sustain you.
Soil, water, sky, the foundation we live by.
Mother Earth, we praise you every day so true.
We come from your womb, we go to the tomb, under your blanketing love.

"You may sit down," said the Archbishop. "Today is the holiest day of our Church calendar. We have come here in holy union, linked by our love for Diversity, to worship the Mother who gives us life and sustains us with her love. The seasons pass, one by one, winter, spring, summer, fall, only because she permits it. We must always ask ourselves, have we earned the right to Mother Earth's favor? Do we deserve to live enjoying her bounty? What have we done to breathe the fresh air, and swim in the lakes and oceans she has provided?" (Malia briefly wondered if she would ever earn enough Social Credit points for the beach vacation she coveted).

"For many years we sinned against Mother Earth. Under the rule of white supremacists, our continent was trampled. The European invaders seized it from the indigenous peoples of the continent, who were murdered by smallpox and fire-weapons. The land was brutalized by the white supremacist farmers, who enslaved the indigenous African to knock down the forests to grow cash crops, particularly cotton. A moment of silence, please, for our Martyred Land and Peoples. The slave economy fueled the foundations of rampant capitalism. The air was polluted, the rivers ran red with blood and brown with sewage, the soil turned into dust in many places. Cities were built, not the efficient towers we live in today, which respect the finite nature of resources given us by the Mother, but sprawling subdivisions, soulless suburban tracts in which patriarchal fathers ruled by fear, all linked by ASPHALT HIGHWAYS AND ROADS on which millions of smoke-belching privately owned vehicles carried individuals from one selfish personal destination to another. Individualism meant people could travel where they wanted, when they wanted. The rich capitalists flew their privately owned airplanes wherever and whenever they wanted. Nobody managed this tangled, disrespectful waste of resources.

"Then, thanks to Mother Earth, the Diversity Justice Republic came into being. It was not an easy birth. The white supremacists fou ght hard to maintain their control over the Diverse Peoples, the racial and sexual minorities of America. They worked their will through their President, a puppet of capital, their Congress, which under evil Republican Party rule always sided with the white property overlords. The supremacists even created a terrible coronavirus in the early 2020s, as they saw the tide of Diversity rise. Our foreparents were wise to take advantage of the chaos to move forward with controls on Christianity, firearms, and False Knowledge. We were granted the beautiful Mask of Safety. Under pressure from the pandemic, we resolved to wash the country Blue. We have reined in False Knowledge by creating the Great Virtual Network.

"And yet today, the supremacists still linger beyond the Appalachians, continuing to abuse Mother Earth." An angry buzz began to rise from the crowds.

"Every day, by expressing love for Mother Earth, we show our love for the Diversity Justice Republic, the choate representation of Her Being…

"We will now rise for the Four Minute Hate."

Malia and other ushers had distributed gobs of clay throughout the crowd, and now strong young men were carrying large papier-mâché effigies of capitalists and white supremacists down the aisles. The powerful beat of a tribal song erupted, and when the Archbishop lowered her crosier, the worshipers recognized the cue, screaming epithets and hurling the gobbets at the effigies. Some of the gobbets hit other worshipers. Foul language filled the assembly. "Damn you, racists!" a young woman near Malia screamed. "You killed my grandfather!"

"Leave Mother Earth alone!" yelled a heavy-set bearded man who looked incongruous in a lace-trimmed pink pussy hat.

The riot slowed down as worshipers tired, and as soon as they could decently do so, they slumped again in their folding chairs. Hating hate was hard work.

"Thank you, Most Earthful and Faithful Assembly," said the Archbishop. They sang another hymn, "Why the Soil is Brown and Not White." Next came the homily, based on the How Dare You verse from the *Book of Greta*:

> I should be back in school, on the other side of the ocean. Yet you all come to us young people for hope. How dare you! How dare you pretend that this can be solved with just 'business as usual' and some technical solutions? You are still not mature enough to tell it like it is. You are failing us. But the young people are starting to understand your betrayal. The eyes of all future generations are upon you.

The Archbishop urged the attendees to devote themselves even more unceasingly to Mother Earth. "You are young," she said. "Our Diversity Nation needs your strength and wisdom more than ever. Strive unceasingly to fulfill your flawed elders' incomplete vision of the Diverse future. Make sacrifices while you have the vigor to do so."

She then yielded the floor to Vice President Kumbaya Peace-Williams, who began by relaying the greetings of the elusive President Avadaughter.

"President Avadaughter wishes she could be with you today, but business has forced her to stay in Anacosta. She sends you special greetings on Earth Day, our beloved holiday so rooted in our hearts." The Vice President then picked up on the theme the Archbishop had laid down.

"We continue to build our strength against the supremacists in the Interior. They are the ones who have prevented us from vanquishing climate change, so we continue to face the deadly threat of rising seas and sweltering temperatures. They are oppressing our brown brethren under their racist laws, and forcing them to live in poverty. Yes, we still are not as wealthy as we would like to be in the Diversity Justice Republic. I cannot lie about that. Why are we not as wealthy as we should be?

"It is because we are committed to equalization of resources. The Republic has succeeded in ensuring that the rich are not as rich as they are elsewhere, so that the poorest among us may live with a sufficiency. We may have fewer rich plutocrats, but we have many more people living without fear of hunger and in decent housing."

Malia here thought of the Esplanade, comparing its forbidden delicacies with her sorry weekly Healthy Eating bag, and then recalled the Street People. Standing near a side entrance, she became aware of shadows of figures outside the tent. Perhaps security officials were closely patrolling the perimeter to protect the great Vice President?

"You know that even the Plores, our traditional adversaries, have been given a basic minimum income and the opportunity to engage in honorable labor. Would the white supremacists have done the same for us? You know the answer.

"What is the solution to the problem of wealth creation? How can we raise our Republic to the heights that would allow all of us to live in comfort? We are looking to our Economic Zones. Our scientists are daily devising new improved means of production that will require fewer hands and less effort, while maximizing yield and production. We are tapping the expertise of our farmers and Eco-Artisans to create exciting new fruit and vegetable yields, and products to make our lives easier and more fulfilling. Yet we still need all hands on deck.

"Unfortunately, the Plores are only willing to do the bare minimum to earn their guaranteed income, and the Treaty of the Red and the Blue that codified the separation of the Diversity Justice Republic from the current United States decreed that we must treat the Plores humanely. We are forbidden from forcing them to work in our Economic Zones. Fine."

"Make them work!" shouted a short bald white man in the section in front of Malia's. "Make the fascists work!" called a dreadlocked black woman near him.

"We do not need the Plores! We have millions of young, dedicated Blues who want to see us succeed! I know you are among them, otherwise you would not be here. I am calling on you to volunteer your talents for service in the Economic Zone. I know you have heard conditions are spartan and unwelcoming, and you may fear the fascists who live across the border. I want to reassure you that these are just outdated rumors. The Zone has become increasingly lively and sophisticated in recent years. The fascists are nearer than they are here, true, but our Antifan Defense Forces have kept them on their side of the border. You would have nothing to fear from fascists. In fact, there are fascists around us here, hiding behind a mask of Diversity! Do not think you are safer here than you are there from fascism.

"Come to the Zone, where your ideas and energy will be used and rewarded. This is a way to rise in our society if you feel your talents are not sufficiently engaged."

Malia's armband phone vibrated urgently. She looked down at the screen. It said:

Do not move. Stay where you are.

She hadn't planned to move at all, especially not along with the first eager volunteers, stirred by the passion of the moment, who were lining up in the aisles ahead of her to pledge their willingness to move. Malia supposed that they would renege on their pledges as soon as they returned to the pleasures of City life.

When you see me, pretend to be shocked.
I'm going to arrest you. Don't worry.

Malia looked around wildly. And there was David, wearing his Antifan black leather uniform, heading toward her with an impassive face. She was indeed shocked. No pretense was necessary. He took her by the arm and said under his breath, "We're getting out of here."

He steered her up the side aisle. Nancy, 125, stepped in their way, unaware or dismissive of the Antifan uniform with the white letters ADF on the back. "This person is under my control," she said firmly, "and her obligation to the service is not yet over this afternoon."

David gave Nancy a steely look as he propelled Malia past her. "I'm Commander Harris of the Antifan Defense Forces, 240, and this woman is my prisoner. She is a material witness in a criminal case. Move aside unless you would like to be arrested as well." Nancy stood aside.

Malia burst into genuine tears, and he pushed her out of the last side entrance, holding her left arm slightly behind her back as if to convey she was indeed a prisoner. To her shock, the entire tent was ringed by Economic Strike Force police, and behind them stood another ring of Antifans. Beyond the Antifans waited long lines of yellow buses and brown trucks.

David said under his breath, "All the people in the tent except the VIPs are about to be herded into those trucks and taken away to the Economic Zones. We're getting out of here fast."

The police officers and Antifans made way for them. A tall, strapping, gray-haired Antifan gave the crossed-arm Antifan salute to David, who released Malia's arm just long enough to return it. Then they were back on the road hurrying toward the main parking lot.

"That was my colleague Commander Steve Rosen of the Economic Crimes Unit," said David as they walked briskly, but did not break into a run that would invite suspicion. "I learned about this operation only this morning—not in my usual area. He understood I needed to get you out of here, even though he doesn't know who you are. I tried to reach you earlier, but they had shut down the communications perimeter so no one could receive or send texts."

Behind them they heard a growing dull roar of consternation as the tent's inmates realized they were being prevented from leaving the enclosure. The worshipers from the pens were already being led out meekly, sheeplike, in single file in between lines of police and Antifans toward the buses and trucks. They still wore their pink pussy hats, which made them an even more pathetic sight than before.

Malia suddenly cried, alarmed, "My duffel bag! It's in the bunk. I need to get it."

"Pointless," said David. "All the belongings have been collected from the barracks and thrown into the trucks. They'll be reunited with their owners in the Zone, maybe."

"My toothbrush!"

"I'll buy you another toothbrush. Do you realize what you're escaping from?"

"What about my Social Credit points?"

"Oh for God's sake," said David. "Like you were going to get them anyway?" They ran the last few yards to the yellow sportscar, and in ten seconds they were rolling back down the road toward Anacosta.

Once a safe distance had been opened up between them and the camp, David said soberly, "Those people are doomed. They may be fools, but I feel sorry for them. The conditions in the Zone are abysmal, especially in the mountains. The bunks here were paradise compared with what awaits them. At least it's springtime and not winter. I give them one winter, unless the government really tries to honor its commitment to them and treats them properly."

Malia shook her head thinking how close she had come to disappearing. "I can't thank you enough. You didn't have to stick your neck out for me."

David turned briefly from the road to smile at her. "Oh, you're a very important material witness. Even if I'm trying to keep you from being one much longer. And it wasn't difficult for me to do once I realized it was about to happen. Steve and I are friends. I almost didn't learn about the roundup in time, that's the scary part."

"I don't know how I will ever thank you."

"I thought you just did," he joked. "But here's a suggestion so my effort isn't wasted. I don't want you going back to your apartment immediately—just in case they start trying to round up some stragglers. Your name is on that volunteer list, but you won't be on the buses, so they might wonder. They might be too incompetent to realize or care, but you can't count on that. You would be safe in my apartment, even if they trace the chip there.

"My suggestion is we go to my place and cook a delicious dinner that nobody will demand Social Credit points for. We'll relax, we'll talk, we'll watch a movie. I have a guest room, and you are welcome to it until this business blows over. You can buy a toothbrush. Hell, buy a wardrobe, and they'll deliver it within a few hours.

"Who's watching your cats?"

Malia was surprised and pleased he had thought of them. "Fern is staying at the apartment. It's a more comfortable place than hers. She has to share with roommates."

"Good. Give her a call and tell her she can stay a few more days."

Chapter 14
Dinner at David's
(Saturday/Sunday, 23-24 April)

The hydrogen-fueled yellow sportscar drove into the garage of the Avalon Tower in which David lived, about one mile north of Beaufort at the City's edge. When time and weather permitted, he bicycled to work. They took the elevator to the 23rd floor, where his apartment was one of six luxurious units. A wave of his armband slid open the door, which closed behind them.

"Oh my goodness," Malia gasped. Her eyes swept over the spacious room. "This is so beautiful."

The curved expanse of floor-to-ceiling windows stretched across the room. The shades were raised, revealing a stunning river view as the sun began its descent. A giant screen was mounted above a fireplace to the left, with a dark brown sectional sofa and a light wood coffee table facing it. A rustic wooden chandelier hung above the coffee table. To the left, she gazed on a large kitchen with marble counters, cocktail bar seats along them, and gleaming steel appliances. To the right lay an area behind another curved set of draperies, through which Malia glimpsed a wide bed with mussed bedsheets. There was a corridor to the right of that curtained area which she presumed led to the bathroom and the guest room.

"My mother says it's sterile," said David. He did not add the usual follow-up comment by Marjory, who had necessarily seen it via phone only, that it clearly needed a woman's touch.

"It's like out of a magazine!" Malia countered.

David excused himself to change out of the uniform; while she waited, Malia stared out the windows and ran her hand over the kitchen counters and appliances. He came out wearing a blue polo shirt and navy slacks. "I've put a bunch of shirts and a bathrobe on the bed in the guest room," he said. "You can make up any outfit you like after you shower."

"Shower?"

"When was the last time you showered?" he asked.

She was sheepish. "There were no shower facilities at the festival. We just sponge bathed with towels. Do I smell?"

"No, of course you don't. But you look a little earthy. Maybe that was the idea. Wouldn't you want to take a shower? I assure you that you'll be wearing more clothes afterward than you did at the festival. I put out a very nice selection. And then you can order some replacements, but I know I have an extra toothbrush somewhere." He dug into one of the kitchen cabinets and emerged triumphantly holding a brand-new toothbrush.

While she showered, he called his mother and asked if he could bring his new girlfriend with him tomorrow to her house. Marjory, looming above him on the giant screen, was cautious. "Is she going to be nice to us? I don't want to deal with anyone who's going to be hoity-toity City and start bragging about her Social Credit points."

"She wasn't like that to begin with," David said. "But after today, I think she'll be even less so." He recounted Malia's near miss at the festival. Fortunately, he could be fairly confident no one was listening to his apartment, and Plores were generally exempt from such surveillance.

"Oh my," said Marjory. "Thank goodness you were there like a knight in shining armor."

"I was lucky to have heard about it in time. Will you give her a chance? She has no family at all, and I think she would really enjoy being with us tomorrow afternoon."

"Of course, she is very welcome. I know you wouldn't bring home anyone who wouldn't be nice to us. Not after that last one, who yelled at us for eating a meatloaf."

David laughed, and as he heard Malia turn the doorknob of the guest room, wished his mother a good evening. Malia came out a few minutes later wearing an oversized T-shirt that fell down to above her knees and an old white bathrobe of David's tied tightly around her waist. She had wrapped a soft green towel beehive-like around her wet hair. In the guest room, she had poked around out of sheer curiosity. In the nightstand she found several old boxes of cosmetics labeled "African Goddess Party Powder" and "Aretha Eye Shadow," both bearing the motto "For the Black Goddess You Are." There were also some brochures for vineyards in the nightstand drawer ("Top Shelf Vineyards, 165 and up only") and on the dresser a miniature wicker basket with real sea shells and a little sign indicating a beach vacation at Punta Calidad, the premier resort of the DJR, in Florida. Propped up against the basket rested a small photograph of David with a leggy blonde woman in a demure one-piece bathing suit.

"How do you feel now?"

"Much better," she admitted, "very comfortable. Was that your mom on the phone?"

"Yes," he said, "and you're invited to her house for dinner tomorrow night. It's nothing special, I go over there almost every Sunday, so please don't worry that you're being invited for any special event. You'll like my mother and sisters. Just don't mention Social Credit points."

Malia was cautious. "Only if you're sure I won't be putting them out. Wait, does that mean we're going to Ploreville?"

"Yes, that's where they live, among the savages. That doesn't frighten you, does it? Didn't I tell you last week they probably won't eat you there?"

"I've only been to Ploreville once," Malia marveled, recalling one night when she and a few college friends had gone "slumming" over to Ploreville, where they drank in a bar under suspicious gazes. It was difficult to visit Ploreville, because the self-driving cars would not take you there, and you had to master the labyrinthine bus system the Plores themselves used to travel to the bridges and back. And those buses were far and few between on weekends, when fewer Plores trudged to jobs in the City. And if you paid your fare with your armband, some ADF monitor might wonder why a Social Crediteer was on the Plore bus system at all.

David resisted the temptation to say, "Don't feed the animals, please."

He set her up on a kitchen barstool with a workscreen, and said, "Go order a few outfits. Whatever you like just to be comfortable through the end of the week, including to go to work. A nightgown or two? Here's my carbon offset number, so just plug it in, all right?"

"That's very kind of you. First you save my life, and now you buy me clothes," she smiled.

"You make them sound equivalent in importance, but maybe for a woman that's the case," he grinned back. "While you're doing that, I'm going to make us dinner." He stared somewhat perplexedly into the coldbox. The coldbox was full, thanks to his grocery delivery on Thursday, but he was at a loss. "Would you prefer a steak or pasta?"

"A steak, please," she said demurely, peering at the screen, her bare feet twining around the bars of the stool. Of course you would, thought David. Four days of vegan food and a spartan diet in general would settle that dilemma quickly. He shouldn't even have asked. He decided to broil steaks in the fast-flash cooking box on the counter, *and* cook pasta with tomato sauce. Malia probably wouldn't need any vegetables tonight, but just to be safe and balanced, he extracted frozen broccoli from the freezer. While everything cooked in the multi-compartmented box, he opened a bottle of red California wine, poured them glasses, and brought Malia her glass, coming around behind her to look at the screen.

She was deciding between nightgowns, and showed him two.

"Get the purple one," he said, and then pointed to a babydoll twin nightgown. "What about that?"

"Oh, I don't know," she said. "That seems a little risqué, doesn't it?"

"Exactly," he said. "Do it to please me." So she added that to the cart, placed the order with the Diversity Warehouse, and was happy to learn the entire order would be delivered by 10 o'clock that evening. That's what happened when you placed your order from the Avalon Tower in Upper Northwest instead of the Rosebud.

He handed Malia her glass, picked up his, and said, "We need to toast to a successful rescue today. I shudder to think of how much inconvenience I would have had if I'd needed to locate you in the Economic Zone and bring you back."

"Would you have been able to find me?"

"Honestly, it might not have been possible. It's a void, nobody keeps records of the workers, and those factory managers don't care if you are calling from the Antifan Defense Forces. They answer to the Economic Tower only. So let's toast to your rescue, and your happiness."

"Our happiness," Malia dared to say. His steady gray eyes locked on her sparkling brown ones, and they clinked their wine glasses together.

He suddenly realized, almost achingly, that he really did want to make her happy, and he had never felt this way with any other woman he had dated. All of them were complete and self-sufficient, armed with Social Credit, the product of a system designed to ensure their satisfaction at the expense of others. What more could he do for any of them? What did they want from him other than a good-looking companion, especially with his raffish Plore background?

Malia needed him, and not just for better meals. Seeing her relaxed and content convinced him that he could make her life better, and she in turn would understand that his status and job notwithstanding, he was an outsider too. Both had lost parents in the wars fighting on the losing side. Malia had grown up in an orphanage, was enduring the grinding semi-poverty of low Social Credit status, and her child had been taken from her, presumably unjustly, perhaps the cruelest thing one could do to a mother. He wanted to ask her about that child, but not at this moment.

After dinner, they sat on the sofa together with more wine, his arm around her shoulders, and watched a 20th century movie from the less-restricted GVN list to which David had access. As the credits rolled, the lobby attendant arrived with the wardrobe package. David went to the door and signed for it. "Here," he said, giving it to Malia. "Go try on the short nightgown."

She came back wearing the old bathrobe over the new nightgown. He didn't ask to see it yet. They sat on the couch, looking at each other.

"I have to ask you something," he said. "I kept waiting for the right moment, but there is no right moment and it's going to be awkward no matter when I ask. Will you tell me what exactly happened to your daughter?"

Malia's smile shrank and the anxiety washed over her face again. "I thought you already knew. I thought you knew everything about me." She suddenly feared that David would drive her home, his face rigid with disapproval, drop her off without opening the door or looking at her, and then she would be alone again, the dream having vanished as quickly as it came.

"Believe it or not, it's not in your file. All it says is that they took your five-year old daughter away." He felt her panic, and he held her head gently on each side, meeting her eyes. "Malia, I don't care what the reason was. I promise I won't leave you. Unless you killed her, and since they took her away, I know that's not what happened. But we can't continue without knowing each other's secrets. It's too big a gap in your story for me not to ask. And if you want to ask me anything about my life, you ask. This goes two ways. But tell me about this before it's too late."

She took a deep breath and told him. How the principal of the school where Isabelle was in kindergarten called her into the school. After dropping Isabelle off, she went to the main office, glancing only briefly at the walls decorated with positive Diversity slogans. The severe-looking principal told her that a disturbing incident had occurred. The children were drawing pictures for "Coronavirus Liberation Day," the June holiday when the nation commemorated the political gains from the terrible epidemic of 2020-2022.

Even more so than the retreat of the illness itself, the liberals celebrated the decision by the left-wing Congress to maintain many of the temporary restrictions that had been placed on church worship, firearms, rightwing assembly, and other activities that the progressive elites had been aiming to curtail or eliminate for years. It was argued that since the country still lacked a safe vaccine against the sickness, the right to assembly needed to be curbed, for the health of the nation, to "flatten the curve." Voters made fearful about safety elected an even more left-wing Congress in Fall 2022; aided by likeminded governors, lawmakers quickly moved to codify the temporary restrictions into law.

The right swung back, with grassroots fervor stoked by the Republican president, who had been under attack for years from the mandarins of the press, academia, and the Deep State of permanent government as he defended the traditional liberty of the people. The corporate sector hesitated, but seeded by educated shock-troop progressives, mostly succumbed under political pressure. The armed stalwarts of Virginia and the Rocky Mountains, the farmers of the Great Plains, and the Deplorables in exurban areas across the country, rose in righteous anger against the diminution of constitutional freedoms two or three centuries old.

The country seethed for another quarter century, with Americans steadily moving to areas that reflected their values. Control of Congress and the White House careened between increasingly polarized factions. Violence erupted in the streets and in the universities. The US Congress held its last in-person session in 2050 after congressmen rioted in the House chamber, killing six.

But generally, the Left lacked the armed force to impose its values on those whom Hillary Clinton had once sneeringly called a basket of "Deplorables." Eventually, it turned to the anarchist gangs collectively known as Antifans and built an army that would begin to seize territory from the Deplorables and drive them either into the Interior, herd them into the coastal Cities, or just kill them. The US military would not strike against political opponents, but neither would it accept control by the Left, so its members retreated into the Interior with the Right, with which it aligned culturally.

By 2052, civil war raged throughout the United States, the DJR was declared in 2055, and the war concluded in 2060 with the signing of the Treaty and the hardening of boundaries between the Blue coastal areas and the Red Interior.

"All right, so they were drawing Coronavirus Liberation Day pictures," said David. He knew at least three or four women named Corona in honor of the liberation. "What was the problem?"

The principal handed Malia a crayoned drawing, saying, "This is a copy of the original, which is in safekeeping with the authorities." The third person in the room was a scruffily dressed man who appeared to be taking notes on a workscreen.

Malia looked at the copy. Four scrawled stick figures seemed to be dancing. It looked like a typical kindergarten drawing. In the upper right corner was the word "COFING."

"I don't understand," she said. "What is the problem?"

The principal arched her eyebrows, "Are you really so dense? Look at the figures on the left."

The two figures on the left were colored in yellow and facing the two on the right, colored in blue.

"What about it?"

"When asked about the painting, your daughter said the yellow figures were from China and they were coughing on the blue figures. The class was expressly taught that the coronavirus was not, not, from China at all, but was part of a United States plot to weaken our adversaries by creating a worldwide pandemic. China was the first victim. This is completely in accordance with the national doctrine of Coronavirus Liberation. How your daughter misunderstood the lesson is inconceivable unless she was being deliberately misled at home. And we also find it very disturbing that she colored the Asian figures yellow."

Malia would have laughed at the nonsense, but knew the moment was turning ominous.

"They're only kindergarteners. I don't think they would understand the complexity of that history lesson at all. And I'm sure she colored those figures yellow because that's the crayon she had at the time. She has Asian friends and knows they are not colored yellow at all."

"Are you saying that the Knowledge Tower and our educational establishment lack an understanding of what five-year-olds are capable of learning? Are you one of those ignorant people who do not understand that when children are not taught early about Diversity, they will fall prey to false doctrines?

"Ms. Jenness, I find it disturbing that you are not taking this incident with the proper seriousness. Nor are you assuming responsibility for your daughter having learned false doctrines. I am not saying you taught her heresy, but you are not concerned about this at all."

"Yes, I am very concerned. I don't know how this happened. We have not talked about Coronavirus Liberation Day at all—"

"Not at all? With the preparations for the holiday having been underway for weeks? Do you not take her to Church and Mother Earth School?" Malia could not deny that she and Isabelle had been sleeping in for many weeks on Sunday. They were night owls and they would play games until midnight and drink hot cocoa together.

"We talked at home. I'm not sure how she misunderstood the story. For Mother's sakes, she's just five years old!"

"I thought you said you did not talk about the holiday at all."

"Well, yes, not in depth—"

"Ms. Jenness, we find your explanation to be very unconvincing, even cavalier."

"I'm sorry. Is my daughter going to be punished? Does she know she did anything wrong?"

"She understands now."

"Thank you." Malia rose to leave. "I'm sorry to have caused you such inconvenience."

The principal fixed her with a gimlet eye. "This may not be the end of the issue," she warned Malia, who did not read anything unusual into the comment. Malia figured that there would be a black mark in Isabelle's book, but what could even the Diversity Justice Republic do to a tiny five-year old with brown bangs and rosy cheeks?

Malia went to pick up Isabelle at the after-school nursery, but the teachers said they had not seen her all afternoon. "She never arrived," one said apologetically to Malia. "We called the school and they said she had gone home sick."

Malia rushed home, but saw no Isabelle, not that Isabelle would have gone home on her own or have been left there unsupervised. The apartment was a shambles. Drawers had been yanked out and left on the floor. All of Isabelle's clothes, toys, and electronics were missing. Even the artwork on the coldbox door was missing. It was as if she had never lived there. She called the police to report a child kidnapping, but after a few minutes, they said they regretted they could not help in what appeared to be a Knowledge Tower administrative issue. The phone at the school rang and rang, since the teachers had gone home. She texted her daughter's teacher but got no response. She had no one else to call. She took perverse hope in the apartment's disarray—whatever had happened to Isabelle was clearly done at the behest of someone in authority so she had to assume that Isabelle was safe and unharmed, somewhere. But of course, crying and distressed.

After a sleepless night of weeping, Malia stalked into the principal's office. Her head throbbed; pains of anxiety shot through her chest. This time an Anacosta Mental Health policewoman waited with the principal. "What have you done with my daughter?" she screamed at them.

The principal looked satisfied. "The authorities have removed her from your custody and she will now be placed in a more suitable home. You are not fit to raise a child in the Diversity Justice Republic." She handed Malia a sheet of paper that was headed "Order #4468—June 4, 2080." She pointed out the section that committed Malia to silence on the issue, lest she become subject herself to criminal penalty.

Malia thought briefly of leaping across the desk and assaulting the principal, but at least they were leaving her alone for now, and a jail term would only seal her fate and that of Isabelle. She called the office of her assemblywoman, and left a futile message. She called the only lawyer she knew, a man she had dated briefly when she arrived in the City. He listened to her story, made a few phone calls, and then apologetically said, "I'm sorry. This is completely out of my range. There's nothing any lawyer can do if it's a Knowledge Tower administrative action."

"There's no appeal process?" Malia asked him desperately. It was like punching air.

"None in this case," he replied, sympathetic but without conveying hope. "In an ordinary criminal case, of course, there is an appeals process. A criminal is usually given the benefit of the doubt all the way through the process, since they are usually a victim of disadvantaged circumstances. But in a knowledge crime, the government is granted the presumptive victory with complete control over the administrative record. That means they have the right not to show you anything regarding the case, let alone where your daughter goes." He paused. "They might return to do another sweep of your apartment. If there's anything of your daughter's they left behind, I'd suggest safeguarding it now. I probably shouldn't even have said that. Good luck, and I am very sorry."

Dazed, Malia began tidying up the apartment. No one could ever guess a child had lived here. Theobald emerged from a closet. To her surprise, she found on a closet shelf two drawings by Isabelle, and she quickly inserted them in the mattress case on her own bed, which proved to be a judicious move, since the apartment was ransacked twice more that month. There was no recourse but to continue marching zombie-like from workplace to home, from home to workplace. Even empty of all Isabelle's belongings, the apartment was full of torturous memories. On her armband phone, someone had mysteriously erased all of the photographs of Isabelle, even when she was only one of several children in the frame.

A psychologist called to set up an appointment, but it quickly became clear that the woman was only testing the extent to which she was accepting her fate. How she would have resisted, Malia did not know. But she knew that anything she said would be reported to the authorities. "I would be happy to meet with you to discuss Diversity-appropriate child rearing techniques."

"Would this help me recover my daughter?" Malia asked.

"No, I'm afraid not, but this would help you be better prepared to raise your next child."

Malia wanted to tell her, "F—k you too," but could not risk her own safety. "No thank you," she said politely.

"Earth Mother be with you," the psychologist intoned. "Let me know if you change your mind."

A month later came the notice of eviction and reassignment to the EcoLand Hostel. A few weeks after she moved into the hostel her annual Social Credit score plummeted to 41, one point more than the minimum required to live in the City. The reassignment to the hostel had been a sure sign that the Social Credit downgrade was coming; normally she would have merited a modest one bedroom. The authorities had docked her 50 points for antisocial behavior involving a child, which fortunately was only a one-year penalty. If she minded her behavior, next year's Social Credit score would rebound 15 points, and so on until she regained whatever score she was otherwise entitled to. It gave her an incentive to plow on, silently and without complaint, except for the nightmares in which policemen came to her home and stole Isabelle all over again, only with her present.

For three years, she lived in a narrow cell with a bed, dresser and small closet, shared a grim kitchenette and toilet/shower with ten slovenly men and women, and trudged to work in the morning at the Depository, and home again in the evening. She constantly attended special Earth Mother services and funerals to boost her Social Credit score. She said nothing to her colleagues, but the framed photograph of Isabelle on her desk had vanished immediately, so they must have known.

At the Depository, she began furtively reading dangerous volumes, taking advantage of the gradually disappearing colleagues and the inattention of the remaining ones. It was risky, but she felt that only to these paper confidants brimming with Truth could she be herself, albeit silently. She learned how to defeat the electronic eye with the cardboard brick that resembled a book and when not in use, sat in a closet with cleaning materials.

The only other solace was she met Fern at the hostel, and the two women bonded over free concerts in the park and the occasional takeout meal. Still, she did not tell Fern about Isabelle until much later.

David shook his head. "How absolutely horrible. What a nightmare. I don't know what I can say." The tears were streaming down Malia's cheeks. He pulled her gently toward him on the sofa and she cried into his strong chest.

"How could they do such a thing?" he asked, incredulously. But in her eyes, he saw the unspoken accusation, or perhaps he imagined it. *You Antifans do terrible things too.* Earlier that same day, hadn't she seen dozens of Antifans helping the police herd the Earth worshipers into the buses? "Antifans have never, ever separated a child from her mother, I can promise you that." He could, however, imagine some of the chilly bureaucrats in the Knowledge Tower mercilessly kidnapping a child from her mother under the rubric of 'law.' Just based on Malia's story, he was glad that Director Ferraro was aiming the ADF's artillery at the Knowledge Tower.

He raised Malia's jaw and placed his mouth over hers, kissing her deeply. David's instinctive reaction was to show that he cared and nothing she had done and nothing she had suffered would change the commitment he had made today to protect her. Words would no longer suffice. She responded diffidently at first, but then the bathrobe and the polo shirt were shed. She had not seen his bare chest before, it was muscled, but not clownishly, and covered with a light blond fuzz. Soon they were together on the great bed behind the curtain. He reached over to dim the lights, and another button released a canopy around them, which created a cozy, brown cave.

The first time he was tender, kissing her everywhere, calling her "beautiful," and "darling." The second time, an hour later, just as she was drifting off to sleep, he mounted her from behind. It was gentler than it would have been in an Antifan detention cell, but no less insistent, and it told her, "I want you again. You." The third time, she rode him so that he could view her breasts from below. They were surprisingly long and heavy, but the nipples turned upward at the ends, and he enjoyed watching them billow and retreat above him. An hour later, she apologetically pleaded soreness, and he forcefully moved her head and mouth down to bring him to completion, turning her around so that his hand simultaneously brought her to climax one more time. Then they finally fell asleep shortly before dawn, backs touching.

When Malia woke up, it was around eleven, the canopy was raised, and she was alone in bed. David, wearing only boxer shorts, and holding a spatula, smiled at her and gave her a chaste kiss as she approached. Something sizzled on the stove. "I'm making us blueberry pancakes," he said, and to her blank look, he said, "It's a Plore specialty. You'll love it."

She looked out the window bemusedly. Strange, yesterday afternoon the view had been of the Potowmack at sunset and today she was looking at the Cityscape to the northeast. Had she really imagined the view? "Didn't you have a river view yesterday?" she asked.

David said, "The penthouse level rotates constantly, but so slowly you won't notice any movement. You get a 360-degree view every seventy-two hours." Malia had never heard of such a thing.

On the screen was the Sunday morning news program, *Diversity Today*. The lead story was about the amazing pledge by thousands of worshipers at the Earth Festival yesterday to commit immediately to traveling to the Economic Zone to lend their talents to building a bulwark against white supremacy. Todd Charles, 270, the famous anchorman, droned, "We are all used to seeing Social Crediteers promise to help build Diversity, but often the reality falls short of the promise. Life is too comfortable in our modern Cities. Yesterday, however, moved by Vice President Peace-Williams' stirring speech, thousands not only lined up to volunteer, but afterward joyfully boarded eighty buses that drove them directly to their new home."

"Imagine," said David. "What a coincidence that eighty buses were waiting for them."

"I think the Earth Festival is going to have a lot more trouble next year with attendance," Malia said wryly. Propaganda commercials then promoted various DJR initiatives. In keeping with the Anti-White Privilege doctrine, Diverse Peoples represented 90 percent of the people in commercials, unless the whites were the butt of some humor or criticism.

When the show returned, Charles interviewed the Vice President and an academic. All three agreed that youth were more enthusiastic than ever in the cause of Diversity, and that the buildup on the frontiers boded ill for the white supremacists. Footage showed the lines of volunteers boarding the buses, but none of the policemen, let alone the Antifans. None of the attendees themselves were interviewed. "We were unable to interview a volunteer," said Todd Charles, "since the buses departed so rapidly. We will bring you a special episode from the Zone this summer to document the amazing transformation taking place on the frontier."

"What a liar," said David. "Let's eat."

Chapter 15
The Director's Office
(Monday, 25 April)

On Monday morning, David took Malia to work, and then hurried up to Beaufort, wearier than usual after the busy weekend. Malia and his family had gotten along so well that the yellow sportscar had left Ploreville later than expected, not that he was complaining about that. After driving back from Ploreville on Sunday evening, he had left Malia scrolling through the half-forbidden movies in his apartment while he went into the office. "If anything strange starts happening or you feel unsafe, call me immediately," he said. He didn't think anyone would dare accost her in his apartment, but ever since hearing about the kidnapped child, even he was shaken. He needed a few hours to prepare for the Director's briefing and wasn't going to leave it for early Monday morning.

The Knowledge Tower investigation dossier was fattening with interviews but David had to admit to himself there was no real smoking gun. Self-satisfied unctuous bureaucrats were annoying, but not in themselves criminal. Everyone claimed that they were not responsible for the Depository, and took credit only for a narrow slice of the Tower pie for whose salutary state they could personally vouch. The Director would likely be impatient with him at the meeting and push for some progress, he knew it.

Walters poked his head into David's office, "Good morning, chief! I hear we're going to see the Director later this morning."

The deputy sat down opposite David and said, "Pinckney completely denies taking anything over to MacMillan other than muffins and cookies. She says she brought the food over to the MacMillans because even though she's a member of the church, it's out of her way and it was more convenient to bring it to the MacMillans first."

"What about the book residue?"

"Just denies any books were in there. I got to admit, it's possible that MacMillan used the bags afterward for his books, but we also had Julie MacMillan send us a bunch of those reusable bags, not just Pinckney's—for a control group, so to speak—and none of the residue was in those. Only in the ones Pinckney used."

"What does the residue tell us about the dates and the possible origin of the books? And are these similar to the ones we found in the MacMillan basement?"

"The chemists are still running the tests, chief."

"Anything from her electronic feeds?"

"A lot of interference on the Tuesday night armband feeds, consistently most weeks when school was in session. And, interestingly enough, the same on MacMillan's feed at the same time. Like music in the background, or deliberate static of some kind. And it wasn't an issue of the neighborhood, since others we picked randomly, including Julie's, had no such problem."

"Could they have been having an affair?" David threw it out, but regretted the suggestion when he saw Walters' mocking face. He did not like that face. "A very unlikely pair, I gather."

"She denies anything of the sort, chief, and I think I'd believe her on that one."

"Have we checked yet for that interference on any of the other suspects' feeds at that time?"

"Not yet," said Walters, making a mental note to have Cheysa and Karlmarx start researching that immediately.

"What's going on with Melendez?" asked David.

"Just a lot of blubbering and nasty comments about the other professors, but he's starting to repeat himself a lot. I'm wondering if we should switch him out with someone who might actually be part of that discussion club MacMillan supposedly started."

Walters came back to Pinckney. "I don't think she's telling us the truth. I've been a real gentleman so far, just a slap here or there, but I'm inclined to take her down to the Red Rooms to see if we can get more out of her, like, *tell us about those goddamned books before we kill you.*" The Red Rooms were a euphemism for the Beaufort physical punishment chambers. MacMillan mercifully had died without ever seeing them.

The two arrived at the Director's suite with ample time to spare. Walters scanned his files while David chatted up the secretary. Then the door to Ferraro's suite opened, and Steve Rosen emerged with several of his lieutenants. David and Steve exchanged quick salutes, and it was now David and Walters' turn to enter the sanctum.

Ferraro was exultant. "Did you hear about the Earth Weekend operation?" he said, "Those drones didn't expect a thing until they were herded onto the buses. I'm not sure how useful they'll be out in the Economic Zone, but they weren't doing us a whole lot of good here either. The Towers should be getting a fresh crop of college graduates any week now to replace them."

David said, "I saw it on TV. Todd Charles made it seem as if everyone had volunteered to go out there and help Diversity."

Ferraro snorted, "People will believe anything. Frankly, we're desperate for labor out there. Plores won't go even if you pay them. What I like about the operation is that here's an example where we, the ADF, cooperated fully with the Economic Tower. But this brings me back to the stupid Knowledge Tower. Let's talk about those pussies."

Walters perked up.

As David had feared, the Director viewed the Knowledge Tower investigation to date as clearly flailing at an elusive target. Yes, the Depository had been poorly managed, but unless it could be connected to more widespread rot in the Tower, it would lead nowhere. If only books from the Depository could be linked to subversive efforts elsewhere—however, David acknowledged that the books seemed to have stayed in the building.

"So, you recommend the librarian stay?" Ferraro was asking him.

"I don't see the harm," said David. "I think the MacMillan incident terrified her. She's competent enough."

On the other hand, the Clinton University investigation seemed very promising indeed. Ferraro chortled happily as Walters ran down the list of subversive and potentially criminal remarks and activities of the Clinton University staff and faculty. The evidence of a club led by MacMillan was compelling, if still vague. Walters explained what they knew about the club, and why the book angle was critical. The next steps were to link the books with the club, and the club with members. "What about the president?" asked Ferraro. "Do you think she could be guilty?"

"No, sir," said Walters, "she's comfortable being the president and doesn't want to jeopardize her lifestyle. On the bright side, she's not going to stand in our way. I convinced her to stand aside, which is what she prefers to do anyway."

"Ha ha!" said Ferraro. "I'm sure you have some interesting convincing techniques, Walters." Walters decided he would tell Ferraro about his trick on Fufuloa when the time was right, like when David was not sitting there, glowering at him.

"Here's how I feel we ought to proceed, based on what you guys are telling me. We're going to strike at the Tower, one way or another. That's my main goal here. They've gotten a little too fat and comfy. I've even had some of them hinting they ought to have more control over ADF policies, like which cases we take on and how we treat our Knowledge Tower detainees. I'm not putting up with that crap. We need to strike at them before they get any more obnoxious.

"But there are different ways to get behind their walls. The Depository isn't their weak spot. We probed it, but there's no give there, at least not with what we've learned. Fine. But they are also responsible for ideological control at all the universities in the DJR. Judging by what you're finding out at Clinton, I think we can make a strong case that the rot is everywhere and that we need to expand the probe into all the universities. Harris, I am going to give you another forty officers to go out to the field, and twenty analysts to work the evidence here at Beaufort.

"All I ask is that you get me the evidence. I'm not going to look at it too hard. If you tell me it's sound, we'll use it. I'm not going to be tripped up by PhD standards here. You understand?" Ferraro fixed David with a steady stare under his heavy brows.

David said he understood.

Outside the Director's suite, David and Walters looked at each other. David said, cautiously, "This is a huge development. I wasn't expecting this. We'll be purging the universities for years." Privately, he thought, at least Malia is now safe.

"Red Room time," said Walters happily.

David went back to his office and signed release forms for two dozen black protesters who had been languishing in the bowels of Beaufort since Halloween after their ill-advised demonstration calling for the right to publish an independent black-themed publication on the GVN. We'll need the room shortly, he thought. He smiled at the memory of how he had flooded the demonstration with white Antifan plainclothesmen to disguise the fact that black citizens specifically had grievances with the government. Ferraro had called that "damn clever."

Chapter 16

Party Night

(Saturday, 30 April)

Cheysa sat on her powder blue sofa, watching a light romantic comedy about black pole dancers, but was distracted. Walters called her several times during the evening to ensure she was staying home, per his instructions. Cheysa knew that because they had identical 185 Social Credit scores, he could not listen to either her armband or her appliance feed, but since he was a demon, he was not bound by earthly or Antifan rules. And he had installed cameras throughout her apartment a few weeks ago, just in case demon magic alone was insufficient.

Yes, a demon. Her mother, a secret Christian who had raised Cheysa and her sister Lisa in a two-bedroom apartment in Southeast Anacosta, knew about such things. She had been hearing Cheysa's complaints about Walters, ever since he accosted her in a Beaufort break room literally two days after she broke up with Arnaud. It wasn't working out with Arnaud, admittedly, even though he was a nice man with a good job at the Economic Tower.

How Walters had known that she was newly available still puzzled her, unless he had overheard gossip at work, but she always tried to keep her private life private around the jovial boys of the KCU. She was heating her leftover pasta lunch in the box-oven, and, when she turned around, he was sitting at one of the round tables, gazing on her. "Hello, beautiful," he said. "Come and have your lunch with me." He was her supervisor, what else could she say? He chewed reflectively on a granola bar and she tried to avoid those piercing green eyes, to the point at which he said, "Look at me. Don't be shy. A woman as beautiful as you shouldn't be so shy."

Cheysa desperately longed for someone else to come in and interrupt them, but it was a late lunch hour and almost nobody appeared. When a weedy-looking analyst showed up, paper sack in hand, Walters curtly said, "Do you mind if we have some privacy?" and the analyst fled.

"Your braids," Walters eventually said, referring to her crowning glory, tightly wound around her head. "They are absolutely magnificent. I would love to see them down. How long are they?"

Cheysa was speechless with shock. But Walters would not be deterred.

"About one meter," she quavered.

"You know, my bed has a head board with iron railings. I've often wondered what you would look like in my bed if those braids were tied to the railings."

She had no alternative but to accept his invitation to a date at Campesino's, the City's most exclusive eco-Mexican restaurant, and no alternative but to mutely accompany him home after their second date, since Walters was not a patient man. The braid idea was less workable in practice than in theory, since the knots kept slipping off the railings, despite Walters' assiduous efforts. But from that night on, they were a couple, and everyone at work except Commander Harris realized it. When she complained about his visits to the brothel, Walters became angry. "Well, you're not there 24 hours a day. What happens when I'm at work late and I need a break?"

Then he would kiss her, saying, "That's just a physical release, like going to the bathroom. You're the one I care about. I don't even know their names." He allowed her to stay in her own apartment, but she was under his eye nine hours a day at work, which was only going to increase now that the KCU was turning on the universities. On weekends he stayed with her.

It wasn't entirely bad, which is why she hadn't appealed to Commander Harris, whom she considered a gentleman and who would probably transfer her if she asked. She had to admit Brian was handsome, his lovemaking was grimly determined at achieving her satisfaction, and others were impressed she was dating him. She hadn't really ever expected to be dating a white man, however, with the possibility of cultural miscues and children whose Social Credit scores would be lower than hers. Arnaud had respected her mother's deep faith in the Lord, but she would never dare mention it to Brian, who might use it as an excuse to separate her from her mother. Along those lines, he didn't understand why she wanted to spend so much time with her mother and sister, or talk with them at least once a night. "What are you, a f---ing Plore?" he sneered when he caught her in another conversation with them.

As for Plores, he was hardened against them, and could not mention Commander Harris for a minute without disparaging his background and sissified love for his own mother and sisters, a love that Cheysa privately thought commendable. Walters was bitter at Harris, who he thought was holding his career back with his "ladylike" approach. This added knowledge of the commander's humanity gave Cheysa greater hope that if she appealed to Commander Harris, he would help her. But at what cost? Walters would know she had gone over his head, especially because she had tentatively asked him once they began dating whether she ought to transfer to another unit. He had looked sharply at her and said, "Don't even think about that."

Walters didn't talk much about his own family, but Cheysa soon learned he was from an esteemed Antifan background. His father had commanded an Antifan unit in western Pennsylvania during the civil wars, dying in an engagement shortly before the Treaty was signed. Walters was proud of the father he had hardly known. Both of his older brothers were Antifan officers in Boston. "We have all served this Republic," said Walters in an unguarded moment, "and I will kill anyone who tries to undermine it. No regrets."

"How many people have you killed?" Cheysa asked him. He looked at her thoughtfully and said, "I have stopped counting. But they all deserved it."

Cheysa lacked that history or the brimstone spirit it invoked. Really, she thought, it would have been much better had she become an ordinary policewoman, maybe with a beat in a City neighborhood of ordinary Social Crediteers like her mother. She could envision herself rescuing a cat from a tree or driving off Street People from the lobby of a retirement home, maybe finding them some appropriate social services. Or just calmly walking her beat, talking with and developing friendly relationships with the old people and the dog walkers and the mothers of small children. Unlike her sister, who was a cardiologist, Cheysa had had little patience for schoolwork, but she liked to help people. When she graduated from high school, she had applied for a social worker program, but her grades hadn't been quite good enough, or so she surmised, because they directed her to the police academy instead.

Two years into her program, shortly before graduation, the Antifans came to the academy and skimmed off the cream of the crop, which that year meant an African-American woman who could meet the stringent physical standards of the ADF, which for a woman were not much less than for a man. Even the Antifans kept a checklist to show the Knowledge Tower they were loyal to Diversity, if only to divert scrutiny from their other less wholesome practices. They cared little whether a recruit was too kind or empathetic to become an Antifan, because they held that anyone could be trained to the required level of brutality.

In her quiet moments, Cheysa had to admit she wasn't a very good Antifan. Naturally, she joined in with her comrades when they mocked prisoners and swung her baton and chain when they rounded up knowledge criminals. She always swung a few seconds later and landed fewer blows, doing just enough to deflect criticism. Any noticeable diffidence in her approach to violence was probably attributed to her femaleness. Sometimes she wondered if Walters would let her become an analyst, so at least she could be spared the violent outside operations. But thinking of Karlmarx and his calm tapping on the screen adjacent to the interrogation rooms, she knew she would still witness hideous deeds. Brian was already telling her, "You need to do a Red Room interrogation. Otherwise you aren't really a true Antifan." She dared not say, "But I am not a true Antifan. And I still am a Christian, in my heart."

On the rare occasions when she could find the time to visit her mother in her modest one-bedroom apartment at the Snowball, she told her all this, sparing her the more gruesome details. They would only talk about the demon when they could stroll outside, where frankness was safer. Her mother agreed that she could not risk leaving Walters or the ADF, which was all one and the same. "It is a real shame that you ended up there," said Reba Conroy, 115, "he is a demon, for sure." Reba Conroy was a fiftyish woman with cropped gray hair and a peppery demeanor. She had worked in the Social Tower for decades, processing income transfers for Plores and retirees. Sometimes Cheysa was not sure how the Antifans had taken her, with her mother's disdain for the official church so easy to uncover by any credible investigator.

When Cheysa, in fairness to her lover, pointed out to her mother that he was good looking, occasionally tender and affectionate, and made sure her performance reviews stayed flattering, her mother said, "That's a demon indeed. If they were only cruel, you would have left by now no matter what. The demon knows how to mix just enough good with bad to keep you around.

"You will just have to wait until he loses interest in you, Cheysa, honey. That's the only way to treat a demon. The harder you try to escape the harder they grasp onto you. And pray with your full heart that he goes soon." They would sometimes sit on a bench and quietly pray the prayers she knew from childhood, but only after Cheysa checked under the metal slats to make sure no listening devices had been placed there.

Cheysa heard the wet clothes moving from the chute from the washer into the dryer. During the week, a Plore woman came to clean the apartment and do laundry, but Cheysa had told her not to bother coming yesterday, instead paying her the full amount owed in honor of the May Day holiday celebrating Labor. She lay on the bed watching the movie. At 9:30 pm promptly, Brian called as promised. She heard men's conversation in the background. In a rare honor, he had been invited with Commander Harris to one of Director Ferraro's Saturday night parties.

"How is the party?" she asked.

"Amazing," he said, "You would not believe the spread. I've been eating lobster rolls and drinking French champagne all evening. I'll bring some of the rolls home if I can. Do you know how hard it is to get French champagne these days? And you'll be happy to know there aren't many women here, and they're nowhere of your quality. I wouldn't let them lick my shoes. Call you in an hour. Be a good girl." *Click.*

A few hours earlier, she had lain on the same bed, propped up on a pillow, and watched him dress for the event. He was a fine-looking man, she couldn't deny it— broad shoulders, a muscular back, narrowing to tight buttocks and powerful thighs, six foot three in stocking feet. A giant Fist tattoo with ADF spelled out above it rippled across his back. Whatever he wore, he presented powerfully. He smiled in the mirror back at her on the bed. He had been in a buoyant mood since Monday, when Director Ferraro practically took the investigation from Commander Harris and endorsed Walters' view. Well, not exactly taken it from Harris, but Ferraro had for all intents and purposes told Harris his side of the investigation wasn't working and then praised Walters' work, concluding that they did indeed need to toughen up with the knowledge criminals. And on Tuesday afternoon, one of Ferraro's aides had personally delivered the party invitations to David and Walters, causing a ripple of pride and excitement in the unit.

"It's all Whiro," said Walters when Cheysa commented that fortune was favoring him this week. "I've been doing the same damn thing for years, but couldn't get past our civilized commander. Nobody cared. What's changed? We've got a goddamn god of evil now helping us."

While Walters was calling Cheysa from the house's porch, David stood in an arched doorway to the living room as Ferraro held court in a low-slung armchair, knees spread beneath his comfortable paunch. It would have been a faux pas to wear a uniform tonight, but he recognized several other commanders, one or two with spouses. Some were sitting on the hobnailed leather sofa or on the high-backed chairs placed around the room, and two young fellows were perched on the staircase with a good view of the living room. David recognized Jim Fielding, 150, from the *Anacosta Post*, and the female executive from the Diversity Warehouse (likely 200 plus) that supplied the City's, and by extension, the ADF's needs.

Ferraro was saying to his audience, "As some of you know, I'm losing patience with the Knowledge Tower. I understand we've got to guard the revolution and champion Diversity, and no one's more on board with that than I am, this has been my life's passion, but are we going to guard something that's rotting from within? It's going to be up to the ADF to make sure we continue to have something worth protecting. Jim, I'll give you a few statements for your article, just make sure to run it by our press office on Monday morning, okay?"

"Thank you, sir," said Jim Fielding. He was a balding man in an old plaid jacket that bunched around his middle. He looked like a sports reporter, but he had been covering the ADF for two decades, or rather, it had been instructing him on coverage. It was a good deal for both sides.

"Sir," said one of the commanders, a mustachioed Latino fellow whom David recognized from the gym, "how bad might this get? Are we looking for a confrontation, or are we just hoping the Tower will back down and allow us to do our thing?"

"The latter, Felix," said Ferraro. "I'm not looking for trouble. But I'm getting a little tired of being lectured to by mid-200 twits with fancy degrees who don't recognize who and what holds their entire Diversity Land fantasy together." Chuckles from the accommodating lobstered crowd. He pointed to David, "Commander Harris is my point person as we clean out the universities. This is an area where the Tower absolutely stinks. Clinton University is full of subversives and we know it isn't the only one. Let's have a round of applause for Commander Harris!" Everyone obliged, with a stray "hear hear" from one corner; David raised his glass to the Director.

At the Rosebud, Malia was enjoying a cozy evening with Ansel and Frida, who seemed happy to have her back at home and cuddled against her as she watched a movie in bed. And then Fern called, frantic. Her aunt was in the hospital again after another mini-stroke and fall, and the medical staff was pressing her to kill herself.

They had placed the death pills and the water by her bed for her consideration, and a physician had visited to counsel her on their ingestion. Fern's aunt had driven him away with energetic curses. "She's perfectly lucid. There is nothing wrong with her except that she's 92," said Fern. "Maybe David could do something?"

"I don't know," said Malia reluctantly. The Social Tower, which dealt with health and death care and income, was a different universe from either Beaufort or the Knowledge Tower. She did not mind herself benefiting from David's generosity, but she sensed he would balk at random favors for friends of hers he hadn't yet met, especially when it involved inserting himself into an unknown arena. What good would it do to flash the Antifan credentials to nurses who wouldn't even recognize them? And she could well imagine David saying, *What do I do the next time her aunt lands in the hospital? Are we going to tell someone else's 89-year-old aunt to swallow the dose instead?* "Can't you take her home yourself?" Malia asked.

"They won't let her leave, at least not alive. They say she isn't fit to leave the hospital. But really, she's fine. I could take leave from my job and stay with her for a few weeks, probably, if they'd only let her go."

Malia had agreed to meet David tomorrow at the National Diversity Cathedral, where they would attend the service. She told Fern she would ask him what recourse Fern and her aunt might have, her aunt being a heroine of the civil wars and all that. She was still puzzled as to why David wanted to meet her at the cathedral, given his Plore disdain for the faith, but trusted he had good reason.

Chapter 17
Imagine the Children
(Sunday, 1 May)

Malia arrived a full hour before the service was to begin, clutching a brand new pink pussy hat bought from the Diversity Warehouse, since the other one had been lost in the Earth Weekend melee. Unlike on the day of the great Councilor's funeral, there were no crowds, and the ushers hadn't yet arrived. A few worshipers already sat in the pews, but Malia, donning the pink hat for fear of reprimand, had the floor mostly to herself.

She wandered around the margins, as if she did not quite dare to occupy central space. A dozen small chapels, each dedicated to a prominent saint of the MED Church, ringed the cathedral walls. A special Knowledge Tower office was responsible for discovering and vetting proposed saints, of which there were now about 220. Above each chapel's gated entry loomed a screen showing vignettes of the saint's life. Inside were glass boxes with relics of the saint meant to inspire worshipers. Rows of votive candles awaited lighting by the faithful.

She stood in front of the chapel of St. Alexandria Ocasio-Cortez, whose image soared above her on the screen. When she pressed a button, videos showed the saint leading the charge in Congress to preserve social advances made during the pandemic. Then a quote flashed on the screen, "Our planet is going to hit disaster if we don't turn this ship around and so it's basically like, there's a scientific consensus that the lives of children are going to be very difficult." Encased in glass boxes were a broken nail relic and a pair of sunglasses worn by the saint.

Then she moved onto the delicately wrought gate and video screen of St. Barack Obama, past the chapels of St. Greta Thunberg, St. Martin Luther King, St. Cesar Chavez, St. Paul Wellstone, St. Harvey Milk, St. Malcolm X, St. Saul Alinsky, St. Ilhan Omar, St. Gloria Steinem, St. John Beaufort, St. Ruth Bader Ginsberg, St. Michelle Obama, and St. Michael Rotzow, who had been executed after having beaten a fascist to death with a skateboard at a mostly peaceful rally in 2020. She lit a votive candle at St. Gloria's chapel and prayed for Fern's aunt, partly to make a good impression on anyone watching. She then lit a candle at St. John Beaufort's chapel, because he had founded the Antifan Defense Forces, which gave her an opportunity to pray for

David's safety.

Just before 11 o'clock, she found the pew in which David had asked her to sit, about two-thirds of the way back in the nave, and under a loudspeaker. She was surprised by how few people were in attendance, but nobody got Social Credit points for normal Church attendance. Also, no doubt many devout worshippers were taking advantage of live-streamed services.

The robed multiethnic multisex choir sang the classic "In Diversity We Are One," and "Death to the Haters," and the Rector announced, "Let us pray, friends." They marched through the liturgy, their voices inaudible except for the loudspeakers. They read responsively:

"Praise Ye Mother Earth, whose blessings are as firm as law.
Destroy the industrialists, the magnates, the fascists, the individualists who rip you asunder,
Preserve the cool waters, the calm forests, do not taint them with a saw.
Imagine the children playing, hear their happy cries as they learn Your Wonder."

David slipped into the pew next to her, greeting her with a quick pat on her skirted thigh and a tired smile. He looked worn, and Malia noticed lines etched under his bloodshot eyes. It must have been a late night after what she knew had been a difficult week for him. He hadn't relayed details so far, but she gathered there had been major changes in an investigation he was leading and of course she knew he had attended the Director's party last night.

He tapped the noise cylinder button on his armband. "How are you, sweetheart?"
She nodded, "How are you?"
"Tough week, I'll tell you more later. After this, let's get some brunch and then we'll head over to Ploreville. I need some coffee."

Malia wondered, why are we here? The organ music swelled again. David said in a hushed voice, "I spent a lot of the week thinking about your daughter. It was painful, not as painful for me as for you, of course. But hearing the story made me question the twenty years I've spent protecting this government, not questioning it, even when I knew about injustices, even when I committed some of those injustices. I'm done lying to myself." She looked at him quizzically.

He stared straight ahead. Anyone watching them would have thought them a loyal pair of worshipers, perhaps married, perhaps fulfilling a premarital commitment to the Church to attend services. Otherwise it was an unusual place to go for a date.

"I want you to know that I am going to find your daughter and bring her back to you."

She turned, her brown eyes wide, "How?" But for the first time in many years, something warm and glowing spread through her. Someone finally cared enough to help. If anyone could rescue Isabelle, David would do it.

He shook his head, "More later. Don't say too much in one place." He tapped the button again, removing the interference. He sang the ugly lyrics with vigor, as if he believed them, and followed the rector's homily intently, as if he were receiving morning orders at Beaufort. Malia followed suit, stealing sideways glances at him.

Outside the cathedral, they tried to find a brunch place, but the first two restaurants were open only to 150 and above. "I don't want to deal with that shit again," said David, exasperated. A third was closed, and a line trailed out the door at the fourth. "There's a good diner in Ploreville. They'll take our money and not ask questions." He didn't want to taint Malia's reputation with too many trips to Ploreville, but they were going out to his mother's anyway.

Twenty minutes later, they were entering the famed Seven Seas, patronized today by churchgoers and late risers in search of a Bloody Mary and that Plore favorite, pancakes. A tall, heavyset Plore behind the counter greeted David by name. "Hello, Frank," replied David, "do you have the special table available today?" Frank grinned, "This time not for business, I hope?" he said, his eyes lighting on Malia.

"Just trying to show my beautiful date a good time in Arlington," David said, "And there is no better brunch than right here."

"You can say that again, Commander," Frank assented. "Give me five minutes— that table is about to clear and we'll have it ready for you in a jiffy."

In five minutes, David and Malia were seated at the special corner table. The small table ordinarily would not have occasioned much interest, situated just before the kitchen doors, but it adjoined only one other table that Frank courteously kept vacant. Next to it on one side was a window overlooking a parking lot where vans and bicycles and one yellow sportscar were parked, since almost no one drove anymore. No one would linger in front of the kitchen doors, and if David sat with his back to the corner, he could see all comers. She stared around them.

"Have you never been in a diner?" David smiled at her, but he knew the answer. He discreetly swept his hand under the table and the windowsill, and eyed the ceiling.

"No," she admitted. "I don't go to restaurants. And, when I do, I don't get to sit down or order from a menu like this one." She held up the oversized menu. "Usually I choose between ten options, not ten pages, and all of the options are various kinds of leafy greens."

He laughed at her, saying, "It's expensive, but for all I know there was a clause in the Treaty of the Red and the Blue about keeping the Plore neighborhood diner open. The government knows its limits."

They ordered a carafe of coffee, mimosas, scrambled eggs, and those now ubiquitous pancakes that Malia had never seen before last weekend. After they had eaten for a few minutes, David hit the interference button, and said, "Well, starting from where we left off...

"I have access to a lot of information and I think I can help you. I can't promise anything, at least not quickly. But after what I've seen this week, if it is possible, I will find your person, and if it is humanly possible, we will retrieve this person. But we cannot do this within the law. Once we recover this person, we have to run for the Interior. And we may not make it."

"And if we fail...."

"Also death, but more unpleasantly."

'What are the chances of our making it across the border?" she asked anxiously.

"Maybe 20 percent. I can probably develop an escape route that will take us to the Economic Zone and over the border. I think the fascists would probably welcome us as refugees and I can make it worthwhile for them."

Malia hadn't thought about the overwhelming odds of first locating Isabelle, then kidnapping her, then making it to the border with the full might of the DJR on their collective tail and very possibly a recalcitrant teenager, and then across to uncertain safety. "David, I know why I want to risk my life for this. But I don't understand why you are risking so much for me. You have so much more to lose—your reputation, your career, your family, your life—and all for me, whom you hardly know yet."

He looked steadily at her. "Malia, in a few minutes, I will tell you why I would risk it now."

She then asked him about the Director's party, a less fraught subject. "I think even his butler is a Social Credit person," said David. In response to another question, "No, there were very few women there. One executive from the Warehouse and maybe several wives or girlfriends.

"The Director did give me a toast, so I suppose it was a successful night for me career wise."

"Really?" said Malia, "what did he toast you for?"

"That's kind of the problem here," said David. He signaled for the check, and paid cash, since the armband payment system was not used in Ploreville. Plores paid with cash or their phones. Each Friday David visited the bank at Beaufort to take out money for the weekend. Because everyone knew he visited his mother in Ploreville on Sundays, it did not attract the scrutiny it would have were he an ordinary Social Crediteer.

Instead of driving directly to Marjory's house, David and Malia left the sportscar at the diner and walked around the block first. Around them was a mix of worn rowhouses, some with barbed wire fences shielding lilac and azalea bushes in full bloom. Because there was little zoning in Ploreville, the rowhouses alternated with small businesses selling electronic devices, toiletries, and groceries (*bodegas*, David called them). The sidewalks were cracked but there was little or no garbage in the streets. On some blocks, kids were playing ball in the streets, confident that few if any cars would pass through. He pointed to a Catholic church, and then a Lutheran church, saying, "That's where my mother goes. Sometimes I go with her."

As they walked along, David became a little self-conscious of Malia's drinking in of the street scene, as if she were in a primitive foreign country on safari.

"It's not fancy, but we take care of our neighborhood. Nobody is going to come and pave it for us," said David, a little defensively against Malia's gaze. "The City does almost nothing. They consider it well done to allow us to go to church and eat fried chicken."

"So how do the streets get paved?" Malia asked.

He smiled. "Who does the paving in the City? When the Plore trucks return home, they keep some of the asphalt and cement and fix what needs to be fixed. Everyone on the block contributes some cash, and the job gets done, somehow."

"Can you tell me now why you are willing to help me?"

He sobered quickly, hit the interference button again, and told her that he was experiencing a crisis of confidence. "For twenty years, I have been sworn to the Antifan Defense Forces. They gave me opportunities I couldn't have had anywhere else. Last year I even went to China to learn from their security services. Who travels overseas anymore? We can be brutal, I don't deny that, but there was always a logic behind our brutality. We are sworn to protect the DJR. The government accepts that we use harsh means to ensure the DJR continues to exist. There is always low-level opposition humming along, and we spare no trouble to wipe it out. But we don't invent opponents and we don't torture obviously innocent people for no purpose at all.

"You know that we have been investigating the security breakdown that happened at the Depository. We could have pursued mismanagement up your chain of command, but there wasn't enough there to strike. All your superiors denied any knowledge; frankly, you're lucky that all the books seem to have stayed in the building. But my Director wants very badly to destroy some of his political opponents at the Knowledge Tower. So, we are pursuing subversion and heresy at Hillary Clinton University."

"Where Professor MacMillan came from?" she asked, but knowing the answer. He had told her that MacMillan had died in his sleep of an undiagnosed heart condition.

"Yes, and that's what led us in that direction. We've been interrogating some of his colleagues, and if we were honest, we would admit that there isn't a whole lot to worry about. Just the usual malcontents and gossips. So what if they read a book they shouldn't, if they can actually get ahold of one, and they don't teach it in the classroom? But our Director wants to strike at the Knowledge Tower and so we are going to purge all the DJR universities and add up all the small infractions to create an inferno. If we are successful, this will ensure that the ADF controls the Knowledge Tower in the future, and not vice versa, which they are itching to do. I can't disagree with the Director's goal—we need to maintain our autonomy.

"From a bureaucratic perspective, this is a windfall for me. I've been given sixty more officers and analysts and more office space for them. But I have to deliver results. The Director doesn't care what evidence my people find, as long as it gives him the conclusions he wants and can use against the Tower. He doesn't care what methods we use to extract that information.

"I'm basically a detective. I'm good at asking questions that will yield real, actionable information from criminals. Even Knowledge Criminals. I don't mind using force to break up an illegal meeting. But torturing people who probably aren't criminals at all isn't my specialty and I'm losing any appetite I might once have had for it. It's now almost the 22nd century and we ought to know better. Maybe I'm getting old.

"Malia, this week I have watched interrogations of various Clinton University faculty and staff we arrested this week. You do not want to know what we do in the Red Room, and I will not tell you. But it has broken my spirit." He added, "It doesn't help that my deputy agrees completely with the Director. He would take my job from me in a minute and destroy hundreds of lives if he could. He knows that my heart is not in this."

They had reached an outlying neighborhood where the houses looked even shabbier, with some broken windows, and youths were exchanging plastic bags on street corners. "Let's turn around here," said David. He was not known here and was not eager to become involved in a confrontation. They headed back toward the diner.

"I can't quit because it would be a criminal offense in itself. If I pretended to go mad, they would send me to a psychiatric hospital and that would be even worse. Once you know the secrets of Beaufort Tower, you will never leave, one way or another. There are many things I still love about the ADF—the camaraderie, the passion for the mission, so many of the outstanding officers I've trained. But this is a bitter mess to swallow and it may consume the rest of my career unless the Director goes first and the new one has a different set of priorities."

"Can't you just ask for another assignment?" asked Malia, being practical.

He considered this. "No. It would be taken as a sign of lack of confidence in the Director. Honey, I took this oath. I am going to continue to serve as I am told to serve. But the main reason to continue is that I can use my access and influence to do some good, and that means helping you find your person. At least it isn't too late to do a good deed and reverse an evil one.

"And Madame," David concluded, "that is why I am now in your service."

This was not a good moment to ask about Fern's aunt. When she raised it, with trepidation, in the sportscar at the end of the evening, David's shoulders sagged and his voice became edgy. She had predicted the outcome, and it was unfair to spring this new problem on him when he was so exhausted and embittered. "Malia, I can't help people I don't even know in places that even I have no influence over, like the Social

Tower or a hospital. If I went into that hospital and kidnapped that poor old woman, I would be disciplined by the ADF and lose my ability to help you. I can't do just anything I want.

"And let's say that I did somehow magically use my influence, which I think you overestimate, to secure her release. How much longer would she live anyway? And what other oldster would the doctors have to kill to meet their financial bottom line? Someone who's two years younger?

"I don't want to use my access and my power to perpetuate systemic abuses. I want to help, but only where it makes sense, and not at the expense of some other innocent person. I'm sorry, I'm sorry that we live in a society where even the doctors encourage the killing of people who have lost their utility for them, and even kill people we consider war heroes."

He was in a deep funk when he dropped Malia off at the Rosebud, and kissed her only perfunctorily. She was sorry she had introduced the subject of Fern's aunt at all, since it had immediately erased the pleasure he was taking in fighting on her behalf. If David felt resistance was futile, he might decide not to risk his life for Malia's daughter, and Malia would not allow herself to lose this chance of recovering her child. She resolved not to mention Fern's aunt again and to avoid Fern's calls for a few days until the matter blew over.

Chapter 18
Red Room
(Thursday, 5 May)

"We do not object to equality as such. It merely happens to be the case that a demand for equality is the professed motive of most of those who desire to impose upon society a preconceived pattern of distribution...we shall indeed see that many of those who demand an extension of equality do not really demand equality but a distribution that conforms more closely to human conceptions of individual merit and that their desires are as irreconcilable with freedom as the more strictly egalitarian demands."
—*Friedrich A. Hayek*, The Constitution of Liberty

The new Higher Education Heresy Task Force had taken possession of three full Red Room suites on Level Seven. It was operating them all day, and often well into the night, because on windowless Level Seven, deeper into the ground than even the regular interrogation rooms, no one could tell day apart from night except by looking at their armbands. The tables, the instrumentation, the torturers, and their victims strapped to the tables or punishment chairs were all bathed in the reddish light that Beaufort scientists contended was itself a form of bodily harm. It was like walking into a glowing furnace.

Virtually all of David's squad had been promoted to supervisory positions with the influx of new officers. So today Lt. Patel was in charge of Room C, Lt. Conor Chung of Room E, and Walters had room G. A physician attended in each room to advise. Undergoing the Red Room were the annoying Professor Renata Yazdan, about whom Walters had said, "Patel, she's yours. I might finish her off too soon," Joyous Smeldring from Engineering, who was not so joyous anymore, and Andrew Leonard of Disability Studies and Sociology. On Leonard, who used a wheelchair, Walters had cheerfully said, "What a shame he's already gotten a head start on our treatment."

But Leonard was the potentially rich motherlode of heresy, because forbidden books had also been discovered buried in his garden—probably secreted right after MacMillan's apprehension. And, even more remarkable, those books bore not just Leonard's fingerprints, but MacMillan's and Pinckney's. There was another set of fingerprints, more faded and of unknown provenance, on the volumes. Regardless of their origin, at least three faculty members had shared these books, which was sufficient to back allegations of a "club." Investigators had also found residue from these books in the reusable bags that Pinckney had brought to the MacMillan house. Now they were determined to find out who else had belonged to this Club and, second, how the Club had gotten the books in the first place.

Smeldring refused to acknowledge that his talks with MacMillan had ever ventured into forbidden territory. "I hold no truck with individualism or liberty absent from the context in which they are exercised. There is no liberty under so-called representative government and capitalism," he tried to reassure his questioners. But his questioners were incapable of grappling with the concepts he raised. The Antifans broke several of his bones in succession as Smeldring steadily refused to sign the form they shoved at him. Chung's amplified voice filled the room, "Professor Smeldring, if you sign this form admitting your participation, we can stop this session."

"But I have never participated! I don't know of any such club. How can I sign this?"

"The same way you sign anything," Chung said, phlegmatically. He signaled for the targeting machine to be brought over. He wanted to show Walters that he was capable of extracting a confession. He was sorry for Smeldring, but also considered that the prospect of relief was in Smeldring's own hands, so any trouble he was suffering was his own doing at this point.

Meanwhile, the initially brash Yazdan had quickly crumbled after they beat her with hangars and used some techniques involving chairs they had picked up from their Chinese counterparts. She willingly signed all the documents they placed before her. These documents affirmed that her friend Kendra Pinckney—now lying half-dead in the infirmary after last week's ordeal—had mentioned a club in which she, MacMillan, and Leonard discussed democracy and capitalism.

In Room G, Walters stood over the misshapen body of the valiant Andrew Leonard, holding a copy of Hayek's *Constitution of Liberty*. When the furor erupted over MacMillan, Leonard had asked his able-bodied wife to bury several forbidden books in the backyard, and although she chose to do so at 2 am, an insomniac neighbor saw her with a shovel by the toolshed that Leonard used as an office. When the neighbor's husband pointed out that it seemed an odd time to be gardening, she responsibly reported it to the police, who in turn contacted the ADF. Walters brandished several volumes that the ADF had recovered in the backyard as Leonard watched sadly from his wheelchair.

"Do you deny these are yours?" Walters asked.

"No, they are mine," said Leonard.

"How did you get these?"

"I don't know." Walters signaled to Cheysa, and Leonard screamed.

"Every lie or attempt to lie will be punished. We know more than you realize. How do you not know how you get a book? There aren't many paper books any more. You obviously cared about these if you bothered to have your wife bury them in the backyard. Surely you can give us a more accurate answer."

"I bought them from a yard sale out in the countryside somewhere."

"Do you remember when?"

"Uh—maybe last summer."

"Where was this yard sale?"

Walters demolished the likelihood of a yard sale near Hagerstown, Maryland selling paper books, let alone heretical ones, alongside chipped china teacups and outgrown baby equipment. A quick check of databases by the analysts proved that no yard sales had been permitted in that vicinity that entire summer, due to the order to requisition housewares and other supplies for the adjacent Industrial Zone.

He pulled over a high stool, and perched on it, leaning over the professor. "Dr. Leonard, you're such an intelligent man. But must you insult my intelligence?" Another shock wave and the professor's broken body quivered. Half turned toward her, half toward Leonard, framed in the red light, Walters truly did look like a demon, thought Cheysa, operating the dials. She feared that God would never forgive her for torturing this saintly man, even at the behest of a demon.

Slowly, but inexorably over the course of the afternoon, Leonard admitted that Pinckney had brought him the books. He fainted twice, but the doctor revived him.

"I think this time you may be telling us the truth, professor," said Walters. "Everyone, let's take a break." They left Leonard strapped to the table, mocking his request for a bathroom break. "What is this, a hotel?" When Walters and his officers came back, they had to remove the soiled pants and underwear lest he be electrocuted prematurely, and Walters had one of the officers slap Leonard with a wire hangar "for causing us such inconvenience. You really shouldn't have drunk so much at lunch."

Cheysa ran from the room, with Walters not noticing until he turned around to command her to turn up the dial. "Where did she go? Cowardly bitch. Mittleman, take her place."

The young woman called the elevator, her hand shaking, and ran outside into the achingly bright sunshine, collapsing at one of the tables near the Antifan statue. It was past lunch hour, and no one saw her slump over the round table, weeping. Most passersby would have assumed she had just been spurned by a boyfriend, or lost a promotion; they would have been incredulous at her revulsion at what was, after all, an unexceptional, albeit harsh, interrogation.

She felt rather than saw a shadow over her, and started, afraid that Walters had followed her. But instead, it was Commander Harris, his tired face full of concern. "Conroy, I saw you run out of the main lobby and I followed you out. Can we talk?"

She nodded, wiping tears from her cheeks. He offered her a clean brown paper napkin from the lunch he had been carrying back to his desk.

"What's going on down there?" he asked her.

"Commander Harris, I just can't do it. It's not right." She explained what she had been watching, and what Walters had demanded she do.

"This was your first time in a Red Room?" She nodded again.

David hesitated. On one hand, this was a normal and routine, or almost routine experience for every Antifan officer. One could not avoid the cruelty, or more precisely, the wielding of the baton, the turning of the dial, the dislocating of the joints of the criminal. He had done his share of torture, never relishing it like those such as Walters, although it was gratifying to extract a confession when it was possibly true. You could not honorably be an Antifan officer while allowing others to do the dirty work for you. As a junior officer, David had had to learn to control his natural revulsion in the Red Room. On the other hand, not everyone was made of the required sterner stuff, and David had seen cases where the officer really should have been permitted to transfer to regular police work or even resign. When forced to stay in place, their lives often descended into the drinking or drug use they needed to survive their workdays. Or they stayed for the prestige, the Social Credit points, and the lifestyle, which turned some of them into worse monsters than the officers from whom they had initially recoiled.

"You didn't want to come here originally, did you?" he asked. He knew that Cheysa had been pulled out of the police academy for the ADF. Sensing her gentleness and her reticence in close encounters, David had occasionally fretted that she was not suited for the hard-edged work. But after several months during which Walters expressed his doubts as well about her performance, he had begun reassuring David that Cheysa was doing fine.

"No, sir," she said, the sobs subsiding. "I thought I would be a good ordinary policewoman, but not this. But I didn't have a choice."

"Hey, neither did I," said David. She stared at him, and he nodded. "They pulled me out of a Plore gym class when I was fifteen, and there was no looking back."

"But you're a Commander, sir."

"Yes, the recruiters may have been right after all," he said, "in my case. But there were things that took getting used to, and the Red Room was hard going. If you are going to be an Antifan officer, you have to learn to accept it. You have to tell yourself, 'I am a good person. I am doing this to protect the DJR from knowledge criminals who would destroy everything we have built. If we did not use harsh techniques,"—he could not bring himself to call it torture— "we would lose everything to the fascists and the white supremacists, who stop at nothing.'

"If you really can't do the Red Room, we can try to find you an analyst position or something else where you would be a better fit. But I would recommend you spend some time figuring out whether you can't really stand it. Too much is at stake to throw it away.

"Think about it for a few weeks," said David kindly, while thinking that she might make a good secretary for Walters, who was finally about to get his long coveted private office. He wasn't sure Cheysa was cut out for the green eyeshade analytic work either.

She assented, her tears finally dried, looking into David's own gentle face, taking a chance. "Sir, I have to confess something that might help you understand where I am coming from here."

He looked at her curiously.

She leaned forward and said softly, "I'm sorry, I'm a Christian." Cheysa may or may not have had the stamina for the Red Room, but it took a great deal of courage to confess her faith to a senior Antifan commander.

David smiled, "I noticed you weren't so eager to join in the Whiro parade on Monday." Although several dozen Antifans, including the newcomers, had marched around the unit behind Walters, who carried the god in his arms, Cheysa had appeared to be on a phone call. Cheysa also knew David did not participate.

"No, sir, Wurro isn't for me."

David had stood in the door of his office, arms crossed, watching the procession snake around the room around 8:15 am. A few of the Antifans began a chant that spread to the whole, alternating between "Wurro is Lord! Wurro is King! Wurro our Lord, give us your BlesSING!" and then "Wur-RO! Wur-RO! Kill more fascists! Make them GO!" After several circuits, the Antifans clustered before Wurro's nook. Cheysa drifted discreetly to the back. Walters faced them, holding the statue high. "Everyone kneel to Wurro, who has brought us good luck!" he called. A bit awkwardly, everyone kneeled. "Repeat after me—thank you, Lord Wurro!"

"Thank you, Lord Wurro!"

"Wurro is the son of the Earth Mother! All hail the Earth Mother! Hail Diversity!" Clever political move, thought David.

"Wurro is the son of the Earth Mother! All hail the Earth Mother!" the crowd dutifully chanted. "Hail Diversity!"

Walters brought over an expensive bottle of champagne that bore a striking resemblance to the brand on offer at the Director's party. "This is my offering today to the Lord Wurro! If you have an offering for Wurro, please bring it up here now."

He placed the statue back on its shelf, and stood aside to mark who brought offerings. They spilled over the adjoining shelves and were placed on the floor beneath Wurro. Walters decided he would ask some of the junior officers to build an altar so the offerings need not be on the floor, which might offend the powerful mana of Wurro.

"We will worship Wurro on Mondays, Wednesdays and Fridays at 8:15 am sharp," said Walters. "May Wurro protect us all! Amen."

"Amen," chorused the group, which then moved toward the center for the 8:30 unit meeting. David chose to ignore the Whiro worship, at least for the moment. The

Earth Mother feint had been brilliant on Walters' part, because it made it virtually impossible for David to oppose the worship. He could allow officers to excuse themselves, but even that would be somewhat suspect now given the deliberate linkage with the Earth Mother, and would trigger some disparaging "typical Plore" remarks that Walters might even encourage. Therefore, he did nothing to stop the worship.

And here he was, several days later, finding unanticipated fellowship with the most junior member of his Suede Fist.

"I don't care for it much either," said David. He took out a small notepad from his pocket, drew a cross on it, and showed it to her, quickly tapping his chest. He would be more circumspect than Cheysa, by not uttering the incriminating words, but he could not refuse to admit his faith now that she had placed her secret in his hands.

She looked at him, astonished.

"Conroy, all I ask is that you think about your next steps carefully. I would not advise that you resign at this time. Here are your options. One, decide you can stay on and endure the Red Room and learn to hurt people who may be innocent. It is the hardest path, but ultimately the most rewarding for an Antifan career. Two, do something else in the ADF that wouldn't require the Red Room. Three, and this might not be doable anymore, become a regular police officer again. We would have to pull strings for that one, because we don't like releasing anyone who has sworn loyalty to us. It poses a possible security risk. In the meantime, I will ask Walters to release you from the Red Room for the next few days."

"Thank you so much, sir, I promise. I will let you know soon." Perhaps Walters would accept her becoming an analyst or a secretary, as long as she remained nearby, she thought.

"Good," said David. Another successful, if bizarre, mentoring encounter, at least for now. He and Cheysa entered the KCU together. It was 4 pm sharp, and the afternoon news was beginning on the giant TV screen across the room. Over a banner reading "Heresy at Universities," the broadcaster was announcing, "The Antifan Defense Forces are investigating subversive activity at Hillary Clinton University, and may extend the investigation to other universities. Informed sources tell us that faculty belonged to a pro-capitalism club that read banned materials and sought to influence students. Director Ferraro of the ADF gave us an exclusive interview today."

All the heads below the screen swiveled upward. David had been hoping for the news to leak in another week or so, so that other campuses could at least finish the school year before the ADF rolled in to arrest professors. But Ferraro had been impatient, and Jim Fielding's *Post* story had run yesterday, giving impetus to other media outlets to cover the issue. Looking into the camera, his jowls moving, Ferraro said, "The campuses have been allowed to do what they like for years, without suitable ideological controls. Now the ADF has to come in and do what we do best, ensuring the survival of the Diversity Justice Republic against a continued threat of fascism and white supremacy. All we ask, is, why isn't the Knowledge Tower doing its job?"

Next on the screen was President Fufuloa, saying, "Clinton University is cooperating fully with the Antifan Defense Forces. If we have subversive faculty members, we want the ADF to root them out. And perhaps there are other universities that also need some ideological assistance." Here we go, thought David. It was a highly pro-ADF segment and he knew Ferraro would be pleased. When the segment ended, there was some scattered applause from the cubicles, after which the broadcaster moved onto President Avadaughter's planned visit to China next week. David knew she would be requesting more financial assistance, in return for an expansion of the PLAN naval base near Say Francisco, but the reporter focused on mutual friendship and a planned visit to the Great Wall. The reporter advised, "The Great Wall kept out barbarian hordes for centuries, much as our Great Wall fends off the fascists of the rump United States. China has much to teach us."

And then Walters appeared. His eyes lighted on Cheysa, but David preempted him by gesturing toward his office.

Chapter 19
Devil's Deal
(Thursday, 5 May)

"**D**o you want to wash up first?" David asked. He sniffed a smoky stench about Walters, whose shirt also sported a bloodstain. The hygiene protocol called for washing before leaving the Red Room level, and a change of clothes, if soiled, for which reason there was an actual eco-friendly dry cleaner on the premises. However, Walters recently seemed to consider ignoring it a matter of masculine pride, and unfortunately some of the men were following his lead. David decided he would mention this at tomorrow's 8:30 meeting, after Wurro worship. Wurro was probably pretty filthy himself, David reflected, but the Antifans were not Maori gods. Not yet.

Walters shook his head. "Not yet, chief. I wanted to give you the report as quickly as possible."

"What did we find out today?" David asked him.

"We..." David caught perhaps a little extra emphasis on that "we" from Walters, as if to say, "not you, you were upstairs," but perhaps he was imagining it, "got some useful information. Yazdan completely caved, and she has already signed an affirmation that Pinckney had told her she belonged to a pro-capitalism book club with MacMillan and Leonard."

David nodded, "That's helpful. What about Leonard?"

"Tough little dude, in spite of the wheelchair. He fainted twice. But his story of buying these books at a yard sale fell apart. We got him to admit that Pinckney brought him the books."

"Very good. What about Smeldring?"

"Refused to admit he was in this club at all, even though Chung's guys broke both his legs and an arm. Maybe he's telling the truth. When we were at Clinton, he actually brought up Pinckney on his own. If he had been in this club, he probably wouldn't have mentioned her at all when we interviewed him initially." David thought angrily, perhaps you should have considered this before you brought him into the Red Room.

David concluded, "So what we don't know at all is how Pinckney got these books. She seems to have been the main conduit. Where were they coming from? And unless there are others hidden around the school, they seem to have been passed on eventually, to somewhere else."

The two men thought of Kendra Pinckney, drifting in and out of consciousness for three days in the Beaufort infirmary, attached to a nutrient tube.

"Now that is one tough lady," Walters said with grudging approval. "I threw everything at her on Monday. Confessed nothing, and we now know she has plenty to confess. I'm just afraid if we bring her back tomorrow, she's going to die on us. And that will be the end of that trail."

"Right," David said. "Let's leave her alone for a while in sick bay. The doctors don't think she's on the verge of dying right now, do they?"

"No, she's okay, by Red Room standards."

"When she's a little better, let's bring her back to a regular interrogation room. Maybe she'll be more cooperative, especially when we tell her what her colleagues confessed about her. If they're all throwing you overboard, what's the point of holding out?"

Walters thought David was being unduly optimistic, not having actually witnessed the frightening stoicism of the gray-haired spinster. But he had no better ideas at this point. He ran over the names of the faculty who would be treated to the Red Room tomorrow, to which David made a few changes, favoring those prisoners who knew Pinckney personally. "I don't mind coming up with a list of offenses against Diversity and insults to President Avadaughter or Governor Farnham," he said, referring to the administrative prefect of the Anacosta District. "It'll be good stuffing for Ferraro's turkey, but I don't think we need the Red Room for that, at least not immediately. I want to nail down this book network."

David moved onto the next subject. "I ran into Conroy outside the building this afternoon. She didn't do too well in the Red Room, did she?"

It took a second or two for Walters to digest that David had actually spoken with Cheysa.

"A cowardly bitch," he drawled. "Couldn't hack the dials."

"I'm wondering whether she is misplaced as a squad officer," said David. "You've given her good reports but she won't survive if she can't handle the Red Room. Do you think you could use her as your secretary? I don't see her as an analyst, she's kind of hands-on."

You're telling me, Walters thought smugly. But it dawned on David, watching Walters' face, that the two were intimate. All the small interactions he had witnessed over the past few months, but not bothered to put together, suddenly made sense.

"Chief, I don't think she can even alphabetize. She'd look good behind the desk. But I have to admit that if she can't handle the Red Room, she can't stay on the squad. You know as well as I do that you can't delegate nasty stuff to others, even if you're a female. What did you tell her?"

"I told her to think about it. She still has some decent options. And, in the meantime, keep her away from the Red Room unless she says she wants to try again. And I don't want you pressuring her one way or the other. She's got to figure this out for herself."

"Yes, sir. One other thing, chief—and then I promise to go and shower. I realize I'm not very fragrant right now. Speaking of letting others do the Red Room stuff for you. Some of the men are wondering why they hardly ever see you in the Red Room."

"Maybe that's because I'm running a staff of a hundred people and running back and forth up to the Director's suite four times a day. Has it occurred to anyone that I've done my share and more of Red Room stuff?" David recognized that he sounded defensive, but there was an ounce of truth in Walters' accusation, even if none of the men really had openly complained, and even if this was just an effort by Walters to goad him. From his earliest days as a junior team leader, he knew that it was unacceptable to expect a subordinate to perform a task you would never be willing to do yourself. No matter how exalted he was now in the Antifan hierarchy, you couldn't rest on your long-ago laurels. "Walters, you could delegate some more too."

"But, sir, the troops want some reassurance you're supporting them in the dirty work. You and I know it's dirty work. They would like to hear something at the 8:30 at least. And seeing you work in the Red Room—not for the whole afternoon, I got it, would be very helpful for morale."

You got me, thought David. First the effing Maori god and now back to playing inquisitor in the Red Room. After all, Commander Harris, didn't you just tell Cheysa that if you can't hack the Red Room, you really can't survive as an Antifan officer? "I'll take Room C tomorrow," said David, "I'll have Vanessa clear my schedule. I hope that will reassure some of our officers."

"Thank you, chief," said Walters. "That would be appreciated. Room C—that will be Jeffrey Bertone—he and Pinckney dated until about a year ago."

"You always leave me with the most interesting cases," said David archly, even though he had picked Room C deliberately. He knew Bertone was a Plore by birth.

"It's my salute to great leadership, sir," said Walters, rising to leave. "Wurro be with you."

"My loyalty and my honor. Take a shower," said David, turning back to his screen. The plan for tomorrow night was to go to the Depository and pick up Malia for the weekend, after spending a romantic hour in the basement, which she seemed to have had a hankering for. He was very willing to oblige Malia. That said, she would doubtless expect him to have done some research on the missing child. He could not disappoint her. After asking Vanessa to clear the Friday schedule, and order him a sandwich before she left, he pulled up several databases that he thought might yield some clues. He would also have to review the Bertone dossier and check in with the Director. It would be a late night. He then called upstairs to report on the progress made this afternoon, running a hand through his blond curls. He did need a haircut, he realized—the barber shop was in the basement down the hall from the brothel, but he doubted he'd find the time before the weekend began.

He was patched through immediately to the Director, who was brimming with satisfaction at the evidence accumulating about the Club. "I agree you've got to figure out where these books are coming from," said Ferraro. "But I hear that Walters is a real master in the Red Room, so I have confidence you'll get what we need."

David was slightly miffed. "I'll be handling a session tomorrow myself, by the way. Pinckney's ex-boyfriend." David wondered how Ferraro would react if he told him that Walters had pinched the champagne, but it was highly possible the Director would chuckle, "a small price to pay for his evil excellence."

"Oh, no worries, Harris. You've got plenty to handle without a branding iron. No offense intended at all. But that should be an interesting opportunity. Did they part as friends?"

"Yes, it was all very amicable, so I gather. Kind of unfortunate from our standpoint."

"Yes. Did you see my interview on Channel Five this afternoon?"

"Yes, sir. That was perfect. Sticking it to the Tower. Let the games begin and all that."

"Can you just imagine the scurrying of the mice there right now?" The two laughed, David more dutifully. "I imagine that Terwilliger"—Ferraro's counterpart—"will be begging to speak with Avadaughter, but she's off to China tonight on Earth Wings One, so good luck with that. We'll make some good headway while she's kowtowing to the Commie Emperor."

Ferraro added, "Speaking of the emperor, what's this about a Hawaiian god you're all worshipping down in the KCU?"

"I wouldn't quite put it like that, sir. Walters brought back a statue of the Maori god of darkness from Clinton University and several times a week they are marching around the room with it chanting slogans. Just a morale boost and a way to bring people together, since we have so many new officers in the unit. And while Walters is asking officers to bring offerings to the god, I understand we'll be drinking them at happy hour tomorrow."

"Excellent, that Walters really is something. And that god is a spawn of the Maori Earth Mother, right? Just to make sure it doesn't create any problems with our ideological cred."

"Yes, sir. I understand that the mother of Whiro is in fact the Maori Earth Mother goddess, very ideologically sound. The Knowledge Tower won't be able to complain."

The Director started to sign off, and then said, "Oh by the way, you should ask Walters to tell you about the prank he played on the Clinton president. He was telling me about it at the party the other night. You don't need to rape or beat someone to have them at your mercy, apparently. Really hilarious. Nice change of pace. Thanks,

Harris, and have a good night!"

"You too, sir," said David as the screen faded out. He ran his hands through his hair again. He just couldn't, couldn't, deal with this new information right now. One of the junior officers delivered a turkey sandwich and organic potato fries.

With the sandwich in one hand, David brought up the Vital Statistics page for District Four, Anacosta, and its subcategories "City," "Near-City Suburban," "Outlying Suburban," and "Industrial Zones." Just out of curiosity, he clicked on Industrial Zones, but the link led to "this page is under permanent construction." Near-City Suburban was urban Ploreville, which stretched from the former Fredericksburg, VA to Frederick, MD. Outlying Suburban was mostly rural, with a majority of Plore residents and some Social Crediteers in positions of authority. Those Plores in good standing were allowed to own one household vehicle, and drive up to 2000 miles each year in recognition of the challenges of rural life.

He clicked on City, births, 2074, July 12.

Five baby girls and four baby boys, each listed with the hospital of birth or street address if a home delivery with midwife. The availability of sanitary abortion as a convenient and Earth Friendly practice had halved the births from pre-DJR days. He clicked again, on the girls.

Harriet Corona Watts, 0518, Obama General
Rex Gretabelle Andrews, 1026, Anacosta Metropolitan
Jasmine Araminta Nunez, 1511, Obama General
Diversity Whittington, 1645, Anacosta Metropolitan
Ocean Gloria Piscatta, 2010, Obama General

No Isabelle Jenness. David tried the adjoining dates, with no luck. He called Malia, who was home eating a kale soybake. "Hi sweetheart," he said quickly, to minimize exposure, "remind me what was the time of birth and the hospital?"

"Hi David. It was Anacosta Metropolitan, 10:26 in the morning on July 12th." Thank goodness women never forgot those things.

"Thanks, I'll see you tomorrow evening—can't wait."

David stared at "Rex Gretabelle Andrews," which was a pretty horrible comedown from Isabelle Jennifer Jenness if these babies were in fact the same. About ten years ago, there had been a flurry of efforts to give boys' names to girls, and to a lesser extent, the reverse. "I'd name a dog Rex," he thought to himself. It was very possible that someone had taken extraordinary efforts to wipe out any reference to Isabelle after her kidnapping. But that should mean it would be fairly easy to trace the above-ground Rex. And if his hunch was correct, it was fortunate that whoever had adopted her was an Anacosta resident, and not living in Pittsburgh or Boston.

He brought up the City residential listing. The trick was going to be that it only named heads of households, and several hundred Andrews popped up. He narrowed it to households with minor children above the age of ten. Now he had eighty-five. He would return to it tomorrow. Under normal circumstances, he would delegate to one of his analysts the job of finding a girl named Rex, but he did not want to show a footprint, and certainly not this soon. He looked up "School age roster," and Rex Gretabelle, from what Malia had described, looked pretty close—dark brown hair and pale skin at least. He imagined he saw a resemblance to Malia herself, but couldn't be sure, since the girl was wearing thick-rimmed glasses. We'll get some DNA samples, somehow, he told himself. They had Malia's on file after the MacMillan incident.

He turned to the Bertone dossier. Forty-five years old. SC 140. Professor of Postcolonial English Literature with a specialty in "marginalized South Asian voices," whatever that was. He knew about the Plore background and that they had lived in the same neighborhood, but Bertone was about seven years older than him. And with the Italian name, it was likelier that Bertone's family had attended the Catholic St. Thomas parish church, not his own Lutheran one.

It was much harder to become a university professor than even an Antifan commander from a Plore background, so David was impressed. On the debit side, multiple assignations with underage Hispanic girls—not Clinton students—that the local authorities had not bothered to pursue, probably from when outraged parents had complained, fruitlessly, against the Social Credited professor. "Those would be marginalized Latinx voices," David muttered sarcastically to himself. How Bertone had gotten romantically involved with the sober Kendra Pinckney given his interest in the younger crowd puzzled David.

The photo of Bertone from his Clinton ID showed a handsome man with dark curly hair and white teeth. The intake photo from Beaufort showed Bertone as a slightly older man, with more gray hair and a glassy-eyed shocked expression that was quite typical of an intake photo. David had once taken a class in face reading, but didn't need those lessons to imagine this man might well quail before a threat to smash his jaw.

David had an idea. "Here goes," he said to himself, heading down to the cellblocks. He hoped that Bertone was made of weaker stuff than his ex-girlfriend. It was a quarter to ten.

The guard on Level Four Antifan-saluted David, who returned it.

"Bertone?"

The guard pointed, "Cell 17." David asked for a plastic stool that he carried down the hall.

David opened the cell with his armband and switched on the lone bulb in the ceiling. On the metal cot with the thin mattress a prisoner in green paper pajamas shrank back, crying, "Don't hurt me, don't hurt me!" Strange, thought David, Bertone supposedly had put up a brave front in the interrogation room, which is why he was headed for the Red Room. But late at night, in a darkened cell in white, black, gray, and metal, with only the toilet bowl shining at you, you were left with your fears of the next day. Bertone could not have taken much pleasure in his defiance when he knew the Antifans would strike back harder.

He sat down. "I'm Commander Harris, the chief of the Knowledge Crimes Unit. We are going to meet tomorrow in the Red Room. I will be handling your interrogation personally." Bertone whimpered. Good, he knew what the Red Rooms were. Candiss Yardley must have mentioned them during her interrogation of Bertone the other day.

"The room in which we will meet has the following features: waterboarding, torture chairs for joint dislocation, electronic shocking, cellular disruption that will turn your brain into jelly eventually, and implements that can break and crush bones and remove teeth and eyes from their sockets. I can use any and all of them and I have been doing so for twenty years.

"Would you like to have me use these on you?"

"No," wept the prisoner.

"Well, honestly I would rather not. I see we both went to Bethune elementary and junior high school in Arlington, but you would have graduated before I did. We're both Plores. I normally am perfectly happy breaking jaws and waterboarding prisoners, but I am prepared to give a fellow Plore a break. Sometimes literally, of course."

Bertone stared at him with shock.

"You dated Kendra Pinckney for three years?"

"Y-y-y-yes."

"Why did you break up last year? Was it the underage girls?"

Bertone nodded fearfully.

"Do you know how Kendra Pinckney got the books she shared with MacMillan and Leonard, and possibly others?"

Bertone shook his head, "No, I don't."

"Did you know she was bringing them these books? Reading these books? Talking about them?"

"No."

"So you dated this woman for three years with absolutely no awareness of her knowledge crimes or her interest in these subversive subjects or her hanging out with other men, even if they were intellectuals and in wheelchairs. Did you not care, or were you completely obtuse? A man should be interested in knowing when his girlfriend is seeing other men."

Bertone was silent.

"Bertone, here's the deal. We know that Professor Pinckney was involved in this club. As you can see, we know some of its members. We know she was the conduit.

What we would like to know is how she acquired these books, and where they went after they made the circuit through Clinton. You say you don't know, which I find peculiar given how long you dated her.

"If tomorrow afternoon you still don't know, we will be resorting to a lot of painful methods to jog your memory. I won't give a damn how Plore you are. And in the end, you'll tell us anyway. And we will throw in charges on behalf of all the little Latinas you molested, and call it Hate Crime. You will never see the outside of a prison hospital again. You know that Hate Crime brings an automatic life sentence."

Bertone sobbed.

"But!" said David, "all is not lost. If your memory miraculously revives, we can arrange a pleasant stay at one of the better psychiatric hospitals, where you can work on your own betterment." He enjoyed lingering over the classic Diversity mantra, "and you might even make it back to Clinton after all this excitement dies down. I won't worry about the Latinas, I'm sure they were absolutely delicious and asking for it.

"But you need to hold out for about twenty minutes in the Red Room. This will be extremely unpleasant. Almost certainly the worst twenty minutes of your life. I suggest waterboarding, as least likely to leave permanent damage, but I may change my mind. Then I will say 'Professor Bertone, it's now or never. Will you tell us how Professor Pinckney got her books?' That will be your final cue for a full confession. If I have to keep working you over after that, this deal is off. I have other things I need to do tomorrow afternoon.

"Are your parents still alive?"

Bertone said, "Yes, my mother, in Ploreville."

"For your mother's sake, so she can see you again, do as I say. In five years, none of this will matter. And you'll still be alive. Don't throw away everything."

He picked up the stool, and at the door, said, "You're lucky I'm such a sentimental Plore," and then, "remember the cue. I need twenty minutes of resistance, so caving early won't be acceptable either. Show that Arlington Plore spirit."

He switched off the light, pushed the button to lock the cell from the outside, and returned the stool to the guard. Bertone lay awake for hours, staring at the cement ceiling.

Chapter 20
Most Excellent Master of the Red Room
(Friday, 6 May)

The morning meeting had gone well. As the unit marched behind Wurro and brought offerings, David pretended to watch while mentally organizing his pep talk. When the room silenced, David said some things he meant and others he didn't, not anymore. But the crowd seemed not to be able to discern between the two, and applauded fervently, so it was a success. "And don't forget that we'll start our happy hour at four," he concluded. Walters nodded to him, as if he were the unit chief and David a promising subordinate, "That was good, chief."

"Thank you, Deputy Commander Wurro," said David absentmindedly, and before the end of the day, to his everlasting regret, the moniker had stuck, to Walters' great pleasure.

The morning went faster than he wanted it to, and there he was in Red Room C looking down at Bertone, strapped to the waterboarding table. Drains were underneath the table, but never quite enough to swallow the splashing flow. Their eyes met briefly. Bertone looked calmer than last night, but that could be a prelude to stiffened resistance, not cooperation, so David didn't read too much into it. He was aware of the other eyes on him, those of the three other officers, at least one of whom was new to the unit, and the doctors, and the analysts in the observation room. At some level, it was a performance that, if it went well—and Bertone remembered his lines—would require minimal suffering from Bertone, or at least a lot less than he would have gotten from any of David's colleagues. "Prepare irons," David told one of the officers, who went over to the branding iron bin and turned it on. This was part of the dramatic effect and he devoutly hoped they would stay unused. The waterboarding apparatus was already in place. He felt numb and distant, as if he were watching from afar.

David asked Bertone the same questions he had asked last night. Bertone kept saying, "I don't know, I don't know." And then, "What do you want from me? Do you want me to lie?"

It was a long twenty minutes. They waterboarded him, the floor was slippery, he struggled futilely and cried soundlessly under the cloth fastened by the officers.

David's lips pressed together. He moved slowly, to run out the clock a little faster. He had forgotten how long twenty minutes could be in the Red Room. After they had pounded the water out of Bertone, and the attendants mopped up the floor around the drain, he asked the questions again. Bertone pleaded innocence of Pinckney's activities. The cloth and the buckets of water came out again. The sodden paper pajamas fell off Bertone, leaving him naked. There were still several minutes to kill. The protocol forbade waterboarding and electrical treatment in that succession, if only for the safety of the torturers, so David had to call for the punishment chair. Bertone needed to be dried off to reach the point at which his limbs could be tied and stretched behind that chair. That took a good three or four minutes.

"Professor Bertone, it's now or never. Will you tell us how Professor Pinckney got her books?"

Several seconds passed. "No, you bastard!" Bertone looked up from the chair, increasing the pressure on his shoulders further, presenting a face of fury to David. David was briefly reminded of when MacMillan had snapped too.

David was incredulous. Here he had been, giving this molester professor every break possible. He had given him specific instructions on how to survive the Red Room and even recover his dissolute life. He had tried to behave like a human being caught in this maelstrom of cruelty, or as close to one as he could. And this was the reward—with disrespect to boot. A wave of anger he had not experienced in years flooded him, warming him as with a fever, and the remoteness he had been cultivating so far completely vanished. He slapped Bertone across the face, then shoved him in the chair to the floor. Bertone howled. And then David darted over to the stand where the irons—rarely used—stood in their metal rack, red hot at their tips, and he spun around and faced Bertone holding one only inches from the prisoner's face.

"Do you want this, you f---ing Plore? Do you want this up your ass, or just on your face? How do you plan to explain that to the little girls? Because when we're done, you won't have anything left to show them."

Bertone at that point must have come to his senses, possibly aided by the reminder of the Latinas, or was actually convinced David was about to assault him with the red-hot iron, possibly on his exposed private parts. He groaned, "Okay, okay, yes, I'll talk."

The chair was righted, the bonds not instantly loosened, and then only gradually, as he talked about how he and Kendra Pinckney would go to Anacosta once a month, ostensibly for theater and dining. But on Sunday morning, Kendra would wake early, and take a car to a recycling plant in a remote corner of the City. She would come back with several books that had been destined for the recycling vats, now hidden at the bottom of her large purse. They would hide them in their suitpods, and take them back home. David mentally noted to have the analysts check chip data on Pinckney's movements in the City on weekends. City trips would stand out from her default data, so it wouldn't be particularly difficult to narrow this down.

David, his heart rate finally starting to return to normal, asked whom she had dealt with at the plant. He asked which books Bertone remembered seeing—Bertone stumbled here but recalled the names Friedman and Hayek. He remembered an orange cover here, a tattered paperback there. They were usually in disrepair, but Kendra would tape them carefully upon their return to Clinton. Bertone seemed to have been a willing accomplice rather than a full-fledged member of the Club, which dealt with philosophies outside his natural sphere of interest. He claimed that after Kendra repaired the books, he never saw them again. "I didn't want the trouble. I was just doing her a favor when we went to Anacosta."

"Did she interact with anyone at the plant, or did she just pick them up from the trash?"

"I don't know. I think she paid someone to leave the books out."

"What makes you think that?"

"Once she came back empty-handed and said that the usual guy hadn't been there that week or he'd been sick or something."

David interrogated Bertone for a few more minutes, but he had gotten what he needed. He was willing to believe Bertone's claim he hadn't seen the books after Pinckney repaired them, at least for now. "Untie him," he told the junior officers. "Give him another set of greens and take him away."

He turned away from Bertone as the junior officers started shutting down the Red Room and attending to Bertone. The last officer to leave the room would switch on the regular lights, and the red furnace would shrink into the corners.

"Hey," said the professor, "are you going to help me now that I'm cooperating with you?"

David's eyes narrowed. "Sorry, you bastard, you missed your cue." The casualness of Bertone's address to him, "hey," rubbed him the wrong way, without a "sir" or "commander," although David would have been more tolerant had Bertone played his part as promised. Not to mention he was risking the interest of the junior officers in exactly what was meant by "cue." He stalked out before Bertone could compromise him any further. His addition of "bastard" had been deliberate, to remind the professor where he had gone wrong. Yes, it would be a pleasure to point the Knowledge Tower in the direction of the professor's Hate Crime against innocent Latina youngsters.

David lathered his hands and changed clothes in the washroom at the end of the corridor. His shirt and pants were both damp. He placed them in the laundry bag labeled Harris. He stared into the mirror, wondering how he could look like a human being after that ordeal.

The one junior officer who wasn't escorting Bertone back to his cell came into the washroom. David knew he was a newcomer to the KCU, on detail from the Economic Crimes Unit. Steve Rosen had said to him, wryly, "I'm lending you one of my best young guys, Odin Valentine. Don't ruin him with your excessive thinking." Valentine was a very young six-footer with a fresh, friendly face and curly brown hair. Seeing the young man with his puppyish mien made David feel old and weathered. And very tired. Thank goodness the weekend was here.

"Sir, that was terrific. Really great to see how to do that kind of interrogation."

David reminded himself to be gentle. "Thanks, Valentine. It paid off today. I'd prefer we don't have to get to the Red Room, of course. Last resort."

"Oh, yes, of course, sir."

David wanted to add, "Because it will just remind you that our methods, with the addition of electricity, have not advanced beyond those of medieval savages." But of course, you couldn't tell this to a Valentine, and indeed not to any sworn Antifan, no matter how senior your status. And then, thought David, you would almost always punish your prisoner for a nonexistent crime, or something that in a civilized society would not be a crime but a virtue; whereas he himself would gladly have smacked Bertone around on his own time for his apparently tolerable (to the government) molestation habits.

Valentine noticed that David seemed distracted, so he turned to the sink and began washing.

Yes, David thought, it had paid off today. And he wasn't being paid to humor his own moral preferences, but to protect the DJR. It wasn't wrong to have tried to make Bertone's life a little easier to extract the needed information. So what was right? On his way out, he clapped Valentine on the shoulder and said, "Thanks for your work today, Valentine. Glad you were there."

Back in the unit, a festive air was building with the advent of the happy hour. Walters and Patel had not yet returned, but the staff members were moving the liquor bottles from Whiro's altar to the main table, amid various snacks—crackers and cheese, quinoa spread, beef satay sticks, pepperoni slices. When David entered the unit, the officers nearest the door cheered loudly, as word of the breakthrough had preceded him. "Congratulations, sir!" several chorused.

Karlmarx, who had recently been promoted to branch chief for the burgeoning analytic corps, stepped forward and said, "I've put the request out on the Pinckney chip, sir."

"Thank you, Karlmarx. Thanks, everyone." David stepped into his office, which he had been told would next week become Walters', as a new, larger one was being constructed for him. In the meantime, he was visible to the whole crew through the glass, so he kept up the façade, pulling up his mail and reading without absorbing it. He would sign off on the interrogation report when the analysts had prepared it, most likely tomorrow morning. It was possible Pinckney would cave when presented with the report, but now David didn't feel her confession would be absolutely essential. The recycling plant was about to undergo unusual scrutiny, once the chip scan revealed which one it was. There were two in the City and two more in Ploreville Alexandria. He wondered what Walters and Patel had found out today, and whether, given the nature of torture, any of it would be reliable.

Walters and Patel came in together, and David could tell from a glimpse at their faces that it had been a mixed afternoon. The beefy pair crammed into his office, which made David realize it was high time he moved into a larger one.

"We heard about your session with Bertone, chief," said Walters respectfully. "Glad to hear we have made some progress. We will run down that recycling plant immediately."

"How about yours?" Walters had continued with Leonard and Patel had interrogated Gina Carladaughter of the Women's Studies Department. The bulky Patel seemed to have luck with women prisoners, to which he always modestly said, "Sir, it's because I'm married."

Patel said, "Carladaughter gave us a lot of trouble initially, which is why she ended up in the Red Room. She was more cooperative today. She still claimed she didn't know about any Club. But she said she had seen Pinckney, MacMillan, and Leonard sitting in a campus gazebo on Tuesday evenings in nice weather. She waved and they would wave back if they saw her, but the one time she tried to join them she didn't feel welcome, so she didn't try again."

"Well, that's useful," said David, "It will probably fit in with the chip and armband data for each of them. Do we have it yet?" Patel responded, "Yes, we'll look at it tonight."

"Monday is fine," said David. "We don't need to ruin anyone's weekend."

David turned to Walters. "So what did you find out, Deputy Commander?"

Walters bit his lip and Patel turned away slightly. "Leonard died in the Red Room today. He went into cardiac arrest late in the session and the doctor couldn't revive him."

David slammed his fist on the table. "Didn't I tell you we couldn't afford another death?"

"Commander," said the chagrined Walters. "We now have thirty-three Clinton faculty and staff here at Beaufort, half of whom are getting the Red Room. It's really not a terrible ratio." He was probably right, but none of those other cases were facing the same scrutiny from the Director.

David glared at him. "Do you realize that of the only three Club members we have identified, two are now dead? And the third one is teetering on the precipice."

"Yes, sir." Walters was unusually subdued. "I didn't ask him who else was in the Club, I just asked him for names of faculty who had shown evidence of sympathy for capitalism and individualism. He insisted there were none. But after about fifteen minutes with the cellular scrambling machine, he gave the names of two economics professors. And then he died."

David cradled his head in his right hand. There was not much point in lambasting Walters further. David hoped this had taken him down a notch, however. Maybe Whiro's mana had already taken a dark turn.

One good thing about today's miserable Red Room session, David thought ruefully, was his own added credibility. He then said, "I've decided we need to have better training for the Red Room and we need to raise the bar for who we bring in there. I was unhappy with what happened to Smeldring, for one thing. If we had given some consideration to the fact he actually brought Pinckney to our attention, why would we have tried to punish him into admitting he was a member of the Club?" And then he explained how he had approached Bertone, by threatening him with the molestation case. "I'm not sure I would have succeeded this afternoon if I hadn't read the file the night before," he said. "We should do a lot more scrutinizing of these dossiers as a senior group beforehand so we can have a strategy in place. This has been too haphazard, especially with our numbers increasing so quickly, and I take responsibility." The new chief of the KCU, Alex Charlton, was reporting for duty on Monday, a prospect that relieved David, who had been acting Senior Commander since January.

To Walters, he said, "Let's find out how Smeldring is doing and make sure those bones are set properly. He doesn't deserve to be crippled for life. Make sure he's in the sick bay and not in his cell. Just keep the Clinton people separate. Then let's move him onto Garrett," which was the topline criminal hospital, most of whose patients eventually returned home.

"Yes, chief." Walters was sounding deferential, for once.

The happy hour was well underway when the men exited David's office. David forced himself to accept a drink and circulate, introducing himself to the new officers, even though they knew who he was. Socializing was usually one of his strong suits, but Leonard's death—even though he had never met the man personally—was depressing. Partly because Leonard had been a key witness, so too valuable to be destroyed like a dog—no, even a euthanized animal would have been treated more gently—and partly because David felt empathy for someone whose life must have been a continuous struggle even before he began reading dangerous books.

"Well," he thought with some grim satisfaction, "at least if this happened, it was in Walters' room. I won't mind too terribly telling the Director."

An hour later, he left his bicycle in the Beaufort garage and took a car down to the Depository. He called Malia, "I'm out here, honey." Once the door closed behind him, they embraced, and he said, "Give me a short nap, and I'll be fine. It's been an exhausting week and today was very, very hard. I'll tell you about it later." Malia set him up in two upholstered chairs in the lobby as an impromptu cot, and he promptly fell asleep, waking up exactly half an hour later. It was an acquired skill. She tidied her desk, occasionally peeking into the lobby.

Back in her office, after his routine checks to make sure the cameras were still broken, he asked her, "How's the research going?" She told him about having just finished *Gone With the Wind,* but now she was struggling with John Locke's *Essay on Toleration.*

He nodded approvingly. "How do you figure out what to read next?" he asked.

"Oh, that's where the *Diversity Scholarship* journals come in handy," she said, "I skim to see who they call the most dangerous, the most often. I have to prioritize." They laughed together.

"Look, I have something for you, too," he said. They sat side-by-side at her desk, and with the cameras off, he placed a finger to his lips and wrote on a sheet of paper what he had committed to memory at Beaufort a short while ago:

Isabelle J. Jenness = Rex Gretabelle Andrews, age 14, family SC 255
Address: The Octavian, 3000 Connecticut Avenue, NW, Anacosta
Adoptive parents (he was careful to write down 'adoptive'): Leighton Andrews and Belinda Barbaradaughter.

He scribbled:

LA Senior Counsel, Inter Tower Relations, KT, SC 260
BB Senior Libraries Coordinator, KT, SC 250

Malia jabbed her finger on the BB, while nodding, mouthing a silent "I know her!" Belinda Barbaradaughter was about two levels above Antelides.

"That's very interesting," David said, aloud, softly. Coincidence, or not?

Malia then pointed to "Rex Gretabelle" and made a face.

"Pretty awful, isn't it?" he replied. He pointed to the address, nodding and rolling his eyes, as if to say "Big stuff." He thought, I'm not sure they'd let ME live there. It was one of the finest addresses in Anacosta. A 19th century stone fortress with gargoyles and towers, the Octavian faced the old zoo across Connecticut Avenue, which was now the botanical garden of Anacosta—now that enlightened views prevailed about caged animals, if not about caged humans. The garden banned Plores outright, with the exception of one holiday weekend a year, and under-120s were permitted to patronize it on weekends.

He then tore up the paper, popped the shreds into his mouth, and ate them.

As he swallowed, he saw four boxes stacked near the door to the lobby. "What are those?"

"Discards," said Malia.

"Discards?"

"Yes, one of my responsibilities is to go through the stacks and put aside any volumes that are no longer in good enough condition for use. Even if it's the only copy, we aren't supposed to keep it. I think they really want to destroy this whole library, eventually, book by book."

David was hit by his second thunderbolt of the day. "So where do those boxes go?"

"A Plore driver picks them up on the second Tuesday of the month and takes them—well, I always assumed he takes them to the Knowledge Tower for review and then recycling."

"But you don't know for sure?" David pressed.

"Well, no. Is it important?"

David thought somewhat impatiently that for an intellectual, Malia sometimes showed a remarkable lack of curiosity.

"It might be, sweetheart. Could he be taking them directly to the recycling plant, without going to the Knowledge Tower first?"

"I guess so, I never asked. I never hear anything about them afterward. You'd think they might send back a book or two as being fit for research after all. But they never do."

"Is it always the same driver?"

"Usually, yes, his name is Peter. Sometimes it's another driver. Am I in trouble?"

"Not at all, just curious, since we were asking a few weeks ago about missing books. Nothing that should be on the shelves is missing, but it just occurred to me there's more than one way out of the building. You're doing your job, don't worry. Let's just have a fun weekend, okay?" They were going to Ada's tomorrow night. David had called to make sure he could bring Malia, but Ada's was used to accommodating the low-Social Credit dates of powerful people.

"Would you like to go down to the basement and investigate how our stacks are doing today?" she smiled at him. He couldn't help smiling back, although he'd had enough of basements for one day. "That's very conscientious of you," he said, and followed her to the elevator. They emerged from the Depository an hour later, Malia locking up carefully for the weekend, and then they went for takeout to bring home. He let Malia wait for the food while he made a quick call back to Beaufort on the deserted street corner. Answering was Night Commander Angela, who made sure to compliment him on the interrogation that afternoon and who was pleased to take down some instructions for an operation for early Monday morning.

Chapter 21
Glitterati Melee at Ada's
(Saturday/Sunday, 7-8 May)

Malia and David came out of the shower. She reached for the new dress, a slinky black and gold sheath with a dramatic V-neck.

"Hope you don't fall out of that," David observed. But she had indeed filled out a bit more in recent weeks, thanks to a higher calorie Social Credit diet than she was entitled to, so the dress clung more than it would have a month ago. He was pleased with how it looked.

Within the hour, they were heading downtown in the sportscar. Ada's occupied a square block near Logan Circle, with ADA's flashing in gold neon from the roof. A long line of supplicants snaked along a plush cord strung between stanchions. David and Malia waved their armbands at the RESERVATIONS window. David signed an "Assurance for Under-130 Guest," in which he promised that Malia would neither assault other patrons nor destroy drinkware. Then they were led into the amphitheater-style venue—just as Malia had seen in photos—anchored by a wooden dance floor, with tiered seating around the floor, and two balconies. The ground floor and the top level each featured a VIP area from which patrons liked to view the dance floor, or display themselves.

David and Malia were seated to the left of the dance floor. David was able to sit in his preferred location with his back to the wall, which he always requested whenever he made reservations at a restaurant. But he moved her chair around the table and beside him so she could also watch the scene. The host handed them menus edged in black and gold.

From their vantage point, they could see the other tables at their level and a glimpse of the VIP balcony across the way. "I'll let you know if anyone interesting shows up," said David. "We're a bit early." For the moment, Malia was satisfied to scan the couples around them, both same-sex and opposite-sex, with a heavy sprinkling of possible New Men and New Women, mostly under 45. It was a snapshot of the Anacosta political and artistic elite.

The waiter requested their preferred pronouns. They ordered a carafe of sangria, and the mezze, including lamb, chicken, grape leaves, and falafel. "No one will blame us for cultural appropriation here," said David. "We've already done the hard work of our betterment."

The music started up again, a mix of slower love songs building into pounding rock. "Like from courtship to sex," thought Malia. Couples began to drift onto the floor.

The food arrived. Malia continued sipping sangria while David switched to whiskey. Eventually, they gravitated onto the dance floor, where dozens of couples and some larger clots of unpaired young people were gyrating to the now more aggressive beat. She realized that they had not danced together before; in fact, Malia had not danced at all in years. There was no reason to dance and no partner with whom to dance. First, she had been rearing a small child, then she hid at home, and most of the safer nightclubs were out of her credit range. The deejay played the current big hit, "Wave at Diversity," whose choruses required all the dancers to wave their arms in sync above their heads.

"Di-VER-si-TY! Di-VER-si-TY !
Fight the fascists, take them down!
Tonight we're gonna get way down!
Our Social Credit gets around!"

The beat is good, thought David. A lot of DJR musicians worked hard on the music and filled in the lyrics with safe restatements of whatever would win them official approval and all the bennies that came along with that. Lyrics with aggressively Diverse themes paid off better than ordinary songs with no offensive words. There was a separate Social Credit scale for musicians and artists, which gave them incentives to conform. In all his years at Beaufort, he had dealt with only a handful of them, accused of performing unapproved lyrics or displaying retrograde oil paintings of white people in out-of-the-way club garages or lofts. It was usually sufficient to administer a beating and close down the space. For the most part, musicians and artists were a docile bunch, especially when plied with Art Diversity Medals and Diversity Art Fellowships.

They returned to the table and ordered dessert. David held Malia's hand. "I hope you're happy."

"I have never been happier than I am now," she said. "I don't think I even knew what it was like to be happy before I met you."

"Well," he said, "if we're lucky, in a year you will be even happier." An eavesdropper would have thought David was referring to marriage, or possibly a baby, but Malia knew otherwise.

David suddenly stared straight ahead. "Oh no." Not Dianne Abimbala, not tonight, please. Malia, who expected trouble at every turn, was alarmed. He squeezed her hand.

A statuesque black woman with an aureole-like Afro was approaching the table determinedly. She wore a bold orange and green wrap print, dangling gold earrings, and a necklace with black and brown wooden beads. Malia instantly knew, this is the African Goddess of the nightstand cosmetics collection. She was almost six feet tall and the Afro added several more inches.

"David Harris, COMMANDER David Harris," she trilled, cooing at David. "I haven't seen you in MONTHS, baby. What have you been doing with yourself?"

"Hi Dianne. Working hard, staying out of trouble. What about you?"

'Well, I got a license for joint ownership with the Tourism Department to open a culturally relevant tourism company, not capitalistic at all, and business has been booming. African cooking classes, whitewater rafting for brown people, things like that. We only take 200s plus, just to stay elite. Once you start admitting anyone, the best people won't be interested."

She bent down to peer at Malia. "And who is this?"

David apologized. "Sorry not to have introduced you first. Dianne, this is Malia Jenness. Malia, this is Dianne Abimbala."

"That's Dianne Abimbala, 260, by the way," said Dianne proudly. "And you?"

"Malia is 196," David said quickly. "I hope that's adequate for you."

"She can stay," said Dianne breezily, "but honey, I hope you can keep up with this very fine man. What beautiful tight white buns, I miss having them for my breakfast."

"I don't think she's joking, she liked to butter them," said David, pretending to be lighthearted but casting worried sideways glances at Malia's impassive face.

"But when I got my 260, well, I moved into another universe, so a girl's gotta find new company."

"Who's the latest beau, Dianne?" asked David, moving into only slightly safer territory.

"Do you know Garrett Bates, 280?"

"Garrett Bates the painter?" asked Malia. Bates was the current rave of the Anacosta artistic scene, currently featured in a major show. Art critics enthused about the slapdash strokes, bold colors and vigorous knife slashings of his canvases. They had titles such as "Rage Against the Interior," "Blak (sic) Feminist Wombs," and "Born Oppressed," and sold for vast sums.

"Look, David, sweetie, she's actually cultural," cooed Dianne.

"I don't recognize the name," said David pointedly. "So is the lucky Mr. Bates here tonight?"

"Yes, they are on the dance floor nearest us, wearing the orange outfit." Dianne pointed to a very tall man in a dashiki and fez. "But they prefer to be known as 'they' and 'Mxist.'"

"Well, thank you for the information, Dianne. It was good seeing you." David stared her down, which was hard when she was staring down at you. "Good luck with the business. Sounds like you're doing great. Good luck with Mxist They too."

"Don't miss me too much, David. I'm not coming back." She flounced off, and not only was Malia not upset, she broke out laughing. Having patiently waited out the unsettling visitor, the waiter brought cups of chocolate mousse.

"At least now I know who she was cheating on me with last Saturnalia," said David. "Although I find it hard to have lost out to a Mxist in an orange costume.

"Can you imagine what it was like to date her for two years? Constant drama. After one fight, she told me she had put a Nigerian curse on my manhood and it would shrivel up. And if you think you fret over your Social Credit scores, you can just imagine Dianne counting up all her chips each year. But she kept getting confused and having to start all over again. It was a lot of chips.

"She comes from an interesting family. Her parents were Nigerians who came here before the war to start a taxicab business. Then they—that's a legitimate use of *they*, by the way—used the cabs to ferry Blue fighters and Antifans to the front lines and drove a fleet of ambulances to bring them back again. Excellent understanding of the concept of the war supply chain.

"When the war ended, her father graciously donated the fleet to the DJR, which was about to confiscate them anyway, under socialism, and agreed to become the first Eco-Transport Secretary of the DJR. So they started with 300 Social Credit points even before you start adding in the race and sex points. And her father then came up with the self-driving car system.

"I thought her last name sounded familiar," said Malia.

"Now she has tried to keep up with the family Social Credit score. She started as an Antifan— that's where we originally met. Yes, can't you just see her storming into a nest of knowledge criminals swinging a chain? It would be like something out of a comic book. That gave her a big point boost; it wasn't easy work, although I'd be scared of her coming at me with the chain, for sure. They let her quit ten years ago and her folks helped her begin fresh at the Economic Tower, coming up with entrepreneurial ideas for Diverse Women to benefit from tourism. Someday tourists will come back. Now she has a legitimate 260, between the job and being a black woman. She thought about becoming bisexual, but realized she could get the ten points just by going to three funerals each year of her parents' friends."

Malia asked, "So did the curse work?"

"The one on my manhood? No, do you think so?" They laughed.

Malia said, "I don't know why you are spending time with me, when you have had so many more exciting girlfriends. Here I am, just the mousy low-credit librarian. You even had to lie just now about my Social Credit score."

David looked at her again, that steady purposeful gaze. "Yeah, I'm not sure why I did that at the last second, but who knows what she would have said in response if I hadn't? Don't run yourself down again. I don't waste my time, and if we're together, there's a reason. It's not just to fatten you up, although I admit that's a noble cause. Finish the mousse, please."

They watched the throbbing dance floor. Inaudible amid the heightening buzz of Ada's close to midnight, he said, "We are both outsiders. We hate the society around us. You hide from it, and I blend with its ugliest side."

"You mean we both serve it," argued Malia. "Neither of us has refused to do anything we were told to do. They told you to become an Antifan, and you did it willingly. And they told me to study Knowledge Management, and to go to the Depository, and I did that, willingly. And they stole my daughter, and I still went to work every day as if it hadn't happened, like I didn't even deserve to have a child. What's the point of being an outsider forever if you don't do anything about it? It just kills you slowly, every day."

"We are doing something about it," said David. "If we're lucky, in a year we'll be somewhere else." His eyes skittered around them, but most of the patrons at nearby tables were on the dance floor. He had also checked underneath the table and chairs, although he knew the sensors were most plentiful in the VIP areas, where the biggest fish fried.

"Is that all?" Malia asked.

"What do you mean, is that *all?* We are likelier to fail than to succeed at this enterprise. This would be the achievement of a lifetime and you say, 'is that all?'"

"No, I understand it would be a stupendous victory, for us. Well, especially for me. But life here would go on as normal. We would be safe, and yet all this suffering would continue here."

"Malia, one thing at a time. We can do nothing here on our own. If we live in a free country, we can work with others to make a difference back here. And let's leave it there." Couples were drifting off the dance floor and back to their section. He was surprised, almost pleasantly, that she cared for more than just her daughter.

He placed his arm around her shoulder and drew her face to his. They kissed deeply, an act in which they were not conspicuous, not at Ada's and not at this hour, when the evening was turning into the middle of the night, and the casual wholesome Diversity fun was intensifying into more ominous notes, whether of pending sexual liaison, drug use, or other dangers.

"I love you," said David. "I will always be here for you."

Malia felt awkward, but she said, sincerely, "I love you too. And I will be here for you."

They went out to the dance floor again, and it was even more crowded than before, and darker, with red and gold strobe lights flashing across the uninhibited bodies. David pointed out Governor Farnham's Chief of Staff and a topless starlet, separately leaning over the VIP balconies to display themselves to the crowd. David and Malia danced within a tight space they made their own near the edge of the floor, and when the music switched to a tender Diversity love ballad, she rested her head on his shoulder, and they swayed gently to the music, ignoring the lyrics as one had to do.

"I love you Non-Binary Boy,
You're my Non-Binary Toy,
I'm just a New Woman looking for a Non-Binary Boy,
Give me your sweetness, don't be coy
Lie down here next to me and stroke me, harder...I swell to meet you."

"Hey, chief!"

David looked up and there was Walters, of all people, crashing toward him, with Jeremy Einhorn, 180, his counterpart deputy on the other side of the KCU, right behind. Both were dressed in civilian clothes, out for a night on the town. "Hi, Commander," said Jeremy. David hoped that Walters would not recognize Malia, but he said, "Hi miss, I remember you from the Depository."

"That's right," said David. "There isn't a problem tonight, is there?"

"Not really," said Walters. "We just came out for some fun. Chief, you'll be glad to know I'm leaving Cheysa alone all weekend. She's spending the weekend with her mom."

Einhorn said, "There's some Knowledge Tower guys here, kind of obnoxious. We're trying to ignore them."

"Good," said David. "Remember that revenge is a dish best served cold."

Walters said, "We just wanted to say hi. Have a good time!" Then Walters and Jeremy disappeared into the throng again.

"That's Walters, if you didn't figure it out on your own."

"Oh!" Malia said, connecting the Antifan who had called her "bitch" at the Depository with the stories David had been relating about the Wurro-worshiping deputy. At least he seemed to have been dealt a setback, judging from David's sanitized account of the Red Room victory on Friday. David had intimidated a prisoner into confessing a crime, which had impressed everyone at work, but he had not used any physical coercion, she was pleased to know.

They continued to dance, but it was not the same as before.

Back at the table, David paid the bill, and they exited into the damp overnight air, waiting for the valet to bring the car. Suddenly, they heard men shouting. A fight was taking place at the street corner. David said, "I'll be right back," instinctively knowing that Walters and Einhorn were facing off against some of those feckless Knowledge Tower punks, who were brave only when they outnumbered you five to one. And Ada's drew them like flies, like an EcoBar with a dance floor.

Just as he had feared, Walters and Einhorn were backed against the brick wall of Ada's, confronted by a circle of foppish but gym-muscled and intoxicated Knowledge Tower guys a decade younger than the Antifans. No one sober would have thought to assault Antifans on the streets of Anacosta. Several girlfriends huddled at the curb. The two Latinos, a black, and three white guys were cursing Walters and Einhorn. "Antifa bastards! You think you can do anything you want! Why don't you stay in your dungeons? I'm gonna smash your f---ing face!" The young women in their high heels and brief skirts were trying to calm down their boyfriends, calling out, "Let's go, this isn't worth it," and "guys, please stop." The bouncers were watching from the door, unsure whether to get involved in what looked like a political fracas.

David waded into the fray, adopting the paternal policeman style. "Okay, guys, what's going on here?"

The Tower guys did not immediately recognize David as an Antifan, possibly because he did need that haircut. "These Antifan bastards think they can grab your girlfriends whenever they want. And they think they're going to take down the Knowledge Tower! We're fighting back against you bastards!" The offense to the Tower and to the girlfriends had become one frothy mix of resentment.

David signaled to the bouncers, who inched toward them reluctantly.

He turned to Walters and Einhorn, "All right, guys, were you bothering their girls?" It was easier to treat this as a typical nightclub incident than as a political one.

"We just were talking. Can we help it if we're interesting guys?" said Walters. Then directing his spite at the mob, "I mean, if you had enough balls to keep them interested in you, this wouldn't be a problem at all." Thanks for helping, Brian, you diplomat asshole, thought David. One of the Tower guys rushed at Walters, but David inserted himself between them.

"I'd be careful if I were you," David said to a Latino guy who was trying to get at the much taller Walters. "This fellow killed a prisoner with his bare hands yesterday. I'm only trying to help you." This was mostly true. The Latino slunk back into the mob.

One of the white guys flashed a knife, but being sober was an advantage, so David disarmed him quickly and pocketed the knife. "Let me tell you fellows," said David, "if we pursue this on Monday, we'll be seeing you at Beaufort. A knife offense is a good fifty points off your Social Credit score, so you won't be coming back here when we convict you."

The Tower mob started to lose its verve, like a thundercloud breaking up, falling into wispy clouds of mutters and grumbles, at which point the bouncers became active and began herding them all down the street.

"Thank you, sir," said Einhorn. "I mean, we could have taken them down, but it would have been messy."

"I did kill someone with my bare hands yesterday," said Walters, "and not for the first time. They were lucky you came along, Commander Harris."

David sighed, "perhaps Wurro was with you tonight as well."

Walters nodded solemnly. "Big mana," he said.

As the deputies' self-driving car lumbered away, he returned to Malia, who was standing next to the sportscar and had seen the confrontation, even if she couldn't hear the words they had exchanged. "What did you say to end that?" she marveled.

"I just delayed things a bit until everyone started to sober up," he replied modestly.

But driving home, he thought, I have never seen any nightclub fight take on this political tone. We are truly striking at the heart of the Knowledge Tower if it's beginning to creep into nightclub brawls. The knife defense class he was taking at the Beaufort gym had served him well against the Tower guy. If I had not been there, it could have gone much worse, he realized.

Chapter 22
Express Deliveries
(Monday/Tuesday, 9-10 May)

Several hours before Monday dawned, at the quietest time of the week, with the sidewalks glistening from a midnight shower, two Antifan technicians let themselves into the Depository. They opened all four boxes destined for the recycling plant and placed virtually invisible tape that were also tracking devices on the inside cover of all the books. Then they carefully repackaged and retaped the boxes that Malia had herself secured on Friday. David told them to imitate the original taping as much as possible, but he was pretty sure that Malia lacked an interest in such details, and would fail to notice any discrepancies, particularly if the boxes were restacked as before.

On Monday morning, David was glad he had notified the Director's office about the confrontation at Ada's, because two other such clashes had taken place in downtown Anacosta the same night. Three men jumped an Antifan who was walking home from a restaurant with his wife, while wearing his uniform jacket; the assailants shouted anti-Antifan remarks before running away. A chip trace at that location had yielded arrests of two Knowledge Tower officers and one Social Tower officer. The trio would be transferred to Beaufort this morning where the assault would doubtless be repaid in kind. In a second incident, two women Antifans whose employment was known to others were roughed up by other bar customers who openly declared they worked at the Knowledge Tower and weren't going to take crap from the ADF anymore. The ADF was investigating that incident too, using chip records.

"Just what you'd expect," said the Director to David and Alex Charlton, David's new boss, who had started that morning. "Cowardly attacks where they outnumber our officers, and against women too. I guess it's best that none of these escalated." He sounded faintly regretful.

"What are we going to do about it, sir?" asked Alex Charlton. David had known Alex for years, and liked him personally, but knew Alex was not going to be a fount of ideas or initiative. He hoped that Alex would at least competently handle some of the bureaucratic minutiae and meetings that had preoccupied him all year as acting chief, KCU.

"I am going to call Terwilliger and remind him that according to the Basic Diversity Law of 2061, the ADF has the right to override the Anacosta police to arrest and detain anyone threatening its officers or interests. I am going to tell him that unless he wants more of his officers taken to Beaufort, he would be advised to rein them in immediately," said Ferraro.

"What should we tell our own officers, sir?" asked David. "Do we want them to stay away from bars or nightclubs for a while?"

"Nope," said Ferraro. "Our officers work hard and they deserve to play hard. We will tell them not to pick a fight, but when confronted, try to de-escalate with honor. And if they feel they are in physical danger, do what they need to do. If we run and hide, other people in Anacosta will start attacking ADF officers too. I'm not pretending we're well loved in this town."

David thought of how many City residents lived in fear of Antifan raids, had seen or felt chains and clubs in use, or knew someone who had fallen under Antifan scrutiny. After nearly forty years, folks on the receiving end of Antifan justice might well be tempted to strike back if they perceived leniency was in style. The Director was right.

After briefing Alex on the latest developments in the university probe, including the recycling plant operation scheduled for tomorrow, David settled in his new office. Vanessa had already moved his belongings into the office. The giant "Are You the Fist" poster already hung on the wall. The view was a northern one, with the Potowmack meandering northwest, shorter towers reaching toward the City limits, and hardscrabble Plore neighborhoods lying somewhere beyond them. David placed his feet on the desk, and then took them down, restless.

He knew that fifteen Garvey University professors were being trucked down from the New York-Schuylkill District today, and ten Sanders University professors would arrive tomorrow. Diverse American University in Beaufort's own neighborhood was also well represented this week. The investigation was beginning to bleed into other universities, which could be expected to yield similar yeasty results as faculty tattled on each other. He was interested in finding out whether the book circuit extended to other universities, and the travel data for Kendra Pinckney had indeed shown monthly visits to Sanders in Baltimore, with no apparent justification. Once or twice a year for a conference would have made sense. David hoped that Red Room rumors had circulated sufficiently so that the Antifans could mostly rely on regular interrogations to achieve results. But he also knew that the fury of the Knowledge Tower would only increase with each new batch of arrested faculty. Could Ferraro hold fast?

David was grateful that Rex Gretabelle's parents were Knowledge Tower functionaries, which allowed him to tuck a request for Malia's cause into the current flurry of operational activity. He applied for a sample of Rex's DNA, along with random samples from four other children of Tower bureaucrats, and asked for matches with several women in the database, including Malia's. This way, he could have an explanation, however tortured, if someone asked why he was running searches on children's DNA. I'm running down a theory that the Knowledge Tower was kidnapping the children of Social Crediteers, he practiced saying. And really, who knew if Isabelle/Rex had been the only victim? He might well be onto something here.

Dominic Farrell, the junior officer whom David had encouraged to join the KCU a few weeks ago, stood in the doorway. Because of the ramp-up of the KCU, David had been able to expedite Farrell's application. He Antifan-saluted, and David reciprocated. "Good morning, sir, just letting you know that I am reporting for duty today. I'm glad to be here."

David stood up and shook Dominic's hand. "Welcome, Farrell. I'm delighted to see you here finally. I understand you'll be accompanying Yardley on the recycling plant op tomorrow?"

"Yes, sir, it'll be great to do something operational so quickly. In my old unit, they'd have you reading files for months first. Not that I want to be a complainer."

"No, completely understood, Farrell. We want a bias for action in this unit. It's to your credit. Where are you sitting?"

Farrell pointed to one of the desks on the platform near what had been Walters' old desk, which Chung had just occupied. "Do you have everything you need? And who's your mentor?"

"Yes, sir, I'm well equipped. And Lieutenant Chung will be mentoring me."

"Then you're in good hands, Farrell. Let me know if I can be of any assistance, and welcome."

Dominic returned to his desk, his eyes scanning the busy KCU floor. The bustle and cheeriness of the expanded staff were heartening, after the lifeless and suspicious Cyber Crime unit, whose introverted officers spent most of their time warding off Interior attacks on the GVN and other DJR systems. More interesting CCU work lay in designing cyber attacks on the Interior, with expert guidance available from Chinese and Russian cyber warriors, but Dominic's supervisors had ignored his requests to join more offensive sections. He had started to wonder whether they were discriminating against him for being black, or if they were just poor managers.

The only jarring moment so far had been the Wurro worship that morning, which no one had warned him about. Noticing his perturbation, Chung had said quietly, "Just think of it as a morale boost. No one's really worshipping that statue. Well, maybe Deputy Commander Walters, but everyone else is just having some fun."

Dominic stood at his desk, looking at the southern view of the City. All the officers at the surrounding desks had introduced themselves, pleased to welcome the newcomer. The only exception was a very lovely sister about four desks away, who he noticed had been taking a phone call at the time of the Wurro worship. Their eyes met, and then she looked away. Nor did she look toward him as he stared in her direction. She had amazing braids wrapped around in a towering bun. Why would she not acknowledge him here, when the number of black officers in this unit could be counted on two hands? He decided perhaps she was shy, despite being an Antifan, because the number of women officers in this room was even smaller, and that he would take matters into his own hands. He walked over to her desk.

"Hi," he said. "I'm Dominic Farrell and I just started today."

"Hi," she replied. "I'm Cheysa Conroy. Welcome to the KCU. Where are you coming from?"

He told her, and they exchanged a few pleasantries. She had only been an Antifan for a year, and didn't seem to be enthusiastic about it, Dominic inferred. Nor was she particularly eager to continue the conversation, so he didn't push it. Strange, he thought, as he returned to his desk and began reading the files on the Knowledge Tower interrogations for background on tomorrow's operation. Before he'd gotten very far, Lieutenant Chung suggested they take a walk to the cafeteria for a cup of coffee. Dominic wasn't going to turn down his mentor's invitation, and they headed downstairs, jogging down all ten flights.

"Look," said Chung, as they sat in the cafeteria, which was mostly empty an hour before lunch. "I need to warn you. You saw Deputy Commander Walters this morning at Wurro worship—he's kind of intense, right?" Dominic nodded, wondering where this was going.

"Be very careful when you talk to Conroy. She's his girlfriend, and he's extremely possessive," said Chung. "Irrational about it. I complimented her work performance a few weeks ago, and he slammed *me* against a wall and told me to lay off, and threatened to do things to me that would get us an extra 30 points as a couple. Mother Earth knows what he does to her at home. It's like she's his enslaved person, if you'll pardon the expression. So as your mentor, I needed to warn you first thing about Conroy. Be polite, but distant."

Oh weird, thought Dominic. Maybe I should have asked more questions before coming here.

"And I don't know whether Commander Harris even cares about their relationship, honestly," said Chung. "He and Walters are kind of at cross purposes anyway. Commander Harris is a Plore, and didn't take to the Wurro worship, but because Deputy Commander Wurro—I mean Walters—linked it to the Earth Mother, he was boxed in. If I were you, I'd try to blend in at first. Parade around and chant, it'll get your blood flowing before the unit meeting."

"Commander Harris is a Plore?" Dominic was surprised. "He's been very decent to me." He thought of Plores as not-very-well closeted white supremacists.

"Commander Harris is a gentleman and a true Antifan," said Chung. "There is no one else I'd rather work for, even though he gave it to me for a Red Room interrogation I botched last week. But he blamed himself as well for not going over the dossier more carefully. That's the way he is, and we have been overworked and understaffed. He recognizes that. You couldn't have a better commander, so don't think you made a mistake."

"Good," said Dominic.

"That doesn't mean he notices everything going on around him, of course." Chung drained his coffee cup. "Even more so now that they gave him a bigger office farther away from the main floor. So, if you're running into a problem, come to me first, okay? He'd expect that anyway. Chain of command and all that."

"Yes, sir. Thank you."

"That's what I'm here for," said the unflappable Chung. "Let's head back upstairs."

Walters was standing over Cheysa's desk with a sheaf of papers needing his signature. They looked up as Chung and Dominic returned. Walters came over, and Dominic Antifan-saluted, which Walters returned, as Chung breathed a sigh of relief. Walters would not initiate a salute with an underling, but would have given Dominic grief for not saluting promptly, new or not.

"So you're our newest officer, Farrell, right?" said Walters. "Welcome to Wurro World. What's with the name Dominic anyway? That sounds awfully Christian to me."

Dominic stiffened. No one had ever talked to him like this in the CCU, where polite disinterest was the default mode. "I was named after my uncle, sir. He was a Catholic priest who was killed during the wars."

"Glad *you* ended up on the right side, at least," said Walters breezily. "Might want to help out with Wurro worship then, just so there aren't any doubts about your loyalties here." He pointed to Cheysa. "And if Chung hasn't explained Officer Conroy's role here, it's to serve me. That is to say, me. Don't think that because you share an—ethnic background—that you're going to become friends with her. Is that understood?" Even Chung was shocked by the outright malice. Walters must have noticed Dominic's earlier overture. "Yes, sir," Dominic stammered.

"Good," said Walters. He picked up a turtle paperweight from Dominic's desk—a souvenir from a beach trip with a former girlfriend—and tossed it up in the air, catching it deftly. "This would be a good first offering to Wurro," he said, pointing to the altar. "You can bring something more substantial on Wednesday. Wurro is good to those who are good to him." He left the papers on Cheysa's desk, and headed back to his new office.

Chung made a big inhaling motion and rolled his eyes, as if to say "that was even worse than usual, I'm sorry." But Dominic was staring at Cheysa, on whose face was a look of total despair. Realizing that Dominic was looking at her, she turned back abruptly to her screen. He vowed that Walters or no Walters, he would help her somehow. How could Commander Harris be unaware of this abuse? Or worse, did he tolerate it?

The afternoon improved when Candiss Yardley, his assigned partner in tomorrow's operation, came over to introduce herself and go over the plans. Dominic was happy to focus on business, since he was still shaken by Walters' remarks, and Cheysa sat in his line of sight, which was very distracting. He wondered if he could rearrange the file boxes on his desk to block his view of her before Walters realized that it was currently unobstructed. He could hardly move his desk around. Or should he ask Chung if he ought to move elsewhere?

Dominic and Candiss went across the hall to the former FCU to sit in one of the new small conference rooms built as part of the KCU expansion. It still smelled new, with fresh paint. Candiss was a 30-year-old blonde with a serious, professional mien. She was acutely aware of her status as the only woman officer on the operations squad, now that Cheysa had been sidelined. Walters' few efforts to intimidate her had not gone well for him, since she had a sharp tongue and an Antifan family background. So he mostly left her alone.

Candiss explained that she and Dominic would wait in an undercover van by the Depository starting at 7 am the next morning. The pickup by the Plore driver would likely take place sometime during the morning, but the exact hour was unknown, so they had to be in place early. The guard came on duty at 7:30, and the driver could appear at any time after then. They would follow the driver, whose route was also unknown. He could take the boxes to the Knowledge Tower for inspection, or directly to the recycling plant. Bertone had claimed Pinckney went to the plant to purchase the books, but it was possible that the books first went through the Knowledge Tower, if the Tower was doing due diligence. It was also possible that the driver would make other stops before going to either the Tower or the plant, although that posed a security risk since the boxes would be sitting unguarded in his van. "So we're basically collecting this information tomorrow," she said. "And we stay out of sight. All the books in the boxes now have tracking devices, so we will be able to see what happens to all of them, or at least know whether they have been destroyed."

She leaned over and tapped several times on the electronic table screen. A map of downtown Anacosta appeared on the screen, and she honed in on 585 G Street SW, the False Knowledge Depository, just south of 395. All the tracking devices were still at the Depository, judging by the dozens of little dots throbbing at that location.

When Dominic arrived at the front entrance of Beaufort at 6:30 am the next morning, Yardley was waiting behind the wheel of the official black van. She rolled down the window to catch his attention. "Hey, Farrell!" He climbed into the passenger seat and was pleasantly surprised to find that Yardley had brought coffee and pastries from the cafeteria. "You don't think about that at 6:30, but you sure will by 9 am, if you don't bring something," she said. Yardley had heard about his encounter with Walters the day before and was determined to show Dominic that everyone else in the KCU wished him well. They swung away from the building and toward downtown.

They were in place by 7 am, about a hundred feet away from the entrance of the Depository. They watched the guard, a middle-aged white man with a paunch, slowly enter the building. An hour later, they watched the librarian, a slender brunette in her mid-thirties, wave her armband and enter as well. "That's Commander Harris's girlfriend," said Yardley.

"You're kidding, really?" said Dominic. He had imagined Harris as comfortably married, or playing the scene with high Social Credit types. The librarian wasn't unattractive, but she seemed like, well, a librarian.

"Yup," said Candiss. "They met when we arrested MacMillan here last month. She's not under suspicion for anything, though, so no conflict of interest there. She has no idea about our operation, and hopefully she won't notice anything different about the boxes she taped up on Friday.

"She's the only librarian there now—there used to be about two dozen, and now it's just her. They might close up this place entirely after we trace where the books are going. Not that it's her fault if the discards don't go where they are meant to, but it's too much scandal for the Knowledge Tower to handle. And you know that Director Ferraro is determined to check the Tower before they check us." Dominic nodded, still mulling the Harris-librarian connection. If he was dating the librarian, she must be all right.

They sat there for another hour, sharing stories of how they had come to the ADF and the KCU. Yardley's father was a veteran Antifan and her mother had just retired from the Human Relations Division. There was little doubt that she would eventually find herself at ADF training school and Beaufort after two years of criminal justice studies at Garvey. "It's like my family, good and bad," she said, shrugging. She had also done a year on a border command, this one in the Florida Panhandle-Alabama region.

Dominic, who had just turned twenty-five, had applied to the ADF out of high school over his mother's objections. But he was determined to serve the DJR, which was fighting for the liberation of black and brown people against the fascists of the Interior. "It's our best hope," he told his mother, whose eyes were sad, perhaps thinking of her brother, the priest. "It's not perfect, but how can I let other people fight for us?" After a stint in the Pennsylvania wilderness facing off against the fascists in Ohio, a lonely experience, on which he and Yardley could agree, he transferred to the CCU at Beaufort.

"If you can ignore Walters, you'll be fine," said Candiss. "I'm sorry he gave you a hard time yesterday. I hope it's reassuring to know that he treats almost everyone that way. Imagine being on the receiving end in the Red Room. And he's bristling even with Commander Harris. Something's going to blow there if he doesn't get a promotion to his own command."

"How does he get away with that?" Dominic asked.

Candiss raised her eyebrows at him. "It's the ADF. Whatever he does, it doesn't break the rule book, not that we really have one, and he works very hard to solve cases and get confessions out of prisoners. The Director likes him a lot. Just try to stay out of his way and ignore it if you can't. It's not personal, he's just a lunatic.

"I feel sorry for Cheysa," said Candiss, as Dominic's heart jumped. "If he treated me that way, I would have shot him by now, that's for sure. Wait, I think that's our guy." A white van labeled "Secure Eco-Disposal Services" had pulled into the open space in front of the Antifans. A thirtyish man wearing a uniform and cap but no armband got out, pulled out the dolly from the back of the van, and rang the doorbell. He emerged several minutes later with the four boxes, packed them and the dolly into the rear, which seemed otherwise empty, and took off.

"Here we go!" said Candiss. She gave the van a few seconds' head start before falling in a hundred feet behind it, just close enough to make the green lights the van made. They were heading toward the Knowledge Tower, which could prove a bit awkward after the hostile weekend, even though they had the credentials to enter the grounds. The van made two more stops before pulling into the Knowledge Tower. The gate guard spent a full half minute inspecting the Antifans' credentials before allowing them through. It was just enough time to lose the van. Candiss cursed, but had had the presence of mind to tag it with her tracker before it disappeared, which allowed them to catch up with the van in the second driveway in front of the main building—fortunately it had not entered one of the restricted garages. They again stayed about a hundred feet back.

Candiss pulled on a regular suit jacket over her blouse and jumped out. She was wearing the regulation leather skirt—Antifan leggings, which she normally wore, would be conspicuous—but the eco-poly jacket and a leather skirt, presumably faux to onlookers, made her look like yet another hip Knowledge Tower functionary taking a break. Dominic started to follow, but Candiss cautioned him, "No, stay with the car. I'll be right back." She positioned herself atop a short stone wall surrounding shrubs and a spindly tree directly in front of the building, and waited. She had a direct view of the van's passenger side. Dominic belatedly realized that a uniformed Antifan should not be seen loitering in front of the Knowledge Tower today, and was embarrassed at his error. He kept his eyes trained on the white van.

A female from Antelides' office came out of the building and approached the van. The driver gave her a box from the back, and she signed for it. Dominic couldn't tell if the box was from the Depository or not. Candiss came back, briskly, and jumped into the driver's seat again. "Got some good pics of her while she wasn't looking."

"Farrell, would you please check the trackers on our boxes? Just to see whether she took one of the Depository boxes or one of the others he picked up." While Dominic was checking, she prepared to follow the van again.

Now they were driving down M Street, onto 695 and across the Anacostia River into southeast Anacosta. "All our boxes are still in the van," said Dominic.

"Good," said Candiss. "Because why one box would go into the Knowledge Tower and the others stayed in the van would be a big puzzle. That we don't need." They drove past 295 and Malcolm X Boulevard, past the old Bolling Air Force base, now the Liberation Eco-Trades School, and then onto Solids Rd SW. "I think this will be the recycling plant," Candiss said. "The smell is the waste treatment plant. This is where Pinckney's chip trail had her going, generally."

Their vehicle pulled up next to a trailer next to a weathered sign lettered "Recycling Plant No. 4." Candiss parked the vehicle under a tree in the corner of the parking lot. "I think we're far enough back not to attract attention. Let's use the telescoping lens." Using the screen in front of them, they positioned the lens toward the open garage doors where Peter, if it was indeed Peter, was headed with the dolly and six boxes. A heavy-set older man approached him, and they chatted pleasantly, judging by the body language, and then Peter handed over the boxes, for which the man electronically signed. "I think that may be the fellow I deal with when I come back on Sunday as Professor Pinckney's representative. This Sunday would have been her regular appointment," said Candiss. In twenty-five minutes, they were back at Beaufort.

As they were entering the building, Dominic's armband phone rang and he vaguely recognized the number as that of a girl he knew who worked at the Knowledge Tower. "I'll catch up with you," he told Candiss, and took the girl's call.

The girl was a marginal acquaintance from his social circle, which consisted mostly of other young black Tower professionals. She was anxious and he had to beg her to lower her voice, since others were looking curiously in his direction. It turned out that her boyfriend's brother, who worked at the Social Tower, was one of the three men who had been arrested in the attack on the Antifan walking home with his wife. "He just got carried away," she said frantically. "He doesn't care about this political stuff." Dominic gathered that she was asking him, a junior Antifan, to somehow intercede to spring her boyfriend's brother from Beaufort. "We haven't even heard from him yet," she cried.

And you're not going to until we're good and ready, thought Dominic, who was now markedly less sympathetic. Still, he didn't want to tell her off, not when he would likely see her again over this weekend or next. He took down the boyfriend's name, and said he would look into it. "Imagine, as if I was Commander Harris," he marveled. He thought he would ask Chung about this.

After he and Candiss reported to Walters on their findings, the deputy nodded amicably, and bestowed a "good work," and a smile on Dominic that was almost as alarming as yesterday's malice. "So, Yardley, you'll be playing a professor on Sunday in need of subversive books?"

"Yes, sir. We have the armband feed from those visits, so I know what to say. This would have been her normal time to visit, so the plant staff won't be surprised."

A few minutes after the meeting with Walters, Dominic asked Chung what he should do about the acquaintance who had called. Chung said, "Let's ask Walters." But Walters now wasn't in his office, while Commander Harris was available. David smiled to see Dominic, asked how the van trail had gone, and seemed relieved to hear the boxes were all sitting at the recycling plant and none had entered the Knowledge Tower. "Too bad for them," said David.

"Sir," said Chung. "Farrell here has an interesting situation to share with you."

David invited them to sit, and heard Dominic out. "Should I have told her off, sir?" Dominic asked.

"Farrell, what would you recommend?"

"She works at the Knowledge Tower, sir, even if the attacker doesn't. I was wondering whether we might be able to use this to our advantage."

"Bingo," said David, which was a Plore phrase he immediately regretted uttering, but this was good news. "Thank you for not prematurely closing off that channel. Do you know where she works at the Knowledge Tower? It's a big place."

"I didn't ask, sir."

"That's fine. I'd set up a meeting with her in some open space where you won't be overheard. If you know a bar where you haven't been with your crowd, that might be all right. You don't want to be recognized. Go in civilian clothes. Find out where exactly she works, and then say your commander might be open to releasing him, but we need something to make it worthwhile. Don't promise anything immediately, but see how she reacts. We might be able to pay her too, if that's motivating.

"We have the guy, we've roughed him up a little, but we can put that on hold for a day or two. I'm not interested in beating up on the Social Tower. You can tell her we're keeping our hands off him for a day or two while we talk with her. She will want to move fast, but we're not in that much of a hurry," David said reflectively. Recruiting sources was one of his favorite parts of the job, but it had gotten lost in the mounting piles of paperwork and meetings in recent years.

The conversation with Dominic reminded David he needed to raise a sensitive issue with Malia. He was happy to see her on the screen before him, safe and comfortable in her office at the end of the day, and at least three pounds heavier than last month. "Honey, you free this evening? Let's take a ride in the car...yes, we can go to dinner. See you at seven, all right?"

PART TWO
THE OCTAVIAN

Chapter 23
The New Concierge
(Wednesday, 18 May)

On her first evening on the night shift as the assistant concierge, Malia stood erect behind the marble-topped counter inside the palatial Octavian on Connecticut Avenue and greeted residents as they came and went, even when they did not look at her. Jorge, 120, the head night concierge, had been kind, maybe knowing she was the Antifan spy, or maybe just being conscientious, and had given her a tour of the premises. He was Latino, an actual immigrant, and a Healthy Eating subscriber.

She wore the dark blue jacket and skirt, with a light blue blouse underneath and a nametag that read "Melia." She felt crisp and professional, if servile, like a flight attendant. She admired the beautiful gilt moldings along the ceilings, the stone and glass fountain in the midst of the lobby, and the plush upholstered chairs and sofas scattered throughout. It was rare to see such beauty nowadays under socialism. During the day, a doorman stood outside the main entrance to discreetly redirect the occasional unsightly Street Person and hail self-driving cars. At night, the residents' armbands automatically unlocked the sliding door for them.

When a light on the console shone, she answered the phone, whether it was from residents who had left their armbands inside the apartment and locked themselves out, who were having trouble figuring out their movie screen controls, or who wanted a delivery of ice cream or liquor from the Octavian's snack bar. She gladly delivered to several apartments, sneaking quick peeks of the interiors. A few residents kindly asked if she was new, and introduced themselves. One haughty late-middle aged lady demanded, "You ARE a Social Crediteer, aren't you?"

"Yes, amba-mam," said Malia. "I'm 96." It was a point of pride at the Octavian that every employee, however lowly, was a Social Crediteer and no Plores were hired on staff. That said, if a 250 Social Credit toilet overflowed in the middle of the night, the resident was not likely to demand that the plumber show his credentials, and it was likelier than not that the repairon was called in from the City emergency service that hired whomever it wanted.

"Excellent," said the lady. "I'm 270. My late husband was the third Councilor on the Supreme Advisory Council." She did not give her name, which Jorge whispered to Malia later. Malia recognized the name of the man whose funeral she had attended for the Social Credit points last month. She wished she could have known this, so she could have said, "Yes, I got three Social Credit points thanks to his funeral. It was so convenient that he dropped dead."

David had warned her this would be the hardest part of the job. You will have to control your emotions and your words, he said. Some of the residents will be fine upstanding people, and others will be infuriating Social Credit snobs. If you think your afternoon visiting Antelides at the Knowledge Tower when she fired you was humiliating, you will have at least one such encounter every day at the Octavian, he told her. Five residents will treat you respectfully and the sixth will make you forget the others existed.

"And the hardest thing of all," he said, "will be when you see your daughter, not just the first time, but repeatedly, in the company of her so-called parents. You cannot, cannot reveal any trace of emotion or recognition, other than as the daughter of two Knowledge Tower residents far more important than you are. Can you do that?"

"I don't know," admitted Malia. They were driving around Anacosta late on that Tuesday night after dinner. David had mentioned to her that the Knowledge Tower would likely be closing the Depository permanently; although he only hinted at some private information to substantiate his conclusion, Malia had no reason to distrust him. "It would be better if you were out of there sooner rather than later," he said, "before they figure out we are connected. And I have a very interesting opportunity for you."

He told her that afternoon that the Rex Gretabelle DNA had come back a positive match with Malia's, "which didn't surprise me, but at least we won't have to wonder if we are doing all this for nothing," he said. And then he had learned the Octavian had an opening for a night concierge. He knew this, because the assistant Octavian night concierge was traditionally on the payroll of the ADF, which valued having an extra set of eyes and ears trained on the high-credit residents, who were disproportionately Knowledge and Economic Tower bureaucrats, with a dash of White Black House. "A little too fussy for our senior Antifans," David said.

David was surprised she wasn't more eager to tackle the challenge. "Come on, Malia, think about this. Your mission is twofold—and finally you have a mission other than reading old books that are very bad for your ideological purity. First, you are going to keep tabs on my Knowledge Tower enemies at a time when the ADF is going to set them back for a generation. That should be enough excitement." He was teasing her, but this was true. "And secondly, here is our real mission. You are going to be patient, and you are going to get to know Isabelle again and get her to trust you. I leave that up to you, but I am willing to bet she is a typical teenager who is pretending to rebel against her parents and will be open to some fun opportunities presented by the cool new concierge. We need to be patient, though. This will take time.

"And when the time is right, we leave, and she will leave with us. But I haven't planned that far ahead yet. Are you willing to go through with this, or would you rather weep for the past?"

"What about my Social Credit points? I'll lose almost 30 points."

David pulled over the car into one of the viewing points over the Potowmack. From the heights, they surveyed a mostly empty glass bridge through which Plores who worked in restaurants or retail were moving along conveyor belts back into Virginia. He glared at Malia. "You know what I think about your effing Social Credit points. Here I am offering you the only chance you will ever, ever get to have your daughter back and all you can think about is a block of cheese. Do you not have a strategic bone in your body?"

"I'm sorry," she said. "You're right."

"Also, if it's any comfort to you, the ADF will pay you so much on the side for your services that you'll be able to buy almost anything you want except prestige. And if you think about it, you're still in the Under 100 category, so you haven't lost any real ground. And fourth," he hammered in, "you have no guarantee that your next job in the Knowledge Tower would have offered you the same amount of points. Do you not remember the MacMillan incident? Do you think that Antelides is eager to have you sitting in her office? Would that be any better?"

She shook her head. "The only thing that bothers me is that Belinda Barbaradaughter might recognize me, or at least my name." David acknowledged that was a good point. "Do you think she'd actually recognize you by sight after ten years?" he asked. "How much personal contact have you had with her?"

"I've sat in an auditorium every few years listening to her lecture us on library ideological purity," said Malia.

"But I bet you sat in the back," said David. Malia agreed, yes, she had.

"We could give you a different name for the Octavian," he said. "But the danger is someone who knows you might call you by your real one. And Malia Jenness isn't a common name."

"No," she said. "But Amelia is, and they could call me Melia."

"Done," he said. "Good catch. Melia the spy." He paused. "The great thing about these high Social Credit types," he said, forgetting he himself was one, "is that if you're not in their circles, they don't make it their business to remember you. Obscurity and meekness will be your friends in this business. Let them think you couldn't be smart enough to be subversive."

He pulled her head down to his shoulder, and they sat there watching the twinkling buoys in the Potowmack. A dinner cruise boat sailed by, with a police motorboat in its wake.

"I have a suggestion for you," he said. "Remember you are playing a role. You are an actor. Every insult you take is part of your role. Look for opportunities to learn more about the others in the building. Be friendly to Isabelle *and* her parents, so they will trust you. You *have* to be sugar sweet to the kidnappers—revenge is a dish best served cold."

A disadvantage, thought Malia, as she updated resident files at 1 am after a break for dinner in a small room off the lobby, was that many Saturday nights would be spent here, rather than at David's apartment. Her schedule would be Wednesday, Thursday, Friday, and either Saturday or Sunday, 9 pm to 7 am.

"These are the best hours to learn the most, when people are at their most vulnerable and most likely to make mistakes," David said. "Rich in material for the attentive spy." He also pointed out the four-day workweek and the proximity of the Octavian to his own building—well, not close by, but certainly closer than the Rosebud.

"This means we finally need to bring Ansel and Frida to my apartment," he said. "So they don't get too lonely." On the few occasions David had visited her apartment, the cats had shown cautious interest in the unusual visitor with the deep voice and brushed up against his slacks.

"I knew this was your ulterior motive all along," she smiled.

The cats reminded him of something else. "Whatever happened to your friend Fern's grandmother?"

Malia frowned. "One morning that week they just found her dead in her bed in the hospital. The pills were gone and she had drunk the water. Or the glass was emptier. I went to the funeral at the crematorium. It was just Fern and myself. Fern was very upset. She was convinced they had done away with her and staged it to look like she had committed suicide."

"Probably right," said David.

"She said her aunt would never, ever have killed herself willingly."

"Not even for the DJR?" His wry words met with a sullen look from Malia.

"Well," said David flatly. "I couldn't have stopped this. I hope you don't think I really could have rescued her. We kill old people and our enemies, and that's just the way it is—goddammit!"

What a Plore, Malia thought, but fondly, as they headed back to the Rosebud.

At 3 am Malia was yawning, despite having gradually adjusted her sleep schedule for several nights before, and her feet were aching in the unaccustomed pumps. Jorge said, "You can sit down if none of our residents are around—just stand up when you see one." She quickly rose when a raffish fifty-something man in a rumpled blue suit, and with curly dark hair with a dash of gray staggered into the building, clearly having had a little too much to drink.

"Hi Jorge," he said, just managing to not slur his words. "Who's the beauty behind the desk?"

"This is Melia, Amba-sah Ross. She just started as our assistant concierge tonight."

Ross reached for Malia's hand, which she could not refuse. He gave it a kiss. "Welcome to the Octavian, Melia. I am 200. I believe I also have a name, but I left it at the bar with my self-respect. Perhaps they will hold it for me until tomorrow." He staggered off toward the elevators. When the doors had closed on him, Jorge said quietly, "Adam Ross, Anacosta Industrial Zone Secretary at the Economic Tower. Drinks too much on weeknights." Malia wondered whether he had a wife or girlfriend. "Divorced," said Jorge, as if he could read her mind. It occurred to Malia that Jorge could also be working for the ADF, although wouldn't David have told her this? More likely Jorge was just being a typical building functionary with a professional interest in knowing who lived under his roof, the better to serve them.

Two residents separately left around 5 am, early risers off to work or to the gym before work. "Have a good day!" she wished them both, although she almost wished them a good night instead. Calls with repair requests started to come in, and she fielded those, with Jorge showing her how to log them for the maintenance staff. She felt lightheaded with lack of sleep.

At 7 am, she left the building via the side entrance, and David quickly crossed the street from the garden entrance to meet her. "I take it you didn't see the party of interest?"

"No," she shook her head. "But just as well. That would have been a little too intense for the first night."

"I went over to your place and fed the cats last night. This way I can bring you over to my apartment and you can spend the day there. I have to get changed for work anyway."

"But the cats will wonder where I am," said Malia.

"No," he smiled. "I let them know about your new job. Anyway, we'll bring them over to my place over the weekend. They'll have so much more room. If I say I have cats, I'll get a gourmet kibble ration for them."

"I never thought about high Social Credit cats," confessed Malia.

"They'll enjoy their promotion," David promised. "I'll get them some fancy cat toys too."

Briefly, Malia wondered what would happen to the cats when the humans took off for the Interior, but that prospect seemed so distant, whatever David thought, that she did not spend any extra time ruminating on it. She entered the self-driving car as if she always had used them, and the door closed behind David. "Good morning," said Gauthier.

Chapter 24
Kendra
(Monday/Thursday, 16-19 May)

Sitting next to each other on David's sofa on Thursday morning, they ate granola cereal, with Malia barely able to summon the energy to lift her spoon. David's eyes were trained on the headlines from *DJR Morning*, just in case it covered the university crisis, and then on the baseball scores from last night. He helped her undress, because it gave him pleasure to do so, and lay down next to her on the bed. She curled up against him, and he tried to give her a massage, with the hope that perhaps they could make love before he had to run to Beaufort. But within a minute, he was deflated by her light snoring. Poor kid, he thought, and within five minutes he had drawn the covers over her, pulled on his uniform, and was out the door. He was sorry Malia had lost access to her books, but the Depository was likely closing anyway. Everything he had told her when he argued for the Octavian was true, he told himself again. Be strategic.

As he walked into the unit, with a few minutes to spare before the 0830, David reflected with satisfaction that everything had been going splendidly for the KCU in the last two weeks. Disguised as a colleague of Pinckney's, Yardley had brought back eight books to Beaufort, including *A Man for All Seasons*, a play about a man who became a Catholic saint; *Revolt of the Elites*, by Christopher Lasch, and Adam Smith's *Wealth of Nations*, all in disrepair. They were now locked in a cabinet. "The guy was asking why Kendra hadn't paid him in advance, so I took care of that," she said. It seemed Kendra had rarely dared to purchase more than three books at a time, but the man at the plant was pleased that Yardley was eager to buy more. He knew they were illegal, and could command a high price from these women who mysteriously wanted them so badly, but as a Plore he was mostly insulated from the ADF. The trackers for the non-Beaufort books had disappeared off the screen, which confirmed that the remaining books had been destroyed.

Yardley had left open the possibility that she would return next month to purchase more. None of the Antifans knew whether the Depository would still be functioning at that point, of course, but it was best to keep the conduit open. If the Depository closed, the entire inventory would end up at recycling plants, which would potentially pose a Knowledge danger as well.

Second, Dominic's acquaintance had turned out to be a junior program officer in the Arts section of the Knowledge Tower. She was very willing to relay a mishmash of Tower gossip that meant little to her—she probably felt it was not particularly sensitive, and well worth springing her boyfriend's brother from Beaufort. Dominic had suggested that he would pay her a sizable sum each month for continued streams of gossip, which he could steer as Beaufort's needs demanded, and which meant that over time she would be deliberately seeking out more valuable information on their behalf. "Great opportunity," David told him, "to already be running your first source." Dominic felt deeply grateful to David for turning a potentially awkward situation into an unmitigated boon.

And now at 9 am, David—with Charlton and Walters—was watching Karlmarx demonstrate the electronic chart of the network that his analysts had painstakingly developed with the infusion of Garvey, Sanders, Diverse American, and now Justice University professors. A red X was placed over MacMillan at the center of the chart, and over Andrew Leonard's name linked to his on the right. Analysts were working hard to identify the connections among the professors and university staff. "If you were Kendra Pinckney, and you were going to Sanders once a month, who would you know best there?" Karlmarx explained. He used the laser pointer to indicate a series of names linking to hers, but there were question marks after each. All of them were now languishing in Beaufort cells, but just because they had attended graduate school with Pinckney did not necessarily mean she had sought them out as part of her network. Professors might be acquainted through shared areas of expertise, or through other ties not visible to the analysts. So far everyone was denying any connection with the gray-haired courier beyond meeting at a conference here or there.

Now that classes had ended for the summer, the ADF faced few constraints on arresting and bringing faculty members to Beaufort, except its own resources. As innocent or useless faculty were permitted to depart for psychiatric hospitals, others were brought, quaking, to Beaufort on the ADF conveyor belt. The interrogation rooms, including the Red Rooms, hummed night and day. David was grimly muscling through his Red Room duties every Friday, but no longer tried to secure anyone's cooperation in advance. His loss of control in the Bertone session after the professor had reneged on their deal had frightened him. David still wondered whether his overture, with the confession of shared Ploreness, had backfired by reassuring Bertone that he could get away with defying his inquisitor.

It was still galling that they had not obtained Pinckney's cooperation. Even though David had breezily suggested two weeks ago that they did not absolutely need Pinckney's cooperation at this point, it would spare them these fumbling guesses as to her contacts at Sanders. On Monday, he had finally met her in one of the regular interrogation rooms. He had ordered a pitcher of juice, and some vanilla wafers. He hoped her spare rations would make her inclined to accept some hospitality. It was obvious that weeks of harsh treatment had taken a toll; she looked much older than 45, which he knew was her actual age. He poured them each a glass, and drank some of his so she need not worry about the contents. "Please have a wafer," he invited her.

She shook her head, "No, thank you."

He introduced himself, so she knew he was not some underling and could deliver on a promise made here. "Professor Pinckney, what is the point now of refusing to cooperate?" he asked patiently. "We know how you acquired these books, and we know how you distributed them around Clinton. We know about your Capitalism Club. Professor Bertone was very forthcoming." Bertone had been discharged from Beaufort yesterday to a middling hospital in Pennsylvania where he could be monitored for any continued signs of resistance. David had eventually mellowed and decided not to follow through with the Hate Crime charges. Too much work to do someone else's law enforcement job for them. And you couldn't blame a man for being a man, even a weak one—the girls had been young but not really children.

"We are interviewing several dozen faculty members from various universities, including Sanders. I would like to know why you went to Sanders once a month. Were you distributing illegal books to faculty members there?"

She shook her head.

"Does that mean you deny distributing illegal books at Sanders?"

She shook her head again.

"So what are you saying 'no' to, then?"

"I refuse to discuss the matter," she said, in a shaky voice. "I have the right to read Truth. I have the right to share Truth with others. I refuse to accept this is a crime." The words sounded vaguely familiar to David, who then recalled what MacMillan had shouted as the squad dragged him out of the reading room at the Depository.

"Actually, it is a crime," he said.

"Why is it a crime to use your brain to read the greatest thoughts in Western civilization and to discuss them with other intelligent, humane people?" she asked him. Even the reference to "Western civilization" was a knowledge crime, which she must know, he thought.

"I'm not going to discuss why the law is the law. In this country, it is the law, and we punish violations severely. You may think you can handle these books, but you're fooling yourself."

"Commander, what are the consequences of 'not being able to handle' books? Would we grovel on the floor drooling and spitting out our teeth? Or would we start smashing each other's heads in? Oh no, I forgot we are doing both those things in this building, so it can't possibly be the fault of the books. Maybe someone would be found wrong, but we would decide that after many hours of civilized and reasoned discussion, not through brute force."

David thought that Malia would have enjoyed sitting in the gazebo with the professors and talking about these dangerous ideas, that could not have really been so terribly dangerous, because he had been encouraging her to sit and read about them in the Depository at that very moment, on her second to last day in the building. Was he a hypocrite, or were the circumstances truly different? Malia wasn't trying to share the ideas with others, he reasoned.

His voice remained even. "Professor Pinckney, you have a choice to make. You can tell us who your contacts were at Sanders. We will find this out eventually, by interrogating every single faculty member at Sanders, most of whom will not be as stubborn as you are. If you save us the trouble, we can send you to a hospital where you will be treated decently and possibly be able to return to Clinton."

"Your deputy told me we would be treated decently here as well," said Pinckney. "That has not been the case, so why should I trust you now?"

"His word was not my word," said David. "If you continue to refuse to cooperate, you will return to the Red Room. And honestly, I doubt you will survive. MacMillan is dead, and now so is Leonard." He saw the shock on her face; she had not known, since it happened while she was in the infirmary. "I really don't care if all three of you die. And don't think that generations of schoolchildren will learn your name and sing your praises; we will dump your remains into a mass composting grave and you will be forgotten. You could have many more years to enjoy, if you would just be sensible."

"Andrew—" she whispered, barely audible.

"This is just about a few books," said David. "Why are you so stubborn? All you have to do is give us a few names and you would be leaving this place in a few days. Wouldn't you like to see some sunlight and breathe some fresh air again?"

The interval gave Pinckney time to regroup. David saw her visibly stiffen her spine.

"Commander, if it was really just about a few silly books and a few names, you wouldn't care either. I realize this is just your job, and you probably don't believe what you're saying, but this matters more than a job to me. This is what makes me a human being and not a savage." The implication was clear that the savages were the ones who destroyed lives for a paycheck.

She continued, "There was a dissident in Soviet Russia, over a hundred years ago. He wrote a very inspiring passage about the great satisfaction he received while in prison, despite all his suffering, from the knowledge that he was in the right in opposing evil. It sustained him through his difficult ordeal, until he was freed and went to Israel."

David said, "I hope you have fun imitating this Russian guy, whoever he was. I suggest you give your decision some serious consideration, because there is no audience out there waiting to quote you and celebrate you. You have twenty-four hours to think about it." He rose, popping a wafer in his mouth as he did so. "See, they're perfectly safe. Please do take one."

She shook her head. She would not compromise even to the extent of eating a wafer offered by her adversary. David thought her both foolish and principled. What was the point of making the ultimate sacrifice when no one but yourself would respect or even remember it?

"Are you a Christian?" he asked, curious about whether she believed in an afterlife. Perhaps Kendra Pinckney was rejecting his perfectly reasonable appeals out of fear of God's wrath on the Day of Judgment. That he could understand, at least intellectually.

"No," she said. "I am an atheist. If there was a God, he would not allow his creatures to cause such suffering." Nevertheless, she attended the First Mother Earth Diversity Church of Clintonia, Maryland, David recalled.

"You have twenty-four hours," he said, abruptly exiting the room, but already knowing that she would not bend. Pinckney's convictions were impervious to his recitation of common sense and threats that formed the building blocks of prisoner management at Beaufort.

When David returned to the unit after his interrogation of Pinckney, Walters was waiting for him. "Chief, we were watching up here. She's a stubborn old bitch. Do you want me to take her back to the Red Room? I've got an opening for tomorrow." David thought irreverently that Walters sounded like a hair stylist hungry for business.

"No, let's just keep her in isolation for now. We might get our answers from the Sanders guys. We can come back to her if the other ways don't work." Is he pouting? David thought incredulously. "You've got plenty of other talent to work on for now, Walters," he said as he strode off toward his office. He said a quick hello to Cheysa, who sat at the secretary's desk in front of Walters' office. He wasn't sure how that was working out—she didn't look happy. In fact, she looked downright morose. But he couldn't worry about that right now.

Chapter 25
Rex Gretabelle
(Friday/Saturday, 27-28 May)

Malia reported for duty at the Octavian on Friday night, perspiring even though she carried her suit jacket. The air was sultry, and she had taken a Diversity Bus from David's apartment after walking ten blocks to catch one, since David had had to work late again. The remote location of the Avalon was turning out to be a disadvantage of moving in with David; it was far from public transportation, and of course she was ineligible for the self-driving cars on which most of the neighborhood relied. "How bad can the bus be?" David asked, showing a trace of impatience when she complained. Well, she explained to him, you had to be patient waiting for one going downtown at 8 pm, and then it stopped on virtually every street corner, and then you were unprotected against weirdos who thought any single woman longed for their company. And since the buses were self driving there was no driver to protect you. If you hit the yellow alarm button, nothing happened, except you revealed your fear to the weirdo, emboldening him. "I'll pick you up when your shift ends," said David.

The night shift had its own comforting routine. For the first two or three hours, especially on a weekend night, residents would be streaming in and out regularly, at first more exiting to the street, but then most returning after dinner out, carrying Enviro-pods whose scent wafted enticingly to Malia. By now, Malia knew most of the residents by name, even if most were still learning hers. There was the autocratic Amba-mam Johnson, of course, and the flirtatious Amba-sah Ross; some celebrities like the interior decorator Vernon Poythress and the singer Scot Gosling, whose brash expletive-laden revolutionary lyrics seemed at odds with the refined Octavian; young families like the Chernow-Lashkys with the adorable blonde toddler twin girls, and others with spoiled teenagers fixated on their armband phones; brusque young Tower professionals encased in their privilege; retired Diversity War veterans who needed little encouragement to recount their brave escapades; severe single women of late middle-age who owned cats and clung to their Social Credit scores for reassurance; insouciant gay men who called her "darling," and bestowed gourmet cupcakes on her and Jorge (she liked these residents best). At Jorge's suggestion, Malia reviewed the residents' files at odd hours to memorize their likes, dislikes, and preferred pronouns.

From about midnight to three, the stream of residents died down, with an occasional partier returning, sometimes with a date. Some who returned alone and tipsy would need assistance finding their apartment, complaining that their broken armbands had failed to open their doors. Jorge or Malia would accompany the resident upstairs to find the correct door. Jorge and Malia took turns eating their meals in the little break room. The quietest time of the shift, from 3 to 7 am, required coffee and conversation to stay awake. Malia found out that Jorge was an actual immigrant from Bolivia. It had been many years since she had met anyone born outside the DJR, at least anyone aged under sixty. "Why did you come here?" she asked.

"I was offered one of the Dreaming Immigrant Fellowships in 2077," Jorge told her. "It was easier than waiting for the United States or Canada, and even though I'd heard things were difficult in the DJR, I wanted to leave Bolivia and see the world. My grandmother had lived in Anacosta when it was called Washington and we only heard good things about it."

"Was it what you expected?" Malia asked.

Jorge was as diplomatic in discussing the DJR as he was in navigating the complicated world of resident interactions. "I was very fortunate to meet my wife. We are very happy together. We aren't very political." Perhaps sensing he was deflecting Malia's question, he said, "It was much quieter than what my grandmother told us."

This Friday night was going much as the previous one had. Malia had still not encountered the Andrews family, and her initial fear that she would see them all too painfully often had virtually disappeared. In fact, in her state of exhaustion, she had almost forgotten that they were her primary reason for serving at the Octavian. On this Friday night, the family chose to use the main entrance because of an unexpected thunderstorm. As soon as she saw Belinda Barbaradaughter, Malia trembled. Even if she hadn't recognized Belinda, she would have known this was the family, because the sullen 14-year-old looked exactly as she, Malia, had as a teenager. However, this teenager was not wearing the orphanage uniform of chinos and blue polo shirt with the Diversity Now emblem on the breast pocket, but overalls and ugly black-rimmed glasses, and green and purple streaks ran through her short-cropped hair. She also wore a nose ring, Malia saw with dismay.

"Hello, Amba-sah, Amba-mam, Mxti Rex," said Jorge. Malia could not have assembled this collection of titles in her flustered head anywhere near as quickly as did her polished colleague.

Amba-sah Andrews was a tall, thin, anxious-looking man with an aureole of golden frizzy curls and a slight stoop. Amba-mam Barbaradaughter had changed little from when Malia had last seen her in a darkened auditorium lecturing on "Ideological Conformity as Liberating Praxis." She was petite, busty, with dark hair and eyes, projecting more confidence than she really felt. Mxti Rex—Malia was alarmed at hearing this non-binary salutation—scowled at both of their parents, griping over their refusal to go for ice cream after dinner.

"Oh, all right," said their father. "Why don't you just get some from the snack bar?" He turned to Malia, "Excuse me, would you please help my dauson pick out some ice cream?" Dauson was the word for a daughter-son hybrid. Malia was in shock. "Of course, amba-sah," she said, and beckoned Mxti Rex into the room behind the concierge station.

She studied the child as they surveyed the ice cream case. The child had gone to some effort to look ugly and awkward, but their hair was thick and shining brown, and they was developing a nice female figure under all the pronouns. They grabbed an ice cream sandwich and said, "Okay, I'm done." Out in the lobby, Andrews waved his armband wearily over the screen for the transaction, and Barbaradaughter said to Mxti Rex, "What do you say to the nice concierge?"

"F--k you," said Mxti Rex. Their mother looked horrified, but rather than correct Mxti Rex, the parents hustled them in the elevator, and they were gone.

Malia was shaking, but Jorge understandably blamed it on the rudeness.

"The family is troubled," he said. "She is an adopted child, and it has not worked out well. When she came here, about eight years ago, she was very sad, and one would have thought she would have been happy to finally have a family and to live in such a fine building. But she has never been happy. I believe they are taking her to a psychiatrist and Diversity counselor. Her surgery is scheduled for next year, before she develops too much."

Malia's eyes began to tear, but she heeded David's warning and willed herself to seem normal.

"Yes, it is sad indeed," said Jorge. "It is dangerous to adopt a child when you do not know its background."

She was a happy, kind, normal child when they stole her from me, Malia thought. She wished she could call David right now and not wait for morning.

Around 2 am, the console lit up and Jorge took the call. He looked over at Malia, who was counting snack bar receipts for the night. "It's Amba-sah Ross. He wants some company. He asked for you expressly."

Malia was alarmed. "What exactly does this mean? I don't like the sound of a request for company at 2 am."

"Your predecessor was very accommodating," Jorge said. "I believe he just likes to talk. If you feel you are in danger, of course you may leave. But we try to meet our residents' needs."

David did *not* tell me about this aspect of the job, Malia thought. The ambiguity of Jorge's phrasing gave her little confidence, especially when Jorge said, "I cannot meet his needs."

"But I can leave, right?" Malia had rarely been in situations where she could make her own decisions about staying or leaving, right down to David's pulling her from the Depository.

"If you must," said Jorge, inscrutably. "Please try to return within the hour."

She took the elevator to the 11th floor, and rang the doorbell at 1104. Amba-sah Ross answered the door, mostly sober, but disturbingly, wearing a silk Chinese-style dressing gown. "Come in, Melia, please," he said. "Thank you for humoring me at this late hour. But this is the hour when I like to talk, and, well, there is no one to talk to. Please remove your shoes. The carpets, you know."

Talk, thought Malia. That sounds manageable.

"What kind of drink would you like?" He moved over to a bar in the corner.

"Oh, I don't think I should drink on the job," she said, but quailed before his steady gaze under heavy brows. "A club soda, please. I still have to count snack bar receipts tonight," she explained. While he mixed her a whisky soda, she looked around the living room. The furniture was old-fashioned, as befitted the Octavian, but Malia sensed he had either inherited it or it had been purchased by someone of different tastes. Exotic sculptures, colorful bowls, and other evidence of privileged trips to foreign lands surrounded them on tables and on bookcases. Real books lined one of the shelves, but Malia could not read the titles at that distance. Above the sofa was an oil portrait of a beautiful woman with an elegant dark chignon, and next to it a drawing of a small girl in pigtails. "That was my mother," said Adam. "And my daughter."

"How old is your daughter now?" Malia asked politely.

Adam said, "She would have been twenty-six this year. She died when she was seven, in the meningitis epidemic that year." Malia, horrified at her faux pas, tried to apologize, but Adam waved it away. Malia now remembered the epidemic that had killed several of her classmates at the orphanage. The hospitals had been overwhelmed and understaffed, and the fascists in the Interior had refused to provide the needed antibiotics, or so the DJR news outlets had claimed.

Adam handed Malia her drink, which she dared not refuse, even after smelling the alcohol. She sat primly at one end of the green sofa, as directed, removing her jacket, also as directed. "Sorry, it just makes me think we're in a business meeting," he joked feebly.

Adam faced her from a winged rose armchair across the coffee table. "Tell me where you were before you came to the Octavian."

Malia had practiced her story with David. When the Social Credit score associated with the Octavian job was minimal, a prior 96 would invite questions. "I was an infotech assistant at the Diversity Warehouse," she said. A lie now enshrined as truth in her records, since Paula Findlay had personally handled that amendment. "But it was lonely and I wanted a job that would allow me to interact more with people, even if it meant a lower Social Credit score."

"That's brave of you," said Adam sincerely. "Since you'll be giving up a lot of points. It's funny, you don't seem like the extroverted type. Have you ever been married?" She shook her head.

David had told her, "You don't have to respond to every question. It's dangerous to try to fill a silence and it can be a trap. Learn to let it rest sometimes."

She gave it a few seconds, and then said, "You seem to travel a lot. I see a lot of interesting art here that isn't from here."

"Yes," he said. "Almost all the furniture was my mother's. My wife got ours in the divorce. But I've picked up the artifacts while traveling for work. Mostly Asian, some Russian." The DJR answered primarily to Beijing, but also needed to acknowledge the Bear that had gobbled up much of Europe as its protectorate since the civil war.

"Where do you work?" She knew the answer from Jorge and the files, but the Octavian residents seemed blissfully unaware that the employees collected information on them.

"I'm at the Economic Tower," said Adam modestly, but he could not resist bragging, since he was trying to impress Malia. "I'm the Chief Administrator of the Industrial Zones in the Anacosta region."

"What exactly do the Industrial Zones do?" Malia asked, wide eyed. "I've heard a little about them, and sometimes I think it might be a good place to live. It sounds kind of adventurous."

Oh, you poor innocent, thought Adam. "The Industrial Zones in the Anacosta region produce almost all the household goods we use here in the City, as well as chemicals and mechanical inputs for heavy manufacturing elsewhere. I don't think you're suited to that kind of work."

Your minions weren't so fussy about that at Earth Weekend, she thought, recollecting the shabby canting festival-goers herded in the long lines toward the waiting buses.

"Stay here with us instead, beautiful," Adam said.

"What about the farms?" she asked, trying not to show any alarm at his having moved over to the sofa, albeit still a few feet away.

"Cabbage, broccoli, cauliflower, cucumbers, beans, sweet corn, tomatoes, potatoes, strawberries, watermelon, apples, peaches, and wine grapes," said Adam. "In their respective seasons. Are you interviewing me for a school report?"

"No," she laughed nervously. "Is your job a hard one?"

The question made Adam think of what was building under his dressing gown. He moved a little closer, and said, "Yes, it's hard.

"It's a big responsibility," he said, as if she were actually interviewing him. "That's why they give me 200 Social Credit points. You have to mobilize thousands of people who don't want to be in the Industrial Zones. You can't use Plore labor, thanks to that stupid Treaty, unless you pay them. We don't have the immigrant talent or the scientific talent we need. The Chinese won't send us experts, or at least not the intellectual property in their heads, even though we basically gave it to them years ago. We don't have the money to buy the high-end fertilizer or other inputs that would allow us to go beyond low-yield agriculture or to manufacture goods that some other country would buy. That's why we're dependent on China for so much." He paused. "It's hopeless. But a pretty girl like you doesn't need to know about all that, right?" He lunged in, and Malia shrank back.

"I'm sorry, Jorge said I needed to return within the hour."

"Jorge knows the score. I tip him well for accommodating me. I can tip you too." Did he think she was a sex worker?

Outraged, Malia pushed him away, but he was on top of her now, and she felt the bulge through the dressing gown. "I have a boyfriend!" she cried. "Please don't."

"A boyfriend!" he smiled, looming above her. She was conscious of his amused pale blue eyes and a day's growth of stubble—he might have spent the day at home savoring a potential conquest of the new concierge. "You didn't mention him. How many points does your boyfriend have?" The subtext was: do I have to worry about this boyfriend?

She had not rehearsed this with David. She knew that she could not mention the ADF, even though that would certainly have proven effective. "He's a Plore," she said quickly.

"That doesn't count," said Adam, inserting his hand under her skirt. "We can share you."

At that point, Malia knew, it was now or never. She was twenty years younger than Ross, if seventy pounds lighter, and she used that to her advantage. Ross was slightly off balance with the hand insertion move. With all her strength, she shoved him sideways with both arms so that he fell backwards over the coffee table, landing on the floor opposite. She scrambled away over the sofa and was at the door before he could rise to his feet.

"You'll be back," said Adam, coldly. "We're going to keep meeting until you see sense."

"I seriously doubt that," she said loftily, grabbing her shoes and running down the hall. Then she realized her jacket was still in the apartment. Should she send Jorge up to retrieve it? Or should she be brave and ring the doorbell again? She chose the latter.

"I see you're back," Adam said.

"My jacket, please, amba-sah," she requested, staring him down.

"Come in and get it," he said, closing the door all but a crack. She waited. Eventually, he handed her the jacket through the crack.

"*Thank* you," she said, and turned and left. She realized her skirt and hosiery were torn, but at least the jacket had been spared. When Jorge saw her, he suggested she go freshen up.

"I think Amba-sah Ross expected a bit much from me, Jorge," she said, finally calming down.

"We aim to accommodate our residents," said Jorge flatly. "I hope you did not disappoint Amba-sah Ross."

"If I wanted to be a sex worker, I would have better options out there," Malia retorted, flinging her arm at the City beyond the plate glass windows, and stalking off to the washroom.

They worked side-by-side, in silence, except for greeting the occasional early-morning jogger, until 7 am finally came.

"See you Sunday evening," she said to Jorge, who waved goodbye without looking at her, and ran out the side entrance into David's arms. He was wearing denim jeans and a windbreaker over a T-shirt, unusually casual.

"What happened to you?" he asked with mild astonishment, looking at her torn skirt and agitated face. "Wait, explain in the car. We'll go home, have a quick breakfast, and we'll be off."

"Off?" she asked. "Where are we going?"

"To the Massanutten!" said David, to her complete bewilderment. "A day and a night in the countryside. The concierge will feed the cats."

Chapter 26
Countryside
(Saturday/Sunday, 28-29 May)

As soon as they left the Avalon garage, Malia fell asleep, and David did not disturb her as they headed into Virginia, and west on 66. He looked at her tenderly, thinking that was a crazy night, all right. But this was the perfect weekend for some reconnoitering, with Malia's schedule open until Sunday night, so off they were. He had packed them roast beef sandwiches, potato salad, and cookies, and made reservations in Staunton for the return journey.

An hour later, they were heading south on 81, between the Shenandoah Valley (Outer Plore) on their left and the Massanutten range (security zone) on their right. Most of the traffic were trucks. Exiting 81 to head west, they stopped at a gatehouse manned by local ADF militia. The gatehouses ran down the west side of the Shenandoah Valley down to the Tennessee border, preventing anyone without a 150 Credit score or higher, or who wasn't a local resident, from accessing the Massanutten region. "Hi guys," said David, seemingly oblivious to the AK-15s as he showed his credentials. Impressed, the young guard saluted David crisply. Nobody objected to Malia in the car.

"That was scary, I didn't expect that," said Malia, blinking. Their eyes followed an observation drone swooping above them, dipping down and disappearing to the southwest, and another that headed due west.

They drove into the mountains from the piedmont, passing shabby Plore farms on both sides of the road, then some dilapidated houses, then one deserted small town. Plywood planks were hammered over the windows of a small brick church retaken by ivy. "Probably everyone was driven away during the wars," said David. They saw no one else, whether in a vehicle or on foot. It was eerily quiet. He turned off the winding paved road onto a gravel one, and after about fifteen minutes, into a small clearing. "From here we walk," he said. David grabbed the coolbox and Malia the duffel bag with the blankets and the binoculars. It was another ten minutes to the overlook, where they were rewarded with a panoramic view of the mountainsides. They sat under some heavy foliage to give them cover from the drones and camouflage against surveillance from below, and placed their armbands at the side of the clearing.

In the distance on the right was a long winding road that led to the ADF outpost responsible for guarding the border; they could see the dusty-looking khaki colored metal buildings. Everything looked sleepy on this late Saturday morning. Several miles to their left was a giant enclosure filled by vast metal buildings and wooden sheds, and fields stretching toward the border. Dozens of people moved among the buildings, some wearing harnesses and pulling giant pallets laden with goods, while drivers steered other pallets on small trucks. "That is Economic Zone Camp No. 4," said David soberly. He pointed out to Malia distant wire fences beyond the camps. "That's what stands between us and the fascists," he said. "Or freedom, your call." Pointing to the ADF base, David said, "My brother Daniel works there as an electrician."

"Really!" Malia said. "Shouldn't we be visiting him?"

"Easier said than done," said David. "Lots of paperwork. And that's with *my* access. But I'm hoping to get myself on an ADF inspection tour this summer and that will bring me here again. I'll be testing the perimeter security...for them and for us."

Having taken a look, he stowed the binoculars in the duffel, and they took out their sandwiches, eating with a good appetite. "Have you ever been out this far west?" he asked her.

"No," said Malia, "I know there are some bus tours that take you to Shenandoah National Park, and those are open to every Social Crediteer. You learn all about the sufferings of the rural people and the coal miners. But I've never done it—they never said how beautiful the scenery was." She chewed thoughtfully. "This is so lovely, even with those awful camps."

"Hey, those are my Antifan comrades you're talking about," said David with mock seriousness.

After they ate, Malia lay on one blanket, pulling David's ADF jacket over her, and slept deeply, secure in David's presence. David pulled out the binoculars, and lying flat and propping himself up by his elbows, he watched the camps. At one o'clock, he witnessed a hanging of three Economic Zone workers, glad Malia was sleeping through it. Even with the binoculars, he was unsure whether the dangling bodies, clad in shapeless denim uniforms, were men or women. They might have been saboteurs, thought David, but it was possible they had committed ordinary heinous crimes not worth trucking them to Charlottesville to try or punish. Discipline was needed, he told himself, but not with any great conviction, since it was likelier than not the trio hanged were more sinned against than sinning. If he had not rescued Malia from the Earth Weekend service, this is where she would have ended up, assembling brooms, or with her small hands, electronic components in one of those giant metal sheds.

Malia awakened, and they lay in each other's arms, kissing and touching each other. The sky was a bright blue, with few clouds, and even though it was breezy and cool, the sunshine warmed them, and they warmed each other. "So beautiful," he said to her, looking into her eyes, so he meant her, and not the scenery. As she rolled over onto her back, they heard the sudden sound of foliage being crushed under heavy boots. David looked up as a squad of local Antifans spilled onto the overlook.

"Up with you, fascists," the squad leader ordered. All the rifles pointed at them. Then a subordinate caught his attention, indicating with his elbow the ADF jacket Malia had cast aside after her nap.

"Your papers, please," the leader said, his tone taking a turn for the polite, just in case. David said, "Certainly," and raised his leather credentials holder. "May I approach, Lieutenant?"

In a few seconds, the lieutenant was apologizing for the disruption. "But Commander, you happen to be picnicking at a very sensitive location. We just cannot take the chance that fascists or other enemies of Diversity are spying on our camp or the Industrial Zone."

"I agree, Lieutenant," said David, donning the jacket, just so the squad could see his battle insignia. "I should have notified Camp Six"—the one below— "and not assumed this would be acceptable just because of my rank. I must say I am impressed with your vigilance, and I will let Commander Agostino at Beaufort know when I return." Agostino was the Headquarters Commander of all the border guards in the Mid-Atlantic region, and it would be easy—and prudent—to do these conscientious guys a favor and send him a note on Monday.

"That would be very much appreciated, sir," said the lieutenant. He cleared his throat. "Unfortunately, we need to escort you to your car. You can't remain here." Ten minutes later, they were back at the yellow sportscar, next to which the black Antifan van had parked. The squad Antifan-saluted David, and watched until the sportscar had begun moving back down the gravel road before jumping into their van, and following them down to the main road. David was certain the conversation in the van was mostly about the sportscar.

"That was a good test of the general level of readiness. I can compliment them to Agostino with a clear conscience," said David. "I wish they'd shown up about twenty minutes later, though."

"Did you see what you needed to see?" asked Malia.

David nodded, "Mostly. If we'd stayed for another two hours, we would have been able to watch the afternoon muster, and that would give us a good indication of the strength levels at Six. Of course, I can research the files for this—I just don't want to attract unnecessary attention to what I'm reading online if it isn't closely related to my own responsibilities. And sometimes the reality doesn't match the paper claims." He sighed.

They arrived in Staunton around 4 pm and checked in at the Governor Northam Hotel, once named for the legendary Confederate general Stonewall Jackson and now honoring the early 21st century Virginia governor whose own racist deeds had been forgiven due to his progressive stances. The elegant hotel with a sweeping staircase was a 120-credit minimum hotel. David signed another form vouching for the behavior of his guest while Malia watched from a precious upholstered armchair.

David spent several minutes dutifully checking their room for surveillance devices, unscrewing and rescrewing an old-fashioned glass cover to a light bulb above the bed. Once satisfied, they showered, and then they lay together on the bed watching a Diversity TV special about a multiethnic posse chasing racist cowboys. Then they completed the lovemaking that the Antifans had interrupted.

Afterward, he turned the TV on again, pulled the comforter over them, and said, "Now we can talk about what happened last night.

"As for Mxti Rex, I'm not surprised. She's got neurotic parents—adoptive parents, I know, don't look at me like that—and no doubt they raised her wrong in every way. This morning you said you weren't sure if you really wanted to undertake the challenge of fixing everything they messed up. I think that was exhaustion and frustration speaking. She is your daughter, and just as if she fell in with a band of criminals, you would want to rescue her. And I told you, I think this is doable. In a better environment, you would find your sweet, kind Isabelle again under that frightening exterior. Don't give up on her."

"But we have to move soon. Jorge said her New Boy surgery was scheduled for next year."

"I hear you," said David. Even though this girl was not his own child, he was angry on her behalf and Malia's against those who would mutilate a child to satisfy their ideological convictions. "Start getting to know her so we don't have to commit aggravated kidnapping." He surfaced from under the comforter to check the armband on the night table for the noise cylinder. Staunton was far from the City's orbit, but he knew it was theoretically possible to tap into his conversations.

"But at least you've met her, and she knows who you are," said David. "So, I consider that progress, even if she told you to eff off. Now for the Adam Ross situation. This is trickier. I'm glad you fought him off, but it would be more helpful if you cultivated him. He is very highly placed in the Economic Tower, and we want to know more about the Zones. We suspect some of the Tower types are embezzling Zone profits. If that's the case, he would know about it. It's not under the purview of my unit, but we discuss it at the Director's meetings. Right now, we're targeting the Knowledge Tower, but eventually we will turn northeast.

"And secondly, he has oversight over the Industrial Zone camp we saw today. We will need to make some inroads here to facilitate our escape, because this is the route I think will work best. My brother will help us, but we could use more connections here."

"Are you asking me to sleep with him?" Malia asked him with astonishment.

"You jump from A to Z very quickly," David observed. "I don't want you to sleep with him. I will be pretty pissed off if you do. But I want you to give him the impression you *might* eventually sleep with him. Haven't you ever kept a guy hanging?"

"Uh, no," said Malia. "This kind of thing has never happened to me before." Indeed, she had had little opportunity to learn flirtation.

"If you didn't break his neck last night, that's a good start. Did you tell him you had a boyfriend? That should have helped."

"He asked what your Social Credit score was. I said you were a Plore."

"Quick thinking, and not exactly false," said David. "The truth would have been a bad idea on a number of levels. What did he say then?"

Malia took some wicked pleasure in saying, "He said it didn't count and that he would share me with you."

"I hate the bastard already," said David, "and will take great pleasure in bringing him down."

He jumped out of the bed and reached for his clothes. "Let's go to dinner."

They strolled around Staunton, a town built on steep hills that was the birthplace of President Woodrow Wilson over two hundred years earlier, just before the first Civil War. It had also hosted the General Assembly in 1781 when the delegates fled Charlottesville ahead of the Redcoats. Few in Staunton knew its history anymore, although they were proud of its current status as an official Diversity Art City. The Wilson birthplace was closed; even though he had been a Democrat, he had been a staunch racist and the local authorities had chosen to shutter the museum rather than grapple with the embarrassing history.

Staunton had served during the Great Diversity War as a staging ground for Antifan raids. The Economic Tower's mid-Atlantic training center now occupied the grounds of the former Mary Baldwin College. The long famous Blackfriars theater had expanded its repertoire beyond Shakespeare—even though many of his plays had lent themselves to revision for the elite masses under the guidance of Diversity literature experts—and now showcased "The Best in Diversity Drama." The main street was lined with cute shops and expensive restaurants that were open to all willing to pay; Staunton was still not wealthy enough to be able to afford a Social Credit hierarchy. Enough Plores lived in the area to serve the stores and restaurants.

As Malia and David passed the theater, a crowd of well-dressed Social Crediteers, mostly visiting from Anacosta, was milling outside before the night's performance. According to the review, which Malia had read to him in the vain hope that David might agree to attend the theater, *Taking America Back* was yet another gripping portrayal of oppression in 20th century America, this time through the eyes of a gay Latino activist, a black janitress, and a mermaid. "A *mer*maid?" David had asked with disbelief. "Are they going to pay us for attending?"

"No, I think it's the other way around," admitted Malia.

"Well, to hell with it then," said David. "I would prefer to be entertained by a prime rib." And so they found themselves in a cavernous old tavern, eating steaks and savoring the casual privacy of a wooden booth with high walls. After the waiter took away the plates, David reached out with his hands for her right one, and played with it, almost absentmindedly.

"How long have we known each other?" he asked.

"Not quite two months," Malia said. "But it seems as if we've known each other longer."

"Yes, it does—you know, you really are beautiful when you aren't anxious."

"Around you I'm not anxious."

"And what happens when I'm not there?"

"Oh, I have to flip guys with only 200 Social Credits onto the floor. It makes me anxious."

"Really," said David. "I would have liked to see that." To Malia, the whole episode with Adam Ross now seemed very far away. "Before your next shift, I'll teach you some other self-defense moves just in case he tries harder next time. You were lucky last night. But I really admire your courage. I bet two months ago you would never have dared do that to him."

"Never," said Malia. "I wouldn't have dared stand up to Jorge. You've been good for me."

"You have imbibed some of that Antifan spirit, if I may say so."

"I think I'm going to need it in the coming months," Malia said. "Given what we have planned."

"Yes," said David. "You're becoming anxious again. Let's see if this will help." He reached into his pocket and brought out a small box. Opening it, he extracted a silver-colored gold ring with a small but perfect diamond and handed it to her between two fingers.

Malia was confused. "It's lovely. Are you giving it to me? Thank you. What kind of jewel is this?" She had never seen a diamond before.

"It's a diamond," said David, hiding his surprise at her complete misunderstanding. "We're engaging in a Plore ritual. When a man wants to marry a woman, he gives her a diamond ring, and asks for her hand in marriage. If he is lucky, she says yes, and wears the ring."

"Oh yes!" said Malia. "I've read about that in some of the books at work. It's very romantic, but I was taught that it was a very sexist custom. It represents a man's ownership of a woman, so we stopped allowing that. Aren't you supposed to ask the girl's father for his permission?" But there were very few fathers of marriageable women around these days, she realized.

David wasn't sure whether to cry or laugh. "Uh—can we bring this around to us?"

"Are you asking me to marry you?"

"Yes! You got it," said David. "I was hoping this would be a little more romantic, though."

"Oh…" Malia said, reverently. "That's lovely. Of course." She placed her hands on one of his, and said, "I love you, David. How sweet."

"I love you too. I'm glad I waited for the right woman." He moved the ring onto what he knew was not the appropriate finger. It gleamed in the dark restaurant.

He paused. "Now for the DJR protocols, which are going to make us wait a while longer. What we are about to do is called an 'engagement.'"

"Yes, I've read about that too. There's usually a lot of excitement during an engagement as the couple fights, but some crisis brings them back together."

"We're not going to be fighting. Normally, as you know, if you become engaged, you have to go to the local administrative office and apply to marry so they can decide whether you are suitable for each other. If you're an Antifan, they will scrutinize your application very carefully. If you are a 240 and you suddenly decide you want to marry a 96, they will be very concerned."

"Will they say no?" Malia was alarmed. "Especially with what happened with—Isabelle?"

"They will almost certainly say no," said David. "And they will push someone else at me." Malia looked like she was about to cry. David squeezed her hand and made a hushing gesture. The restaurant had largely emptied out, but patrons still were within earshot of a crying scene. David recalled when Ferraro had warned him not to let the Depository librarian "become your type." This is what the Director, in his rough but realistic discernment, had foreshadowed.

"I have a plan—don't you know I always have a plan? Would I be proposing to you now if I thought it was completely futile?"

Malia nodded, wiping away a tear.

"The plan is that you and I know we are engaged to marry, but we are not going to tip off those in charge." His voice dropped to a whisper. "Just as we are not letting them know other things we plan to do. I promise you, as soon as we are in a safe place, we will get married. Not by a DJR judge, not by a Mother Earth freak, but by a proper minister. I swear this to you, by God."

"But what if we don't make it across?" Malia fretted.

"Then we're not going to get married," David said dryly. "So now you have another incentive to keep plugging away at the Octavian."

"We don't have to take Isabelle with us," said Malia, fearful that bringing this impossible child would destroy her chances at a happy future with David in a free country.

"How could I leave my fiancée's daughter behind the lines?" said David. "Now that I have proposed to you, and you have accepted, she's my family too.

"But wear the ring, which I've placed on the wrong finger on purpose. No Social Crediteer will really think of it as signaling an engagement unless you tell them. Maybe

Ross will know enough so that it deters him, slightly. He'll find it an amusing Plore custom and won't take it very seriously, but maybe it will slow him down."

David's behind the lines comment had made Malia's thoughts turn in another direction. "But we would be leaving your mother and sisters behind the lines."

David frowned at her. "Their lines are different from our lines, or Isabelle's. They would not be punished in the end for really not knowing what we were doing. They're Plores, so they are protected somewhat, assuming they really were innocent of our plans. And so, we will say nothing, ever, to them. Do you understand?"

"Yes," said Malia. "You see, they are now becoming my family too, so I had to ask."

David was moved. She enjoyed seeing that serious gray gaze that always told her when she had impressed him. "That is just wonderful. I hadn't seen it from your point of view. I love you for thinking like that. Thank you, Malia." They looked tenderly at each other, and the waiter brought the bill. You could pay with cash in Staunton, and they covered their tracks with a thick wad of bills, tipping the waiter generously, since tipping was legal here and David always helped a fellow Plore when he could.

Chapter 27
Coronavirus Liberation Day, Observed
(Monday, 6 June)

"The health crisis has come as a boon for some
authoritarian leaders, empowering them to introduce the
kinds of controls on their citizens they could only have
dreamed of before the spread of COVID-19,"
—Washington Post, *20 April 2020.*

Along with 200 million other DJR citizens and Plores, David and Malia were watching President Avadaughter's Coronavirus Liberation Day speech the night before the holiday. Most of the speech would serve as predictable scaffolding to protect the DJR's vulnerabilities and lash out at opponents, but as David said, to discern the political winds, it was worthwhile comparing each year's speech with the previous one, so they watched intently.

President Avadaughter, looking more vigorous than expected in a red silk pantsuit, ("She got a face lift in Beijing," David remarked) reminded her listeners that the pandemic of 2020-22 had ultimately been a blessing to the world. Yes, several hundred thousand people had died in the then United States as the virus struck populations beyond those thought to be most vulnerable. "A tragedy?" she shouted. "But it became a triumph. As every schoolchild knows…"

David pulled Malia into his embrace. This was a painful time of the year for her, but this year he was determined to share it with her to the extent he could.

"…the crisis allowed progressives to seize the initiative and impose public safety laws that in the end undermined the individualistic, racist, and wasteful ways of the former United States. Governors cracked down on church services that had been the right-wingers' organizing node—this so-called worship, in the patriarchal and racist mode of the times, was preventing the Diverse Peoples from achieving their rightful goals. Protesters who valued money and property above the health of their fellow citizens were unmasked, and learned the hard way that the safety of the collective is supreme. We closed gun ranges and then deprived them of their weapons. We freed prisoners from the jails, citing coronavirus. We closed the schools until we could ensure proper teaching, and campaigned to give everyone a basic minimum income if they were unable to work from home. Most importantly, we were able to postpone and eventually cancel elections that were going to be decided wrongly in favor of racists. The switch to a mail-in voting system allowed us to curate the elections to ensure a fair outcome. Coronavirus proved that life in old America was unfair, disproportionately killing the marginalized and Diverse, while wealthier white people sheltered at home. And Americans learned that what once had been calling 'snitching,' was in fact a noble cause when practiced for the right reason, to keep fellow Americans safe. We love our Karens!" said Avadaughter, referring to the female busybodies who enforced the Cult of the Mask.

"Mother Earth, thank you for the Coronavirus pandemic. As Archbishop Mountainspring said today at our service of Thanksgiving, 'From tragedy comes exaltation in Mother Earth.'"

Only if it's someone else's tragedy, thought Malia.

"Fortunately, our friends in China helped us recover from the coronavirus that epidemiological research has shown originated from a lab run by rightwing fanatics in Nebraska...."

"Last year, it was Kansas," David observed.

Avadaughter continued, "The fascists thought that they could peddle the lie that China had created the virus and sought to profit from it. Thank goodness China was wealthy enough to send us the supplies we needed to overcome the crisis. And then over the next forty years, the People's Republic, in its goodness, helped us institute a Social Credit system that replaced the twisted incentive system of capitalism and money grubbing, and made sure those who contribute most to Diversity reap the most rewards.

"Of course, the fascists retreated into the Interior, and they continue to war against us today. Thus we have not yet been able to achieve the kind of prosperity we deserve under socialism; the defeat of climate change and rising oceans remains elusive. Thus, we must remain vigilant. One thing we cannot do is fight each other..."

"Uh oh," said David, leaning forward.

"No one admires more than I do the fighting spirit and dedication to Diversity of our Antifan Defense Forces. Without the Antifans, where would our revolution be? Yet the Antifans are not the keepers of the flame. The Knowledge Tower is where the ideological heart of Diversity lies. The Antifans protect the keepers of the flame and should not turn on their revolutionary leaders. Because without intellectual leaders, who knows the direction we should take? Such confusion over proper roles can only serve to undermine Diversity."

"Ferraro is having a coronary right now," David said gloomily, but without noticing the pun.

"The ADF must remain mindful of its proper role and serve at the direction of its ideological superiors," Avadaughter primly concluded.

"The Tower must have gotten to her," said David.

"I urge all lovers of Diversity to unite, and remember who our real enemies are. We'll see you at the parade tomorrow. Mother Earth bless you all and good night."

As soon as the broadcast ended, David's phone rang. "Yes, sir, I most certainly heard that. I agree, it's unconscionable. Yes, sir, I'll be there shortly."

David stood up, stretching.

"Do you have to go into work?" Malia asked. "Because of what President Avadaughter said?"

"Yes," said David. "I'm sorry. Don't wait up for me, I may not return tonight. But I promise I'll come back in time to get you to the parade, okay?" He kissed her absentmindedly, already thinking ahead. He bicycled over to Beaufort along the deserted roadways—a few minutes of fresh air would clear his head for the challenge ahead. But one thought crowded out the others. Unless the Antifan Defense Forces voluntarily relinquished its monopoly on violence, no one would be able to control it. And we will stay firm, he said to himself, pedaling steadily.

As he walked into the building, he thought that the greatest political advances of coronavirus had in fact been technical ones. The heat-seeking technology intended to find infected people, once married to information available from people's phones and filtered through artificial intelligence algorithms, allowed authorities to identify the location of specific persons of interest. The chip inserted behind the ear of every adult DJR citizen was the direct descendant of the heat-seeking technology advances. So if you were tracking down an illegal poetry circle that you knew met somewhere in Northeast Anacosta, you had at your disposal myriad databases, that when asked, would list the names of all 20-somethings who had downloaded poetry from the GVN and were congregating in the suspected vicinity, and your men could be at their doorstep in ten minutes. The ability to integrate surveillance into almost all household appliances—the Internet of Things—had vastly simplified the ADF's ability to monitor the population. Even the utterance of specific suspicious phrases would trigger an alert at Beaufort. An entire team at Beaufort was charged with running down these utterances and linking them with other relevant data about the person. Sometimes, of course, a phrase might just have gotten mangled; "hate the president" might actually have just been "take the depressant."

It also occurred to him that Avadaughter's point about the DJR having legitimized snitching was a good one. Only in Plore neighborhoods was tattling on one's neighbors' private activities still considered disreputable, unless of course they were engaged in truly criminal acts.

"Hey, chief," said Walters, who seemed to spend most of his weekends at Beaufort. "The Director's asking for us." They hurried upstairs to the executive suite.

Seven hours later, Coronavirus Liberation Day dawned bright and sunny; it would be a hot day, but fortunately the authorities were prepared. Below the bleachers lining

Corona Avenue (the former Constitution Avenue) were tables laden with water boxes for marchers. Volunteers dressed in covid red would spray them with a cooling mist as they passed, wearing masks that bore various slogans, such as "Safe at Home," or "Hate Hate." Many marchers brought their own masks, often decorated with cute cats and fish; the DJR was not opposed to citizens bringing a small playful touch to their political message, which complemented government-sponsored severity by showing that grass-roots elements, and especially women, embraced the promise of perpetual safety. Everyone wore masks of some kind, since the parade monitors would evict one otherwise; slyer attendees poked small holes in theirs to enable breathing.

The main first-aid station was ready for marchers, volunteers, or spectators who became sick in the heat or were overwhelmed with patriotic excitement. Bleachers catering to the 150-above element were still mostly vacant, but crowds were filling up the open-seating bleachers. Everyone was given a paper bag with a free healthy meal to eat while waiting, as long as sufficient quantities remained, making early arrival prudent for the lower classes. Even Plore families came into the City for the festivities, which would be followed by street fairs and musical entertainment all afternoon. One saw them hurriedly pulling homemade masks over their faces several blocks away from the bleachers, at the secured entrances.

Directly above the first-aid station jutted out the glassed-in security control center with a three-sided view of the parade route below and the adjoining streets. ADF and police analysts staffed the workstations, monitoring numbers and threats, and receiving reports from the volunteers and police officers. Snipers sat midway up the glass towers and on the roofs of lower buildings, eyes and weapons trained on the parade route. Every decent citizen was overjoyed to celebrate the virus that had finally tamed them of rampant individualism and taught Americans to embrace safety over freedom, but as the ADF officers knew, there would always be malcontents eager to embarrass or strike at the DJR.

At the end of Corona Avenue the authorities had set up stages on which the musical entertainment would take place. Chief among the scheduled talent was the all-girl group "The Karens," who would sing their new hit, "Stay Home With Me," and the urban rockers, "The Vegan Cannibals," first on the charts this week with "Diversity Mix."

David circulated through the security center, checking with each of the officers on their feeds. As the mid-range commander with the second highest seniority—the first was recuperating from a knee replacement—he had been selected as the deputy to an Alex Charlton equivalent for managing the center. It was an honor; Ferraro could have jumped over him to the next in line given the KCU's workload. David had dedicated the entire week and weekend to the security preparations and rehearsals, while back at Beaufort, the analysts doggedly continued plotting out the network by which books had left two recycling plants via other trusted faculty members, not just Pinckney. He was grateful to have skipped his turn in the Red Room this week. Like a nun having taken vows of silence, Kendra Pinckney stayed mute and solitary in her cell, he was told, eating just enough to avoid the ordeal of forcible feeding.

The usual reported threats from assorted white supremacists and fascists at the beck and call of the United States and eager to disrupt the CVLD festivities were David's main preoccupation today, although he personally did not give the reports much credence, and would not have been surprised if they had been imaginatively generated by some DJR agency even more secretive than his own. He also knew that the Chinese Ambassador was going to sit with President Avadaughter in her enclosed box, and one had to track threats to his safety posed by Chinese renegades who might be at loose in the DJR.

The only other reported threat was from a group called the Free Marketeers that planned to hack into the Corona Day site and spread seditious alerts on attendees' armbands. David was confident that if they did so, the ADF would quickly trace the location of the hacker, but it would spoil the day. David had brought Dominic at the last minute because of his cyber expertise, and because he wanted at least one of his own people in place.

David knew that somewhere down there was Malia, who had been impressed into the marching unit organized by the otherwise mysterious "Apartment Workers Union," even though it should have been her day off. "They're making me hold a sign that says 'Safety Trumps Freedom,'" she told David mournfully. The Octavian would not spare its day shift, since enemies of Safety might choose that day to make a run at its residents.

"Be glad you aren't one of the street cleaners who will have to wear the Coronavirus spore costumes," he responded cheerfully. "It's going to be a hot day and a few of them will probably faint."

"Very fitting," she snapped irritably. But she was cheered up when he returned from Beaufort at 7 am to bring them both down to the parade area. She was profoundly grateful to David for having found a loophole that allowed him to book her a regular ride with an Antifan driver to and from the Octavian.

Since she rarely went to her Rosebud apartment now, she had arranged for Fern to retrieve and consume her Healthy Eating bag each week, which pleased Fern and her hungry roommates. It was already becoming clear that the information she brought back to David from the Octavian was personally lucrative, as he had promised, and she could now buy all the seeded rolls and cream cheese she craved.

Her only concern was that Adam Ross seemed to have gone missing days before the holiday. She wondered whether he was taking the back entrance to avoid her, but David confirmed that the Ross household feed had been silent all week, and afterward ADF analysts relayed that Ross had gone to China on an official visit following President Avadaughter's. Jorge maintained a studied reserve all week; Ross must have told him that Malia had not met his needs.

Down at Corona and 5th, the 150 volunteers from the Apartment Workers Union shuffled in place. Malia was spinning her sign upside-down on the upper point of its stick. Next to her was Jason, one of the building engineers, who, shrugging, said he didn't mind a change of scenery from the Octavian's basement. "Everyone wear your mask NOW!" called one of the organizer women from the union, even though the parade would not begin for another ten minutes. There was grumbling, because the air was already sultry, and the heavy cotton masks that proclaimed a bold red SAFE on black backgrounds made it difficult to breathe. Most of the marchers shoved the masks below their noses when none of the minders were looking. Behind the Apartment Workers milled about a hundred round red coronavirus spores, presumably the street cleaners.

Behind the coronavirus spores—which when twirling would make a brilliant red picture from above—glided the most magnificent float of the parade, donated by the People's Republic of China. Against a background of tender green leaves surged a friendly-looking dragon, and standing before the dragon at the head of the float was a clutch of giant animatronic dolls representing China. Next to the Chinese dolls stood a Diverse assortment of DJR dolls—one white, one black, one Latinx, one Asian, and one indeterminate. The dolls sang in both English and Chinese a paean to friendship while the dragon's fire breathed red corona spores in a steady circle fifty feet high. A banner alongside the dragon read "Thanks to Our Chinese Friends," while the other side read, "Victory After Coronavirus." Chinese workmen—presumably not DJR Asians—swarmed over the float doing a final test of the mechanical system. Behind the dragon, pairs of dancers engaged in an exaggerated "Social Distancing" dance in which they shunned each other and then drew together in wild ecstasies.

In front of the Apartment Workers Union were contingents from the League of Karen and the Cult of Ruth. The former wore their trademark eco-spandex leggings and fanny belts, and the latter wore long black robes and lace jabots. Some of the Karens, proud of their stewardship of the Cult of the Mask, were admonishing some of the Ruths for their allegedly too-casual mask wearing. This was creating some ill will between the two leading women's organizations of the DJR on the festive day.

A hundred other different entities were marching that morning. Each of the Towers fielded a contingent, except the ADF, which would anchor the celebration of National Security Day later that summer. A float from the Economic Zones, which featured no actual workers, displayed a cornucopia of lush ceramic produce and manufactures. High-level Economic Tower officers aboard a tractor on the float wore denim overalls and sun hats. Groups from the politically beleaguered universities were more subdued than usual. The Clinton University marchers had surrendered their sign to the organizers and fell in meekly behind Justice University. Also lined up to march were groups from the Diversity Warehouse, Socialist Self-Driving Taxis, the Social Credit Petty Tradesmen, and Anacosta Waste Management. The salacious float of the Anacosta Sex Workers United showcased members demonstrating their various specialties. The float of the Anacosta Bakeries featured a gigantic baker's hat and mixing bowl on whose rim heroic bakers perched to beat fascists with wooden spoons. And then would come the Health Workers Union, the heroes of the event, for whom everyone would stand as they passed.

As the parade lumbered into movement, everyone finally and reluctantly pulled up their masks, and the dragon gave its first official noisy corona belch. Malia, walking a hundred meters ahead, waved her sign, but gratefully relinquished it to Jason when her arms began to ache with its weight. Around her bobbed hundreds of other signs, all manufactured by the Knowledge Tower Art Department:

"ALONE TOGETHER"
"THE VIRUS IS CAPITALISM"
"CAPITALISM KILLS, CORONA FREES"
"RISING TOGETHER FROM CORONA"
"THANK YOU, PRC, FOR OUR SAFETY"
"SHELTER IN THE DJR HOME"
"WE ARE NOT SELFISH"
"FLATTEN YOUR CURVE"
"SAFE NOT STUPID"

The crowds roared:

"Do not defy ,
You must conform,
The mask, the chip
Are now the norm!"

And then following it,

"Safety first,
Freedom last,
Fascists' time
Has surely passed!"

Their roaring chants rippled all the way back to the final group, "Victims of US Fascism." The victims aboard that float were a somber but sincere-looking clump of citizens of all ages, some in wheelchairs and others leaning on crutches. In their midst stretched a giant DJR flag, with its round green earth juxtaposed against a black background. Nestled in the center of the group, in a bed of greenery, was a beautiful beaming little black girl of about four with chubby cheeks, wearing a red smocked dress, the sign below her declaring, "Orphaned by US Fascism."

The Apartment Workers Union marched past the first-aid station. Malia took a surreptitious upward look at the glass box where she knew David was working hard to keep everyone safe. Then they approached the enclosed reviewing stand. The minders had told them to salute crisply at the count of four, but they were not soldiers, and became distracted, so the salutes were ragged and incidental. The coronavirus balls drew the eye instead. As they passed beneath the security box, two of the street cleaners fainted from the heat and dehydration, and their paper mâché costumes rolled toward the bleachers with their unfortunate occupants inside. Volunteers quickly ran to prod them away from the route. After that, several coronavirus spores were lost every hundred feet for the remainder of the parade, including right under Avadaughter's eyes. David pressed his lips together to avoid laughing at the sight.

Finally, the Victims of Fascism float glided by the president's box, its occupants waving wanly. Three hundred meters ahead, the marchers were dispersing at the end of the parade route, scattering into the crowds, and dropping their signs at the first opportunity. Then the float exploded in a fiery ball, black smoke billowing into the sky above, and everyone began screaming one long scream. "Dear Earth," David said, gesturing to Dominic as they ran out to the scene. "Secure Ballerina!" he shouted into his special event armband. President Avadaughter, a.k.a. "Ballerina," was already being spirited into the interior of whatever building was behind her box, and out to safety.

By the time they reached the scene, the firefighters were spraying the smoking ruins of the float. Most of the survivors had staggered over to the sidelines, where first responders were treating them, and others were being extracted from the wreckage. Fortunately, not all the wheelchair-bound Victims had actually been handicapped, and some were able to sprint to safety. About half a dozen bodies lay on the ground, unrecognizable, except in one case by shreds of a smocked red dress. The orphaned Victim of Fascism had been sitting closest to the float core in which the explosive device had been secreted.

David and Dominic stood looking at the debris, the younger man visibly aghast. "The fascists—" he said to David, unable to finish the sentence or the thought.

David nodded. "Yes, most likely, Farrell. Let this inspire us to even greater efforts against our adversaries." He put his arm around Dominic's shoulders, and that was the photograph that made it into the *Anacosta Post* evening online edition, with the caption, "Antifan Defense Forces Commander David Harris, 38, comforts Private Dominic Farrell, 25, after the cowardly bombing of the Victims of Fascism float at the CVLD parade today." A second shot by Jim Fielding's photographer had captured a slight sickly smile on David's face, but Ferraro had snapped, "For Earth's sake, not that one, Fielding. Are you trying to make us look bad?"

Chapter 28
Checkmate at the Octavian
(Saturday, 11 June)

Mxti Rex presented themself at the concierge counter at 10:10 pm on a quiet Saturday evening. They was holding a board game. "Can you play this with me?" they asked Malia, who had just finished totaling up receipts for the health club.

Malia looked over at Jorge, who shrugged. I'm meeting her needs, she wanted to say. She had been especially kind to the child during their trips to the snack bar, which seemed to have increased in the last week or two. Now that school was ending for the year, she was able to ask Mxti Rex about their summer plans—apparently Mxti Rex was going to an LGBT camp for a month ("great," said the prospective stepfather sarcastically when Malia told him) and the family would spend three weeks at their beach house ("Not good from our standpoint").

As they sat down at one of the seating groups, a sleek blond coffee table between them, Malia recognized the game from a glowing review in the *Post* last weekend. The Knowledge Tower Teenage Entertainment division had just produced its latest board game, "All Gender Victory." Players decided at the outset whether they would be the gay man or lesbian, New Man or New Woman, cis-man or cis-woman, pansexual, bisexual, or asexual. Your character had to move around the board collecting affirmations from a majority of the other gender/sexual types, which you would do by landing on their spaces, picking up a card from their pile, and answering the question correctly. Sometimes the answers were different depending on whether you were a cis-man or a New Woman, for example, so there were some entertaining tripwires. If you answered incorrectly, you would have to begin all over again. Some of the questions were quite sophisticated, and one really needed to have had benefited from college-level indoctrination to answer them correctly. Malia chose "cis-woman" and Mxti Rex chose "New Man."

"My mom brought this home from work yesterday," said Mxti Rex. "But she has a headache and can't play with me."

"I'm happy to play with you," said Malia. "Where's your dad?"

"He's working hard," said Mxti Rex. "He's writing up the plan against the Antifans who bombed the parade."

"Why would the Antifans bomb the parade? Wasn't it the Fascists?"

"That's what the newspapers said," said Mxti Rex. "But my parents work in the Knowledge Tower and they know better. You can't always believe what you read online."

"That's for sure," said Malia. "Your parents are probably really smart." She excused herself briefly. David thanked her for the call, and within ten minutes Beaufort—by authorization of Director Ferraro himself—was monitoring the Andrews household feed. Stroke of luck, thought David, since Andrews would likely be reading snippets aloud to himself, or to his wife, or over the phone to a colleague. "How did you find this out?" said Ferraro, looming large on David's screen as he electronically signed the authorization at home.

"Remember the librarian at the Depository?" David said. "Well, sir, she's now working for us at the Octavian. She was playing a board game with the Andrews daughter who just chirped it out."

"You don't say," Ferraro marveled. "Well, perhaps I underestimated our librarian. Maybe she is your type, just a little."

The game took longer to play than Malia expected, what with all the ideological twists and turns. Once Malia had to go back to the beginning, when she failed to refuse the proposition of the New Man with sufficiently abject apologies. As she sighed, inserting the card in the bottom of the pile, she felt a shadow over her, and she looked up to see Adam Ross towering over them. She hadn't realized how powerfully built he was until her eyes ran up his thighs to his blazer. He was holding an Enviro-pod and was alone. His smile was thin and grudging.

"Mind if I watch?"

Malia said, "That would be fine, amba-sah." But Mxti Rex blurted out, "Who are you?"

"I'm Mr. Ross, and I live in this building. But I'm a little lonely so I would enjoy watching your game if you don't mind." One did not use "Amba-sah" or "Amba-mam" unless there was a significant Social Credit difference, and you were both adults. Plores ignored these salutations altogether. Using it, with its various permutations, was a sign that you were versed in the Social Credit equivalent of court language, but of course it was mostly the responsibility of the lower Social Crediteers to know it.

"Fine, have it your way," said the rude teenager, and Adam settled down in the armchair perpendicular to the game board. Mxti Rex suggested that now that they had three people, Adam could play the role of the arbiter, who would decide in close cases whether the player's answer was sufficiently correct. "I would love to be your arbiter," said Adam.

Mxti Rex successfully answered a question about the best way for a New Man to invite an asexual on a date. Answer: do not just request sex. Find another interest you have in common such as bicycling or gourmet dining. On their next turn, they faltered, but Adam decreed in their favor. To her irritation, Malia then landed on the cis-man spot. The card asked, "The cis-man does not ask for your permission, but you secretly do want to have sex with him. How do you answer?" Adam gave a short blunt laugh, causing Mxti Rex to look curiously at him.

"Insist that he ask for your permission," said Malia curtly.

Mxti Rex looked at the answer, "It says something about whether his Social Credit score is higher than yours or not. If it is at least twenty points higher, you should forgive him the omission and have sex. It says he may have forgotten because of his important responsibilities so you need to be understanding of the Diversity factor."

Mxti Rex looked to Adam. "What is your decision?" they asked.

The arbiter looked coolly at Malia. "I think Ms. Melia definitely got it wrong."

"Ha!" said the child, who cruised to victory on their next turn. As they packed up the game, with Malia's help, they said, "Thank you Ms. Melia—can we play again tomorrow night?"

"You're welcome, Mxti Rex. If Mr. Jorge permits it, we can play. I know we also have a set of checkers and chess here in the lobby." Please don't make me play this horrible game again, at least never again with a virgin and satyr at the same time, she thought.

Ross had already disappeared into the elevator.

Malia resumed her position behind the counter while Jorge took his dinner break. "Hello amba-wah. Hello amba-sah and amba-mam! Welcome back, amba-wah—how was your trip?" The flow of residents began to slow around 11 pm, and Malia did some carpet sweeping. As the witching hour of 2 am approached, Malia became anxious, thinking that Amba-sah Ross would certainly call her upstairs. But he didn't. He will let me stew all night, she thought around 4 am, he's playing with me. Upstairs, much earlier, Ross had mixed himself a final cocktail of the night, thinking with satisfaction how he had taught that Low Credit slut a lesson, but not as soundly as she deserved. Next time, he thought before he fell asleep, his sprawling thick body taking up most of the bed.

After getting the call from Malia, David was too restless to watch TV or play a video game. Might as well go into the office, he thought, just for a little while. Beaufort's proximity meant that he spent far more time at work than was probably good for his health. But he grabbed the bicycle and in ten minutes was greeting the junior guards who typically got the weekend graveyard shifts. It was 11 pm.

Up in the Unit, David greeted the skeleton crew, caught watching the fascist National Basketball Association finals out of Omaha. They scrambled to switch the channels, but he waved that off. "Who's winning?" he asked.

"Cleveland Lakers, sir."

"Good," said David. "My family's originally from Ohio, so I'm happy to hear that. As you were, please."

"Thank you, sir."

One young officer, Caroline Ramirez, was monitoring the Andrews feed. "What are you finding out, Ramirez?" asked David. Ramirez showed him the feed:

Lee: Belinda, can I run some of these ideas by you? I know you have a headache, darling, just give me five minutes of your time so I don't sound like an idiot in front of Terwilliger. Here's where I want to point out that only the ADF could have planted that bomb. All the floats were being guarded the night before by the ADF and Anacosta Police. The police wouldn't have the capability to plant the bomb or the motive for that matter.

Belinda: What if the bomb was planted there during construction? Why would it have to have been the night before?

Lee: (silence) I think they must have been doing bomb sweeps before last night, don't you think?

Belinda: Well, why don't you place a call over to Beaufort and ask?

Lee: Honey, don't be sarcastic. I'm trying to help our director.

Belinda: And why don't we think it was some fascist group? Aren't fascist groups constantly trying to take down the DJR?

Lee: The ADF hasn't come up with any. Shouldn't they know who might have been responsible? Isn't it their job? If the ADF did the bombing, you'd think they'd attribute it to some group, even if it's fake.

Belinda: So give the Director a statement in which he demands clearer answers from the ADF about what we know and don't know about the bombing. I'm sure Avadaughter would support that.

Lee: I've been looking at the Basic Law of 2061. It does say that the ADF will be permitted to administer its own affairs and its Director is not responsible to any other member of the government other than President Avadaughter. It's explicit that the president approves the ADF's appointment of the Director of the ADF, but it seems only the ADF can dismiss him.

Belinda: If Avadaughter dismissed him, would the ADF allow it?

Lee: Maybe if the Supreme Advisory Court told them to? (silence) Well, thanks, honey, sorry to have bothered you.

"That's it so far, sir," said Ramirez.

"That's plenty so far. Can you send that to me so I can take a closer look? Thank you, Ramirez."

An hour later, at midnight, he was presenting the findings to Ferraro in the director's living room, where he had attended the party only last month. Ferraro sat in the same armchair, and David on the hobnailed sofa, leaning forward over the papers arrayed on the table.

"So they think Avadaughter is going to tell me to go, and I'll just slip quietly into the night?"

"Sir, they seemed somewhat naïve about the resolve of the ADF, the wife a little less so perhaps." The two chuckled, but a little anxiously.

"I know that Basic Law better than any of those Knowledge pussies," said Ferraro. "There is absolutely no way that they can tell us how to do this investigation. The intention of the Basic Law was to prevent the administrative agencies from being corrupted. Antifans are trusted not to try to become the government, just to protect it by the means we see fit."

"I think President Avadaughter will probably ask for more clarity on where our investigation stands, sir. It would behoove us to have some prospective fascist groups to identify as the focus of our efforts."

"Do we have any, Harris?"

"We could pick a few out of the files, I guess. There's some group operating out of West Virginia that would at least be in plausible proximity to Anacosta. Not that we've seen any of them south of Martinsburg in five years. We could invent a group out of thin cloth, and maybe get someone in our cellblock to confess to belonging to it in return for favored treatment."

"I forget—how many arrests did we make on Monday?" Ferraro asked.

"Ten total, sir. Mostly for excessive alcohol consumption, very unwise in that heat. Several made subversive remarks within earshot of our officers. We booked them all at Beaufort, but all but two have been released with a warning. Two for assault, arguing over a woman. And one man who was assaulting a young girl under the bleachers. Some Plores brought it to our attention. We think he was mentally ill. Those three are all in the custody of the police."

Ferraro closed his eyes meditatively. David knew better than to rush him, and sipped the whiskey Ferraro's Social Credit butler had made for him before turning in.

"Harris, let's assume that Avadaughter will demand to know where our investigation stands. Let's give a full account of what kinds of explosives were used, how we think the terrorists might have placed the bomb. We know that information really well," he chortled. "And then who those terrorists might have been. Let's bring in the mentally ill guy. He can be the fall guy. You know, kind of like the Reichstag Fire." David must have looked blank, so the better-educated Ferraro explained.

"And then if he disappears in the next few weeks, no one will miss him."

David was appalled. He knew the Antifan justification for the float bombing, in the consternation at Beaufort after Avadaughter's rebuke of the ADF, was to show the public that the ADF was needed more than ever. It had been a dangerous move, because it risked creating an impression of ADF incompetence. He himself had expected the bomb would be far less powerful, and that perhaps no one aboard would actually be killed, perhaps the back of the float would have been nicked, but he had not been in charge of the technical execution of the plan. That had been the Technical Operations Unit. He did not have the stomach to frame and execute an innocent man, but what about a child molester? Would that be acceptable?

"Harris, don't look so horrified. Did you show up at Beaufort yesterday?"

"Sir, may I offer a compromise? Let's stick with defending our rights under the Basic Law for now and informing the public what we've found out about the bombing so far. I can have our disinformation team start pulling together a prospective terrorist group that we can blame for the bombing in a few weeks if we're still getting pressure to find the culprits. Frankly, we could invent several bombers and execute them all without the Knowledge Tower ever knowing any better."

Leighton Andrews had all but acknowledged the ADF could do as much, and it didn't seem the Tower would have much recourse if Beaufort chose that route. It would be hard for the Knowledge Tower to unpack the invention, and by the time it did, public interest in the bombing would have waned. But the ADF would be able to point to how the Knowledge Tower—the parade's organizer—needed the security service.

"Maybe Fielding could run the story for us in a week or two?" Ferraro mused. "It's true, who needs real criminals if we can invent some? Hey, what if we even produced several for the press, and they are really just our guys roughed up a bit? A little disguise, some filters for the media release, who would know any differently?"

"Sir, I think this kind of strategy can be played out until the excitement has died down."

Ferraro beamed at David, "Now I know why I like having you around—no need to be more brutal than necessary, right? You're very clever, and you're right, let's not kill anyone if we don't have to. Let's have another drink to celebrate our victory over the Knowledge Tower."

David sighed, since he had bicycled over, and was already slightly tipsy. But relieved at the outcome, he would not refuse the Director a small celebration. Ferraro could easily have bawled him out for his lack of Antifan spirit.

"So Harris, you didn't know about the Reichstag Fire. What about the Night of the Long Knives? That was in 1934—no? I'll explain it to you, and keep this to yourself for now, would you?"

Chapter 29
Various Kinds of Love
(Sunday/Monday, 12-13 June)

David slept fitfully Saturday night, perhaps due to the liquor downed at Ferraro's house, but when he awoke, Malia was making lumpy pancakes. She thanked him for having sent a car to pick her up when her shift ended, which he had arranged before leaving Beaufort for Ferraro's house, knowing he would not want to make the trip to Connecticut Avenue at 7 am. "Anything for you, sweetheart," he said, giving her a kiss.

"I have to tell you about last night," she said. "Isabelle and I played the board game together for hours! It was a horrible, nasty board game, but we played together and when we were finished, she asked if we could play another time. That was progress, don't you think?" He agreed.

"That board game killed two birds with one stone," he observed, thinking of the Andrews feed. Malia looked confused at the arcane saying, so he explained what he had meant.

Then she told him about that awful Adam Ross and his comments, which required explaining how nasty the board game was. David agreed the board game was disgusting, and so was Adam Ross, but optimistically noted, "He wouldn't have bothered saying this or hanging out in the lobby watching your game if he weren't interested in you, so I'd take this as a good sign."

Malia fell asleep in the car to Ploreville, but awoke when the car halted in front of Marjory's house. Marjory appeared in the doorway, drying her hands on an apron. She received their news with joy. She hugged both of them at once, then kissed each.

Sitting at the kitchen table, she asked, "Isn't this going to be a long process? Don't you have to ask for permission?" Naively, she assumed that since Malia was a Social Crediteer, permission would come eventually. The intricacies of high and low Social Credit were beyond her.

"Yes, Mom, this could take a long time. But we're prepared to be patient. We just wanted you to know as soon as possible that this was our intention."

"I'm so happy to hear this," she said. "Malia, you're a lovely young lady. I'm so happy for both of you and for all of us. I hope you'll start thinking of us as your own family."

Marjory decided that to commemorate the occasion, they should all attend the 2 pm service at St. Paul's. They looked cautiously at Malia, who nodded willingly.

"You don't have to do anything you don't want to, dear," said Marjory. "But it would give me so much pleasure to have you both with me celebrating our special happiness today."

"If Malia can attend a Mother Earth Diversity service without laughing, I'm sure she can get through a Lutheran one," joked David. They all became sober, thinking of the Earth Weekend service from which Malia had so narrowly escaped. The 2 pm service was a casual, contemporary one, so David and Malia at least were appropriately dressed, and the three headed down the street. Occasional passersby greeted them respectfully. "Mom," said David, "one favor, please. Don't introduce Malia as my fiancée, not today."

"Why not?" Marjory asked, surprised. "Won't the authorities know when you apply for your permission?" Even though a Plore, she knew that informers attended church services, mostly to ensure that preachers avoided even implicit criticism of the DJR. The informers would relay back to the Knowledge Tower, the keeper of religion, any gossipy tidbit that might interest authorities.

David said, "I don't want to get ahead of the paperwork, please. If it gets back to Beaufort prematurely, it'll look like I'm trying to deceive them. Please, for now."

"Of course, David," said Marjory. But she was disappointed. The ushers greeted them, handing them the bulletins. Malia noticed with some surprise that Marjory addressed them by name.

They sat in their usual pew toward the rear. Malia puzzled over the paper bulletin, with its list of volunteers and resolute "Saved by God's Grace in Declaring Faith in Jesus Christ." She could only compare the plain church with what she knew of the Mother Earth Diversity churches, which indulged in lavish decor to mask theological poverty. The walls of this church were bare and whitewashed, the pews a deep brown wood. The windows had stained glass, but pictured scenes from the Bible, not the passionate contemporary political dramas of the MED churches. Marjory pointed to a thirtyish man in a white robe bedecked with a green stole and a gold cross, who was climbing the stairs. "That's Pastor Denman."

They rose for the invocation, calling on the Savior Lord and praising Him with songs. Then came the confession of sins:

"Holy and merciful Father, I confess that I am by nature sinful and that I have disobeyed you in my thoughts, words, and actions. I have done what is evil and failed to do what is good. For this I deserve Your punishment both now and in eternity. But I am truly sorry for my sins, and trusting in my Savior Jesus Christ, I pray: Lord have mercy on me a sinner."

215

More than usual, David thought of all his sins. "I have done what is evil and failed to do what is good." He typically accepted it matter-of-factly, and packed it away in a mental closet as soon as the service ended. What alternative did he have? Wasn't everyone a sinner? He wasn't sinning of his own volition. But this week he had grievous sins on his record, he acknowledged, more even than the Red Room. He briefly saw a red smocked dress and smelled burning human flesh. Oh, stop it, he thought. God would show him mercy on faith alone and he was doing good works—helping Malia find her daughter, mentoring young Antifans, generously tipping Plore waiters—he faltered. Yes, helping Malia find her daughter.

He looked at Malia, who still seemed very puzzled. It must seem very strange to her. Of course, the MED Church assumed its adherents were also sinners; this seemed to be required by churches, she was thinking. But for the MED Church, worshipers' sins were political and environmental, and more about responsibility toward the collective than about one's own soul. They centered on racism and the waste of earthly resources.

She was intrigued to hear the pastor announce the forgiveness of sins won for the believers by the perfect life and innocent sufferings and death of Jesus, the Savior. But, she wondered, if sins were forgiven, what was to keep a believer from committing them with impunity? She decided the hymns were much more beautiful than the awkward screeds of the Mother Earth Diversity Church. "Gloria in Excelsis," David whispered to her after she was visibly moved by one such hymn. "Glory be to God on high. The angels sang it over Bethlehem when Jesus was born." Malia was glad when she realized that this service would contain no Four Minute Hate.

She listened attentively to the sermon, which was more focused than the standard MED rant against the DJR's enemies. It was on the parable of the Good Samaritan, which she had never heard:

Jesus told a skeptic, "A man was going down from Jerusalem to Jericho, and he fell among robbers, who both stripped him and beat him, and departed, leaving him half dead. By chance a priest was going down that way. When he saw him, he passed him by. A Levite also ignored him. But a Samaritan came where he was and compassionately dressed his wounds. He brought him to an inn, and took care of him. On the next day, when he departed, he gave money to the innkeeper, and said to him, 'Take care of him. Whatever more you spend, I will repay you when I return.' Now which of the three was the true neighbor?"

The skeptic said, "He who showed kindness and mercy to the man."

Then Jesus said to him, "Go and do likewise."

Pastor Denman's sermon was about loving your neighbor, not just the people around you in Ploreville, but the "people in the City." The pastor said, "We might not have the Social Credits of the people who live in the City, but we all have Social Credit in Christ Jesus. We are all equal in God's eyes." Flirting with trouble, thought David, but probably marginally acceptable for a Ploreville congregation.

"Some of you may have attended the parade on Monday in honor of Coronavirus Liberation Day. You all know about the dreadful bombing of a float called 'Victims of Fascism' that took place at the very end of the parade. Now some of you might have reacted with satisfaction because the people on that float or their parents might have been our enemies in the war. No Christian should respond this way. Among the victims were small children who did our people no harm, cripples, and elderly grandmothers. Every one of those people was made in the image of God and is beloved to Him. We must always love and pray for our enemies. Nor should we forget that whatever sins these people may have committed, you too—and I, your pastor—are also sinners and deserving of condemnation before God were it not for the forgiveness that comes through the blood of the Lamb."

Out of the corner of her eye, Malia saw David tense. How unfair, she thought. He is berating himself for not having stopped the attack. She reached out to touch his arm, but he impatiently shrugged it off. She wondered if she had committed a faux pas in church.

Pastor Denman continued. "We must treat every human being as the Samaritan treated the robbery victim, created in the image of God, and thus our neighbor. You might ask, 'Why should I do so when the City resident does not treat me likewise? When he holds me in contempt? When he keeps me sequestered on one side of the river and he lives in glass palaces on the other?' We cannot ignore the lesson of the Good Samaritan because someone else fails to live by it, any more than we can ignore the Commandments or the teachings of Jesus because others fail to live by them. It is not always easy to be a Christian. But violence and coldblooded murder can never, ever be condoned or excused because the victims or their families were once our adversaries. As Christians, we must wish good luck to the Antifan Defense Forces in tracking down and bringing to justice the killers of these innocent people." No mistake, thought David. He is looking straight at me.

Scripture readings followed from Isaiah 42.

I am the Lord, that is my name: and my glory will I not give to another, neither my praise to graven images...The Lord shall go forth as a mighty man, he shall stir up jealousy like a man of war; he shall cry, yea, roar; he shall prevail against his enemies. I have long time holden my peace; I have been still and refrained myself; now I will cry like a travailing woman; I will destroy and devour at once....

But this is a people robbed and spoiled; they are all of them snared in holes, and they are hid in prison houses: they are for a prey, and none delivereth: for a spoil, and none saith, Restore. Who among you will give ear to this? Who will hearken and hear for the time to come?

Now it was David's turn to stare at Malia. Her eyes were closed and she was shaking with silent sobs. He put his arm around her. What is this? he thought. In a minute or two, she had composed herself again, answering his concern with a reassuring nod. He would ask later.

Eventually came the Lord's Prayer, and the communion. David indicated to Malia that she should wait for them in the pew, while he and Marjory moved to the front to receive the sacrament. Again, she looked confused. Why could she not eat the cracker and drink the juice?

The service ended, and Pastor Denman stood by the door to greet the parishioners. "This is my friend Malia Jenness," David introduced her to the pastor. The armband told him immediately that she was also a Social Crediteer. Marjory looked on proudly.

"Welcome to St. Paul's, Ms. Jenness," said Pastor Denman. "Was this your first Lutheran service?"

"I think it was my first Christian service ever," Malia said.

The pastor nodded. "Perhaps it won't be the last." The couple moved on.

Down in the social hall, holding a cookie and a paper cup of tea, David asked, "Why were you so emotional when we read the Scripture? You know, the passage from Isaiah?" Marjory was circulating among her friends, answering, but not as fully as she would have liked, questions about David's girlfriend. David had said it was all right to refer to Malia as a girlfriend.

Malia hesitated. "I felt as if I had lost consciousness, or awareness of my surroundings. Could I have fallen asleep for a moment? I saw myself as a child in an unfamiliar house. I was on a lap, maybe an aunt's? Not my mother's. I had heard these words before, in this house. Then something dark and evil, like a towering wave, flowed over us. It was as if we were drowned. Then I woke up, or maybe more correctly, I became aware of my surroundings again. I don't think I actually fell asleep. But I have never felt such a powerful emotion in my life."

"Could this be a memory from your very early childhood?" David wondered.

"Who knows?" Malia shook her head. "But nothing like that has ever happened to me."

Pastor Denman came by to chat, and David urged Malia to tell him about her experience. The pastor said, somewhat clinically, "I noticed you seemed overtaken by some kind of emotion." He listened to her, then said, "I'm not qualified to speak about dreams, or of course, your childhood. As a pastor, all I can say is that sometimes the soul cries out to speak its truth. It cuts through our daily existence, our usual thoughts, the apparatus we construct to protect our ego from harsh realities. How does the soul speak to us? Artists have visions, and so do madmen.

"But if it is your soul crying out, it must reach out to you in a way or place so it breaks out from the everyday clutter. Here you are, in a true church of God, which you say has never happened to you before. Perhaps after many years, your soul chose this moment to reach out and say, 'Here is where you belong. Listen to what I am telling you.' You would not be the first person who came to this church and told me something unusual had happened to you while hearing the word of God."

"What should I do next?" Malia asked him.

David half expected Pastor Denman to suggest Malia immediately accept Christ as her Lord and Savior in front of the lemonade pitchers, but the minister was patient.

"My dear young lady," he said, although he was only a few years older than her. "I would advise you to think deeply about this incident. Do not do anything rash. What a shame that I cannot give you a Bible. The Treaty forbids us to give religious literature to Social Credit citizens. Perhaps David here can help you think about the meaning of this incident."

"I could go to a Mother Earth Diversity church meeting, Protestant division," said Malia. "Would that help?"

"No," said the pastor sternly. "It is nothing but idolatry and abomination. You have begun to enter on a path to possible righteousness and salvation. Avoid the temptation of easy, but false, answers." Malia looked taken aback, so the pastor softened his tone. "It is not your fault."

David asked, "What if she read these materials at my mother's house?"

The pastor replied, "I am forbidden by law from recommending a Social Credit citizen access a Bible or Christian literature in any manner whatsoever. That said, if Ms. Jenness is visiting your mother's house, and she finds such materials, and chooses to read them, I certainly would not discourage it." He winked, shook hands with David, and moved onto the next group.

"You're so clever," said Malia.

David grinned at her, "Another reason to spend Sundays at my mother's house, I suppose." He paused, almost teasing her, "I mean, how many more points can they take away from you?"

The previous week Malia had received her notification that with her reassignment to the Octavian, her Social Credit score was now down to 70. She had received the minimum 30 now that she was working in a category classified as "Menial Labor." Five points for being a cis-woman, three for Martin Johnson's funeral, 20 for the abandoned Healthy Eating bag, and believe it or not, eight points had come through for the awful Earth Weekend. And her volunteer activities had accumulated so that her score reached 70.

"I guess they're going to take away the apartment now," said Malia. "And stick me in a hostel again." The minimum credit score for an apartment was 85.

"Do you need the apartment anymore?"

"What if you get angry at me and send me home?"

"Never," he said, leaning over on the sofa and kissing her tenderly. "At worst, I'll stomp out and walk around in the rain by myself. When I get home, completely drenched, you'll forgive me and we'll make passionate love. Like this...."

"You're seeing too many movies," Malia said, but she then wrapped her arms around his strong back.

After the service, Christine, Emma, and their husbands, Larry and Kevin, came over for dinner. Larry drove a bus in Ploreville, and Kevin painted houses. They all embraced Malia warmly and congratulated the couple. Then came a cozy family dinner of pot roast and potatoes in Marjory's tidy dining room, with lively conversation about the neighbors and the baseball season. The sisters and their families went to baseball games, sitting in the Plore sections. "The seats are just as good," said Larry, "and I don't want any trouble with anyone else." Malia was persuaded to tell them a few stories about the beautiful Octavian and its eccentric residents. Marjory had no idea that the lost child lived there, let alone that Malia had met her. "They will know nothing when we disappear," said David severely.

Before they left to return to the City, David pointed out to Malia where Marjory kept her Bible and her devotionals. "No obligation," he said. "I'd hate to contribute to your moral degradation." He left it at that. After the service David had told himself that if anything, his spiritual development was well behind Malia's, whatever that dream had meant.

David dropped Malia off several safe blocks from the Octavian, telling her, "Don't forget the jujitsu!" He added, "If he calls you upstairs, text me, even if it's 2 am. If I can get into the office, I'll listen in on his appliance feed, or your armband feed, whichever comes in clearer. Move a little slowly, so I'll have a few extra minutes to get there." Fortunately, he had forty more points than Adam Ross, the bastard. David dozed on the sofa with the TV on, just in case he would need to be awake later that night, but the call never came.

At the 8:30 meeting on Monday, David confided that they expected the Knowledge Tower to demand that the ADF make arrests in the float bombing. For the first time, he lied consciously and brazenly to his subordinates. "We do not yet know who committed this atrocity," he said, "but I have no doubt that the Terrorist Crime Unit is painstakingly investigating all the likely suspects. We may be asked to assist." He and Walters were going to be meeting with their TCU counterparts that afternoon to follow up on Ferraro's directives.

Walters followed him into his office and closed the door behind him. "That was good, Chief. I can't say I enjoy being in this position, though."

"Me neither, Walters. It's an ugly business. I hate lying to our people."

"Sir, are we going to be able to stick this to the Knowledge Tower?"

"Possibly, but we're going to muddy ourselves in the process. It could end up being what they call a Pyrrhic victory—we win but at such a cost it wasn't worth it. By the way, what's the latest with Kendra Pinckney?"

Walters perked up. "Oh, she's still rotting in her cell, chief. It's been almost a month since you tried to make her see reason."

"What else do we need from her at this point? I mean, is there anything she could tell us that we haven't figured out from the Garvey professors?"

"It would be more evidence on top of theirs."

"But we don't absolutely need it, Walters, do we?"

"No, sir."

"All right then. Let's do one more civilized interrogation on the off chance she's willing to unburden herself. I doubt it'll make a difference, but maybe she's gotten lonely. And then if she still won't cooperate, let's just send her off to Markham." Markham, a towering pile of stone near Shenandoah, was a middling psychiatric hospital for those recovering from Beaufort. "Have Cheysa bring me the discharge and transfer authorization to sign, would you?"

"Chief, you're too nice to that traitorous hag."

"We've got other fish to fry," said David, in one of his Plore-isms. "She has been very courageous, which I respect. Maybe she was doing this for posterity, and too bad she's doomed to disappointment on that score. If she cooperates, offer her Garrett"— the best of the psychiatric hospitals. "She can hang out with Smeldring there. She doesn't have to know he's the one who turned her in, not that he meant to."

Outside Walters' office, Cheysa dared to open once again the little red ceramic apple that had been left on her desk. She had walked in on Monday and seen it there among the manila files, the stapler, the pencil holder, and the paper clip dish shaped like a duck. It took her awhile to realize that it actually opened, a darling little box. She unfolded the scrap of paper inside it.

I love you
Be strong

It wasn't Brian's handwriting and it certainly wasn't his *modus operandi*. When Cheysa looked up, afraid that Brian might be watching from David's office, her eyes locked with those of Dominic, across the room. Trim and intense, he stood at his desk, on the platform near the window, looking slightly abashed. He smiled at her, and this time she reciprocated.

Chapter 30
Maneuvers
(Tuesday, 14 June)

By the time David and Walters met with Ferraro, it was a full day later. The ADF had learned—thanks to the providential Andrews household feed—that the Knowledge Tower would not issue its statement on the bombing until Tuesday morning. On Tuesday morning, the entire KCU watched the news broadcast at 8:30, which led with "Salvo on Bombing from KT." The turbaned Knowledge Tower spokeswoman, Xochitl Ferdinango-Ahmed, pointedly noted that the ADF had been responsible for security at the event, and had guarded the floats the night before alongside the Anacosta Police. The Tower demanded a full accounting from the ADF for what it called "lapses in security," and "derelictions of duty."

Xochitl said fiercely, "If the ADF does not produce an explanation of the atrocity, and accept responsibility, we will begin to ask whether the ADF knows something about the bombing that it has not shared with the public." The KCU officers looked at each other and David in consternation.

"Rabbit noise," said David to his officers after the segment ended, ordering the technical control officer to turn off the video. Privately, he was alarmed. The ADF operation against the parade risked backfiring unless they could seize control of the narrative.

When Charlton, David, and Walters entered the Director's conference room at 2 pm, Ferraro was sputtering over the just-received Avadaughter letter, on official White Black House stationery. Already at the table were TCU chief Valerie Marzullo, and her deputy, Rob Rivera.

"The arrogance! The absolute nerve!" Ferraro exclaimed. "Asking me to step down so that the country can regain confidence in the ADF! Can you believe this? Welcome to the table, KCU."

"She's not actually forcing you to resign, sir, is she?" asked Marzullo.

"No, she knows that there is no provision for that under the Basic Law," said Ferraro. "We appoint our own, even if she signs the paperwork, and we step down on our own timetable. This is how we keep the Towers honest. But the very fact that she's even daring to suggest this shows how arrogant these Privilegeers have become.

"My initial intention was to just find some likely suspects, even if we had to invent them and report that we'd executed them in our basement. But after today, I'm inclined to be more aggressive, if we can." Surveying the blank faces of the commanders, he inquired, "Can we construct a credible case that lays the blame for this on the Knowledge Tower itself?"

"You mean that alleges the Knowledge Tower was responsible for the bombing?" Alex asked.

David gloomily thought to himself that this entire mess was the old man's fault. Nobody was openly challenging the ADF before the parade fiasco. Now the ADF had handed the Knowledge Tower a club with which to bash it. It was going to be very hard to claim that the Tower would have a motive to attack its own parade—let alone the technical ability—to conduct such an attack, unless it did so through one of its university science departments.

The five were silent.

"And you're the best we have in this building," Ferraro roared. "If you have no ideas, we are truly lost."

Walters spoke up, "Sir, may I make a suggestion?"

Ferraro breathed a sigh of relief. "Of course, Walters. Sometimes our younger officers are the most creative and insightful."

He's just a few years younger than I am, thought David resentfully, and his only talent is his bloodthirstiness. Marzullo also looked aggrieved.

Walters said, "We have about fifteen professors in this building from Garvey, Sanders, Justice, and Soros-Bloomberg Universities from science departments. For example, we have Professor Drew Hannaford from the Sanders chemistry department, and Professor Georgia Wang from the Justice mechanical engineering department. We could make a case that they came up with the bomb mechanism at the behest of the Knowledge Tower."

"Who in the Knowledge Tower?" Ferraro fired back.

David said, almost simultaneously, "We're going to say they plotted from Beaufort?"

Walters said smoothly, "Wang and Hannaford have only been here a week. We arrested them on Monday and transferred them to Beaufort on Tuesday. Plenty of time to have connived against the parade. We could even say that we arrested them on suspicions of plotting against the parade."

Damn, thought David.

"Okay," said Ferraro, "who do we blame in the Knowledge Tower? What's their motive?"

"To make us look bad, sir," said Walters. "I would claim that they were seeking retaliation for our exposing their carelessness at the Depository. Remember that story ran nonstop in the media last month? They were throwing away dangerous books without even bothering to track them safely after they left the Depository. Dozens of books left the control of the state and found their way to various universities. Didn't they look bad?"

"Ah yes," said Ferraro. "Who's in that group supervising books?"

"That's the Government Libraries Department, sir. Elofea Antelides, 190, is the Depository Director with responsibility for seditious books; she reports to Bruce Smeton-Capitello, 200, the Physical Libraries Director, and he reports to Belinda Barbaradaughter, 250, Senior Libraries Coordinator. She reports directly to Terwilliger," said Walters, who had done his homework.

"It's hard for me to imagine them planning to bomb the parade," Ferraro admitted. "They seem like pretty typical deadweight types. Not a lot of imagination." The group looked at him inquisitively, and Ferraro added, "Men with hyphenated names. Tend to have small penises." Marzullo started choking, and Rivera quickly passed her a glass of water.

"They don't have to be the ones who were directly avenging the Knowledge Tower, sir," said Walters. "But perhaps they complained to someone else more motivated to act against us."

"True, Walters, good point."

David interjected. "Sir, I'm afraid we are becoming very elaborate here. It strains credulity to claim the Knowledge Tower would bomb its own parade, even to embarrass the ADF. We run the risk of creating a tissue of lies and false confessions that can't hold up, that even the Knowledge Tower could rip apart, embarrassing ourselves further."

"Further, Harris? Are we embarrassed yet? *I'm* not embarrassed."

"Yes, sir." continued David. "Right now at worst we look as if we failed at the security mission of protecting the parade. It could start to look as if we really are covering up for ourselves by accusing the Tower of conducting the attack.

"Even if we do nothing else, our attack still serves the purpose of reminding the Tower whom they rely on for security. That was the original intention of our operation. We could have been even deadlier. It's okay if they think we did it. We're not going to convince them otherwise—they know they didn't bomb their own parade.

"I would remind you, sir, of the advice I gave you Saturday night. We can fob off the public—and even the White Black House—with lists of prospective suspects and promises that we are investigating. We can spin this out for weeks. The public will lose interest eventually. President Avadaughter will lose interest and move on. But we have made our point clear to our main audience, the Knowledge Tower. That's why we're seeing the anger and hysteria from them. They know they can't do anything about it."

"Perhaps," Ferraro said silkily, "the KCU is overloaded. I wouldn't blame you for avoiding an even bigger workload, Harris."

"No, sir," David responded. "That's not my motivation. It's my loyalty and honor to carry out any mission from you. But I would caution that we should not overextend ourselves unnecessarily. We aimed to tell the Knowledge Tower who is boss. We succeeded. Even Avadaughter is rattled. We should not walk into the Knowledge Tower's attempt to set a public relations trap for us."

"I think Harris makes good sense, sir," said Charlton. Marzullo and Rivera nodded vigorously.

"All right," said Ferraro. "Let's spin out an investigation, dropping nuggets here and there. And it wouldn't hurt if we occasionally placed a rumor with Fielding about the Knowledge Tower still being angry about the Depository business."

Walters sullenly followed David and Charlton from the room. He knew that the Director would have approved his plan had they, the cowards, not interfered. Where had the Antifan spirit gone, he scowled to himself.

Back in the office, David asked Walters, "Do you have the room reserved for Kendra Pinckney?"

"Yes, chief, for Thursday at 3 pm. I was going to send Patel, since we're not expecting much anyway."

"I'll go instead." He wasn't sure why he had suddenly volunteered.

"Yes, sir. I wouldn't expect much. Personally, I'd just as soon break her neck for causing us this much trouble."

David did not take his remarks entirely figuratively.

"Well, don't, please." David turned back to his screen. "I have some respect for the courage she's shown. Courage must salute courage. See you later, Walters."

Vanessa poked her head into David's office as Walters stalked out. "Sir, your reinvestigation interview is scheduled for Thursday at 10. The investigator will be coming here."

"Thanks, Vanessa," said David. He had deliberately scheduled an early reinvestigation rather than wait for them to notify him. He wanted this five-year review over before he started committing illegal deeds. In any security organization, the counterintelligence/security officers were the scariest, and with the least sense of humor. Even a veteran Antifan commander did not approach a reinvestigation lightheartedly.

David called up the highly restricted weekly bulletin of US news. Until recently, he hadn't bothered doing more than skimming it, but he was taking an increased interest in affairs on the other side of the militarized frontier. Were we to actually make it over the border, what kind of work would I do in the US? he pondered. He knew that the US had no ADF, but instead what seemed to be a confusing gaggle of intelligence, law enforcement and security agencies. An instructor at the Antifan Defense College had once explained that the US valued individual liberty, so the seemingly inefficient division of responsibilities was actually intentional, by avoiding concentrating power too heavily. The various agencies with shared powers engaged in something called "checks and balances." The instructor made it clear that the DJR could not afford this laxity. David remembered the heads nodding in front of him like birds drinking from a pond. Power, concentrated power, was good, they all acknowledged.

David skimmed the headlines:

"President Thomason Signs Free Trade Treaty With Mexico; Treaty to Senate for Ratification."

"Economy Expected To Grow 3.5 Percent in Second Quarter." Agricultural exports and heavy manufacturing were driving good numbers.

"Charity Concert to Raise Millions for Hunger Alleviation." David had heard there was a great deal of poverty in the US, but thought it remarkable that celebrities and ordinary people felt responsible for addressing it themselves. The government must certainly be deficient in addressing the needs of the people.

"Mayo Invents Medical Devices Capable of Destroying Cancer Cells From Home in Several Days." Had to be propaganda, thought David. This could not be possible. The DJR censors had probably cleared this for consumption due to the sheer ridiculousness of the claim.

"All US States Now Permitting Open Carry; Supreme Court Reaffirms Second Amendment Rights in Court Case." In the DJR, any private possession or use of firearms was a capital offense. David wondered how safe the US could be if any adult could easily acquire and openly carry weapons.

"Deputy Secretary Fired for Improprieties." A bureaucrat had misused official resources for private purposes. In the DJR, this was nothing unusual. That's what resources were there for.

He exited out of the document, not wanting to give his reinvestigators any reason to ask why he was showing increased interest in this weekly publication.

A few minutes later, elsewhere in the Unit, Dominic was fingering a miniature green and orange shellacked box left on his desk during lunch. He turned it over and over. When he opened it, a note fell out onto his desk.

I love you too, C

He looked across the room toward Cheysa's desk, but she was away. By coincidence, he locked eyes with Walters, who was standing over her desk, but broke off before the deputy could read any offense into his stare. He brought over some paper files to the disposal box, and made sure to insert the incriminating note between them. He always liked watching the ultraviolet ray incinerate the smoldering papers on the other side of the plastic window, but this time he felt the ray must have scraped his heart as well, since it was suffused and shining with warmth.

Chapter 31
Volleying
(Wednesday, 15 June)

Adam Ross had summoned Malia to his apartment at about 11 pm, earlier than she had expected, perhaps because it was a weekday night. "Well, hello, Melia," he said as she entered, as if she had surprised him with a neighborly visit. As he had last time, he ordered "Shoes off, please—you know, the carpets." This time he was wearing slacks and a burgundy T-shirt, which revealed muscular arms. He seemed to be growing a beard, judging by the aspirant stubble.

"A drink?"

"No, thank you. I shouldn't drink on the job."

But also as last time, he ignored her plea and went behind the bar, "Come and watch me mix your drink. I don't want you suspecting that I've spiked it." She complied, and took the glass with some relief. She removed her jacket, which was uncomfortable. She had gained another three pounds since last month.

He sat on the armchair, as he had last time, and watched her on the sofa, with her knees purposely together. Still wearing the nylon stockings, he thought regretfully. "Let's talk," he said. "What shall we talk about?"

Malia was hoping David would turn on the armband feed from Beaufort shortly.

"Anything you like, amba-sah." Then, as his eyes lit up, she added, "Anything decent."

"How about if we go back and forth, and ask each other questions. This way we can learn more about each other. You can go first."

Malia gave it a few seconds. "Please tell me where you grew up and where you went to school, and how you came to work at the Economic Tower."

Adam responded, "That seems to be three questions. I was born here in Washington—that was before it became Anacosta—at Sibley Hospital, in Upper Northwest. It's closed now. I grew up in a house several blocks away from here, when we still had single-family houses and not giant apartment buildings everywhere. I went to Duke University, which is now called Justice."

"I went to Justice, too!" she exclaimed.

"How nice that we have something in common," said Adam. "When I entered Duke in 2052, it was still called Duke, but by next year, with the DJR forces finally in control of the area, they renamed it Justice. He was a racist tobacco tycoon, you know. So I matriculated at Duke, but graduated from Justice. The civil war was in full force by then and everyone—at least the men—gravitated into the Antifan forces, or sometimes, got behind the lines and managed to join the fascists if they were minded differently. We could see that the DJR was coming into being, and everybody realized it would be in their interests to commit to the Republic."

"What did you do?" Malia asked.

"I didn't join the fascists." Adam smiled thinly at her, running a hand through his graying dark curls. "I joined the Antifan militia. We were stationed in the Charlottesville barracks, and our job was to round up Deplorables and other resisters who were still at large, and herd them into the DJR. We needed bodies, especially young people, although it was sometimes easier just to shoot them. I'd like to say I participated in heroic engagements, fighting hand to hand against fascists, but mostly it was shoving women and children into trucks and bringing them to the Plore camps for resettlement. Every once in a while, some old granny would take aim at us with an ancient firearm—once my commander got shot in the arm—which didn't end well for the granny. I did learn to serve as a medic, and I learned how to break someone's neck. I guess those skills cancel each other out.

"Then the war ended, we had the DJR, and after a few years, I realized I didn't want to spend my whole life as a secret policeman. I didn't want to salute and say 'yes, sir' all the time, and I wanted to make money. The Tower system was being put in place, and the Economic Tower needed expertise in setting up socialism. My degree was in economics, but because I'd served loyally as an Antifan, they didn't object. They offered me a position as a junior officer building the Industrial Zones, and I've been in this field ever since.

"My turn?"

"Yes, amba-sah."

"Tell me about your Plore boyfriend. What's his name, where does he work, and did he give you that ring you're wearing?"

"His name is Dave, he works on an asphalt paving crew, and he gave me this ring because we want to get married at some point."

"You do realize that's a diamond? That's awfully expensive for a mere Plore."

"It was his grandmother's," Malia said stiffly.

"They're not going to let you marry him, you know. And he doesn't have a last name?"

"I'm not going to give you any more information about him than absolutely necessary. I don't trust you to leave him alone."

"Bravo," said Adam. "Your turn."

"Why did you and your wife get a divorce?"

"That's easy. Our daughter died, and I said I never wanted another child. She said that was unacceptable. Counseling didn't help. So that was that...my turn."

"Do you have a photo of your boyfriend you can show me?"

"No," said Malia.

"How long have you been dating? And you don't have a photo of him?"

"I didn't say that," said Malia. "You asked me whether I had a picture of him to show you. And I'm not showing you any photos of him since I don't trust your intentions."

Well done, thought David, listening in from Beaufort. If Malia showed Adam any photographs of him, it would be obvious he was no ordinary Plore. And it would box them in. They had to manufacture some boyfriend evidence pronto.

"My turn," said Malia. "Would you be able to get me a job at the Economic Tower?"

Adam showed some surprise. "Really? You? Why?"

"I did work for the Warehouse, remember. I just got my Social Credit demotion. They put even less food in my Healthy Eating grocery bag than last month, I can tell. I'm ashamed to be just a 70." Malia thought that introducing the Economic Tower into the conversation might make it easier to ask some questions about the Zone.

"You should be ashamed," said Adam lightly, as she glared at him, "when you have so many options to improve your status—if only you were more compliant."

I've been too compliant, all along, she thought, to no good end. "You're not answering my question, amba-sah."

"The answer is maybe. But you have to give me a reason to want to do you any favors, because you haven't been doing me any." Adam was transactionally minded. "All right. My next question is whether you have any children."

"I had an abortion," she lied.

"Good," said Adam, "that's the easiest way to deal with those situations. You wouldn't know how many women I've had to drag to the Abortion Palace. They tell you they're all for reproductive choice, and then when they carelessly get pregnant, they want to exercise it—the wrong way."

"What happens when a woman gets pregnant in the Economic Zone?" she asked, genuinely curious, but it was a shot in the dark.

Adam fixed her with a hard stare. "What do you think?"

"That's not an answer," she said.

"This game is rather fun," said Adam, "or at least it was until you started asking about the Economic Zones." Dial back, Malia, thought David. "Next question. Why are you so interested in that awful non-binary Andrews offspring?"

It took Malia a moment to process what Adam meant. "I feel sorry for them. They've got two high-powered parents who don't pay much attention to them. Even if

I don't have a child of my own, I still can take an interest in other people's children."

Adam looked skeptical. "All right," he said. "If it were one of those cute blond twins, I'd understand. You get one more question tonight."

"Should my boyfriend Dave start worrying that you're going to round him up and send him to some Zone?"

"He should worry that I'm going to take you from him. Because I don't think you'll be able to hold out forever against my virile charms and my Social Credit score. Or Jorge's greed."

David hurled a rubber paperweight at the wall.

"That's not my question, amba-sah."

"Oh, he's probably safe. We need Plores to fix our roads." Adam dismissed her question airily. "And now I get the final question of the night. I'm sure Jorge is waiting expectantly downstairs to see if he'll win a big tip tonight from me. Do I get a kiss?"

"Too bad, amba-sah," said Malia. "It wouldn't be professional." Good girl, David thought. But would she have said yes if he, David, weren't listening? If she were any other Antifan informant, he would have counseled her to become more pliable, but she was not any other Antifan informant.

Next time, David thought, perhaps she could turn the subject toward money. Was Adam Ross, who had spurned the Antifans for the supposedly more lucrative Economic Tower, actually making extra money under the socialist regime? And exactly how one might do that? Ideally, Adam would view Malia's curiosity as finally indicating an interest in practical affairs and his wealth that would be conducive to seduction, at least in his twisted mind.

David knew he would have to find someone who could play Malia's boyfriend, since Adam would start demanding more evidence that he existed. Fortunately, David knew a young Plore acting student named Tom who might be pleased to accept the gig.

Chapter 32
Human Sacrifice
(Thursday, 16 June)

David stood up and saluted the reinvestigator. "Welcome to the KCU, Commander Ulansky." They shook hands. Mark Ulansky was a tall, cadaverous veteran with a mournful expression, as if to say, "Nobody really deserves to be cleared. We are all guilty." In a previous era more attuned to original sin, he might have been a particularly gloomy Calvinist preacher.

They sat down. "As you know, Commander Harris, I am doing your reinvestigation slightly ahead of schedule at your own request. I understand this is in connection with the increasing workload of the Knowledge Crimes Unit."

"Yes, Commander. It just keeps growing, and while I am eager for the challenge, I'm trying to look strategically at my calendar and do what I can while it's summer."

They ran efficiently over the usual questions, such as current address, travel, finances, and Mother Earth Diversity Church affiliation. David participated in the sole permitted investment fund, which gave you a guaranteed 1.75 percent each year. The lack of other options simplified finances considerably, for both the investor and the investigator.

"I see you still attend a Lutheran church in Arlington?" Ulansky inquired. This was always asked.

"Yes, with my mother," said David. "Just to please her." This was how he always answered.

"How often do you go to MED church?"

"I was at the National Cathedral last month and I attended the annual Earth Weekend service that the Archbishop presided over," said David. "But I have to admit I am not a big churchgoer." This was not unusual for an Antifan, so Ulansky moved on.

"I see you're currently involved with a 70-pointer," said Ulansky. This seemed an unfair characterization of Malia, as if she were a prize pig at a state fair. "How long has this been going on?" Informants are everywhere, thought David. Not that we've been keeping this particularly secret.

"Since mid-April," he said. "It's still pretty early."

"She's moved in with you, I gather."

"More convenient. I don't have the time to run downtown to her place for romance."

Ulansky said, "You are aware that such a union will almost certainly not be approved if you petition for marriage. If you are ready for marriage, the ADF is prepared to introduce you to more suitable candidates. It's not in your favor that you are involved with such a low-level Social Crediteer."

David's eyes narrowed. "Well, she is a Social Crediteer. That should count for something. And my last two romances with high-level Social Crediteers crashed and burned."

Ulansky asked, "You are aware that a child was removed from her custody about ten years ago for ideological errors?"

David said, "I know the child was removed, but I have no information about the case other than what you've just told me. It's a very painful subject for her." By the time the truth serum was administered, he would confess to having asked her for more information.

Ulansky said, "The only other item of interest right now is your trip to the Massanutten last month. You were traveling with your 70-pointer, and not on official business. One of our militia units found you on a ledge overlooking the Antifan border camp and the Economic Zone. It seemed odd that you were unaware of the sensitivities of that location."

"Ah, yes," David leaned forward. "Commander Ulansky, do you have a wife or girlfriend?"

"My husband," said Ulansky primly. "Ten years in August."

"Ah yes, sorry, sorry. And congratulations on your impending anniversary. Have you ever been out to that area yourself?"

"I thought I was asking the questions."

"Apologies again," said David enthusiastically. "I just want you to know that this spot where the militia unit found us is gorgeous. You are surrounded by mountainsides, except for the camp part, admittedly. It's lush and green at this time of the year and the sky is so blue and the breeze is just right and only a little cool. It is an absolutely perfect location for making love to your girlfriend. I'm sorry, of course it could be your boyfriend, and if the militia hadn't shown up when they did, I would have nailed her right then and there. She was half undressed when they showed up. Do you know how hard it is to find places to make love outdoors?

"They ruined it for us," said David, as Ulansky blushed scarlet at this prurient revelation of heterosexual behavior.

"I would recommend keeping it indoors," said Ulansky severely. "Or at least find a location not within sight of the Economic Zone and our border camp. Just so you know, they were watching you both from the Antifan camp."

"They should get their own girlfriends," David said, quickly adding, "or boyfriends, of course."

"As long as you are aware of the impediments to a more permanent relationship with this person, and you are primarily doing this for your personal gratification and release, this will probably not be an obstacle to renewing your clearance. I see you are going out to the same area next month."

"Yes, Commander, as part of a security inspection crew. Fulfilling one of my corporate responsibilities. One of those summer requirements I'm getting out of the way."

"Official business is fine. You have a brother who works at our base?"

"Yes, he's the senior electrician."

"Are you planning to see him?"

"Yes, Commander, out of brotherly duty. We might go fishing."

Ulansky said, "I understand that Plore family relationships are very profound. It's hard to inculcate a true socialist perspective of love for one's fellow Diverse Citizen when these primitive family bonds persist. But this will not be held against you in this reinvestigation."

"It's never been a problem before."

"Commander Harris, we never hold one of these individual concerns against an employee, but when there are multiple concerns, and more issues have surfaced compared with the previous reinvestigation, then we are obliged to pay greater attention. It is actually more concerning when the officer is more senior. Generally over time we find fewer complications, not more."

I'm getting more complicated as I become older and wiser, David wanted to say. Instead, he nodded, and said "All right, Commander, I understand."

Ulansky took his leave, promising they'd be in touch to schedule the final truth serum session. Watching Ulansky's retreating form, David mouthed obscenely, "Reinvestigate my dick." Which Ulansky might have been willing to do, come to think of it. It had been a useful session, though, not just in terms of speeding up the process, but in confirming for David that his relationship with Malia would almost certainly not be tolerated in the long term, let alone marriage.

After Ulansky left, David noticed a clump of officers near the Wurro altar. Several inches taller than most of the others, Walters was visibly up to something in the middle of the throng. David went to see what new mischief was afoot. He thought of the verse from Isaiah 57:20, "But the wicked are like the troubled sea, which cannot rest, and whose waters cast up mire and dirt." Yes, that was Walters all right.

Stripped to the waist, Walters had painted his bare chest and face in blue, red, and orange zig-zags and was raising a wooden board flat above his head. "Wurro, also known as Tu, we of the KCU make homage to you! We bring you our human sacrifice!" He seemed unaware of anyone around him. When he lowered the board, a red blob the size of a man's fist was visible. It took David a horrified few seconds to recognize it was an actual human heart.

"Deputy Commander Walters! What is this?" David shouted.

Walters turned to him, eyes glazed. He has taken something, David thought.

"Commander," he said, "We are sacrificing to Wurro. We are making a human sacrifice such as he is accustomed to. These are dangerous times for the ADF and we must ramp up our offerings accordingly. Our lives and fortunes, our loyalty and honor, are in Wurro's hands." He paused, "Don't worry, chief, this heart is from the morgue downstairs. I'll bring it right back."

David didn't know whether to laugh or cry, but either way, he was appalled.

"Wurro would also accept a dog in lieu of a human sacrifice, but nobody would give me their dog," Walters lamented.

"Walters, please meet me in my office when you've calmed down. Clothed, please." He looked around the group. "Holdeman, please return the organ to the morgue." He returned to his office, where he stared dully at the wall. All he could hope was that the heart had already been separated from the body by the pathologists for an autopsy or some other legitimate reason, and not carved out of a corpse by a manic Walters. No one from the morgue had called, which was encouraging.

By the time Walters appeared at his door, in uniform, and looking somewhat abashed, David had collected himself as well.

"Sit down, Walters. What the hell was that about?"

"Sorry, chief. I was just trying to improve morale. I think Wurro's mana needed a little bit of help, given what's going on with the Knowledge Tower. So I had Cheysa paint me, I took a few zingos, and borrowed the heart from the morgue." Zingos were shorthand for zingothene, an amphetamine that was used by Antifans to stay awake long hours or before a violent operation.

"Did they really give it to you?"

"Yes, I came in and said, 'I need a human heart, and I need it fast!'"

You're not kidding, thought David. "Don't do that again. We'll be the laughingstock of the entire building. I don't think the Director would care for it, either. It won't help to have better mana against the Knowledge Tower if the KCU looks like fools to the rest of our building." Walters looked sullen once again.

David had a feeling of dread. "Kendra Pinckney is still okay, right? I'm meeting with her at three."

"Chief, don't worry, this isn't Kendra Pinckney's heart. As far as I know, she was fine at noon."

"Good." Nothing would have surprised David when it came to Walters and Kendra Pinckney. He wanted to see Professor Pinckney gone from Beaufort, alive if not well, as soon as possible.

At 3 pm promptly, David entered the interrogation room to find Kendra Pinckney sitting at the same table where they had last talked. This time there were no refreshments. Two guards sat along the wall, and he dismissed them to the corridor.

"Professor Pinckney," he said, "here we are again."

Kendra Pinckney looked gaunt, perhaps from the near-hunger strike. Her eyes were listless. "Yes," she said.

David decided not to waste time. "We have decided to release you."

"Back to Clinton University?" she asked.

He shook his head. "No, to a hospital where you can recover from your experiences here. And perhaps learn to be the agent of your own betterment."

She responded, "Trying to do that got me here in the first place, I am afraid. But if you could not destroy my mind or my soul here, I doubt they will succeed in any so-called hospital."

"Not all these hospitals are the same. It is within your power to secure a better placement.

"Mind you, we have extracted all the evidence we needed from faculty at Sanders and elsewhere who were not as courageous as you were. You can remain silent if you want about your role in the conspiracy—or you can speak. Either way, the ADF can prosecute this case. But at this point, you can improve your own circumstances. Do you understand me?"

"Commander Harris, it is all the same to me at this point. You and your henchmen have destroyed my life, my health, and my dearest friends. I know I too will die soon. What difference does it make in which anteroom I await death?"

David felt as if he were in some alternate universe where people spoke precisely and profoundly about unspeakable truths. He was painfully aware of the stark poverty of his mealy-mouthed "working on your own betterment" statements compared to hers.

"Professor Pinckney, please give me something to allow me to send you to a better hospital. I have respected your courage and your fidelity to your principles. We rarely see that here."

"Commander, if you give me paper and pen, I will give you something that I hope you might find of value. I would text it to you if I still had my armband."

"Of course," he said. He sprang up, opened the door to the hallway, and ordered the guards to bring him pen and paper. She scratched painstakingly at the paper, as if both pen and writing were now unfamiliar. David noticed, almost irrelevantly, that she was lefthanded.

"I'm not lefthanded," she said, noticing his stare. "Or I wasn't before I came here."

When Pinckney was done, she carefully folded the paper twice, and pushed it across the table at him. "Please read this when you are alone," she said, "and you can decide whether this is worthy information." That queer phrasing. "I have had a lot of time to think about this."

"Thank you," he said, turning the folded square over and then placing it in his inside jacket pocket. He rose to take his leave. "I hope you recover fully and that you can return to the classroom someday. I won't apologize, since we are keeping our oath to protect the country."

Kendra Pinckney inclined her head at him, in one long nod. "I wish you all the best, Commander Harris, in keeping with your conscience."

Back in his office, he curiously unfolded the paper square. She had written two sayings by someone named Marcus Aurelius. In parentheses after his name was (Roman Emperor, c. 180):

Waste no more time arguing about what a good man should be. Be one.

The general wickedness of mankind cannot injure the universe; nor can the particular wickedness of one man injure a fellow-man. It harms none but the culprit himself; and he can free himself from it as soon as he chooses. (Meditations)

I should not have been surprised, thought David. He called for Vanessa. "Would you bring the Pinckney discharge papers please? For Garrett Medical. Yes, Garrett."

Chapter 33
Fight Back
(Friday, 17 June)

The KCU staff watched proudly as David and Alex Charlton stood behind Director Ferraro at the news conference in the Beaufort auditorium at 11 am. The session was timed to give the media enough opportunity to post their coverage of Beaufort's response to the Knowledge Tower (and Jim Fielding enough time to vet his with the ADF media office), but not enough time for the bumbling Tower or White Black House functionaries to rebut it, certainly not before everyone left town for the Midsummer-Beltane holiday weekend.

"I was very disappointed in President Avadaughter's letter," Ferraro intoned sadly. The president had publicly issued her letter when Ferraro had not obediently stepped down. "Here we have been, the Antifan Defense Forces, fighting sedition steadfastly. We have been rooting out corruption in our universities, which I stress are under the control of the Knowledge Tower. We have exposed complete lack of oversight by the Knowledge Tower in the False Knowledge Depository, which allowed dangerous books to circulate surreptitiously among faculty members, further underscoring the rot infesting our universities. Who guards the revolution, the Diversity Justice Republic, when the functionaries"—he spat out the word— "fail at their jobs? It is the Antifan Defense Forces." Ferraro then outlined several delectable heresies that the university investigation was continuing to uncover.

David listened to the stream of KCU achievements, wishing he could share Ferraro's confidence that the confessions were genuine. Once the ADF—analysts spitballing on a Saturday night, perhaps—determined that professors might theoretically be contacting their counterparts across the border, it was a short step to seeking to elicit exactly those revelations in interrogation, in the Red Room if necessary. And then someone would almost certainly confess. In fact, this afternoon he was scheduled in the Red Room to torture a mathematics faculty member from Malcolm X University suspected of clandestine communications with a professor at Case Western in Ohio. Ostensibly, they had discussed only trends in numerical weather predictions, but even that was forbidden.

Ferraro continued, "What kind of thanks is this to the Antifan Defense Forces?

We do not expect gratitude, but we demand respect. We urge President Avadaughter and the Knowledge Tower to purge their own ranks of time-servers and sycophants, so that the ADF need not do it for them." He opened the floor for questions.

In their spacious living room at the Octavian, the Andrewses were temporarily diverted from Mxti Rex's distressing end-of-year report card by the ADF Director's news conference.

"Can you believe that?" Belinda bubbled angrily, her ample chest heaving. "How dare he mention the Depository? So what if a few books went astray? We sent them to the recycling plants for destruction. Is it our fault if the workers illegally sold them?"

Leighton's golden head bobbed, making him resemble a dandelion floating in the breeze. "I hope President Avadaughter stands firm. She shouldn't forget about how the ADF botched the parade security. I still think they might even have done the bombing themselves.

"It wouldn't surprise me if they invented this George Washington Brigade," he fumed. "They just want to run out the clock. What do they care if our parade was ruined?"

"Those illiterate savages couldn't care less about people's lives," agreed his wife. "I'm so glad we're getting out of town." The family's car was already awaiting them in the garage entrance, loaded with everything needed for a carefree week at their beach house in the Outer Banks. "We need to have a serious talk with Rex this weekend about those grades."

"I know," said Leighton. "Next year they start counting toward Social Credit scores. They probably haven't realized how serious this is." They had muted the audio and were now staring disconsolately at Ferraro's agitated jaw.

Belinda read the grade report from her armband. "C in Diversity Math; D in Diversity History; D in Introductory Physics; C in Gay Diversity Literature; C in Spanish. At least she got a B in Art."

"Those were good vulvas," said Leighton, referring to the final art project. "Very deep pink."

"I don't know how you can't get an A in art if you hand in the projects," complained Belinda. "I mean, there are no objective standards for art, right?"

"Where is she, I mean they? We need to leave soon."

"They're in their room, like always," said Belinda, "playing video games."

"Well, they seems to have made friends with the new night concierge," said Leighton, "They're always playing board games on her duty nights. Must be kind of boring down there." He felt illiterate when he said things like "they seems," but it was the politically correct locution. And if you were a high-level Knowledge Tower official, you could not let down your side.

But they could not quite bring themselves to move yet. They sat comfortably together in their gloom, twenty years of marriage behind them. They had met in 2067 as new, recently graduated functionaries at the Knowledge Tower. Belinda was assigned to the Great Virtual Network effort, working to vet the entire realm of literature to decide what was worthy of inclusion for the new Diverse People. Leighton had graduated with the last law class at Yale (now Malcolm X) and was busy bringing successful lawsuits by the new government against the remaining independent media outlets. In the wake of the Diversity Revolution, it was a heady time to be young and progressively employed and watching your rising Social Credit scores. All agreed that Social Credit was a much fairer system for distributing resources than rampant capitalism. Even the Plores were happy to be serving them behind takeout counters and fixing their toilets, or so they imagined.

Twenty-two years ago this weekend, they had traipsed to the Midsummer-Beltane rites in the Botanical Gardens with friends. Belinda had pulled Leighton down to the ground with her; she was still busty, but less stout in those days, and he stooped far less. After that, they were a couple, and when they married two years later in the National Diversity Cathedral, they chose Ishtar, the Mesopotamian goddess of sexual congress, fertility and war, as their patroness, as was the fashion. In your kitchen you would build a small altar to whichever pagan god you had chosen as your household deity, and it would be a conversation piece for company.

Ishtar failed them, because despite expecting they would round out their rapidly perfecting life with a child they could mold to be a properly Diverse citizen, nothing happened. Leighton wondered whether they could approach the Abortion Palace to find a woman willing to let them adopt her baby. "That's a great idea, Lee," enthused Belinda, but all they got was a stern lecture from the Abortion Palace receptionist about allowing women to exercise Choice. They briefly considered adopting a Plore baby whose mother might not be able to afford to keep him or her, but were afraid to contact the Ploreville churches that usually ran such programs. Only New Men and New Women and same-sex couples were permitted to harvest babies from the human hatchery where poor Plore women lived while renting their bodies for surrogacy.

Time passed, and then someone else at the Knowledge Tower who knew that Belinda and Leighton wanted a child advised them that a colleague ran a private adoption agency for high-level Social Crediteers. It would be pricey, but nothing they couldn't afford.

The colleague assured them that the babies and children were the offspring of young Social Credit college students who couldn't afford the responsibility of a child during their studies, but wanted to give them a chance at a good future. Belinda and Leighton passed what was called a character investigation, and excitedly awaited their baby.

When a sullen five-year old was pushed at them instead of the infant they had expected, they couldn't quite bring themselves to protest. The child was angry, but quite pretty, with dark bangs and brown eyes. "At least she looks like us," said the blond

Leighton, a code phrase for "at least they didn't give us a Hottentot."

"I want my mommy," said the five-year old.

"This is your new mommy," said the matronly colleague who ran the agency. She made a good living on the side, even after the bribes to principals who cooperated in stealing children.

"No, she's not."

"Your old mommy died. Now you have a new mommy."

The child burst into tears, and then was silent for weeks despite Belinda and Leighton's awkward efforts at kindness. But it was hard for either to think of this strange and distant child as their own, and they lacked the patience to draw her out. They had sought a compatible accessory to their own successful lives, another badge of their easy success, and instead had been presented with a disturbed child. They responded to the challenge by hiring a succession of patient and less-patient nannies and sending her to the best schools possible.

The sole condition of the adoption was that the child no longer use her given name, but Leighton and Belinda did not spend much time wondering why. Gender-fluid names were popular, so they called her Rex, as if she were a dog from the humane society. They compromised by giving her the middle name of "Gretabelle," which honored Leighton's mother Greta. The child refused to answer to Rex until they began ignoring her otherwise. Belinda and Leighton never considered returning the child to the colleague, but they also never considered therapy or any extraordinary efforts to learn about her needs, let alone meet them. They did get a cat when the child mentioned "Tobal, my cat."

"Maybe she needs a cat?" Leighton had asked. But the cat died of a mammary tumor three years later, and they did not replace it.

As Rex Gretabelle entered her early tween years, and the nannies disappeared, the situation did not improve and she began referring to herself as "non-binary" and demanding appropriate pronouns. At school, where children had strictly limited spheres of autonomy, they could at a whim decide they were another gender, or neither, and put into play a process that would end with surgery to match what they considered their real gender at 16. Rex Gretabelle applied for the trans surgical program on her 13th birthday, delighting in the consternation this caused their parents, along with their inability, for ideological reasons, to resist their decision. The hormone treatment had started, and a light fuzz had begun showing on their chin and cheeks. But Leighton and Belinda were perhaps not as alarmed as they might have been had they been their biological child, and moreover, high-level Knowledge Tower functionaries needed to applaud such bold affirmations of transsexual identity. "Yes, thank you so much," said the couple when complimented on Rex's bold and modern choice.

Belinda and Leighton reasoned that at least an operative New Man would receive 70 extra Social Credit points. If Rex could go to a decent university, they could find them a respectable Tower job, and then they'd be set with at least 120 points. The couple would do all they could to keep them over 100 points, below which Rex would be at the mercy of the authorities. They felt they owed Rex that much. But what if Rex refused to earn the grades required for a decent university? The Andrewses were not quite elite enough to pull those strings.

Eager to escape the oppressive heat and politics of the City for the holiday weekend, they finally extracted Rex from their room, and they were soon off to the shore on the delightfully empty highways. Despite their aversion to Plores, the Andrews always stopped at the fruit stand after the North Carolina border to stock up on peaches and berries for the week.

Holiday weekend or not, David was headed down to the Red Room. He had hoped the press conference would go overlong, but it ended at 12:30. He decided to eat a granola bar for lunch, experience having proven to him that a full lunch and torture were a risky combination. Was it his imagination, or could he already smell burned flesh in the Red Room corridors as he strode down to Interrogation Room C?

Waiting for him was Walters, who had been poised to proceed with the interrogation had the press conference detained David. Unlike any normal person, thought David, Walters seemed inclined to stay regardless. Perhaps Walters was staying to pick up some techniques. David had been successful in most of his Red Room sessions, so possibly Walters was simply curious.

Today's victim was Professor James Evert of the Malcolm X University math department. Evert was a tall black man with a dome-like forehead and a severe countenance that so far had revealed nothing but disdain for his Antifan interrogators. Yes, he admitted to corresponding with mathematicians in the US, saying, "how else can we maintain any level of competence in math in the DJR? They are far ahead of us, and unless we learn from them, we will fall behind, with disastrous consequences for DJR science, technology, and even our economy." David had read this statement in the briefing book, and privately agreed this seemed a reasonable assessment. It was hardly treasonous to want to improve DJR mathematics by learning the enemy's secrets. Perhaps the opposite would have been a betrayal of the DJR, but in few cases did the US seem interested in DJR intellectual achievements. Well, in none, really.

As David could read for himself, the United States press routinely mocked the DJR's low levels of academic and literary output. A recent review of *Amindala*, which Malia's book club had read, was titled "My Grandmother Was A Tree: More Woodenheaded Diversity Delusions."

David decided that he wanted to elicit the names of Evert's correspondents. Evert had confessed to using an encrypted system to communicate with, it seemed, two other academics. He would not share the keys to the system, nor the names of the other men. If the ADF could break the encryption, they could identify the men, but that had proven fruitless so far.

Mittleman was at the dials and Yardley and Olivieri were in attendance. Evert was sitting, tied akimbo, in the punishment chair. This was the at-rest position. "Good afternoon, fascist," David greeted Professor Evert, having learned to his regret in the Bertone affair that civility was a waste of time. "I'm Commander Harris, and I'll be serving you today."

"Good afternoon, savage," Evert responded. David smiled, and delivered his first punch of the afternoon. Then he explained to Evert exactly what he wanted from him. Really, it was not asking much to tell him the names of two US mathematicians who were not subject to DJR arrest and punishment, was it? Sometimes when a prisoner made an initial confession, it lowered the barriers to revealing more. But Evert was stubborn. He seemed to consider it a matter of professional courtesy not to reveal his correspondents' names. David thought, if the United States tortured me to reveal the name of the Chinese fellow who taught me the latest improvements in the use of the punishment chair, I would gladly admit it was the snake-like Li Yi-feng of the Ministry of State Security.

A few minutes later, David decided to forgo the punishment chair to turn to the cellular scrambling device. He liked to explain each device before its use to the intended victim. Professors were particularly alarmed at any torture that threatened to destroy brain cells, understandably enough.

Yardley and Olivieri had applied the pads to Evert's forehead, torso and legs, and Mittleman was beginning to adjust the dials when the door to the room opened. A bright yellow light from the hallway spilled into the red furnace. Framed in the yellow light was Cheysa, wearing her old uniform. She walked over to Mittleman and stood there beside him. "May I?" she asked David.

Astonished to see her there in the Red Room, David looked at Walters for some explanation. Walters shrugged his shoulders and opened his hands. He was equally perplexed. "Thank you, Conroy," said David. "You may relieve Mittleman. Mittleman, you are excused." Mittleman left the room gratefully, and Conroy sat down in his place. Well, thought David.

He recovered his poise, and an hour and a half later, he had extracted the names from Evert, who slumped unconscious in his bonds, David having worked hard to convince him this was hardly a secret worth keeping. Of course, now this would assist the cyber analysts who were working on the decryption, and possibly open the avenues to finding other DJR mathematicians who had been illegally communicating with their US counterparts.

Perhaps Evert could now be sent onward to one of the rapidly filling psychiatric hospitals overseen by Beaufort. David had begun to joke that the university faculties might as well take over the hospitals and open satellite campuses.

He left Evert in the squad's hands, and left for the washrooms. Walters followed, doing David the courtesy of washing even though he had just been a spectator.

"Conroy seems to have made a decision to rejoin the squad," David said while toweling down. "Were you aware of this?"

"Not at all chief," said Walters, "although she hasn't been a very good secretary. She's away from the desk a lot. I'm answering my own phones most of the time."

"Any idea why she wants to come back, what with the Red Room?"

Walters shook his head. "I guess it's better than being my secretary." Neither man discerned any connection between Cheysa and the handsome young newcomer sitting on the platform next to the window. She and Dominic were spending lunch hours discreetly wandering the far perimeter of the Beaufort campus. When it seemed safe, they exchanged affectionate notes in a special code. Cheysa had calculated that returning to the squad would return her to her desk near the window as well, and proximity to Dominic was worth returning to the Red Room. Just in case Commander Harris had any doubts, she had shown her mettle by deftly manipulating the dials to cause great suffering to the professor.

Chapter 34
Looking for Help
(Wednesday–Sunday, 22-26 June)

Belinda and Leighton were smoking joints on the deck after a day on the beach. Leighton had grilled steaks, and all had eaten with a healthy appetite. They were all as relaxed as the Andrews family could ever be. When Rex pulled out her workscreen, Belinda had asked, "Do you have to play video games here, too?"

"Mom," said Rex haughtily, "I am not going to play video games. I am going to read."

"Oh good, what are you reading?"

"A book that Ms. Melia recommended."

"Melia? Oh, right, the night concierge," Belinda recalled. Then curiously, "What did she recommend?"

"It's called *A Wrinkle in Time* and it's about a girl named Meg who's good at math and she travels into another dimension to rescue her father from a rightwing conspiracy." It was an abridged DJR version that made IT into a certifiably conservative white-supremacist villain.

"Excellent," said Leighton, aiming his long draught toward the beach. "If it's on the GVN, I wouldn't worry, Belinda."

But Belinda was a worrier, and she began fretting again over the grades, pot or no pot. "What are we going to do about those grades of yours, Rex?"

Rex said, "They're my grades, not yours," which showed a naïve view of the situation.

"Next year the grades will start counting for your Social Credit score," said Belinda. "You won't be able to benefit from our score forever, you know."

"Oh, they'll give me 70 points when I have the surgery," said Rex breezily. "That'll make up for a lot of D's."

"But imagine if you had the surgery *and* you had all As and Bs," coaxed Belinda. "You'd be ahead of everyone else."

Rex was unimpressed, which caused Belinda to ramp up the anxiety. "You won't be prepared for the makeup exams. I think we need to find you a tutor or a coach."

"I bet Ms. Melia could tutor me. She's very smart, and she has a college degree."

"Really?" said Leighton. "But isn't she only like a 70 or so? You might as well find some Plore." He chuckled at his own wit.

"That doesn't mean anything. It's just because of her job. You know, sometimes really smart people don't have high Social Credit scores."

If she were really smart, thought Belinda, she wouldn't be fetching ice cream from behind the desk of the Octavian. Still, if Rex was willing to take coaching from Malia, that would be better than nothing. It would certainly be convenient. She'd have to pay Malia extra, which no doubt the girl would appreciate, being low Social Credit. When they returned to the Octavian on Saturday, Belinda went immediately to sound out Malia. "Perhaps you could tutor Rex before your shift twice a week?"

"Of course. I'd be happy to help, amba-mam."

"May I ask what your degree is in?"

"Knowledge Management, at Justice University—on campus," said Malia, referring to the more prestigious degree, before wondering if she had ventured too closely to Belinda's territory. "But I went to work at the Diversity Warehouse after I graduated."

"We do hire a lot of KM grads at the Tower," said Belinda. "An excellent major." She was reassured. "How much would you like to be paid?"

Malia named an amount far below what Belinda had been willing to pay, not that Belinda was inclined to correct her. Perhaps it was an honor to work for their household, Belinda convinced herself, or Malia was conniving at a job at the Knowledge Tower with a good recommendation from Belinda. Unknown to Belinda, money was not a motivation here, as Malia was now rolling in Antifan cash. She and Belinda agreed that at least for the duration of the summer, she would tutor Rex on Wednesday and Friday afternoons before her shift began, except during the family vacation and LGBT camp. During her break, Malia called David with the news. He was sitting shirtless on the sofa watching reruns of World Wrestling championships, available on the restricted GVN, and to Plores willing to pay. Frida nestled next to his thigh as he stroked her fur.

"That's great, honey. A breakthrough."

"Amba-mam Belinda said that Rex herself suggested I tutor. Apparently, her grades this spring were abysmal. They're very worried about her Social Credit score. She gets her own after tenth grade, you know."

"The kid's probably thinking that the mutilation, sorry, the surgery, will help on that score."

"David!" she uttered, distressed.

"I know, I know, sorry." David was watching Uxildor Thierry pinned to the mat. He had placed a bet on Thierry against some Antifan colleagues who backed the opponent, and Malia could tell he was distracted, but didn't hold it against him.

"By the way," said David, remembering something he had meant to tell Malia. "Your new boyfriend will be meeting you from now on when your shift ends, starting tomorrow. You have my permission to do whatever you need to convince anyone else that this is genuine, okay? Within reason. God-dammit." The referee had upheld Thierry's opponent's chokehold.

"Okay, that's Tom?" she asked. They had been introduced earlier in the week and spent several hours chatting at the Ploreville diner to make sure their stories were consistent.

"No. As far as you're concerned, it's Dave. You got it?"

"Yes, amba-sah," she said archly, and they said goodnight affectionately.

David had taken some steps to help Malia as Operation Octavian, as he called it, moved into another stage. An Antifan librarian had researched book recommendations for Malia to make to Mxti Rex, and would help shape the tutoring curriculum. He had also ventured down to the gym to find the female trainer and request a favor. "I have a female informant," he said, "who's getting hit on by her target. I can't let her give in too soon. Can you show me some moves she can use if he's forcing himself on her?" Kate was happy to oblige, knocking David over to the side and on his back, or swiveling out of a headlock she requested he try on her.

Kate added, "I would recommend she do physical training if she isn't already. These moves will all be more effective if she's in good physical shape." David realized that aside from pedaling absentmindedly in the Avalon gym while reading a book onscreen, or wading through the indoor pool, Malia didn't bother much with exercise. Perhaps it was time to begin gaining strength for the physical demands that lay ahead of them. He arranged with Kate to come over to the Avalon on Saturdays and Monday evening to train Malia.

"Thank you for beating me up just now. Very reassuring." As he left the gym, he surreptitiously massaged his now-aching shoulder. He felt every one of his 38, almost 39 years.

"Anytime, Commander!"

Finally, he paid a visit to Steve Rosen. The Economic Crimes Unit was on the 39th floor of Beaufort, in spacious and hushed spaces, in contrast to the evil-god jocularity of the KCU. The handsome steel gray-haired commander came out to greet him and usher him personally into his office. "This is really nice," said David.

"Please don't expand into our spaces," said Steve, a wry reference to the KCU's growing footprint. "But we don't have a god of evil like we hear you do." Steve had a pleasant gravelly deep voice.

"You've heard about our Wurro?"

"You've got to tell me, did that deputy of yours really steal a human heart from the morgue for a human sacrifice?"

"He *borrowed* it," said David, "and returned it promptly."

He turned the conversation around to the intended purpose of his visit. "I remember you mentioning at a staff meeting a few months ago that you were curious about some possible Industrial Zone schemes going on at the Economic Tower."

"Self-dealing, I'd say," Rosen said, leaning back in his chair, knitting his fingers behind his head. "Some of these guys have gotten very wealthy—bank accounts in Mexico. But there's no solid information here about where the money is coming from. We suspect the Zones because we can't really track the production. Some could be siphoned off by Tower functionaries, but it's just guessing at this point."

"Would an informant around Adam Ross be useful to us?" David always found phrasing these proposals in the first-person plural tended to work better.

"You've got one?" Steve now leaned forward.

"Remember that girl we rescued from the Earth Weekend?"

Steve nodded. "Yup."

"She's now working as a concierge at the Octavian, where Adam Ross lives. That wouldn't be particularly promising on its own, except he can't leave her alone. He keeps calling her up to his apartment. Apparently, the senior concierge is concerned that they 'meet Mr. Ross's needs,' as they call it. I think Ross pays him a finder's fee, or a pimping fee, if you prefer."

"Well, does she meet his needs? And are you saying that we could arrange a little trade here between them for some information? It seems she's already given up what she can."

"No," said David emphatically, "she hasn't. Once she had to knock him across a coffee table, but so far she's kept him honest." Steve frowned a little—he'd only glimpsed the girl during the Earth Weekend melee, but she hadn't seemed very glamorous. Of course, that crowd wasn't particularly appetizing, and in the land of the blind, the one-eyed man was king. Steve Rosen himself was married to a plain, but adorable woman, so he didn't speculate about David's reason for his love interest.

"Then why does she keep going up to his apartment?"

"The senior concierge is hopeful, and so is Ross, that eventually she will see the error of her ways. So he insists that she come upstairs at least once a week, in the middle of the night."

"Harris, what's your connection to this girl? Are you dating her?"

"Yes, since you ask. That's one reason why Ross isn't getting anywhere. I've had to train a Plore actor I know to pretend to be her boyfriend, since I can't show up at the Octavian myself if we are going to take a professional interest in Ross."

"Steve, would you be interested in running her as a joint informant?"

"What's the KCU's stake here?" Steve was blunt. "I mean, I'll take your money, but I'm not sure why this is a KCU affair."

David looked up at the ceiling, then down at Steve's tilted, curious face. "Just because she's my affair, I suppose. She would have never thought to help us if it weren't for me, and she wouldn't do it otherwise. She's a complete novice, and I want to make sure she stays safe and motivated throughout. I'm happy to lend you analysts if you want extra support.

"And Adam Ross is a complete asshole, and I would be very pleased to welcome him to Beaufort someday, on legitimate grounds."

"Well, there we go!" Steve laughed. "Thanks for your honesty, Harris. Yes, I'll take you up on your offer, including a few analysts. Let me tell you what I think is going on with Ross and his cronies, and the analysts can come up with some questions and topics for your girlfriend. First, tell me a little more about her so we can get her file started." And that was how it all began with Malia and the ADF, at least officially.

That Saturday night was Beltane. The pagan fertility holiday that in ancient days had traditionally been celebrated midway between spring and summer had been conjoined with Midsummer for convenience. Malia was glad to be working that night. In past years, after losing Isabelle, Malia had twice gone to the Beltane celebration in the Botanical Garden, once at Fern's urging, and once just drawn to the fires out of boredom and loneliness. In neither case could she remember years later with whom she had partnered. With no Social Credit points to be gained, Malia saw little point and no pleasure in the adventure.

A stream of younger Octavian residents were clearly heading to the festivities, judging by their dress and general silliness. "Have a good time, amba-sah! amba-mam!" she repeated, at least two dozen times. A few older couples also headed in that direction, more tentatively. It was one way to spice up a long marriage, if only once a year.

Mxti Rex came downstairs with a video game they wanted Malia to play. Jorge let Mxti Rex come behind the counter so Malia could still be attentive to residents while playing the game with them. Another product of the Knowledge Tower, this game involved intercepting fascists who were attempting to sneak over the border from the United States and wreak havoc on the City. It was called, "Save Our City." This is definitely better than the "All Gender Victory" game, thought Malia, but distracted, she eventually lost.

Around 12:20 am, Adam Ross entered with his arm around a slightly chubby thirtyish brunette, her mascara smeared. Both had had a little too much to drink, perhaps the historically authentic mead served in tankards at the festivities. After coupling, it was delightful to quaff mead and eat toasted nuts either with your friends or perhaps a new lover under the lanterns.

"Mr. Jorge, Melia," said Ross, deliberately dropping Ms. "Happy Beltane to both of you! I'm sorry you must tend our fire here, and not enjoy the festivity in the gardens."

"That is all right, amba-sah," said the domestically content Jorge. "We are happy to serve you here."

"Well, not everyone is happy to serve me," said Adam, giving Malia a quick, resentful look. "But here is Amba-mam Laura, who has been of great service this evening."

Amba-mam Laura giggled, tossing her mane of black curls. "Oh, Adam, you've been serving me, too! So many times!"

Adam circled Laura's waist with his arm and steered her to the elevator bank. "The festivities will continue upstairs. Good night, loyal servants!"

When the elevator door closed on them, Jorge turned to Malia. "You see, Amba-sah Ross does not need you to serve him. You are just throwing away a good opportunity."

"I could never do that to my boyfriend," Malia said.

"Boyfriend?" said Jorge. "Please show me his picture."

Malia turned on the armband and found the photographs of Dave that the ADF had just added to her camera roll. They were doctored to show him and Malia on a park bench; on a sofa with his arm around her; on a rowboat at a lake. "Hmmm," said Jorge, "he is a Plore, right?"

"Yes," said Malia huffily, as she had been coached to react. Keep the boyfriend, but always leave open the possibility you might exchange him for a Social Credit version. She was not trying to sever the relationship with Adam Ross. Just a little defensiveness would lead questioners to assume she was not completely committed to keeping the Plore boyfriend.

"Then he does not count," said Jorge. "You should do better. Amba-sah Ross will probably still take you if you apologize properly."

"Thanks for the advice, Jorge," replied Malia, and turned to counting the health club receipts. Fortunately, Adam Ross did not summon her to a post-Beltane threesome. In the morning, Tom/Dave made his appearance just before her quitting time. They had arranged for him to show up at the front entrance this time only, as if he did not yet realize Malia was required to leave from the side entrance. Otherwise, Jorge would probably not see him. Dave walked straight into the lobby, in front of Jorge's alarmed eyes, embraced Malia, and gave her a long passionate kiss. She bent backward pliantly.

Dave Mitchell was a nondescript but pleasant looking man in his mid-thirties with wavy, chestnut colored hair. He had just enough musculature to be convincing as a shovel man on an asphalt crew, but a deft makeup job would keep street facial recognition cameras from identifying him as Tom Peters, Plore actor, illegally roaming the City.

"I'm sorry, Jorge. This is my boyfriend, Dave Mitchell," she said.

"Hello, Dave," said Jorge. "Please, in future greet Melia by the side door," pointing in the general direction. "We do not allow Plores and deliverymen to use the front entrance."

"Oh, shoot, did I mess up?" said Dave. "I don't want to get my Melia in trouble here." He reached for her hand and squeezed it while smiling.

"Oh, Dave, I'm so happy to see you. See you Wednesday, Jorge." They exited hand-in-hand, a conscious skip in Malia's otherwise tired walk. She was confident that Jorge would give Ross a description of the boyfriend.

They strolled out the side door together and walked a few blocks to where the black Antifan car, which looked plausibly like a self-driving car, was waiting for them. It would drop Dave off at the Memorial Bridge tunnel and then shoot up Rock Creek Parkway to the Avalon. "Good morning, miss," said the Sunday driver, Charlie. She and Dave discussed the arrangements for next Thursday morning, when Dave would greet her dressed in his putative work uniform.

At the Avalon, she entered the apartment, and smiled to see David sound asleep with Frida and Ansel also snuggling on the bed. The cats greeted her, meowing for breakfast. She fed them the high-grade Social Credit cat pate, and took advantage of their distraction to replace them in the bed while they ate, enjoying the warm spot they had created through their soft catness. "Welcome home, beautiful," said David, turning over and falling back to sleep, which was fine by her, too. Soon they were both sound asleep in the morning light.

Chapter 35
Lessons
(Wednesday-Saturday, 6-9 July)

When Malia arrived at 6 pm, Belinda and Leighton were still at work. Mxti Rex let her in, overjoyed to see her. Malia noticed that the purple and green streaks in their hair were growing out. Mxti Rex heated up a mini-veggie lasagna and gave Malia vanilla wafers and a cup of tea, and they settled themselves at the kitchen table. They each scrolled down on their workscreens to "Diversity Literature Review, 8th grade." Last week they had soldiered through the outline of the classic Diversity play, *Kofi Komes To Amerikka*.

This week, Malia, impatient with the play's sheer awfulness, decided she would give Mxti Rex a cheat sheet for how all such children's literature worked. She knew this well from her own college class in Children's Literature Management. One was supposed to determine the suitability of a children's play or storybook by applying this framework. Why make Mxti Rex figure this out on their own? It was much more interesting to analyze what the authorities wanted you to know, category by category, and then Mxti Rex would be amply prepared for the makeup exam in September.

"Look at this," said Malia, drawing a table. "Here are six categories—subject, intersectional background, diversity challenge, adversary, key to solution, moral. This is really all the teachers want you to know. Then you just have to remember two or three anecdotes from the story to illustrate them. That's all you need to regurgitate. We'll go through all the books you read this year in Diversity Literature and see how they fit into all the boxes. Let's start with Kofi."

Mxti Rex frowned at the screen, fiddling with the straps on her child's armband. "Let's see. He's from Ethiopia, which is a country in Africa, so he is African-American. And he decides he is gay after he meets the nice man in the bodega, Juan, who shows him the magazines."

"Very good," said Malia. "What is his diversity challenge?"

"His mother is a Christian and disapproves of Kofi's gayness. Also she is a single mother and loses her job because her employer tries to make her sleep with him and she refuses."

"Is that part about his mother's job Kofi's diversity challenge, or is that something else? Is the employer the adversary?"

"Not for Kofi," agreed Mxti Rex. "What about the teacher who is the secret white supremacist?"

"Yes, that's the main adversary. Do you have some examples that you can give to show he is Kofi's main adversary and how he tries to keep Kofi down? The employer is the mother's adversary, by the way, but I can see how you might think the employer is Kofi's problem, too."

Mxti Rex listed a few examples, and Malia nodded approvingly. "Very good. And what's the correct Diversity solution here?"

"Is that when the gay teacher saves Kofi's mother's life by donating a kidney and the mother repents of her wickedness and accepts Kofi's sexual orientation?"

"Yes. Notice the use of the dramatic altruistic gesture to win over the opponent. You see that a lot in Diversity literature. But what is the solution to the white supremacist?"

"The Antifans invade the school during the Diversity War, and torture and kill the supremacist. And then Kofi joins the Antifans. And his mother becomes a priestess in the MED Church."

"What's the moral?"

Mxti Rex said triumphantly, "Love conquers all. One should not put one kind of love before another, although gayness is better than straightness because it is less likely to lead to overpopulation that stresses the earth. Also, Christian faith is opposed to Gender Awareness unless within the MED church."

"Perfect," said Malia, secretly wincing. "Let's try this framework with the other books." Mxti Rex caught on quickly, and Malia was pleased. This was a much more analytic and enjoyable way to approach the subject matter. They moved onto the math lesson. Soon it was nearly 9 pm and Malia excused herself to go downstairs to the lobby, via the back stairs of course.

"That was almost fun, Melia!" said Mxti Rex.

"That's as much fun as we can have without actually having fun," Malia deadpanned back at them.

"Melia, will you come to my birthday party on Sunday? I'm going to be fifteen on Monday. Then I get my grownup armband!" The armband issued at fifteen to all Social Credit citizens was capable of all the required surveillance functions.

"It's a big birthday," agreed Malia. "Please check with your—parents—and make sure it's all right with them. And would you text me the details, please, so I know when to arrive?"

"I will, but I'm sure it will be fine with them. We're going to be in the party room." The party room was on the rooftop patio. Malia had often signed in various deejays and catering help hired for weekend evening parties. "Can you bring your boyfriend?"

"Oh, I don't know if he would want to come. He's a Plore and he might be uncomfortable with all these Social Credit people," Malia hesitated.

"I would like to meet some real Plores," insisted Mxti Rex. "It's not fair how we're kept so separate. That's how you have misunderstandings." Rex didn't know that Tom would be breaking the law by visiting the City if he were not actually at work. But of course, neither did they know that were the police to arrest him, the ADF would have him freed in half an hour.

"Look, ask your parents," said Malia as she slipped out the door, wishing she could hug her child. "If they specifically invite him, I'll ask him to come. But I can't make him come if he doesn't want to. Thanks for the invitation either way!"

Adam called for her on Friday night sometime after 2 am. Possibly because of her new jujitsu training, she went upstairs with more confidence than before. Or possibly it was Adam's unslakable interest in bedding her that gave her confidence, as it might any woman not accustomed to male attention. When she entered the apartment, she noticed his stubble had become a genuine if short beard—dark with some flecks of gray. It was not unattractive—he resembled some second-century Roman emperor, hopefully, but not likely, one of the more enlightened ones before the empire fell to pieces.

"Are we going to play the question game again?" she asked brightly after she had settled onto the sofa. Last time they had played the question game she had asked earnest and plausible questions about the DJR economy and its trade relations with China and Russia. The ECU analysts had given her an innocuous list aimed at establishing her interest and credentials. Adam had asked her about her childhood and her first sexual experience, which had happened at the orphanage with an older Plore workman. "You seem to like Plores a lot," he commented, to which she had retorted, "because they behave like gentlemen."

"No," he said. "It got boring last time. If I wanted to recite a lot of economic statistics, I could just stay at work. Also, I'm getting tired of talking."

"Well, amba-sah," she replied sweetly, "I'm not ready for the alternative."

"Let's listen to some music," he said abruptly, reaching for his armband and selecting some instrumental music clearly aimed at romance. He stared directly at her, so that her eyes dropped. The dulcet sounds swirled around them.

"What happened to Amba-mam Laura from Beltane night?" she asked.

"Just a Beltane fling," he said. "Her husband came home from his business trip."

"Look, why are you so interested in the economic stuff anyway? It's pretty dry. I don't see a lot of women who care about this, honestly. It makes you less attractive, if you want my opinion."

"Well, that's some protection," she said tartly, at which he laughed.

"Not much protection." He went to mix her another drink, but didn't remember to ask her to watch. Malia assumed he had just forgotten or he felt he had proven his integrity in this matter.

She sipped from the glass. It tasted all right.

"I want you to take off your blouse," said Adam. "I won't touch you. I just want to see what you look like when you're not covered up like a Christian nun."

Malia said, "If you pop by Mxti Rex's birthday party tomorrow afternoon on the roof, you'll see me wearing normal summer clothes. And you can meet my boyfriend Dave."

"Really? That sounds like quite a wild party," said Adam, but he was genuinely curious about this boyfriend. The child was a horror show, in his considered opinion, and he thought Malia a fool to be tutoring her for next to nothing. Some aspiring economist. He paused, "Are you really interested in economics? You're not pretending to be in order to flatter me, are you? No, I see you do have some intellectual interest in the matter. That's rather pathetic. Well, my interest in economics was mostly to become rich, and I have succeeded."

"But you don't earn any more than someone who works in the Knowledge or the Social Tower at your grade level, do you? I don't understand how you could become rich. I mean, we're all investing in the same fund. We're all living under socialism. How would you do it?"

"Sweetheart," drawled Adam, humoring this naïve female. "There's a lot you don't understand about economics. Maybe sometime I will reveal all to you, when I've gotten a little more satisfaction from you."

Malia smiled, remembering David's threat to bring Adam Ross to Beaufort someday, where he would indeed reveal all.

"I'm not sure what you think is so funny. Take off the blouse," he ordered her.

For some reason, this now seemed like a completely reasonable request, and she giddily unbuttoned the blue blouse, tossing it on the sofa. She was glad to be wearing one of her prettier lace bras, a recent purchase involving a heavy carbon offset. She thought David would probably grudgingly approve of her having conceded this much to Adam tonight.

"That's very pleasant to look at," said Adam. "You're bigger on top than I thought. But it looks a bit silly as long as you have that skirt on as well."

Her fingers hovered over the waist of the skirt before she recovered. "Well, I'll just put the blouse back on," she said. "It's really not decent to be sitting here like this."

"Just pretend I'm one of your Plore boyfriends. I bet you don't stand on such ceremony with them. Seriously, would it be any different from wearing a bikini on the beach?"

Malia pulled on the blouse and rebuttoned it with shaky fingers.

"I wouldn't know, amba-sah," she said haughtily, "because my meager Social Credit doesn't permit me to take a beach vacation. I qualify for Earth Weekends and maybe a bus trip to Philadelphia. It would be nice to have a beach vacation someday."

"Really!" said Adam, with mock concern. "If all you want is a vacation, I'd be happy to take you on one. The beach, you say?" If he heard her mention the Earth Weekend, he gave no indication of it, let alone asking how she had escaped the roundup. Perhaps it had been tactless of her to have mentioned Earth Weekend in front of the man who had most likely organized the roundup of the attendees.

Suddenly waves of nausea overcame her and she vomited, while summoning the presence of mind to spew mostly over the coffee table and not her skirt. She began to cry. Adam was quick to bring towels and a glass of water, but didn't seem particularly alarmed. She wiped her face with the towels, and lifted the glass to drink, but then put it down, warily.

"What did you put in that drink?" she hissed at him.

"Just a little bit stronger than usual," he said cheerfully, "but not calibrated quite properly, I'm afraid. Chemistry was not my best subject at Justice. Better luck next time. Would you mind cleaning my coffee table?" He handed her a clean towel, which she threw back at him.

This time she grabbed her jacket and her shoes, and stalked out into the hallway. Her throat was raw. Jorge tsked sadly when he saw the stained skirt, and said, "Please try to stay behind the counter for the rest of the shift."

Sorry, Jorge, no tip for you tonight either, she thought grimly.

David dropped her off shortly before 4 pm a few blocks from the Octavian. In a bittersweet decision, he had recently traded in the sportscar for a beige sedan. "Too conspicuous," he said sadly, "especially now. Or I am getting old and decrepit." Malia was holding her gift for Mxti Rex, a backgammon set wrapped in cheerful balloon paper. Diversity Warehouse had delivered it, with the paper and a card, yesterday afternoon, in about an hour. It seemed an appropriate present from a tutor. She had insisted on wrapping it herself, while David watched bemusedly. "They would have done it for you, you know," he said, to which she responded, "I've missed out on a lot of her birthdays. This is a pleasure." She signed the card, "Affectionately, Melia."

Tom was waiting for her on the corner. He was wearing a plausible Plore-goes-to-a-Social-Credit function outfit—slacks in a shade of blue a touch lighter than fashionable, a light plaid button-down shirt with short sleeves, and a tan jacket. He wore cloth sneakers. "I want you to know that I would not normally wear this combination," he said. "I am downgrading my fashion sense for this assignment." Once the car was safely gone, he gave her a kiss and put his arm around her as they headed toward the Octavian. It was one thing to be believable as a couple and another to antagonize David. Malia wore a yellow sundress; she hated herself for thinking about it, but Adam Ross might see her and it was a flattering color.

"Too bad about the sportscar," he said to Malia. "It was famous on the streets of Ploreville."

To avoid complications with the front desk staff, they took the staff elevator to the roof. An electronic sign flashed, "Happy 15th Birthday Rex." Round tables with white tablecloths were scattered around with teak eco-chairs. About thirty guests, mostly adults, were already milling around, but Malia was pleased to see several of Rex's peers sitting in a circle with her in the corner. A bartender was mixing drinks and several workers were setting up long buffet tables. "See, my people," said Tom, nudging her discreetly.

"Let me introduce you to the guest of honor," said Malia, leading him over to Rex and their friends. She was confident Tom did not know about her true relationship with the girl. "She wanted to meet you. I apologize in advance if she says something odd. She seems to think she needs to meet more Plores for mutual understanding."

"Uh-oh," said Tom amiably, but agreed to be steered in that direction.

Mxti Rex and about five girlfriends were together, mostly toying quietly with their armbands, occasionally tapping the arm of another to show her an amusing video. When Mxti Rex saw them, they jumped up and ran over, giving Malia a hug. "Happy birthday, Mxti Rex," said Malia, handing them the gift, for which Mxti Rex thanked her and placed next to their chair.

"Is this Dave?" Mxti Rex asked excitedly. "Hi Dave! I'm so glad to meet you." The girls looked at him skeptically, the eyes trailing down from the mussed hair to the cloth sneakers. "I'm glad you were able to come in from Ploreville for my party." The girls started whispering to each other. Malia wished she could slap them.

"Miss Rex, it's an honor," said Tom. "Thanks for inviting us. I wish you a very happy birthday."

Belinda and Leighton glided toward them. Malia introduced them to Tom, knowing they would almost certainly use the episode as fodder for a running narrative of, "Of course we have nothing against Plores. We even invited some to Rex's birthday party. Well, one, but we think he was very representative."

Leighton said to Tom, "I don't know what we would have done without Melia here. She's been tutoring our dauson for the last month and Rex has really started showing an interest in their schoolwork."

And so much better behaved too, thought Belinda.

Belinda said to Malia, "Would you be interested in coming to the shore with us next month? We'd go away for three weeks. All you'd have to do would be hang out with Rex, and we'd pay you whatever your salary is here." She paused. "Then there wouldn't be an interruption in Rex's tutoring. You've been a goddess-send!"

Mxti Rex squealed, "Melia, I hope you can come! That would be so great."

Tom thought, they think they can do anything and disrupt people's lives if they're paid for it. But I guess that's pretty much a fair assessment, isn't it? After all, I wouldn't be here if David weren't paying me.

"Thank you for the invitation, amba-mam," said Malia in a dignified manner. "I'll have to check with the building management," and she caught herself, "and with Dave here." She looked up at him appealingly, and he smiled down at her fondly.

"I'm sorry we wouldn't be able to bring you, too," said Belinda quickly.

"No, ma'am, I understand completely. Summer's the big season for our road repairs anyway. My crew chief would be pretty upset if I suddenly disappeared on him! You wouldn't want your car to fall into a pothole because I spent several weeks at the beach." Everyone chuckled with relief, and the hosts wafted away.

"Oh, Melia, could you come? Dave, you wouldn't make her stay here, would you? It would be so much fun. We would spend all afternoon on the beach and then go into town and get ice cream at night. My dad barbecues too."

"I'll think about it, Mxti Rex, promise." Seriously, Malia thought, that does sound good. David wouldn't object to a few weeks of mother-daughter bonding at the beach, would he? If anything, it was a coup. And personally, she knew that the Outer Banks would normally have been off limits to her, with its 175 Social Credit requirement to keep the crowds away.

She looked up to see Adam Ross walking out onto the patio, but he didn't see her, at least not initially. He presented a gift-wrapped box to the Andrewses, introducing himself, apologizing for the intrusion, and explaining that he lived in the building and spent many evenings playing games with Rex in the lobby. "Rex is so delightful. When I heard it was their birthday," Adam said, "I had to pay my respects. I apologize for my rudeness, but I won't stay long, I promise."

"Not at all!" said Leighton. "I'm sorry we didn't realize that you already knew our dauson, or we would have invited you specially. Please stay as long as you like!"

Adam sauntered over to Malia and Tom. "Hello, Melia. Is this the boyfriend I hear so much about?"

She had warned Tom about Adam, and the Plore actor had asked, "You don't think I'll have to fight him, do you? My persona really is more aw-shucks than fisticuffs."

Malia had said, "He claims to know how to break necks from his Antifan days, and I don't think he was referring to chickens. I'd do the deferential Plore thing."

Malia pretended surprise at seeing him. "Hello, amba-sah. This is Dave Mitchell."

"Adam Ross, 200," Adam said, offering an unduly firm handshake. "I'm at the Economic Tower."

"Nice to meet you, sir," said Tom. "I'm on the asphalt crew that's been paving most of the downtown streets this summer. I'm the assistant crew chief," he added proudly.

"Well, that's very nice," said Adam. "I don't know what we'd do without our streets, especially since we can't all ride around on drones quite yet. Do they pay well?"

"Yes, sir," Tom responded. "I mean, not bad for manual labor, although you've got to have people skills around the crew too, of course. I'm trying to save up money so maybe Melia and I could buy a house at some point."

She won't be allowed to marry you, Adam thought, not unless she goes Plore, and who in their right mind would do that? "You gave her a lovely diamond ring," he said.

"Yes, that was my grandma's. She was wearing it when they brought her here from

Kentucky. Good thing they didn't steal it from her along the way." Tom could not resist the risky dig at the Antifans, which was slightly out of character, but he guarded his voice so that he sounded almost cheerful at the lucky break at keeping the ring rather than resentful at the thieves.

The guests were called to the lavish buffet, and Adam made sure to sit with some other residents from the building, whether to underscore his superior social status, or as an intermission between approaches to Malia and Tom. Malia and Tom sat with an elderly male couple from the building— "retired from the Knowledge Tower" they said proudly—who did not seem to recognize Malia as the night concierge even though she knew them. When she told them, they seemed taken aback. "Well, you are certainly out of context!" She explained how she had been tutoring Rex, and they nodded, but she had the distinct impression they considered themselves to have made an impolitic choice in sitting with her.

Adam came over and politely asked Tom if he wouldn't mind stepping aside to chat for a few minutes. Malia watched them head toward the edge of the roof, grateful that a ledge encircled it and that Tom could probably fend off any efforts to push him over the side. She watched Adam put his arm around Tom's shoulders as they approached the edge of the patio.

She turned back to the elderly couple. "If the tenant in 403 is causing difficulties with the late night parties, we could do something about that. But you would have to file a complaint."

"Oh, no," said the older of the two men, "we wouldn't want to complain about an African-American resident. It would be politically incorrect."

"Please let us know, amba-sehm, if you change your mind," she said, using the polite plural.

Tom came back, looking somewhat amused and aghast at the same time. "Later," he said.

Out in the street finally (she was not working that night), he said, "He offered me a thousand dollars if I would let you go on a vacation with him. Can you believe that?"

"I think Amba-sah Ross assumes that everyone can be bought, especially people like us," Malia said. "Did you take it?"

"I'm going to ask David," said Tom. "You know money's always tight for our folks. I decided not to be offended. By the way, do you know how much that girl resembles you?"

"Really?" said Malia, both pleased and alarmed.

"Well, maybe it's just me," Tom said, "but if you don't want others to notice, you might want to use a little light disguise in these situations."

David pulled alongside of them in the sedan, looking slightly gloomy. "It's just not as much fun as the DragonFire. I feel like a dad."

They went to a bare-bones Chinese restaurant open to all in a dingier neighborhood of the City near the Social Tower. With his reinvestigation underway and not going so smoothly, David was limiting his excursions to Ploreville, although its Chinese restaurants were better. A blonde Plore girl took their order. Actual ethnic Chinese waitstaff were reserved for the higher-end establishments, if you could find any Chinese-Diversans willing to serve customers instead of work in a Tower. But it was relatively safe here. David switched on the noise cylinder, as well as the recording device, and they reported their findings. The waitress brought egg rolls, kung pao chicken, and sautéed gai lan with noodles. "This is practically a Plore place," said David approvingly, as they tucked in. "No concerns with cultural appropriation here."

"Beach with the Andrews family—yes, absolutely," he said. "They are top level, and you can learn a lot in two weeks hanging around them about Knowledge Tower people. We'll bring in your predecessor to staff the desk in the meantime." He wasn't going to mention the Mxti Rex recovery angle around Tom, who might be highly reliable, but in the end you never knew whom else he might be working for.

David looked grimmer as he contemplated Adam Ross's offer, which he would normally have celebrated as an operational advance. On one hand, Ross might well reveal what the ADF was looking for, or at least some of it, if he were less guarded on a holiday break with Malia. On the other hand, Malia wouldn't be able to keep resisting Ross's advances if he were treating her to a vacation and they were presumably sharing a bed. He certainly would not hold back if he were in Ross's position. His face clouded, which troubled Malia, who had already run through these complications in her head. "Tom, take the money from Ross; it's well earned. We'll figure out how to handle the vacation."

Tom shared some of the tidbits he'd picked up while standing at the bar or when several women had flirted with him, even in proximity to their husbands. He made sure to have gotten their names and Social Credit numbers. "They all seem eager to sleep with a Plore," he said ruefully. "They seem to have some idea that we have incredible sexual prowess."

"Well, isn't that true?" smiled David, who exchanged a quick glance with Malia. She was relieved he seemed to be cheering up again. "And Tom, that's with your wearing that godawful plaid outfit."

"Amazing, huh?"

PART THREE
THE ZONE

Chapter 36
Invitation to the Zone
(Sunday/Monday, 10-11 July)

They slept late, then nestled in bed. David drew the bedcurtains back so the daylight streamed in and he could track the Sunday news shows. "Lies or not," he said, "it tells you what the Knowledge Tower is thinking." They sat up against the dark plush bolster, and he pressed the command on the signaler that brought the smaller screen down in front of the bed for more convenient viewing.

To their surprise, on this sleepy midsummer morning, Todd Charles was finally delivering on the promised special on the Anacosta Industrial Zone, including the camp they had viewed from afar that day in the Massanutten. Wearing a baseball cap and a jaunty camouflage jacket, to show his unity with the wilderness, Charles intoned into the camera, "Today we will report on the amazing socialist Industrial Zone that produces 80 percent of all of Anacosta's manufactures, and half of the climate-appropriate produce consumed in the Anacosta region. Camp Number Four achieved record production growth rates last year and is on track for double-digit growth rates again. I am speaking with Barry Mattison, the Commander of Camp Number Four, 180 miles southwest of the City of Anacosta." Barry Mattison was a short, broad man in his mid-forties with a receding hairline. He was wearing the brown uniform of the Economic Strike Force that ran the camps.

"He's a commander too?" Malia asked. "Of what?"

"Thousands and thousands of slaves," said David irritably. He clearly didn't think much of that kind of commander. "Fields and factories."

"Commander Mattison, Camp Number Four has seen tremendous production levels this year. To what do you attribute it?"

"Todd, in the fields we have been using a new fertilizer developed in our own factories that has yielded remarkable results. We are growing larger apples and grapes than ever, with no loss in taste. In the factories, we are working 24-hour shifts. Under socialism, we don't need to prioritize automation, which leaves people without meaningful work."

"Effing can't afford the computerized machinery," snarled David.

"Commander, tell us about what the people bring to the process. How does the spirit of Diversity improve the workings of Camp Four?"

"Todd, everyone in Camp Four realizes that their work makes the DJR stronger and better able to fight our enemies in the United States. Our work force includes all genders, races, and sexual orientations, guided by our shared faith in Diversity. We have services each Sunday in which all our workers joyously participate. We do not tolerate intolerant views, and remove such workers from the camp before they can taint our Diverse progress."

David and Malia gave each other a worried look. "Not sent home, I imagine," Malia said.

Todd said, "And now we are privileged to speak with some of those workers. Here are Mollie and Jim, who arrived in late April. Mollie works in the fruit orchards, and Jim works in the plastics factory. Would you both tell us what labor in a Diversity environment means to you?"

"How much do you want to bet they're local Plores?" said David, as much to Todd Charles as to Malia. "Or ESF officers?" Indeed, they both looked ruddy, healthy, and most significantly, untroubled. Local Plores could work in the Zone as paid employees, as David's brother did, but labored separately in the fields and factories from the Social Crediteers.

Todd Charles then returned to tell the audience that Economic Zones, soon to be renamed Economic Strike Zones to underscore their frontline role in fighting fascism, were also increasingly becoming hotbeds of scientific research. "Labs at Camp Four are engaged in chemical research with important dual-use defense medical implications," he said vaguely, before signing off. "Come learn a new scientific skill at the Zone's vocational training centers. All citizens are urged to volunteer at your local Economic Service office!"

"Now that," said David, "I'd like to know more about. Without volunteering." His phone rang. He rolled over and picked up on audio. "Hi, Steve. Yes, I saw that too." A few seconds of silence. "Yes, I see what you meant. Ten o'clock tomorrow in your spaces? See you then."

"What was that about?" asked Malia.

"Something I'd like to find out from your friend Adam Ross," said David. "But not today." He leapt out of bed. "Let's get those pancakes going." Malia's pancakes were a valiant effort, but invariably lumpy; he preferred his own. Later they would head out to Ploreville. Malia liked to curl up with one of his mother's devotionals if they didn't attend church; he was pleased to see that. Pastor Denman had baptized her, secretly, soberly, in his basement over a sink of water the weekend after the service she had attended with him. Two weeks ago, he could congratulate himself on having brought her to a safe place and supplied her with ample cheese for herself, and kibbles for the cats. But now he was beginning to worry that maybe he should have left her alone in the Depository, for her own sake if not his.

On Monday morning, after the Wurro worship, David began the 8:30 meeting. He reminded the group that thanks to the work of the KCU, the ADF had regained the momentum against the Knowledge Tower. "Eighty faculty members and staff have been interrogated here since April," he noted, "Twenty-one still in the building, 57 at various hospitals still available if necessary." The late MacMillan and Leonard brought the total to eighty, but David did not mention them.

David continued, "We are tracing the path taken by illegal books from the Anacosta recycling plants to several different university communities—a shout out to Sergeant Yardley for her great leadership on this front." Candiss waved modestly at the group.

"The Knowledge Tower is under pressure to close the Depository permanently, so these books will never again see the light of day, at least not in the DJR. The lack of control exercised by twhe Knowledge Tower over our universities was made clear. The bombing of the parade showed everyone that the country relies on the ADF for our security. We have produced a group—the George Washington Brigade—that we say committed the bombing, and we have punished the perpetrators."

Anacosta elites might mutter that the Brigade was fictional, but how would they prove a negative? The ADF had actually broadcast a purported confession from the ringleader, whom ADF insiders might have recognized as one of the Infotech staff members if they were perceptive at recognizing faces behind heavy makeup, including a skillfully applied black eye. Avadaughter now knew that Victor Ferraro intended to stay in place.

Normally, the room would have exploded in cheers, but David's tone was subdued and somber. The enemy he alone saw approaching was more daunting than the chastened Knowledge Tower. Would that he could vanquish the Economic Tower as easily as they had dispatched the George Washington Brigade.

The interrogations would continue because the self-satisfied elites of the DJR's universities provided a steady stream of offenses, mostly verbal, against the very apparatus that sustained them in comfort. Academics were now vying with each other to inform on their colleagues lest those colleagues attack them first, just as David and Walters had predicted. David would be visiting California at the end of the month to confer with Beaufort West, in Los Angeles, as their counterparts began their own investigations. Confucian University, Jerry Brown University, Angela Davis University, Hemp University, we are coming for you, thought David.

David signed several more release forms, briefly wondering how Kendra Pinckney was faring. He drank several cups of coffee. Vanessa came in to run over some details for his trip next week with the investigation review committee to Antifan Camp Six. Before he knew it, it was nearly 10 am and time to head up to the ECU.

David wished the secretary a polite good morning as he walked into Steve's office. He and Steve exchanged crisp salutes, and then sat down. Steve leaned forward, his body language tighter than it had been last week.

"That was an interesting segment yesterday," Steve began. "The closest thing I've heard in public channels to what we've been suspecting about laboratories. I mean, laboratories doing defense-related chemical research. At a bare-bones worker camp that you wouldn't think could handle anything more sophisticated than food processing." The Economic Tower, which had responsibility for higher science, and the ADF, with responsibility for defense, jointly ran research and testing institutes for conventional defense in remote areas of Southern California and upstate New York. Whatever was happening at Camp Four was going on purely under Economic Tower auspices.

"Why did they come out and say it?" David asked. "Wouldn't you think they'd want to keep this a secret?"

"Maybe they're close to achieving whatever they plan to achieve. I mean, overall, I figure this is aimed at the US, and announcing it now might be a warning to St. Louis"—the US capital— "to step back from its aggression." That was the most hopeful view, an outcome that any loyal DJR citizen would view with pride.

Rosen then said, "But the Director called Pernella Smith yesterday to ask what this was all about." Pernella Smith, 360, was the Economic Tower chief, a fiftyish PhD in international economics and Knowledge Management from Confucian University in Say Francisco. A tall elegant African-American woman with a stately hair bun, Smith spoke fluent Chinese and favored colorful silk scarves that trailed behind her as she marched quickly down a hallway. She was rumored to be the lover of Chinese President Shang Chang-lin.

"Smith told him it was none of our business."

David stared, openmouthed. Rarely had anyone told the ADF something was not its business, since ultimately, everything tended to be, and it was prudent for others to make the assumption earlier rather than later. Not to mention, if this project were truly aimed at national defense against the US, it certainly would have been relevant to the ADF mission.

"Yeah, we'll be meeting with the Director at 2 pm this afternoon. You probably ought to come along, since you've got a stake in the game. I think he's actually forgotten about the Knowledge Tower, at least for today.

"So, Harris, I want to suggest a small change here. We know Adam Ross is a vulnerability in the Econ Tower defenses. Your girlfriend's job has positioned her to extract the kind of information we need from him. But she's hit a brick wall, I think, if she's not willing to move forward. Can I suggest we—the ECU—move one of our female informants into that assignment? I promise we'll find something just as good if not better for your girlfriend in another building."

"She can't leave the Octavian," David said flatly. Rosen's eyebrows rose.

"And," David continued, "I would object to the notion she's not positioned to extract that info. In some ways, by not giving into his pressure this soon, she's kept him engaged. I'm not sure that interest would still be there a week after she slept with him. She's also convinced him that she's interested in economics because of her alleged Warehouse job, so it's plausible she could ask him questions. If your female informant also starts asking, it will be suspicious—he has young women pegged as not interested in economics. That's too many young women concierges asking him about economics."

"Okay," said Steve, digesting this.

"And hear this," David said triumphantly. "Last night he asked her to travel to the Zone with him. He's going to a big meeting there a week from Friday." He had already arranged for Malia's predecessor to take her shifts for her. The woman was now working a sleepy overnight shift at a loading dock of Antifan interest and was happy to fill in at the Octavian.

"Oh wow," breathed Steve, now truly impressed.

"He first asked her to go to the beach with him, but she's already going to the Outer Banks with the Andrewses from the Knowledge Tower, to tutor their daughter. So when that failed, he offered the Industrial Zone. Not glamorous, but pretty views, and apparently a guesthouse that accommodates senior Economic Tower personnel."

"You realize what he plans to do in that guesthouse, don't you?" Steve said, "He's not taking her there for a school trip."

"Yes," said David, looking down briefly.

"Look, Harris, I agree that your girlfriend is in the best position of anyone we've had so far to collect this information. I have sent in one informant and two officers, and I have lost them all. They all just disappeared. Their chip trails ended in the camps. I'm losing my appetite for losing my people. If you don't mind sending her, let's see what she can come back with—without taking too many chances. I'm thinking she'll at least come back.

"But I want to warn you: Ross is not an average guy who will take 'no' for an answer there. He'll be on his territory. Our psychologists say he is a psychopath who is willing to kill anyone who stands in his way. As you know, he learned how to kill during the war as an Antifan soldier. If your girlfriend breaks character, or spurns his advances in a place where she is completely at his mercy, I really don't want to contemplate what could happen. I don't think he's going to just pop her in the car and return her to the City. You understand?"

"Yes," said David dejectedly.

"Look, Harris, it's just sex, right? She's not a virgin, she can handle it. It will make Ross think he's in control, so maybe he'll say something out of sheer goodwill after winning the round in bed. Just be glad you'll likely get her back. For goodness sakes, don't be…so old-fashioned."

David grinned at him, finally. "You were about to say 'don't be such a Plore,' weren't you?"

"One and the same," admitted Steve, "not that it isn't a very fine trait in some ways.

So I assume she is going to go with Ross to the Zone?"

"Yes, she's definitely willing. She understands this is important. Of course, three months ago, she would never have dreamed of being mixed up in these things."

Steve grinned back. "It seems you have given her some of that Antifan spirit." As David rose to leave, Steve suddenly asked, "What did you mean by her not being able to leave the Octavian? Why couldn't she go to another building?"

David briefly considered lying, but he felt he could trust Steve Rosen, up to a point. The man's basic decency was his shining hallmark. "Her child lives there. The one they took away from her ten years ago. It gives my girlfriend comfort to see the child occasionally."

Steve sighed. Some people, not himself of course, just led very complicated lives. "Okay, Harris, your secret is safe with me. We owe your girlfriend something in return for her help. See you at two, upstairs." He wondered if the child in question was the Knowledge Tower daughter she'd be tutoring at the beach next month, but decided it really wasn't his business and he'd rather know less than more in this case. "My loyalty and my honor."

"Same to you, Steve."

The conference table in the Director's suite was full at 1:57 pm. The issue of Economic Tower malfeasance struck at many ADF portfolios.

David looked around the table. Rosen sat to his left, and Gary Garnett, the ADF commander in charge of joint defense efforts, sat across from him. Ferraro's deputy Valdivar Montoya, 300, sat at the Director's right. He also recognized Lefever, from ADF Camp Six; and Lefever's superior, General Derek Agostino, who commanded all the ADF units in the Mid-Atlantic. Robert Van Worden, FCU Commander, faced him slightly to the left. Relations with Van Worden had been a little strained since the FCU had been forced into more cramped quarters by the KCU expansion. Strictly speaking, David was junior to all these commanders, and KCU Senior Commander Alex Charlton should have represented the KCU. However, Alex had agreed that, as Rosen put it, David "had a stake in the game," and that KCU equities per se were not in question, so David could attend as long as he stuck to Malia's role in the operation.

Ferraro bustled in and took his seat at the head of the table. It was 2:01. The electronic door slid shut and "Top Secret C-Level" flashed from the electronic display, along with the times in today's selected locations: Anacosta, St. Louis, Beijing, Moscow, and London. "C-Level" meant that only unit commanders or their authorized deputies could participate.

"Sorry for being late, gentlemen…ma'am," as he noticed Gemma Carpenter, 315, the Commander of the CIU, or the Counterintelligence Unit. As a panracial lesbian who was a senior commander, she actually outranked Ferraro in Social Credit. Ferraro behaved cautiously around her, whether for that reason or for the radioactive

CI portfolio. Carpenter was one of the few at Beaufort with the authority to singlehandedly imprison any Antifan officer in the cellblock downstairs.

Rosen and Van Worden laid out the concerns about the Economic Tower that had emerged in recent weeks, and that had accelerated with the *Diversity Today* segment yesterday and Pernella Smith's brushoff of Ferraro. "Can you imagine?" fumed Ferraro. "We could arrest them all tomorrow, and this is what I hear to my face."

Until a few days ago, the ADF's main interest in Economic Tower malfeasance had been the rumors of self-dealing by Tower leadership. The FCU had identified six Mexican bank accounts belonging to named Tower leaders, with balances ranging from $1,300,000 to $25 million, USD. "And that counts for something," said Van Worden, reluctantly acknowledging the enduring strength of the US dollar. The Mexican economy had just exceeded the DJR economy in overall GDP, which DJR outlets had studiously ignored, but everyone at the table knew it was regarded as a good investment arena. However, it was illegal for DJR citizens to hold foreign bank accounts. So just based on the existence of the bank accounts, the ADF would have been within its rights to arrest all six of the leaders. But Van Worden said that the FCU was curious about where the money had originated—how were the Tower leaders acquiring their illicit fortunes? The accounts seemed to have started about two years ago, and most had rapidly expanded beyond what you would expect even from non-DJR investments.

Van Worden noted that one thing all the six leaders had in common was that they shared some oversight for the Economic Zones.

"How did we learn about these accounts in May?" asked Ferraro.

"The Mexican service brought it to our attention," said Van Worden, "when we arrested the head of the Oaxaca Jimenez cartel in Miami and extradited him to Mexico. So it was kind of in gratitude, like a thank you note. They just said, you guys might want to know, and pointed us in the right direction. Then we confirmed the existence of the accounts, even if we don't know which account is whose."

"Why didn't we just arrest all six of them immediately and get them to tell us how they got the money?" Ferraro asked impatiently. "And how they managed to open accounts in Mexico without our knowing? Is there a cutout they're using to transfer the funds?"

Van Worden puckered his lips. "We wanted to have more information before we started interrogations. You can't count on these guys ratting on each other, unless they think you know more than about the bank accounts."

Pretty sound, thought David, but Ferraro looked displeased. "I guess Pernella Smith isn't one of the six, is she?"

Van Worden said, "No, sir."

"Too bad," said Ferraro. "And none of them have any idea we are aware of their bank accounts?'"

"No, sir," said Van Worden. "We have not been in contact with anyone in the Econ Tower, yet."

Ferraro turned to Rosen, "So now we turn to the moneymaking opportunities in the Industrial Zones, which may or may not be connected to these secret laboratories there."

Rosen said, "Sir, under the principle that the usual solution is the most obvious one, until a week or two ago our operating assumption was that the six were profiting off of illicit sales to either US buyers or maybe Plore neighborhoods. You know, produce falling off a truck, or a shipment going missing. But we realized that shipments here or there wouldn't be fattening the accounts that much, not in only two years. We had started to wonder what else could be going on at these camps to allow for such steady enrichment.

"So when we saw that *Diversity Today* segment yesterday, we realized it might be a pointer to something more profitable going on in the Industrial Zones, or at least in Camp Four. Sir, may I show you the location of the camp?" Ferraro nodded, and Rosen brought it up on the screen. "On the left is Camp Four, near the abandoned town of McDowell, Virginia, in the Massanutten region. Our ADF base, number Six, is on the right. Commander Lefever is here with us."

Lefever saluted and said, "My loyalty and honor, sir."

Rosen said, "We estimate this camp has about 7,000 Social Credit workers, mostly brought in from Anacosta. I must warn you, sir, we have low confidence in these numbers."

"We picked up a few thousand at the Earth Weekend, if I remember," said Ferraro.

"Yes, sir, we assisted in the transfer. The Economic Strike Force carried out most of the actual apprehensions, but we stood by in case there was any significant resistance."

"Why do they need so many people? I don't understand why with these numbers, the Tower is always begging for more workers."

Rosen answered, "The conditions are extremely primitive, sir. Unheated barracks with wooden and metal bunkbeds. Food is very basic and not adequate for heavy labor. Both areas are at high elevation. Maybe three or four medics for the entire worker population, usually nurses and physician assistants caught up in the roundups. Doctors would have too high Social Credit to be forced to go. Workers labor six days a week for 12 hours, and six hours on Sunday. We suspect that the zones lose about 20 percent of their population each winter."

"Good Goddess, sounds like Adolf Hitler, or something," said Ferraro.

David thought, sickened, can I send Malia into this inferno?

Rosen inclined his head. "It is reminiscent of Nazi concentration camps, sir. I do not think they are deliberately murdering workers, but neglect and overwork take their toll."

"Really, it makes our cellblocks look pretty good, by comparison. Warm, dry, and regular meals. No work required." Ferraro mused. "I mean, until you get into a Red

Room, we're definitely superior." The group contemplated the comparison.

"So how are we going to find out what's going on here? Other than just dragging the six of them in here right now?"

Rosen cleared his throat, "Sir, I have sent in one informant and one officer to Camp Four in March and another officer in May. The chip trail disappeared completely within two weeks for all of them, leaving me with the unavoidable conclusion that all three were killed. And that was when we were investigating a much more mundane issue than we are now.

"We now have another informant, who works at the Octavian and has gotten to know Adam Ross, one of our six, very well."

"That's your librarian girlfriend, Commander Harris, if I remember correctly?" Ferraro asked.

"Yes, sir," said David, as others wondered why the Octavian employed a librarian.

"How are we so sure that Harris's librarian isn't going to disappear as well? She's not even a trained informant, let alone an Antifan officer." At Ferraro's words, David felt sick again.

"This is a different kind of infiltration, sir," said Rosen. "Adam Ross has invited her as his guest to Camp Four on the weekend of the 23rd."

"Ooo la lah," joked Ferraro, at which some attendees, even Gemma Carpenter, chuckled.

"There's going to be some high-level meeting between Adam Ross and some unspecified colleagues, who I gather are bringing spouses or girlfriends, so she won't be out of place," Rosen gamely persevered. "All she has to do is sit there and listen. We don't want her trying anything risky. We expect just by going to this gathering, she will pick up something useful."

"That sounds like a good start," said Ferraro. "That's very generous of you, Harris, sending her off with that lunatic Adam Ross."

David smiled weakly. "She wants to help, sir."

"If she pulls off something amazing, I'm inclined to make it easier for you to marry her," said Ferraro. Turning to the others, he noted, "Low Social Credit issues."

"Thank you, sir." Color returned to David's face. But they would marry on the other side of the border, he promised himself.

"The least we could do—if she returns alive from all this," Ferraro noted amiably.

Chapter 37
Go West, Antifans
(Tuesday/Wednesday, 19-20 July)

Very early on Tuesday morning, just after daybreak, David was shaving, wearing only a towel tied around his waist. A tan duffel bag lay unzipped on the sofa, awaiting a few last-minute toiletry items before his visit to Antifan Camp Six. Malia had cured him of the disgusting habit of shaving over the kitchen sink, so he was dutifully scraping his chin in the bathroom.

To his surprise, he saw her watching him from the doorway, wearing the babydoll nightgown. She rarely woke up on Mondays or Tuesdays, her days off, before he left the apartment for work. But of course he would be gone for several days at Camp Six, and when he returned on Friday, she would be gone to the Industrial Zone Camp Four, in the company of that bastard Adam Ross, and how they had gotten to this point was still a source of self-recrimination for David. She could have just fended off Adam Ross at the Octavian until he lost interest, had not he, David, the big Antifan commander, gone strutting to Steve Rosen with her findings. But how could one ignore the threat to the DJR from its own sworn functionaries? Which leaving Malia alone would effectively have done, unless one held to Ferraro's preferred—and not particularly effective—method of arresting and beating out confessions?

So goodbyes more meaningful than the typical weekday farewells needed to be said. And in David's case, he needed to rein in his trepidation lest it infect Malia. She also needed to be warned, however. He was still unsure whether she truly understood the risk she was taking.

"Good morning, sweetheart," he said to her reflection in the mirror. She was far more beautiful than she had been when they met in April, the result of greater confidence and more calories. Curves had softened her angular frame. Her brown ringlets were longer, tumbling beneath her shoulders, and she was using cosmetics to enhance her dark eyes—she hadn't been wearing makeup much at all in April. As she told him later, "Who would I have worn makeup for?" All of these changes had made her look less like a librarian, and more like, well, David thought, an Antifan spy. David could not blame Adam Ross for his interest in Malia, but it didn't mean he was going to just roll over and let him have her. Or maybe he was.

"Good morning, lover." She smiled at him.

He washed his hands free of the shaving cream, came over to her, and gave her an affectionate hug. She ran her arms around his waist and pulled him closer. Their lips met, and then he said, "Let's talk." He brought her over to the bed, and rather than push her down on it, which she had expected, they sat on the edge together and stared straight ahead.

"You're worried about me going to the Zone, aren't you?" she asked. She had started referring to the Economic Strike Zone as if it were a hot new nightclub.

"Yes, honestly," said David. "Remember, do nothing to attract attention. Do nothing beyond what Adam Ross's girlfriend would be expected to do. You must, must, stay in character. You will learn a lot just by sitting there quietly and listening. Let them think you're a nonentity. But for God's sake, don't be a hero, please.

"I don't trust Adam Ross," he said. "I think he's potentially very dangerous. In the Octavian, he's bad enough, but when he's in the Zone, he's on his own territory, which is lawless. He probably thinks he can do whatever he wants, and get away with it. Do you understand what I mean?" He did not want to use the word "psychopath" around her.

"I won't give him any reason to be angry with me," said Malia cheerfully.

"I don't suppose he's booking a separate room for you?" David said with some asperity.

"Oh, I see what you mean!"

Good Lord, girl, David thought.

"What should I do?"

"No jujitsu," said David. "No screaming. Nothing that would provoke him to be violent. Because I don't think he'd hesitate to physically hurt you if you stood in his way this time."

"So are you telling me that if he tries to seduce me, I should go along with it this time?"

Well, that's your price of admission, David sighed to himself. "I don't want you to be hurt," he said. "Whatever gets you back home safely, I'm all for." He could not bring himself to echo Steve Rosen's "it's only sex" line.

"Remember, stay in character," he repeated. "No heroics. No efforts to sneak around. If he even suspects you're a spy, he would probably just dump you among the workers. Your Social Credit number wouldn't stand out there at all. Nobody would believe your story, and if they did, they'd think you'd gotten what you deserved for lording it over them when you arrived with him. They can't revenge themselves on Ross, but they could take it out on you. Prisoners are vicious to each other.

"And that's if he doesn't just break your neck outright." David still felt Malia was being slightly cavalier, and wanted to instill some caution in her.

"But if he killed me, wouldn't the police come looking for him?"

A lot of good that would do you, he thought. "Honey, *I* would come looking for him and that would be the end of Adam Ross. But then I would be all alone. And your daughter would never be reunited with her mother, or even know she had met her again. And you would be dead, by the way. Wouldn't it be better just to play it safe and dumb?"

"Yes, I understand," she said. "I promise not to do anything rash."

"That's more like it," he said. "Do you realize we'll both be in the same neighborhood on Thursday night?"

"So you don't want me to call you to rescue me when Adam Ross attacks me on Thursday night?" Malia was being coy, but it hit a raw nerve. David knew he might well be just a few miles away but unable to help her at all. Angry, he turned away from her.

"I'm sorry," she said. "That was in bad taste."

He buttoned the light blue shirt, and pulled up and fastened the black cloth dress pants suitable for the inspection tour. Then he donned the slip-on leather shoes and the leather jacket. In the DJR, only Antifans enjoyed the privilege of legally wearing actual leather. Now fully dressed, he looked at her, unable to help softening at the sight of her, tearful and just a little fearful now. "It's only that I care for you so much," he said. "We are so happy, and I am afraid of losing it all.

"But" he said, "you gave me an idea. I'll call you from the office with a number code that you can use from your armband if you are truly in danger. It will ring in my Unit, and our night commander will relay it to the ADF post near you. But I can't promise that the rescue would come in time, and when the ADF shows up at the Zone camp demanding your release, it will tell the ESF who you really are, so only call it when there is nothing left to lose. It may be futile, but let's not leave you without any defense whatsoever."

They embraced for a good minute, before saying "I love you" and promising to talk the next two nights, provided the armband signals worked over the miles. Reception across the mountain range was iffy. But they would not talk on Thursday night.

By 10:15, the ADF inspection team was heading out of Anacosta in a chauffeured van, since the more remote roads were not reliably navigated by self-driving vehicles. The team consisted of David, Cyber Security Unit Deputy Commander Peter Zheng, SC 220 (bisexual Asian Healthy Eater) and Senior Commander Valerie Marzullo of the TCU (275; cis-woman Healthy Eater), who was the team leader. David didn't know Valerie very well, but she turned out to be a cheerful sort with an ironic sense of humor.

As the van rolled down 81, David stared at the abandoned fields in the Shenandoah Valley. The farmers had long ago been evicted. A crumpled silo here, a collapsed fence over there. At one point, he saw a lone horse grazing in a field and wondered whose it could be. On the right, billboards that once had advertised commercial products—so that businessmen could make profits and feed their families and pay workers so they could feed theirs--now blasted propaganda that suggested the loyalty of local populations was not taken for granted:

CELEBRATE CORONAVIRUS LIBERATION DAY

GET YOUR ANNUAL CHIP CHECK AT THE AUGUSTA COUNTY FAIR

NEW WOMEN AND NEW MEN ARE WOMEN AND MEN, REMEMBER UNDER PENALTY OF LAW

REPORT HATERS, a billboard sponsored by the Harrisonburg Police. A hotline number for hate reporting was below.

SOCIAL CREDITEERS ARE YOUR FRIENDS. TRUST THEM TO KNOW BEST!

TRY GAY SEX, IT'S EARTH FRIENDLIER! Profiles of a male couple and a female couple, each outlined in a heart shape, looking lovingly at each other.

They exited 81 at exit 256, just as he and Malia had done. The driver waved at the militiamen at the gatehouse, whom he seemed to know well, but otherwise there was no need to roll down windows; all three armbands signaled and confirmed the presence of high-level Antifan officers. David noted that for future reference. He recognized the abandoned village, but where he had instead taken the gravel road, the van continued on the winding paved road. After another twenty minutes, they came out on the fine paved highway that he and Malia had glimpsed from above. In another fifteen minutes they were arriving at the camp and dismounting from the van to be greeted by Commander Lefever himself.

"Welcome to ADF Camp Number Six," Lefever boomed, giving them a vigorous Antifan salute, which they all returned.

"Two hundred and twenty troops here," he regaled them as he escorted them to the guesthouse. "Plus twenty-two officers, including myself. The militiamen outside the camp are another three hundred. We've got this region locked down pretty well!"

We'll see, thought David. He deposited his duffel bag in a spare but clean room in the two-story guesthouse, freshened up, and met the others outside. He would call Daniel later and see if they could make the fishing expedition happen. Lefever then led the trio on a tour of the camp.

Back at the guesthouse before dinner, David called Daniel. From the one time he had visited the house, David could envision Daniel moving around the shabby one-room kitchen and parlor in the wooden frame structure that would be a shack had not Daniel been handy with tools. The bedroom was upstairs, in the attic. It was big enough for a solitary man who had lost his wife, Marie, to cancer a year ago. They had not had children.

Daniel was happy to hear from David. "We can go fishing on Friday afternoon. The trout and the rockbass are doing well in spite of the heat." They agreed to meet at the camp entrance on Friday at noon when the inspection tour officially ended. Daniel owned a small pickup, and would drop David off in Harrisonburg, "which is as far as they'll let me go, being a Plore." It was almost as if he no longer remembered that David, too, was a Plore, in sentiment if not in law. David would not allow himself to feel hurt, but it stung a little. From Harrisonburg, David could order a self-driving taxi to bring him back to Anacosta.

The next morning, Lefever's deputy, Herbert Collingswood, 220, a thirtyish African-American, took the team on a tour of the border fortifications. Collingswood looked vaguely familiar to David. Collingswood reminded David that he had been one of the young arrivals whom David had mentored ten years ago, steering him away from a suffocating desk-bound assignment, and in the direction of the military services. He said the change had suited him, but it was hard to find suitable spouse material "out here in the backwoods," so he was considering transferring back to Beaufort. Not an uncommon complaint.

They stood on a ridge overlooking two parallel barbed wire fences, both electrified. "Our goal is twofold," said Collingswood, pointing to the other side. "We keep them out," he said, and then pointed back toward the camp. "And we keep our people safe here." The camp also positioned artillery on the hills above the fence as an additional deterrent.

"How many times do you get intrusions from the fascists?" asked David. And then, "How many times do you apprehend Diversans trying to leave?"

"We don't see any attempts to infiltrate from the other side, sir," said Collingswood. "They know our defenses are good. As to the other half, about two years ago, we caught a family trying to sneak through the fences. They somehow got past the first one, since it was in the middle of the night and it didn't alert us. But then one of the children was blown up by the mines between the fences, and another was electrocuted at the fence. After that, they just waited for us to come pick them up before they lost any more of their children."

"That's a shame," said David. "Such foolishness." Everyone nodded, and he continued, "What kinds of overnight and weekend defenses do you have against escapees? Let's say a group trying to escape knew about the electrified fence and the mines—is that enough, or are we patrolling regularly as well?"

"Good question, sir," said Collingswood. "We have regular patrols along the fence, every 15 minutes on the hour, by jeep." He pointed to a lone jeep on the horizon alongside the fence to the south. "That's the day patrol, with a sergeant and two privates."

"And what about at 3 am, for example?"

"Then the patrols are on the half hour, sir, 3 am, 3:30, 4 am, etc., north to south and then back again. That's the time they start from the base, by the way. It would take them about 15 minutes to reach the point at which we are standing."

"And what kind of operations center do you maintain at that hour? If the patrol needs to communicate a problem to base, what kind of presence is awake back there?"

"Sir, we have a non-com and three privates monitoring the video camera feed along the fences 24/7. There are cameras every 150 feet with high resolution and motion detectors."

"Deputy Commander, are we able to call on the ESF if we needed extra support here?"

"I can't imagine we would call on them," said Collingswood with a touch of affronted dignity. "They're really not trained troops. If they need help from us, of course, we could respond."

"Excellent," said David. "Thank you, Collingswood." All electrified, he thought, all dependent on an electrical grid to work. Except for the mines. It would help to know the chief electrician here. And there was no protocol for ESF forces supporting the Antifan border effort, whether out of misplaced pride or lack of crisis planning, or both.

"My loyalty and honor, sir."

David then let the others ask their questions. This is doable, he thought. But not if you were a simple family with no connections that just wanted to live in a free country and made the mistake of assuming that a fence was just a fence.

Chapter 38
Just the Girlfriend
(Thursday/Friday, 21-22 July)

The Antifan driver dropped Malia off at the Rosebud after her shift ended Thursday morning, since Adam had said his car would pick her up at home at 10 am. It felt strange to be moving around in the oddly unfamiliar apartment, as if she were a guest. She saw a few items Fern must have left, including a frayed toothbrush and a beige bra, and Fern had mostly filled the closet with her own clothes. Last weekend, Malia and David had brought over what she would need for the trip, and her small wheeled bag was ready to go. She took a shower, ate a breakfast from the fresher odds and ends left in the coldbox, and then lay on the bed for a quick nap with the armband alarm set for 9:45 am.

At 9:35 David called her with the emergency number from the Antifan camp. As he was about to say goodbye, he asked, "By the way, does your friend Fern live at the EcoLand pen?"

"Yes," she responded, somewhat sleepily.

"Tell her to stay at your apartment for the time being."

"All right, I think she does most of the time. Is there a reason for insisting on it?"

"Just tell her you feel better with someone staying there while you're away."

"But what's wrong with the EcoLand?"

"Just do as I say," he said shortly, and hung up. A minute later, he called back to apologize and wish her a good trip. "See you on Saturday, sweetheart, love you."

"Love you, too."

She left a message for Fern, who couldn't be reached at work. "Hi Fern, please stay at my apartment as much as you can. I'm out of town until Saturday, and I feel much better if you're watching things." But she couldn't say, "Stay away from the hostel."

A few minutes after 10 am, Adam's car pulled up in front of the Rosebud, exciting great interest from the Street People loitering in front of the building. "Woo wee!" said one man, "that limo ain't at the right place, that's for sure." The driver came out to take Malia's suitpod and open the door for her. The Street People cast some muttered innuendos in her wake, but not loudly enough for the driver or the exalted unseen passenger to intervene. One particularly foul woman howled something clearly obscene, but her toothlessness ensured that Malia couldn't quite understand the insult.

"Fine neighbors you have," said Adam as Malia settled herself on the synthetic leather seat and the car began moving. To her surprise, he was wearing a dark brown uniform with a shoulder patch that read "ESF."

"That's one reason why I need a vacation, amba-sah," she replied.

"Like I always say, you could improve your situation if you only were more realistic," he said impatiently. He pressed the button for the worktable that slid out of the seatback ahead of them and spread out some papers around the workscreen, indicating that he did not intend to engage in casual conversation with her. "Sorry, I need to take care of some business here."

"Of course, amba-sah," she said meekly. She dared not ask why he was wearing the uniform. She had no idea that an Economic Tower functionary not in the ESF would be uniformed. A holster hung from a hook with a 9-millimeter pistol and a short whip. Weren't firearms illegal if you weren't an Antifan or a police officer?

As the car accelerated along 66 West, she sneaked a few glances at Adam. For the first time, she saw him wearing reading glasses, which with the short beard, gave him a slightly bookish look. She had to admit he was handsome, in a darker, heavier way than the fairer, light-footed David. Fifteen years older than David, Adam Ross wore his years and his authority well. The image he projected at the Octavian of a dissolute playboy wounded by personal traumas fell away as soon as he arrived at the Economic Tower, where he was all business.

In acknowledging to herself that Adam Ross really was quite attractive, she wondered why David cared so much about whether she slept with the Economic Tower bureaucrat or not. It was just sex, wasn't it? If it would help her obtain the information David and the ADF sought, wouldn't that just be capitalizing on one of her few advantages over Ross, namely his lustfulness? He had all the other advantages, especially in the ESZ setting. She pouted that it really wasn't fair of David to send her to the ESZ and expect her to evade Ross's advances, while giving her only a last-ditch emergency phone number with which to protect herself.

Perhaps David simply could not shake the influence of those Ten Commandments that his family seemed to think were so important. She suddenly recalled her Diversity Ethics class in high school. Mx Tiffany had deconstructed the Ten Commandments, which they called a foundational apparatus of racism and oppression. "The Jewish fascists say the Ten Commandments were given by God to their prophet Moses," they said, rubbing their light beard with a soft manicured hand. "But of course, they were written to keep Diverse Peoples down." One by one, Mx Tiffany went down the list showing the hypocrisy behind each. "Adultery?" they said. "The same men who wrote the Ten Commandments usually had multiple wives and concubines. 'Honor thy mother and father' when your parents, especially your father, could exercise the right to execute you for disrespect? Again, a tool of control. You are all fortunate to have escaped the tyranny of parents and to be able to think for yourselves."

Malia tried to remember the other Commandments, which she had come across in her reading at the Depository as well. "Thou shalt not covet" and "thou shalt not steal" were clearly meant to keep the downtrodden and impoverished from acquiring the goods they deserved. "Keeping the Sabbath Day holy" was a form of thought control, and not having a graven image to worship made it possible for the fascists to substitute the patriarchal monotheistic God and the masculine Jesus, when, as Mx Tiffany said, "we all know that the tangible Mother Earth, who you can feel with your own hand at your feet, is the true object of worship."

Having recently become a Christian, Malia had at least reached the point where she was prepared to accept that the Ten Commandments were superior to the Five Commandments of the MED, which she still knew better, and which were recited each Sunday in services:

1. Thou shalt worship our Mother Earth
2. Thou shalt honor Diversity as the source of all earthly goods
3. Thou shalt know that Gender is variable, and all Its ways are good
4. Thou shalt honor Social Credit as a sign of Mother Earth Godliness
5. Blessed are the meek, for they shall build Diversity

As she stared out of the window, she asked herself, it's not adultery, is it, when we're not married? She suspected she would not like Pastor Denman's answer.

She discreetly edged two or three inches closer to Adam. He was not so consumed by his work matters that he failed to notice. He took off his glasses, putting them, the table, and its contents away in a deliberate manner. He then placed his hands on her shoulders and began pressing his mouth against hers, inserting his tongue in her mouth. She felt his beard scraping her soft cheeks, but she didn't mind. His hands slipped under her blouse and bra, fondling her breasts for the first time. When he emerged for air, he smiled and said, "I'm glad that a vacation is making you more reasonable already. We should have done this earlier." Were the car a self-driving vehicle, he might have pressed his advantage, but he was prudent enough not to want the driver to see anything that might make its way back to gossips in the Tower. "Every man is a hero except to his own valet," he remembered reading once.

Malia recognized the gatehouse where she and David had stopped to present his credentials. This time the driver presented Adam's, and they were off again with barely a full stop. She also recognized the abandoned village, but missed the turnoff they had taken onto the gravel road. Within half an hour, the imposing "Main Gate, Economic Strike Zone Camp Four" loomed above them, with the slogan underneath, "Produce for Diversity." With everything in order, the limousine continued onto a neat compound with tidy one and two-story administrative buildings flanked by well-tended lawns. The car pulled up in front of a two-story whitewashed mansion with pillars. Commander Barry Mattison, who Malia had seen on the *Diversity Today* segment, came out to greet them personally.

Mattison saluted Adam, who reciprocated, and then turned to Malia. "And who is this lovely lady you have brought with you this time?"

"Commander, this is Melia Jenness, 70. She has an interest in economic issues, so I thought she might find this an interesting learning opportunity." The "70" signaled to Mattison that he could humor Malia like a bright child, since she was a Social Crediteer, but need not take her too seriously. Malia bubbled that she had seen Mattison on the *Diversity Today* segment, and "I was so impressed with what you are accomplishing here!"

Mattison beamed at her. "Is that so? I'm sure you'll learn something here. And keep our Adam from being too serious, with your charms. He's really too serious." He beckoned them into the building. "We were holding lunch for your arrival, so don't be too surprised if everyone welcomes you with enthusiasm."

The crowd was waiting for them in the side parlor off the lobby. All the men and two of the women were wearing the dark brown uniforms. The uniforms included holsters in each of which were inserted a pistol and a short whip.

"Everyone, Adam finally made it!" Scattered applause erupted, and Mattison said, "Lunch is served!" at which point the group migrated into the dining room. Mattison sat at the table's head, and Mrs. Mattison, a thin, anxious-looking blonde, at the foot. To her relief, Malia was seated next to Adam, which meant she only had to engage with one stranger, a tall fellow named Will with a narrow face, aquiline nose, and slicked back brown hair. Fortunately, he was amiable, and not put off by her admission that she was the night concierge at the Octavian. "That's a really nice building," he said kindly, "even though Adam lives there. I'm sure you can learn a lot about human nature from that kind of job."

"Not the better side of human nature," Adam said in his saturnine way, and the two men shared a knowing smile over her head.

"What do you do at the Economic Tower?" Malia asked.

"Will is the quartermaster for all the Anacosta Region Economic Strike Zones," said Adam.

Malia's eyes widened as she turned toward Will. "Does that mean you're responsible for all the supplies coming in here?" She made herself sound a little breathless.

"Yes," he replied. "Everything we're eating that we didn't grow or make ourselves. And all the inputs that we need for the fields and the factories. And Henry over there—" he pointed at a roundfaced fiftyish Asian man with a receding hairline, "is the sales manager of the Anacosta region camps. So I take care of what comes into the camps, and Henry is responsible for making sure we can properly distribute what we produce, namely what goes out. We achieve a nice balance that way, which is what you're supposed to do under socialism, right? No profiteering."

Malia calculated that the Six were present, assuming that the five of the brown-uniformed officers were Adam's cronies in self-enrichment. She marked the woman, a handsome middle-aged brunette with a sallow complexion and confident laugh, chatting with the final brown-uniformed man, who seemed to be of Middle Eastern extraction. On Will's right was a fair woman in a brown uniform, who turned out to be Mattison's deputy, Taryn Bulmer, and who was chatting with Mrs. Mattison.

"Oh my," Malia said to Will. "I do feel under-accomplished compared to all of you."

"No worries," said Will, "you're definitely the prettiest, so you're doing your part."

Waiters served salads with pear halves and berries, and then came plates of Chicken Kiev, new small potatoes, and asparagus.

"How often do you meet for these offsites?" she asked Will, since Adam was conversing with Mattison on his left.

"Quarterly," said Will wryly. "I don't think we could stand it more often. But seriously, it's good to get away and talk with our counterparts who are actually on the ground here."

Since Adam had turned toward Mattison, she could not quite hear what they were discussing, but she heard the words "output," "labor force," and "optimize." Then she was suddenly aware of Adam's hand running up and down her left thigh, kneading it under the table. Will took advantage of her obvious distraction to politely turn to Taryn Bulmer. At that point, she looked up at the waiter who was removing her plate, saw the hatred in his eyes as he stared at Adam's moving hand and her squirms, and realized this was no private, but a prisoner. What David had warned her about became horribly real in that one second—the prisoners would treat her as the enemy, not as an ally, should she fall into their hands.

When the chocolate mousse dishes and empty coffee and teacups were removed, the group minus Mrs. Mattison headed out the door and into three jeeps to tour the facility. Adam told her this was customary on the first afternoon, since there were always noteworthy changes to see. She and Adam sat in the backseat of one vehicle, with Mattison and the driver in front. The jeeps were reinforced plastic with giant inflatable resin tires. "They're manufactured here, for export to Mexico and Central America. We could export to China if it weren't for the complications in shipping," said Mattison proudly, obliquely referring to the giant hostile obstacle of the US between themselves and the Pacific Coast. "These are great all-terrain vehicles and dirt cheap." He pointed out the administration buildings, the parade ground, the barracks for the ESZ troops, and bungalows for the married troops. They turned around and drove past a fence behind which were about four dozen metal and wooden longhouses for the female worker population. Behind them was the main gate.

Mattison pointed at the sheds. "You see these are perfectly habitable buildings. Each houses about fifty workers and has two indoor toilets. There are also outhouses and showers."

"What's that big open area on the other side of the longhouses?" asked Malia. "Is that for exercise?"

Mattison looked solemn. "I'm afraid that's our execution ground. Despite our very favorable treatment of the workforce, we occasionally have cases of sabotage. And sometimes we have rapes or murders. It's really much easier to take care of the problem here ourselves rather than truck the criminals to Charlottesville." The jeeps then headed toward the fields, stretching endlessly off to the right. At the end of the fields, about two miles straightaway, were additional bungalows for the married troops and beyond them, the fences at the frontier.

"The compound is almost 100,000 acres, or 155 square miles," he continued, mostly for Malia's benefit. "About 60,000 acres are farmed; we just came out of the onion and spinach season, so right now we've got ripening tomatoes, beets, cucumbers, green beans, and blueberries and raspberries. Most are going straight to Anacosta for restaurants and personal consumption, but we also trade with other regions to take advantage of their own specialized crops. We just sent a shipment of berries to New York in return for marijuana and corn."

They jolted down one long aisle. In the distance were hundreds of kneeling figures engaged in harvesting. "The tomatoes," said Mattison.

They pulled up alongside a bronzed ESZ sergeant, also armed, who called up the overseer, a Plore. The Plore explained the fertilizer and hybrid improvements that were increasing yield, much as Mattison had told Todd Charles. As they drove off, Mattison said, "All the workers in this field today are local Plores—they are about 10 percent of our agricultural workforce. Of course, you have to pay them, but they tend to be more efficient."

"Will we get to meet the regular workers?" asked Malia, "you know, like Mollie and Jim from the program last weekend?" Adam looked up at the sky.

"I don't think you want to meet the regular workers," said Mattison. "They're kind of scruffy and desperate characters." Malia wished she could tell him that she had come within a hairbreadth of joining their ranks. "Mollie and Jim are from our Plore workforce, but they actually represent us better." Just as David had guessed, Malia thought.

The vehicles eventually emerged from the fields and headed into the industrial compound. About two dozen armory-sized buildings were scattered along various streets. "This is where we build the jeeps...the furnaces and air conditioning units... housewares and furniture...our timber crew brings in all the wood for the furniture... both low end for Plores and low Social Crediteers, and fancier stuff for better folks... computer accessories...food processing...hospital supplies...chemicals." They halted, and Mattison and Bulmer led them into a protected viewing box overlooking the furnace factory floor. Mostly men in shapeless denim overalls and long-sleeved T-shirts and heavy work gloves manned the conveyor belt on which furnace parts glided steadily. Malia was surprised they were not equipped with protective eye gear, since even from the observation deck they could see sparks and bits of metal flying under drills. "They just need to be careful, that's all," said Mattison in response to her question, "and we passed the infirmary, by the way, where our medics can take care of any injuries."

When they emerged from the factory, they watched workers filling trucks at the loading dock. "Most going to Anacosta," said Mattison, "but some going to Florida, New York, and Boston, because of all our exchanges. No profits, of course, just making socialist trade more efficient."

"How do you coordinate these exchanges?" asked Malia. "I mean, how do you know that Boston might want hospital gowns, and that they might be able to send us fish, for example?"

"Now that's a good question," exclaimed Mattison. "The Economic Tower is our brain trust. Adam's people know who is manufacturing what. Each region inputs what it needs and the Tower facilitates the trade, and arranges for the correct deployment of the trucks. We'd never be able to manage all these transactions from the ground level."

The tour concluded with a circuit around the eighty or so men's barracks, also fenced off from the rest of the camp, and then through the central square again before arriving at the guesthouses next to the execution ground. Someone had thoughtfully planted a row of high pines between the execution ground and the guesthouses, so visitors would not inadvertently glimpse any upsetting scenes. Malia and Mrs. Henry were dropped off at their bungalows, and the jeeps darted off with the uniformed functionaries, who would have a meeting before returning to prepare for dinner.

Malia found her suitpod and Adam's in their guesthouse. One entered into a tiled foyer. To the right was a kitchenette area with a metal table and chairs and appliances. Straight ahead was the bedroom with a king-sized bed covered in a brown chenille quilt, an armoire, a desk and chair, and a screen that raised and lowered. The walls were painted light beige. Malia took off her armband and wrapped it around stalactite-shaped spools that grew upward from the night table. Mattison had mentioned that this item was a specialty of Camp Number Four and very popular among Social Credit families. The master bathroom—in mushroom and white—also opened into the hallway. A cast iron table and three matching chairs stood on the patio outside the sliding doors of the bedroom.

She decided to take a shower before Adam returned and complicated matters. She was toweling off in the bedroom when he walked in, to which she gave a little shriek and covered herself. He waved it off, saying "I'm not ready for that now." Then he sat, watching her dress in the blue pantsuit she had worn on her first date with David.

"Lovely," he said. "So wasted on Plores."

An hour later, a van took them and the others back to the main house for dinner. Adam and the other visiting officers had changed into civilian outfits. Dinner was Indian paprichaat, roast beef or salmon, and ice cream sundaes. Afterward, they exited onto the lawn, where small colored lanterns strung along the eaves of the building relieved the darkness. The party sat at various scattered patio-style tables, served wine and cocktails by wraiths in the dark. Mattison announced they would be serenaded by two of the workers, a man and woman who possessed extraordinary voices. "They could be at the symphony in Anacosta," he said by way of introduction, "but I think we'll keep them here a while longer for our entertainment."

As they listened to the indeed talented singers, Malia ran through what she had learned so far. The ADF presumably knew what the camp manufactured and grew. They would be interested to know who was present for this offsite; she had learned the sallow-faced woman was Connie Milliband, 260, the Economic Tower's Chief of Manufacturing, and the Middle Eastern-looking man was Ghazi Mafani, PhD, 250, in charge of the DJR's Chemical Engineering Program. His PhD was from Malcolm X University, but he had done post-graduate study in Tehran as well. Malia was impressed to meet someone who had actually lived abroad. She asked him whether he was in the camp to check on the chemical production, and he smiled. "Some very interesting projects, yes. Perhaps you will hear more tomorrow." She decided not to press. Finally, she knew the ADF would find it of great interest that the ESF officers carried firearms. Even the infuriating Knowledge Tower did not presume that much on Antifan prerogatives.

Eventually the program ended, the group applauded vigorously, and the evening concluded. The officers would meet at 10 am at the main house, then Malia and Mrs. Henry would join them for lunch. "After that, a very interesting afternoon," promised Mattison.

Adam and Malia entered the guesthouse, where the lights came on automatically to greet them. He closed the door behind them firmly, and locked it.

In the bedroom, he said, "All right, Melia. I'm done waiting. Get ready for bed."

The ADF had given her an ointment that she could rub into the doorknobs in the room, or on Adam's glass if she got an opportunity. It would enter his system through his skin pores, dull his libido and make it difficult or impossible for him to maintain an erection. It would be less risky than trying to slip a pill into a drink of his, since Adam obviously was familiar with those subterfuges. "That said," David had said mournfully, handing her the tube, "It would probably also make him extremely angry, so I wouldn't risk using it, frankly." Down the road, at that moment, in his spartan room, David was wondering whether Malia had dared to use the ointment, but the possibility sharpened rather than eased his fears.

Malia undressed and joined Adam in bed, where he was ready for her. The second and third time he went more slowly, but he was not particularly interested in her needs. Still, she climaxed, he figured, judging by several "amba-sahs" and one stray "Adam" that he tolerated under the circumstances, and her thrashing beneath him. Not that he really cared. He finally let her fall asleep.

In the morning, he took her again, warning her that he was going to teach her to enjoy being penetrated in the ass. "I prefer sex that doesn't risk a trip to the Abortion Palace," he said. She protested and wept, but he shrugged and said, "You'll get used to it. They all do. I would be gentler, and more patient, but you've given me such trouble that I'm really not inclined to make your life easier at this point."

"Dave isn't going to allow me to continue with you like this. He only gave permission for this trip because you paid him."

"Dave is going to get a nice hefty severance package," said Adam, "which he'll take because the alternative is losing you and getting nothing. Or maybe I'll just arrange for him to disappear if he gives me too much trouble as well." He said this with such quiet confidence that Malia truly feared that he would not be deterred once they returned to Anacosta.

"Dave at least wants to marry me," said Malia.

"Dave isn't going to be allowed to marry you, unless you want to move to Ploreville," sneered Adam.

"Maybe I'd rather live in Ploreville," Malia retorted.

"That's great. You can go to church, be poor, eat junk food, have a bunch of kids, if you like that kind of thing. Sing to Jesus."

"What do you think my life is like as a low Social Crediteer? Except it's Mother Earth and I don't get any kids."

The doorbell rang; Adam went to let in the servant with the breakfast trays, and directed him to place them on the outside picnic table. He had the young man return with him through the bedroom, and he directed Malia to throw off the blankets and show herself naked to the young man, who averted his eyes.

"I want you to look," said Adam, "because this is what you're not going to get. Ever. Melia, stand up and turn around. Goddamn it, turn around, you bitch. And you, look at her."

When the young man had hastily escaped, and they were eating breakfast outdoors, she asked him angrily, "Why did you do such a mean thing to that poor young man? I'm prepared to be abused by you, but that was just cruel. All he was doing was bringing our breakfast, and you couldn't treat him decently. What is wrong with you?" *Out of character,* David would have warned her darkly.

Adam put down his fork, sat back, and looked at her with cold blue eyes. "There are people who win in life and people who are born to serve those who win. If you're lucky, you can latch onto a winner like me. Or you can just join—" He waved toward the barracks. "Your choice.

"And I'd strongly advise you to watch your language when you talk to me. I haven't heard a single amba-sah all morning, and I can't say I'm pleased at your impertinence."

Don't make him angry, she thought. "I'm sorry, amba-sah."

"That's better. Do you know who Genghis Khan was?" She nodded, and he said, "Yes, I'm not surprised. My favorite quote was one of Genghis's, where he says 'The greatest happiness is to vanquish your enemies, to chase them before you, to rob them of their wealth, to see those dear to them bathed in tears, to clasp to your bosom their wives and daughters.' So now you know my operating principles. You stand warned, Melia."

Chapter 39
Chemical Factory
(Friday, 22 July)

A jeep came to pick her and Mrs. Henry up at noon and bring them to lunch at the main house. Mrs. Henry turned out to be named Roxanne, and was friendlier when separated from the larger group, around which she was painfully shy. "I don't have any advanced degrees," she said, "and I was low Social Credit until I married Henry, like you are now. I only had 95 points, working in the Economic Tower in accounts receivable."

"I'm glad it all worked out, amba-mam," said Malia, who even out of sight of Adam was scrupulously obeying his admonition to show proper respect to the others.

"Please call me Roxanne. It's so nice to have someone to talk to here."

Fortunately, lunch was a buffet and they were allowed to seat themselves anywhere in the two parlors. Various tray tables placed around the room allowed the diners to avoid balancing plates precariously on their laps. Roxanne brought her plate over to a corner where Malia sat in one armchair and asked to join her.

"Of course!" said Malia, now afraid to call her either amba-mam or Roxanne. "Please do." Roxanne took the other armchair in the corner. A servant placed a tray table in front of her.

Malia remembered the guidance David had given her. "People love to talk about themselves. You can never go wrong asking questions if they are not obviously sensitive ones. Egotistical people will think nothing unusual about your interest in them. And shyer and insecure people will open up even more if they feel they can trust you. Don't think cultivating the lesser lights is a waste of your time—they will be more likely to reveal interesting information, just through sheer lack of awareness that they have useful knowledge to impart.

"By the same token, never underestimate the lesser lights. They may be targeting you and pretending to be humbler than they are."

Malia asked where the Henrys lived in Anacosta. They lived in the Marina Parade skyscraper overlooking the wharf in Southwest Anacosta. "We moved there after our last child went to college," said Roxanne. "Downsizing, you know." The youngest son was a sophomore on campus at Malcolm X. Roxanne emphasized that he was not one of the large cohort of students who were allowed to study remotely. The remote learning degree was awarded by the same school but less prestigious than one earned on campus. This was another consequence of the Coronavirus epidemic, when colleges learned they could expand their student bodies—and thus income— by introducing remote learning. It continued after the Diversity Revolution, as the government sought to reinforce social stratification while on the surface pretending to be more democratic by widening the number of degree holders.

Malia could not resist making it clear she did in fact have an on-campus degree from Justice University, although technically she had finished it off campus after Isabelle was born. David would have cautioned her against revealing unnecessary details about herself. "And frankly," he said later, "it undercuts the humble and low-level persona you're trying to project."

"Are you getting close to retirement," she asked, "what with your downsizing and all?"

Roxanne said confidentially, "We've begun to discuss possibly retiring in Mexico. Nice weather, friendly people, we could have a house instead of an apartment. I would love to read *any* book or magazine." She looked around her anxiously.

"Is that possible? I didn't know we were allowed to move out of the country."

Roxanne was uncertain. "It must be all right, if my husband was suggesting it. But we probably won't do that, since we'd want to stay near our children and grandchildren."

Lowering her voice, and glancing at Adam, whose right arm was just visible in the next room through the doorway, Roxanne added, "If you and Adam get married, all your troubles would be over. And think of all the cute curly-haired children you could have for Diversity."

Malia smiled, looking downward, as if she were too embarrassed to even entertain such a marvelous fairy tale ending. "I hope so, amba-mam."

At that point, Adam stood in the doorway between the two rooms and called out, "Melia, would you mind joining us here?"

Malia excused herself, and went into the other room, where Adam was sitting in a comfortable foursome with Mattison, Will, and another brown-uniformed man she didn't recognize. Adam said, "Tell these gentlemen how you escaped the Earth Weekend dragnet. They're a little sorry they don't have you here in the fields picking their tomatoes."

At one point, Malia had mentioned the Earth Weekend fiasco, and Adam had asked her how she had avoided the mass kidnapping. She struggled to remember her answer—it had been one of those late-night tennis volley conversations.

"I just walked out of the tent as soon as I saw something was wrong, but while the attention was at the front of the tent, and I walked back down the road. Then I walked ten miles to Say Michaels and caught a bus back to Anacosta." St. Michaels had been renamed when all non-MED saints had been proscribed and towns named for saints were no longer permitted.

Adam looked up at her skeptically. "Didn't you mention a local police officer helping you?"

Oh yes, that's what I told him, Malia remembered. "I walked about halfway, and then he came along in his patrol car, and brought me into the town."

The fourth officer, a black man in early middle age with deep eyes and short beard, asked her, "Do you remember the name of the police officer who helped you?"

"No, amba-sah, we didn't introduce ourselves."

The black officer said to the others, "So our nets aren't as tight as they could be. And it's going to be really hard getting attendees to come to next year's Earth Weekend. We need to move to housing pen roundups. There's about 2,000 people under forty living in each of these pens—"

Will changed the subject smoothly. "Well, Roland, please don't let's give Ms. Melia the impression we're disappointed to see her here alive and well this afternoon, and in the company of our friend Adam."

Roland laughed ruefully. "Yes, sorry if I seem disappointed in our failure to arrest you. You're here under much more congenial circumstances today."

Adam said, "That's fine, Melia. You can return to the other room."

"Yes, amba-sah," she said. "Good afternoon, amba-sehm."

When she had retreated, Will grinned at Adam. "What do you have going on there with Miss Melia? She's amba-sahing and amba-sehming like she's your personal maidservant."

Adam frowned, "Nothing. I just think she ought to keep in mind who her betters are. Otherwise she gets too fresh."

"Adam runs a tight ship, there," Mattison chortled. "His own little two-person command post."

Turning to Will, Adam said, "I don't see your love life going too well." He wasn't going to comment on the wan Mrs. Mattison.

"My heart is broken," said Will. "I wish I had your sweetheart. She would just have to remember to call me Will."

Roland said, "I think we need to have a more serious discussion of next steps. The labor situation in the Anacosta Region Zone is increasingly dire. There are only so many Plores who will work here. And what's going on in the chemical building isn't helping—" Mattison raised a cautious hand, as the waiters cleared the plates and brought over coffee and carrot cake.

"Later, Roland," said Adam. "We hear you." They turned to a safe discussion of baseball rankings. The Anacosta Raptors were struggling, but a steroid-laden New Woman pitcher brought up from the minors offered some hope for the team.

After lunch, they piled into the jeeps for the short trip to the industrial park. This time Malia and Adam sat behind Taryn Bulmer at the wheel and Dr. Ghazi Mofani. Walking into the chemical factory, they were given hazmat suits and bubble helmets to wear. Once everyone was safely attired, they walked through inflatable hallways through the plant. Behind plastic windows workers moved in similar protective garb, some tapping at keyboards, others stirring vats, and a few carrying screenboards. Malia wondered why several workers were simply wearing plastic white ponchos, rubber gloves, and goggles. Mofani, now accompanied by Chief Chemical Engineer Thomas Retsinger, 180, explained they were now viewing the ethylene factory. "We use ethylene here in the Zone for our fruit orchards and to control ripening, as well as for resin used in the jeep tires and ordinary household furnishings. We produce ethylene for the entire Anacosta region."

Malia longed to ask about the different protective garb, but was aware of Adam's looming presence behind her. Fortunately, Commander Milliband asked instead.

"The special PPE isn't cheap, Commander," said Retsinger. "We of course give the full protective equipment to our staff members and outside workers, but it's a bit iffier for our inside workers." No one seemed to object, least of all Will the quartermaster.

They reached the end of the main factory tour, and now stood at an elevator bank. "Now for the highlight of our entire enterprise, ladies and gentlemen. You'll be able to take off the hazmat suits once you reach the lowest level, which is where some very cutting-edge experimentation is taking place." He answered a muffled question from one of the Henrys. "No, it's perfectly safe. You'll just be observing from the conference room."

The elevators descended six stories, and they emerged into a lobby area with benches on which they sat to remove the suits. A gloved worker collected the suits as they were ushered into a large conference room. Retsinger stood at the podium waiting for everyone to sit down.

"Good afternoon, commanders, visitors. I am about to show you some of our latest research in the area of truth serum development. Before we begin, I note that this briefing is classified Top Secret. You are enjoined under penalty of death not to reveal any information you hear here today." Malia looked nervously at Adam, who shrugged.

Who is going to administer the penalty, wondered Malia. Surely not the Antifans?

Retsinger talked about the age-old search for a working truth serum, which would guarantee complete control of a society. The perennial challenge for rulers had always been uncertainty about what their population really believed or thought, no matter how firmly governments exercised control with their armies, spies, guillotines, and prisons. Even governments "such as ours, which have succeeded in reversing a millennium of oppressive and pernicious values, and replacing them with Diverse and liberating ones, need a method to ensure that the population is truly in conformance. Otherwise we are forced to continue to use coercive methods when they might not even be necessary.

"If we succeed in our efforts to invent the first reliable truth serum, all we may need to do is give everyone a single truth serum dose and exam once a year, much as one goes to one's physician for an annual exam, or to the local police for your chip check. It would also have the benefit of showing our ideological enemies that the DJR is truly a society built on consensus."

"What would we do with those who fail the truth serum exam?" asked Will. Malia had been wondering the same thing.

Retsinger replied, "These are political and police matters of little concern to me. But once you have identified these outliers, you can decide whether they need to be cured in hospitals, jailed in prisons, or simply removed permanently from the society, like a wart on a foot."

He went on to explain how in the past most efforts at a truth serum had stalled, such as with sodium pentothal, at the level of dulling central nervous reaction, or loosening inhibitions. "This makes it harder for someone to lie, because they cannot quickly produce a convincing lie. But it also makes it possible for them to completely fabricate stories. Those so-called truth serums paradoxically can produce lies, especially when the subject wishes to please the interrogator. So interest in truth serums faded in the early 21st century.

"About ten years ago, we were fortunate to begin informal consultations about truth serums with several members of the Chinese Academy of Political Medical Science in Beijing. The People's Republic has similar motivations. But their scientific expertise was admittedly superior to ours, as were their financial resources. At this point I would like to introduce my lead Chinese collaborator, Dr. Ling Li-hua, of the Academy, who is heading our clinical efforts here."

Dr. Ling stood up and joined Retsinger at the head of the table. She was a poised woman in her mid-40s whose attractiveness was enhanced in this setting by her white lab coat, severe bun and fashionable wire glasses. She uttered some pleasantries, and then continued.

"In the last several years we have also made progress in the development of the truth serum that is so important to both of our countries. We made our first breakthrough three years ago when we learned that by mapping AI knowledge about subject activity across brain activity linked to decisionmaking processes, we could identify differential patterns that we have since looked to influence. We knew that by activating the anterior prefrontal cortex, we would make it harder for subjects to lie. But how could we create conditions in which the subject would be unable to process an untruth? Since that insight, we have worked constantly to develop chemical stimulants that would excite the prefrontal cortex in just the right manner to shut down the ability to speak untruths by causing great pain."

"But the subject could remain silent, correct?" asked Adam.

"True, but that would be an indication of regime antipathy. And the subject could theoretically develop an answer that was truthful, but not material or irrelevant to our purposes. This would not fool us. Unfortunately, calibrating the right chemical composition is extremely difficult and this has been a very dangerous process. It has failed with approximately 830 subjects so far."

"What does failed mean?" asked Henry.

"It means they died while under observation," Dr. Ling responded. "About 1,500 others have been injured in the course of the experiments, usually brain injuries. Some have recovered, but most eventually need to be euthanized."

Malia wondered why Adam and Henry were exchanging almost satisfied nods. Surely wasn't this a bad thing? No wonder the Economic Strike Zone was short of workers.

Dr. Ling spoke for a few more minutes about the challenges the laboratory team faced, including the relative absence of regime opponents among the subjects. Since most of the subjects had been Social Crediteers, they generally held positive views of the DJR, despite their travails. "It would be helpful to begin testing on actual regime opponents, but you would need to bring them from your psychiatric hospitals. It is very helpful that you have such ability to collect subjects here in the DJR—we face more barriers to our work in China."

"Good luck getting the Antifans to send us their prisoners," Adam commented.

Dr. Ling then announced it was time to view an experiment in progress. A screen rose behind one long side of the conference table, revealing a wide glass window that looked into a laboratory room. Facing them, but not seeing them, was a young man in denim overalls and a white T-shirt, who was strapped to a padded wooden chair.

"This is a young man, twenty-six years old, from Baltimore," said Dr. Ling. "He was a graduate student at Hillary Clinton University in Diversity History. He volunteered to come to the Zone last year after hearing patriotic speeches. Then he volunteered for our program because he no longer wished to work in the fields. He is an intellectual."

Two mistakes, Malia thought. Never volunteer for anything in the DJR, let alone twice.

"In our intake interviews, we collect information about beliefs and behavior, so we have something to test against. We have administered a cocktail of two relatively recently derived chemical compounds with proven success at depressing the thalamus while stimulating the anterior prefrontal cortex." She named the compounds, which meant little or nothing to the group. "In five minutes, we will ask the preset questions of the subject.

"This week we have gotten satisfactory results twenty-four times with no injury, have lost fourteen patients outright, and five others within the following two weeks. This chemical mix tends to destroy nerves connecting to other parts of the brain, but women seem more resistant to it for reasons we do not know. In some cases, the subject's heart fails due to the stress."

Malia looked at the screen. Two masked lab technicians were hovering nearby, waiting for the moment to ask questions. An offscreen male voice was giving them directions of some sort. The young man stared at the camera, eyes glazed.

Aware of Adam's eyes on her, she tried to look bored. She picked at her cuticles. She realized it was very dangerous for her to be here, and Adam probably had not realized the extent of the briefing before they sat down in the room. Admittedly, the uncleared guest of a fully cleared functionary could legally attend, but this was generally meant for spouses and other close partners who could be trusted to protect the interests of the functionary. While Adam certainly did not know her Antifan links, he could not fully trust her not to gossip about the demonstration or experimentations back in Anacosta, most likely to other low Social Credit peers. It was in her interest to show boredom, and if possible, obtuseness or a lack of understanding of Dr. Ling's remarks.

The technicians began reading questions to the young man. "Were you born in Baltimore?"

"Yes," he answered.

"Were you a student at Hillary Clinton University?" "Yes."

"Were you a math major?" "No."

"Did you like working in the fields here in the Zone?" The young man struggled, and seemed to be trying to say, "Yes," but screamed with pain.

Dr. Ling said, "This is a good result, since we can tell he is lying here. Lying will cause pain that will be noticeable to the observer."

The examination continued for another ten minutes, at which point the young man slumped forward in the chair, restrained by the straps. Another technician entered and took the subject's pulse. "Gone," he said. "Heart failure."

Dr. Ling tsked tsked. "Such a shame. It was going very well. The cocktail may have been too strong in this case."

Meanwhile, about ten miles to the north, the Harris brothers were canoeing down the Bullpasture River. They had caught some rainbow trout in one of the smaller tributaries, since summertime heat made the main river channel unfavorable for fishing, and now they were looking for a shady spot to gut, clean, and cook the fish.

If the men hadn't been wearing baseball caps, any observer would have recognized them as brothers. Daniel looked every year his ten years over David. Both were blond—Daniel's hair was thinning, but not much, and they shared the gray eyes and facial cast that Marjory had told them they had inherited from their father. Daniel was in good shape because as the ADF camp's chief electrician, and an outdoorsman, he never stayed still long.

Daniel remembered their father, but this also meant he remembered the hardest years of the civil war, and the cruel treatment they had received at the hands of the

Antifans. By the time they were resettled in Ploreville, he was nearly grown and learning a trade was the most practical option. He was taciturn and pessimistic by nature and experience.

They pulled the canoe up on the pebbly shore, then prepared and cooked the fish. Daniel quickly took over the job from the citified David. But within a half hour, they were eating their catch and taking long swigs from their flasks. Daniel unpacked a chopped beet salad to share. "They're in season at the Zone, so we can buy some of the produce," he said.

When they finished eating, it was time for the talk they knew was coming. "I'm sorry about Marie," said David. Even though Marie and Daniel had been married 25 years, he hadn't known her well, because he hadn't seen them often, except at Christmas when they ventured to Ploreville under special holiday leave.

"Thanks," said Daniel. "She's not suffering anymore. By the time we got an appointment for the scan, it was too late. She just wasn't a complainer."

Another minute passed. Daniel said, referring to Malia, "Mom says she's a nice girl even though she's a Social Credit type."

David nodded. "Yes, I think this is for real. She's coming to church with us and fits in well. She doesn't have airs. Her name's Malia, and she was orphaned during the war. We're the first family she's ever known."

"Are you going to get married?" asked Daniel. "A wedding would be nice."

David unfastened his armband and tossed it into the bushes about fifty feet away.

"Not as things stand, not in the DJR. I've got too much Social Credit compared to her. They don't let Antifans marry just anyone. They've already pushed other women at me, women who would make sure I didn't stray too far from the straight and narrow. Mom doesn't know this is going to be a problem. I didn't tell her, because she was so happy we were engaged."

"How're you gonna fix this?"

"We're going to cross the frontier. I'll take my chances with the fascists. I've got a lot of useful stuff I can tell them. I'm sure they've got Lutheran pastors there who would marry us."

"I hope you're not planning to cross around here," said Daniel. "Oh, you are, I can tell. You're going to need some help, aren't you? I should have known."

Daniel confirmed what David had learned about the electrified fence that week. "If we could identify a spot for crossing, I could arrange to dismantle the wiring in advance, but not too far in advance, because eventually even those half-asleep guys in the guardhouse would realize that a section was broken. I'm not sure what you'd do about the mines, though."

"I'll think about that. Maybe I can work that from Beau—from work. I might even be able to get some intel on how they've laid out these mines."

"That would be good. I'd hate to see us blown up."

"Us?" David asked.

"Yeah, because once I shut down the boxes all around camp and in the ops center, and you escape past that electrified fence, and they remember that you're related to the chief electrician, my goose is cooked. You know that, don't you?"

"Well," said David. "I'd like to have some more relatives with me in the US."

"I don't have much keeping me here anymore," said Daniel. "Honestly."

They exchanged a long look. "Brother, I'd be honored," said David. He paused, "By the way, there will be four of us."

"Who's the fourth?"

"Malia's daughter, who was taken away from her ten years ago. I was finally able to locate the daughter, and Malia got a job in the building where the family lives. She and the kid have become friends, but the kid still doesn't know Malia's her mother."

"Oh boy. Life is much simpler out here," said Daniel.

Chapter 40
Return Home Safely
(Friday/Saturday, 22-23 July)

Back in the guesthouse before dinner, Malia was pleased to see another message from Mxti Rex at LGBT camp. "What are you smiling about?" asked Adam. She told him, and he grimaced. "I don't get your interest in that girl, or whatever it is at all."

"But, amba-sah, they have learned how to climb the rope adventure structure. It's very good for building their strength and their self-esteem."

"Let's not spoil the evening. By the way, you were calmer than I expected about that whole experiment business at the chemical factory. Weren't you upset at all? A lot of other women would probably faint. Henry's wife had her eyes closed the whole time."

Malia looked up. "No, amba-sah, I didn't really understand a lot of it. I know they are trying to develop a truth serum, and it's very risky. I was sorry for the young man, but I'm glad the woman who came after him was all right. I'm sorry, amba-sah, I'm just not good at science."

Adam looked at her levelly, as if he was measuring her sincerity. I'd like to use a lie detector on her right now, he thought. Did she really not grasp how many people we are killing here every day? And how close she came to being one of these test subjects? But why would she lie about it? "A lot of people are being killed to get this truth serum, so we can protect the country," he said. "Did you not understand that part?"

"Yes, amba-sah," she said. "The country needs this serum, that much I understood, and how can we have it without testing? As long as these workers are in the Zone, they're here to serve Diversity, right? If they were smarter, they'd be back in the City, not here. So I guess if we need to test it, we ought to test it on them." She met Adam's eyes without flinching.

"Remarkable how reasonable you've become in just a few days among your betters," he said.

"I've learned a lot," she chirped brightly. But in a moment, he had crossed the room and placed his large hairy hands around her neck. She cried out.

"One thing," he said. "You will never, ever tell anyone about what you have seen here today, or I will kill you with these hands. You won't be the first." It had been thirty years since he had strangled his last resister in an abandoned house near Lynchburg, but he could still recollect that moment, and feel the older man's rough stubbly skin under his hands, while watching him turn blue and then collapse to the floor. He recalled, we were told to save the ammunition that day, we were waiting for a shipment, but we still had to do our jobs.

She looked gratifyingly panicked. "Yes, amba-sah, I understand! I know it is a secret!" Her neck showed red marks from his hands, but they would fade fast.

"Good," he said, undressing. "Come take a shower with me now." She followed him into the bathroom, disrobing behind him. He turned on the taps and they stood face-to-face under the steamy flow, their torsos touching, her belly pressing into his groin. She soaped him, and herself, and then she washed her face with the special oatmeal facial scrub she preferred and could now afford to buy. She could no longer claim she was unattracted to Adam, but everything in her training and raising had taught her that monogamy was at best a holdover from a more selfish and individualistic era, at best to be mocked in all the movies and books she read, so she felt little guilt, except in an intellectual way, knowing David would be upset. And whatever guilt she may have felt was alleviated by her satisfaction that David would be astonished at what she had learned here. No one else could have accomplished this, she said to herself, as Adam sat on the bench in the shower and she took him in her mouth. I did this myself. Now all I have to do is return home safely tomorrow. She did not think about the day after tomorrow.

She was wearing the yellow sundress with yellow sandals, and a gold necklace with the Diversity symbol "D" superimposed on a globe with matching gold earrings in the shape of Ds. She looked the part of a meek low Social Credit helpmeet who would never trouble the higher-ups with a contrarian question. "You're going to be the best, most loyal Diversan at the offsite," David had said. "Every little thing can help establish your persona for the people you need to deceive." The crowd was larger tonight in the main house—it was a final reception for the honored guests from the Economics Tower—and all the ESF officers in the camp were present, some with spouses. Only Commander Lefever and Deputy Commander Collingswood had been invited from the ADF camp, and she prudently avoided their black uniforms.

Adam brought her a gin and tonic, and then was diverted by some ESF officers who sought to make a good impression. Feeling somewhat neglected, she gravitated toward the back porch with her drink. "Hello, beautiful," said Will, who had been stretching his long legs in a rocker while drinking whiskey. "What did you think of today's entertainment?"

"The visit to the chemical factory?" she asked blandly, sitting on the adjacent straight chair.

"Well, that, and the lab experiments that don't seem to be going so well." She noticed he made sure that no one was within earshot.

"Oh, I'm just not good at science at all," she said, embarrassed. "I felt very sorry for the young man, but everything else just went over my head. I hope they come up with the serum, because it would be good for Diversity, wouldn't it? People would just believe in Diversity and not suffer thinking differently from everyone else."

"Indeed," said Will. He noticed the ideologically chic earrings and necklace. "You're a good Diversity girl, aren't you?"

She nodded, "Yes, amba-sah."

"Even though you came close to being a prisoner here yourself. But now you're mingling with the elite. It's a crazy world, isn't it?"

He waited a moment and then asked, "May I ask where you live in Anacosta? Just curious, I promise not to find you in the City. Adam would kill me if I tried."

"The Rosebud," she said, "At H and 10th."

"So not one of the hostels," he said. "Not like EcoLand, or TerraCity?"

She shook her head.

"I'm surprised you can get your own apartment with a 70. Adam must have pulled some strings for you. I'm glad to hear that—it might become a little unsafe to live in the hostels."

She would have drawn him out on the subject, except that Adam had come out onto the porch, placed his empty highball glass on a table, and dropped his hands heavily on her bare shoulders, and then into his pockets.

"What's that about hostels?" he said, moving in front of them and leaning against the railing.

"I was congratulating Melia on having an apartment in the City even with her Social Credit score, and not having to live in one of the housing pens."

"Hmmm," said Adam. "That's probably a lag from when she had a higher Social Credit score. Once the bookkeeping catches up with the concierge job, the housing level will drop accordingly. But I'd certainly hate to see her have to share an apartment with some of those nobodies. It doesn't make me look good. We'll figure out a solution." Malia beamed at him.

On her right side at dinner sat a young ESF captain with an agriculture degree who complained discreetly about inefficiencies in Zone farming. "If only we could order some of those combines from the US," he said, looking around anxiously. "I hear we might open diplomatic relations soon. That would allow us to buy some equipment we really need. And then we wouldn't need to use so many Social Crediteers as workers. We've got too many Plores here, and they talk back too much." Malia gave him a sweet smile and continued poking at her peach soufflé. She didn't dare confess that she was afraid of Plores herself, for fear Adam would overhear and know she was dissembling, although it would have been a good opening for a more revealing conversation about the state of affairs in the Zone. The captain, who was lonely, wished he could ask her to talk with him more intimately on the porch, but one glance at Adam, who was engaged in conversation with Taryn Bulmer on his left, dissuaded him.

When they returned to the guesthouse, Malia told herself, "Just one more night. In 24 hours you'll be back with David." It was hard to stay one step ahead of Adam and the other Tower functionaries, while at the same time staying several steps behind, or at least pretending to be stupider than you really were. What if she were talking in her sleep?

She started wishing she had actually applied the ointment to the door knobs as Adam began assembling an array of devices and tubes from his suitpod. "Get ready for bed," he threw over his shoulder. "Tonight we'll start doing things a little differently." This did not bode well, Malia thought, but she removed her makeup and brushed her teeth, trying to delay.

"Hurry up," she heard from the bedroom. And "don't bother with the nightgown, not yet."

He tied a gag around her mouth. She had asked, "Do I have to wear that? I promise not to scream."

"Do I have to wear that, what?" he asked irritably.

"Do I have to wear that, amba-sah," she corrected herself.

"Yes, you do. Because you will scream and yell, I know this from long experience in these matters, and Will is just next door. I'm afraid he may have a slightly chivalric streak and come to rescue you." The gag went on, tightly. I can't breathe, I'm hyperventilating, Malia thought, but perhaps it was just panic. It's just panic, she laughed at herself. Imagine what he'd do to you if he thought you were an Antifan spy. Count your Mother Earth blessings. She submitted.

At around that moment, David was finally arriving at Beaufort. He and Daniel had lingered on the shore, delighting in the beautiful sunlit evening, returning to the truck just before darkness set. Much of their conversation was about their different childhood experiences. The ten-year age difference meant everything given the tumult in the country at the time. Daniel remembered the hunger times in Toledo, when the aunt and uncle regretfully said they would need to leave. Because he was already fifteen, and nearly a man, he remembered with particular humiliation and anguish the mistreatment by the Antifans. He remembered being herded in a long convoy of Plores into Pennsylvania by the black-clad Antifans, who confiscated and destroyed their Bibles in front of them. "That's why you can be easier about the Antifans than the rest of us can," Daniel said, without recrimination.

David's first memories were of a spare dinner table, covered by a worn floral tablecloth, which Daniel confirmed was their aunt's, and waking up hungry in the middle of the night, but knowing full well it was pointless to ask for more food. Then he remembered cots in a huge tent, and sharing one with his toddler brother, who subsequently died. Daniel told him of the day he and Marjory had taken George, shaking with fever and gasping for breath, to the hospital tent, where the Antifan medics refused to treat him until Marjory and Daniel swore the Diversity Confession. "For myself, I would never have done that," said Daniel. "But for the baby, of course we would lie, and we did. But we came back in the morning, and he was gone anyway." He paused. "He was a sweet baby, long blond curls, just wanted to follow you around all the time on those chubby legs. Not that they were chubby by then."

"Tell me about our father," David asked Daniel. Daniel had last seen their father during a furlough in 2053, when he was thirteen.

"He looked like us. He liked to read newspapers online and discuss current events. He had great faith. He said that if we always did the right thing, God would take care of us in the long run even if it didn't seem so in the short run. Once when Mom asked him to stay with us, he said we were engaged in a great battle to keep our rights and save the country, and if he was capable of fighting, he couldn't delegate it to someone else. 'It wouldn't be right,' he said."

The two were silent for a few moments, contemplating his sacrifice. "I hope we can be worthy," David said.

Daniel looked at him, asking calmly, "While you work for Antifans?"

"I've done honorable things as an Antifan too," said David, "We protect the borders. We keep the real bastards in check." Daniel looked skeptical.

"What the hell," said David. "We're getting out of here. And Dad would approve, right?"

"Surely," said Daniel. "He'd ask what took us so long. I'm glad you're giving me an excuse to escape to the decent side of the border." They began packing up the picnic and cleaning the fish knives. "It's getting late."

David walked into Beaufort around the time Malia and Adam were returning to the guesthouse from the farewell reception. It hadn't been as easy to secure the self-drive taxi from Harrisonburg as he had expected, and occasionally the vehicle had erupted with odd squealing noises. He feared being stranded on 66, but fortunately the car had creaked on, and there he was, ready to type his notes out, even on this Friday night, because waiting until Monday would make it much harder. He greeted the night shift in the Unit, and had them give him a quick rundown on what he had missed. He felt good being among his young people again. Wurro looked at them steadily from his nook, as if to say, David, my mana still holds for you.

Before typing anything, David closed the door to his office, went to the armband feed site, and found Malia's signal. Getting clear reception from the Zone would be challenging, but he could not resist. He told himself he was concerned about her safety, which was true, but then acknowledged he could do nothing to protect her tonight, which was also true.

He heard mostly Adam Ross's gruff voice, but Malia's muffled imploring sounds were impossible to decipher. Well, at least she's alive, he thought. Then he heard clearly, "that Plore boyfriend will disappear, if he knows what's good for him." Hmm, what to do about Tom?

Chapter 41
Warning
(Saturday, 23 July)

The chauffeur pulled up in front of the Rosebud around 4:30 pm Saturday afternoon. It had taken longer to leave the Zone camp than Malia had expected. First, she and Adam had enjoyed a leisurely breakfast—delivered without incident—outside. It was a lovely morning, promising heat, but still detaining the cool breeze of the sunrise. They sat in an almost comfortable silence, Malia salting and cutting up a fried egg, nibbling at fruit salad, drinking black coffee. She was still wearing her nightgown and the purple silk bathrobe she had bought with her Antifan largesse, and Adam was wearing a polo shirt and long tan shorts while reading the news on his phone. Will emerged briefly, waved to them over the short hedge, then disappeared inside.

As she was packing her suitpod, mostly with dirty laundry, Adam, who had been tapping on his armband phone, said to her, "Go over to Will's."

"What, amba-sah?" She wasn't sure she had heard correctly.

"Go over to Will's for a little while. Meet his needs. I'm just doing him a favor, since he doesn't seem to find women on his own."

"Amba-sah," she said, becoming upset. "This isn't fair. My boyfriend had no idea you would do something like this. This isn't part of the deal."

Adam glared at her. "Don't make me angry. Go there right now."

I can't make him angry, she thought, so close to escaping this place and returning to Anacosta and David with everything I've learned. So close. At least Will seems to be a gentleman.

"Does he know I'm coming over, amba-sah?"

"Yes, I just told him I was sending you over as a farewell gesture. He wasn't surprised; he knows I'm not selfish in these matters. Just be back by noon, please, we need to get going."

Malia trailed over to Will's guesthouse in her nightgown and robe and rang the doorbell. He smiled down at her and beckoned her inside. His guesthouse was a mirror image of theirs, only with the kitchenette and sitting area on the left side. He ushered her into the bedroom, sat her on the bed, and gently undressed her. She was still wearing her gold Diversity earrings from the previous night, which jangled pleasantly.

"You really are beautiful," he said, joining her on the bed and kissing her warmly. "It's very generous of Adam, really. He's a little stingy with money, but not with his women." Will was a considerate lover, for which Malia was grateful.

While infuriating, Adam's dispatch of her to Will's bed had yielded unexpected fruit. Will had followed up on his initial remark about the hostels, since Adam had implied Malia might end up in one. "In all good conscience, I need to tell you. There will be a roundup against EcoLand in the next several weeks. It'll happen in the middle of the night, to catch as many people as possible. Try to delay any move there. I couldn't stand you coming back here as a prisoner, after you've already escaped one roundup."

"Thank you, amba-sah."

"It's Will. He's not listening to you right now."

"Thank you, Will."

"You bet," he drawled. And then he said, "It might not be easy, but without giving you more than you need to know, it might be worth sticking with Adam. He's becoming a very rich man." In response to Malia's tilted head, he smiled and said, "No more information at this time. We're all following in his greedy wake, that's all. Let me kiss you one more time. Thanks, sweetheart, that will keep me going all week."

There was an extra spring in Malia's step as she exited the limousine. Finally, free of Adam! She would wait upstairs for David, and they would go for a nice cozy dinner. How utterly grateful she would be to luxuriate in the normalcy of her real romance, with a man who treated her like a human being worth caring for, and not an object with an inferior numerical rating. It was still nightmarish to think about last night, and it still hurt. It wasn't going to happen again if she could help it. Tom/Dave was just going to have to stand up for his presumptive rights.

"I'd like to come upstairs and see the apartment," said Adam.

"Really, amba-sah? It's not much. You'll lose even more respect for me when you see it."

"I'll come upstairs. Just for a few minutes." Adam went to give instructions to the driver and she frantically tapped on her phone:

Don't come now. Adam coming up.

She pulled her suitpod into the building, waving the armband at the sensors. Adam followed, observing the peeling paint in the hallway and sniffing the goat curry scent emanating from the apartment of the Somali family that had replaced the Guatemalans. "Charming," he said. "I'm glad you're the ones who get to welcome newcomers to our lovely country." *I hate you,* she thought.

She should have known, especially after having invited Fern to stay in the apartment, that Fern might actually be there. But who would have thought Adam would request to see her apartment this afternoon? Why on earth would Adam Ross even want to step foot in the Rosebud? And then she realized that she had never told Fern about Adam at all, or about finding Isabelle, although she had necessarily confided in Fern about her new job at the Octavian. She had explained that she needed to meet more higher Social Credit people who could help her get a better job.

Fern was painting her toenails on the coffee table while watching the new movie adaptation of *Felicia: A Rap Artist Finds Socialism and Love.* In her surprise to see Malia, and in the company of a strange man, she toppled the nail polish bottle. Fern grabbed one of Malia's yellow hand towels, dabbing at the growing purple pool.

"I'm so pleased to meet you finally!" said Fern. "David, right?"

Adam did not take her outstretched hand. "No, do I look like a Plore?"

"This is Adam Ross, Fern," Malia said quickly. "Adam, this is my friend Fern Potts, who was staying here while we were away."

"Adam Ross, 200," said Adam, finally extending his hand.

"I'm only a 75," she said meekly. "It's a great honor to meet you." Then to Malia, "I should have known better. You've told me David is blond and about our age. Sorry about that." Malia thanked the Mother Goddess that Tom/Dave was reasonably close to blond. She could only hope Adam would not take umbrage at the age comparison.

At that point, Adam began touring the apartment, opening the kitchen cabinets, and peeking in the bathroom and bedroom. One would have thought he was considering renting the property.

"What is he doing?" Fern wondered. Malia put her finger to her lips, shaking her head.

Adam came out, observing, "You don't keep a lot of clothes here, do you?"

"No, amba-sah," she said automatically, but was grateful that Fern had brought over hers, since she had left little or nothing behind when she moved to the Avalon.

"Oh, most of them—" Fern began, but Malia cowed her with an angry look. She was sure Adam would not overlook her slip. One foolish remark might now ruin an excellent trip.

"Well, darling, that was very interesting. As an expert in economic affairs, I like to get snapshots of ordinary people's lives. It reminds me that I never want to be ordinary again," said Adam. "Give me a farewell kiss and when will I see you next? Are you working tomorrow night?"

"Yes, amba-sah," she said, tiptoeing to meet his lips. "Thank you for the fun trip."

"The fun was all mine, I'm sure," said Adam. "See you tomorrow night. Nice to meet you, Erin." And then he was gone.

He descended in the elevator to the street. Consumed by his own thoughts, particularly that something had not been quite right about the apartment setup, he barely paid any attention to the beige sedan with the blond man in the driver's seat.

While it was rare to see private vehicles, especially parked outside the Rosebud, Adam recognized neither the car nor the driver, and for all he knew, the man had his own mistress at the Rosebud. The limousine driver opened the door and Adam slid in. "Back to the Octavian," he said. "Thank Mother Earth."

Back in the apartment, Fern said, "Malia, I have no idea what's going on. I'm sorry if I said anything wrong."

Malia was relieved that Fern hadn't called her Malia, instead of Melia. That could have been explained, but it would have registered as another discordant note.

"No, no, I'm sure it seems confusing. This is someone I met at the Octavian from the Economic Tower and he invited me to spend the weekend with him. He thinks I have a boyfriend named David who is a Plore, so that's why he took offense when you called him David. That's a separate David from my real David, who should be here any minute. But don't worry about keeping Adam secret from the real David. The real David is fine with my having gone on the trip with Adam." Fern blinked hard several times. "You can be normal with the real David."

A few minutes later, the real David appeared in the doorway. "Well, Malia!" The gray eyes sparkled, partly happiness at seeing her again, and partly relief that he was seeing her again. The last few days had been stressful. He had planned to greet her at the Rosebud entrance but held back when he saw Adam follow her into the building, even before he saw her text.

She ran into his arms. They hugged tightly for a good half minute. If Fern hadn't been watching, Malia would have cried openly with relief. She pulled him into the living room and finally introduced him to Fern. David was kindly to Fern, which Malia appreciated. "I've heard a lot about you!" he said to her, smiling broadly.

Fern looked grateful. "Same about you!"

Even though David was dying to know what Malia had found out, he knew they needed to eat dinner. He had planned to whisk Malia off to the Avalon and talk in relative confidence. But, he thought, let's grab a quick dinner, bring Fern along, do her a favor, and then Malia and I will head home. Malia was surprised when he suggested the threesome, but he said, "We can talk later." They went back to the Chinese restaurant that was good enough to be in Ploreville.

After they had dropped an effusively grateful Fern off at the Rosebud, they drove up the Tubman Parkway as the sunset dipped over the horizon. David pulled the sedan into one of the overlooks just before the Esplanade. "I've got to get my sportscar back," he said, "this just isn't working for me." All the private vehicles came from the same government supply house, so it would be an uncomplicated transaction provided no one else had purchased it.

He turned to her. "Okay, in terms of explosive findings, with one being not worth the trip you took, and ten being of immediate interest to the ADF Director, where would you place yours?"

"Definitely ten," said Malia.

"Seriously?"

"Seriously," she responded firmly.

"Okay, we're not talking here then. Would you come with me to Beaufort tonight?"

"I can come into Beaufort?"

"With me, yes." He would also call Steve Rosen and give him a chance to hear Malia firsthand.

"That big?" was Steve's only response.

"Yes, so she says."

"See you in 45 minutes," said Steve. In the background David heard a woman's voice. He was probably disrupting a congenial domestic evening, but David suspected that Steve would bring home ice cream afterward to make up for his sudden departure. He was that type of guy.

To David, Beaufort by night was nothing exceptional. It was his second home. But for Malia, who had never visited—which was a good thing—but who had heard only ominous stories until she met David, the 80-story spire splayed in the moonlit darkness above them, puckered by office lights, was a dramatic sight. They parked in the garage, and David signed Malia into the building in the lobby in front of the curious night officers.

An analyst who introduced herself as Calla met them at the entrance to the ECU. "Commander Rosen asked you to wait for him in the conference room," she said, escorting them. "I'll be joining you to take notes." Calla was the ECU's Karlmarx, from what David had gathered.

"Calla's absolutely reliable," said Steve Rosen when he joined them about ten minutes later and shook Malia's hand. "No worries. And you are the lady who escaped from the Earth Weekend and now you've survived the Economic Zone itself. Quite remarkable. Are you ready, Calla?" The microphone went red, and Calla began typing. David had already told Malia that Steve was among the most decent Antifans he knew, and she felt instantly reassured by his open, friendly face and warm voice, as his demeanor at the festival had reassured her at a distance.

They went over the circumstances that had brought Malia to the Economic Strike Zone. Steve asked her to relate the schedule of events of the offsite. When she got to the tour, Steve asked sharply, "Can you draw us a map later?"

Malia nodded, "roughly."

"That would be very helpful," said Steve with relief. "Okay, please continue."

When he had finished questioning Malia, Steve said, "So, what I see here are several worrying developments, in rising order of concern. One, the ESF definitely plans to close down the EcoLand hostel in downtown Anacosta and deport its residents to the Zone. Mind you, we're possibly two weeks away from that happening, and the ADF has not been notified. Two, we have armed ESF officers who are actually Economic Tower civilians, in violation of Basic Law Number Six, which says only Antifan officers and Zone camp guards, and a few police officers, may be armed in the DJR. Three, and most alarming, they are killing thousands of Social Credit citizens in pursuit of a truth serum, in conjunction with Beijing, with absolutely no notification to the ADF, which you think would be essential or at least prudent, for several reasons. If any DJR agency would have an interest in a truth serum, it would be the ADF.

"Are we sure that no ADF entity has been contacted about this?" Steve asked. Beaufort, like most of the Towers, was notorious for stovepiping in which one silo might have little knowledge of the activities of others.

"If they had, it should have come out in the meeting with the Director on Monday, right?" replied David. "Garnett would have known. Everyone who mattered was in the room, but no one spoke up. And in that room, the silos come down."

Steve continued, "And what eludes us, is that so far we cannot make a connection to those Mexican bank accounts. But there must be one."

"Oh!" Malia suddenly said. They all turned to look at her.

"Mexico came up in one of my conversations. I'm sorry I didn't realize it might be important. Henry's wife said that her husband had suggested they retire to Mexico in the next few years. I asked whether it was legal, and she said if her husband was suggesting it, she assumed it was."

"It's not," said David, "although you could defect if you could travel there in the first place."

Malia then remembered Will's remark about Adam becoming a rich man and the others "following in his wake," which she mentioned to the Antifans.

"Did anything else happen that seemed peculiar, or not easy to explain?" Steve asked.

Malia relayed, "One thing that still puzzles me is that when the Chinese doctor spoke of all the dead subjects, Henry and Adam exchanged glances that if I had to describe them, seemed satisfied. It was as if they were happy about the deaths, but why would it make them happy? Getting the truth serum, yes, but lots of dead inmates?"

"Was there any mention of the ADF or Antifans at any time?" asked Steve.

"Yes," Malia recalled. "When Dr. Ling was regretting that there was no proper control group, such as real dissidents they could test the serums on, Adam said 'good luck' in getting Antifans to give up their prisoners in the hospitals." Steve then confirmed that no one at the meeting had followed up on that remark, for example, suggesting they reach out to the ADF. For him, it was confirmation that the Economic Tower had no intention of partnering with the ADF.

"One member of the group said that a successful serum would put the Economic Tower in a powerful position over all the other towers, permanently," she recalled. "That was Will Kendall. He's the quartermaster for the Anacosta Zone."

"Good enough," said Steve. "There's a motive." They had been sitting there for two hours. "Perhaps Ms. Malia would like a break." Calla offered to escort her to the washroom. As the women left, Steve said to David, "Harris, I'm really glad I said yes when you asked me to help your girlfriend escape at the Earth Weekend. I almost brushed you off."

"My mother always said that a favor granted is a favor repaid."

"I think we need to tell the Director immediately," said Steve. They called Ferraro's assistant, who confirmed the Director was playing *Risk* with his bodyguards as he typically did on Saturday nights. "They want to know whether he needs to come into the building?"

"We need to use his safe room if we go to his place. He's got servants and— others—roaming around the house, especially on weekends." David realized that Steve had not yet visited Ferraro at home. Steve wasn't the kind of Antifan commander whom the Director would invite to his parties, or who would be inclined to accept.

They called for a driver to take Malia home. Before David walked her out of the ECU, Steve said, "Ms. Malia, on behalf of the ADF, we are very indebted to you. I admire your courage. What you have found out, at great risk to yourself, is worth a great deal to the country and to the Antifan Defense Forces. If I may, I would like to give you an Antifan salute." Malia smiled shyly as he did. "Harris, I'll see you back here in a few."

Then they were in Steve's sport van heading for the Director's house. Even Steve has a cooler car than I do, David thought ruefully.

At Ferraro's house, they found the Director in the living room defeating the remaining opponent and refilling a glass from a decanter. "Hah!" said Ferraro, placing another several dozen armies on the board as the bodyguard sadly awaited the final blow. "You shouldn't have chosen pink. It sapped your *Risk* manhood. Do we have to use the safe room? Jermaine, where's the code for that room, dammit?"

Jermaine, who had been vanquished earlier, found the code; they trudged down to the basement, briefly glimpsing a pale young man clad only in a thong bathing suit standing at the sink in the kitchen. They entered a room that held a small round table and several chairs. In this room, one could talk as confidentially as in the Director's office at Beaufort.

Ferraro listened without interrupting to Steve's account of Malia's visit to the ESZ. He could be a blowhard, but he also knew when to become deadly serious. When they were done, Ferraro shook his head. "Gentlemen, I never saw this coming. It pains me to think of the monstrous treatment of our young Social Krediteers. I thought them foolish, but in no way deserving of murder. This is evil, something you would expect of the fascists, but not from our side. And then being cut out of this proposition—if anyone should be pioneering this truth serum, it should be us. Maybe instead of fighting the Knowledge Tower, we need to turn our attention to the Economic Tower.

I'm still angry at Pernella, she should have known better—should we show her the info about the bank accounts yet? I don't want to reveal our hand too soon.

"And the firearms—these guys are pretending to be Antifans. What's the end goal here?"

"Maybe to become the next Antifans," said David. "If they had the truth serum, and the Chinese backing, what is to keep them from telling Avadaughter the ADF has outlived our purpose? It's all about economics, today, and control is all about science, and what could be more telling than Beijing placing the Economic Tower of a socialist country at the fore?"

"I doubt the Knowledge Tower would object," said Ferraro, "that's for sure."

He looked at Steve and David. "Thank you for coming out here tonight, even though I won't sleep that well. Let's have a commander meeting tomorrow afternoon at headquarters. I don't want to wait for Monday." David realized he would have to cancel his visit to Marjory, and Steve knew that he would have to bring flowers as well as ice cream home tonight. But this was truly important.

They returned upstairs to the living room, Ferraro complaining about his old knees. As the commanders prepared to step outside, the Director said to David, "I'll send you both invitations to my next party, next Saturday night. Harris, bring that girlfriend of yours. I want to meet this brave young lady—she showed true Antifan spirit in going out to the Zone."

"Yes, sir," said David. "We'd be honored to attend."

Chapter 42
Basic Law Lesson
(Saturday/Sunday, 23-24 July)

When David entered the apartment around 1 am, Malia was soundly asleep in bed, having only dimmed the lights, presumably waiting for him to return. He quietly made himself a snack in the kitchen, washed, and still too alert to fall asleep, read news on his phone while stretched out on the sofa, a chenille throw blanket over his midsection. He was engrossed in an article, allegedly written by a Plore, called "How I Realized That the DJR Was My True Homeland," which ended with the Plore being granted Social Credit citizenship and a job at the Social Tower. The article made David uneasy, since he suspected no real Plore had written this, or if he had, then he was betraying his side in some way. A few careless telling words revealed the hand of at least a Social Credit editor if not author.

When he looked up, Malia was standing there. He made way for her on the sofa, drawing the throw blanket around them.

"What did the Director think?" she wanted to know.

"Very impressed, actually shocked. He never thought we'd have any kind of challenge from the Economic Tower," he said. "We're having a meeting tomorrow. I hope you don't mind if we skip going to my mother's."

"I think I need to rest anyway, and I'm on duty tomorrow night. You realize I'm going to the beach with Rex a week from tomorrow."

"Maybe just as well," he said. "You need a longer break. It'll take us weeks to digest and run down what you brought back. I'd rather you stayed away from Adam Ross for a few weeks. By the way, the Director is inviting us to one of his parties next Saturday."

Malia nodded, and then she burst into tears. Alarmed, David put both arms around her and held her until the sobs stopped.

"Talk to me," he said, as he turned on the noise cylinder.

She told him, in no real order, about Mollie and Jim being Plores, just like he'd guessed; the helplessness of the young man strapped to the chair; being constantly terrified they would discover she was an Antifan spy; the angry look the waiter had given her at that first lunch; the execution grounds looming on the other side of the pine trees from their guesthouse (David recalled the execution he had witnessed while

Malia slept on their day in the Massanutten); the casual and cruel comments she had overheard about Plores and also about low Social Crediteers—"like they were some kind of farm animals, not human beings, not even fellow DJRers—they euthanize them...." This was awful enough to David, but he sensed this was not all. When witnesses revealed details in this kind of jumbled way, there was usually something more central looming behind it that the speaker needed help to approach coherently.

"What else?" he asked, with a harsher tone than he intended.

She lowered her voice, and afraid to meet David's stare, which was both angry and caring at the same time, told him everything, including about being sent to Will's guesthouse, as well as about Adam's cruel treatment of the young man who had delivered their breakfast on Friday (a girl had shown up the second morning). Except for Friday night, it had not been entirely unpleasant, but under no circumstances could she confess that to him. Plores were so sensitive.

She watched him pivot to a facing forward position on the couch, lean over, and put his sandy head in his hands. "I'm sorry, Malia, I should not have sent you there. It was not right, no matter what you came back with. I didn't realize what kind of monster you were dealing with."

Now it was her turn to comfort him, kneeling next to him on the sofa, putting her soft arms around his muscular shoulders. She was wearing the babydoll nightgown she had bought her first night in this apartment, the one David liked so much.

"I promise you, Malia," David eventually said, "that someday soon, I will make Adam Ross pay for all of this." He was thinking of a hulking gay Antifan named Otto who would gladly give Adam Ross some of his own medicine when the time came. "Thanks to you, the noose is tightening around that gang." In the morning, when they once again made love, with him especially tender, he was relieved to see that the time spent with Adam Ross had not unduly traumatized her, nor did she hold against him the sins of more wicked men.

The Commander Executive Session began at 1 pm sharp on Sunday. This time Charlton was in place, representing the KCU, with David sitting against the wall behind him. Steve Rosen sat at the Director's right and Montoya, the Director's deputy, on his left. A black and gold banner with the official ADF slogan for the upcoming National Security Day, "In It To Win It," hung from the window, jauntily, as if it were already Saturnalia.

Ferraro opened with, "Over the weekend, we began to realize that despite all our efforts focused on the Knowledge Tower, the Economic Tower has also been up to no good. We have also learned, thanks to our informant, who spent several days at ESZ Camp Four, that the Economic Tower is secretly developing a powerful new indoctrination serum—much more powerful than the truth serum we use here at Beaufort. In addition, they have killed about 2,300 Social Crediteers in these dangerous experiments, whether during the experiments themselves, or afterwards by euthanasia. Let me remind you, the victims are not fascist enemies, nor even Plores, but Social Crediteers in good standing. Second, of concern is that the Economic Tower has kept this effort secret from the ADF. If anyone has standing here to supervise such a project, it is ourselves. Garnett, let me confirm—the Economic Tower has made no effort to reach out to us at the scientific enterprise level on this matter?"

"No, sir, none at all," emphasized Garnett, the coordinator of Antifan national security research with the Economic Tower.

"The active sidelining of the ADF casts the Tower's motives into question, but we'll return to that later," said Ferraro. "Third, we have evidence from our informant that Econ Tower bureaucrats are carrying firearms, which as you know violates Basic Law Number Six. Finally, they are planning a roundup at the EcoLand to seize more victims, but unlike at the Earth Weekend roundup, we have not been notified, let alone requested to provide backup.

"Commander Rosen, would you please apprise our colleagues of the details regarding each of the four concerns?" asked Ferraro.

"Yes, sir," said Steve Rosen. He reminded the group that the inquiry had begun with the Mexicans informing the ADF of the six illegal bank accounts, all in the names of Economic Tower functionaries met by the informant during her stay at the Zone camp. He underscored that their informant had been an eyewitness to the experimentation, and to the Chinese doctor's own admission of the roughly 2,300 deaths as a result of the experiments. This was first-hand information and not hearsay in any respect. "The prisoner population of the camp is normally about 7,000, to the best of our knowledge." He noted Adam Ross's remark about Antifan prisoners in psychiatric hospitals, which could be interpreted either as casual regret that those possible control groups were out of reach, or more likely, that the Economic Tower wasn't planning to approach Beaufort.

"What we need to discuss today," said Ferraro, "is whether we confront the Economic Tower with what we already know, or if we just arrest the six with the bank accounts and press them for more on the experimentation. But the arrests, along with my asking Pernella Smith for more information on the laboratory, would put them on notice we're connecting the two."

"Director," said Montoya, "This might depend on what we think the Tower's ultimate goal is here. Why would they engage in these experiments without notifying us? If it were just an oversight, then Pernella Smith wouldn't have told you off like that when you asked." Ferraro bristled at the reminder.

One of the commanders observed that the bearing of arms by Econ Tower civilians well away from the Zone was an ominous sign. And the implication that the ESF felt it needed no coordination with, let alone support from the ADF on the planned

EcoLand raid suggested that the ESF was confident in its own capabilities, and felt no need to defer to the ADF.

"The worst-case scenario," said Montoya, a shrewd and lethal deputy raised in the Counterintelligence Unit and Gemma Carpenter's former boss, "is that the Econ Tower is putting itself into a position to absorb Beaufort's responsibilities."

A hubbub broke out. "That's impossible!" Charlton said.

"Not impossible," Montoya responded. "They don't have to put Econ bodies in every ADF seat at Beaufort. All President Avadaughter has to do is transfer some major ADF responsibilities and functions to the ESF, and seed their people throughout our building. Maybe they'd leave us the Border Patrols and the Coast Guard. The proud heritage of the Antifan Defense Forces would wither to a few quasi-military units."

The Director turned on Montoya. "How is that possible? The Basic Law gives the ADF responsibility for keeping the other towers in check."

"Victor, where does the Basic Law say that? Explicitly?" Only Montoya could get away with calling the Director "Victor."

"Implicitly," said Ferraro, who demanded that the assistants pull the text of the Basic Law up onto the screen. Half a minute later, he was scrolling through the Tower Responsibility section of the Basic Law:

One. The Antifan Defense Forces exercise military, law enforcement and counterintelligence responsibilities for the Diversity Justice Republic. Other Towers may exercise limited such functions internally. ("That's the justification for the ESF," Rosen pointed out.) The ADF may name its own Director, subject to formal written assent from the President of the Republic, and dismiss at will. ("I never thought that assent part would be more than a formality," grumbled Ferraro.)

(Basic Laws Two and Three dealt with the responsibilities of the Social and Knowledge Towers, respectively).

Four. The Economic Tower is responsible for: the conduct of routine diplomatic and trade affairs with foreign countries; the production and distribution of all goods and agriculture; the conduct of scientific inquiry, in coordination with other Towers as overlapping with their spheres of responsibility. ("Hah!" grunted Ferraro)

Five. Unassigned functions as they arise will be granted to one or several Towers by the President, advised by the DJR Advisory Congress. ("Potentially problematic," Montoya noted.)

Six. The use and carrying of firearms are restricted to members of the Antifan Defense Forces, authorized units of the Community Police, and members of the Economic Strike Force performing guard duties exclusively on Industrial Zone grounds. Violators are subject to the death penalty.

Seven. Arrest powers are reserved to the Antifan Defense Forces and to local police forces under the general direction of the ADF. Economic Strike Force arrest powers are for economic violations only, as authorized by the ADF; and unilaterally on Economic Zone grounds.

Eight. The President of the Diversity Justice Republic, as advised by the Supreme Advisory Court and the DJR Advisory Congress, may adjust these responsibilities.

"I never really paid attention to Eight," lamented Ferraro. "It just seemed like boilerplate. I mean, who would give military and law enforcement responsibilities to the *Economic* Tower, after all those Antifan sacrifices in the service of this government? I mean, would we ever try to run factories?"

The commanders recalled the now-ominous confrontation with President Avadaughter after the parade bombing. This was a pissing contest that had done the ADF more harm than good.

"I'm worried about going public when all we have is the word of one informant," said Ferraro, "even a credible one. I'm inclined to see how much more the informant can find out for us about the Tower's ultimate intentions." He paused. "I can see a situation in which the bank account holders are prosecuted, and yet the Econ Tower goes ahead with the larger scheme because we can't stop it. I'm not sure that uncovering the bank accounts will do much for us if we can't link it to the broader plan, assuming there is one."

David thought, we wasted too much political capital with the Coronavirus Parade bombing. We don't dare attack the Economic Tower now, not directly. He suddenly leaned forward and whispered to Charlton.

"What is that, Harris? Do you have something to say to the group?"

"Yes, sir. The informant, who as you know is a private citizen, has already put herself in grave danger to find out what we have already learned about the illicit activities in the Zone. I doubt she would be able to find out more without jeopardizing herself further."

"The informant is also your girlfriend, correct, Harris?" Ferraro asked. "Well, it's commendable that you are seeking to protect her. A little old-fashioned, if I may say so." With that one word, he reminded the room where David came from. "Under Diversity, there are no private citizens."

"She didn't have to do as much as she has for us," said David, "sir."

"Harris, your girlfriend is earning a sizable sum of money from her job at the Octavian, which has led us in this direction. She now has a moral, if not legal obligation, to see this assignment through. No one else is in a position to do so. If we make this public now, or even approach Avadaughter, we may not be taken seriously."

David thought bitterly to himself that he couldn't remember the last time he'd heard the words "moral" and "obligation" uttered jointly in this room. But he had to acknowledge the Director's rebuke was not entirely harmful to his and Malia's cause.

Adam Ross would likely suspect how the information got out, thought David, so soon after her visit to the Zone. Perhaps Malia is safer with a more long-term strategy here. She'll be gone for three weeks at the beach anyway.

"Yes, sir, she is a loyal Diversity citizen and will gladly continue serving the ADF. I apologize for the appearance that my personal equities might be interfering with the ADF mission. My loyalty and my honor, always."

"Not at all, Harris. Perfectly understandable," said Ferraro, thinking that this was the usual Plore Achilles' heel showing itself again.

"What about the EcoLand action, sir?" asked Rosen.

"Let's see if they do it," replied Ferraro. "Maybe they'll regret having tried it on their own. If they come to us, let me know. Anything else, folks?" He pulled himself to his feet, a little unsteadily, and said, "Thank you. Dismissed."

Back in the Director's office, Ferraro and Montoya sat glumly. A bias for action was the hallmark of the ADF and it was painful to sit there and watch the Econ Tower steaming ahead with its devious plots. It would have been much more satisfying to round up the usual suspects. "We're lucky we had that informant in place in the Zone this week," said Montoya. "Otherwise we'd know nothing other than the bank accounts. Harris is really dating her?"

"She's the former Depository librarian," said Ferraro, "Harris met her then. Then when it got too hot there, he found her our slot at the Octavian and this Adam Ross took an interest in her, so things started moving from that point."

"Yeah, I could see that being a problem for a Plore. Personally, I'd just as soon share my wife with someone else."

"He wants to marry her, but her Social Credit score is 70 now that's she's working at the Octavian," said Ferraro. "Normally this would be impossible. Fine for other Towers, but not for an Antifan. I'd have to petition the Knowledge Tower and the Archbishop, who aren't inclined to do me any favors these days. I'd rather not bother—it would be a lot of work and some humiliating crow-eating."

"Well, maybe the Econ Tower guys will take care of her after she's gotten us what we need," said Montoya. "From what I hear, Adam Ross is a ruthless bastard. He was one of ours during the civil war. In the report we got, he brags about having learned to break necks during that time. His must have been a wild unit, because I was a clean killer myself. We used knives when the ammunition was short."

"You're kind of ruthless yourself, Valdivar," Ferraro joked. "You're already finishing off our informant even before we've gotten what we need from her. Let's find out what we can and I'll worry about marriages later. I'll let Harris and his girlfriend think that marriage is a possibility. It might motivate her to work harder and Harris to encourage it."

"We're such bastards, aren't we?" said Montoya, rising to return to his office.

"We're in it to win it," Ferraro concluded, turning to the workscreen. He called for his car, but not before sending a voice note to his secretary to summon Brian Walters first thing tomorrow. As Montoya departed, Ferraro called after him, "Why we even still allow marriage in the DJR is beyond me. I guess it's the women's influence."

Chapter 43

Southern Shores

(Sunday/Monday, 31 July-1 August)

As the Andrewses' self-driving car approached the causeway from the mainland, Malia stared out the back window, reverent at the sight of so much water. An hour earlier, she had gazed on the vast expanse of water at Hampton Roads in southeastern Virginia, but the rusted hulks littering the abandoned once-great Norfolk Naval Station had inexplicably saddened Malia. She was quickly brought back down to earth as the local police flagged down the car on the causeway. "What's this about?" grumbled Leighton. "Never happened before."

The officer bent down to address them. "Good afternoon, amba-sehm. Do you have the waiver for the person in your vehicle who is unauthorized to cross the causeway?"

Belinda was grateful she had gone to the effort to put in the waiver for Ms. Melia, without which they would have lost precious beach time this afternoon. "Hello, officer. Yes, we have the waiver." She tapped at the armband, and leaned over to show the waiver to the officer.

"Thank you very much," the officer said. "Enjoy your stay." He moved away and Leighton restarted the car.

"Honey, thanks for taking care of that," said Leighton, like millions of husbands before him. "That just never occurred to me." He looked in the back seat at Malia, next to Rex, "Hope you don't have to deal with that all the time, Melia."

"Oh, I've learned to avoid those situations," said Malia. "I know where I belong."

The couple did not pick up on her remark's morose undertone, and Leighton even said, "Glad to hear that." But Rex reached over and squeezed Malia's hand.

Malia had slept for several hours in the car, exhausted after Director Ferraro's party last night. The Director couldn't have been nicer to her, she thought, bowing over her hand and thanking her effusively, vaguely, for her "service to the cause." Malia had eaten so much seafood and drunk so much that she had felt slightly queasy on the way home, causing David to say, "Don't throw up! I'm about to trade in the car." Nonetheless, she was back at the Octavian promptly at 10 am. Leighton had wedged her suitpod into the trunk, which was crammed with boxes of food and bedding. The Diversity Warehouse did not operate dependably on the Outer Banks.

Within the hour, the family had settled into their beach house in Southern Shores, for which they paid a substantial annual carbon offset. Malia was pleased to have her own room, with light wood paneled walls, and a full-sized bed covered with a seashell-themed quilt. She hadn't known what to expect. Rex's very similar room was next to hers. Across an airy wood-paneled living room and kitchen with breakfast bar was Leighton and Belinda's bedroom.

"Let's go to the beach right now," said Leighton. "It's a perfect summer day."

The Atlantic Ocean lay before them, today flat, shimmering and blue. For hundreds of years these notorious waters, roiling in winter, had swallowed ships, tankers, German U-Boats, and small craft. But today it presented a calm expanse, with even the surf less crashing on the sand than landing politely, invitingly, so quietly that you could hear the distant squeals of small children. A line of pelicans bobbed across the horizon.

The Outer Banks of North Carolina were a success story, at least by the usual Janus-faced DJR standards. Beset by climate change (the official version), or just by the implacable ways of the ocean, the Outer Banks had already shrunk by half in the decades before the DJR's triumph. After the war ended, the DJR had undertaken a massive expenditure to preserve the northern half of the Banks and down to Nags Head, since so many of its elites clamored for its rescue. But the price of its preservation was to restrict access to high Social Crediteers who understood that the Earth was delicate and could not be trampled by humanity, particularly those without sufficient levels of Social Credit. For those Social Crediteers able to visit, the reward was a relatively isolated and quiet stretch of tan sand and paradise. "My grandmother said this place was a zoo before the wars. You couldn't even cross the highway without running," said Belinda with satisfaction, referring to the main north-south conduit, Highway 12. "Anyone could come here, and it showed. Fortunately, we've become much more environmentally aware."

They set up their shade pavilion a good hundred feet away from the nearest other party, and took out the sunscreen. Leighton began offering to help Malia with hers, but Belinda's fierce look caused him to ask, "Rex, would you put some sunscreen on Melia, please?" The armbands were placed in a pile next to the cooler with the drinks.

To Malia's surprise, Rex was wearing a pink girls' two-piece swimsuit. "It just looks prettier," said Rex, who said they had brought their boys' swimshorts as well, but their father would probably make them wear a T-shirt with them. Malia noticed the down on Rex's cheeks had receded slightly. She wondered if Rex had stopped taking the hormone blockers, but didn't dare to ask, not yet. She was relieved to see that Rex had a modest bust, hormone blockers or not.

The next day was rainy, so Malia and Rex walked into downtown Duck after their Diversity History lessons were over for the day.

"Is that a bookstore?" Malia asked excitedly. The marquee at the roadside said, "OBX Elite Progressive Books." They approached, but the sign on the door said, "ONLY 150 and over."

"They have real books in there," explained Rex, "and I guess they don't want Plores wandering in and reading dangerous materials. Or you."

Malia sent Rex into the store while she sat on the covered porch. They texted back and forth, Malia asking Rex to look for certain titles. She had briefly thought of daring to enter herself, and test the store's defenses, but most such enterprises had sensors that would detect an unauthorized visitor, and she neither wanted to risk more humiliation or draw more attention to Rex. Eventually Rex emerged with five books. "I had to show identification and write down our address at home," they said. "They put tracking strips in all the books too, so I don't know if you'll be able to take them back to your apartment."

Malia sighed. A 15-year old, high-Social Credit child could buy any books on offer, but a grown librarian couldn't. She still considered herself a librarian. She had encountered all these titles in the Depository, where they were held under advisory but were not strictly banned. As Belinda contended, it was best not to expose the ideologically fragile to readings outside the GVN, but more enlightened Social Crediteers could handle the mixed messages contained therein.

The two sat in the Beachcomber Café over tea and scones and handed the books back and forth. The Plore-owned café was open to all.

"I guess I'll have to read these while we're on vacation," said Malia. She would not admit to having read them before in the Depository. "I'd heard these were classics, once upon a time."

Rex looked at her with sympathy. "Or you can read them when you come to tutor me," they said. "You know my parents aren't usually home at that time."

"We should read them together," said Malia, "so we can discuss them, too. That's part of the pleasure. Too bad none of them are going to be on your makeup exams."

"I'll work especially hard at the real schoolwork," Rex promised, "so I'll have more time to read these." They paged through *The Mists of Avalon,* and Malia explained the Arthurian Camelot legend to them.

"It's too sexist for modern times, especially the notion of chivalry," said Malia. At Rex's request, she explained chivalry, at which Rex sighed softly. Malia suddenly recalled Adam's sardonic comment about Will coming to her rescue. Adam was old enough to remember the word, if not old enough to respect the spirit behind it.

The Plore proprietress of the café looked approvingly at the Social Credit mother and the boyish girl she assumed was her daughter engaged in deep conversation. "You don't see mothers and daughters so close to each other around here, not that type for sure," she thought to herself, "and even though the daughter has straight hair, she's a spitting image of the mother." She also liked how polite they were to her, even though she was just a Plore, with no armband.

Afterward, Malia and Rex trudged back to the beach house. The rain had stopped and the sun was peeking out behind clouds. "How do you know so much about books?" asked Rex.

"I had a very good education at the orphanage," said Malia.

"But how do you know about these books? I thought only people who worked at the Knowledge Tower knew about these kinds of books, like my mother."

"Like I said, I had some good teachers," said Malia shortly, afraid of inadvertently revealing her connection with the Depository. "And I did go to Justice University, the real campus. I might not have a lot of Social Credit, but I had a lot of education."

"I want to go to Justice University too," said Rex enthusiastically.

"Then we need to get your grades up this fall," said Malia, but she smiled at her daughter. When they reached the beach house, she excused herself to call David at the office. He was glad to hear from her, but she could tell it was busy at Beaufort. Once or twice David silenced the receiver and on the small screen she saw a man's hand pass him a sheaf of paperwork.

"It's beautiful here," she said.

"So are you," he said. "I see you got some sun. How's Operation Kidlet going?" This was their mock name for the program, because it was easier to explain than "Operation Kidnapping."

"We had a lovely afternoon. It was raining so we went downtown to a bookstore and then out for tea and scones in a café. Lee and Belinda are thrilled I'm taking her off their hands, and she's not moping around the house."

"Very nice," said David. "You're not planning to bring any of these books into my apartment, are you?" Like a man with a mate inclined to alcoholism, he was on the lookout for any recidivist tendencies from the former librarian. Someday, he thought, she will have all the books she wants, and I will just complain about tripping over them.

"No," she said, but hesitating. "They all have trackers, and they'll stay at the Andrews'. They're mostly for Rex. I can't stand her reading garbage like Kofi the Diversity Boy."

"Got it," he said. "Hey, give me a call tonight if you can. Maybe after nine?"

"Sure. Love you, honey."

"Love you too, book babe."

The days passed steadily, one much like the last. The Andrewses were not early risers, so by the time the family arrived on the beach, it was usually slightly after noon. Leighton and Belinda would take a quick dip, then retreat under the pavilion to read their armbands. After swimming and jumping in the waves, Rex and Malia would towel off, have a snack, and pull the books out. Rex had finished *The Mists of Avalon* and had moved onto Marcus Zusak's *The Book Thief,* switching with Malia. As the sun began to dip westward, they would bring their low metal-framed chairs just beyond the reach of the surf and read there. Then they would put the books out of sight and go for a long walk along the shoreline, like a married couple.

As they watched Malia and Rex head north along the beach, Leighton and Belinda were silent. "I'm not so sure I approve of those books," Belinda finally said as the pair disappeared into the cluster around the lifeguard's chair. "I hope no one's noticing."

"Oh?" Leighton stretched, his ribs visibly shifting under his bare chest. "How bad could they be if they bought them at the bookstore in town?"

"These are all books under advisory," Belinda informed him indignantly. "They shouldn't have sold them to a child or to a low Social Credit person. Rex said that Melia couldn't go into the bookstore, so she told them what to get."

"What's so bad about them?" asked Leighton, who was remarkably cavalier for a senior bureaucrat at the Knowledge Tower. He was steeling himself for stern instructions to confiscate the books, although he hoped he could reassure Belinda before they had a confrontation with the delightful Ms. Melia. Belinda was an expert in navigating matters of ideological purity, which he respected. Working for Terwilliger, he was aware he needed to know just enough about these intricacies to properly advise the Director.

"First of all," said Belinda, "it looks bad to be reading paper books if you're the dauson of a couple like us. We need to set an example, and reading online is far more ideologically hygienic, since it's much more strictly under the control of the proper authorities, namely ourselves. Second, these books are under advisory for a reason. The messages are mixed. The one Melia's reading is good because it is pagan-friendly. But the chivalry of the Arthurian Era is dangerously sexist. The one Rex is reading is good because it's set in Nazi Germany and is clear-eyed about fascism. But the burning of books might make ideologically fragile readers compare it with our own restrictions on books, which would be completely nonsensical, but of course that's why they're ideologically fragile."

Wow, thought Leighton, this is complicated. He remembered Terwilliger's State of the Tower speech last fall in which he had hailed the women of the Knowledge Tower as the "most resolute guardians of pure and correct thought." Including the New Women, of course, Terwilliger had hastened to add.

"It's ironic," said Belinda, "since we'll be destroying the Depository in a few weeks. But you can see how some Low Credit types might become confused."

Leighton nodded. "I'd hate to offend Melia," he said, "since she's done a lot of good for Rex. Have you noticed they has stopped taking the hormone blockers?"

"Not that that is necessarily something to be happy about," Belinda instructed him, "if they is doing it for the wrong reason. If they feel like they is really a woman, that's acceptable, but now we're going to have to explain it to our friends. We really got a lot of credit from the wokists when Rex decided they was—were non-binary and then a boy." Speaking such ungrammatical English made both of them feel like uneducated buffoons, but even between themselves, they felt incumbent to set a good example for each other. No wonder we avoid talking about Rex, thought Leighton.

"And their hair isn't colored weirdly," said Leighton. "Have you overheard their lessons? Melia really knows what's she's doing."

Belinda was in partial agreement. "I can't say I approve of all the shortcuts that are aimed at acing the test. It seems a little cynical to start parsing the different aspects of Diversity literature. That makes it seem like we produce every story or novel out of the same machine."

"Well, don't we?" laughed Leighton. "Look, do you want Rex passing these tests or not? Whatever Melia's doing seems to be working. And Rex is actually doing the work."

Belinda agreed, but her lip stuck out slightly, a pout that informed Leighton the conversation was not yet over. "You'd think she was Rex's mother or something. The waitron in the restaurant last night assumed Melia was the mother, did you see that?"

"What do you expect from a stupid Plore?" asked Leighton. "So there's a slight resemblance. They were sitting on the same side of the table. She really looks more like you." He was already slipping on the Rex terminology.

Belinda brightened. "Our hair is the same color, true. I guess I shouldn't be so sensitive."

Leighton was relieved that she wasn't harping on his difficulty in keeping his eyes off the curvaceous Ms. Malia even in her modest, one-piece bathing suits. Dark sunglasses helped him greatly in this regard. He especially liked how her body stretched when she reached up to tie her abundant dark curls in a ponytail before entering the water. He idly thought about whether she might welcome a visit in the middle of the night, but the recollection of the Plore boyfriend and his dauson's room next door stopped these ruminations cold. "Who knows how a crazy Plore would react," he thought, assuming that Malia herself would behave like a grateful low Social Crediteer.

Chapter 44
Revelations
(Monday, 15 August)

Their last Monday at the beach house dawned hazy, a marine layer that would burn off by late morning. Leighton and Belinda slept. Malia and Rex sat at the wooden picnic table on the screened porch with a partial view of the ocean, breakfast plates pushed to the side. They peered at today's Diversity History review lesson, about the American Revolution. The Knowledge Tower framework, which had originated in the 1619 Project started by the *New York Times* in 2019, had correctly attributed all major events in US history to race relations, namely the blight of slavery and the desire of the whites to preserve their supremacy in the fabric of the new nation, even post-slavery. Malia had learned early in life to stop asking questions that cast the framework's veracity into doubt, while the authorities awaited the death of older historians who asked inconvenient fact-based questions. The Knowledge Tower historians reasoned that not every fact needed to be absolutely correct to create a convincing discourse of oppression, especially when the goal was to explain the emergence and triumph of the DJR. Context was all.

Rex was making unfortunate connections from the previous unit, on black Americans, with the current one. "But if Crispus Attucks was killed in the Boston Massacre, why was the Revolution all about protecting slaveowners? Surely he would not have wanted to defend such a cause."

Malia had to explain that as a former slave, Attucks probably mistakenly thought that serving the Revolutionary cause would help free his brethren. False consciousness has always been the standby excuse of revolutionaries disappointed in the objects of their affection. "That's the answer for passing the test," she said.

"What's the real answer?" asked Rex.

"Because he was a patriot and loved America, and he hated how the British were muscling their way around Boston," said Malia. "But don't you dare answer that on the test. I hope you can keep the two sets of answers straight."

"Oh yes," said Rex. "I'll remember them. Whichever makes America look bad is the right answer—for the test." Malia nodded with relief. She knew a lot was riding on Rex doing well on the exams next month, including her own relationship with them.

Her armband buzzed with a text from David. She was surprised, because she knew he was in California today for the long-delayed visit to Beaufort West. Given the time zone difference, he must have just awakened.

Watch the news. Love u.

Rather than fiddle with her armband, which was in the bedroom, she switched on the main TV, keeping the volume low to avoid disturbing Leighton and Belinda. Rex looked at her with puzzlement. "Just a second," Malia said. "I need to see the news headlines."

To her shock, the screen was filled by an overhead view of EcoLand. Plumes of smoke rose from a charred section of the massive building. The banner read, "EcoLand Raid Ends in Fire." The announcer was saying, "Overnight, Economic Strike Zone forces entered the EcoLand Hostel at Fairmont and 11th St NW to evict known criminal elements for transportation to the Zone, where they will begin the process of their own betterment. Some of the criminals, when cornered, started a fire that destroyed the northwest corner of the pen and killed ten residents. The entire building has now been emptied for the safety of its residents. The fire continues as of 10 this morning, but firefighters have rescued several residents who were hiding and handed them to the authorities for further action." The newscaster then cheerfully added, "Eleven cats were rescued and can be adopted at the Anacosta Humane Society."

The newscaster asked, "Tejas, what have you heard about a similar action at the Rosebud?"

Malia gasped, and Rex looked at her curiously.

The reporter responded, "ESZ forces also went to the Rosebud, at H Street and 10th NW, which is home to 300 slightly higher status Social Crediteers, on a similar report of illegal activity. They arrested the 172 residents under the age of 40, and are questioning them at ESZ camps Four and Five in western Virginia. It is believed that the criminals at the hostel may have been under the direction of masterminds living at the Rosebud. However, immigrants living at the Rosebud under the New Friends program were spared."

"Oh, no, Fern!" Malia said. She reached for her armband, only to see, in her despair, a series of attempted calls from her friend at around 3:30 am. The last one was at 3:43 am.

"What's wrong, Melia?" asked Rex.

Leighton emerged from his bedroom, tying the belt of his bathrobe. He looked at the screen. "What's this?"

"The Economic Strike Force raided both the EcoLand Hostel and my building," said Malia, still in shock. "They took away hundreds of people; they took away my friend."

"Really? What was the reason?" Leighton began scanning his armband phone for the news coverage. "It says they were criminals."

"Hundreds of people in the EcoLand were criminals? My friend was a criminal?" Malia nearly shouted. "And 172 people in my building? All they had in common were they were under forty."

"Please calm down, Melia," said Leighton.

"If I hadn't been here, they would have taken me too, in the middle of the night. Am I a criminal?" She slumped down on the sofa in front of the screen, her brown cascading curls shielding her face as she stared at the floor. Rex sat down an arm's length away and looked on with concern, but dared not come closer.

"Perhaps it's all a misunderstanding," said Leighton, his stock of comforting phrases quickly evaporating. "Let's give it a day or so, and the authorities will sort it out." Despite the early hour, he began mixing Malia a stiff drink, which was his usual last resort when Belinda lost her self-control or was suffering from hormonal imbalance.

Malia could not strike from her mind the picture of the young man, strapped to the chair in his worker's clothes, a young man whose faith in the DJR had outweighed his common sense. He was no exception, but the rule, another Low Credit sheep headed to the slaughter. And yet she could not tell this well-meaning, but ignorant family what lay in wait for all these alleged criminals, who diligently went to work each day in their Tower cubicles, ate their Healthy Eating foods, prayed to Mother Earth, and trusted the government. She wept bitterly.

"It's just a work farm," said Belinda, coming out from the bedroom. "Don't be so upset."

"But Mom," said Rex, "the police took away all the people in Melia's building. They would have taken her, too, if she wasn't here."

"Well," said Belinda with a determinedly cheerful mien. "Isn't it terrific that she's here and not there?"

"Here, Melia, have a drink," said Leighton. "It's mostly orange juice."

Malia grabbed her armband on the table and ran out the house and toward the beach. Leighton sighed and drank the contents of the glass himself. "I think I need one too, Lee," said Belinda. "What drama." They began rummaging in the cabinets and coldbox for breakfast.

"Isn't it horrible, Mom, Dad?" Rex asked, their forehead furrowed.

Leighton took the signaler and scrolled back to watch the news report from the beginning. Their parenting style was to avoid upsetting Rex, and for all of them to evade any unpleasant realities in connection with imposing Diversity in the DJR. When Isabelle had come crying to their home, they had behaved as if nothing were amiss, and they had waited out her trauma, or pretended to. When a friend from Rex's school disappeared, likely to an orphanage because her parents had committed some knowledge crime, Leighton and Belinda refrained from commenting on the girl's fate even though Rex was clearly troubled. This morning's events also fell into the category of "stay happy at all costs," and only because Malia's building was involved, did they even think she was justified in exhibiting some distress.

"It'll all be sorted out," Leighton said lamely as he mixed Belinda a drink.

"If the Economic Tower says they were going after the criminals, they must have had a reason to arrest these people," Belinda said severely. "They don't just arrest people for no reason at all, like the Antifans do." Both parents nodded in agreement.

"Is Melia a criminal then?" asked Rex coldly.

"No, of course not!" said Belinda. "I'm sure they would have released her by now. But how wonderful she doesn't need to bother with all that."

Rex stared at them, aghast. "You're horrible people! Don't you have any feelings at all?" They grabbed their new, grownup armband and a box of water and went running after Malia.

Leighton and Belinda looked at each other, and Leighton asked, bewildered, "What did we do?"

Malia ran about a hundred yards onto the sand before she stopped, breathing heavily and crying. An elderly couple standing by the water with a dog looked at her curiously. Her voice shook when she spoke "David" into the armband phone. He was sitting at an outdoor café, sporting dark sunglasses and basking in California sunshine. If it were not for the ADF jacket, one might have thought him a moderately famous producer of action movies or possibly a stunt actor. Scrawny orange trees clustered behind a low brick wall. A blonde waitress with heavy eye makeup gave him a meaningfully flirtatious glance as she passed by to serve another table.

"Hello, Harris here."

"David? They went to the Rosebud!"

He looked around anxiously, but a few tables separated him from the nearest other customers, and in keeping with Angeleno unconcern about serious matters, nobody seemed particularly interested in his conversation. "Yes, I saw."

"I got several calls from Fern around 3:30 am. I turned off the phone when I went to bed, so I didn't hear any of them. Imagine her calling my name into the armband again and again, and not getting any response while the ESF gestapo were pounding on the door. Oh, it's so awful."

"You couldn't have done anything even if you had answered the phone, and I wouldn't call them by that name," said David matter-of-factly. "Please get yourself under control. You're not going to ask me to go after her, are you? It's pretty hopeless, you know."

Malia burst out crying so loudly that the customers three tables away looked over at him. He covered the microphone, and mouthed, "Women," at them. They were not surprised that such a handsome man would be dealing with crying women. She cries a lot, he thought, but as a Plore, he regarded it as a somewhat commendable testament to her emotional feeling.

"How could you not tell me? You knew, didn't you?"

David jumped up, gestured to the waitress that he would return, and put a healthy distance between himself and the tables by crossing the street and standing in front of what looked like an abandoned warehouse with the faint lettering "Pena Auto Repair and Junk." Los Angeles was a strange flattened cityscape for someone used to Anacosta's soaring towers.

"No, Malia, I did not know. None of us in—my building—knew the Rosebud was on their list. We did not help at all with this operation because we were not asked."

"But you knew they were going to go after the hostel, didn't you?"

"Look, Malia, I'm not going to stand here and discuss operational issues. Did you know anyone at EcoLand? Is there someone else you want me to rescue?"

She hung up on him, which was a partial relief, as he didn't want to have to ask the waitress to reheat his fried eggs that were now visible on the table. He would deal with Malia later, after his meetings, after he and his Beaufort West counterparts had drawn up the list for the West Coast purges. Thank goodness she had been at the beach, although he doubted that even the malevolent Adam Ross would have approved the Rosebud raid had she been in town. He chewed on his baguette, his cheeriness at the warm sunshine and the unfamiliar surroundings sorely diminished.

David took a self-driving car to Beaufort West, which resembled its eastern counterpart, though only about one-third of its height. Nonetheless, a 25-story building stood out here. And there were orange trees and exotically colorful plants in garden beds. It was like being in a foreign country. He had about twenty minutes before his first meeting, and while pacing near a grouping of resin benches, called Steve Rosen. No answer. Against his better judgment, he called Brian Walters, who was entering his third week as Steve's deputy.

"Walters here."

"Walters, this is David Harris, calling from Los Angeles."

"Hi, Harris!" No more chief or sir anymore. They were now peers. "What can I do for you?"

"You heard about the raids on EcoLand and the Rosebud?"

"Yeah, the Rosebud was a surprise, wasn't it? Isn't that where your girlfriend lives?"

"Thank goodness she was away at the beach," said David. "But a friend was staying in her apartment. Any chance we could do something to rescue her from the Zone camp?"

There was a long silence. Here was Commander Harris, finally asking for a favor, not talking down to him for once. He had known the day would come, and here it was.

"Is she one of ours?" asked Walters. He knew that Steve Rosen had facilitated the rescue of Harris's girlfriend from the Earth Weekend, but that was a bonafide girlfriend, who had since proven her mettle on behalf of the ADF, librarian or not.

"No," David admitted.

"Sorry, I think not," said Walters. "Like they'd listen to us anyway, you know. We're Tower toast these days, it seems."

"How's Wurro doing in his new spaces?" David wanted to end on a high note.

"Great. Everyone's getting into Wurro worship," said Walters. "The ECU is benefiting from some serious Wurro mana."

"That's terrific," said David. "Give my best to Steve."

"Will do, cheerio." Walters stretched and, unknown to David, smiled with satisfaction. Cheysa was standing in the doorway. He couldn't wait to tell her how he had humbled Commander Harris, although he would then rebuke her for what he perceived as her muted reaction.

Cheerio? David wondered, as he entered the building. The Antifan guards were impressed to receive a senior visitor from main Beaufort but still seemed sleepier than their East Coast counterparts. Sunshine seemed to have an enervating effect on the Antifan spirit. He wished that he had not met Fern so recently, because he could not erase from his mind's eye the thought of her roused out of Malia's bed by resounding knocks on the door and scrambling in fear to throw a few items into a duffel bag before the shock troops pushed her out of the building and into the waiting yellow buses. The only fact that comforted David was that if they had not caught her at the Rosebud, they would have found her at EcoLand, and maybe she would have instead been among those who died choking in the fire. Nothing he or Malia could have done would have made a difference. If anything, they had done their best by insisting that Fern stay at the Rosebud.

Would Avadaughter tolerate this brutal raid and mass kidnapping in the center of Anacosta? When it happened at Earth Weekend, it was mostly out of sight, and did not require emptying entire buildings in front of the rest of the City, or cause a conflagration in the middle of the night. David hoped that Ferraro and the ADF would bestir themselves to protest what was indisputably an evil deed. This would be the honorable reaction if the ADF's mission truly was to keep the other Towers honest. But here he was in Lotus Land, feeling helpless himself, with thin confidence that the ADF would assert its prerogatives this time.

Malia saw Rex running toward her. Her first reaction was to flee, but she reminded herself, "This is your daughter. She cares about you. Even if she doesn't know why, you know why."

"Melia, Melia!" Rex stopped in the sand just before her. "I'm sorry! I'm so sorry!"

Instinctively, they reached out for each other, and hugged. It felt so natural to Malia, who usually avoided personal contact, that she let the moment linger. Rex thought, why doesn't it feel like this with Mom? Both cried.

They began walking down the beach in a tense, but companionable, silence. Rex was glad they could just be there for Malia, and they sensed Malia was happy they was there. Eventually, tired, they spotted a completely deserted section of the beach, and dropped down on a shady spot just in front of a wooden wall separating the beach from an oceanfront property. It was high noon, and both were now sunburned and getting thirsty. They shared the water box, passing it back and forth. I gave you life, Malia thought, and so what are a few germs?

They sat for a few minutes before Rex asked, "Melia, why did the troops raid the hostel and your apartment building? They can't all have been criminals."

"Nobody was a criminal," said Malia sharply. "They just want more slave labor for the Industrial Zone camps. So now they will even kidnap Social Credit citizens from their beds in the middle of the City.

"They also raided the Earth Weekend service in April, and I was very lucky to escape," she said.

"How did you escape?"

"Someone helped me," said Malia. "But no one was there to help the others."

"Who helped you?"

Malia looked at Rex severely. "I won't tell you, because I want to protect him—and you. But out of thousands of people at that service, I was the only low Social Crediteer who made it home that day. Otherwise we would certainly not be here, talking."

Rex gave a deep sigh. "I'm very lucky, aren't I? My family doesn't have to worry about being treated like this."

Malia could not help herself. It was going to have to happen eventually, and why not on this beach? She wasn't going to wait for David, a continent away, brutally spurning her feelings, to give her permission. "Your current family."

Rex stared at her.

"You've told me you know you were adopted, right?" Malia stated.

"Well, nobody's ever said it to me. But that's what I assume, because my first memories aren't about my Mom and Dad. I remember sitting at a table with a lady in an apartment, playing a game and drinking hot chocolate. I also remember a picture of a rabbit on the wall." She remembers the Peter Rabbit poster, Malia thought with a giant happy pang. "But my mother says we never had that poster, and I must have just made it up."

"No, you didn't make it up," said Malia grimly, crossing the Rubicon. "We had the poster of Peter Rabbit in your bedroom." It had disappeared in that first brutal raid, probably ending up on a junk heap. I should have checked the recycling dumpster that afternoon, she thought ruefully. I could have hidden it somewhere in the basement until the raids ended.

Rex stared at her again, open-mouthed. "Are you the lady in that memory? Are you saying that you're my real mother?"

"Yes," said Malia, "and if you are ready, I can tell you more about what happened.

But before I say anything else, anything, you must swear by Mother Earth that you will not tell anyone. Because if you so much as hint to Lee and Belinda what you know, they will never let me see you again. They will either send me away or have me arrested, and that will be the end. Someday it will be all right to tell the truth but not yet."

"I swear!" said Rex. "I swear by Mother Earth I will not breathe a word of this."

"Not to your friends, either," said Malia. "To nobody."

"Nobody!"

"And you must not hold this against your current parents. They do not know that you were stolen. They think it was an ordinary adoption and that your mother could not keep you. There must be no resentment. They did their best for you." High road, thought Malia. It was mostly true, and she could not poison Rex's last few months with them, if only because it would signal that something was wrong and that secrets had been revealed. Rex promised they would not blame Lee and Belinda.

Then Malia finally told Rex about themself. "Your real name is Isabelle Jennifer Jenness. I had you when I was a student. I can tell you about your father sometime, but all I remember is his first name, Peter, and he was a Plore who was working on a building at my college. After I gave birth to you, we lived in an apartment in the City, and I was working as a librarian at…"

"I knew it!" Rex said triumphantly.

Malia smiled tolerantly, and continued, "while I finished my degree online. You were in kindergarten, and the class was drawing pictures in honor of Coronavirus Liberation Day. Your principal called me in and said that you had drawn a subversive picture that slandered our friend China and Asian people in general. She accused me of raising you wrong. Later that day, you disappeared from school. I ran home, and the authorities had ransacked the apartment and taken everything of yours. They came back twice, in case they had missed anything. Someone even took the photo of you I kept on my desk at work."

"Why didn't you complain? Didn't anyone want to help you?"

"Of course I tried to complain. Nobody wanted to help because I was nothing, and the Knowledge Tower bureaucrats were in control. They could steal my child and threaten *me* with prison. Let that be a lesson to you about how this country works."

"I thought we looked a lot alike," Rex said. "Remember the waitron thought last week that you were my mother? Mom was really mad about that afterward."

"We will do nothing different. For now," said Malia, "it's enough just to know who you really are. No written communication, no texts between us that refer to this. Other people can read your texts, you know. Do you remember we had a cat named Theobald?"

Rex frowned. "No, I don't remember any cats. My parents got one, but it died." She paused. "Is it okay if I call them that for now?"

"Yes, please. Keep everything normal so we don't awaken any suspicions. I'm still

Melia," said Malia. Or Malia. But that's another layer of deception you don't need to know about for now, my precious. "We'd better return to the house. Your parents must be worrying."

"I really like the name Isabelle," Rex confided. "Can I use it again someday?"

"Yes, but again, don't mention it to anyone. It would not be a safe thing to do. Your parents probably know it was originally your name, but they changed it."

As they walked back across the sand, Rex suddenly sprang forth and started twirling in giant circles, kicking up sand, and singing, "I'm a real person! I'm a real person again!" Malia didn't recognize the lyrics from a current hit, "Real Person," by the New Man singer Kelly Morgan, but later she heard it on her armband radio and it suddenly made sense.

> "I'm a real person, honey,
> I'm a real person again,
> True to myself,
> I know who I am!"

As with many Diversity songs, it was better to overlook the lyrics.

As they approached the turnoff to the Andrewses' house, and were about to exit the beach, they recognized the family's blue and yellow pavilion, and reluctantly trudged over, kicking up sand. Belinda was wading in the surf. Leighton waved at them from behind his dark glasses, relieved that Malia and Rex seemed to have recovered their equanimity.

"Are you feeling better?" he said. "I'm sure that was very upsetting news."

"Yes, thank you," said Malia. "That was a little too close for comfort. I'm sorry to have lost my temper. That was inappropriate."

"Not at all, not at all," said Leighton. "I'd be discomfited too. But I'm sure the authorities will sort out the whole matter. We need to trust they have everyone's interests at heart." He returned to his armband screen.

As they climbed the wooden steps to the asphalt path, Rex turned to Malia, and said, "My dad's a little naïve, don't you think?"

"A little!" snorted Malia, but she would say nothing more to disparage Rex's parents, who had brought her here to the Outer Banks and enabled the reunion with her daughter. Meanwhile, Rex was digesting her lesson on truth and power in the DJR.

PART FOUR

THE ECONOMIC
TOWER/REHOBA

Chapter 45

Plore Boyfriends

(Sunday, 21 August)

"I'm nervous about the Andrewses dropping you off at the Rosebud," said David. "I don't know whether your apartment is still yours or in livable shape, or if someone's waiting for the real you to make an appearance. Text me when you're half an hour away, and I'll meet you there."

When the Andrewses dropped Malia off, she got her own suitpod out of the vehicle. As she waved after their car—frankly, she was not sure they even remembered that the Rosebud had been raided a week ago—she heard David's voice behind her. She spun around and met his kiss enthusiastically. "You look like a sun goddess!" he said.

"And you look like my sun god," she replied sweetly, since after several days in Los Angeles, he too was bronzed. It was hard to tell initially, since he had pulled a baseball cap over his forehead and wore the kind of plaid short-sleeved shirt and jeans favored by Tom as Dave.

"Let's get into the building quickly," he said, grabbing her suitpod strap and ushering her into the lobby.

"Why the hurry?" she asked. "And why are you dressed like Tom?"

"Because I think we're being watched," said David, "at least outside the building, which I guessed might happen." David had spent the day with his family in Ploreville. He had parked the now-recovered yellow sportscar several blocks away from the Rosebud, and had been waiting about a dozen yards from the entrance, just another illegal Plore hanging out on a street corner. It gave him time to assess the surroundings. Ostensibly it was another very sleepy Sunday in late August as those privileged enough to leave town enjoyed one of the final beach weekends of the season. National Security Day on September 12th would officially mark the end of the summer, and children would return to school the following morning.

David spotted a black car that looked like an Antifan vehicle, but he was confident that no Antifan surveillance unit needed to be loitering in front of the Rosebud today. Standing a good distance behind the car, David could just glimpse some movement in the front seat. But if not an Antifan surveillance unit, then who else but the ESF, possibly checking out returnees to the building, or ensuring no suspicious activity was taking place in the aftermath of the raid? For that reason, he was glad he had not worn his ADF jacket, and had protected Malia's cover by sparing her interaction with recognizable Antifans. Even though the day was uncomfortably warm, David wore a long windbreaker over his armband and his holster.

The couple went upstairs in an oddly silent building, encountering no one, then walked down the hallway to Malia's apartment. Yellow tape crossed over the door in a giant X and a sign read, "Property of the ESF." Technically, thought David, it should be property of the Social Tower. "At least no one's inside," said David as he tore down the tape. "Why don't you stay outside for a moment while I check it out? Just in case."

A minute later, he called, "You can come in," and Malia entered with trepidation.

The apartment was emptied of all personal items, as if cleaning and painting crews were due shortly to prepare it for the next tenant.

"This time you at least have your toothbrush," David said, joking grimly.

"It's as if neither Fern or I ever lived here," said Malia slowly. In some ways, it was more disturbing than if they had found the apartment in disarray. Under the shadow of the papasan chair lay a nail polish bottle, which she picked up and popped in her purse.

"You didn't get your Healthy Eating delivery on Tuesday either, I bet," said David, peeking in the empty coldbox. The cabinets were empty as well. They departed the building by the back basement entrance, which was closer to the sportscar. They saw no one else in the building the entire time, although half the tenants had supposedly been spared deportation.

Malia was relieved to return to the Avalon, even if the question remained of where the government thought she lived. The question was answered the next day, when she awoke to a buzzing armband and a notice that she was assigned to the TerraCity Hostel, effective immediately, "pursuant to Social Law 45," which housed under-85 Social Crediteers in socialist "solidarity pens." Malia was invited to check in during business hours. "Individual rooms at TerraCity are small, in keeping with Diversity socialist spirit," advised the letter. "Please only bring a minimum of personal baggage." Malia snorted at the double meaning, even in her dismay.

"To hell with that," said David when he came home that evening, but then reluctantly agreed that it would be prudent for Malia to pretend to live at the hostel, if only because the government might otherwise try to track her whereabouts. First thing on Tuesday, he escorted her to TerraCity before they both went to Beaufort, where Malia would be debriefed on the Andrewses and then briefed by Cheysa for her next encounters with Adam Ross.

"Oh, David, I'm frightened," she said sincerely as they pulled up in front of the block-long stone façade, atop which sat the giant "TerraCity Hostel" sign. No self-driving cars needed to park here, except perhaps for the hostel manager herself.

"I'll come in with you," said David. He had already requested that his new deputy

Helen Zhu, whom he had got in the trade with Steve Rosen for Walters, handle the 8:30. David stowed the holster with its electronic firearm and knife in the safe compartment under the seat and exchanged the ADF jacket for a simple blue blazer.

To avoid looking conspicuous, Malia had brought a few canvas bags of unneeded personal items. They marched up the staircase with the bags and took a moment to get their bearings in the lobby. A sign to the left with an arrow said "Intake This Way." A sign on the right said, "Cafeteria This Way." Directly in front of them, the sign said, "Authorized Personnel Only." A heavyset female in a guard uniform sat before that sign, uninterested in helping them, mesmerized by the screen on her armband. It was probably time for the morning chat shows.

Inside the intake office was a high counter with a few plastic chairs along the wall. A ponytailed young woman came over. "Name?" she demanded. Malia gave her name and the woman spent several minutes retrieving the record. She looked at Malia as if to confirm this was not some impostor seeking to seize a coveted cell at TerraCity. "We need to take your fingerprints, eye prints, and a new photo," she said. Malia complied, sensing that David, who would not sit down, was beginning to bristle. As a Plore with a high Social Credit score, he was unaccustomed on both fronts to socialist manners.

"He's not staying here, is he?" said the young woman. "You can't have sexual partners in your rooms." Malia was sure that was not the case, from her previous experience, or more precisely, that of roommates at EcoLand, but she said, "He's only helping me move in."

"Good," said the young woman. "Keep it that way." Malia knew that the only thing keeping David from lambasting the clerk was the fear that any protest would ultimately make both of them late for an important morning at Beaufort. The sluggish female guard would no doubt be summoned, resentful at the interruption, and possibly even a manager who might call the police. Showing Antifan credentials wouldn't help here.

She was given Suite 583, Room C. "Is that a good room?" David asked, as if they were checking into a hotel. "It's what we have," the young woman responded, almost deferential to his mantle of authority. "We've had a lot of new people recently." Nobody said "EcoLand," but all understood what was meant. The clerk gave Malia a brochure that listed times for meals, laundry pickup, the marijuana dispensary, and Mother Earth Diversity services.

Malia's fingerprint would open the suite door and her cell. She and David took the large freight-like elevator to the fifth floor. The faint smell of marijuana suffused the hallway. This is how you keep the inmates sedated, thought David. Walking down the long corridor, which went around the entire rectangular compound, David was reminded of some of the dingier Antifan psychiatric hospitals he had visited. The interior suites looked into a dank courtyard in which nobody ever sat. Unfortunately, not that it really mattered, Suite 583 had an interior view.

The door slid open at Malia's touch to reveal a small sitting room with wooden lounge chairs with dirty orange cushions, and a rickety wooden table or two, much like a college dorm lounge, only smaller and far more dispirited. Malia and David hoped all the residents would be at work, and they could place the bags in Room C and disappear. But the door to Room A was open, and the distinct smell of marijuana smoke wafted out. Malia opened Room C before Occupant A could emerge.

"Good God," said David. "What did you do to deserve this?" The room was truly a cell, seven feet wide by fourteen feet long, with a small high window that overlooked the courtyard, if you were tall enough to look down, which Malia wouldn't be. There was an iron bed with a thin stained mattress and pillow, and a folded set of clean sheets. The cell also contained a square chest-high wooden cabinet for clothing, and a small table and chair. The mixed-gender showers and toilets were down the hall. They dumped the bags onto the bed and turned to flee, but Occupant A now stood between them and the door. He was an unshaven, bare-chested white man about forty dressed only in worn pajama bottoms. Malia saw that his toes were dirty. The fastidious David was visibly repelled.

"Hey, which one of you is the new one?"

"Me," said Malia.

"Good," said the stoned man. "Real pretty. Welcome to TerraCity. Ha, ha, I made a poem. You're real pretty; welcome to TerraCity!"

"Why aren't you at work?" demanded David.

"Work?" asked the stoned man, bemused. "Maybe when they catch up with me." Now Malia knew where Street People came from.

"We're going," said David. "Excuse us."

The man stood before them. "Uh, uh," he said. "That's not Diversity manners. If she's going to live here, you need to be friendlier. I want a kiss."

"Not from me," said David, finally at the end of his patience with the whole depressing experience. He took the man by the shoulders and flung him against the back corner of the room, where he crashed into a chair, and they escaped. Behind them, they heard, "You can't do that to me! I'm a Social Credit citizen!"

"He'll be fine," said David as they hightailed it to the elevators. "Pot makes you spongier. He won't have broken any bones."

Back in the sportscar, David slumped against his seat, closing his eyes for a moment. "Malia, that was the worst thing I've seen in my whole life. No wonder Fern was thrilled to stay in your apartment. And you lived like that for three years?"

"Yes," she said. "But I really think EcoLand was better than that. Or maybe I was younger and more clueless." She realized, to her mixed pleasure and shock, that in some ways she was tougher and more attuned to DJR realities than was David, who did not much remember his early childhood and had been protected by Ploreville and the Antifans ever since.

"I want you to know," he said, "that our Antifan psychiatric hospitals are more comfortable than that, definitely more orderly, and the patients are far saner than that fellow. So if you get a choice between being a low Social Crediteer or a knowledge criminal, I'd go with the latter.

"Can you imagine what it would have been like to sleep there?" David shuddered. "I'm sure rapes happen there all the time. I mean, you could lock your door, but then you'd have to go to the bathroom in the middle of the night—" Malia, who was a light sleeper and usually made several such trips in the course of the night, leaned over from the passenger seat, and gave David a long hug, which seemed to restore his fortitude. "And now for a normal day at the office," he finally said, unlocking the hydrogen engine, and they moved into traffic, and into the better living lane of the DJR. It was 9:45 am.

Once inside Beaufort, they went directly to the KCU. He was proud to show her his Unit. "You have a nice office," said Malia, transfixed by the "Are You The Fist?" poster that David mostly didn't notice. "But you don't have a photo of me," she said, indicating the console.

"I'll fix that," David promised.

Karlmarx came in to interview Malia. David sat and watched as she answered Karlmarx's precise questions about the Andrewses' daily habits, reading tastes, political inclinations, and friendships—the last mostly discerned from the attendees at Rex's birthday party. Strangely, thought David, she seemed incurious about why the KCU was asking about the Andrewses, but she probably thought it was just a routine accounting in keeping with her role at the Octavian.

What David would not tell Malia was at some point the ADF would probably arrest key Knowledge Tower bureaucrats, and he would make sure the Andrewses would be swept up in the fray. Any doubts he had about targeting them evaporated when Malia told him about their reaction to the Rosebud raid. He was incredulous that they could treat it so dismissively even after learning Malia herself had barely escaped. "High time they got some lessons in empathy," he told himself. Now that Rex knew their real mother and seemed genuinely open to a permanent reunion, he felt safe taking down the information, or more precisely, evidence, for the next stage of the process.

After the KCU interview, David decided to take Malia to the cafeteria for lunch. He was now unconcerned about who might see them. The ADF should be damned grateful she was on their side, whatever other purpose she might have in serving them. "This is really nice," she said, as they sat alongside the floor to ceiling windows in the warm sun, eating fried chicken (David) and steak salad (Malia). Steve Rosen came over to say hello.

"How's my protégé Walters doing?" David joked.

Steve rolled his eyes. "He's quite the character. But it's clear the Director is favoring him these days, so I guess it's good for the ECU." And then, "I'm not sure how I feel about the god of evil—I mean, I'm a pagan, at least officially, but that's a real ugly statue."

David smiled, "Malia wants to see Wurro. We'll be up shortly for her meeting with Cheysa."

"I've been looking at this wrong," said Steve. "Maybe it's an opportunity to increase the tourist trade. See you later." He gave a quick Antifan salute and left.

"Oh, wow, that is ugly," Malia said as she approached Wurro in his new corner nook. "Steve wasn't kidding." The ECU officers peered at them, since Malia's low-credit, non-Antifan armband had activated flashing red lights to alert the unit that a non-authorized person was in the vicinity. That said, the red alternated with short greens to indicate she did have some kind of semi-official status vis-à-vis the ADF and was not simply an intruder. "Commander Harris from the KCU," they whispered and messaged each other.

Walters suddenly appeared with Cheysa in tow. "Hello, Harris. Hello, Ms. Librarian." The narrow green eyes that had frightened her that day at the Depository were now glinting amiably at her. "The mana of Wurro is powerful and constant."

"Jenness," said David, a little irritably. "Malia Jenness. Who is helping us a great deal."

"That I know," said Walters. "Conroy, why don't you two ladies talk in the conference room?" Malia turned and gave David a little wave before the women disappeared around the corner.

"Looking good, Harris, looking good," said Walters, giving the now-empty corner a hard look. "She's definitely improved under your influence."

"How are you enjoying the ECU?" said David. As competent as Helen Zhu was, he felt the KCU had lost a little of its edgy verve since Walters' departure.

"Can't argue with the title," said Walters, "and I could bring both Cheysa and Wurro. It's a little sleepier here than the KCU. But I think the Director's keeping a sharper eye on the Econ Tower now that we've set the Knowledge Tower back on its heels."

"So you think we're going to let the EcoLand raid slide this time?" David asked. "And the experiments?"

"Gotta figure out what they're really up to," said Walters. "Your girlfriend will help there. And I've got some of my own sources. What a mess. Just a little early to be cracking down."

"Sources in the Econ Tower? High-placed?"

"Can't tell you everything, Harris. Need to know and all that."

He's become even more insufferable, thought David. Not just the promotion, but the lavish favor of the Director had inflated Walters' ego. David suspected Walters had become a regular at Ferraro's soirees. "Can you have Cheysa bring Malia back to the KCU when they're done?"

"Sure, my former boss."

Cheysa introduced herself to Malia, building some initial rapport over mutual compliments on hair and jewelry as women did. She was happier with the ECU assignment than she had been in the KCU. The ECU did very little Red Room activity, which she knew disappointed Brian. "I feel like a f---ing bureaucrat these days," he said, but it suited her perfectly. No one was telling her to turn dials that killed people. She learned that she did indeed have talent for handling assets. Instead of getting to know people along a police beat, she was developing sources so that they came to trust her, and that was building a relationship, too. If sources felt they benefited from their relationship with her, and she in turn could bring valuable information to the ADF in the interests of some kind of justice, wasn't that good?

Her romance with Dominic had also deepened. Perhaps Brian was less possessive now that he had the kind of assignment for which he'd been angling for years, but he didn't seem to mind when she disappeared for a long lunch hour and he had loosened his grip enough so that when he attended a Director's party, she could spend the night at her mother's. Cheysa had even brought Dominic home to meet her mother and sister on one of those nights, to everyone's approbation. She hoped that eventually Brian would meet someone more high-powered whom he would deem more fitting for his new status than Cheysa Conroy. Then everyone could be happy. "Your sister and I are praying hard that this happens soon," said Reba. "Dominic is a good man, and we would love to see you together." For now, Cheysa was beginning to enjoy her corner of the Antifan universe.

"We need to find out what the goals of the Econ Tower are, both with the experiments and toward us," she told Malia. "They're starting to pull out of their lane. What do they want? Are they trying to influence President Avadaughter to sideline the ADF? Were they happy with the EcoLand and the Rosebud raids? Do they plan any more?"

Malia squinted, mentally etching the questions, which she dared not write down, on her brain.

"So you'll see Adam Ross tomorrow night?"

"Not sure," said Malia. "It's only when he calls me upstairs. Sometimes he does, sometimes he doesn't. It's been nearly a month since we've seen each other, so I'm betting it'll happen sometime this week. That said, I'll probably have to fight him off. If you folks hadn't given me the fake Plore boyfriend, I'd be at his mercy. He respects—just enough—the boyfriend." Malia realized that she needed to restart the training with Kate before she fell out of practice or out of shape. Adam would probably try to get her to go on another trip, she said. He had mentioned a beach house in Rehoba Beach.

"Tom has his instructions," said Cheysa. "He will take money from Ross to let you go away for a weekend, but not permanently." She explained that the ADF calculated this would keep Ross interested and make him more likely to take Malia to locales, including the ESZ camp, where she would be privy to other Econ Tower folks and information. "Your having debates in his apartment won't help us much."

Cheysa went over to a bookcase and brought over a cardboard box. "Here are a few items I've put aside for you," she said, "some of which might come in handy dealing with Mr. Ross. And if you don't need them, they're perfectly ordinary looking. He'll never suspect anything."

The first object was a square metal object half an inch long that looked like a computer drive. It was an electronic metal cutter. "Completely silent," said Cheysa, demonstrating its use on an old bracelet in the box. The cutter's edges glowed briefly, and the bracelet fell into two halves.

"This," said Cheysa, giving her a small vial of blue pills, "will counteract any sleeping drug or date rape drug he might give you. You would need to take one within a minute or two for it to work, but at least you can pop it into your own drink or mouth quickly. I doubt he'll realize such a drug exists so you could probably claim it's a pain reliever if he asks. I find if you say it's connected to your period, no man will question you further." The two laughed knowingly.

Cheysa reached into the box and brought out another item, two small cloth patches wrapped in plastic labeled 'beauty aid.' "Each contain enough relaxant to temporarily paralyze a grown man," she said. If you unwrapped a patch and then pressed it against your victim's skin, he would swiftly lose control of his limbs. The poison would immobilize him for about half an hour but do no permanent harm. "A whole hour if you use both. Enough to escape if you need to," said Cheysa, "but make sure you escape because it's definitely going to make him angry."

She said, "We can't give you a firearm, but here's a knife, so you aren't completely unarmed." It was a seven-inch knife in a pink suede sleeve. "He'll probably think it's a nail file. And here's a chart that shows you what to aim for if you have to defend yourself with the knife. Memorize it, so you can attack instinctively." It was the same chart that the knife-fighting instructor had given David.

She continued, "If you don't want it, just give it back to us. You have to be willing to use it, lest it be used against you. But all the other items, you can put them in your toiletry case and no man would be the wiser, even if he's nosy." She then gave Malia a number to call if she felt under immediate threat. It replaced the one that would have contacted the KCU night team from the ESZ. It would completely destroy her cover but might save her life. "No promises, though," said Cheysa. "If you're in Rehoba or the Zone, I doubt we'd reach you in time."

With the interview mostly over, Cheysa turned to more personal matters. "I know Commander Harris is a Christian. I've told him that I am too. Are you also a Christian?"

"I don't know," Malia lied. She had been baptized in June, but was leery of confessing her faith in the interior of the feared Beaufort Tower. "I think I was when I was a child. I think I'm moving back in that direction. I know I couldn't worship a Wurro."

"Commander Harris is a great leader. I just want you to know how loved he is here."

Malia was touched. "Thank you for letting me know."

Cheysa inclined her head, "Surely. Good luck."

At about the same time, on the 55th floor of the Economic Tower in northeast Anacosta, Adam Ross was examining photographs on his screen that the ESF surveillant had taken of Malia and David on Sunday. The ESF had posted the surveillant for a week after the raid, just in case any residents tried to return or cause trouble. Of course, the ESF had immediately dispatched the vast majority of the young Rosebud residents to the ESZ, although it had grudgingly released the few who worked at Beaufort or for the City police. It had been a quiet week and this was the final day of the surveillant's watch. Adam had asked the surveillant to look out for Malia returning from the beach and see whether she actually entered the building, and with whom.

Adam's assistant Daisy stood next to him as he sat there. "Is that the Plore boyfriend?" she asked. Daisy was a fortyish divorcee who had long ago given up her slight crush on Adam. Too self-absorbed and sinister for love, she thought, but basically a fair boss. In return, Adam respected her efficiency and intuition.

Adam frowned. "The outfit looks familiar. Awful Plore fashion sense. The baseball cap isn't helping, but yeah, he seems to be blond, like I remember. A little taller than average, not tall though. I guess that's him."

"Why is he wearing that windbreaker?" Daisy asked. "Sunday was a really hot day, especially in the afternoon."

They peered at the grainy photo. "Let's zoom in," said Adam.

"Seems there's a little bulge on the right side," she said.

"Armed?" Adam whistled. "A Plore? Sometimes they carry knives."

"The left sleeve seems a little snug too, compared to the right one," she said. Righthanded Social Crediteers wore their armbands on their left arm so they could tap the keyboard with their righthand fingers, and vice versa.

"Maybe not a Plore?" Adam wondered. "Could have fooled me." To himself, he mused, "maybe she's sleeping with more than one guy. Naah, I think that's him. I wonder if we could have him arrested on weapons charges. That would get him out of the way quickly—and permanently."

Daisy went to answer the phone in the anteroom. She came back tense with excitement. "Adam, that was Director Smith. She wants to see you immediately."

Chapter 46
Econ Tower On The Move
(Tuesday–Friday, 23 and 26 August)

Adam stopped by the washroom on his way up to the Director's suite. He gave a hard look at his reflection in the full-length mirror. A nice-fitting dark blue suit, blue tie with pink stripes. The pink showed he was a woke, hip guy, not just some stolid middle-aged bureaucrat. He felt the short beard was more flattering than his indecisive chin. All in all, quite presentable for whatever would come next. A curvy fortyish woman gave him an appraising look as she headed into a stall. Adam wondered what would happen if he followed her into one—it had happened before, at off hours. But no, not now, not today.

He was ushered promptly into the round office of Pernella Smith, PhD, on the 80th floor of the Economic Tower, with its sweeping view of downtown Anacosta. Dr. Smith rose to greet him, her neatly manicured hand extended. She was a teetotaler, but partial to tea, so she offered him a porcelain cup of genuine Oolong from her sideboard, which he accepted. Adam saw Smith once or twice a week, but mostly in large meetings where he did not present or take the lead, so he was curious as to what might have caused her to invite him here.

He was used to scrutinizing women—well, he scrutinized men too, he had to admit, as part of the eternal game of status determination. They were about the same age, and Adam had to admit, about the same height. Pernella's exotic Asian scarves softened the severity of her own blue suit, and she examined him frankly from almond-shaped eyes set in her café-au-lait complected oval face. Adam could see why, despite her age, the austere but still lovely Pernella might appeal to the dissolute Chinese President, Shang Chang-lin. She seemed the type of woman who would divulge no secrets to anyone but a lover, and then give him too much. If Shang wanted to know about the status of Economic Tower projects, or curtail any possible outreach to the United States or other foreign countries, Pernella would provide and comply. But to her own subjects in this glass tower, she was determined and implacable.

"Adam," she said, "we have reached a crossroads."

He cocked his head at her, waiting for her to explain.

"The Antifans know about our experiments at Camp Four. Not everything. But they know about Beijing's help."

"How?" he asked. "We have maintained the utmost secrecy."

"Ferraro went and told the President," she said. "I wish we had included the ADF from the beginning, but Beijing ordered us to keep this within the Tower." Adam knew that the ADF, with its harsh integrity, would never have permitted him and his closest colleagues to siphon a generous fee from each accidentally murdered victim, in compensation for the loss of the victim's services to the Economic Zone. Somewhere in Mexico, his bank account was fattening with each failed experiment, with each dead Social Credit fool. He himself had negotiated this with his Chinese counterpart, arguing about the youth and the promise of each victim. The Chinese wanted to go full speed ahead with the development of the serum, and nowadays, Chinese lives were too valuable to spend on such fanciful experiments. He just hoped that the Antifans were not monitoring foreign bank accounts in Mexico.

Even Pernella Smith had no idea that some of her senior officers were enriching themselves at the expense of the DJR, the Chinese, and yes, the Social Crediteers themselves, who paid with their lives. It had never occurred to the elegant Pernella Smith, PhD, that opportunities for self-dealing thrived in the crevices between the Tower's noble goals and Beijing's ruthlessness. The Chinese cooperated handsomely with Adam, dispatching the funds through cutouts to Mexican banks offering high interest rates. Adam knew that when he arrived in Mexico City, ostensibly as a tourist, he would embark on a comfortable retirement as a free, wealthy man.

"What exactly did Ferraro want Avadaughter to do?" he asked.

"He wanted her to tell us to stop the experiments. He lashed out at us for the EcoLand and the Rosebud raids—he said we weren't acquiring workers, but corpses. He even knew—roughly—how many of the workers had been killed."

Adam pressed his lips together. Not good. And anyone working in that building, any ESF officer in the Zone might have known this information, if secondhand. "What did Avadaughter say?"

"She said the truth serum was too important to the DJR to abandon the experiments. She suggested we have our scientists find more efficient methods, to be less wasteful." Adam knew that "less wasteful" meant less income for the project from Beijing, as well as less income for Adam Ross, and frankly, a slower time frame for development of the valuable serum. The Chinese might want to back off entirely if the venture looked in jeopardy.

"What if we offered to let the ADF get involved? Or is it too late?"

Pernella shook her small fine head. "It's too late. The ADF would rather avoid being tainted by any scandal. They probably figure they would benefit from the truth serum eventually. But Chang, I mean, President Shang does not want the ADF to be involved." The following was hard for her to admit, but she said it. "He sees the ADF as a truly patriotic corner of the DJR that would not allow our youth to be killed for a truth serum for the Chinese. They might be biding their time for now, but they would never agree to participate in such experiments."

"At least Avadaughter is letting us proceed," said Adam, estimating what this might mean for his Mexican bank account in the short run.

"The Antifans have an intelligence system," said Pernella. "They know far more about us than we do about them."

True, thought Adam. It was the ADF's job to track the other Towers, and ensure their bureaucrats served the interests of the DJR by carrying out their Diversity mission. It was Adam's good fortune that so far he had evaded the scrutiny of the ADF, at least as far as he knew. He definitely did not need the ADF nosing around the chemistry building.

"Madam Director, are you proposing we start taking steps to defend ourselves from this ADF spying? Or actively resisting the ADF's right to intrude on our affairs?"

"I don't know," she admitted. "At the very least I think we need to have our own intelligence service. Nothing prevents a Tower from policing its own. We can carry out our own offensive operations and intelligence collection from under that rubric. Not openly, not yet."

She paused. "The Chinese have always had what they called a Control Yuan, or something similar, whether under the emperors, or the Nationalists, and even the Communists. It was charged with policing the government and fighting corruption..."

"Uh-oh," thought Adam.

"Not that it worked well in the long run, because each dynasty eventually rotted and collapsed from internal decay. But the purpose is noble."

She looked at Adam. "I know you were in the Antifans early on"—his was an unusual background for an Econocrat—"and so you must understand the way they work. I've been very impressed with your command style over the Anacosta Zone, our most important Zone. Would you take on the responsibility of starting our Control Yuan? We need to learn who is telling the ADF about us. We need to start developing our own sources. We need to develop the intelligence architecture to protect our own people and projects. We will sell it to the public as a way to combat the United States which seeks to destroy our socialist economy."

Adam reflected on this. "In addition to my current duties? This seems like a full-time job."

Pernella said, "You can hire an additional deputy for the Economic Zone management job for the meantime. And your current Social Credit score is 200? I have the authority to bump you up immediately to 250. Would that be acceptable?"

Adam's eyes lit up. But he didn't want to lose the Economic Zone job at any cost. "Madam Director, that sounds very enticing. One more request—I don't want to be chasing after everyone in this building for various infractions. We need to be able to count on managers to identify incompetence or corruption among their own workforce. I want to be able to focus on the counterintelligence threat you've identified, since we are under assault from at least the ADF, and maybe from the White Black House. Will you let me do that?"

"Yes, completely," said Pernella. "And you'll need a staff—I'll give you 20 officers to start, with the understanding that your staff will increase as the workload does. You will be the Director of Intelligence for the Economic Tower, reporting directly to me, with secondary responsibility for the Anacosta Economic Zone for the duration. The ESF will be at your disposal. I will announce all this on Friday afternoon. Congratulations, Director Ross." They shook hands.

Over the next few days, Adam spent most of his time assembling a staff and scrubbing the list of possible or actual ESF informants. Will agreed to serve as his deputy, likewise maintaining his quartermaster role for now. Daisy would continue as his assistant. He called in his chips from the days of favors done, assuming the officers in question had the intellect and temperament for the job. In a politically savvy move aimed at the Tower's Diversity Inspectorate, they carefully included the requisite mixes of colors and sexualities and gender identities given that he and Will were unapologetically heterosexual white cis-males. "Little Antifa," he and Will privately called their new unit.

On Friday morning, Adam watched a handyperson mount framed pictures on the wall of his new office in the new Intelligence Directorate spaces on the 79th floor. He had asked the Diversity Inspectorate to select motivational posters, which won him goodwill with the sober matrons in charge of its art department.

One proclaimed "Diversity For Better Living." This poster neatly aligned with the Economic Tower's key economic and scientific missions, showing children of various races wearing protective eyewear and circling a set of glass laboratory tubes. Not caring for children, Adam asked for that poster to be hanged to the side where his eyes would not casually light on it. Another poster, titled Diversity, listed the characteristics of a Diversity regime: Equality, Trust, Inclusiveness, Respect, and Sharing, all of which Adam devoutly believed were antithetical to the effectiveness of Little Antifa. It was kind of ugly, and Adam wondered whether the Art Department wasn't just cleaning out its attic. On the other hand, a large Impressionistic painting of, presumably, a flower looked remarkably like a pair of female buttocks, which mollified him. He asked for that to be placed on the wall directly ahead of his desk.

That afternoon after the press conference, Will showed up to check out his adjoining office and to meet with Adam and one of the intel officers to discuss the informants at their disposal. "Wooh. Impressive. You've got a view of downtown!"

"Yours isn't bad either," said Adam, pleased at the indirect accolade.

"Yes," said Will, "but who chose your art, man?" He pointed to the Diversity poster. "I've got black and white photos of industry and farming on my wall. You know, from when we really had manufacturing in the cities. It all looks rather grim, but appropriate because it's pre-DJR."

"I let the Diversity art people choose," said Adam.

"Oh well, that's what you get, then. I'd switch those out as soon as the honeymoon ends."

After the profoundly disappointing meeting with the incompetent CI officer, they began discussing the development of a stable of assets. "Going to have to start from scratch here," said Adam. "Damn."

"I was in a bar last weekend near Beaufort," Will said. "A lot of Antifans watching baseball and track. We could start there." They decided there were one or two Intelligence Directorate officers who would make plausible sports fans. Nor did Will mind applying his affability to the task, either, at least as long as the baseball season continued.

When Will took his leave, Adam remembered that it was Friday, and that Malia would be on duty at the Octavian. He had been so preoccupied this week with work that she had skipped his mind. A concierge at the Octavian would be an excellent source of intelligence, at least on his Knowledge Tower neighbors, if not Beaufort, and he resolved to press his advantage.

Chapter 47
The Double Agent
(Friday, 26 August)

Malia stood at the counter next to Jorge greeting the residents who were headed out to restaurants and bars, and wishing a good night to the others returning. These were mostly older couples carrying Enviro-pods, since overeating now gave them indigestion. The Andrews family returned from Jolly Cholee, the new Cambodian-Indian fusion restaurant (150 minimum), and bestowed kind smiles on Malia, who had tutored Rex earlier in the day. Rex, trailing behind them, turned around to give Malia a long sweet glance. Jorge had been kindlier to her since Adam Ross had indicated Malia was meeting his needs sufficiently. The tip from Amba-sah would allow him to take his wife on a vacation to Miami and Key West, and to book sleeping berths on the train. If you couldn't fly, you might as well make the best of it. Amba-sah Ross had even given him a coupon from the Economic Tower for a discount on the condo in Key West. "I won't be able to use it, Jorge," he said. "Too busy these days."

Ross had not called for Malia since her return from the beach the previous weekend, which was unfortunate, she thought with some vanity, since her bronze glow had begun to fade. David's call on Friday afternoon, waking her up, solved the mystery of Ross's silence. "Turn on the TV," he said. Malia quickly turned to Diversity Channel One, where the headline was, "Economic Tower Names First Intelligence Director." Dr. Pernella Smith said she was naming Adam Ross, longtime senior bureaucrat, to the position, noting that his "frontline service to Diversity in the civil wars and his expertise in building socialism makes him the consummate choice for this demanding position." The newscaster informed the audience that the DJR would be ramping up its efforts to acquire US economic secrets and intellectual property.

Alex Charlton poked his silver head in David's doorway. "I expect the call from the Director any moment," he said. "We didn't know about this, did we?"

"Completely unaware," said David, "but not surprising."

"Do we really have anything to worry about from this guy?" asked Charlton.

"Yes, he's a highly competent cold-blooded killer who doesn't like Antifans, even though—or maybe because—he was one of us," David said.

"Great," said Charlton. Vanessa announced that they were expected in the Director's office immediately. Ferraro, flanked by Steve Rosen and Gemma Carpenter, awaited them, fingers tapping impatiently.

"Hello, gentlemen," he greeted them. "This seems to be a shot across our bow, does it not?"

"Nothing was said about the ADF," said Charlton, looking to put a positive gloss on the situation. "It seemed to be mostly targeted at the US."

Ferraro looked incredulous. "That's too hard. If they were going to do it, it would have happened years ago. Who else are they planning to spy on? Not the Chinese. Pernella's been their concubine for years and it's only to our disadvantage. She wouldn't have dared made this move without checking with Beijing. And Beijing doesn't trust us—meaning the ADF. They know we're actually defending the country's interests."

"Well, it's not all bad news," Rosen reminded them. "We have a very reliable informant close to Adam Ross."

Ferraro grinned, "That's true. What a great break. That girlfriend of yours, Harris. We are really going to be counting on her to deliver."

"It's getting more dangerous," said David, his brow furrowing. This morning, to his alarm, he had spotted several distinctly gray hairs on his sunny head.

"Well, that's just because you're looking at it from your own narrow personal interests. If you adopt an Antifan perspective, you'll recognize the opportunity here," Ferraro rebuked him.

"I think we are giving our informant a great deal of support," said Rosen, outlining the devices and phone number she had been provided. "Just because she is not a trained intelligence professional, doesn't mean she can't protect herself and operate effectively. In some ways, the implausibility of her being a spy—her humble status, her demeanor—may make her safer."

"Harris here does not look convinced," said Ferraro, inviting him to wander further into the trap.

David thought, I'm sorry I ever told Steve Rosen that Adam Ross was pursuing Malia. But he also recognized that without Rosen, Malia would have disappeared months ago into the Zone vortex. He summoned enough Antifan spirit to respond. "Sir, I recognize the great opportunity for the ADF. And Commander Rosen is correct, the ECU has done everything possible to ensure her safety." He knew if this informant had been anyone but Malia, he would have eagerly egged her on, regardless of the peril.

"That's the right attitude, Harris," said Ferraro. "Now we need to think about how the Economic Tower plans to target us. Our workforce knows about the threat from the Knowledge Tower, but in practice they can't spy on us. The average Econocrat has 20 more IQ points than his or her drone counterpart in the Knowledge Tower, and if they are daring enough to set up an Intelligence Directorate, they have probably figured out how they want to use it."

Gemma Carpenter said, "We will start scrutinizing our officers' ties with their counterparts in the Economic Tower. We already keep sufficient records to do a social network analysis on any Antifan officer, including with Plores. This will include college and family ties. Anyone who has reported they are currently dating an Econocrat will come under special scrutiny, if only to warn them of their vulnerability. We will not ban such ties at this time, however, unless you want us to do so. I think doing so would force such relationships underground.

"All this will take time. I would also recommend sending out a note to the workforce, notifying them of the Economic Tower's start-up and what it means. Hopefully our officers can exercise some caution in their social interactions."

"Thank you, Gemma," said Ferraro.

The meeting ended in sufficient time for David to begin his delayed Red Room session for the week. A month ago, the steady march of university professors through Beaufort had begun to flag. David wondered whether the KCU might be approaching a point at which it could begin to digest its findings for Ferraro, but Beaufort West had started shipping its faculty prisoners east via special chartered planes. Ferraro's theory was that the Californians lacked the stomach for interrogation ("Lotus eaters!" he had charged) and were all too willing to let the main Beaufort KCU do their dirty work. The ADF had not found any evidence of illegal book transfers on the West Coast, but some faculty had participated in an intriguing encrypted electronic network that shared subversive comments on Avadaughter, and the entire routine had resumed.

Meanwhile, Cheysa was sending a car to the Avalon to pick up Malia for a quick meeting. They met not at Beaufort, which always carried an element of risk, but at a coffee shop nearby where two women would not look out of place gossiping on a Friday afternoon in late summer over iced coffees. Cheysa, of course, wore civilian clothing. That evening, Malia would tutor Rex at the Octavian before her shift began.

Around 10 pm, Rex came downstairs to the lobby with a new video game from the Knowledge Tower, Parvenu. The goal of the game was to interact with a dozen different ethnic and racial groups and celebrate each other without causing offense. You could not interact with your own group and had to cobble together a coalition of Allies who would agree that you were Woke. However, it was the kind of game where everyone could aspire to be deemed Woke, and so it was not zero-sum. One could continue playing until one either became Woke, or until the other players lost patience and went to bed. David rolled his eyes at Malia's description of these Knowledge Tower games, grateful that the KCU kept a technically illegal store of old war games such as *Call of Duty*, *Risk*, and *Battleship* that tended to inculcate rather than sap the proper Antifan spirit in his troops.

It was hard for Malia not to want to wrap her daughter in her arms, and she was achingly aware that Rex was equally longing for contact with their mother. They dared to sit shoulder to shoulder on the sofa as they played the game, with Malia aware that Jorge was looking disapprovingly in their direction.

But it comforted her to think that they had hugged deeply when she had arrived for tutoring, and Rex had said, "Let's have cocoa just like we used to in the old days." Malia boiled the water in the hot box, they drank the fine French cocoa with a dinner of leftover stir fry, and pored over the Diversity History lesson about the civil wars. The Troubles of 2020-25 were a giant mishmash for Rex, what with impeachment trials, coronavirus, riots for racial justice, and even locusts all plaguing the country in quick succession, or from the distance of seventy years, all at once.

"This was when the first Antifans came out into the streets," said Malia, "but they were not yet a single organized force. That had to wait another twenty years until the Diverse Peoples realized they needed an army to fight the US government. And then John Beaufort began organizing the various Antifan units throughout the country to fight."

"Why did all this happen at once?" Rex wanted to know.

Malia knew that the Antifans were listening in on the Andrewses occasionally, but David had said she was probably safe if the parents themselves weren't home, and he would fix any misunderstandings that occurred. "It was less that everything happened at once, since there was always trouble before socialism, but the Diverse Peoples were finally able to capitalize on these crises. A famous man named Rahm Emanuel, who served the great President St. Barack Obama, said that 'You never let a serious crisis go to waste, and what I mean by that is that it's an opportunity to do what you could not do before'.

"So the forces of Diversity kept hammering away at people's confidence in their government. They impeached the president at the time, although he was able to survive and finish his term. They destroyed the economy by forcing everyone to stay home during coronavirus, including the people who could not afford to do so. Then when a black man was wrongly killed by the police, Antifan forces roused the righteous anger of the poor and the excluded, and they rioted throughout many cities. It was a brand-new concept of tactics in the service of revolution."

"Can I say that on the test?" asked Rex. The Diversity History makeup exam would be on September 23rd.

"Yes, you can mention all the destruction and hate and death, but make sure you praise it because it led to the foundation of the DJR. You already know how coronavirus helped the victory of socialism." Malia had told Rex that the final essay question this year would almost certainly address the importance of the Troubles; David had learned that from one of his Knowledge Tower sources. He had laughed at the thought of asking sources about test questions, but one couldn't deny the operational imperative here.

Around 1 am, the call came from Adam. Malia stopped in the toilet to freshen up and not give Jorge the satisfaction of seeing her care about how her makeup looked. She texted David.

She knocked on Ross's door. The door opened but all she saw was the dark room within. "Come in," she heard him say. With some trepidation, she entered, her eyes adjusting to the dark. Her eyes caught a single lamp lighting the living room area. Then before she quite realized what was happening, Adam had grabbed her shoulders and was pinning her to the wall behind the door, lifting her off the ground. His mouth closed insistently over hers as she struggled to break free. She couldn't get the space she needed to punch him either in the face or the solar plexus. The element of surprise had been entirely to his advantage, as he slid her up the wall, tore the stockings, and had his way with her, her fists flailing without impact.

Afterward, he let her down, grinning at her. "My arms are pretty sore now. That's a workout."

"I hate you," she said. "That was completely unfair and uncalled for. And you've ruined another pair of stockings." Oh, you liked that, he thought, I'll let you pretend you didn't.

"I'll give you my carbon offset number and you can order replacements. Or you could just think ahead and not wear them. They're a huge inconvenience to me."

He went to mix her a drink, which she felt under the circumstances of his victory she could probably trust. He let her weep silently for a minute on the sofa and then placed her drink on the coffee table, while he sat at the other end of the sofa. "I thought that given the events of the week, you might want to be especially nice to me."

She had practiced the blank look beforehand. "What events?"

He responded with mock astonishment, "Are you the only person in the whole City, in all of the DJR, who doesn't know that Adam Ross was appointed this week to become the first Director of Intelligence for the Economic Tower? It was on TV this very afternoon—our director gave a press conference to announce it, and I was standing right behind her. I thought you Low Credit types were supposed to get a good dose of propaganda each week."

How pathetic, Malia thought, this pride in titles and advancement and standing in front of the cameras. The Christians were right to warn of the delusory perils of worldly goods and fame.

"That's very impressive," Malia said, still managing to look clueless while sniffling slightly. "Do you get a Social Credit increase?"

"Yes, you silly thing. Is that all you care about?" Adam chuckled condescendingly at her lack of sophistication.

If you were a 70, and eating soybake casseroles, that's all you'd care about too, Malia thought bitterly. She hoped that her unknown roommates, including the pothead, were enjoying her Healthy Eating groceries that presumably still arrived regularly in the grocery mailroom at TerraCity, or that they were being siphoned off by the workers. It didn't matter which. She couldn't afford to lose the 20 extra Social Credit points by cancelling the deliveries.

Adam reached over and took her shoulders in his hands, and looked intently at her, ignoring her flinch. "This is the most important thing that has ever happened to me, and you should recognize this can be a good thing for you too. My director gave me complete control of the Economic Strike Force. That's our version of the Antifan Defense Forces, or it will be soon. She wants me to use my experience as an Antifan to build our own military and intelligence counter to the ADF. We aren't going to be pushed around forever. We are the center of economics and science in the DJR. *We* should be in control, not a bunch of brutal policemen. And I have been trusted with making sure that happens eventually. It's a great honor."

"Wow," said Malia, finally allowing herself to show reluctant awe. "But I don't think the Antifans would allow this to happen, would they?"

"Honey," said Adam, "by the time we're ready to take over, they won't know what hit them. You saw that we are arming ourselves, and outside the Zones as well.

"But you can be a great help to me here, and you can help yourself too. You're probably learning a lot about the residents just by staffing the desk downstairs. I want you to keep me informed about what you hear. In return, we can pay you, depending on the information you give us—it needs to be significant and helpful, not just any scrap of gossip."

"But we don't have any Antifans in the building," she said, deliberately misunderstanding. "Wait, there's Deputy Commander Gerhardt in 407, but I think he's the only one." She thought irrelevantly, at this rate, I'm going to become the richest woman in the DJR who can't go to a fancy restaurant on my own.

"You don't have to bring me information about Antifans," he said, "since you're right, there are hardly any in the building. We also need to know what is going on with the Knowledge Tower. We expect that they've been so bruised by the Antifans this year that they will gladly unite with us against the ADF. I want to know who in this building might be sympathetic to this kind of undertaking. Maybe you'll hear a stray comment against the ADF, for example. I'd want to know who said it and under what circumstances."

"Look," Malia said with a flash of manufactured anger, "you rape me and now you expect me to help you? I should probably call the police on you instead."

"They won't come, especially now. They might arrest you for causing all of us inconvenience. Come on, this is good for you too."

"All the money in the world won't get me out of the TerraCity Hostel. You know that's where I'm living now, you realize?"

"Oh yes," said Adam loftily, inching toward her again. "Well, that's what happens under socialism. Resources, including housing, must be directed toward society's most useful members, not just those who become rich by oppressing others. Think of how you're helping Mother Earth by consuming fewer resources."

Infuriated, she tried shoving him away, but he grabbed her wrists and pushed her down to the sofa. She tried to flip him over as she had that first time, but he laughed, saying, "I know that trick by now." But he unexpectedly released her and sat up. "Lucky for you that I'm middle aged, and I need to take breaks in between assaulting you.

"Seriously," he said, "what's TerraCity like? If it's that bad and you're inclined to be cooperative, I could move you to something better. Maybe even your own place—in my name, of course."

Malia realized that pretending to live at TerraCity was a better and smarter deal for her than pretending to live in an apartment owned by Adam while actually living at the Avalon with David. "No, that's all right, amba-sah," she sniffed. "I can take care of myself."

"Sure you can," said Adam. "So I'll assume you'll be helping me. By the way, I've offered that Plore boyfriend of yours a very sizable sum to disappear. He'd be advised to take it. The next offer is going to be a lot less friendly. I'm getting tired of spending money on him."

"I don't think your crackerjack Economic stormtroops would know how to find their way around Ploreville," she sneered at him.

"We can track down his crew in the City, so I don't have to risk catching a contagious disease by going to Ploreville," said Adam. "I've always wondered what it would be like to crush someone under one of those rollers." Then seeing her aghast face, he said, "Oh, I'm just kidding, come on, Melia! Too much trouble." He amusedly let her fend off his next set of advances. "By the way, would you happen to know whether your Plore has a firearm or a knife?"

She glared. "Like I would tell you. Are your valiant troops that afraid of a mere Plore?"

He laughed again, in an unusually good mood. "Just curious. How about coming with me to Rehoba Beach after National Day?" he asked. "I've got a beach house there. Beaches seem to agree with you—I can see that you got some very nice sun down in the Outer Banks."

She consented to go to Rehoba with him, provided that Tom/Dave agreed. "More money," said Adam gloomily, but seemed to accept the terms.

Chapter 48
Buster Frog's
(Saturday, 3 September)

Malia left the Octavian at her normal quitting time, 7 am, but now she was starting to take greater precautions before meeting her driver. She followed a circuitous route away from the Octavian, looking backward a few times to make sure no one was following her. One self-driving car passed her, but turned right at the corner and disappeared. Grant, the new weekend driver, was waiting for her at the designated spot, the location of which would now change each day.

When she entered the apartment, she was surprised to find David awake and sitting up in bed reading his armband, with Frida and Ansel grooming each other at the foot of the bed. She undressed, put on her purple silk nightgown, and joined him. They kissed. The cats shifted position as Malia pulled the covers over herself.

"I couldn't gain access to the armband conversation," said David, reaching over for the armband on the night table and activating the noise cylinder. "Could not hear a word. And then I checked and realized Adam had gotten a very quick Social Credit boost this week, one that pushed him ahead of me. By the time I found someone in the building late last night who could access Adam's feed, the cyber unit commander, it was mostly quiet. But we heard the threat to Tom and his invitation to you to go to Rehoba."

"Yes, that was the end of the conversation, for all intents and purposes," said Malia. "And he told me a lot that validates your concerns about the Tower's intentions."

David placed his fingers on his lips. "Let's have breakfast in the sunroom today." They ordered from the restaurant downstairs and he brewed a pot of coffee. Within 20 minutes, they were laying out their breakfast on the table in the sunroom off the kitchen. At any other time, David would have lowered the cheery yellow walls to create an open pavilion so they could enjoy the morning breeze while eating. The view at this point of the building's orbit showed northeast Anacosta, specifically the Economic Tower, which loomed hulkingly over its neighbors. Instead, he switched on the Diversity Rock station to further drown out their conversation. He did not think Adam Ross's henchmen could listen to their conversations, not yet, but he would not take any chances. Under the circumstances, they would adopt security practices so they would become practiced before the need became acute.

In a low voice, just audible enough to be heard by David against the rock music backdrop, Malia relayed what Adam had told her. She told him Adam now expected her to give him information on the Octavian's residents. She did not tell him how Adam had greeted her last night; she knew that David simply did not want to know these things anymore since he could do nothing to protect her. So he did not ask, and she did not tell. Eyes on the prize, revenge a dish best served cold, those Plore phrases beloved by David now had crept into her vocabulary. She spread cream cheese on an onion bagel. For all she knew, the onions probably came from the Economic Zone. Then Malia hoped Fern was all right, and tried to imagine her friend wearing denim overalls and a sunhat in the fields, picking strawberries. Someone still had to grow the crops, right? The image of the young man strapped in the chair came back to haunt her at these inopportune moments, diminishing the sunny cheer of this new morning.

David chewed his plain bagel with its more sparing dab of cream cheese. He wasn't surprised by the revelations Malia brought back, although they were welcome evidence. One would have to be dense not to grasp the threat and the reasoning behind the Economic Tower's move, with all due respect to Alex Charlton. In some ways, the smaller details were the most worrisome. Joking about Tom being crushed under his own imaginary paving equipment. The question about whether the Plore boyfriend was armed. This could simply be proof that the ESF had indeed staked out the Rosebud the night Malia returned from the beach and had detected suspicious bulges under the ill-fitting windbreaker, but nonetheless encouraging in that the disguise had convinced Adam Ross. Or perhaps Adam was looking for an excuse to rid himself of the inconvenient Plore. A capital crime would be just the ticket. Either way, it was exposing Tom/Dave to more danger than David had ever intended. David pondered whether it was time to cut the boyfriend loose, for his own sake.

"Just show us what you think might be all right to tell him, and we'll vet it first. It'll be good for your credibility to provide him the info. But," David added with some satisfaction, "perhaps not all of it will be true.

"Did you see Rex yesterday?" he asked.

Malia told him about the tutoring session and how useful it was to know the exam questions.

"In another day and age," he said, "it would have been called cheating and would be thoroughly dishonorable. But in a dishonorable age, anything you can do to survive is all right. I'll get some more information about the test questions. I mean, she still has to write the exams, right?"

"She's stopped taking the hormone blockers," said Malia. "And she no longer wants to be addressed as Mxti. It's progress, we're winning her back for the normal side."

David had never met the girl, but he already thought of himself as a stepfather-in-waiting. "Glad to hear that." He needed some good news. The serious conversation mostly over, he turned down the volume of the rock music, which was beginning to give him a headache. He would let Malia sleep, while he headed over to Beaufort to relay her findings.

Buster Frog's was hopping on the first Saturday evening in September. Two big games were playing on the giant screens around the restaurant, although each table was equipped with its own screen so no one could complain about a bad view. In baseball, the suddenly ascendant Anacosta Raptors were battling their rival the Miami Genders in a late season game, and in women's rugby—men's rugby had been abolished in the DJR years ago—the beefy Anacosta Butches were about to tackle the strapping Los Angeles Amazons.

In the blond wood and brass railing atmosphere of Buster's, comfy booths lined the walls, and long kitchen block tables occupied the center areas, to foster conviviality. Despite its location in elite Upper Northwest Anacosta, Buster's was democratically open to all sports fans, regardless of Social Credit or Plore status. Plore sports fans were sometimes the most knowledgeable, and lent a gloss of working-class authenticity to the premises. To cover all its bases, Buster's alternated sports photographs on the walls with inspirational Diversity posters. "Be Green Be Mean," said a poster of a fierce-looking basketball player by the restrooms.

Walters and Cheysa were occupying their preferred seats at the center of the longest table, drinking pints of Diversity Stout. Both had ordered the fish and chips special. Seats were filling up sooner than usual, probably on account of the high-profile games. When a rangy white man with slicked-back blond hair and a friendly face, and his African-American friend with a round face and deep calm eyes politely requested to join them, Walters expansively declared, noting their fan gear, "Only because you're Raptorites!" Will and Tony quickly admitted to the charge, and introductions were made. It turned out they both worked at the Social Tower, Will in supplies for the hostels and low-Credit residences, and Tony ran a unit that disbursed payments to Plores. "Think of me as a quartermaster," Will explained. "Supplying sheets and pillows to the hostels. Also, cookware." Walters' eyes began to glaze over slightly.

Will and Tony quickly ingratiated themselves with the Antifans at the table, the former by buying two rounds of drinks, and the latter by revealing vast knowledge of Raptor and baseball statistics in general. "Tony, you're keeping us from arguing about anything tonight," Walters said amiably. A spirited discussion followed about whether Armando Duras, the star pitcher of the Raptors, would recover from his arm injury in time to pitch during the playoffs. Will resisted the temptation to share with the group his inside knowledge that Duras was heading to Mexico City for an operation next week, and would be out for the rest of the season. The Economic Tower controlled the baseball industry.

Tony overheard someone to his right confirming, "These guys are with the Social

Tower, right? Not the Econ Tower, right?" The din was loud enough for him to pretend he hadn't heard the exchange. "We'd have to report this if they were Econ Tower."

By the time the evening ended, with a resounding Raptors victory, Will had invited everyone, but especially Walters and Cheysa, to a playoff party at his apartment at the Argonne Tower near the White Black House in two weeks exactly, on September 17th. Everyone devoutly hoped that the Raptors would make it that far in the series competition, but as Will pointed out, two teams would be playing that night, regardless, and it was still going to be worth a celebration. "Two bars, folks! And catering from Zabaglione's," he said, naming the trendiest new caterer in the City. "My girlfriend said they were the best—I don't know much about these things myself, just like to watch baseball."

"The Argonne Tower," said Cheysa to Walters privately. "That's a big deal." Despite Walters' recent promotion, their social circle had remained static. Walters had expressed to Cheysa it was time they began moving among some bigger fish, but neither was certain how to go about it. Walters was regularly attending the Director's parties, but always encountered the same Antifans at them. This seemed like a promising opportunity, even if it was just with Social Tower officials. Cheysa knew her mom, the Social Tower employee, would be impressed, however.

Will gave his address to everyone, including some strangers farther down the table who didn't know the Antifans at all. After another round of drinks was consumed, Will and Tony rose to leave. "My girlfriend gets pretty angry if I get home too late or too drunk," said Will.

"You need a new girlfriend," said Walters, "or need to lay down the law more."

"Are you kidding?" said Will, "she's the lawmaker. But a good idea—someday!" They all chuckled. "Nice meeting you guys—see you all on the 17th!"

"That was easier than I thought it would be," said Tony as the two headed down the street toward the self-driving car depot. "Your makeup was pretty good, by the way. You really look different with the brown contact lenses and the blond hair."

"It helped that we waited until we really needed to sit in that area to sit down at all," observed Will. "Otherwise it would have looked a bit obvious. And nobody objects to free drinks."

"But you don't live in the Argonne Tower," Tony said, "and you don't have a girlfriend."

"I just got a long-term rental there," said Will, "paid for by our generous Intelligence Directorate. And Olivia Amberdaughter is going to play the role of girlfriend." Olivia was the tall shapely blonde who had just joined the Directorate yesterday. Olivia was thrilled to negotiate with the Diversity Warehouse over furnishings and had indeed insisted on catering from Zabaglione's, the government's new high-end caterer, Italian/Mediterranean division. If Olivia wanted to stay after the party and spend the night with him, Will would surrender gratefully.

"We're on the move, aren't we?" said Tony.

"Not missing a beat here," Will said. "These Antifans are getting sloppy. If I were them, I would have asked a few more questions about exactly what we do at the Social Tower. But I have noticed nobody ever seems to be interested in whatever the Social Tower does. It makes most people sleepy. I lost Walters at 'cookware.'"

"It always helps to talk baseball," noted Tony, the consummate fan, as the two men parted ways at the depot.

Chapter 49
Rehoba
(Saturday, September 17 and 24)

The self-driving car crossed the Bay Bridge and plowed steadily into Outer Plore country. Adam darkened the windows and awakened the sleeping Malia, who was recovering from her night shift. He had decided to have his way with Malia before they reached the Delaware border, figuring he might as well get his money's worth as soon as possible. Long self-driving car rides were notorious for trysts, he knew. As the lead passenger, you were supposed to remain alert in case you needed to override the car's controls, but in thirty years Adam had never experienced such a crisis, and he calculated it was unlikely to happen in those ten minutes. The self-driving cars were more reliable than those driven by humans, he contended. He could easily have bought his own private vehicle, but as he told Malia, it was cheaper and more convenient to rely on the self-driving cars if you didn't leave the City often.

Afterward, he let her fall back to sleep. He stared irritably out of the window at the Plore farm collectives they passed in the countryside. It was offensive that such inefficient entities were still permitted to survive, and for no reason connected with economic rationality. The DJR had relented when these farmers, or more precisely their parents and grandparents, had demanded the right to preserve their artisanal and earth-friendly lifestyle, in fact bragging about its unprofitability, in claiming it posed no threat to socialism. Yet the DJR authorities knew full well that these farmers harbored anti-regime sentiment. True, the farmers did not dare to take overt political stands, but their real sentiments were discernible through their insistence in maintaining some level of cultural independence, their primitive faith in God and His judgments, and their refusal to trust the new government. Whenever forced to take a side during the war, they had resisted the Antifans and for that reason alone, judged Adam, their communities should have been destroyed and all the inhabitants herded into urban Plorevilles.

Efforts to woo their children to a more progressive viewpoint and a Social Credit future were largely unsuccessful. But at least the land was under cultivation. The farmers had been willing to make the compromise of sacrificing their individual landholdings to a larger cooperative with their neighbors, supervised by the Collective

Farm Office of the Economic Tower, which was infuriatingly uninterested in cooperating with the Anacosta Economic Zone division.

These disturbing sights faded as they approached Rehoba Beach, renamed from Rehoboth in 2057 during the Great Naming when religious-origin place names were struck from the map. The car wended through streets with comfortable homes, each occupied, as law required, by 120-plus Social Crediteers. Plores were not allowed in town between May and September unless they were employed by a local business, and then only during working hours. Three blocks from the boardwalk, the car stopped in front of a bright blue frame house with a spacious high porch. "Welcome to my second home," said Adam. They clambered out and extracted the luggage. Adam dismissed the car, which trundled down the street.

"It's so cute," Malia exclaimed. Adam rolled his eyes at the thought, but it indeed was cute. It was not one of those sprawling mansions masquerading as a beach house so common in the Outer Banks. Inside was an airy living room with cream walls, light oaken floors and a ceiling fan, furnished in a contemporary style, with a blue and white striped rug. The kitchen was in the back, with a walkout to the deck and the hot tub. Off to the right were two bedrooms and a large luxurious bath. Downstairs were the rooms Adam cared about, including a newly constructed secure room for private work conversations. He had bought the house from his wife in the divorce fifteen years ago, and the credit for the upstairs decorating was hers, wherever she was now. A Plore cleaning crew visited biweekly during the summer, courtesy of the Rehoba Area Amenities Authority. As a newly minted 250-pointer, Adam had just learned to his joy that the service would now be free for him.

"Let's take a walk," he said. The season had officially ended two weekends ago with National Security Day, but the weather remained fine and warm. Families were still coming out for weekends and all the restaurants and ice cream stands were serving throngs of customers. Malia quickly changed into a baby-blue sundress with matching crocheted cardigan and sandals, and Adam into a burgundy polo shirt and tan Bermuda shorts and faux leather sandals that exposed his solid hairy legs. In their dark sunglasses, they looked like typical high-Social Credit summer residents, the woman perhaps a second, trophy wife.

Malia stopped several times on the boardwalk to watch the ocean. Adam tolerated the stops, but when she decided to buy herself an ice cream cone, he said, "No."

"What do you mean?" she asked. "I'm buying it for myself."

"I don't want you eating more ice cream," he said. "It's starting to show. Maybe you can have one tomorrow."

She gaped at him, both outraged and mortified. He strode off, and just to defy him, she stood in line and bought a vanilla cone, and then ate it slowly, licking it contentedly, as she trailed in his general direction on the boardwalk. She looked for a glimpse of the burgundy shirt, but he had disappeared. This was mildly troubling, since

Malia was unfamiliar with her surroundings, not good at directions, and wasn't exactly sure how she would find the house again.

At the end of the boardwalk, she sat down on a wooden bench and patiently waited for him to reappear. To while away the time, she read a novel from the GVN about a clinically depressed lesbian couple struggling for equality during the civil rights movement. An hour later, he sat down heavily next to her, without speaking. "I'm sorry, amba-sah," she said meekly, the ice cream safely eaten but now weighing on her conscience. He leaned back, placing his left ankle on his right knee, and his left arm around her shoulders, looking like any vacationer enjoying the sunshine. Then she felt his fingers at the base of her neck, pressing at each side. "Ow," she said, trying futilely to squirm away.

"It would be really easy to snap your neck," said Adam. "Don't try me." It had occurred to him that the legal authorities, such as they were, would probably be fairly tolerant of a manslaughter committed by a 250-pointer against an insubordinate 70-pointer, although one might expect some annoying paperwork.

She was starting to feel faint when he relented. Her palms were sweaty. "Time to go back to the house," Adam said. She was careful to memorize the route back to the house.

Back at the house, she unpacked her clothes and toiletries carefully. She placed the darling new toiletry bag, with its cats and puppies against a pink background, under the sink, out of sight. When she came out, Adam was watching the 4 pm news. She sat next to him and watched the segment about a Social Credit teenager who was bringing a new Diversity program to Plorevilles. Plores would be taught about Aztec and Mayan cultures and to eat empanadas and maize tamalitos. The plump dark-skinned teenager, herself presumably of Aztec or Mayan descent, since the banner read, Cecilia Munoz, family230, chirped at the camera, "This way we can reduce hate in the Plore community toward Diverse Peoples. We'll also bring them toiletry items and cleaning materials to improve their hygiene and to show our goodwill." It did not seem that Cecilia planned to demonstrate human sacrifice a la Azteca to the Plores.

"I hate Plores," grumbled Adam. "Let them choke on the empanadas." He paused. "And I especially hate *your* Plore."

He told her to go down to the basement and bring them two bottles of beer. "The coldbox is in the room to your left after you go down the stairs."

"Yes, amba-sah," she said, relieved to escape his relentless fury at Tom/Dave. How angry would he be if he knew that Tom/Dave was just a fiction?

She had descended the stairs, and walked into the room on the left when she heard the upstairs door close firmly and Adam's heavy tread following her downstairs. She didn't switch on the light, mostly out of laziness, but looked around vainly for what she assumed would be a white coldbox glowing in the dark. Then, standing in the doorway, he switched on the light.

"Oh!" she said. "Is this your gym, amba-sah?"

He laughed, not pleasantly. "Take a closer look."

She flooded with embarrassment and then alarm as she noticed the tables with restraints and stirrups, the cages, the stockade with restraints, the wooden box and oddly shaped structures with holes, the open display case with the handcuffs and clamps; the rack with the whips and scourges. "Mother Earth!" she breathed audibly. Now she was truly frightened. Adam had brought her here to murder her. She should have never, ever gotten involved with Antifans, even David. Six months ago, she was safe. Childless, hungry, but not in physical danger, or at least not in a beach dungeon.

She tried to flee the room, but Adam stood in the doorway. "Let's have some fun," he suggested, his forearm leaning on the door frame.

"This is not fun!" she shouted at him. "This is absolutely awful. You dragged me here without giving me any warning whatsoever. Dave would have *never* let me come here if he thought you were going to try to murder me."

"No one is going to be murdered," said Adam. "When I said I'd killed people, that was just during the war. I've been mostly peaceful and law-abiding ever since."

"You said you were going to snap my neck just an hour ago, amba-sah," she reminded him.

"I just said I 'could.' That was a statement of capability, not intention. We'll pick a safeword and when you can't take it anymore, just use the word and I'll stop."

She looked at him wildly and he let her run from the room. Then he heard the basement exit door to the back yard open and slam. She left her armband upstairs, he thought, she won't be gone very long. If she's not careful, someone will report her for not having the armband, and she'll be arrested as a suspected Plore or for violating the armband laws. The human leash laws in Rehoba, as Adam liked to call them, were quite strict, to protect the serenity of the Diverse community. He calmly locked the basement exit from the inside, trudged upstairs, mixed himself a very stiff drink, and went to wait for her on the porch. It was very pleasant to sit with one's Old Fashioned in one of the two brown resin rocking chairs that Alyssa had bought just before she left him. The house faced west, and the descending sun filtered through the chestnut trees on the sidewalk. He drank a second and then a third drink.

Much as he suspected would happen, Malia showed up around twilight in the company of a Rehoba city policewoman. "Amba-sah Ross?"

Adam acknowledged the name.

"This woman says she is your friend and you brought her here. She isn't wearing her armband and claims she isn't a Plore. She was identified by one of our drones as not in correct order. Can you confirm which is the case, Plore or armband infraction, so we can cite her?"

"I'm sorry, officer," said Adam pleasantly, kinglike, from the elevation of his porch. "She is not a Plore. We had an argument and she ran out of the house without her armband. She probably couldn't find the house again when she remembered she'd left the armband behind. She's not terribly bright."

The officer wrote the electronic ticket for the failure-to-wear-armband offense. "This is a $1,200 ticket, payable to the Rehoba City Council, with a $100 surcharge for an under-100 Social Credit offender. A second infraction will lead to a mandatory one-week jail sentence."

"Thank you, officer," said Adam as the policewoman departed, "Melia, dear, come up and have a drink." He had mixed her a vodka gimlet half an hour ago, and it sat on the table between the rocking chairs, the ice slowly melting. She sullenly climbed the steps and sat down.

"That was smart," he said to her. "Now you have to pay a pretty hefty fine. I hope you don't think I'm going to pay it."

"I can pay my own fines," she sniffed. Adam thought privately that for someone on the bottom rungs of City society, she seemed remarkably unfazed by the prospect of such a penalty.

"Did you think you were going to run back to the City?" he asked her. "You realize that you can't get here except by private or self-driving cars? There's no bus service except for the workers. Not that you could even pay for a bus ticket without your armband."

"I don't know what I thought," said Malia.

"I'm very disappointed that you think I would lure you here to murder you," said Adam. "I thought we were friends—of a sort."

She gave him a reproving look. "Friends don't do that kind of thing to each other, amba-sah."

"You need more interesting friends," he said. Malia, of course, had only one friend besides David, namely Fern, whom she still felt she had betrayed in some way. Malia had already berated Adam for the Rosebud raid, to which he curtly had said she should be glad she wasn't around that weekend herself, which he had thoughtfully taken into account. He had offered to ensure that Fern had a decent job in the Zone if she, Malia, would dismiss Dave from her life. But Malia was desperately clinging to Dave, or more precisely, the chimera of his protection.

"If I…if I go into that room with you, will you make sure Fern doesn't get sent to the chemical building?" she asked pointedly. "And has a halfway decent job assignment?"

"That's two requests," said Adam, draining his third whiskey. "But sure, if she's still alive, I'll make sure they put her somewhere easier than the fields or the factories." He gave her a hard stare, "and in return, I want complete obedience. I didn't care for the ice cream episode this afternoon. Look at me, damn you."

"I'm sorry, amba-sah."

"I doubt it, but let's see if your behavior improves. Starting now." He began to rise.

"Amba-sah, can you call the Zone now and ask? I'm just afraid if we wait a few days, it might be too late." Adam had to admit Malia had a good point, given the turnover at the chemical factory. Even with Avadaughter's caution, Beijing was insistent on progress. The laboratory had slowed down and was conserving its human material more carefully, but the experiments were still claiming almost two dozen lives each week.

Adam nodded, and went into the house. She heard him speak on the phone, probably to Mattison, she hoped. There was a long silence while Adam waited, presumably for Mattison to track down the prisoner's whereabouts. Eventually Adam reemerged, as she was signing for a delivery of Thai food for dinner that he had ordered while waiting for her.

"Done," he said. "Your friend is still alive and starting tomorrow, she begins working in the kitchen in the main house. Commander Mattison personally guaranteed it."

"Thank you, amba-sah," she said with relief, both for the favor and for the good news.

"Let's see some gratitude," he said. "First, dinner." They brought the large Enviro-pod into the house and unpacked the larb gai, beef with basil, and mango with sticky rice for dessert. The restaurant, like others of its kind, sported a sign in its front window asserting its status as a "Culturally Non-Appropriative Restaurant," which the authorities could grant after extensive inspections and background checks of the owners' ideological credentials. It did not guarantee that the food would be tasty.

After dinner, Adam led the way downstairs, promising her that each day she avoided using the safeword, he would buy her ice cream on the boardwalk. At least that first night, it was not too awful. Twice Adam disappeared to take calls in the adjoining secure room, during which she lay there, almost comfortable in the restraints, despite the occasional spasm in her right leg, her mind wandering. She realized that her entire life had been one of restraints on which she had relied to avoid making choices. It was not necessarily bad to avoid making choices and to have others, perhaps more knowledgeable and wiser, make them for you. And even if this was a rationalization, her relief that Fern was safe made it all worthwhile.

The days took on their own rhythm. Adam let Malia sleep in each morning, while he jogged on the beach, and then worked in the living room, tapping on the workscreen or taking or making phone calls. When she awoke, they took sandwiches and an umbrella to the beach, coming back mid-afternoon for some basement recreation. Around evening, they went for a walk on the boardwalk, finishing with dinner in an upscale beachside restaurant. Adam was partial to French and Italian cuisine. She got her ice cream every night. When they returned, they lounged in the hot tub and Malia's sore muscles relaxed. The nights went late; Adam needed far less sleep than she did.

To her surprise, although perhaps her whole life had trained her for this moment, she turned out to be inclined to the submissive role. "It's your low-credit DJR existence made flesh," Adam taunted, but his voice had an almost-gentle, reverent quality. "Yoga with pain," he called it. Through the slits in the mask, she watched him, heavy but purposeful, warming wax on the hot plate or selecting a device. As the week went on, he tested various machines and apparatuses in the room on her, or more precisely, he tested her. She turned out to be alarmingly claustrophobic, panicking at the close of a lid or a jangling door, so the boxes and cages largely stayed in the corners, but not always. He liked dressing her in masks and faux leather and tying her in odd positions.

On Wednesday, Adam said that Will would be joining them for the weekend. On one hand, she was afraid of Will disturbing their cozy, if metallic, domesticity. ("Don't worry," said Adam. "There are no secrets between Will and me in these matters.") Yet it offered the appealing possibility of picking up useful intelligence that would justify her trip to Rehoba. Surely Adam and Will would have to discuss some business-related matters, and they would not always be too fastidious about retiring to the secure room. Malia had already learned from a triumphant Adam that Will had held a party at the Argonne Tower on Saturday to which Antifans had been deliberately invited. Perhaps he would openly tell Adam what he had learned from them.

On Friday morning, Adam altered the schedule somewhat by having them start the day with a walk along the beach, and then descending into the basement. Around noon, he came upstairs to prepare lunch, leaving Malia in the dungeon to reflect on her various offenses against him, which he had thoughtfully listed for her. Will's Chinese-made DragonFire sportscar pulled up—he had purchased the vehicle with his own recent Social Credit promotion to 220—and he bounded up the stairs with his duffel. "Hey, Adam! I made good time."

"Great," Adam said. "Why don't you go grab us some beers in the basement? Take a look in the rec room while you're down there."

Will gave the figure tied to the stockade a good hard look. "Well, is that you, Ms. Melia?" The Antifan-like black leather mask made positive identification a challenge, especially when the victim was tightly gagged. Odd muffled sounds emerged. "No worries, I'll ask Adam," and he disappeared upstairs with the bottles of beer.

"That's really quite beautiful, Adam," said Will, who had an aesthetic appreciation of the bondage arts. "I assume that's our Melia?"

"*My* Melia," Adam said, but he smiled.

"I suppose we should release her for lunch, then?"

"She can have hers later. Let's have ours now." They ate with the basement door wide open so that she could hear them eating and drinking. The mask tended to make it harder to hear, since it covered almost the entire head, so Malia regretted she was probably missing out on some useful intelligence. She was quite hungry, but they didn't seem to care.

"Absolutely lovely work," said Will about Adam's stockade presentation. "I would call it 'Splayed DJR Butterfly,' or something like that. It's too bad it's politically incorrect, otherwise you could have a show at the art museum on the Mall. Maybe if it were the other way around, and she tied you to the stockade, the authorities would swoon over it."

"Be serious, Will," said Adam. "Feel free to go untie her if you like and finish the job. We've got some work to do this afternoon." His mind was already on the tasks awaiting discussion.

They enjoyed dinner at La Chatte Noire, the new bistro on the boardwalk. Adam ordered a fruity cabernet sauvignon for the table, beef bourguignon for himself and coq au vin for Malia.

When they returned to the house, they poured the remainder of the third bottle and took the glasses to the hot tub. As Malia had hoped, the men talked work matters, probably what they considered more mundane matters in the Intelligence Directorate. Five more officers had been seconded into the Directorate; Malia remembered the names as best she could. Dr. Smith was urging them to consider a list of unspecified collection tasks suggested by Beijing. At one point, Will looked uncertainly at Malia, and then questioningly at Adam.

"That's all right," said Adam, watching her body stretching luxuriantly in the tub, her eyes closed. "She's not paying attention to anything we say." The undertone was, "She's not smart enough to understand anything we're saying."

Eff you, I am, she thought.

But then they steered the conversation to general DJR matters. "Did you hear they blew up the Depository yesterday?"

Even Malia was visibly shocked, sitting up straight in the tub. "Isn't that where they keep all the old books? That's..."

"Awful?" teased Will. "Since when have you been you such a big reader?"

"I read quite a lot," she said huffily, "of course, only books on the GVN. I just think it's horrible to blow up a whole building full of books, even if they are dangerous books. What if the government decided some of these books were all right after all? What would we do then?"

Adam said, amused, "Then we'll just buy them from foreign countries and reintroduce them. But they're no good to anyone here, now. Terrible backward ideas. Most of the books in the Depository were quite old—modern books are much better, or much safer, anyway."

She was silent as the men moved onto other conversational topics. She had given 13 years of her life to the Depository, and had believed in its mission, at least until the very end of her tenure. Even if she had come to believe that John MacMillan was right, and human beings ought to read whatever they liked, and to find Truth, or more precisely, to search for it among full storehouses of human knowledge, it was hard not to be sentimental about her days in the building, her colleagues, and really, as often was the case in these matters, her youth.

"Good Lord," said Adam, "are you crying over a shed full of subversive books? You must have had too much to drink tonight. Why don't you just go into the house and get ready for bed?"

They were all planning to leave on Sunday by noon. Malia was due to work her shift on Sunday night, and Adam's mind was already preoccupied with the workweek ahead. But it was a full Saturday, albeit an unseasonably cool one, and they walked along the beachfront in the morning rather than swimming. Adam invited Will to join them in the basement during the afternoon, and they emerged to go to dinner at Henry's, a posh pizzeria near the boardwalk.

Back at the house, the men clearly wanted to go over some files in the living room and not be shut in the secure room. Malia said, "I can sit out on the porch if you like, amba-sehm."

Adam said, "No, you can take this instead. Go get a glass of water." He handed her a blue pill from a jar on the coffee table, "You'll be out for a little while."

She obediently took the pill in front of him, and then disappeared into the bathroom, emerging two or three minutes later, having taken the counter-pill Cheysa had given her. "Go into the bedroom," he said. She dropped her armband on the console with theirs and went into the bedroom. He checked five minutes later to find her snoring gently on the bed. But shortly after he closed the door, she leapt out of the bed and placed her ear against the door to the living room, overhearing what she could. The armband was also recording the conversation, but could only record for an hour.

When Adam returned to the living room, he and Will covered what would be the discreet recruitment and deployment of ESF troops outside the Zone and the process of importing arms and distributing them to the units. Will's network of contacts outside the DJR was quite willing to turn from selling heavy equipment to selling firearms and even artillery to him, as he presumably still represented a DJR governmental arm. Some of those contacts were even in the US, and not all of them were savory, but this did not trouble Will unduly, as long as the transactions were honestly completed.

"We need to locate warehouses where we can store weapons until the moment comes," said Adam, "but the troops also need to be able to drill and practice." Will identified several empty old armories on government grounds, and warehouses that might be repurposed for ESF use, mostly in Outer Plore areas. "Antifans stay in the City," said Adam, "They don't have a lot of interest in what goes on outside the

City, so this will be to our advantage. When the moment to strike comes, we will be everywhere, and they will be bottled up in the cities."

"And we have the Knowledge Tower on our side?" asked Will.

"The Knowledge Tower has indicated it will stand to the side," said Adam, "not that they have any choice. But it will give them a great deal of pleasure to see the Antifans humbled. We will absorb the parts of the ADF we want to keep and abolish the rest. Three towers are enough, and in a socialist society the economists should be wielding the security power."

He added, "Avadaughter is getting feeble. According to our source in the White Black House, her physician is prescribing zingothene for all her public appearances. And she's sleeping ten hours a day."

Will said, "Might be a good time to work with Peace-Williams more. He could be a friend when the time comes. Maybe we can encourage him to take over a little earlier with our support."

The two men looked at each other. Despite the 15-year age difference, they had become fast friends years ago, and they always spoke frankly with each other.

"What happens if we don't succeed?" said Will. "I don't underestimate the Antifans."

Adam said, "We'll have a plane out at the Zone ready to head to Mexico. Just in case. Flying south along the frontier until we reach Texas and then heading straight for Matamoros. If I can't be a rich hero in the DJR, I don't plan on being a dead rebel either."

He looked levelly at Will. "But remember, that's the worst-case scenario. And my plan is to make the best-case scenario the one that happens. As Genghis Khan said, 'If you're afraid, don't do it, and if you're doing it—don't be afraid.'" He slammed his fist on the end table for emphasis. Malia leapt back into the bed.

Chapter 50

Just Say No

(Sunday, 25 September)

The self-driving car dropped her and Adam off at the Octavian around 5:30 pm. He had offered to take her directly to TerraCity, but she had declined, saying it would be easier to nap in the back of the concierge breakroom before her shift began. "Suit yourself," said Adam, who was neither inclined to great chivalry, nor to having to gaze upon that depressing pile of bricks containing society's losers, Diverse or not. At the Octavian, he left her in the doorway as she apologetically said, "Since I'm staff, I need to enter through the side door." He shrugged, gave her a final casual kiss, and said, "See you later, but maybe not tonight."

As he disappeared through the front door, Malia leaned against the brick front of the building and texted David. Within ten minutes, the sportscar was waiting for her several blocks away, on Albemarle. She slid in, relieved to see David's handsome and smiling face. No games here. They kissed deeply, finally a kiss of soulmates, not adversaries. Warmth flooded her body. She lay back against the passenger seat and beamed at him.

"I'm glad you're alive and well," he said. "Thank God." And then she realized that even though she had flirted with danger, David had been in the even worse position of not knowing how she was faring. For all he knew, she could have been lying in a ditch, strangled by Adam Ross after he discovered her Antifan ties. "Actually, you look pretty good."

"Thanks," she said sarcastically. "Just pretty good?"

"Gorgeous," he said, lighting over her mouth again, his hands roaming through her hair. A minute later, he lifted his head, and said, "Home? We should get dinner before you have to show up for work, although I'm inclined to tell you to call in sick."

They fixed themselves a quick dinner of sautéed chicken breasts and bagged vegetables. David poured a French chardonnay into their glasses, not Diversity-grown at all. Malia drank plenty of water, knowing it would help her survive the long night ahead. Her sleep schedule was completely awry. If Adam Ross called her upstairs at 2 am, she would likely fall asleep on his couch while he did whatever he liked.

"How was your week?" she asked him.

"Kind of boring, except for wondering how you were doing. Tell me what you found out."

He hit the noise cylinder, turned on the Diversity alt-rock station to high volume, and she told him her findings. "I've got about an hour recorded on my armband from their Saturday night conversation. He gave me a pill to knock me out, but I took the counter-pill and made sure my armband recorder was turned on before I went into the bedroom, so I could listen a little just in case the recorder didn't work."

David took her armband, and listened for a minute. "Amazing, just what I'm hearing. Let's transfer what you have on there to my armband. Just in case Adam Ross starts wondering what you have on there and comes down at midnight to check." Transferring the file and deleting hers took only a minute.

Then she told him about the plans to deploy and arm ESF troops, to smuggle weapons, and to stage a coup against the ADF when the time was right. "It should be on the recording," she said, adding, "President Avadaughter is on zingos and sleeping ten hours a day." She told him about the party Will had hosted on the 17th under the guise of being a Social Tower baseball fan, and that Walters and Cheysa had attended and bragged about how the ADF had cowed the Knowledge Tower. The Econ Tower's Intelligence Directorate was taking collection instructions from Beijing. The lab's consumption of Social Crediteers had slowed after pressure from Avadaughter, but Beijing was insisting on maintaining the pace of experimentation.

"So, Kendall was visiting you in Rehoba the past few days? What was he like?"

"Easygoing except when he and Adam were discussing work. He and Adam are almost like brothers. Adam treats him much better than he does me. He's from Atlanta originally, has a slight southern accent."

"Did he also—"

"As Will told me, Adam might be selfish with his money but never with his women."

David looked anguished.

"But I have good news," she said. "I was able to convince Adam to call Mattison at the Economic Zone and get Fern transferred to a job in the kitchen that will keep her from being sent to the chemical factory lab."

"That's good," said David, with genuine relief. Even though technically he and Malia had done their best to help alleviate Fern's situation, he felt they had just sent her from one frying pan into another. It was nothing to be proud of. "What did you have to do to get Adam Ross to agree? I thought he had been pressuring you to drop Tom in return for helping you with Fern."

"He just agreed to help," she said lamely.

David looked up sharply. "Don't lie to me. Adam Ross doesn't just agree to help. You gave him something, and I know it wasn't just sex, because that horse has left the barn."

Horse? Barn? Malia wondered.

"You've already given him that, is what I'm trying to say. What did you give him this time that was worth him picking up the phone and calling Mattison?"

"You're not going to like this," said Malia, "but he was going to force me anyway, so I figured I'd get something from the transaction." She explained about the dungeon.

"Holy God," said David, in full shocked Plore mode. And then, with some genuine interest, "Did you like it?"

"It wasn't as bad as I thought it would be," she admitted, "and then Adam bought me ice cream on the boardwalk every night because I didn't use the safeword." Like a child, he thought, almost amused. "On the first night he was angry that I bought my own ice cream when he'd told me not to, because I was getting fat."

"You? Getting fat?" David was momentarily diverted. "The bastard." Having finished dinner, he steered her toward the bed. "I know you're probably exhausted, but I'm determined to rid you of the stink of Adam Ross. And his friend. This way you'll know you're really home."

She pulled away from him. "Do you realize what I've been dealing with all week? Do you think I might have a night off to recover from all that?"

David stared at her, stunned. She turned away. He hadn't thought about it from her perspective, that even his approaches might fall broadly into the same category as those from Adam Ross and Will Kendall, at least tonight, in a lesser degree of evil, but still compelling her compliance. He was a fair enough man and still Plore enough that he could acknowledge and respect her feelings in the matter.

"All right," he said. "I'm sorry." He felt a little ashamed.

Malia was pathetically grateful. She did not take for granted his kindness to her, and she had feared rejecting any advance because, at some point, might David not impatiently walk away and leave her bereft again? She gave him a warm hug and said sweetly, "Thank you. Just not tonight." He reciprocated, with rueful understanding.

David's car pulled up at the Director's house and parked in the driveway. As he exited, Steve Rosen, who had been waiting for him, got out of his car. With his sportscar restored, David felt he could look Steve Rosen in the eye again. "That's more you, brother," Steve said approvingly.

Ferraro was waiting for them in the living room, drink in hand. They hastened down to the secure room, with the Social Credit butler bringing several Old Fashioneds on a tray behind them. The door closed firmly behind the butler as he exited.

"What has your girlfriend brought us now, Harris?" Ferraro said, deadly serious.

"It's as bad as we thought, sir," said David. "I have an hour-long recording that she caught on her armband when they thought they'd knocked her out with a pill and she was out of the room. The ESF are being deployed and armed; the deputy of the

Intelligence Directorate, who's also the quartermaster of the Anacosta Economic Zone, is acquiring weapons and even artillery launchers. Trainers are coming in from the People's Liberation Army under the guise of scientific personnel. Moreover, they are trying to recruit our own Antifan officers—several attended a party the quartermaster held under false pretenses last week at the Argonne Tower, including, I must say, Commander Walters." He was gratified by the shock on the faces of the other two. "They are confident they have the Knowledge Tower on their side, if only by inertia, and now that they, like ourselves, think President Avadaughter's health is fading, will be trying to recruit Vice-President Peace-Williams to their side."

They listened to the recording, which ended with Adam saying, "Three towers are enough, and in a socialist society the economists should be wielding the security power. I'm not sure how the White Black House would stand on this." *Click.* David added, "Malia says she overheard the comment about Peace-Williams afterward, and then something about Mexico. But she jumped back into the bed when she heard them finishing up in the living room."

"Can we trace these arms purchases, Rosen?"

"Yes, sir, we can work with the Cyber Unit to see what is going out under Economic Tower requisitioning. I would expect that the purchases are being line-itemed under other descriptions, but we can use algorithms to determine patterns that would be consonant with arms purchases, rather than, say, for the heavy machinery. And for unusual expenditures, or unusual sellers. If some of these are being acquired in the United States, I would also alert our border stations, since some would have to be smuggled overland."

"The question is going to be whether we crash down on them immediately, or wait until they've started to put forces in place and arm them," said Ferraro. "They aren't expecting to move anytime soon, it seems. I'd rather have the evidence in front of my eyes so we can point it out to the whole country.

"But Mother Earth, I never thought we'd see such treachery. This isn't what we fought for during the war—we'll have to have another commander meeting tomorrow."

At about the same time at the Octavian, Malia was counting spa receipts after Rex had come downstairs to say goodnight. The Diversity History exam would be on Monday, Diversity Lit on Wednesday, and Diversity Math on Friday, so Rex would be buckling down this week. Malia texted:

Let me know if u have any questions b4 the tests and let me know how each test goes when u come home, ok?

She remembered laughing after David had asked her, "When is the Diversity Diversity test?" But then he had more seriously reminded her, "not too long ago, math was objective and not political."

To which she had said, "Math is whatever the Knowledge Tower says it is. I assume they teach objective math before the student becomes a civil engineer and builds bridges."

David had responded, "I bet the Chinese are building our bridges these days."

Rex gave her a hug, and walked by Adam Ross, who had exited the elevator. "Hello, Mr. Ross!" she chirped.

"Hello, Rex," he said, thinking that the child was becoming almost personable.

"Melia," he said at the counter, "I want to see your armband."

"My armband, amba-sah?" She feigned astonishment. "Why on earth?"

He extended his hand, and she obediently unfastened the armband from her left arm and handed it to him. He checked the recording feature, which was empty, and her texts from the week, most of which she had quickly and prudently erased. A few exchanges with Rex were left for authenticity. He sneered at these, with their affectionate greetings and concerned questions about studying and sleeping and eating well. Did she think she was the child's mother or something? Kind of pathetic. But nothing for Adam to worry about. "Thank you, Melia. Just checking." And he went back upstairs.

Malia was grateful for the sturdy counter to lean on. Her legs were shaking. David had saved her again.

Chapter 51
Wait and See
(Monday, 26 September)

The "In It To Win It" banner had finally disappeared from the Director's conference room two weeks after National Security Day, by which point it had begun to visibly sag at one end. This seemed fitting for what had been a more lackluster celebration than usual, at least from the ADF's perspective. No one could fault the extravagant floats, or the crisp marching lines of ADF units from across the country, or the regimental bands that could play current pop, hip hop, and rock favorites, as well as martial but politically correct standards. Nor had anyone bombed the Antifan parade, for sure. But the bleachers were only mostly full, and the crowd was less enthusiastic than usual despite the promise of barbecued meat. Riding on the KCU float, and waving manfully to the crowds, David felt a sense of unease—was it lingering guilt over the orphaned girl in the red smocked dress? He was positive that, at several points in the procession, he had heard boos or jeers, although no arrests were made that day. The KCU float, which featured a looming black Antifan officer with multiple arms and hands, like a Hindu god statue, each hand protectively cupping a different intellectual entity—musicians, artists, authors, professors—was technically impressive. Yet, so Fall 2088.

"By next year, it may be our parade," Adam had said cheerfully to Will as they watched the festivities on the screen in his office, their feet on his desk.

The commanders who filed into the room for the meeting were also more subdued than at the previous meeting exactly two months earlier. Those who had read the files knew that the situation was even more serious than before. The experiments continued at the urging of the Chinese, and now they knew the Economic Tower was aiming at supplanting the ADF. If the Economic Tower gained the upper hand with a monopoly on a working truth serum, combined with effective armed troops, the White Black House, enfeebled itself by the ailing Avadaughter, would defer to the stronger party, Basic Law be damned. Ferraro had used all the Antifans' political capital this year on slapping the Knowledge Tower, which had turned out not to be Beaufort's most dangerous threat. On top of it all, the Economic Tower was launching its own spies against Antifans, reversing the usual prerogative of Beaufort.

After the initial briefing by Steve Rosen, Ferraro laid out the options. "We could arrest several dozen Econocrats tonight, including that skunk Adam Ross, but then they'd keep building up their forces outside the Cities.

"We could arrest half the Econ Tower and nip the takeover plan in the bud, before it becomes obvious to others what they're up to. But then we couldn't assume we'd gain access to the lab or the truth serum. And I'm not sure we'd convince the White Black House to back us.

"So, I don't think we can go in halfway. It's possible that arrests would put an end to the bigger plans because they'd know we were onto them. But it would be like cutting off parts of a snake and leaving the head writhing and the body parts regenerating.

"Do we want to let them continue until the crime becomes sufficiently monstrous so that if we strike, no one will question what we did?"

"What do we think the time frame is for the Tower?" asked Valerie Marzullo of TCU.

Steve said, "They want to have the truth serum in hand before they strike. They need to build ESF forces from about 3,000 troops now to probably 50,000, which is what you would need for a coup. We don't know how close they are to having the serum. If lying kills the subject, then they may be quite close. As for the troop numbers, they would probably need another year." He then acknowledged that the ADF might not be well positioned outside the main Cities to track these developments, if the ESF was mobilizing in Outer Plore and Zone areas. "We can increase drone surveillance, but it's not particularly discreet."

"I saw two uniformed ESF troops near Ada's on Saturday night," said Gemma Carpenter. "Not armed, though."

"Very concerning about the sightings of ESF in the Cities," said Ferraro. "We should advise our forces that if they encounter armed ESF, they should arrest them, if they are themselves uniformed at the time. Otherwise it looks like a brawl. Arming ESF troops outside the Zones is definitely against the Basic Law. It will become worse if we seem to tolerate it."

Two hours later, the debate was continuing. Montoya requested sandwiches and drinks for the table. At 2 pm, Ferraro made a decision. "We will increase our surveillance. We will continue to try to link the bank accounts with the Econ Tower without showing our hand. Maybe our informants will hear something." He looked meaningfully at David. "One month from today, we will meet again. I am not looking to delay this decision until it is too late. We need to act. I do believe that we can increase our credibility and our effectiveness by gathering more information, especially since we have such an excellent informant so close to Adam Ross.

"Who's going to Will Kendall's party on Saturday?" Once he had learned of the Economic Tower's efforts to recruit Antifans by pretending to be Sociocrats, Ferraro decided that the ADF would capitalize on it by sending Antifans to recruit the Econocrats. If there was a single actual Social Tower guest present, Ferraro said, he would be astonished. But the final Diversity National Series game—formerly called the World Series, which the United States selfishly and ethnocentrically had retained—would be played on Saturday night between the Anacosta Raptors and the Atlanta Antiracists. It wasn't hard to find some reliable ADF officers willing to eat lavishly and watch the game on giant screens at the Argonne Tower while engaging their hosts in discussion on the sidelines during breaks. "I mean, who are the real intel officers?" asked Ferraro, with Gemma smiling beside him.

Steve Rosen listed the officers who would be in attendance, including Brian Walters and Cheysa Conroy, both of whom had gotten severe lectures from Gemma's officers and Steve Rosen about their carelessness that first night at the bar. But once the relationship had been established with Kendall, it was too good to disrupt. "We'll play it back on him," said Montoya.

And Ferraro had been inclined to dismiss Walters' naivete as not having resulted in any harm. "In fact," he said cheerily to Steve and David, "this has given us a great opportunity to strike back at the Econ Tower. All in all, I'm inclined to commend Walters."

David wished he had the courage to shake his head in disbelief. Wurro's mana remained strong and constant.

Chapter 52
Positive Result
(Saturday, 1 October)

O n Saturday evening David and Malia went to Deep Fried State, the latest hot restaurant. David was dubious of the "Hip. Woke. Authentic. Delicious." mantra, but it was hard to refuse Malia anything. And it was possible, faintly possible, that the cookery might be worthy of the hype; "fried" was promising. Fortunately, this restaurant allowed any above-120 Social Crediteer to bring any guest, the checking of which had become part of the restaurant reservations routine for David since he started dating Malia. An accommodating response tended to vault any restaurant to the top of the list for them.

He ordered the fried chicken, and she ordered non-culturally appropriative tempura. "Vegetables? Okra?" he asked. "Really?" That was unlike Malia.

"I don't know," she shrugged, "Just feel like it somehow." Halfway through the meal, she excused herself, and came back to say she had vomited the okra.

"Uh, has that happened at other times recently?"

She admitted to throwing up in the washroom once or twice at work this week.

"Do you think you're pregnant?"

"I don't know," she said. But, when pressed, she admitted that she hadn't had her period in seven weeks. David's first reaction was, we will have to move the whole escape timeline up, faster than I expected. That means before winter sets in. It will never happen with a baby, nor with a heavily pregnant woman. His second reaction was, also predictably, is it mine? He had tried to be a modern, Diverse man, who was a credit to the ADF, by accepting her work-related liaison with Adam and now Will Kendall, but very few men would gladly protect with their lives the offspring of another man. And particularly the offspring of either of two very wicked men.

When they got home, David asked, "Do you want to do a pregnancy test right now?" He reassured her, "I'm with you, no matter what. But we need to know, for our own purposes."

She nodded. He took out the home health device, which not only took temperatures, but various other biorhythmic and medical data. He didn't use it often, since he always felt vigorous and in no need of confirmation from a mechanical device. Checking the instructions, he placed the tongue suppressor attachment onto the device and said "say ah," to Malia, who opened her mouth and closed it around the device. Three minutes later, David declared, "You are definitely pregnant. It says six weeks." Every week was precious now. They both remembered the passionate lovemaking after she had returned from the Outer Banks, glorious with joy at telling Rex the truth and Rex receiving her news with love. It was an auspicious time to conceive another child, or should have been.

Despite what David had told her, Malia still wondered whether he would stay with her if the child was Adam or Will's. The GVN stories Malia had read about such predicaments invariably concluded with the right man becoming the father, with "right" meaning upright by DJR standards, politically correct, and often from a different race, sexual identity, or disabled. The high Social Credit expectant mother generously lowered her expectations to welcome the disadvantaged father, who was never a Plore. Sometimes the mother went to the local Abortion Palace if the complications were too difficult for the author to untangle. The child would never be taken from her, if she avoided the Abortion Palace. Marriage was rare, except as a plot device. In general, the GVN's perception of happy endings seemed at variance with Malia's own experiences. On the other hand, the timing favored David, not Adam, and certainly not Will, who had slept with her in July and then in mid-September.

They looked dejectedly at each other. "Do you want to test tonight to see if I'm the father?" he asked her. She shook her head. "That's fine," said David, "we'll sleep on it. I just want you to know, regardless of who is the biological father, I am not leaving you. We are going to see this whole adventure through together."

She cried with relief, again burying her face in his strong shoulder. But in the middle of the night, she awoke, drenched in sweat, shaking from a nightmare in which Adam Ross pursued her with a butcher knife. David held her tightly, saying over and over again, "It's just a dream. It means nothing. You're just afraid of him. You are safe here with me." To himself, he wondered, should she go to the Octavian tomorrow night? Should she refuse to see Adam Ross if he summons her? He recalled what she had said about Adam's determination to never see fatherhood again, but he couldn't force her to go to the Abortion Palace, could he? Would Adam Ross care less if the child were ostensibly that of the Plore, Tom/Dave? Or was any pregnancy in his vicinity offensive to him?

After Malia fell back to sleep, it was David who stayed awake, feeling guilty that he had not yet called Tom/Dave about ending his assignment as Malia's Plore boyfriend. He would call tomorrow, he vowed, before they went to Ploreville.

While Malia slept in the morning, David sat in the sunroom, feet on an adjoining chair, and called Tom. He was relieved that Tom answered, and apologized for calling so early, saying it was urgent. Tom had already rebuffed Adam's offer of a final payment to break up with Malia, but didn't seem afraid. "How is he going to find me in Ploreville, anyway?" he said. "He can look for an imaginary asphalt crew in the City, but he won't find me." Tom was highly satisfied with the money he had been making giving Adam permission to take Malia out of the City. "I have to tell you, this has been a very profitable assignment for me. A lot of money for several in-person acting engagements, and a lot of back and forth texting with Adam Ross."

"You might want to cut it off now," said David. "It's been useful for us to have you play her boyfriend, but I think it's becoming dangerous. We don't need to lose you now. You've done good work for us. Take the final payment and run."

"The next time he calls, I will," said Tom. "Thanks for the good times."

David hung up with a sigh of relief. As a handler, you owed your informants your utmost effort to protect them. They risked their lives for you when they need not have done so, and you needed to ensure their safety, even above your own. It was a sacred obligation.

When Malia awoke, they ate a quick breakfast and then headed to Ploreville. "Don't tell my mother or sisters about the baby," David urged, as they drove across the Potowmack. "I don't want to raise expectations. And then my mother will ask why we aren't getting married yet."

"Are we going to get married?" Malia asked, uncertain.

David said, with some asperity, "Do you doubt it?"

Malia said slowly, but quickening as her doubts mounted, "No, but it seems very far away, and this baby is very near. And what if it isn't yours? And I don't trust your Director to give us permission to get married."

David said shortly, "Take the paternity test and you'll see whether I remain true to you. I promise it doesn't matter whose child it is. I will marry you and treat that child as ours. And I don't trust Ferraro either to give us permission, which is why we aren't applying to get married here, but only when we reach a free country. And finally, because you're pregnant, we are moving up our plans fast. You're not crossing the frontier eight months pregnant, or during the winter, or with a baby. So, in three months, we will be free and married, or dead. Or worse.

"You need to start preparing Isabelle for our move. Do you think we can trust her to keep this secret?" They had switched to calling Rex by her real name, if only to protect her.

"Yes," said Malia. "Absolutely."

Chapter 53
Abortion Palace
(Sunday-Thursday, 2-6 October)

(Planned Parenthood Founder Margaret) Sanger said,
"Well, I think the greatest sin in the world is bringing children
into the world that have disease from their parents, that have no
chance in the world to be a human being practically—delinquents,
prisoners, all sorts of things, just marked when they're born.
That, to me, is the greatest sin that people can commit."
—(ABC *interview, September 21, 1957*)

Malia reported for work at the Octavian on Sunday evening, elated by David's promise to her the previous night. She felt as if she were stepping on buoyant pockets of air, not the mere ground. For the first time, her regulation blue skirt felt snug. Oh, I will have to go to a seamster, she thought, and have this let out. It gave her joy to think of David's child growing inside of her. Although she hadn't taken the paternity test yet, Malia's calculations gave her confidence that the child indeed was David's.

Rex came down to greet her shortly into the shift. "Melia, look!" She thrust her armband forward with the test results. She had earned a "Very Proficient," the highest score, on both the Diversity History and Diversity Literature exams. "I wanted to show this to you in person!" Malia came out from behind the counter and they hugged joyfully. "I haven't gotten the math results yet. But I felt good about that test too. My parents are thrilled. I haven't seen them this happy in a long time. They're planning to come down and thank you later."

Malia wondered how she was going to talk to Rex about the escape plans, since she would neither commit them to the text chat nor whisper in the lobby. Even the apartment was unsafe, what with the Antifan feed. Perhaps they could take a walk in the Botanic Gardens across the street on a weekend when it was open to low Social Crediteers. By the time Rex had returned to the apartment, Malia had texted her, inviting her to stroll in the Gardens next weekend, "and go for ice cream to celebrate, my treat!" Rex accepted instantly, with a big heart symbol.

Even the summons from Adam at midnight could not disturb her good mood. She texted David, but finding someone with a high enough Social Credit number to overhear Adam's feed on a Sunday night at Beaufort wasn't easy anymore. He opened the door, indicated she should enter, and closed the door behind them. He was fully dressed in chinos and a button-down shirt, which boded well for a professional encounter. She smiled at him, and then ran for the bathroom. Adam heard the sound of her retching and when she emerged, he demanded, "has that been happening recently?"

She dropped her eyes. "Just a few times."

Adam brought over the health-o-meter, almost identical to David's, but well into middle age, he was more inclined to use his, especially for blood pressure and pulse readings after a jog. He adjusted the settings and wiped and presented the meter to Malia, who opened her mouth and closed it around the stick. Three minutes later, the same results as yesterday.

Adam cursed. "Dammit. I told you not to get pregnant. Weren't you using birth control?"

She looked at him. "Of course, amba-sah, but it's not fool-proof. Anyway, the baby's probably not yours, amba-sah. I'm sure it's Dave's, which is far better for me and for the entire world, frankly." Adam looked as if he were weighing whether to slap her.

"It doesn't matter whose it is," said Adam, which confused her. "And I wouldn't be so proud of having a Plore's baby. Let's do the paternity test, just to get that out of the way."

He adjusted the settings, and inserted the meter into her mouth again. Several minutes later, his printer issued a single sheet of paper. Each Social Crediteer had a 12-digit identification number followed by three letters, and each Plore, a 14-digit number only. The number printed out was not the 14-digit number he expected, nor was it his or Will's. It was another 12-digit number entirely. But never having administered a paternity test, Malia was unaware of these intricacies.

"How many men are you sleeping with?" Adam snapped at her. "This isn't a Plore number."

Say nothing, she heard David's voice.

"You really are a slut," said Adam, ignoring all the Diversity lessons about not "slut-shaming" sexually active women. Her promiscuity didn't particularly bother him, since in some ways he was a modern Diversity man. It complicated his plans, though, which did bother him.

"I could find out whose number this is," said Adam. "If I cared. But it's going to be moot in a few days. We'll make an appointment at the Abortion Palace for you this week. They can see you in the VIP section, so be glad you know me."

She stared at him, aghast. "I'm not going to the Abortion Palace. I'm having this baby. It's not even yours, so what right to do you have to tell me to abort it?"

"No, you're not having this baby. You do that and you're jeopardizing our future together."

"What future? I wasn't planning on spending the rest of my life in your dungeon—amba-sah," she added quickly for insurance.

"When your boyfriend, the one who can't even impregnate you, it seems, is no longer in the picture, we ought to think more permanently. I'm sure I can get a dispensation from my Director to marry you, despite your low status. Then we can live openly together. And your Social Credit number will rise to mine, or close enough to make it respectable."

I wouldn't call that living, she thought to herself. You've mistaken my coming up here and undergoing your abuse as a sign of love for you, or of my willingness to endure this treatment for the rest of my life. I'm only a masochist for professional reasons. Then she reminded herself, live your cover.

"That's not a very romantic proposal, amba-sah."

"It's what you deserve," he said. "You should be grateful." Then he said, "You've seen how fast I've risen in the last few weeks. I am one of the top people in the Economic Tower. I report directly to Pernella Smith. By this time next year, I may be in charge of an even bigger portfolio. You would be the wife of one of the most important people in the whole DJR. This is your best chance to live a comfortable life in this country, and you want to throw it away on the potheads in TerraCity." A lightbulb switched on. "Don't tell me the father is some TerraCity derelict."

She looked down at her lap. Not a deception flattering to her, but better than his looking in the direction of Beaufort.

"The child would probably be an imbecile, then," said Adam with finality. "And I'm not going to raise some pothead's kid. How about Thursday? I don't have to be in the office until mid-morning. I can drop you off there after your shift."

Then he added, "It's not just the Social Credit score and the lifestyle I can offer you. I have a sizable bank account outside of the country. I won't tell you where, but we might be able to retire there when I'm done here."

"I'm not that close to retirement, amba-sah," she said, reminding him that she was twenty years his junior. He marked that clever retort down for punishment later.

"Just be sensible," he said. "Any other woman would jump at this offer, particularly someone in your predicament."

What am I, a maiden in distress, she thought? But she admitted to herself, a year ago she would have gratefully accepted this grudging offer of rescue, whatever the price. She also had to admit to herself, were David not in the picture, she would accept Adam's offer, for the sake of survival. Even if Adam didn't know the particulars, he sensed that Malia must have some other alternatives, or she would have thrown her lot in with him sooner. He was making it his business to eliminate the alternatives.

When Malia went home on Monday morning, she discussed the situation with David. "Some proposal," he said. "Glad you prefer me." Leave it to Adam Ross to combine a marriage proposition—not quite a proposal—with a statement of his political ambitions. David was relieved by the results of the paternity test, even though he had fully intended to follow through on his promise to raise another man's child as his own.

"He can't force you to go to the Abortion Palace," David said practically. "If he dragged you there somehow, you'd just say no, right? They can't do this to you if you don't consent. Choice is enshrined in the DJR Basic Law." This comforted Malia, and she fell asleep in his arms. He disentangled himself gently, to dress quickly and make it to the 8:30 am unit meeting. She rolled away from him, cradling her head in the crook of her right arm. He drew the curtains around her, blew her a kiss, and was off to Beaufort.

Malia enjoyed her two days off. She swam in the Avalon pool, worked out with Kate, and felt more conscious of her body and how beautifully it served her. It was not the first time she had been pregnant, but now she felt as if she was pregnant for the first time, or that, in the bloom of youth, she had not really understood what was happening to her body or what it all meant. When David came home each night, she had cooked dinner for them, and he did not complain.

On Wednesday afternoon, she stared at herself in the full-length mirror before dressing to go to work. Yes, something about her abdomen seemed softer and heavier. She was glad that the Avalon seamster had altered her Octavian outfits.

It was an uneventful night, except for Leighton and Belinda stopping by the desk to thank Malia. Belinda gave her a small gift-wrapped box that contained a beautiful silver bracelet. Malia slipped it over her wrist after the couple had gone back upstairs, thinking to herself, you gave me something you could never imagine. You gave me my daughter back. And I will be taking her from you soon. Because she's mine, not yours.

At 7 am she finished her shift, and, tired, headed for the side staff door. The Antifan driver would be waiting for her several blocks away. But as she pushed open the exit, a strong arm encircled her from behind, and a wet cloth with a sickly-sweet scent covered her nose and mouth. She had no time to resist before she lost consciousness. When she awoke, she was in the back of a self-driving car with Adam and they were pulling into a garage that was the back entrance of what she quickly realized was the Abortion Palace. The sign said, "VIP Entrance."

"Good morning, Melia," Adam said. Two plainclothes ESF troops in overalls had been loitering in the staff lobby, but she had walked by them, assuming they were workmen waiting for their assignments for the day. At that hour, after an overnight shift, she was less alert than usual.

"What the hell is going on?" Forget any polite amba-sahing.

"What the hell is going on, amba-sah," he reminded her.

"No, this is outrageous. No, we are not going there." In her happy cloud, she had entirely forgotten about Adam's intention to schedule an abortion on Thursday. She had not agreed, and she would not agree to go; therefore, she had mistakenly assumed that he would not proceed. "I'm not going in there."

"Yes, you are," he said, as the car pulled up to the sliding glass doors. "I've arranged everything. You'll be treated like a queen." Two nurses in crisp white uniforms—one Asian man, one white woman—met them with a wheelchair. Malia struggled, but he pulled her out of the car. Neither of the nurses seemed surprised, and they cooperated with Adam to strap her arms and legs to the wheelchair. If she was a queen, it was probably Boadicea of Britain or Marie Antoinette. Paradoxically, in the regular Social Credit section of the Abortion Palace, nobody arrived under duress and Choice was grudgingly permitted. Some of the patients might have been ambivalent, but they made their own calculations—would they want to raise a child at TerraCity on its family floors? Could they afford to raise a child as a low Social Crediteer? Were they good citizens who did not wish to overpopulate the Earth? Would the father support the baby? In the VIP section, on the other hand, a good number of low Social Credit women were brought in by high Social Credit lovers, who were determined not to suffer the inconvenience or the indignity of a child, or the revelation of an affair. Tensions sometimes ran high.

Adam followed them into the glaring white lobby of the VIP section. "Please sign these papers, amba-sah," a clerk behind the desk requested.

"What about me? Do I sign any papers?" Malia yelled. "This is my body, and I don't want to be here. I want to have my baby!"

"Possibly violent," Adam advised them. "I'm authorizing you to knock her out, if necessary. I just want this done sooner rather than later."

"This whole building is built on violence!" she shouted.

"We have her down for a 10 am surgery," they promised him. They untied her left arm to remove her armband, and she struck a glancing blow at the male nurse. The other nurse produced a large needle. Realizing that she did not want to fall unconscious here, Malia suddenly said, "I'll behave, I promise," like a naughty child about to be deprived of a treat.

"That's a good girl," said the male nurse, rubbing his jaw. They reattached the bindings to her now-bare left arm. Adam crouched down in front of her wheelchair, smiling through his Roman dictator beard, "I'll see you tonight. Have a GREAT time." The Palace would send her in a self-driving car with an attendant to the Octavian, a rare exception for a low Social Crediteer, in time for her shift. The justification for the added expense was that she had served Mother Earth by not bringing another greedy human life into the world.

She looked directly into Adam's eyes. "I hate you. And I will have my revenge, someday. I promise." The nurses did not seem particularly fazed by this exchange either.

"Oh, you'll feel better later. You don't want to be fat, do you?" And then he was gone, hurrying off to the Economic Tower before his meetings began.

As the nurse pushed her wheelchair along the corridor, Malia frantically calculated how long it would take for Beaufort to realize she was in trouble. The driver would probably wait up to an hour before calling the ECU to report that she had not shown up. Then Cheysa would try calling her, and maybe fifteen minutes later she would call David to see what was wrong. But David would be in his 8:30 am meeting. It was already 8:15 am, she saw as the wheelchair swept by a wall clock, and then he might be in another meeting. This was important enough to call him out of any meeting, wasn't it? Wasn't it? For the first time, Malia was grateful for the chip. Beaufort would find out almost immediately where she was, and would rescue her. But only David would know she did not want to be in this frightening place. An ordinary Beaufort employee might just assume she had forgotten to notify them of her abortion appointment this morning. Too many moving parts needed to work in sync for her rescue to happen in time. And they had confiscated her armband, so she would not be able to contact David directly.

They arrived in what looked like an upscale spa area, painted a soothing sand color. Women in terry and silk bathrobes were lounging on chaises, and drinking cocktails, perhaps mimosas, or just juices. They wore white terry slippers labeled, "The Spa at the AP." Manicurists and pedicurists were tending to hands and feet. One woman was even getting a massage at a padded table in the corner. A hulking New Woman had shown up for her monthly abortion appointment, which involved no surgery but lots of play acting. At intervals, a nurse would summon a woman for her surgery. A buffet table was laden with breads, muffins, and fruit. On an adjoining sideboard burned vanilla and lavender-scented candles. The lights were dimmed, as if it were evening, not morning. "Would you like a joint?" one attendant asked an anxious woman near Malia's wheelchair. The patient accepted, and took a deep drag.

"Can you be trusted to be released?" the female nurse asked Malia. She nodded, and steadied herself as she stood upright. They handed her a bathrobe and slippers and pointed to the changing area. She left her blue suit in a cubicle and tied the terry cloth cord of the bathrobe around her waist. The attendant then indicated an egg-shaped chair and she sat down again. They offered her a muffin and a mimosa; she requested the muffin and juice. She declined a manicure and pedicure. She tried to think clearly. Looking around the room, she saw a restroom door. It was too much to hope it had a window from which one could escape. "I need to use the restroom," she said, heading in that direction. An attendant accompanied her inside. There was one stall, a sink with fresh flowers, and no window whatsoever. So much for that.

When she emerged, it was time for the hourly film. The room darkened further, and a younger, more vibrant President Avadaughter was shown. The film easily could have been fifteen years old, or perhaps they had photoshopped the younger

Avadaughter. "Congratulations," the President said. "As a woman like yourself, I have faced the consequences of an unwanted pregnancy. And I exercised my right to remove the fetal tissue—not once but three times. Think of all those generations of women under fascism who were deprived of this right and forced to bear children, or who underwent illegal abortions and died in agony. In the DJR, we are resolved to enable all women who wish abortions to have them in safety and dignity. In fact, by choosing to terminate your pregnancy, you have engaged in an unselfish and noble act and demonstrated fealty to Diversity. Mother Earth herself thanks you for reducing her burden. When you leave today, the staff will give you a bag of gifts from the White Black House in gratitude. Thank you for your unselfish act."

The video faded out, and was replaced by a series of gauzy photos set to music showing women and New Women of all races holding hands, drinking from long stemmed wine glasses, laughing, swimming, hiking, enjoying social gatherings, and looking romantically into the eyes of partners, the first one male, the second a female partner. Like that couple had to worry about an unintended pregnancy, sniffed Malia.

The video ended, the lights came on, and Malia realized it must be at least 9 am. Time is getting short, she fretted. "May I call my partner?" she asked a nurse. The nurse looked at the screen in front of her, "No, he has requested not to be disturbed." "What about another partner? If it's really his baby?" "Sorry, that's against our regulations, and we use the word 'embryo' or 'fetus' here, please." Malia decided not to become more conspicuous and sat down again. She took a clump of red grapes and ate several, but she lacked any appetite. When she asked politely, they gave her black coffee. She was afraid she would fall asleep in the comfy egg chair, her slippered feet elevated on an ottoman, but her adrenalin was spiking.

She started watching the nurses escorting the women from the room for their surgeries. They always turned to the left. When Malia had arrived in the wheelchair, she thought she had seen a door labeled 'exit' at the far end of the corridor, which would be to the right. Next to it was a tall window, with the curtains drawn. It was about twenty yards away from the entrance to the spa room, she estimated.

At 9:15, Malia thought, he's not coming this time. The rescues are over. I'm on my own. She wandered over to the console with candles and pretended to sniff them, while holding her paper cup of coffee. As several women hovered over the buffet table, effectively shielding her from view of the nursing station, Malia grabbed a small candle and thrust it upright in the right pocket of her robe. It burned her fingers but she made no sound.

At 9:35, a nurse called her name. Malia sized her up—slightly taller than her, a little chubby, not inclined to fitness workouts. Doing her best to muster a smile, Malia met her at the door. "How are you?" she offered. "Fine, thank you," said the nurse. The nurse turned to the left, but Malia turned to the right and kept going. "This way!" hollered the nurse, but Malia was already running, halfway to the exit door, her slippers kicked off. She grabbed the candle, which was still burning, shoved the drape corner into the candle and set the curtains in the window on fire, hurling the glass, which shattered across the floor. Another nurse came out of a room and grabbed at her, but Malia instinctively used the technique Kate had taught her, delivering an upper cut under her jaw and then slamming into her solar plexus. The nurse slid to the ground.

Other attendants were coming, but now the curtains were truly afire, and they were yelling, "Fire! Fire! Extinguisher!" The sprinklers would eventually come on, but not so quickly at the end of the corridor. Hearing screams behind her, Malia disappeared down the stairwell, thankful that the exit door was unlocked. She heard the door open above, and steps above her, but they stopped quickly, as if the person had changed her mind. Another attendant, a black man in green scrubs, leaning on a mop next to a bucket, was on the landing below, having heard the commotion. "You go, sister!" he said, clearly on the side of the baby. "Two more floors!" She was glad she hadn't had to attack him, too.

Then came the final door, labeled 'Lobby,' and she hurtled through it, into a more institutional setting, with women crowded onto colorful eco-plastic chairs, staring open-mouthed at her. The security guard approached her, and she gave him a good kick in the area that had caused all these women so much trouble. He doubled over, staggering, and before he could react, she had pushed through the revolving door and was in the street, barefoot and dressed only in the bathrobe, underwear, and the silver bracelet. She ran toward the nearest intersection, which turned out to be 12th and G, not far from the Rosebud. She kept running, calculating that it was better to fall into the hands of the Anacosta Police than into those of the Abortion Palace staff. Passersby stared at the half-dressed, barefoot woman.

She stopped to catch her breath on 10th and H, having turned right before she reached busy New York Avenue. The early October day was sunny, but seasonal, and she began to shiver. Somewhere behind her, she heard sirens, and began running again, but soon she darted into a doorway, panting. An unmarked black van pulled up alongside her, and she decided it was useless to run further. These could not be Abortion Palace staffers. A tall ADF officer emerged.

"Well," said Walters, grinning at her. "You're under arrest." He was accompanied by two other ADF officers.

"Thank Go—Mother Earth," she responded.

Before the crowd could grow, he had pushed her into the van, trying to look authentic. "Nothing to see, folks," he said. "This woman's wanted for a pretty bad crime. Disperse, please." He jumped in after her, as did the two other officers, who slid the van door shut after themselves, and said to the driver, "Headquarters."

Walters turned to Malia on the seat next to him. "What the hell was all that about?" She explained how she had been kidnapped by Adam Ross that morning and forcibly taken to the Abortion Palace, where she was scheduled to have an abortion, despite her insistence that she did not want one. She then told them how she had stolen the candle, run away from the nurse, attacked another nurse, dashed down the stairwell after setting fire to the curtains, and kneed the security guard in the balls before running into the street. "I didn't think David was going to come this time," she said, "and I realized I needed to have my own plan." She was still breathing heavily, almost hyperventilating, as the suppressed fear had rushed in behind the adrenalin.

Walters nodded with genuine admiration, his lips pursed. He turned behind them. "You hear that, guys? She's put us all to shame this morning." Then, to Malia, "Now that showed true Antifan spirit." He spoke into his armband, the static crackling, "Bo 3, Walters here. Subject recovered, safely. Heading to base."

"But how did you know where I was?" Malia asked. "Did the driver let you know I hadn't shown up for the ride this morning after my shift?" And what she wanted to know, was, would you have arrived in time if I hadn't escaped myself?

"This is what happened," said Walters. "The driver called at eight, but just left a message with our secretary, because we were in our morning meeting. Cheysa saw the message at 8:50, and contacted Commander Harris, but he was in the KCU meeting until about 9:10. We looked up your chip, and saw the Abortion Palace. None of us would have thought twice about it—it's like getting your nails done, right? But Commander Harris said, she is there against her will. It's Adam Ross's doing. We have to rescue her.

"So, we piled into two vans. Commander Harris led a detachment into the side entrance of the Abortion Palace. He got to the VIP floor where your chip had been showing, but there was a huge commotion because someone had set a fire. They said you'd run away, and so he said, Walters, track the chip, she's out there on the streets. So that's how we found you."

"Do you think he'll ask for my armband?" Malia asked shyly. "And my clothes?"

"They're probably gone now," said Walters, "it was a flash op." But he switched on the radio, "Harris, do you have her armband? Clothes?" Malia heard David's voice, but indistinctly.

He turned back to Malia. "They gave him the armband. No clothes. They sure weren't going to allow you to call for help, were they?"

"It was like a nightmare," she said. "But I wasn't waking up. I couldn't wait any longer."

"Don't blame you one bit," said Walters. "I mean, we're the ADF, but this is crazy."

Malia gave a huge sigh, and stared out at the streets of Upper Northwest. In ten more minutes, they were at Beaufort, and the second black van pulled in behind them in the garage. The driver opened the van door, and she stepped out into David's arms. "I can't stand this much longer," said David, an ambiguous comment to all but Malia. Upstairs, the Beaufort seamster took Malia's measurements and delivered a new blue suit within hours while she slept in David's office all afternoon on a cot. David brought up sandwiches for them. She was afraid to return to the Avalon alone.

"We'll just stay home tonight," said David. "It'll be easy to send your substitute, and Ross probably won't be surprised. We told the Abortion Palace to tell him that the operation was successful, so he'll be preening on his own." Malia didn't argue with him. She asked him to take her down to the gym to thank Kate, who was on duty. Kate was gratified to hear that her lessons had saved the baby's life, and maybe even Malia's.

"I wouldn't have thought you'd use it to fight off nurses," said Kate, "but that shows you never know when you'll need these skills in this business."

Chapter 54
Banana Floats
(Friday-Sunday, 7-9 October)

Tom cheerfully said, "That's fine. Happy to help," when David called apologetically to ask him to play the boyfriend for a few more days. But David wondered whether he should have disguised himself instead to pick up Malia. If ESF police or troops harmed Tom, David knew he would not be able to forgive himself. He smiled ruefully, thinking, "Malia seemed to take care of herself pretty well at the Abortion Palace. Maybe she doesn't need either of us."

Now that he knew the baby was indeed his, he told Marjory and his sisters about Malia's pregnancy. They congratulated him excitedly, and wanted him to bring Malia to the phone, but she was working that night. He also sensed that Marjory was holding back, and guessed correctly that she wondered why on earth they weren't planning to marry yet. "Mom, we don't have permission. It's complicated." But he knew that he sounded like the archetypal commitment-phobic bachelor.

"Will you at least bring Malia out with you on Sunday?" Marjory asked. "And we'll go to church?" He promised. He hadn't dared mention the Abortion Palace escape—it would be impossible to explain how this had come about without revealing things his family ought not to know about, such as Adam Ross. And if it still unsettled *him*, they would be completely horrified.

Malia came home promptly on Saturday morning, ate a bowl of cereal, and then went to sleep, assuring David she had heard nothing from Adam Ross at all. She slept until almost three, knowing she would be meeting Rex at the Gardens at 4 pm. It was a beautiful, crisp fall afternoon, with the leaves beginning to turn and the bravest among them twirling lazily to the ground. Sweater and light jacket weather. David drove her to the Gardens entrance, which would save him a trip to the Octavian later. They had discussed whether it was time for Rex to meet him but ultimately he demurred, saying "You're going to lay a lot on her today. Let's not complicate things—she might balk."

A few minutes early, Malia waited by the entrance. Rex showed exactly at four, thrilled to see her. She happily told Malia that she had received a "Proficient" in Diversity Math, which was enough. If you were too proficient at Diversity Math, it might spoil you for real math, and then the buildings you constructed might collapse on Social Crediteers. They strolled down the walkways toward the restaurant pavilion, Rex telling her of all the things that had happened at school this week, including her invitation to speak at the annual Renounce White Privilege assembly. "Do they renounce white privilege every year?" Malia asked her slyly. "If so, why does it keep coming back?" Rex looked at her uncertainly, so Malia quickly reassured her that she was truly proud of Rex's invitation to speak and hoped she would tape her speech so she, Malia, could hear it later. Malia gladly agreed to read and edit Rex's speech beforehand.

At the pavilion, they ordered banana floats. Malia looked proudly at her daughter, who had shed the last remnants of boyishness when she replaced the odd black glasses with cute blue frames and grown out her hair so it resembled a straighter and slightly lighter version of Malia's curls. She could not quite remember Peter's features, so saw little or nothing in Rex's face reminding her of the young Plore father.

"Why are you looking at me that way?" Rex asked curiously.

"I'm just thinking that you're becoming a beautiful young woman," said Malia. "I'm sorry we didn't have the last ten years together, but I am so happy we are together again at last." Her eyes teared a little, possibly the result of genuine emotion mixed with pregnancy hormonal swings. Rex was pleased, but a little embarrassed. It was nice to be told you were beautiful, but she was unaccustomed to such compliments and it seemed vaguely lookist.

"Let's go find a bench," said Malia, "I have something I would like to tell you."

They found a secluded spot, and Malia quickly, if oddly to Rex's eyes, ran her hand underneath the bench. "Just for good luck," she explained to Rex. "First, promise me that you will keep everything I tell you secret. You don't need to agree, you can do what you like, but I would get into a great deal of trouble if you told anyone what I am about to tell you." Rex fervently promised "total" secrecy.

"What would you say if I offered you the chance to live with me permanently?" said Malia, "and we would be openly mother and daughter? We wouldn't have to hide anything."

"That would be amazing," said Rex. "Do you think my parents would let us do that?"

Malia sighed. "No, they wouldn't. We would have to leave this country and go live somewhere else. Later you could send them a letter to let them know you were safe."

Rex frowned. This was inconceivable, and she knew of very few foreign countries, except of course, the evil United States, the benign People's Republic of China, and maybe Mexico and Canada. The DJR had little interest in teaching its children about geography and other places, with their other, usually dangerous customs. Diversity had its limits. "Where would we go?"

"We would go to the United States," she said. "Where we could tell the truth."

Rex was alarmed. "No, that's a very dangerous place! They're all fascists and white supremacists."

"That's not true," Malia said. "Our government tells us that so we don't all flee there. It's a free country and we can read and say what we want to. Everyone is equal—they don't use Social Credit points to keep some people high and others low." Their kitchen table conversations had opened the girl's eyes to exactly what she, Rex, could do that Malia, by virtue of her 70 Social Credit score, could not. The test prep had served more than one purpose. Rex had been dripping with sympathy for the oppressed Plores, but weeks ago Malia had presented her with the revolutionary idea that in some ways, the Plores lived much more freely than many City residents, such as herself.

Rex stared at the ground. "How would we go there?" she asked.

"We would cross the border secretly. But I have friends who will help us do it."

"Is Dave one of them?" Rex always asked her about Dave the Plore boyfriend. It was her one brush so far with raffishness, so she treasured Dave, or more precisely, the idea of Dave.

"Not that Dave. I have a friend who is also named Dave and he is planning it. I can't tell you anymore, because it isn't safe."

"Would the Antifans try to kill us if we were escaping?"

"Possibly," said Malia, "but the whole point of planning is to make sure we can escape safely."

"I was thinking," said Rex, "that when I grew up, and graduated from Justice, we could live together in a nice apartment in the City. I would have a very high Social Credit score, and you could live with me. We could share my Healthy Eating groceries, so you wouldn't be hungry. Wouldn't that be a lot safer?"

"It would be safer," said Malia, "but what if I wanted to marry Dave?"

"Oh," said Rex, her face crestfallen. "I wasn't thinking about that. He's a nice guy but I can't see us living with him permanently."

"And what if I wanted to read whatever I wanted? What about reading a real book? What if I wanted to go to a real church, and worship God? What if I wanted to fly on a plane, even to a foreign country? Why shouldn't I? They let everyone do that in the US, not just high Social Crediteers." She realized that were David's colleagues here, they would have to arrest her.

"But Melia, you just need to get another job! My parents would get you another job in the Knowledge Tower and you'd be over a 100, easily!"

Perhaps it was unreasonable for Malia to expect a 15-year old reared in privilege to understand why she needed to leave. Admittedly, the thought would never have crossed her mind were it not for David and the resources he could bring to a project that would be impossible left to her own devices. Adam Ross also had invited her to leave the country, someday, presumably as legitimate tourists—another subterfuge exploiting the differential resources of the well-placed high Social Crediteer. But if you were a high-ranking Social Crediteer, why would you want to leave?

"In school," said Rex slowly, "we read a magazine article about the Antifans who defend our border from the fascists. We learned how they have all the latest weapons to keep out the fascists. They didn't say it, but I could tell they also use those weapons to keep us in here. I don't want to die, Melia, I've hardly begun to live!" They fell silent as a pair of young male joggers holding hands loped past them and around the bend.

"If you call this living," thought Malia. But all she said to the girl was, "Just think about it. You don't have to join us, but you have to keep this a secret, or they will kill me." Rex nodded vigorously. "And," Malia dared, "if they kill me, they will kill your little brother or sister," pointing to her belly.

"Wow!" Rex said, "really? You're pregnant? Is it Dave's child?"

"Yes," said Malia, for strictly speaking, it was not a lie. "Only about six weeks along. You will have a little brother or sister, but that's a secret too. Wouldn't it be nice to all live together?"

"I'll think about it," said Rex. "But Mom, I'm not as brave as you."

I'm not brave, thought Malia, just desperate. But she settled for having planted the idea in Rex's brain. For now. Rex had not rejected the idea outright, which gave her some satisfaction. She only worried briefly about whether the ADF had been listening to her armband or Rex's.

Standing at the counter, Malia's feet began aching a few hours earlier than usual, which she attributed to all the walking in the Botanic Gardens. She froze when Adam Ross entered the lobby with an Enviro-pod shortly before 9 pm. But he planted himself in front of her, while Jorge gave them a curious side glance. This was not typical of Amba-sah Ross.

She looked up, resentfully.

"How are you, Melia dear?" he purred, most likely taking pleasure in her helpless fury. How she wished she could tell him that both she and the baby were fine. David had nixed any such idea. "If he thinks it didn't go as planned, he will ask the Abortion Palace people, and they will tell him that the Antifans stopped them. That would be a giveaway that we're protecting you. Someday you will tell him the truth, even if it's in a letter from the United States. You can send him a photograph of the baby. Revenge is a dish best served cold."

"I'm fine, thank you, amba-sah," she said curtly.

"Lovely," he said. "Here's a small gift for you, sweetheart." He handed over a flat medium-sized pink-wrapped box.

"I'm sorry, amba-sah," she said coolly. "I'm not allowed to accept gifts from the residents."

You'll accept it later, all right, he thought, even if I have to shove it into you. "That's very professional of you, Melia. I regret having imposed on you." He disappeared into the elevator. Malia was shaking, whether with anger or fear, she wasn't sure.

"You should have accepted the gift from Amba-sah Ross," Jorge lectured her. "It is perfectly all right to take it. It is a bad thing to offend him."

Tell me about it, she retorted silently.

Adam summoned her around 11 pm, and she stalked upstairs, prepared for blows, assaults, or gifts. But he was genial, insisted that she take a drink—which she dared not refuse—and sat opposite her in the paisley armchair. He brimmed with self-satisfaction.

"See, that wasn't so bad, was it?" he asked. "Didn't they treat you well?"

"Other than their ripping me open, seizing my child and throwing it in the trash, it was great, amba-sah," Malia sneered. She figured that Adam would graciously let her vent. He had won the Abortion Palace battle, or so he thought. "I guess in a month or two it would have been sold to China for some medical remedy, right?"

He laughed, and finished his drink in one great joyous gulp. "Probably. Did it hurt at all?"

"I don't think they used quite enough anesthetic, amba-sah. I was conscious the whole time," she said, knowing this would probably please him. She hoped he wouldn't notice her drink was mostly untouched.

"Good, let that be a lesson to you," he said airily. If she hadn't feared he might attack her with a pair of scissors to finish the job, she would have been sorely tempted to tell him the truth. For now, she prayed that the nausea stayed at bay while she was in his apartment.

"Look," he said, seriously, "I don't want you to think I asked you to do this on a whim. This was important because it impacts our future. I meant it when I said I would marry you. I told you I don't want to raise another child, even my own, even Will's, not at my age. So, thank you for having the abortion."

"I don't know where you get the idea that I would marry you," she said, "I said no. I have a boyfriend."

"Maybe not for much longer," Adam said. "For goodness' sakes, be practical. In ten years, do you want to be one of those low Social Credit spinsters stuck in your TerraCity cell? You'll rue to your dying day not having married me. At least in the old days you could have joined a nunnery. But in TerraCity, you'll live with the pot smokers until they pack you off to a nursing home and then the Euthanasia Palace. But with me, you'd be in a sunny hacienda in Mexico, with a pool and servants. Oh, well, I gave it away. Yes, Mexico."

"Why Mexico?" she said. "Couldn't we just retire here?" Let's play this out a little, she thought.

He mused, "Well, yes. But our money would go farther in Mexico. I have bank accounts in Mexico, but I couldn't access them from here."

She did her best to look bored and irritable at once. "I guess you can have foreign bank accounts if you're a senior bureaucrat at the Economic Tower. Not if you're a poor little TerraCity mouse like me."

"Yes," said Adam. "You'd be amazed at what you can have and do. Do you realize that even my cleaning service in Rehoba is free now that I'm a 250?"

Her eyes widened, as if to say, "Oh, I hadn't thought about a free cleaning service."

"So does the government just put money into your Mexico account? Is that how it works? Because you're a 250?"

Adam pulled back. "I notice you're not drinking tonight. You realize it's safe to have alcohol now, don't you?"

"I don't trust your drinks, amba-sah," she said.

"Maybe 'some' government puts money in the accounts," he said, unable to resist flaunting his influence. "And that's all I'm going to say."

"All right, amba-sah, be mysterious," she replied. "But I'm not going to spend the rest of my life with you if you keep secrets from me."

He sat down next to her on the sofa. "If you marry me, I'll tell you more. Until then, I've got to have some secrets. So get rid of the boyfriend."

"Maybe," she finally conceded, which encouraged Adam greatly. He leaned over and planted his lips on hers as she leaned her head back on the wooden ridgeback of the sofa. She opened her mouth and his tongue entered it. No boyfriend objections this time, he thought. Finally, she's beginning to see sense. Women like cleaning services. He took her jacket and placed it on the adjoining chair, and pushed her down to the sofa, lying atop her.

"Ow!" she said. "Oh, it hurts."

"Hurts?" he asked, puzzled. He hadn't really even tried anything yet.

"I had surgery on Thursday! Do you not remember?" Now she was truly angry. "It's very painful."

"Oh, right," he said. He didn't want to have some female wound opening and infected in front of him.

"That's it," she said indignantly. "I'm going downstairs. You're being sadistic. You just want to celebrate how much you made me suffer this week." She grabbed the jacket and slipped on her shoes. "I'm going to have my secrets too."

"Wait, wait," he said. "Take the box." She was about to refuse, and then thought, let him think you compliant. She gave it to Jorge for his wife.

At 7 am on Sunday morning, she was waiting outside the side entrance for Dave. He had been there yesterday morning dressed in work overalls, saying a cheerful "Hello, sweetheart," before bestowing an airy kiss on her cheek. He had placed his arm around her affectionately and walked with her to the van, both practicing the usual security protocols. It looked convincing, even though in her blue suit and his overalls she was clearly dating someone beneath her.

It was now 7:10 am. No Dave/Tom. She frowned. Should she head for the van on her own? Five minutes later, she decided not to wait. Perhaps he had overslept. He enjoyed a lively social life with other theatrical types in Ploreville and surely Saturday night had gone late. It was unlike him, though. As she walked into the Avalon, she realized that she should have called David immediately. Once in the apartment, she hurried over to the bed, rubbed his shoulder gently, and then he started awake.

"Tom never showed up," she said apologetically.

David looked at the armband clock, and then leapt from the bed. "Not good," he said, alarmed. He tried calling Tom. No answer, but he wasn't expecting one. Tom was totally reliable. He began throwing on his uniform, saying "Steve Rosen" into his armband. Contrary to what one might have expected given his wholesome demeanor, Steve seemed not to be an early riser. "Steve—Tom didn't show up this morning at the Octavian, wasn't like him…not returning calls…Ploreville…going there now." She heard a somewhat groggy assent on the other end. "Walters will meet me there," said David. "I'll be back later. Go to sleep, honey."

Chapter 55
Ploreville Wedding
(Sunday, 9 October)

When David returned to the apartment several hours later, he changed into shorts and a T-shirt and began brewing coffee, frying eggs, and toasting bread for breakfast, as quietly as possible, letting Malia sleep. He did not want to tell her the bad news. A man that she had kissed, even in pretense, but who had been clever, talented, and good natured, and just a little bit greedy—but honestly so—had been brutally murdered. Of course, he, David Harris, had killed and gravely injured people in the course of a long ADF career, and yes, some of them had been innocent of any real crime, but never had it been turned against him or those he loved.

As he finished, occasionally looking mindlessly at news headlines on his armband, ("Industrial Zone Output Rises Modestly," "President Plans Trip to Russia," "Economic Tower Arrests Food Hoarders") David sighed heavily. The sunshine flooding the enclosed porch might normally have cheered him, but today it constituted an additional affront. A murder had taken place in a cramped, dark room in a dingy corner of Anacosta, and the radiant sunrays by shining forth so exuberantly seemed to deny such a deed had ever happened. "Forget it," said the sunshine. "I am here. Nothing happened last night. Move on."

Malia stood before him in her bathrobe. "Was it bad?" she asked fearfully.

David nodded, indicating she should sit down. He turned the music to the Black Power Liberation Symphony, played by the Mexico City Philharmonic. Most classical music had been banned as part of white supremacist culture, but some pieces with strong Diversity messages, authored by non-whites, or played by Third World orchestras had slipped through. David felt the moment called for a bold symphony, not another insipid pop song.

"He's gone. It was as bad as I had feared," he said simply.

"Violent?" she asked.

He nodded again. "A horrible scene. He was knifed in bed, face down. The knife is missing, his phone is missing, the place was ransacked for the cash he got from Adam Ross. I just hope the ESF doesn't start wondering why there was a lot more cash than just Ross's.

"A very dangerous man," said David, and Malia knew he was referring to Ross, not poor Tom. "I don't think you should continue to work at the Octavian after this."

"No, I need to be near Rex," she said. "The time is coming." She was cryptic, but they knew she meant their escape plans. Her resolve had grown since Thursday.

"Take a short leave of absence," he begged. "I ignored my intuition before Tom was killed. Don't let me make another terrible mistake."

She was sufficiently moved by his distress to agree to two weeks away from the Octavian, starting Wednesday, while the eager substitute filled in for her. She was expected to show that night and, in good conscience, it would have been unfairly short notice. "Okay," said David, but he would call and tell the complicit daytime manager at the Octavian that Malia would probably not return. The manager assured David that the decision could always be reversed if operationally required.

David's spirits revived as they left the Avalon for Ploreville. It was another brilliant fall day, with deep red and orange color along both sides of the Potowmack. He was not yet old enough to have suffered personal losses, at least none he could remember, and thought briefly how unfair it was that the day after someone died, the world continued just as if nothing had happened. He would not say this to his mother, of course, since she would all too well remember how injustice and sunshine followed the family's losses, hand in hand.

As they pulled up in front of the house, Marjory, Emma, and Christine all came out to greet them, congratulating and hugging Malia. David had warned her they knew nothing of the Abortion Palace debacle, and it needed to remain that way. Malia was delighted. Finally, the unborn child was receiving the natural and uncomplicated goodwill he or she deserved.

All the family headed for church, even the less-religious brothers-in-law. Pastor Denman looked surprised to see the large contingent, but in the social hall afterward, David told him that he and Malia were now expecting a child. Marjory looked on proudly, only hesitant because of the lack of a wedding. In Plore circles, this was still not regarded favorably, and the civil war had entrenched the cultural and sexual morality of the losing side.

"Your mother told me already," said Pastor Denman. "Congratulations. I know the circumstances are not ideal." He beckoned David and Malia outside, into the small garden where a breeze whipped fallen brown leaves around a stone bench. "She asked me to perform a marriage for you." David switched on the noise cylinder, saying, "This will help keep the conversation private, Pastor."

"You know this would be illegal. I am forbidden by DJR law from performing any marriage ceremony involving a Social Crediteer, and I need not remind you that both of you are Social Crediteers. If this were discovered, I would lose my church and possibly be imprisoned. There are not many pastors these days. It would harm this congregation, perhaps permanently."

"Please don't do anything that risky, Pastor," said Malia. "We don't need to be married." As much as she wanted to marry David, she still bore the stamp of her orphanage upbringing in which heterosexual marriage was slightly discreditable, a reluctant concession by a progressive society to old mores, and certainly no requirement for bearing or raising children.

Pastor Denman gave her an owlish look. "I do believe you need to be married, for the sake of this child, so that your own commitment to each other is as secure as can be, and to avoid knowingly committing a sin. But if you cannot marry in the DJR, I feel I have an obligation to do what I can to redress this in the eyes of God. You are all welcome to come to the parsonage after our service and I will marry you, if you are willing."

David smiled at Malia. "Will you marry me? Today?" He turned to Pastor Denman. "I want you to know I proposed back in June and she accepted. I don't think she's changed her mind."

"I haven't changed my mind," she beamed.

"Good, I'll let you know when we head back to the parsonage," said Pastor Denman. "I'll tell your mother and hopefully she won't tell anyone else."

There would be no marriage license, no wedding cake, no bouquet or wedding dress, and no one would dare take photographs. The family filtered into the parsonage through the back door several at a time. When they assembled in the living room, where the drapes were closed, they numbered a respectable fourteen—Malia and David, Marjory, Christine and Emma and their husbands, the four children, all sworn to secrecy, and Pastor and Mrs. Denman and their teenage daughter, who played Bach's 'Jesu, Meine Freude' on a slightly out-of-tune piano as Malia joined David at the front of the room. Pastor Denman stood before the drawn curtains, holding his Bible. The noise cylinder was very much on.

"Welcome to you all," said Pastor Denman. "To Malia, who has found her faith after all these years in the wilderness; to David, who, like Malia, has found his partner for life; to Marjory, who has a new daughter; to Christine and Emma, and their families, who are welcoming a sister and aunt into their midst. We convene here to marry Malia and David in the sight of God, and among believers, amid trying times for our faith. Like the early Christians, we are hiding today. We hide from the eyes of the community what should normally be a joyous occasion witnessed by all. This ceremony will not be recorded in our church records, nor reported to the authorities, but let me underscore, these vows will be as binding on you as any made in our church, or before a government judge. Perhaps even more so, because the outside world will not hold you to them. Do not let the trials and tribulations of your everyday existence convince you that somehow, these vows are not truly made. God will watch you, and will watch over you, and if you are loyal and faithful to each other, He will protect you."

Pastor Denman was cautious about this illegal wedding, but not so much that he would stint on the proprieties. His wife passed out the house Bibles, and they read Matthew 19 together:

"Haven't you read," Jesus told the Pharisees, "that at the beginning the Creator 'made them male and female,' and said, 'For this reason a man will leave his father and mother and be united to his wife, and the two will become one flesh? So they are no longer two, but one flesh. Therefore what God has joined together, let no one separate.'"

Pastor Denman then read about the wedding at Cana, and then Colossians 3:12-17:

"Therefore, as God's chosen people, holy and dearly loved, clothe yourselves with compassion, kindness, humility, gentleness and patience. Bear with each other and forgive one another if any of you has a grievance against someone. Forgive as the Lord forgave you. And over all these virtues put on love, which binds them all together in perfect unity."

"The rings?" he asked. Malia had handed back to David the ring he had given her in June, and Emma's Larry was lending David his own gold ring for the ceremony. Someday David would be able to wear his own wedding ring.

They made their vows to each other, with Marjory audibly sniffling, and Pastor Denman giving her a discreet, heartening smile.

"I now pronounce you man and wife," he told them. No hint here of the dampening, politically correct, "You are now married person one and married person two in the Diversity Justice Republic." It was permissible to have up to four persons in a marital relationship, although only a few brave polygamists, sometimes celebrities, ventured it.

"You may kiss the bride." David bent over and Malia stretched upward, and everyone applauded, cautiously. "Congratulations!" David flashed his family a truly relaxed, joyous grin. The Denman daughter played "Clair de Lune" for the recessional. The family celebrated with sponge cake and fruit punch left over from the church coffee hour, and David gave the children a ride around the neighborhood in the yellow sportscar, a rare treat. They walked home from the parsonage, David and Malia holding hands, and his beloved family surrounding them.

Chapter 56
Collars Tightening
(Sunday/Monday, 9-10 October)

Malia showed up for her shift, thinking, how could you have just gotten married and then have to pretend nothing unusual happened that day? And likely go up to Adam Ross's apartment as if it were any other Octavian night shift? What a strange wedding night this would be.

When Ross called for her around 11 pm, Malia squared her shoulders, saying to herself, "This will be the last time for weeks. Whatever he throws at me, I can deal with it."

"Melia," said Adam, even more smugly than last night. "What did you think of my gift?"

"I gave it to Jorge for his wife," she said airily.

Adam blanched. "I'll be right back," he said, and returned with the box, minus its wrapping. "Jorge said it was clearly meant for you, and it was."

She reluctantly took it back, and, with Adam's eyes on her, opened the lid and unwrapped the silver tissue paper. It was a thick silver choker, with a charm that, squinting at it, she could not believe, even from Adam. The charm read "Property of Adam Ross." But her first reaction was to laugh uproariously.

"You think it's funny," Adam said malevolently.

"I'm thinking of poor Mrs. Jorge opening her gift," said Malia, and at that even Adam had to laugh.

"Put it on," he said.

"No," she said, suspecting it would be easy to put on and then not easy to remove, and then testing him, "You really don't care that I have a boyfriend."

"Have you heard from your boyfriend today?"

"No," she admitted.

"And was his name really Dave, or was, it, shall we say, Tom?"

She stared stupidly, deliberately, at him, buying time. He switched on the TV, went to local news, and scrolled through the stories until he came to the one labeled, "Brutal Stabbing in Ploreville." The announcer said, "In another frightening criminal incident in Ploreville, a young actor was brutally murdered overnight by what authorities say was a sexual encounter gone horribly wrong. The killer remains at large after robbing the apartment of all its spare cash."

Watching Malia's face as the story ran, Adam was a little surprised at her stupor. "So his name was Tom Peters, not Dave. He was an actor, not an asphalt worker—you know, Melia, I had trouble believing that asphalt story. And did you know he was gay? That must have been so annoying. You know, whatever my faults, I am only attentive to your side of the gender aisle."

"He went by Dave," she said, "and he acted at night. That wasn't his full-time job. How can you make a living being an actor in Ploreville? And he wasn't gay. He was a very caring lover." But she knew she sounded unconvincing.

He requested her armband, and checked it to make sure the recording light was off. He placed it on the end table next to the paisley chair in which he sat.

"My representative who finished off your friend—frankly, I don't know what to call him, since he wasn't ever your boyfriend let alone the father of your dear departed embryo—said he was notorious in Ploreville for his gay appetites. My guy had no trouble encouraging your Dave or Tom to bring him home, where things went sour rather quickly. My officer's tastes run to men as well and he has a remarkable physique. So gay guys don't turn down his propositions."

"You sound very intolerant," said Malia lamely, as she had been raised on state propaganda about all sexualities being equally noble, except heterosexuality.

"Not at all," said Adam. "I just know what I like. Aren't you going to mourn your Tom? No? Now that he's gone, can we just move on and focus on ourselves?"

"Dave," she said fiercely. Now, when she really ought to cry, why could she not cry? "Since the news story said the apartment was robbed, I hope you got all your money back."

"Strangely not," lied Adam. "I probably let my officer keep too much for himself. But that reminds me. I see you're still wearing that engagement ring from Tom's family. Shouldn't you give that ring to me to defray some of my expenditures when he pretended to allow me to take you out of town?" He leaned over and grabbed her wrist.

At that point she burst into tears. "He loved me and we were going to get married. And I will give the ring back to his mother, which is the right thing to do."

"Good luck finding his mother," said Adam sardonically, but he wouldn't press the point that evening, and let her go. "We'll go to Rehoba next weekend. I'll make sure the building brings in your usual substitute." He thought, ten days, really? That's a lot longer than usual. She'll pay for that lie.

As he watched her leave an hour later, having consented to remove the collar from her neck for now, he frowned again. Something was not right. Had this fellow really been her boyfriend? And, if so, how had he deceived her about so many things? Why had she not been surprised by the news, and why had she seemed almost tranquil until he threatened to take the ring? He did wonder, however, how this Plore actor had amassed so much cash in his apartment. Even after splitting it with the ESF officer, Adam had been surprised by the windfall. He knew Malia was right—no one made a living on the stage in Ploreville. Who else was paying this actor, and why? But whoever he had been, this fake boyfriend was no longer an obstacle to his plans.

When she got off work the next morning, David met her himself at the side door, a baseball cap pulled over his face. Back in the apartment, she told David about Adam's coldblooded admission of murder and attempt to seize the ring. "I'm not surprised," he said, "and let's leave the ring here for now in a safe place. Don't wear it again until things blow over." The mention of the collar particularly irked and alarmed him and he was relieved she had left it behind at Adam's. Some wedding night, he thought. Who was the bridegroom?

He thought it would be safe enough to leave Malia at the Avalon during the day, at least at the beginning of the week. But what would Adam Ross do when she failed to show up for her shifts later in the week, and especially with the promised weekend in Rehoba looming? With victory so close, and having committed murder to secure Malia for himself, Adam Ross would certainly not accept losing her now. Thank goodness that the ESF did not yet have access to chip and armband data, at least as far as he knew. Perhaps Steve Rosen would have some ideas for handling the situation, having slept in on Sunday and rested *en famille*.

Steve leaned back in his chair and knitted his large hands behind his head, a pose that David had learned to interpret as, "Let's think about our premises a bit."

Steve said, "We know now, thanks to your girlfriend, that Ross is probably getting his Mexican money from China. He told her it's a foreign country, we know that China's the logical source, and my analysts and the Cyber Unit have figured out that the money is going to those accounts from the Shanghai National Bank. Good. But the sums are so variable and yet specific—down to the cents—and remember, we can't tell whose accounts each are—that it suggests they are payable for various reasons. In other words, it's not just simple bribes to keep the experiments going. But it's related to the experiments somehow, I am betting.

"Harris, I would like to answer this question before I'd let Malia go. I think this would give us the final ammunition we need to finish off Adam Ross and his friends. He doesn't suspect her of working for us—"

"Yet," said David, but Steve chose to roll over it.

"And after all this trouble he's gone to on her behalf, or to win her over, why do you think he would harm her? I'm sure she's safe as long as she's living at your place."

David said, "Psychopaths kill even those they claim to love. The desire for control and stimulation is such that, even after having won control of a woman, they need to raise the ante. Didn't he force her into the Abortion Palace even though he knew the baby wasn't his? You took Me Too criminal psych classes too. I can't predict what he would do next.

"I keep saying she has gone above and beyond for us, which is true, but nobody here seems to take that seriously."

"Well, if it weren't for us," said Steve, "me specifically, she would be spending her seventh month at Industrial Zone Camp Four right now. Come on, David, it's not a lifetime commitment. And she's earning kudos from the Director. If she can see this through, I bet he'll approve your marriage. You're going to have a baby together, that'll help. Just a few more weeks, probably. Don't give up now."

Steve rubbed a little salt in the wound by suggesting he could avoid some trouble by not keeping Malia from working her shifts at the Octavian. If she showed up as normal, Adam Ross wouldn't be alarmed or try to track her down. "It's just sex," Steve smiled at him. "Haven't we all gotten beyond that now? After you marry her, then you can worry more." But then the smile faded, and he said, more harshly, "We need her now. Stop being so damned selfish."

David left Steve's office dissatisfied. Steve always sounded so reasonable, but David didn't see him offering Vicki Rosen for operations or sex with psychopaths either. That was the ADF for you, utilitarian to the core. Back at his desk, he reviewed a printout of the mine defenses at Antifan Camp Number Six. He had printed it out when it was relevant to the inspection survey this summer, and after reviewing it one last time, he would dispose of it in the ultraviolet shredder. He had allowed it to sit in a pile of other documents relevant to the now-closed base survey, since it seemed more innocent in that context than surreptitiously filed in a drawer.

Having passed his truth serum test last month, he was less concerned about the printout than he might have been. He had to admit, though, that test had been rocky. He hadn't expected a slew of questions about his relationship with Malia, nor about his trip with her to the mountains, although after the first interview with Ulansky, he should have known they would reappear. CI commanders did not react well to humor.

And then there were questions about what he had talked about with his brother during the fishing trip. "Family!" he blurted, against the haze that suggested he instead say "Help me escape." But even family was complicated with your older Plore brother and his implacable memory of Antifan abuse. On several occasions, the tester had said aloud, "positive result," which meant signs of physiological distress, followed by, "Would you like to tell us more?" David had forced himself to slow down, and use breathing techniques to fight the impulse to share more. Thank goodness the truth serum test had taken place a week before he unexpectedly married Malia. He was grateful that his mother hadn't warned him beforehand about her plans to enlist Pastor Denman.

When he opened the electronic mail, he was relieved to read, "Congratulations, you passed! You are hereby reinstated in the Antifan Defense Forces until your next reinvestigation." He did not take this result for granted, not this time. Of course, if he had not passed, he would have been notified in person. And if you failed a second reinvestigation, you would not be allowed to resign. The consequences were more dire than those John MacMillan had faced. You would find yourself in the cell block until the ADF had determined the exact nature of your transgressions, and then more than likely, deprived of your Social Credit and dispatched to a psychiatric hospital for an indefinite stay. David knew no one who had been dismissed from the ADF and was living a normal Social Credit life afterward. By then, you knew too much to wander about polite society.

Chapter 57
Terra City Redux
(Friday, 14 October)

Adam didn't worry much on Wednesday when Jorge said Malia was taking the night off. He only worried a little on Thursday night. But when he came in late from work on Friday, deliberately through the front entrance, only to find her substitute there again, he asked Jorge when Malia planned to return. "Oh, I am sorry amba-sah, but Melia is no longer working here."

"What do you mean? She quit?"

"I believe she left, amba-sah, yes."

Adam furiously phoned her, several times, with no response. He texted her. He texted Will. When Will called him back, Adam fumed at the presumption, the nerve of this low-Social Credit slut to simply disappear, just before their Saturday trip to Rehoba.

"Well," drawled Will, "If you really want to track her down, you can go to TerraCity and beat off the potheads. That's where she is, right?" Adam's silence suggested he might actually do that, at which Will said, "I wouldn't go alone if I were you, especially on a Friday night."

"Okay, let's go tonight," said Adam. "Wear the uniforms so we look more official. Call over to the Tower and have two troops meet us in front of TerraCity at 9 pm."

Will sighed. He had been settling down in front of the TV with a plate of meatballs and pasta. Basketball season was just beginning.

"And print off one of those requisitions we have from the Social Tower that shows you're on official quartermaster business on its behalf. Be sure to sign it with your counterpart's name. That'll help us get into the building. Whatever moron they have on duty won't likely understand it anyway. We're going to arrest her for economic crimes. Hoarding. That's all over the news this week. Very plausible."

Will sighed again. "Do we have her exact address there?"

"No, it won't matter. They'll give it to us. And stop sighing. For God's sake, I thought you were my friend."

Adam and Will, dressed in their brown uniforms but unarmed, met in front of TerraCity. At 10 pm, the red neon TerraCity sign would flicker on, just when the denizens of the housing pen came to life, like the mice in the walls, excited by the heady promise of a late night and the opportunity to sleep in, perhaps after a lucky sexual encounter. The two privates met them, and Adam explained to them they were going to arrest a TerraCity inmate for hoarding violations. They marched into the building and requested assistance from the sleepy guard, who found it easier to look up Malia's suite and room number than to object to the uniforms and the official-looking paper. They didn't pay him enough to read, he surmised, and the two gentlemen had higher Social Credit scores than he could even fathom. He directed them toward Malia's suite and went back to watching movies.

The cafeteria was closing but a long line snaked into the marijuana dispensary as residents paid for their weekend supply. Adam took a close look in both directions to make sure Malia wasn't finishing dinner or buying pot, although he figured she was probably one of the few abstainers in the building. They took the massive elevator to the fifth floor, and walked along the same corridor she and David had trod two months ago. Unlike that quiet morning, however, the wide corridor was lined with lounging men and women engaged in conversation, many holding joints. A couple was going at it in the corner where the hallway turned. Most looked haggard, whether because of a hard week or a hard life. The smell of marijuana permeated the hallway. EcoLand had been high class compared to this, thought Adam.

"This is it," said Will, looking up to check the number. "583, Room C." The door was closed. They rapped roughly.

"ESF!" the soldiers shouted. "Open up!"

The door opened, and they burst in to find a conversational grouping of two men and two women, both topless, all inebriated. An empty bottle of whiskey already lay on the floor and another would join it soon. The middle of the five rooms was C, and it was the only closed door of the five adjacent cells. A small crowd of spectators gathered behind them in the hallway.

"Hey, man, what's up?"

"We're looking for Amelia Jenness in Room C. We have a warrant for her arrest." said Will.

"Ain't no one lived in C for a long time," said the second man. "Ooowee—a warrant."

Adam and Will looked at each other. Will signaled to the two troops, and they broke open door C by main force.

"Hey, man!" One of the women shrieked with feigned fear.

The room was virtually empty. A set of dust-covered sheets sat on the stained mattress, and there were only a few lonely outfits in the closet. No toiletries at all, which both men knew would have been the sure sign of a female presence.

"Where the hell is she?" asked Adam. His skin was crawling just being in this hellhole. He would have to check for bedbugs before he walked into his apartment.

They turned to the group. "Did any of you ever see this Amelia?" asked Adam. The four became cagey, as marginalized characters do in the presence of a vengeful and mysterious authority. "Maybe in August? Anyone try to move into the room?"

Will pulled out a small bag of white powder. "Better stuff here than pot for someone who wants to tell the truth. But we're only paying for the truth."

A scruffy white guy said, "There was a pretty girl with long dark hair who came by in late August with a few bags. They dropped them here and left. And the bastard she was with threw me against that wall—" he pointed to the distant corner where a rickety wooden end table listed— "just because I tried to get a kiss. Really stuck-up asshole."

The women giggled, and one said, "we ain't giving you enough yet?"

"Was this the guy she was with?" Adam showed a photo of Tom taken from his apartment, clearly an audition head shot.

"Nope," said the scruffy guy. "He was also blond, blonder than this guy, but acted like he was in charge. Not really tall, but taller than medium. Very built. Blue jacket. Really stuck-up. I coulda beaten him up if he'd given me some warning."

"Did you get a name?"

The man shook his head. "Hey, I was real stoned. It's amazing I even remember this."

"Did he have an armband?"

"Yeah," said the man. "You don't think I'd let a dirty Plore in here, do you? Even TerraCity got to keep up appearances."

Will tossed him the bag and said, "Thanks buddy. You're helping Diversity." The man oohed at the unexpected prize, holding it up, and the group of friends cheered. The four ESFers hightailed it out of the building before, as Will admitted on the sidewalk, the group discovered that the bag only held dishwashing powder. Adam gave him a disgusted look, to which Will said, "Look, I'm not giving these losers my good stuff."

"What, like the baby powder?" Adam teased him. They dismissed the privates and took a self-driving car back to the Argonne Tower, where Will switched on the basketball game, ostensibly for background noise.

"Stop looking at the screen," ordered Adam. "What the hell is going on here? Where is she?"

"Not a good thing when your asset disappears like this," said Will. "But you don't think the Knowledge Tower offed her? She's been giving us a lot of dirt about the KTs in your building."

"The Knowledge Tower? They couldn't off a duck in a Chinese restaurant," said Adam. Will chortled, and snuck another look at the game. "But what I'd like to know is who that blond Social Credit guy is. I'm sure she was pregnant with his kid."

"Maybe you scared her with that whole Abortion Palace escapade, and then offing the fake boyfriend," said Will. "All in one weekend. She probably thinks if she shows up again, you'll finish her off personally."

"Nonsense," said Adam. "I don't know why I have to keep reassuring her I'm not going to hurt her. I told her we'd retire in Mexico. Does that sound like someone who'd murder you?"

"Oh, shit, you talked about Mexico?" wailed Will. "What else have you told her?"

"Why not?" said Adam, contemptuously. "Who's she going to tell? She doesn't know anyone who matters. Kind of pathetic to have to pretend a gay guy is your boyfriend, don't you think?"

"Well that probably gives you a bit of an advantage," jeered Will, "since she's not actually familiar with humanity." Adam hurled a throw pillow at Will, who caught it, laughing, and threw it back at Adam. But then they fell silent, wondering where Malia could be and who that blond fellow could be.

After five days entirely encased in the Avalon, Malia was restless. She had an extra lesson with Kate, swam and worked out several times, read two novels online, and watched a comedy about space aliens interacting hilariously with a DJR space exploration mission. She cooked three dinners for herself and David, two of them, involving chicken, quite passable. But by the time the weekend rolled around, she was ready to leave the building. She curled up in David's lap on Friday night, put her arms around his neck, and drew herself close to his kisses.

"That's really a nice welcome, honey," he said, leaning back so his gray eyes scanned hers. "You must want something from me." He seemed more sober than usual and in need of some lighthearted diversion, she decided.

"I was looking at the weekend section of the *Post*," she said. "There's an Indigenous People's Day concert at the Kennedy Center, and a new play they're recommending. It's a romance between a cis-woman and a sea serpent in her bathtub. It's transgressive."

"No, unless she finds a man to join her in the tub," said David decisively. "Hey, you need to get out of the building, I get it. Let's go do some light hiking tomorrow?" But he understood her need for a change of scenery. They went to a seafood restaurant along the Wharf that had no Social Credit minimums, a friendly staff, and good food. They had to avoid restaurants near the Avalon, which was near Beaufort, and upper Connecticut Avenue was dangerous because of the Octavian clientele.

Late that night, in bed, Malia rested her head on her right palm, and looked down tenderly at David. He still seemed stressed even after their dinner, which he insisted he had enjoyed, and their lovemaking. "What's wrong?" she said. "Please tell me. Did something happen at work?"

David turned his head to look at her, pulling himself up on the bolster. She admired the curve of his strong shoulders peeking above the blanket.

"Not exactly at work," he said. He explained how he had driven out to

Charlottesville to visit a professor who had been arrested during the Clinton University purge. "I really shouldn't have gone." He had expected Kendra to be in good, or at least better, health after four months at Garrett, the jewel in the crown of the Antifan-run psychiatric hospitals. When they wheeled her into the visitor room, he was shocked by how she had become even frailer—and she was not much older than him. The hospital administrator and the chief nurse told him privately that she ate the minimum needed to avoid forced feeding, as she had at Beaufort. She spent most of her day in the wheelchair on the porch, looking over the grounds in the direction of the piedmont. Sometimes at night they heard her call out for an Andrew.

Kendra acknowledged and quietly greeted him, but she seemed neither pleased nor curious that he had visited. What did you think would happen, he berated himself. You ruined her life and she's supposed to be grateful that you're coming to inspect the damage you've done?

The nurse suggested they go sit on the veranda, for it was a pleasant fall afternoon, and she wrapped Kendra in a red wool poncho.

"I tried to start a conversation," he said, "about the beautiful view, about how she liked the staff, the conditions, but it was pointless. We sat there in silence. At one point she said, 'I miss Clinton University. I miss my friends. I miss my students.' I tried to tell her she could return eventually, but she wouldn't believe me, and rightfully so. I am a trained liar, but not trained well enough. She then said, 'I think I will be gone by this time next year,' and of course she didn't mean Clinton.

"Was it my fault it ended this way? Why don't people want to live? When all this began—the purges of the universities—it seemed like a perfectly reasonable idea. I was just carrying out my oath to defend the DJR from its enemies, and it seemed to have enemies. I said to her, 'Thanks to you, I realize what I have done. I am no longer unaware of my crimes against innocent people.'

"But even as I said that, I remembered I had willingly carried out a Red Room session the previous Friday. So do my deeds not conform to my heart, or is it the other way around?"

At that moment, he told Malia, Kendra had perked up. She told him about a play called *Man of All Seasons* about Sir Thomas More, later St. Thomas, who defied Henry VIII by refusing to acknowledge the legitimacy of Henry's casting aside of his first wife, Katherine, for Anne Boleyn. She said, "A perjurer, once More's friend, laments to Cromwell, More's persecutor, that he has lost his innocence. Cromwell answered, 'You lost that some time ago. If you've only just noticed, it can't have been very important to you.'" David then remembered this book had been among the several purchased at the recycling plant by Yardley.

"I think she was insulting me," David admitted to Malia, "but she was probably correct. Was I looking for some absolution from her? Some thanks for having sent her to Garrett instead of a worse hospital? I couldn't help myself. I said to her, 'In a year, I may not be here either.' I hope that nobody overheard."

Malia was not sure what David wanted her to say either. "I'm sure she took some comfort from your visit. Just by visiting, you were saying that you had been in the wrong. And she has no relatives to visit her, so it was a kind deed."

David stared into the curtain surrounding them. "I shouldn't have gone. Once we send someone to those hospitals, we close the book. It's a mistake to open it again."

PART FIVE

BEAUFORT

Chapter 58
Under Suspicion
(Monday-Friday, 17-21 October)

"What the hell is going on?" Ferraro asked indignantly. "Are you telling me that Harris has unilaterally decided his girlfriend is no longer going to help on our priority threat here?"

It had begun as one of Ferraro's regular Monday meetings with Steve Rosen and Brian Walters about the progress in developing the case against the Economic Tower. Rosen and Walters brought up on the screen the various training areas under use by the ESF, and the estimated numbers of troops and recruits, now approaching 30,000. The newly unleashed drone fleet was proving its worth, with the ESF completely oblivious to the Antifan use of the skies overhead. Plore informants in the surrounding areas also contributed to the ADF's knowledge of its adversary's doings, such as exactly how much the ESF was paying recruits, even Plores.

Eventually, they reached the subject of the truth serum experiments, about which the pipeline had seemingly dried up. "What's Harris's girlfriend up to?" asked Ferraro. "We haven't gotten anything from her in a while."

Steve reluctantly explained that David had withdrawn Malia from the case for now. "He's worried about her safety. Ross forced her to go to the Abortion Palace—if you remember, she escaped—and then he had the informant who was playing her boyfriend killed the following weekend. She was able to claim the boyfriend as the reason she could keep Ross dangling a bit. Then Ross called their bluff, in blood."

"So Harris was worried about this girl's safety." Ferraro pronounced each word with disdain, the red spider on his forehead visibly throbbing atop a vein. "Gentlemen, the Antifans I served with in the war would have been disgusted to hear this. The Antifan Defense Forces would never have survived if all we thought about was the safety of our girlfriends. Or boyfriends. The DJR would have never gotten off the ground. We'd still be living under white supremacy." The three white men looked at each other. "What gives Harris the right to make these *insubordinate* decisions that don't belong to him at all?"

Ferraro tapped on the table screen, "Nina, please send Gemma Carpenter up with the Harris file. Yes, David Harris, KCU." Oh good, Walters thought vindictively,

Commander Harris is no longer the golden boy. He had seen David's star dimming each time he stupidly opted to defend his librarian at the expense of the ADF. He, Walters, would never make this mistake. If the Director wanted him to dump Cheysa, Cheysa would be gone in a minute, no matter how much she would cry and wail. The ADF was bigger than either of them. That Plore fool Harris didn't realize it, not even after all these years.

While they waited for Gemma, Ferraro spoke about this mésalliance between a senior Antifan commander and this low-Credit librarian. "This is why we don't allow these marriages," he said dismissively. "A high-Credit woman would understand why Diversity needed to come first.

"If he wants to get married," said Ferraro, "I can think of several excellent candidates. Beautiful women, smart enough, well over 150. Wasn't he dating Kate Langley?" The photo of slender blonde Kate Langley—the daughter of a retired Environmental Crimes Unit chief—was still in David's night stand, forgotten. "I heard she's still upset over that breakup. What's he slumming for?

"In general," Ferraro continued, "I wish we were like the Spartans. The men lived in barracks in their youth and just visited their wives occasionally to impregnate them. I'm not even sure they had wives. And now that (vile word) Avadaughter thinks she's going to make half of us women," referring to the announcement made at the Diversity National Series championship game that had created an uproar at Beaufort. Ferraro had fended that off, at least temporarily.

Gemma Carpenter interrupted his disquisition by entering the room with her precious thick files. They were too dangerous to be entrusted to a computer system. Ferraro was not sure it was politic to discuss women or their impregnation in front of a lesbian whose Social Credit outranked his, so he subsided.

"Gemma, we were talking about some odd behavior by Commander Harris. Rosen here tells me he actually pulled his girlfriend off of the Adam Ross detail, when as you know she's our main informant on him. He is supposedly concerned about her safety." Ferraro spat out the hated word again. "I think this low-Social Credit woman is addling his mind. Until he met her earlier this year, I thought he was one of our best men. But he seems to be obsessed with her, and now he's afraid she's going to get hurt. If he were really a solid Antifan, he wouldn't be behaving like this. He would know ADF priorities came first.

"But after what you told me yesterday, perhaps the situation is more dangerous. Is it possible that Harris is actually a threat to our organization?" He explained to the others, "Harris almost failed his reinvestigation."

"He passed," Gemma said. "But yes, there were areas of concern including his relationship with this woman and their trip very close to the border, and not very well explained to our investigator. If you want to make love in the outdoors, you don't need to do it on an outcrop in western Virginia overlooking the border and our Antifan camp. His answers to these questions led to a lot of false positives."

"It's always a bit of a risk when you bring Plores into the organization," mused Ferraro philosophically. "Some of them are our bravest men, but they are often too attached to their families, and those families have histories, which sometimes they start remembering. The attachment to family becomes attachment to women and to safety."

Gemma said, "I don't think he's disloyal, at least not consciously. But yes, this relationship has unsettled him. I don't think we could tell him to break it up at this point, though."

"She lives with him," said Walters. "Otherwise she'd be in TerraCity. He won't let her go there."

"And for some strange reason," said Gemma, "He actually went out to Garrett on Friday to visit Kendra Pinckney, that professor from Clinton who spent two months here at Beaufort. The administrator reported that he brought her flowers."

Walters gasped angrily. "I spent months working that traitor over, in the Red Room at that, and she didn't cooperate at all. He really went out there to visit her? Whose side is he on?" He was shaking with fury. Ferraro raised a cautionary hand in Walters' direction.

"Now, Walters, thank you. That is the correct spirit. But let's discuss this calmly," said Ferraro. "I hope our Harris is not losing his sanity. And he'd better not think of crossing that frontier. We haven't seen an Antifan officer try to defect in twenty years, and it ended very badly for him. It would be a disaster if someone at his level got to the US." The beaten corpse had been displayed in Beaufort's lobby for three days before guards on duty began fainting from the stink. Ferraro and Steve Rosen both remembered marching past the open coffin; David's training academy class had been bussed down to Beaufort to view the mangled body.

"He's on borrowed time," concluded Ferraro testily, "and he'd better get his girlfriend back on the job. Rosen, call him immediately and don't take no for an answer. And don't tell him we're watching him a lot more carefully now. I just want to see this Econ Tower business through and then we'll assess Harris's situation. Gemma, don't throw him in a cell just yet, all right?"

On Wednesday night, Malia was back at the concierge desk. Really, she didn't mind. It had been boring and lonely after the first few days alone at the Avalon. You could only read so much, she had discovered, at least off the Great Virtual Network. She had finished the entire "Great Latinx Fiction" series in two days. David would come home tired and hungry, and she would be bursting with pent-up energy. He wouldn't even dare let her walk around the building or over to the coffee shop a few blocks away. "There are ESF plainclothes everywhere these days," he said, "and they've started putting up facial recognition cameras that are better than ours. Believe me, Adam Ross is looking for a snapshot of you getting a cup of coffee."

He came home on Monday, hangdog, having been told sharply by Steve Rosen that the Director expected Malia to return to the Octavian pronto. "We're too close to a breakthrough," he explained to her. "A lot is riding on you. I hope you're proud of your contribution." To his relief, she looked pleased, or at least made no objection.

On Tuesday, she met with Cheysa at Beaufort again. Cheysa told her that she needed to accept any marriage proposal that Adam Ross made if that would lead him to tell her the truth about the Mexican bank accounts. "After he's gone," Cheysa pointed out, leaving *gone* undefined, "the promises you made won't matter."

Jorge must have texted Adam Ross, because the summons came shortly after 10 pm. She hesitatingly knocked on Adam's door, not knowing whether he would be angry or relieved.

"Come in, Melia," he said, almost pleasantly. He mixed the drinks, turned on loud and currently popular Bee-fa percussion music from West Africa, or more likely from the Knowledge Tower's West African Music Manufacturing Division in Los Angeles, gestured to the sofa, and sat down next to her. "What happened to you? You didn't return my calls or my texts."

She had rehearsed her story with both Cheysa and David, the latter playing an exasperated and then angry Ross. "I was afraid, amba-sah. You kidnapped me and dragged me to the Abortion Palace, and then you had Dave killed. I didn't know what else you were planning."

"So you were at TerraCity the whole time, hiding from me?"

"Yes," she said, but unable to meet his cold gaze.

"I think not," he said. "Will and I made a special trip to TerraCity on Friday night to find you. The sheets on the bed were gathering dust. I don't think you've ever lived there." He paused, "And from the dregs that were hanging out in the living room area, if you call that living, I can't say I blame you."

She said, "I don't spend much time there, amba-sah."

"I don't think you spend any time there. Where were you this last week?"

She squared her shoulders and looked directly at him. "I was staying with my aunt, amba-sah."

"Oh, now we have an aunt," Adam mocked her. "I thought you were alone in the world." He leaned toward her. "Tell me about this aunt."

"She was married to my mother's brother, who died in the war. We found each other two years ago after she looked me up. She lived with us near Ruckersville before the Antifans evicted us." She knew enough about her background thanks to David to concoct a reasonably plausible story. "She works at the Social Tower."

"You are such a disgraceful liar," said Adam coolly, completely uninterested in this ethereal relative. "I am going to have a delightful time extracting the truth from you this weekend when we go to Rehoba. And don't think I was happy about having to skip last weekend, by the way. You forced me to move around my whole schedule, and when you're me, that's not a trivial business." He decided to postpone asking about the mysterious blond man.

"I'm sorry, amba-sah, but you frightened me."

He reached for her wrists with both hands and pulled her onto his lap, and kissed her hard, holding her head slightly above his with those two hands. She straddled his legs with her own, kneeling on the sofa. They ended up on the floor, Malia on the rose ottoman, her face just hanging over the far end, since Adam had decided he didn't want to mess the comforter and sheets that the Social Credit maids had straightened earlier in the day. Good thing she no longer needed the gag, he thought, just as he had told her would eventually come to pass. The Bee-fa drums thumped encouragingly in the background.

Sometime that Friday afternoon, Fern sat at a wooden table in the subterranean kitchen in the Main House at Economic Zone Camp Four, peeling potatoes and cucumbers for an Indigenous People soup that would serve a hundred officers and guests at the annual Indigenous Peoples Day reception that evening. The Antifan officers next door had also been invited, it was rumored, given the importance of the holiday. When she had peeled a bowlful of either potatoes or cucumbers, she passed it to another woman wielding a utility knife for chopping them. Around her were other prisoners in their denim overalls, chopping, slicing, mixing, filling the industrial-size vats and baking dishes, under the supervision of an ESF mess corporal. He had a unerring eye for using exactly the right amount to feed the honored assemblage. Rarely did enough remain for distribution to the kitchen workers even though they were permitted the leftovers.

Fern longed to sneak a bite of a cucumber, but having once been beaten for nibbling a carrot, like a naughty rabbit, was loath to risk another bout of punishment. Before her banishment to Camp Four, she had been chubby, but now she was much thinner and much hungrier. She missed her armband and the constant, if bowdlerized, entertainment it had provided.

All said, though, she knew to be grateful. Upon arriving at the camp, she had spent a month weeding and manuring strawberry fields, her skin browning and cracking under the fierce summer sun. When they came for her in the barracks one night, she was terrified. Most people who were summoned that way went to that mysterious chemical factory, which constantly needed new workers. But they brought her to the women's kitchen barrack, which had its own bathhouse. Even though she wasn't fed much more than in the fields, at least she could conserve her energy. The privates who deposited her in the barrack said, "You've got a friend in the City," which told her all she needed to know. But sometimes she still woke drenched in sweat after nightmares about that final hour at the Rosebud.

Most of the workers went upstairs with the corporal to start arranging furniture and set the long tables. Two women in the far corner were beating cake batter for the Indigenous Carrot Cake. A middle-aged, medium-sized blond man in jeans and a flannel workshirt came in carrying an electrician's toolbox. Fern thought he looked vaguely familiar. He apologized to Fern, but he would need to check the wiring in the light fixture above the table. She found him a stepladder and pointed out the switches. Before he did the work, he asked, "Are you Fern?" She nodded, not surprised by anything anymore.

"David and Malia say hello," he whispered, lifting his finger to his lips. "They haven't forgotten you."

Fern's face dissolved in happy tears. "Are you David's brother?"

He nodded back, "Yes, Daniel."

Daniel explained that he was the chief electrician at the Antifan camp next door and had been dispatched to check the sound system for Commander Lefever's speech tonight when he would share his insights about the great contributions of the Native Americans to Diversity. Since Lefever was at least one sixty-fourth Native American, no one would question his standing to lecture on the issue.

The sound system was fine, but the corporal had asked him to check out the lights that had been flickering all afternoon in the kitchen. That suited Daniel, since he knew exactly what he had needed to do to cause the lights to flicker in the first place and give him an excuse to approach Fern in the kitchen. Daniel finally climbed the ladder, inspected the fixture, and descended as the corporal reentered the kitchen. "This won't give you any more trouble," he announced cheerfully, giving her a shy smile as he said goodbye. "It'll be better from now on."

Chapter 59
Rehoba Again
(Saturday-Monday, 22-24 October)

When Will arrived around noon on Saturday, Adam and Malia were busy in the living room. Adam, glasses perched on his nose, was peering at his workscreen, tapping away at orders and directions and strategic plans, even writing a coded electronic mail in Chinese to some counterpart in Beijing, and Malia, wearing the silver collar under an open-necked tan T-shirt, was painting about a dozen cloth masks with a child's watercolor set and colored markers. "Isn't it a little late for Coronavirus Day?" Will observed. It was full autumn, and outside the picture window in back of the room, mature trees blazed exuberantly with color.

"I'd like to see her wearing these masks around more," said Adam. "Maybe when she forgets her amba-sahs. So I thought I'd do her a favor by letting her decorate her own masks, you know, like those Karens did during the pandemic. They enjoyed their own subjugation too."

Adam put away the glasses and closed the lid of the workscreen. "Let's have lunch," he said, going to the coldbox where the chicken salad he had made this morning was chilling. He wasn't inclined to let Malia cook for him after the first few attempts. Once he realized the sabotage was accidental, not deliberate, he mostly took care of food preparation himself. "You'd think you'd have learned to cook something by this time in your life," he reproved her, to which she responded, "Amba-sah, all I do is heat up soybakes from my Healthy Eating bag." He told her to slice the tomatoes and wash the grapes.

As they ate the chicken salad with a fresh baguette and drank herbal sodas, Will told Adam about having attended the Anacosta Underground basketball game last night with Brian Walters. They seemed to be becoming fast friends, Will said happily, with Walters having no idea about the Economic Tower net closing in around him. "He told me that the ADF has gotten really bruised this year in its scrap with the Knowledge Tower," he said. "The Antifans know that the Economic Tower is up to something, but Walters said there's not much they can do about it. All their political capital is gone. Walters blames their director for bothering with the Knowledge Tower at all, when it wasn't even a real threat.

"I definitely don't think we need to rush our plans," said Will. "They're clearly way behind us. Let's take the time to do this right." The men had become a lot more comfortable discussing their plans openly, including in front of Malia, who looked, seemingly bored, at her plate.

"Pernella said this week that Avadaughter was considering signing some legislation that would enlarge the ESF mandate officially," said Adam. "Our president is so gaga that I think we could probably get whatever we wanted, if it wouldn't tip off the ADF. If their director had any brains, they'd be working whatever influence they still have in the White Black House."

The conversation then shifted to the likely impact of the pro-women decree on the Anacosta Underground. "They'll have to use New Women," said Adam. "How many real women are six foot five?" In addition to her failed attempt to impose gender parity on the ADF, Avadaughter had announced at the final game of the National Diversity Series that in the spirit of socialism, all professional sports teams would be half female next year, to counteract the remaining harmful influence of testosterone. Even at the Argonne Tower that night, the high-Social Credit men had grumbled.

With lunch concluded, Adam suggested they repair to the basement.

Twenty minutes later, Adam looked down at her on the table. "Melia, tell me about your blond boyfriend."

"The one you had killed, amba-sah?"

"Not that fake one, the one who helped you move into TerraCity."

Her brown eyes stared at him over the mask. Adam thought, she looks frightened. There's something there. The mask made it harder to disguise one's reactions by turning the observer to focus on the eyes alone.

"There's no other blond boyfriend," she said, groaning, and shouting, as he retaliated by tightening the clamps.

"Maybe your aunt helped you move into TerraCity?" he sneered. Silence. "So who helped you move into TerraCity? The main pothead in your ahem—suite—was very sure that a blond guy, well built, threw him into the furniture when he tried to kiss you. Of course, the pothead couldn't have known you only kiss Plores."

Malia seized on that. "He was a Plore workman I met in the street when I was taking stuff over to TerraCity. He saw me struggling with all my bags and offered to help."

"Well, why didn't you say so before?" Adam exclaimed. "We could have avoided all this unpleasantness.

"Unfortunately, our pothead was absolutely sure your helper was a Social Crediteer. He definitely remembers the armband."

Malia yelled as Adam raised the ante. Then he said, "Okay, enough of this. You'll tell me eventually. Let's do some role play." Will went upstairs to watch basketball while Adam and Malia re-created his youth by playing civil war Antifan trooper and innocent Plore resister. They only emerged from the basement around dinnertime.

Adam and Will took a walk before dinner, leaving the exhausted Malia on the sofa to take a nap. Adam locked the coldbox and the cabinets containing food before they left. "Put some makeup on before we go to dinner," said Adam, referring to a red stripe across her cheek. "I don't want anyone wondering what kind of accident you had."

As they strolled down the boardwalk, Will asked, "Why don't you run a camera search on her face? We've now got literally 5,000 facial recognition cameras throughout Anacosta now. Doubled them just in the last month. Surely one of them will pick her up with this guy, if he's really someone in her life."

Adam agreed that would be a great idea. Will was a smart guy.

Meanwhile, that same evening, the Harris family was convening at the best restaurant open to Plores in Harrisonburg to celebrate Marjory's seventy-fifth birthday. Since it wasn't yet Saturnalia, it was harder for Daniel to get a travel permit to Anacosta than for David to get permits for the rest of the family to take a day trip to Harrisonburg, where Daniel could legally travel. David didn't know that Gemma Carpenter herself was approving what would ordinarily be a routine request to visit Harrisonburg for dinner. "Just Harrisonburg?" Gemma asked her assistant, who explained the family party. "Okay, then. But he'd better go no farther and return immediately." The assistant said he would place an order for the chip tracker. If David's chip showed him going anywhere except to Harrisonburg, the ADF would know immediately. David had reserved a 10-seater self-driving car to bring them to and from the City.

"It's a shame that Malia can't be with us tonight," said Marjory, who looked pretty in a mauve floral dress and a matching silk scarf. "What a shame she had to work." The restaurant had given the party of ten a private room, and Emma and Christine had decorated it with the teenagers' help.

"Malia said she wanted us to have a good time and not worry about her," said David, secretly perturbed thinking about her in the hands of that known murderer and sadist, Adam Ross, at that very moment. "She bought this for you." He handed Marjory a small box, "and she made sure I would tell you, not from me, not from us, but from her."

Marjory unwrapped the box and sighed with pleasure at the beautiful silver bracelet inside. "I hope she didn't spend too much," Marjory said. However, Malia had simply regifted the bracelet from the grateful Andrewses, less out of stinginess than because she felt guilty looking at it, let alone wearing it.

After dinner, they sang "Happy Birthday" to Marjory and then to David, whose thirty-ninth birthday would be next week, on October 27. As the party began winding down, David requested his mother's forbearance for him and Daniel to take a short walk around the block. "How nice that you can catch up," said Marjory serenely. "We'll wait here for you." In the meantime, he activated the noise cylinder, whose interference could be explained as a result of scratchy connections from 140 miles away. He did not know that back at Beaufort, Gemma Carpenter had authorized an armband feed, but after an hour of listening to the family party, the analyst, bored out of her mind, had given up finding anything incriminating.

As they walked around the quiet downtown streets, Daniel told David he had talked directly to Fern. "Thanks to you, she's still alive."

"Thanks to Malia," said David. "She has friends who are even more powerful than mine these days. I don't know how we'll get Fern out of the camp, let alone across the border. But I'd like to have the option of rescuing her, too."

"See how it goes," said Daniel placidly.

Will departed for the City on Sunday morning; Adam and Malia would return on Monday, Indigenous Peoples Day. Adam had little interest in participating in the official Econ Tower celebrations.

Malia continued painting and wearing her new masks. When she ran out of ideas, Adam gave her some. "A pair of lips," he said. "A whip. A fish with large eyes, because that's what you remind me of." She dutifully drew these in pencil and painted them in with the markers.

They took a walk on the boardwalk in the afternoon. It was well past the summer season, and while some restaurants were open, the crowds were decidedly thinner, and mostly locals. Plores were permitted on the boardwalk after October 1st, and one could pick them out easily because they were mostly families, and lacked the well-tailored clothes and anxiety more typical of Social Crediteers. Adam's face visibly tightened under his sunglasses when he spotted another Plore family. Malia's face was almost entirely obscured under her fish mask and sunglasses. When one storekeeper asked about it, Adam snapped, "She's got a disease. Do you mind?"

They sat on a bench at the end of the boardwalk, in fact the same one on which they had sat the day Malia had defied Adam by eating the ice cream cone. Malia wistfully remembered that ice cream cone, perhaps because now she had no hopes of eating one in Adam's presence, at least until she lost some weight. And she wasn't going to be losing any weight, not anytime soon.

Adam encircled her with his arm. Despite all her fears, Malia had to admit she felt warm, comfortable, and protected at that moment, although she probably needed to be protected from him more than from anyone else. She looked up at him, thinking him handsome in a brooding way, with the close-cropped beard and the sharp nose, and he smiled down at her, removing her sunglasses and her mask for her and placing them next to him. This was as relaxed as Adam Ross could get.

He still couldn't figure out who that blond guy was. Maybe he really had just been a helpful Plore, despite what the pothead had claimed. After all, how could you believe a pothead? He couldn't tell if Malia was being honest about this new aunt, but he could make her introduce him to the aunt. Where was she living when she wasn't tending desk at the Octavian? At the Plore's, and now at her aunt's?

He might never resolve the issue on his own, but at some point it occurred to him that were he to propose marriage, all that would fade away. She would live with him, and secrets would be impossible to keep. Whoever the blond guy was, he would be gone. That's all that mattered.

"Will you marry me?" he asked Malia. She looked shocked, although he couldn't imagine why. It wasn't the first time he had mentioned the possibility, including moving to Mexico. Hadn't they grown closer in these five months since meeting at the front desk of the Octavian? She had cuckolded the fake Plore actor with him, willingly. Even when he had raped her, she continued to come upstairs, when she really could just have ignored Jorge's implorings.

"I'm just a low-Social Credit girl," she said, stalling. "Aren't you wasting your time with me? Isn't there someone more suitable for you?" But she had talked over this with Cheysa and she knew what her answer would have to be. In any case, she wouldn't be following through, as Cheysa had pointed out. He didn't need to know she was already married. Of course, Cheysa herself had no idea she was already married. How confusing life had become.

"You're suitable for me," said Adam. "Precisely because you're my inferior. So lovely, and so soft and yielding. And not completely unintelligent. I love your breasts; when you're lying down, I always think they're shaped like whales, you know."

Oh, I forgot for a few minutes, Malia remembered, that I'm going to kill you eventually. If David doesn't do it first. But first I'll promise to marry you.

"Think of the wonderful life we could have together," he continued. "You'd be married to one of the senior Econocrats in the country. Getting richer every day, thanks to my connections. Right now, the Intelligence Director of the Economic Tower. When we finally bring the ADF to heel, really, I could be the national security chief of the whole country. We could do whatever we want. No more soybakes for you." He chuckled at his mention of Malia's most frequent complaint.

A year ago, thought Malia, I would have gladly made this deal with the devil.

He actually got down on a knee in front of Malia, and proposed, as a cluster of Plore families grew around them, at a respectful distance. "Look at that big scratch on her face," one of the kids whispered to another.

"Melia, I request your hand in marriage."

She smiled shyly, "Yes, of course." Everyone cheered.

He raised her to her feet, and he kissed her passionately in front of the enthusiastic crowd. "I love you," he told her, in a low voice.

"I love you too," she said, falsely. Because when the moment was right, she really would kill him, she swore.

They brought an Italian takeout dinner back to the house, and Adam was in such an expansive mood that he didn't even mind that she ate seconds. She even was permitted to have sorbet from the gelaterie that was so upscale she couldn't eat it inside. They brought the container home. "This will change after we get married," said Adam, referring to the Social Credit humiliations. "Your Social Credit score goes up to two-thirds of mine, and then 100 percent after we've been married ten years. And when you've been married for another ten years, that change becomes permanent." It occurred to her that would be quite a golden chain—who would want to risk going from a 250 Social Credit score back to 70? How could you walk into TerraCity again, having tasted the best that the DJR could offer you? Adam would hold that sword of Damocles over her every day.

It also occurred to Malia that if anything happened to David, she really would marry Adam. In a minute. If Adam was still alive. Who knew how these machinations would end? She contemplated, hazily, that Adam was promising her security and safety, albeit inside his dungeon, whereas David was offering her true love, freedom, and her daughter, but only at the cost of great danger. If one was risk averse, the first option was definitely better.

"All I ask is to meet your Aunt Paula," said Adam. "I feel I must ask her for permission to marry you." He thought, if there is such a relative, perhaps I can trust her on the blond guy.

"I'll ask her immediately, amba-sah," said Malia, texting on her armband phone. "Do you want to meet her tomorrow when you drop me off at her place?"

Adam was surprised at her alacrity. "Yes, that would be great." He had expected excuses.

The following afternoon, the self-driving car deposited them at the California Tower, a 50-story residential tower for mid-to-high Social Crediteers in the Dupont Circle area.

Paula Findlay, the close support guru of the KCU, and David's longtime "work sister," answered the door. She was thrilled to have been asked to help shore up Malia's cover story, and to have an opportunity to step aside from the computers to serve in an operational role. Malia's having blurted out an aunt to Adam required the quick manufacture of such an aunt, with an impeccable back story. ADF management endorsed the plan quickly. "Paula Findlay, 120," she introduced herself, shaving a good thirty points off her Social Credit score to be more believable as Malia's aunt. That would just qualify you to live at the California Tower.

"Adam Ross, 250," was his response. "I'm at the Economic Tower."

"I know, honey," she said in her soft Southern drawl, "I saw you on TV when you were named. You're the top security guy at the Tower, right?" But there would be no amba-sahing here. That wasn't Paula Findlay's style, and it wasn't the Antifan way either.

"Well, not quite—chief of intelligence," Adam corrected her. But it was a flattering mistake. He thought this aunt was attractive, in a somewhat Deplorable way, with her exuberant mane of teased hair and purple eyeshade. Adam thought she looked younger than her age. He didn't see much of a resemblance to Malia, but Paula explained that she had been married very young to Malia's uncle, Rick, who had died in the war. That was convincing, since everyone had lost a husband or a father or both in the war. Then she had remarried, to an Antifan veteran who became a schoolteacher, but they had divorced. The ex-Antifan schoolteacher had indeed been her husband, but her one and only.

She served them cookies and iced tea, and talked and talked and talked, about her neighbors, her job as a computer specialist at the Social Tower, her husband, who was Malia's Uncle Rick, and how on a whim she had decided to see whether she could locate dear Malia. "The Antifans drove us out of the Lynchburg area. I knew that Malia and her grandma had been sent to Charlottesville, but we lost track of them. Then I heard her grandma had died in the Charlottesville camp and Malia went to an orphanage...."

"Wait," said Adam. "How come you're calling her Malia? I thought you were Melia."

Malia replied, "No one ever gets Malia, so I've been going by Amelia for years. So my relatives know me by Malia and everyone who's known me since I've grown up calls me Melia."

"And then," said Paula, "I was able to track down some of the orphanage records, because after all, I'm at the Social Tower, and we run orphanages, right? Good thing that it wasn't a common name. And then I got a text number, and the rest is history," she concluded triumphantly.

Adam wanted to see where Malia was sleeping, and Paula pointed out the sofa bed on which they were sitting. "It's not fancy," she said, "but we can't let our Malia live at TerraCity, can we?" If he had expressed an interest in seeing where Malia kept her clothes, she would have shown him a closet with clothes brought over by David.

Adam responded, "It won't be a problem for much longer. Melia and I are getting married. I proposed to her this weekend in Rehoba."

"Oh honey! Congratulations!" Paula clapped her hands together and kissed Malia, then insisted on hugging Adam. "Our family is growing again after all these years. I am so thrilled for both of you! Do you have a date yet?"

"Maybe early in the new year?" Adam guessed. He hadn't quite gotten that far yet.

When Adam finally took his leave, he felt more reassured by the existence of the aunt, at least. The blond guy seemed to be receding quickly by contrast with the vibrant Aunt Paula. Talks way too much, he thought to himself, we won't be spending too much time with her.

Once he was gone, Paula turned to Malia and said, "We'll give it an hour, which should be safe enough, and then I'll take you home in a car. You want to watch a movie? That's a nice choker you're wearing, by the way." Adam had said the choker would have to suffice for now until he could find a ring, as he had proposed impulsively. Malia's heart had sunk, as she knew her wearing it would anger David, but she had no reason to refuse Adam anymore.

Malia and Paula didn't dare talk about Adam Ross between themselves. Among Antifans, it was now assumed you could no longer be sure that the Economic Tower wasn't listening to your armband and household feeds. The Tower had been held back not by lack of scientific or technological expertise, but by political convention and will, which no longer restrained it.

Chapter 60
Our Girlfriend Now
(Friday, 21 October)

T he warm glow of Marjory's birthday party vanished abruptly for David after he dropped the family off in Ploreville and he was riding in the car headed back into the City, where it belonged. For a few hours, surrounded by those who loved him best, he had managed to stave off the memories of Friday at Beaufort. In the early afternoon, Alex Charlton had popped his head into David's office and requested he come by for a talk. David expected this would be a sterner reminder about the need for the preliminary university investigation report.

It was embarrassing that for the first time ever, he was flirting with a performance reprimand that would go into his file and might stymie any further promotions. But how could he focus on an investigation that he now freely admitted to himself was a chimera, and even worse, had destroyed the lives of dozens of conscientious DJR citizens, many of whom were loving and kind parents and spouses? Yes, he would tap out onto a screen the numbers of such lives, their various false and true confessions, and how he had connived at the destruction of all involved. But each keystroke was an indictment of himself. No wonder his mother refused to listen even to the tamest news of his work.

When David walked into Alex's office, he was surprised to see Steve Rosen. Well, this isn't about the professors, David thought. But Alex had excused himself from the Economic Tower business on the grounds that the KCU had no equities in the matter other than David's girlfriend's involvement. So what was this about?

"Close the door, would you, Harris? Take a seat," said Alex.

Steve asked, "How are you, buddy?"

"Uh, fine," said David.

Alex said, "We've asked you to come in to make sure that everything is all right. We've noticed a drop-off in your attention to the KCU business, particularly the university report. But in general, you just seem less engaged."

David nodded. "Maybe it's just that I feel the excitement is behind us now. Yes, I should finish that report. But now I'm not sure what's next. Steve, you have the Economic Tower business, but what's next for me? I know this shouldn't be bothering me. How many times do we close out cases? But for some reason, I'm down."

"Would it help to speak with a MED therapist?" Steve asked.

David shrugged. "If that would reassure folks," he said, meaning *you*, "I could do it."

"Perhaps you're having a midlife crisis?" suggested Alex. "Aren't you about to turn 39?"

They all stared at each other, then Alex ventured forth again. "Harris, you won't like hearing this, but as good as your girlfriend might have been for this organization, I don't think she's been particularly good for you."

David gave them a hostile look. "What do you mean?"

"You were fine until you met her," said Alex. "There's a reason we discourage relationships between high and low Social Crediteers. If you're high level and you start dealing with low-levels, you might start resenting on their behalf how they're treated. And when you try to redress those inequalities, which are necessary for Diversity, you cause trouble for yourself.

"After all, how many morning meetings have you missed in the last few months because you were picking up your girlfriend somewhere and bringing her home? You've even brought her into the KCU, where she had no business, honestly. This isn't the family store."

"I didn't mind her coming to the ECU," Steve broke in, "but that's legitimate, given her focus on Ross. Cheysa had to pass her the various devices, which doesn't work so well in a coffee shop."

"Look," said David, "she didn't have to do anything for us. Given how much she's contributed to our investigation of Adam Ross, the Director ought to be giving us permission to marry, and gladly. That's been part of her motivation, and frankly, mine. I'm getting the impression you don't think that will be happening."

"I wouldn't count on it," said Alex. "He doesn't understand why you're so enamored of her, and he was turned off by your defense of her interests rather than ours at various junctures. This is exactly what we're saying about letting your personal wishes override the organization's.

"Look, what's the big deal? You've had your fun with her. Let someone else have a turn. We'll find her a decent job when this is over, somewhere where you won't run into her. We won't turn her into the street. We can find her someone more appropriate, too, if you want. In the meantime, we'd like to suggest you reconnect with Kate Langley. Great Antifan family, a looker, she'd be a credit to you. What happened there, anyway?"

"I was bored," said David flatly, wishing he could punch Alex for the "let someone else have a turn" comment. It wouldn't be Alex himself, who favored the "other side of the aisle," as Adam Ross put it. There was a Mr. Alex Charlton at home who wasn't Alex Charlton himself.

"Bored?" said Steve. "If she showed an interest in me, I'd have to reconsider Mrs.

Rosen, at least temporarily."

"Yes, bored," said David. "I've interacted more productively with flower vases."

"Interesting comparison," grinned Alex, with his lascivious mind. "Well, bored or not, you'd better reconsider. The Director himself came up with a list of potential partners for you, and she's at the top of the list."

"Who else is on the list?" asked David curiously.

Alex picked up a sheet of paper from his desk with several names scrawled on it, and put on his reading glasses. "Dianne Abimbala—"

"She's also history. I don't have the patience for her drama anymore."

"There are several other Diverse choices for you here, all of whom have been sounded out on their interest in you. The Director says you can redeem yourself by at least picking a Diverse partner. You don't need to be in love, you know—that's just a Plore superstition." Alex smiled superciliously at him. "Georgina Batterford, 290, one of our deputy commanders in the Criminal Unit. A New Woman, post-surgical, don't worry." Redeem myself, David thought, uh-oh.

"You're kidding," said David. "Maybe better for you than me." Alex's eyes narrowed, but he persisted.

"Carolina Cruz, 230."

"The singer?" David was astonished. Carolina Cruz was a sultry Latina temptress who regularly appeared at ADF functions and the annual parade entertainment. Her association with the ADF was longstanding because her grandfather had served in one of the elite brigades and after the war had briefly been Deputy Director.

Alex and Steve smiled at what they perceived as the sudden spike in interest. "Yes, she's really into you, by the way," lied Alex. "I think she's ready to settle down, but will only marry an Antifan." Steve thought to himself, he likes brunettes, this isn't a bad idea.

"Vanessa Hodges, 250," Alex read. David knew Vanessa, who was deputy chief of finance, a petite African American about his age, with a sweet round face and serene demeanor. She'd been helpful a few years ago when he needed to arrange covert financing for a subversive arts group that he wanted to give some rope to hang themselves, which they had conveniently done. He had appreciated her efficiency. But he couldn't see it going home. He knew there were teenage children in her house.

"And finally, what about your own Helen Zhu, 210?" said Alex.

"Helen?" David uttered. "Our Helen?" It was disturbing to think of his deputy looking at him with lust. Whatever his other flaws, such as purloining body parts, Walters had at least shown no interest in dating his commander.

"She's ready," said Alex. "We'd simply transfer one of you if it worked out."

"I wish she'd just write the report for me," said David, completely unnerved. Helen was a profoundly anxious type. "She makes me nervous."

"Do you want to go on a date with Carolina this weekend, then?" Steve asked. "Your girlfriend is away with Adam Ross in Rehoba, right? She'll never know you did it. And keep in mind, she's not being so chaste herself this weekend. Don't you deserve a little fun?"

Yes, David thought tiredly, I deserve a little fun. I deserve to live in a free country with the woman of my choice. But he needed to hold off this official ADF pressure, just for a little while longer. The sudden scrutiny was alarming. What else did they know about him? That reinvestigation had been a close call, he knew it. On the other hand, he was still above ground and not in a cell. "Sure, I'll go on a date this weekend with Carolina." He knew most of his male Antifan colleagues, the heterosexuals at least, would envy him. Maybe even the gay guys. Even the placid Steve Rosen looked a little envious. Within half an hour, Alex had arranged a date for David with Carolina on Sunday evening.

David walked into the atrium and to the elevator bank with Steve. "I just want you to know, Steve," said David bluntly. "You shouldn't assume Malia's going to be as helpful on the Tower investigation if we're no longer together. She only did this because we were dating."

Steve's previously mild expression hardened. "David, she has no choice. We'll be taking over from here. It wasn't the KCU's business in the first place."

Now it was David's turn to stiffen. "She won't be happy about that."

"What she wants isn't relevant," said Steve. "Harris, where do you think you've been working for the last twenty years? This isn't a Ploreville high school dance." Steve's elevator slid into the berth and he made ready to enter it. "She isn't your girlfriend anymore. She's *our* girlfriend."

Steve entered the elevator, and as the doors closed, he gave David an Antifan salute. It might have been his normal courtesy, or mockery, or a reminder, David wasn't sure.

David watched Steve's elevator shoot upward through the glass tower toward the ECU, and then he wearily returned to the KCU. Running through his head, for some odd reason, was the chant from the Coronavirus Liberation Day parade, *"Do not defy, you must conform; the mask, the chip, are now the norm!"*

Having given up on productivity for the afternoon, David decided he could at least work out in the gym. That improved his mood somewhat. But as he pounded on the elliptical machine in the gym, he acknowledged to himself the walls seemed to be closing in. He couldn't use his best argument with his ADF matchmakers—"I'm already married, guys." Malia's pregnancy, which was already known, was irrelevant to them. By admitting to an illegal marriage by a Christian pastor, and thus anti-Diversity knowledge crime, he would doom Malia and himself as well as Pastor Denman. Winter was approaching. Malia's pregnancy wasn't reversing itself, Adam Ross's best efforts notwithstanding. The ADF was swirling around them, trying determinedly to separate them.

As he strained at the weight machines afterward, the refrain ran through his mind, can we do this? Can we do this, soon? Various aspects of the escape plot began to join in his mind, giving him a jolt of energy that despite all his misgivings, cheered him slightly. The memory of the bloodied corpse of the Antifan officer who had failed to escape troubled him only a little. That was a long time ago, he reasoned, we were wilder then.

Chapter 61
Carolina Cruz
(Sunday, 23 October)

On Sunday afternoon, David worked out at the Avalon, showered, and carefully chose a polo shirt, jacket, and slacks combination that would serve for Ada's, which Carolina had chosen for the destination. Or maybe the ADF had, who knew.

In his distraction, David nicked himself with his razor while shaving. The instant-heal tube was empty. Where might he have put another? The medicine cabinet yielded nothing. He went into the guest room, remembering that he had shoved some extra toiletry items into various cabinets and drawers at times.

Looking in the deep single drawer of the night table, he saw Dianne's dusty cosmetics, and decided to finally toss them. It was nice of Malia not to have complained about them, since she had certainly come across them in her somewhat sneaky but harmless way. He saw the photographs of him and Kate Langley at Punta Calidad, looking carefree and happy in their swimsuits against palm trees and on the beach. That was before I began to think for myself, he reflected. God, she had been dull.

Digging further, he wondered, what's at the bottom of this pile of stuff? His hand felt a few layers of carefully folded T-shirts. Hmmm, I didn't fold these, he said to himself. He almost stopped, thinking a fresh tube would certainly not have slipped down this far, but now he was curious. And then he was afraid. Very afraid.

Sweating, and with dread, David pulled out four books: *Gone With the Wind*; *The New Class* by Milovan Djilas; *Modern Times* by Paul Johnson; and *1984* by George Orwell. The first and last he quickly recognized as the greatest heretical books that one could possess in the DJR, aside from the Bible. The Depository watermark was still on the first sheet of each book, which at least Kendra had been smart enough to tear out of the Club volumes when she bought them at the plant. Fortunately, the books the KCU had recovered were in such disrepair that missing pages attracted no undue attention from the Beaufort analysts. Eager to shield Malia, David had not pointed out the consistent absence of sheets on which a Depository watermark would have been present. Even bright analysts tended only to see what was visible, not what was missing.

He was unfamiliar with *The New Class*, but the back cover read:

This is one of the great political documents of all time. It is a shattering analysis of Communism…(it) tells why, instead of creating a workers' paradise, it has brought forth a slave state in which the ruling class devours itself while holding down the masses in abject material and intellectual poverty.

Oh my God, thought David. That's us too. He didn't have the time to peruse the thick Johnson volume, but as a KCU commander, he knew Paul Johnson was proscribed, so that was that. And just when he thought he had reached the bottom of the drawer, he drew forth a copy of *Homage to Catalonia*, also by Orwell.

She brought all these into my apartment, David thought to himself, with horror and then anger. For months they have been sitting in this apartment, vulnerable to any casual search. David knew he had been fortunate that the ADF had not conducted a search of his apartment as part of his fraught reinvestigation. Owning any of them would have been a knowledge crime of the first order. He knew that Malia would likely have been executed after a very brief spell at Beaufort, and he would be languishing in the deepest level of cells had any ONE of these books been discovered in his apartment, while they decided what to do with him and how far this knowledge crime had spread among his ranks.

Worrying about the consequences of escaping the DJR almost seemed quaint by comparison with this crime, David thought, and all this while I was persecuting Kendra Pinckney and her friends for acquiring and sharing books far less explosive than these. "I'll burn them right now." He carried the books to the kitchen sink, placed Orwell's volumes in the sink and held the lit match to them first, while the others dejectedly sat face down on the side, awaiting their turn.

He was finally burning *Modern Times* atop the pile of ashes in the sink when the lobby attendant called. "Is everything okay in your apartment, Commander? There's smoke in your kitchen."

"Everything's fine," said David. "I just forgot about something I was cooking and put it out when it started to burn. Thanks for checking." They knew when you were home, of course. Thank goodness they had not sent anyone upstairs to put out the fire. He let the ashes cool, considering the most discreet way to dispose of them. Regular trash, he guessed. He could sneak a bag out of the apartment, but might well be spotted disposing of it in a park or along the river. He knew that criminals sometimes foolishly revealed their hand by making extra efforts to disguise their crimes. And he was now a criminal, well, even more of a criminal.

With a spasm of anger and self-recrimination, he realized, "this is why the ADF wanted to protect me. You brought this low-credit person into your house, this secretive, low-credit person who was committing knowledge crimes all along in her Depository job, and you really thought she would change her ways because you rescued her from the Economic Zone and brought her home and fed her cheese? The mouse ate the cheese, but she did not change her ways. This is why the ADF tells you to stay with your own kind." But it was too late. The damage was done, the baby was coming, his mother was proud they had married.

For a moment, he hated and despised Malia for doing this to him, and then he shrugged it off.

At least he would go on his date with the famous Carolina Cruz with a slightly eased conscience. Perhaps the ADF knew best. They would know how to deftly extract Malia from his life like a tumor, while, he hoped, respecting her contribution to the mission with a job or a payoff. Somewhere a child who might resemble him, maybe even a boy, would wonder who his father was and why he had not married his mother. In ten years, he could retire comfortably.

David picked up Carolina in the yellow sportscar, a flourish he knew she would appreciate. He had waited for her in the lobby of her building, the Azteca Tower, where the Latinx elite liked to live because of the various cultural flourishes, such as the murals of Southwestern pueblos, now of course unfortunately under fascist Texas rule. Each apartment had its own tortilla maker and guacamole press, he had learned with a quick online search while checking the Tower's address, and on your birthday, a mariachi band serenaded you at your door.

"You must be David!" Carolina greeted him, dressed in a skin-tight, black-and-gold accented sheath and gold bangles and earrings. One gold bangle encircled her black armband, which for some reason David found enticing. Her long black curls cascaded around her mocha-complexioned face; she would fling them around with abandon on the dance floor. He guessed she was approaching thirty, which would explain the interest in marriage, although she was several years older in reality. David could see himself sleeping with her later. Yes he could, married or not, baby or not. The ADF was not stupid.

On the way to Ada's, Carolina asked him questions about himself and praised him for his service to the mission in a way that suggested she saw it as part and parcel of his masculine appeal. At the very least, it made David resolve to report to work on Tuesday after the holiday with renewed commitment. Her exuberance and extroversion were a welcome relief from Malia's reticence, but not as jarring as Dianne's volatility. He had to remind himself that Dianne had initially been an enjoyable experience, too. Even as he drove, in the corner of his eye, he saw the sheath sliding up her thighs as she moved around lusciously on the seat. Oh God, he thought, how am I going to last four or five hours before she can take me home?

The valet took the car at Ada's as cameras flashed and they were ushered to a prominent table in the lower VIP deck. No forms needed to be signed this time, David noticed with relief. They gave their pronouns, and over their steak dinners, Carolina continued to flatter him and ply him with questions. "You have such beautiful gray eyes, they are like the ocean on a winter day. Tell me about your workouts—I am trying to build strength but it's so hard, as I am just a woman. What would you recommend? You have such strong arms." Her soft hand with its bright red nails lightly sailed down his bicep.

On the dance floor, Carolina allowed David to take the lead, but in ways that made him look like a better dancer than he was. An hour later, she seemed willing to sit down again at the table.

"I'm sure they told you that I am starting to think about settling down," she told him. "But I can't settle down with just anyone. My family—my grandfather—it must be an Antifan, but not any Antifan. I cannot just marry a policeman, but a hero. My husband needs to be a hero, a warrior, someone who loves Diversity and would kill for it.

"I know you were born a Plore—I apologize for mentioning this to your face—but this makes me even more attracted to you. Here you are from Ploreville, yet you love Diversity. I feel that if we were together, it would be a true symbol of the greatness of the DJR."

David thought, she doesn't know me at all. But am I still capable of living up to the ideal she is drawing for me? It is too late? Have I thrown away my chance to become a hero? It was flattering to think of himself as a still-young warrior, flattering that someone like Carolina Cruz saw him that way. He said, awkwardly, "Thank you, Carolina, for your confidence in me. I know with someone like you at my side, I could do great things for Diversity." She leaned over and gave him a deep and passionate kiss, to which he responded in kind.

David signaled to the waiter, and ran his armband over the screen the waiter had promptly brought, recognizing full well the urgency of the customer's departure. David drove the yellow sportscar to one of the overlooks along the Potowmack, where he stopped, then reached for her, aching with lust. "We need to return to my apartment," she said, just before the moment of no return. "This is not comfortable."

"Oh—Mother Earth!" he said, but he threw himself back in the driver's seat and they returned to the Azteca. He was driven mad with lust and passion, just as the ADF wanted him to be. With another woman, he would have pressed his advantage at the overlook, but you couldn't do that to Carolina Cruz. David hadn't thought about Malia in hours. Once the door closed behind them in Carolina's apartment, he did what he had wanted to do all evening.

Chapter 62
Rainy Night
(Monday, 24 October)

Malia let herself into the apartment, which was surprisingly still. She wondered about the faint acrid smell of smoke in the air, but nothing seemed to be amiss otherwise. The curtains were still drawn from the night before, and David was nowhere to be found. She texted him, "*Hello! Just got home,*" but five minutes later, he had still not replied. Malia was confident he must have gone into Beaufort despite the holiday and she settled down patiently on the sofa to wait. The evening news was enthusing about a movement of young Diversity activists nationwide who, in honor of the holiday had erected paper mâché statues of Christopher Columbus so they could tear them down and burn them. "Never forget," the anchor intoned gravely. "Greet your indigenous comrades today, and apologize for the fascist nation's sins against them."

Bored, Malia, who didn't know any indigenous people to whom she could apologize, at least not at the Avalon, scrolled through her news feed. Today it was heavy on gossip and lifestyle developments—recipes for nourishing harvest season soups; tips on upholstering your own chairs; instructions on how to use filters on your GVN to receive what the Knowledge Tower recommended for Social Crediteers' reading this fall. Then she stared in shock at a photo of David, her husband, walking into Ada's last night with a striking Latina woman. The caption read, "Antifan heartthrob and songster Carolina Cruz partying last night with a handsome date."

She zoomed into the photo. Yes, that was David, his face partly averted from the camera, but definitely with this exotic creature. And he had always told Malia that he avoided Ada's, and after their last visit, had said, "It'll be a long time before we return."

Malia felt small and mousy compared with Carolina Cruz. Did she even have a right to object, given that David had already saved her life? Given that she was off in Rehoba Beach accepting marriage proposals from Adam Ross? But she cried out to herself, "We're married! I'm pregnant with his child! And he's already cheating on me."

Then she asked herself, perhaps there was an operational reason for him to visit Ada's? Was he on a protective detail for Carolina Cruz, who was sufficiently famous that even non-Antifans such as herself knew about the singer? Don't jump to conclusions, she warned herself.

Hungry after the weekend with Adam, she went into the kitchen and cooked dinner, carefully leaving David two sautéed chicken breasts and the lion's share of the fried potatoes. Out of obligation to the baby and David, she filled a bowl from the salad dispenser.

David walked into the apartment about an hour later, after Malia had eaten a pint of mango ice cream and was finally beginning to worry. Malia could tell he had not returned to the apartment last night. Normally fastidious, he was slightly disheveled— his slacks were wrinkled and his hair mussed. He looked tired. The smell of a woman's perfume, heavy and floral, followed him.

Instead of greeting Malia with the warm embrace and loving words she expected, David gave her a measured look, and went into the kitchen, where he poured himself a glass of water from the automatic carafe and drank it in a few gulps.

"David?" she asked. "Are you all right?"

"Yes," he said. "I've never been better."

"I saw a photo of you at Ada's last night with Carolina Cruz," she ventured, tentatively. His next response told her all she needed to know.

"And why not?" he said. "Do you expect me to sit here watching TV all weekend while Adam Ross has his way with you? And his friend does, too?"

She shook her head. "But I have no choice," she replied sadly.

That was mostly true, so David hesitated. He was starting to feel guilty, just a little, about the gymnastic lovemaking that had lasted most of the night on Carolina's platform bed, and that had resumed around noon after they had slept and eaten brunch in bed, delivered from the restaurant in the Azteca Tower. "*Rompe colchon*, which means mattress-breaker," said Carolina, feeding him the oyster meat by hand, "it's a *ceviche*, good for lovers."

Then she poured them little shot glasses of *mamajuana*, a mixture of rum, red wine, honey, and herbs. He rubbed some on her breasts and licked it off. They had napped in each other's arms, awoke to make love, napped again, all afternoon, until the shadows grew long.

"I know you slept with her," Malia said. "I can tell. I smell her perfume."

"And so what?" he said. "Maybe sometimes I need a change of pace. What are we, Plores?"

He turned on her, defensively, "Maybe you need to improve your technique a little. You could learn from Carolina. You're not dealing with a Knowledge Tower drone, you know, but an Antifan. Our standards are higher."

Malia began to weep, and David, in all fairness, acknowledged his anger at her was largely because of how she had endangered them. He pulled her by the wrist into the guest room, signaled silence with a finger to his lips, and opened the drawer of the night table with his other hand. Then he pointed to the now-empty drawer and flipped his hands wide, as if to say, "What the hell? What did you do?"

She scrabbled in the drawer, and then realized all her books were gone. He mouthed angrily, "how COULD you? Here?" She then realized that the acrid smoke smell was her burned books.

Malia broke out into wails and ran away from him, through the living room and out of the apartment. This time she grabbed her armband and her jacket from the sofa.

David thought, she'll be back soon, it's raining heavily. She won't go outside; she'll sulk for awhile in the lobby. He gravitated over to the skillet, speared a now-rubbery chicken breast and ate it off the fork, and then each of the potato slices in a rough order from largest to smallest. He left the second chicken breast for Malia to eat upon her return. With each swallow, he expected Malia to reappear, embarrassed, but she did not.

I guess I'd better go downstairs and retrieve her from the lobby, he thought. He regretted his unkind words about her technique. He had never had any reason to criticize her lovemaking before his nearly 24 hours with the singing Latina siren. He felt in some ways, he had been under a spell, one that had taken control of his body and numbed his feelings toward anyone but Carolina, who was indefatigable. If there was an Antifan Sexual Corps, she would be a general officer. He hoped he had not disappointed her either, because he needed the affair to continue, at least for awhile, as he conciliated his superiors.

David stepped out of the building into a blustery wet night. If anything, it had gotten worse since he had returned home. He decided to get in the car and cover more ground. The yellow sportscar crawled north on tree-lined Massachusetts, but David bleakly realized that he was far more visible than any of the passersby huddled in their raincoats under their umbrellas. He turned right on Yuma, reasoning that Malia might have gone over to Wisconsin Avenue where she could shelter in a coffee or sandwich shop. She was not answering her phone.

As recently as a week ago, he would not have hesitated to call Beaufort for a chip locator check, but now it would be viewed another mark against him for using Antifan resources for distasteful personal ends. Nevertheless, desperate, he called Night Commander Angela.

"Oh, hello David," she said, slightly distant, listening to his request. "Look, I'd love to help, but I can't take responsibility for this. I mean, she's your girlfriend, not a subject of ours, right? Do you think she's in any danger?"

"Well, possibly," David equivocated.

"I'd call the Anacosta Police," she advised. "They're the ones who have the mental health units and they can intervene effectively."

She was clearly resistant to being convinced otherwise, so David said "thanks, anyway," and hung up, thinking "F--k you. A few months ago you were telling me how inspiring my 8:30 speeches were."

How many Antifans now knew that he was tainted, he wondered. In another time, and in another place, he could have just quit his job and taken another one working for some corporation. But now the only corporation was the government, and for him only the ADF. Conform or else. He continued driving up and down the streets between Mass and Wisconsin Avenues, not far from Beaufort, scanning the streets like the good cop he might have been, somewhere else.

David had been driving for about an hour when he spotted Malia hurrying by a McVegan outlet on Wisconsin Avenue. He parked behind her, and got out of the car. The rainstorm was abating, but the sidewalks were slick with rain. He could see she was drenched and shivering.

"Honey," he said, but she didn't hear. Or perhaps she thought he was a lecherous Street Person.

"Malia!" She turned around and saw him. He reached out for her, and he encircled her—and their baby—in his strong arms on the street. "Let's get you home before you catch cold."

Once in the car, she said simply, "I'm sorry. It was foolish of me." He knew she meant the books, but no one listening to them would realize it.

"I understand," he said. "And I'm sorry that I did what I had to do." He meant the books, but he could have been referring to Carolina, too. When they got home, he asked about the choker, and inspecting it, saw that it could only be unlocked by someone who knew the four-digit combination. Malia offered to sever it with the metal melter that Cheysa had given her, but David shook his head. "No, he'll be suspicious if you do that." Perhaps strangely, since it came from another man, he found it very appealing, but all he planned to do tonight was watch TV with Malia snuggled next to him.

"Hi, Uncle Victor." Carolina's chirpy voice on the phone brightened Victor Ferraro's evening as he sat with a whiskey and a book, an actual bound volume, titled, *Concepts of Masculinity in Spartan Life*. The book would have given coronaries to dozens of Knowledge Tower apparatchiks had they known it was circulating, but it wasn't really, except in Ferraro's house. Victor Ferraro had a black-market dealer in antiquarian books at his disposal, and for a price, the Director could acquire virtually any volume he wanted, most of which were stolen or purchased from foreign libraries. When he was finished with a volume, he could trade it in for another one, so as to avoid keeping a collection that might bring even him under suspicion.

"My dear Carolina!" said Victor. He wasn't really her uncle, but the relationship between him and her father was so warm that he indeed thought of her as a niece of sorts. "How did your date with Commander Harris go?"

"It went for almost 24 hours," Carolina said proudly. "If you know what I mean."

"I certainly do, precious child," said Victor. "I've been watching some of your footage with my bodyguards. You really ought to enter the Olympics in some fashion or another. Thanks for humoring my dissolute tastes."

Carolina giggled. "You should have seen him struggling to control himself all evening. When he started in at the overlook after we left Ada's, I cut it off at the very last moment to insist we go back to my place. He cursed, but what could he do? I'm not some low-Social Credit girl."

"No, my dear, you are a princess to us, indeed," purred Victor. "How was the conversation when you finally got around to it?"

"I talked a lot about the cause of Diversity and how I wanted to marry only an Antifan warrior, someone who would kill for Diversity and the DJR. I know you said he's insecure about his Plore background, so I made it seem like to me, that was an advantage. You know, the great unity between Social Credit and Plore under the Antifan banner. He swallowed it, completely."

"Good, good," said Ferraro. "I'd like to win him back for the cause if we can."

"How long am I going to need to date him?"

"Just long enough for him to dump his pregnant girlfriend, and for us to spirit her away somewhere, all right? Was it that terrible?"

"No, he's all right, but he's a little old for me. And I've got my eye on someone else, in the ECU."

"Understood, absolutely," said Ferraro. "A few weeks should do it. And you can still see others, provided that you're a little discreet. He's a Plore, he'll read your extracurricular dating the wrong way. To us, it's a sign of your good health and Diverse character.

"Wait, who are you fancying in the ECU?"

"Do you know Commander Brian Walters?" she queried.

"Yes, a remarkable physical specimen. A family heritage Antifan. I have been promoting him for a while, because he has the makings of a great leader. Why don't you come to my party this Saturday? I'll be inviting him too."

"Oh, thank you, Uncle Victor."

"No problem at all, dear. You can sing a little for the crowd, they'll love it. Just be a little patient, all right?"

Ferraro hung up the phone, chuckling at dear Carolina's charming appetites. Yes, she and Walters would be perfect together.

Chapter 63
White Black House
(Wednesday, 26 October)

Victor Ferraro's limousine sat in the half-circle driveway in front of the West Wing of the White Black House. The middle-aged black chauffeur, leaning against the vehicle, basked in the noontime sunshine as he reflected upon the zebra striping of the stately building. He was old enough to remember the festive repainting and christening, no, celebration would be a better word, of the newly named White Black House in 2060. It had been long overdue vindication for the enslaved peoples who everyone knew had designed and built the historic mansion. Now the building truly served the Diverse Peoples of the DJR and reminded children of the Safari Lodge at the Diversity World theme park.

Ferraro had finally managed to outflank the eunuchs of the Knowledge Tower and secure a private meeting with President Avadaughter. This would be his last effort to convince the doddering woman that her government was threatened by the resurgent Economic Tower.

Unfortunately, his private meeting was not as private as he would have liked, since Vice-President Peace-Williams also participated. Ferraro knew that Peace-Williams was in the indirect employ of the Economic Tower, which had sounded him out on easing him into the presidency once their coup was launched. For all he knew, Peace-Williams was also nurturing a Mexican bank account. The imposing, sixtyish African-American with the walrus moustache sat like a boulder on the side of the table between Ferraro at one end and Avadaughter at the other.

Unlike many DJR men his age, Peace-Williams had not served among the Antifans, but rather as a community organizer in New York. He had become mayor of the city in 2060 on a wave of pro-DJR euphoria, and had presided over its integration into the Hudson-Schuylkill Region a year later. After a brief stint as Regional Administrative Director, he had become Knowledge Tower Director and then slid gracefully into the Vice-Presidential slot when Avadaughter needed a Diverse complement for her presidential run. Not that she needed to run against any other ticket, since of course all DJR presidents were now selected in advance of the election by the Central Diversity Committee, but it was considered desirable to run up the popular vote to demonstrate societal affirmation on Election Day, which took place every four years. Only Social Crediteers could vote for President and the Advisory Congress.

Ferraro had not wanted to reveal some of his best evidence to Peace-Williams, since the Vice-President would likely relay it to his cohorts in the Economic Tower. The likelihood of Avadaughter sharing with Peace-Williams had been a deterrent all along, but Ferraro now reasoned the risk might be worthwhile. The damning accusation came from the intelligence collected by Harris's girlfriend, and perhaps the ADF had reached the point at which it could afford to position Malia Jenness above the trap door.

He once again told Avadaughter that the Economic Tower was deliberately killing young Social Crediteers in the bowels of the chemical factory at its Camp Number Four, not that she remembered the previous time. But he now told her the Chinese were paying the Economic Tower's intelligence director and five other functionaries for their complicity, funneling funds into their illegal Mexican bank accounts.

Avadaughter's head visibly drooped to the right, but she said, "That's terrible. Michael, what are we going to do about that?" Michael was Kumbaya Peace-Williams' nickname, or strictly speaking, the name on his birth certificate. He had declared himself to be "Kumbaya" when he had presided over a mostly peaceful rally that had ended in the death of fifteen policemen and forty-six anti-fascist protesters during the civil war.

"Madam President, I have visited the chemical factory myself and have seen nothing unusual there. The work is entirely in laboratories and all the human subjects are volunteers who are covered by strict safety procedures. Director Ferraro has gotten bad intelligence."

"Oh, that's good," said Avadaughter as she dozed off. Ferraro wondered why she hadn't gotten her zingos that morning.

"Peace-Williams, you know you're lying," said Ferraro angrily.

"Who will they believe, you or me?" the Vice-President said, in his buttery tones. "Everyone knows the ADF is scrambling to salvage its reputation. People want more prosperity, and the Economic Tower is poised to deliver. The next president will get the credit for the next vibrant stage of our revolution. What can your ADF deliver today, except death and destruction?"

"Without the ADF," said Ferraro, his spider tattoo throbbing again, "your revolution would be over. The US could walk into this country and kick you out of here."

"I don't see any fascists around today, do you?" smiled Peace-Williams.

A few minutes later, a grim-faced Ferraro stalked out of the White Black House. The cluster of waiting bodyguards began to stir and move in his direction. One alert guard saw a figure move around from the portico with an electronic gun and raise it in the direction of Ferraro. The swarthy young man fired just as the bodyguard tackled him, aided by the gun's recoil. The electronic beam hit an oak tree branch, which broke off and crashed onto the lawn. Two guards hustled Ferraro into his car, which sped back to Beaufort. The others dragged the assassin into the second car, landing blows as Secret Service agents watched calmly from the portico.

"Holy Mother of God," said Ferraro, wiping his forehead with a handkerchief. Under stress he returned to the instinctive sayings of his youth. "That was close. Who the hell was that?"

The commanders' meeting convened the following morning at 11 am, moved up a day because of the assassination attempt on Ferraro. "Level-C" flashed on as the door slid shut, and Ferraro took his seat.

Ferraro told them, in clipped, contemptuous tones, about Peace-Williams' cynical dismissal of his concerns about the Economic Tower experiments. "He surely is getting a cut himself, if not through Mexico, and he is counting on the Tower to push Avadaughter aside and make him President. She slept through most of our discussion."

Montoya said that the assailant was a Knowledge Tower officer on rotation at the White Black House. "He said his motive was to defend the honor of the Knowledge Tower against what he called the aggression of Beaufort." The young man still had not given the ADF a convincing account of how he had acquired the electronic gun, but regardless, he was doomed because unauthorized use of a firearm was of course, a capital offense. "So we're going to start moving to more aggressive questioning," said Montoya. "Since he cites our aggression as having provoked him, we might as well live up to it."

"Could the ESF have provided the weapon?" someone asked.

Montoya shrugged, "Who knows? They're bringing weapons in for their own forces. It wouldn't be hard for one to go astray, on purpose or by accident."

"We still don't know where the truth serum development stands," said Steve Rosen. "If they were close, we might expect to see a sudden upward bump in the bank accounts. But they have continued growing steadily, not dramatically. And we still don't know the exact connection between the experiments and the bank accounts."

"Harris, what's your girlfriend up to here? Has she been asking?" Ferraro asked him impatiently.

"Yes, sir, she's been trying to find out, but they've been discreet, and any direct questions about this topic would cause them to look at her with suspicion. But last weekend Adam Ross proposed to her, and she accepted, so we hope this will make him more willing to divulge more to her."

"Well, congratulations, Harris!" Ferraro said sarcastically, and the room exploded in laughter.

"My expectation is that their engagement will not lead to marriage, sir," said David coolly.

"The standards of the Economic Tower in these matters are lower than our own," said Ferraro, now deliberately goading David.

Ferraro proposed they strike first against the Knowledge Tower, citing the assassination attempt as the pretext. "Not that it isn't a damned good one," added Montoya. "And when we get the KCU report on the university investigations, it will be an indictment of the Knowledge Tower's traitorous mismanagement of the education sector." David told himself he would seize the report from Helen today and finish it himself.

Montoya said, "We've had Walters tell our Econ Tower friends that we don't feel strong enough to counter them, and Harris's girlfriend has confirmed they believe us. If we go after the Knowledge Tower now and leave the Economic Tower alone for now, it will make them even more complacent. It will confirm their assumptions. They'll just assume we went after the opponent we felt we could handle."

Ferraro waved at the screen, and all eyes turned to look at the TOP SECRET C-LEVEL slide deck that appeared. "Operation Purple Storm—5 November 2089" the first slide declared. The following slides indicated targets for roundups in Anacosta and each major City from Boston to Miami, as well as Seattle, Los Angeles-Say Diego, Say Francisco, Phoenix, and Las Vegas. Each City was broken down into so-called action areas, which then were broken down further into action wards containing Tower targets housing senior Knowledge Tower personnel. David saw that the Octavian was listed in Action Area Three, Action Ward Six. The crack Antifan paramilitary squad, the Loyalty and Honor Brigade, would seize the Knowledge Tower itself.

The KCU would be charged with drawing up lists of key Knowledge Tower personnel for detention at Beaufort, including Terwilliger and his whole family. All Knowledge Tower officers at 180 and above would be arrested. Those with Social Credit scores between 130 and 180 would come under scrutiny. Some might be useful to leave in place, and some might have been hankering for promotions and thus would cooperate with Beaufort to win them.

"And what will the White Black House do in the morning?" asked Ferraro. "Nothing. What will they be able to do? If we wait a few months, they could loose the ESF on us. So either the ESF can heed the lesson, which I don't think they will, or they'll be our next game."

"What will happen to Knowledge Tower functions?" asked Valerie Marzullo.

"Most of them are useless, or at least their absence won't be noticed for a few weeks," said Ferraro. "We'll ask the KCU to absorb the critical functions, at least at the senior managerial level. Good thing the KCU had a personnel uptick earlier this year, right, Alex?"

"What about children?" asked Marzullo.

Ferraro sighed at this petty obstacle posed from one of the few females in the room. "Take them if they're under fifteen and there's no one else who can supervise them. They can go to orphanages until their parents can pick them up. I don't need to be bothered by children." Rex could stay at the Octavian. This might be a godsend, David thought. The Antifans would carry her parents off to Beaufort that night. He would make sure Malia was working the concierge desk that night, and hopefully they would entrust Rex to her custody.

"What are we supposed to do with all these Knowledgeers once they're here at Beaufort?" asked another commander.

"We let them cool their heels for a few weeks. We're going to come up with a loyalty statement in which they can acknowledge the supremacy of the ADF, just as the Basic Law demands, or they can stay in prison. I'm counting on most of them wanting to get back to normal and their EcoBars," laughed Ferraro. "Or even their kids.

"I'm not looking for any harsh interrogations, unless we think someone we've detained knows something we need to know. But most Knowledge Tower types know precious little, so I wouldn't waste the Red Room on them. It wouldn't be fair to the cleaning staff. In fact, I imagine they'll be eager to offer us gossip to get their sorry butts out of here sooner."

Back at his desk, David curtly told Helen that he needed the report.

"Oh," she said, "I was just reading it over again."

"I'll take it from here, thank you," he said, and heard the "ping" of the electronic arrival as he sat down at his desk. He couldn't attend to it immediately, though, because Carolina called him. "David, why haven't I heard from you yet this week? Do you not love your Carolina?"

David almost stammered, partly because his mind was racing with the details of Operation Purple Storm. "No, of course I do, honey—"

"Now I already have engagements for this weekend, but how about next Saturday? I have a lovely new Italian restaurant in mind." He agreed to pick her up at the Azteca at 7 pm on November 5th.

Chapter 64
Breakthrough at the Breakfront
(Friday/Saturday, 4-5 November)

"Let's give your aunt a break," said Adam. "When you come over for your shift on Friday, just bring clothes for the entire weekend. Now that we're engaged, I think we ought to spend a little more time together, at least on weekends."

"Yes, amba-sah," she said. "But won't the building management object?" She knew the Octavian had strict rules against staff staying in residents' apartments, even as guests.

"Those don't apply to us," said Adam, "and if anyone complains, I will remind them that as a co-op board member, I should know what the rules are." He paused. "Just keep taking the back stairs and elevator, and it should be fine."

Having warned David that she would be with Adam all weekend, and David having warned her about his date with Carolina on Saturday night, the score was even. "What can we do," said David. "This is temporary. Let's just try to be transparent with each other." But even he could see the slight changes already taking place in Malia's body, the subtle thickening of her torso. She had started taking anti-nausea drugs, but how long would it be before Adam Ross noticed? David called Daniel a few times, using the codes they had devised between themselves for escape-route planning. And he gave Malia a discreet warning that she shouldn't be surprised by anything unusual that happened on her Sunday night shift. "Just make sure that Rex is all right, and stays at the Octavian," he said.

"Why shouldn't she stay at the Octavian?" asked Malia. David shrugged in a way that conveyed, "don't ask me anything else." She knew better than to press.

Malia was glad when Rex came downstairs around 9 pm to visit. Rex told her about a retreat for Knowledge Tower youth she had attended the previous weekend. "It was palatial, Melia! It was like being at a hotel. They told us all about how the country was looking to us for guidance. I was thinking about working in the Diversity Art department. We're opening up an art museum in Ploreville to bring the message there." Malia felt a pang. She had rescued Rex for normality, but that seemed to entail more normality than she had envisioned. Now Rex was seeing herself as part of the "we," the "we" that neither Malia nor David belonged to.

Rex saw the cloud cross Malia's face. They sat down in a corner of the lobby.

"I love you, Mom," she whispered, "but I can't do anything dangerous. I don't want to die. I don't want to leave my whole life here. It's safe and it's comfortable."

"I understand," said Malia softly, herself timid about the whole enterprise. "Maybe when you grow up, you can join us." To herself, she thought sadly, if she doesn't come with us this time, I will never see her again.

They played a Diversity card game in which you tried to clump together all the same colors, and then acquire mixed sets of everything. But Malia was distracted by Rex's defection, and what might happen at the Octavian on Sunday night that would require her to protect the girl. Rex knew that her words of rejection, however sweetly worded, had disturbed her mother. What could you do, she thought, you had to live your own life. Maybe not everyone was able to lead Diversity forward. But she was. She understood her mother's low Social Credit made her life harder, but why should she, Rex, suffer because of her mother's bad luck?

Adam let Malia sleep most of the day, or so he thought. He went jogging mid-morning and then met a friend for coffee mid-afternoon. Malia was stirring, so he called in the direction of her pile of blankets, "I'll be back in about two hours," hearing a sleepy "yes, amba-sah" in response.

She watched the street below, and seeing him stride purposefully toward the coffee shop on the corner, she got out of bed and began looking for cameras. David had taught her what to look for. All she saw in Adam's dresser were neatly folded shirts, shorts and underwear. The closet was also well organized. She began investigating the living room. If only she could open Adam's workscreen, but it was protected with a four-digit combination much like her choker's. The breakfront in the living room, clearly an inheritance from Adam's mother, featured assorted china that might not have been used since the civil war, including a floral teapot that seemed incongruous in this man's home. She pulled out each of two thin drawers. One contained coasters and the other his mother's death certificate, which read "Lauren Wilson Ross, May 21, 2067. Cause of death: breast cancer. Place of death: Euthanasia Palace."

Underneath the breakfront were three cabinets. One contained a set of china dinnerware and the second sheets and tablecloths. So far, boring. In the third cabinet sat a stack of old envelopes and papers. Adam wasn't likely to keep his deepest, darkest secrets in a poorly hidden stack of old papers, but she was curious, so kneeling down, she sorted through them. Malia knew some older people preferred to print out emails to study them more carefully or to keep them. Lots of anodyne communications from the Octavian Board of Directors. Coronavirus Day celebrations in the recreation room. A warning about a gang of Plores that had reportedly been committing thefts in the vicinity. Under those letters were several sheets that contained only dates and numbers, mostly in the double digits, and then cash amounts. She dared not take any of the sheets, not with another thirty-six hours left in his apartment, for fear he would find the stray sheet among her belongings, or find one missing from the stash, but she scanned them quickly for patterns. The higher the numbers, the higher the cash totals, which made sense. Perhaps it had nothing to do with the Economic Zone, but she wouldn't risk losing the opportunity. She made sure to close the cabinet door tightly.

By the time Adam returned, she was curled up on the sofa reading a book from his shelf, still in her nightgown.

"What are you reading?" he asked.

"It's about the Chinese economy, amba-sah," said Malia. Adam grunted, sat on the sofa and reached for the signaler. Nothing worth watching. He reached for Malia instead.

As the early November dusk fell, they finally stirred from the bedroom, preparing to go out to dinner. Malia wore a long-sleeved purple wool shift dress, and a new pair of black boots. In the bathroom she applied makeup, far more expertly than she had done in April. Adam nodded approvingly as she emerged. She was eager for dinner at the new Italian restaurant praised in the *Anacosta Post* for its cuisine and progressive farm-to-table procurement practices. "Each garlic bulb is lovingly cultivated by a Diverse person," the newspaper trumpeted. As Adam said, "they convince the chicken to go to the Euthanasia Palace. It's a loving farewell."

She descended via the back elevator, and met him outside the building's side entrance, which Adam called "the dog door," where the ESF privates had kidnapped her that morning. They walked two blocks to the restaurant. It was their first restaurant meal together in Anacosta.

Malia had expected that Adam would have checked with the restaurant beforehand about its Social Credit policy, as David always did, but when her armband triggered the credit sensor, it was embarrassing. "You mean my fiancée can't eat here?" Adam said, in apparent shock.

"Yes, sir, I'm afraid we don't serve anyone under 150."

"Goodness," said Adam, "she's only half that. Couldn't you just serve her a half portion?" The young Plore hostess looked sympathetic but was helpless. Violating the Economic Tower's Restaurant and Eatery division's policy on Social Credit requirements could lead to a restaurant's closure. It was even worse than a health or safety violation. Even Adam knew better than to exploit his position at the Tower by threatening the restaurant with dire consequences. Other diners waiting to be seated looked on them smugly. One less table to wait for, some thought. Adam decided he would not give them this satisfaction.

"Very well," he told the hostess. "I'll be dining in. My date will sit outside."

Malia's head swiveled in his direction. The hostess looked confused. "But it's very cold, sir."

"She's from Canada, she'll be fine," said Adam. "Hold the table for me, I'll be right back."

Malia numbly followed Adam outside where he indicated she should sit on the decorative wooden bench with iron trim. Behind it was a plate glass window through which one could see couples lifting their glasses of wine and their forkfuls of humanely killed chicken or veal, illuminated by the yellow flames of candles. "Are you really going to leave me out here in the cold while you have dinner?" Malia asked.

"Amba-sah," he reminded her. She repeated her question.

"Well, why should we both suffer because of your Social Credit deficit?" Adam responded. "I am determined to have the veal piccata tonight. And a Tuscan cabernet, 2087, which was a good year for that vintage. If you behave, I'll order some veal to bring home for you."

He pulled a cord out of his pocket—Malia suddenly recognized it must be a dog's leash—and reaching behind her head, fastened it to some hook on the choker, and then wrapped and tied the leash tightly around the back of the bench. "Just so you don't go wandering off," he said cheerfully. Nobody would see it except for possibly the couple sitting behind her in the plate glass window. One of the two men was already pointing at her back, while the other laughed with disbelief. At that point, Malia realized he must have planned this all along. He owned no dog; why would he be carrying a leash? And he knew perfectly well that most of the restaurants along this stretch of Connecticut were highly restricted, and that she was low Social Credit, because he couldn't go an hour without reminding her. "I hate you," she said aloud.

"I hate you, amba-sah," he grinned, and disappeared into the restaurant.

The first fifteen minutes were tolerable, but she began to realize that a mid-length cloth coat sufficient for the walk to the restaurant was not warm enough for the November evening, especially now that the sun had set. She shivered miserably, close to tears. The horrified hostess brought her a paper cup of tea, saying, "that's some bastard, isn't he? Don't you marry him." Squeezing her eyes shut, Malia tried to distract and warm herself with thoughts of tropical climates, the Rehoba boardwalk, jungles she would never see, the heater in the Depository that hissed steam and made the room far too hot and uncomfortable in the shoulder season. The coat sleeves were too tight for her to extract her armband, which might have provided some diversion. She could at least stick her hands in her coat pockets. Tears welled in the corners of her eyes, but she would not cry in front of the diners leaving the restaurant with their Enviro-pods, let alone the passersby. At most, they gave her a curious glance, but not one expressed any sympathy.

She ran over the few lines she had memorized of the financial documents—or at least what she thought were such—in Adam's apartment. After several minutes, she was certain she had committed them to memory:

13 June-19 June	8k	7.67	14k	1.000	3k	1.234	$69,045.04
20 June-26 June	11k	7.67	21k	1.000	6k	1.234	$103,562.76
27 June-3 July	4k	7.67	16k	1.000	4k	1.234	$76,667.11

She knew some Christian prayers, memorized during the long Sabbath afternoons from Marjory's devotionals; she silently recited them.

"I can do all things through Christ, which strengthens me." She had just finished repeating this ten times, when she looked up, and who was approaching her but her own David, with his arm around the waist of Carolina Cruz. How awful, she thought. Here she was, at her lowest ebb, shivering and weeping. No doubt her mascara had run. David was wearing his new long camel-hair coat, which suited his blond hair and fair complexion; Carolina Cruz was even more beautiful than Malia had imagined in a faux-fur jacket and a black cap and matching faux-fur gloves. They looked like Hollywood stars and she was the Little Match Girl, a story she had read in the orphanage about a poor girl who froze to death in racist pre-socialism days.

They stopped at the restaurant, and David was about to open the door for Carolina when he saw Malia sitting there, hunched over only slightly, because the leash was holding her back. His eyes blazed with gray fury at her predicament. "Give me a minute," he muttered to her.

Carolina looked at him. "What?" she asked, assuming the comment was directed at her.

"I'll be right in. Can you just go in and ask about our table?" Carolina looked dismissively down at Malia, and then swept into the restaurant.

"Is this Adam Ross's doing?" David spat out. She nodded. "It's a 150 minimum. Adam decided he would let me sit out here while he ate."

David cursed roundly. He took off his coat and placed it over her, inserting her arms into its sleeves, and tucking the coat tenderly around her torso. "What's this behind you?" he asked, feeling the back of the bench. His eyes opened wide. "He's tied you to this bench? With this dog leash?

"Well, sweetheart, I always say revenge is a dish best eaten cold, but I have to admit he is trying me sorely. Is this a little better?"

"Yes, thank you," she said, almost formally.

"This won't last much longer," he promised her. An onlooker might have thought he was referring only to her suffering on the bench. He then followed Carolina into the restaurant. Now Malia was comfortable and even dozed slightly, like a Scandinavian baby left in the carriage outside the restaurant, which she had heard was their custom.

"Aren't you the perfect gentleman?" said Carolina as he sat down at their table. His date didn't seem altogether pleased that he had lent his coat to the shivering woman outside.

"What else could I do? She's freezing out there," said David shortly. He realized with dismay that their table was next to Adam Ross's. The bearded Economic Tower intelligence director was reading his armband news feed while leisurely eating what seemed to be veal piccata. He raised his wine glass and inspected the light shining on its contents.

"Well, what IS she doing out there, anyway?" asked Carolina, annoyed. She knew David's girlfriend worked as an informant for the ADF but wouldn't have recognized her. She just assumed David had come to the rescue of an unknown humble young woman.

"I guess her Social Credit number is too low to eat here. I'd like to beat up the bastard who did this to her." He would not confront Ross directly, but could not resist a dig that he knew Malia's tormentor would overhear.

"Take back your coat," ordered Adam.

David was incredulous. "What did you just say to me?" Carolina reached out, placing her manicured hand with the long this-week-blue fingernails on his armband.

Adam locked eyes with him. "I said take back your coat. It's none of your business. If I want her to freeze, she's going to freeze."

"No, she is not," said David calmly. "If you lay one hairy paw on that coat, you'll be in the gutter, I promise."

"If you want to mess with the intelligence director of the Economic Tower, be my guest," said Adam. "I strongly advise you to take back your coat before I call ESF personnel to cart you off."

"Which would be a violation of Basic Law Seven," David observed, "in which the ESF has no arrest authority outside of the Economic Zones. The travesty of EcoLand and Rosebud notwithstanding." His pointed but dry response had defused the mounting conflict. Adam turned back to his armband phone. David, who had not wanted to bring the Antifan Defense Forces into the fray, was relieved. All he needed was for Beaufort to find out that he had beaten up Adam Ross on Connecticut Avenue or countered with a threat from the ADF, just to defend that pesky girlfriend informant.

Ross finished his meal sooner than might have been expected, signaling for the check several minutes later and declining dessert. The waitron brought an Enviro-pod with what David assumed was Malia's meal. Ross paid, and left; David followed to retrieve the coat because Ross would likely dump it on the sidewalk if he didn't steal it outright.

Adam was untying Malia from the bench when David came out. "Allow me to retrieve the coat," David said, lifting it off her lap before it could slide to the ground.

"Thank you so much, amba-sah!" she gushed at him. Color had returned to her face.

"At your service, madame," said David, winking at her. Faces in the window looked at them curiously. Why was the handsome blond man taking an interest in the situation?

Adam glared at him. "You'd better be careful who you mess with. If I make the effort to find out who you are, you'll be sorry."

"I'm not even interested in who you are," said David coldly. "All I needed to hear was Economic Tower before I started to fall asleep. Have a good evening, ma'am," and he reentered the restaurant, handing the coat to the attendant. Carolina was visibly peeved at his absences and his distraction by that strange little woman on the bench. Why did he have to meddle in other people's business? David spent the rest of the meal courting her back into good humor, but now he couldn't have cared less whether she took him home to spend the night with her. Even though she occasionally reached under the cozy table to massage his knee, which was admittedly distracting.

"Thank you so much, amba-sah." Adam mimicked her harshly as they headed back to the Octavian.

"What was I supposed to do? I was freezing. If he hadn't lent me his coat, I'd have gotten pneumonia by now—amba-sah."

"No, you wouldn't have. You're just incredibly weak. Pathetic. You showed me disrespect by allowing him to put that coat on you. And then he gave me grief in the restaurant in front of other customers. I'm going to remember that when we return to the apartment."

"Who treats their fiancée like this? Is this what I should expect for the rest of my life?"

Adam looked hard at her. "Yes, until your behavior improves. Or maybe your life won't be as long as you think it will be." Who would notice or care about a missing Diversan-American dependent in Mexico?

"What did he say to you in the restaurant, amba-sah?" she asked curiously.

Adam ignored her, striding several paces ahead with the Enviro-pod. He disappeared into the front entrance of the building, leaving her to return to the apartment via the side entrance. When she reached Adam's apartment, she stood outside, breathing deeply, collecting her strength before she knocked. The door opened, he pulled her into the apartment, and she saw he had already placed the whips, handcuffs, and the dreaded steel headbox on the coffee table. She hoped that after he had sated his anger, he would at least let her eat the contents of the other Enviro-pod. She could smell the veal and she was very hungry.

Chapter 65

Death and Destruction on Connecticut Avenue

(Sunday/Monday, 6-7 November)

Around 10 pm Sunday evening, Beaufort was humming. Were it January 1st, Adam Ross's intelligence division would have opened its 24-hour alert warning center, which would have noted a flurry of activity on the roads around Beaufort and investigated accordingly. But it was only November 6th, and only a skeletal overnight staff was on duty at the Economic Tower. Its job was to monitor communications from Economic Zones and overseas, and to compile a digest of important economic developments for the senior leadership to read in the morning. No one had told them to pay attention to breaking developments in their own City.

Adam Ross was preparing for an early bedtime, luxuriating in the thought of reclaiming his bed from that low credit fiancée-strumpet, who was downstairs tending the concierge desk whence he had rescued her in June, not that she appreciated it one whit. He was still smarting from the insult on Saturday night, which admittedly was entirely of his own making. Even beating Malia and withholding her dinner until after midnight, and then feeding her a few bites of veal while finishing the majority of the second portion himself, had done little to assuage his wounded pride. He experienced a bout of severe indigestion toward morning. Malia did a poor job of hiding her satisfaction, which led to more recrimination.

David had shown up at Beaufort around 9 pm after trying to nap most of the day, back in his own bed. He had left Carolina's apartment as soon as possible Sunday morning, over her somewhat mechanical protests. He convened with other action commanders in the ready room down the hall from Ferraro's office.

The ADF had divided the City into ten action areas for Purple Storm. David would serve as Commander for Action Area Six, which turned out to be a swath of Northeast Anacosta, a less prestigious area without many targets. Walters was deputy to Steve Rosen in Action Area Three, which covered the Octavian, as well as the largest chunk of high-end Knowledgeers in Anacosta. David studied his list of towers and names, which totaled forty-three at five towers: Emerald, Silver Spring, Lamberton, Arcola, and Kemp Mill. Only several names on the list were over 200; most were at the 150-175 level. He was glad that his force consisted mostly of his own KCU officers, including Chung and Patel as deputies. They had already met to discuss each of the Towers and the tactics to follow so that no one could escape the cordon at each building. Just in case someone at one tower under attack sought to warn friends at another of the Antifan raid, several ADF officers would be discreetly stationed around each building to prevent unauthorized departures before the Antifan squads could arrive. Vans or passenger trucks would deploy to each building in an area just before the specified raid time to cart the prisoners off to Beaufort. Several officers would peel off after departing each building to accompany those detainees to Beaufort, so the towers with the greatest number of targets were scheduled first. Before dawn, the Antifan mortuary crew would patrol the affected streets to dispose of any corpses, presumably those of the Knowledge Tower officers.

David looked around—there was Rosen, who Antifan-saluted him with a smile. Walters next to him was tense and eager, like a hound prepared to spring forward with the hunt. Valerie Marzullo, whose question about children had irritated Ferraro, would cover Area Four, Friendship Heights and Rockville South, formerly Bethesda. Van Worden was assigned Area Five, downtown Anacosta, north of the destroyed Depository. David wondered whether his assigned territory in a somewhat obscure corner of Anacosta reflected his plummeting status, but he reminded himself that he was technically Charlton's deputy, and being handed an area at all was to his credit.

Ferraro entered the room with Montoya by his side. Gemma Carpenter was home tonight.

"Antifan commanders, I have an order for you tonight!" he began, in the now-traditional phrasing. The entire on-duty workforce was watching from their units.

"Our loyalty and honor!" the commanders responded, saluting faithfully. The workforce echoed the salute.

"Tonight, and into the morning, we will arrest most of the senior officers of the Knowledge Tower. This is the culmination of seven months of hard work by the Knowledge Crimes Unit." Ferraro waved gracefully in David's direction. "Since the beginning of the Diversity Justice Republic, the ADF has been charged with maintaining of the integrity of the other Towers. This responsibility was given to us because of our struggle during the civil war, without which there would be no Republic. Who shed their blood for the revolution? Who gave up their youth?"

"We did!" called the commanders, although few were old enough to have experienced the war themselves as combatants.

"Even though the third President of the United States was a racist and a slaveholder, I wish to quote him. He said that the tree of liberty needed to be refreshed once in a while with the blood of patriots," said Ferraro. "Let me suggest that every few decades perhaps we need to refresh the tree of Diversity with the blood of its enemies, the timeservers, the Privilegeers, the bureaucrats for whom the revolution means comfortable living. Tonight is that night. The assassination attempt against me by a Knowledgeer was the final straw.

"You will bring the officials on your lists back to Beaufort tonight. We aim to avoid bloodshed, but you are authorized to meet resistance with deadly force. Under no circumstances should anyone on your lists be at large by tomorrow morning, whatever this requires from you. No Antifan conscientiously discharging their duties should be punished.

"Most of our prisoners will be gently treated, but we will not permit them to leave—let alone resume their jobs until they have signed the Diversity Statement of Antifan Supremacy, drawn up by myself personally with the assistance of the KCU and General Counsel. All Tower officials in our custody will undergo reinvestigation before being allowed to resume their duties. We are also drawing up a list of Knowledge Tower officials whom we may deem suitable to replace others. Some of the lower-level detainees may be fitting to take over the jobs, and I need not remind you they will likely be grateful to those who appointed them. Any questions?"

"Sir," asked Van Worden, "when do we plan to notify the White Black House of the operation?"

Ferraro looked upward, his eyes trailing along the ceiling. "Oh, I imagine around 5 am." The commanders laughed, and applauded him for half a minute before dispersing.

In the ECU, the staging area for Rosen and Walters' force, Walters conducted a Wurro service. Soldiers filtered into the packed room from other units, sensing this was not a night to appeal to tender Mother Earth. Walters stripped to the waist, although there was no time for body paint, and raised the statue above his head, so that it hovered nearly nine feet above the floor.

"The mana of Wurro is powerful and constant! The mana of Wurro is with the ADF tonight! Let us bow to the great Lord Wurro and plead for his continued favor on our mission!"

The troops chanted, stomping fiercely in place while popping their zingos. Walters had added a new chant in honor of tonight's operation: "Kill the traitors, bring them in, Wurro power's here to win!" It could be heard on the first floor in the atrium, thirty-nine floors below.

Adam Ross was sound asleep at 2 am when he received a frantic call from Will. "Adam, there's an ADF operation tonight, they're rounding up Knowledge Tower personnel. At least I think only Knowledge Tower personnel. They're rampaging through this building right now. They're taking away my neighbor."

Adam called Pernella. "Do you want to activate the ESF tonight?"

Pernella hesitated. "If we can't stop the ADF, I'd rather not lose our forces in a hopeless cause." Adam had proposed sending the 23rd ESF, based in Laurel, MD, into the City. This was the best equipped and largest unit the Tower had, but the ADF didn't necessarily know about it. Yet.

"Keep our powder dry, then?" he asked her.

"Yes," she said. "But now we really have to keep moving forward, because otherwise, we'll be next. Tonight is proof that our steady course of action has been the correct one."

He heard pounding on doors down his hallway, and one door was knocked off its hinges, the noise resounding through the night. The retired ladies next door were spared. No one answered his call to the front desk. He found his 9mm in the shirt box in a drawer where Malia had not looked carefully, and sat in the living room cradling it in his hands, prepared to return fire if Antifans came crashing through his door. Even if Knowledgeers were the primary target, Adam had no great confidence that the Antifans would leave him in peace given his prominence. Under no circumstances would he go to Beaufort alive.

The Octavian, with its dozens of Knowledgeers, was the first stop for the ADF in Area Three. At 2 am sharp, Walters had opened the door to the Octavian with a slashing wave of his armband, followed by a wave of black-uniformed, balaclava-wearing Antifans who swarmed up the stairs to their designated targets. Jorge showed them how to prop open the wide sliding door, lest they shatter the lobby plate windows. Here was the cold, narrow-eyed Walters of the Depository raid back in April, not the more amiable comrade who had praised Malia's Antifan spirit to her face. He pretended not to recognize her. "Go sit in that corner," he said to her and Jorge. An Antifan trooper took their armbands for temporary safekeeping, probably a precaution to ensure they did not alert any residents. The ADF unit occupied their desk and lobby as a staging area. Steve Rosen was down the block managing the raid at the equally prestigious Hamilton. The goal was to be out of both buildings and onto the third in twenty minutes.

Walters was fielding calls from the troops upstairs. "No, not 1205," he said. "1207." Apparently, the lists had confused a retired Econocrat with a senior Knowledge Tower religious functionary. "Seize the workscreens," he told the troops in a particularly sensitive apartment. "We'll send a stretcher up," he said on a third call. That functionary was allegedly recovering from an operation and the troops were sufficiently convinced to call for clarification. Thirty seconds later, two auxiliary troops—pulled from the academy ranks—came running to the elevators with the stretcher. We have doctors at Beaufort, Walters thought grimly to himself.

Within five minutes, residents in hastily donned slacks and shirts and jackets, their hair awry, were exiting the elevators, hurried along by shouting Antifans. Troops slapped or struck the few who tried to argue or plead their case. But most of the detainees were in shock, in complete disbelief that anything inconvenient or troublesome could happen to 'them,' let alone be dragged off from their homes in the middle of the night by crass Antifans.

One of Walters' captains found a Knowledgeer hiding in the spa locker room. For that sin, he would be forced into the van wearing only his workout clothes in the chill overnight air. Back in the lobby, Malia stood, arms crossed, watching the exodus of Octavian residents, who only hours ago had breezed by her with their customary arrogance as she chirped "amba-mam" and "amba-sah." Only last night had not some of these same people walked by her as she huddled, shivering on that bench? Some of the detainees had even been among the restaurant patrons who had ignored her suffering. "A little sweet, isn't it?" said Walters to her, reading her face, as he consulted with the female troopers marking off one apartment after another. The selected apartments were emptying out quickly.

Then Malia saw Leighton and Belinda stumbling out the main stairwell into the lobby. Leighton looked even paler than usual. Belinda's eyes lit up when she saw Malia. "Melia! Melia! Take care of Rex, please!" she called as a trooper pushed her forward. Malia called back, "I will, amba-mam! Don't worry!" To herself, bitterly recollecting Leighton's austere reassurance after the Rosebud and EcoLand raids, she said, "I'm sure it'll all be sorted out by the authorities."

"That was 808," said Walters. "Are we closed out?" Another captain confirmed that fifty-eight persons had been located and were now in the vans. Two were traveling and one was not at home. When asked about the whereabouts of Mr. Cordero, Jorge confirmed that he might be with a girlfriend at her apartment at the Argonne. Walters called Van Worden, the relevant area commander, to relay that information.

"OK, we're outta here," Walters spoke into his armband, "Octavian close out. All units heading out, one minute to launch." Rosen's crew was finishing up at the Hamilton.

A minute later, the building was quiet again. Jorge and Malia refastened their armbands, and began straightening up the lobby. Jorge's quick response to prop open the door had spared the plate glass in the lobby. Residents had dropped items here and there—a small notebook, a toothbrush, a comb—that Malia stashed behind the counter for when people returned to the building. She took a quick look at the notebook to see whether it was worth passing to David. They heard the screech of vehicles moving out at high speeds; a minute later the remaining residents began calling the front desk in fear and anger. Jorge took a walk through the hallways to note obvious damage or needed repairs. Adam Ross fell asleep with the firearm in his hand on the end table, waking just before 7 am with the dawn.

Chapter 66
Aftermath
(Monday, 7 November)

The sun rose harshly over the bruised and sullen Cities, reflecting not just off the glass towers but the glass shards littering some streets.

By dawn the activity hive at Beaufort had gravitated down to the intake and jail cell area, as prisoners were marched off to their cells, their belongings and armbands confiscated and tagged, and their clothing traded for the green paper pajamas. Protests and insults from the privileged Social Crediteers were met with raised eyebrows, then stony glances, then blows if they imprudently continued. The Knowledgeers who were not already sleeping, or lying morosely on their bunks, brimmed with anger as they contemplated the treachery of the brutal Antifans, or, a few hours later when adrenalin subsided, with fear. The most enterprising among them were already calculating how to most efficiently appease their captors and return to their homes. Knowledge Tower Director Terwilliger and his family were in VIP prisoner quarters but Terwilliger would be the first to sign the Diversity Doctrine of ADF Supremacy and go home that night. The kitchens were preparing the first meals for distribution at 8 am.

The commanders convened in the ready room once more before disbanding. The operation had been an unalloyed success. Anacosta had seen the most intense roundups, but no East Coast City was spared. On the West Coast, more surgical raids timed to coincide with main Beaufort's had apprehended about forty senior Knowledge Tower bureaucrats, mostly connected with Hollywood and the technology sector. In total, the ADF had arrested 568 Knowledge Tower functionaries with 150 or above Social Credit scores. One's credit score did not necessarily condemn one, though. Ferraro had set aside some who seemed sympathetic to the ADF, or who had some talent he thought worth protecting. Left alone, for example, were Hollywood stars who regularly appeared in pro-Antifan movies such as *Capture of Charlottesville* and *Dawn at the Border*, and their director, as well as the chief engineer of the Great Virtual Network, whom Ferraro thought could be easily steered to projects of interest to the ADF.

Three Knowledgeers in Anacosta and one in Boston had been killed when they resisted; Candiss Yardley on David's squad was knifed by a Knowledgeer. As of 6 am Beaufort's medical staff was patching up the wound to her torso, and she was alert, much to David's relief.

The handoff to the Octavian day shift took longer than usual. Workers were already heading upstairs to paint and repair and erase memories of the brutal night. Malia deliberated whether to go to Adam's apartment and retrieve her clothes, or to see how Rex was doing. She texted Rex, "Will be there soon. Stay put." As soon as the Antifans restored her armband, she had called Rex to reassure her and tell her to go to back to bed. She took the main elevator—David had been right about nobody caring about such proprieties on this Monday morning—and approached Adam's apartment carefully. She texted him, "Outside your door," but after a minute, he had not responded. She knocked tentatively, partly because she was scared and partly because he would presumably not see an Antifan behind that timid knock.

"Who is it?" he called out.

"It's me, Melia," she responded. When he opened the door, Malia first saw his bloodshot eyes, and then the weapon in his hand. He pushed her aside to look up and down the hallway, decided it was not a trap after all, and gestured her inside.

"I'll be staying with Rex," she said. "Her parents were taken away."

"You do too much for that brat," he said. "What was it like downstairs? I assume you couldn't answer the phones while the Antifans were in the building."

"They took Jorge's and my armbands," said Malia, "and had us sit in a corner. At least they didn't ask us for anything. They seemed to have all the information they needed." Only now did she realize how important her information, her nuggets of gossip relayed over several months, had been to enabling the ADF to proceed smoothly through the building last night and discern between important and trivial Knowledgeers. She had provided many of those same nuggets to Adam, once Beaufort vetted them for passage to the Economic Tower, but he had no real use for them at this stage of his empire building. They had just allowed him to pretend he was overseeing an intelligence apparatus.

"Only Knowledge Tower?" he asked her.

"Yes, amba-sah," she said, remembering her manners, although he seemed too preoccupied to care.

"All right," he said, "at least I know where to find you. You might as well move your stuff downstairs." He seemed to know where the Andrews apartment lay. "I have to go to work."

"Today, amba-sah?"

"Today, more than ever."

Adam decided to walk from the Octavian to the Economic Tower, which would normally have taken about fifty minutes. He had expected to see more damage; however, except for the piles of glass shards in front of the Hamilton, the most disturbing thing was the hushed quiet instead of the normal bustle of a new workweek. Except for Plores heading to their menial jobs, he saw few commuters on the street. Perhaps the Plores hadn't even realized what had happened overnight, not yet. He took a slight detour around Dupont Circle, and on one side street passed by a disheveled woman in a faux fur coat weeping bitterly in a pocket park between two towers. Perhaps she had fled her own tower during the night and was afraid to return home. Maybe her friends who lived here had disappeared and she was uncertain where to go next. Adam shrugged it off.

Adam went up to his office, and began scrolling through the electronic mail. Pernella was calling a meeting for 9:30 am. The group would look to him for authoritative summaries of the night's events. But what did he know, other than that his own building had been ransacked by Antifans like foxes raiding a chicken house?

He called Will into his office. Will closed the door behind him when he entered. He was carrying a folder with a sheaf of photographs, from what Adam could see.

"What are your Antifan friends saying?" he asked Will. If all that partying with Walters had a purpose, it should be apparent now.

"I can't reach Walters. Maybe he's sleeping off the raids at home," said Will. "I reached Jeff," one of the Antifans who had attended his party, "and all he told me was don't worry, it's not about the Social Tower. You can sleep tonight."

"Great," said Adam, now realizing the limitations of his thin informer network.

"Look, I have something to show you," said Will. "Remember you asked me to check the street cameras for Melia just in case they caught her with that mysterious blond guy?"

"Yeah, you never got back to me on that," said Adam.

"That's because we didn't catch her with any guys, blond or not. She's not out and about much. But I kept the routine requirement out, and look what came in late on Friday."

Will had printed off several copies of the photograph, zoomed and otherwise, in which a blond man in a dark jacket folding an umbrella was opening a sportscar door for Malia. In another photo, they were kissing on the sidewalk, the man's arms around her protectively. "Wisconsin Avenue, October 23rd," said Will, "Remember that really rainy, blustery night?"

"That was the night after I proposed to her, that bitch," said Adam, but not angrily, almost reflectively. She looked like a drowned rat, the umbrella must have been the man's. Only Malia would be dumb enough to wander Anacosta in the rain without an umbrella. But his attention was captured by the man. "Holy Mother Earth, that's the bastard who caused me trouble on Saturday night at Pulmonella!"

"What?" asked Will. Adam explained about the blond man who insisted on covering Malia with his own coat while he, Adam, was trying to enjoy a simple Diversity-provenanced dinner inside and who then rudely resisted Adam's suggestion he take back his coat. And did not seem intimidated at all by Adam's mention of his position as the Econ Tower's intelligence director.

"You've got worse problems than competition for Melia," said Will. "Do you know why he couldn't have cared less about your job?"

Adam looked up at Will sullenly.

"Because that's Commander David Harris of the Antifan Defense Forces. He's the deputy commander of the Knowledge Crimes Unit at Beaufort. You're lucky he didn't brawl with you in the street, because I'm afraid you would have come out the worse, my friend. Now we know who went with her to TerraCity, which tells us this relationship has been going on a long time.

"But now we have to worry about how much we've told her or she's picked up from us that ended up in Antifan hands. Maybe this is how they heard about our experiments in the chemical factory? At which she was an honored guest in July? And my guess is that it's no accident she's become acquainted with you, and with us, because he didn't seem in the least surprised she was with you, did he? He didn't admit to a relationship with her? He was just pretending to be a strange gentleman concerned about how cold she was on the bench?"

Each new fact from Will hit Adam like a blow. He held his head in his hands, looking down at the desk. "I thought she was OUR informant!" he moaned.

"Adam, you're my friend, but I think we've committed a serious security faux pas here. Or two or ten. You're lucky that we're our own guardians, or someone would be within their rights to clap us in security jail." Will thought, they dangled her like a dog treat in front of Adam and he snapped at it. How many women would have put up with this sadistic nonsense from Adam without another agenda?

"But Antifan commanders don't date low Social Crediteers," Adam objected lamely.

"What makes you think she's really a low Social Crediteer?" Will countered. "She could be a 200-pointer using the identity of a low Social Crediteer just to fool you. I mean, I don't know that's the case here, but it would certainly be within the ADF's ability to create that identity and give her the armband of someone with 70 points. If that's the case, our Melia is a great actress.

"Do you know who this woman really is?" asked Will. "Look, it's time for the staff meeting. Let's just get through it and then we'll figure out how to save our necks."

Malia remembered after leaving Adam's apartment that she needed to check in with Beaufort herself. She knocked on the Andrewses' door, wheeling her suitpod behind her. Rex opened the door, and threw her arms around Malia, sobbing. Before anyone else could see or hear, Malia edged her way into the apartment. Things were still in disarray. Desk drawers had been pulled open and computer workscreens confiscated. Apparently the Andrewses were of special interest to the ADF. "I was afraid to touch anything," said Rex, "what if they come back?"

"It must have been terrifying," she said to the girl.

"Weren't you frightened?" Rex cried, "but you weren't asleep when they came. They almost knocked down the door." She described how four Antifans had piled into the apartment, shoving Leighton into a corner, pulling the cowering Belinda from bed. "You have three minutes to get dressed," the leader said. "You won't need much. You're going to Beaufort."

The leader asked her, "How old are you?"

"Fifteen," she said, to which he replied, "good, you can stay here." Younger children were being gathered in the basement recreation room for transport to local orphanages.

As they shoved her parents out the door, Belinda had called back to her, "Look for Melia! Melia will take care of you!" And then they were gone, perhaps forever. Rex sat on the sofa, pulling her knees to her chest, crying. She was afraid to venture forth from the apartment. Her armband phone wasn't working, at least not during the raid. She was afraid to go back to bed, not that she could have slept. She stared out the window, watching vehicles flashing red sirens moving silently up and down the avenue in the darkest hours before dawn. Eventually she ate a bowl of cereal. As she ate, Rex was thrilled to finally see Malia's texts pop up on the screen. *"Don't worry, they're gone. Your mom said take care of u."*

Malia excused herself, and went into the parents' bedroom, closing the door. She called David. He had only slept about two hours, but was glad to hear from her. She told him about the papers in the cabinet. "I don't know if they mean anything, but they were hidden under stuff that clearly didn't matter."

"He's gone to work?" said David. "I'll notify Steve and they'll send a crew down here. In all the chaos, nobody will think it's odd. They can copy on site and leave everything in place when they leave." He was glad to hear how efficiently the Octavian operation had gone under Walters. He told Malia that his crew had finished by 4 am, and, except for Yardley's injury, it had been uneventful. "They're Social Crediteers, they know how to obey," he said ironically. He had assured his captives that they would just be facing a routine administrative interview and if they cooperated, would go home quickly. "I don't mind lying to keep the peace," he told her.

Within forty minutes, a crew of outside painters showed up at the Octavian, breezed by the witting day shift manager, and spent twenty minutes in 1104, presumably touching up spots that had been scraped during the tumultuous night. If any residents wondered why they were painting in the apartment of the notorious Economic Towercrat, who presumably had not been detained, no one dared ask. Adam was sufficiently disliked that no one would risk their own freedom to inform him later. As they lingered over breakfast, the elderly ladies next door, hearing the painters, discussed the joyous possibility that the scowling man who played Bee-fa music late at night might have been mistaken for a Knowledgeer and carted off to Beaufort. They had never dared even rap on the wall, so intimidated they were, even though he was only a cis-white male. They knew he brought up that poor sweet night concierge on occasion in the middle of the night to abuse her, because they heard her cries. This saddened them. "As feminists, we really should defend her," they would say, and then lapse into silence again.

The news programs were finally broadcasting from the studios at the Knowledge Tower, so everyone knew what had happened the night before, at least from the ADF perspective. The ADF media officers were now in control of the studios.

"ADF Launches Surgical Strike Against Knowledge Tower," said the Diversity One Channel. The newscaster, local celebrity Figaro Akinaba, 250, was in his usual place, but he looked visibly nervous. Antifan troops stood in the studio to make sure he cooperated. "You can keep your job, as we define it, or you can go to Beaufort," said the Antifan media commander—apparently his new boss. Figaro preferred to read what he was given, which was his usual procedure in any case. Knowledge Tower, Beaufort Tower, whatever. When you had such a handsome face and gleaming white teeth, and women left flowers and themselves at your door several times a week, you should not tinker with the formula for success.

"Responding to the attempted assassination of Antifan Defense Forces Director Victor Ferraro, the ADF last night struck at the Knowledge Tower, which was behind the attack," read Figaro. "A Knowledge Tower official attempted to shoot Ferraro last week, but the Tower refused to cooperate with the investigation and the White Black House refused to intervene."

Footage rolled of large towers lit up against the early morning sky; knots of Antifan officers standing in front of another building; Candiss Yardley sitting upright in a Beaufort infirmary bed summoning a dazed look at the command of the camera operator before tucking into her breakfast; and a group of Diverse citizens thanking Antifan soldiers for protecting Diversity.

Figaro vaguely referred to "several hundred Knowledge Tower officials in temporary detention," and said, "they will be asked to sign affirmations of ADF supremacy per the Basic Law of the Republic," and then released. "The ADF says no one will be harmed but Diversity and the Republic must be protected."

The ADF had located a dozen or so Knowledge Tower officials who were willing to complain on air about having been discriminated against. They were looking forward to "new, fairer management," according to a young black woman who seemed to be the spokesperson. Malia thought she had seen one or two of the group around Beaufort, but was too tired to think any more about it. She lay down on the Andrewses' sofa and fell asleep. Rex brought two blankets and gently laid them over her. "I'll go anywhere with you," she whispered.

Director Ferraro had returned to his Beaufort suite by 10 am, where an Antifan media camera crew was waiting to record a grimly triumphant statement to the workforce. "Whether you serve as an analyst, a secretary, a guard, a doctor, or a soldier on the front lines of fighting for Diversity, I salute you. Last night our combined efforts made possible the detention of over 550 Knowledge Tower officials. It was the culmination of our work all this year.

"Our only goal is to ensure that the Knowledge Tower adheres to the Basic Law that affirms the preeminence of the Antifan Defense Forces as the guardian of the revolution. As each Knowledge official here at Beaufort signs the affirmation, and we have no further need for interrogation, they will be released and may return to their homes and workplaces," said Ferraro. Aha, thought David, watching with the other KCU officers. A bit ambiguous on whether we in fact have no need for further interrogation, basically permitting us to detain individuals as long as we see fit. Knowing that the Director would ask the KCU for such confirmations, he thought he could exercise his authority to keep the Andrewses in Beaufort for several weeks.

"You may be interested in knowing that I spoke with President Avadaughter this morning," Ferraro continued. "She congratulated us on the result of the raids and herself said that the ADF was the cornerstone of the Diversity Revolution. So, when our detractors say otherwise, remember the words of our great President and carry on." It had been wise to call Avadaughter shortly after dawn, her most lucid moment of the day, and before Peace-Williams could make his way to the White Black House. When an angry Peace-Williams called Ferraro afterward, he accused Ferraro of taking advantage of poor Avadaughter, to which Ferraro smoothly said, "I thought that our dear President Avadaughter was in fact in charge of our government. So, it was to her I directed my call. Have you taken over yet, Michael? I didn't think so."

After hanging up on Ferraro, Peace-Williams then called Pernella Smith, and said, "You need to keep pushing forward on our plan. If you don't take this seriously, the Antifans will be dragging you off to Beaufort." With the Vice-President's instructions ringing in her head, the Director of the Economic Tower went into her 9:30 am staff meeting. Adam Ross seemed unaccustomedly rattled by the events of the night, his hand shaking as he lifted a coffee cup. However, his deputy, Will Kendall, promised her that they would expedite the ability of the Econ Tower to assume its rightful place at the forefront of the revolution, Basic Law be damned.

"When Michael takes over from Avadaughter," said Pernella, "he will sign an amendment to the Basic Law. But he won't do that until we are ready to assume power, otherwise the ADF will strike first."

"I'll be meeting with our main Beaufort informant Wednesday night," said Will. "I'll make sure the Antifan line hasn't changed. Before this week, he was telling me the

ADF might strike the Knowledge Tower, but they were leery of attacking us. So far, that's playing out, but last night might make them more confident."

"Thank you, Will," said Pernella serenely. Even as they spoke, a hundred shipping containers were arriving at the Port of Baltimore after a six-week voyage from China, ostensibly with self-driving cars and turbines, but in fact with tens of thousands of electronic rifles and missile launcher parts. Pernella's Chinese lover had agreed to send covert shipments of arms and weapons to the ESF that would be disguised in shipping containers of heavy machinery.

Under the direction of the ESF units charged with guarding the port, the containers were swiftly unloaded in secret warehouses. By the time the Antifan informant at the port reported to his Beaufort handler, the contents would have reached ESF units throughout the East Coast. By day's end, Pernella decreed that the Economic Tower would ramp up its self-defense measures and with the tacit support of the White Black House, build its Economic Strike Force to achieve parity with the ADF by next spring.

Chapter 67
What We Don't Know
(Tuesday/Wednesday, 8-9 November)

Adam and Will were doing a damage assessment of what Malia might have told the ADF. They agreed that whatever she had told them, it wasn't enough, not yet, for the ADF to reach out and arrest them. The ADF knew about the experiments, but Econ Tower sources in the White Black House had confirmed the President's lack of interest in following up, or more precisely, her incapacity to be interested, especially with Peace-Williams wielding the real decision-making power. If Social Crediteers had to die to achieve this extraordinary scientific and security breakthrough, so be it. Malia might have mentioned private bank accounts in Mexico, which were illegal, but Adam doubted the ADF would have the ability to locate them. And if the ADF couldn't access the bank accounts, they wouldn't know how much was secreted there or how the account holders had acquired the funds, right? "China," said Will, "she would have mentioned the Chinese angle here."

"But" said Adam, "she knows nothing about what the Chinese are paying us for."

"I hope so," said Will, "otherwise we are doomed."

"If they knew now," said Adam, "we'd be in Beaufort." The pair contemplated this frightening possibility. "Should I just break her neck tonight? I know where she's staying."

"For goodness sakes," said Will. "And then don't you think the Antifans are going to drag you off and beat you to death in their basement? They might even arrest me. I hate to think of her getting away with having done this to us."

"So we're just going to wait around until the ADF puts together the pieces?"

The Chinese shipment that had arrived at Baltimore yesterday would normally have been welcome news for Adam and Will, but could they afford to wait another four or five months, they wondered.

Will said that he had arranged to meet with Walters at the bar on Wednesday; maybe he would be able to get a sense of the ADF's current posture toward the Economic Tower.

They were now inclined to keep the small jet plane in the hangar at the Zone on ready alert for a flight to Mexico. The pilot was an ESF officer of Mexican ancestry who was ready to live in a more agreeable country. For half a million dollars, he would fly them to Matamoros. The DJR and Texas had a mutual extradition treaty that made fleeing to Texas a risky proposition. From Matamoros they would travel to Mexico City.

"Take Melia on that plane," suggested Will, "and we can dump her overboard into the Gulf of Mexico—don't tell me you want to keep her after all this!"

"I don't know how much harm she's really done us." said Adam. "She's not that bright. I find her submissiveness delightful. And her tits are beautiful. I don't know how easy it would be to find a Mexican girl like her."

"For a few million dollars, you'd be surprised how easy it is. They have tits in Mexico."

"I'd be more convinced if you could manage to find tits for yourself here," retorted Adam.

"She's only submissive because she's figured out this works to keep fooling you, and me too," said Will. "She's no more submissive than I am."

"What if we at least brought her out one more time to the Zone?" suggested Adam, "That's our territory. We've got the truth serum and we could find out exactly how dangerous she is to us. Then we'll figure out whether we can afford to stay in the country, or leave her alive. But she doesn't have to leave the Zone again. We could dump her with the workers." They agreed that if a truth serum was near completion, it would be a shame not to test it on a genuinely deceptive subject.

Will arrived at Buster Frog's a few minutes early. Thanks to it being a Wednesday night with no major game on air, he was easily able to snag a private corner booth. He refrained from attaching any listening devices, knowing full well that Antifans swept restaurant tables before they spoke confidentially. In fact, he hoped Walters would take such precautions, which might indicate a willingness to talk frankly. He was pleased that Walters had been almost eager to meet him on a weekday night with no real sports incentive.

"Hey, Will." Walters slid his large frame into the booth. "How you doing, buddy?" He ran his armband arm under the table, discreetly, the Antifan thought.

"Great, Brian, thanks. Really amazing work you guys did on Sunday night. I guess we're agnostic at the Social Tower on these issues—hey, I'm just buying cookware for hospitals, remember—but that showed real spirit. I'm glad someone still remembers what the revolution was all about," said Will. Walters seemed pleased.

They ordered hamburgers—neither worried about having to pay the carbon markup—and several rounds of beer.

"You're not coming after us next, though, are you?" asked Will. "I don't think the Social Tower gives you guys any problems, right? We just do our jobs." Because Walters looked a little inquiring, Will added, "Just some idle conversation this week, but a few people who don't really follow politics were worried."

"No one has to worry," said Walters, taking a long draught of beer. "We got who we wanted." He smiled at Will with his narrow green eyes. "Now, maybe the Economic Tower will have to worry in a year or two, but we're a little busy finishing the business we've started."

Eventually, Will managed to move the conversation around to Commander Harris. "Do you know this guy? He caused a sensation at a restaurant I was at on Saturday night. There was some young woman who'd been left in the cold on a bench by her date, and he insisted on giving her his coat until the date finished eating and came out again."

Walters had gotten an earful about that night from Carolina, but pretended otherwise. "Hadn't heard that, but it sounds like him. Yeah, he's a Plore by birth. They're always going around being nice to women. It's that kind of softness that'll destroy the revolution if we're not careful." Will enthusiastically voiced agreement.

"Does he have a girlfriend or a wife?" Will was curious.

Under normal circumstances, Walters would have clammed up at this obvious interest in a senior commander in the ADF. He knew Will knew Malia was Adam Ross's mistress, but he had his own reasons for not admitting it, and it didn't seem particularly dangerous. "A low-credit girlfriend. She's the night concierge at the Octavian. We're trying to get rid of her because he can't marry her and our Director thinks he needs to find someone more appropriate." Walters sighed, thinking that Carolina's official dalliance with David was standing between them. She had promised to be his once the Director was satisfied that David had been detached from Malia permanently, but David was balking, just as you'd expect from a Plore. Carolina lamented that David seemed distant, even while he had sex with her and said all the right things. And meanwhile, her luscious curves and pouty red mouth were off limits to him, the heroic Brian Walters, or so she claimed.

"So, if she disappeared tomorrow, the ADF wouldn't be sorry?"

"No, she's nothing to us, except she's ruining a good commander. After all these years in the ADF, you'd think he'd put the organization's interests over his own. Plores." Walters took another bite of his juicy hamburger.

Will digested this information. She might not have told the organization much if anything of what she had learned from him and Adam. After all, the ADF had plenty of ways to find out what the Economic Tower was doing without relying on someone who did seem to be a small fry after all. Will admitted to himself that Malia hadn't really shown interest in things that would have been a klaxon alert to anyone with a higher IQ. Second, if Adam wanted to take Malia to Mexico or dump her in the Economic Zone, not only would the ADF not pursue her, it would be grateful. Will knew that if the ADF didn't want Commander Harris to find his girlfriend in the Zone, he wouldn't be able to. The picture Walters was painting of Malia conformed to his and Adam's view of her insignificance, so he readily believed it.

Will briefly felt sorry for Malia. Mixed up with matters far above her competence or intellect, he thought, and now she might pay for it. But they wouldn't know for sure how to deal with her until they tried the truth serum on her. And given the vagaries of the experiments, she might perish regardless of her guilt or innocence. They were still several months away from developing a reliable product, but each casualty fattened his and Adam's bank accounts, so "either way we win," Will concluded.

If Malia had been an Antifan informant, presumably Walters would not be effectively handing her over to them. Will was reasonably content that Walters was telling him the truth, or at least the truth as Walters saw it, which was good enough. Walters felt, contentedly, that he had served both the Antifan cause and his own that night, which was beautiful when you could make it happen.

Adam was relieved when Will reported that, despite her Antifan boyfriend, Malia might not have harmed them much after all. "Walters says the ADF wants to get rid of her," said Will, "I mean, not necessarily kill her, but just get her away from the boyfriend. I guess she's low credit after all. Sounds like she's been a bit of a pest for them. I'd still get her out to the Zone one way or another to see how much damage she's done us.

"Aren't they having some kind of awards ceremony out there next weekend?" Will suggested that Mattison would be pleased to have senior representation from the Tower. It would be the kind of event to which one could bring a date. Adam said he'd call Mattison in the morning.

"I'll try to be very gentle," he said, regarding Malia. "I know last weekend was a bit rough—I don't want to make her suspicious, just get her out there."

"Yeah," said Will, "you might even apologize for that bench stunt."

"What bench stunt? Oh, that one. If it would help—"

He called Malia up to his apartment on Thursday night. On the surface, the Octavian had returned to normal. But there was no denying a fifth of the residents were gone. Even residents who had been spared were staying home if they could. The building management was permitting Malia to stay with Rex, since the Andrewses had authorized it. The complicit daytime manager had pointed out it was better than dealing with an impromptu teenage party.

The first thing Malia noticed was that Adam seemed worn down. Gone was the buoyant arrogance of last weekend. For the first time, he did not begin their encounter with the offer of a drink, whether tainted or safe. From what she guessed, the Antifan strike against the Knowledgeers had brought home to Adam that the ADF could just as easily dispatch its forces against the Economic Tower, at this point. Listening to Antifans rampaging through the Octavian, through his own hallway, must have been a chilling experience.

He sat on the paisley armchair and indicated she should sit on the sofa.

"Melia," he said.

"Amba-sah."

"Adam," he said. "That's all right, it's been a tough week. I wanted to apologize for what happened at the restaurant last weekend. We should have just ordered takeout and brought it back here. I was very selfish."

Malia was shocked at his apology, but she graciously accepted it. Is this what happened when psychopaths had mid-life crises?

By the time she left, she had agreed to accompany him to the Economic Zone the weekend after next. Adam was going to be presenting awards at the Zone's Fall Awards ceremony and it was perfectly acceptable for him to bring her as his date. "You'll brighten up the room full of brown uniforms," he said. And then a little more cagily, "We can use the facilities this time. I know mid-November isn't exactly golf weather, but if there's something you'd like to do or see, we can arrange it. For people like us, it can be like a resort."

"It might be nice to drive around the camp," Malia said.

Chapter 68
Nobody's Getting Out of Beaufort
(Friday, 18 November)

As Malia was heading west on 66 with Adam Ross, David accepted an invitation to lunch in the cafeteria from Alex Charlton. David was inclined to humor authority figures this week, even ones like Alex who didn't exactly exercise their authority much.

"How is your romance going with Carolina Cruz?" Charlton asked once they were seated. David thought, I should have known Alex would have an agenda. All I wanted was a sandwich.

"I don't know," said David. "I don't think she's really interested in me." He pretended to sound despairing, but privately he was relieved to see that her acrobatics had become a little more mechanical and her attention was focused elsewhere, on what or whom, who knew. But as long as he continued to dutifully see her, nobody could fault him.

"Maybe she's a little upset that you still have your girlfriend in your apartment," suggested Charlton. "Maybe she doesn't think you're serious."

"Come on," said David. "Isn't she the ultimate Diversity girl?" Like the ravishing Carolina Cruz would worry about another woman. The experience on Saturday night had appalled him, admittedly, especially after she scored him after dinner for paying more attention to that Low Credit nonentity on the bench than to her. He could not pretend this callous siren was a woman with whom he could spend a week, let alone a lifetime.

"The Director wants to see results," said Charlton frankly, showing his hand.

"Am I supposed to propose to her?" David asked irritably. "What counts as results?"

"Progress. Any progress. The Director isn't going to approve your marriage to your girlfriend, Harris," said Charlton, now impatient. "And you'd better get used to that."

"Fine, then we won't get married," said David, thinking with petty satisfaction that he was already married.

"Look, we won't turn her into the streets. We appreciate what she's done for us. We can find her a partner. You can even pay child support if you want. Not that it's the

Antifan way.

"It doesn't look good," said Charlton, meaningfully. "The Director doesn't like to be thwarted. He takes these issues more seriously than you might think."

David spat out, "Yes, I imagine that someone interested in underage boys might not really grasp heterosexual love." When this conversation finally made its way to Ferraro, embellished by Charlton and then via Steve Rosen and Montoya, it would seal David's fate.

David returned to his office to better news. Steve Rosen called. "We deciphered the documents from Adam Ross's apartment, Harris. Come upstairs and you can give us feedback before we go to the Director with it."

ECU analysts had pored over the documents since the day after the Knowledge Tower raids when the fake painting crew had made copies. They could have been worthless, Steve said, maybe the results of some Economic Tower Zone purchasing algorithm of no interest at all to the Antifans. But the analysts had compared the regular increases in the bank accounts on the specified dates with the numbers given in the lists.

"What we think we have here is a price list," said Steve. "The total number of deaths as a result of these experiments is about 2,300, according to what Malia found out this summer. We see about that number, as of late June, on this list. These numbers are broken out into varying numbers each week, and fall into three different subcategories. The digital multipliers are identical every week, for each category." He passed a sheet across the table to David. "So take the week of 20 June, for example:

20 June-26 June	11k	7.67	21k	1.000	6k	1.234	$103,562.76

"Initially, the analysts thought that the small 'k' referred to thousands, but then we had to ask, thousands of what? Not of people. Thousands of units of the truth serum? Possibly this was a cost sheet, but who is paying for these units? It is a joint undertaking between the ESZ factory and the Chinese Government.

"Then the analysts asked, what if the 'k' refers to people killed? And some price is being paid in return for different groups of people? The numbers—11 here, 21 there, six there, when you add them up, brings you to about 2,300 in late June, not including the ones between July and October."

Steve explained that the total amounts in the final column, when added, approximated the size of the six Mexican bank accounts. "So, this money—the number of deaths times a certain set rate—is going into those bank accounts. But then why the three categories?

"Malia told us that there were three types of casualties. Those who died outright, those who had to be euthanized, and those who were injured, perhaps not catastrophically. Or these different rates could refer to victims who were valued differently, whether by Social Credit number or education or other qualifications. Victims with more credentials might be compensated at a higher rate. Honestly, we don't know. But we think this is the accounting presented to the Chinese for the human cost of these experiments in the factory."

Steve sat back, satisfaction and disgust mingling on his face. "I can see the Chinese paying more for victims with higher education, for example."

"So," David said, slowly, "If I understand you correctly, Adam Ross is profiting off of each dead Social Crediteer in the laboratory."

"Yes," said Steve with finality.

"Malia had said something puzzling happened when she sat in on the experiment," David recalled. "She said that Adam and Henry exchanged satisfied looks when the Chinese doctor was telling them how many people had died. She knew that Adam was callous, but there was still no reason for him to be satisfied at hearing about these deaths, so it was puzzling."

"It would be puzzling if you were a decent human being, yes," said Steve.

"Do we now have what we need to arrest him?" David asked hopefully. Just this morning he had authorized releases for a dozen Knowledge Tower officials who had signed their Diversity Affirmation of ADF Supremacy, and knew there was room in the cells below for deserving newcomers. He reminded himself that the forms for extending the Andrewses' stay another two weeks were awaiting his action on the screen. Two more weeks should do it, he calculated.

"Yeah, we could just arrest him and the others, if the charge was corruption. You know, there's nothing in the DJR legal code that says you can't make money off of killing your fellow citizens." Both Steve and David thought to themselves that most high-end Social Crediteers indeed profited off the labor and the privation of lower-end Crediteers and Plores, so this new atrocity was worse only in the degree, not the type. But you couldn't say that aloud. "These activities constitute illicit private gain and the foreign bank accounts would put them away for about twenty years each, easily, in a criminal prison, not a psychiatric one." And those were grimmer than Garrett, or even Markham.

"However," Steve continued. "I don't think the Director will be satisfied with treating this as a criminal case. This is so horrific that we need to close down the operation, and use it as an example of Economic Tower excess. Maybe cast a light on the operations in the Zone generally. I suspect this would put the Economic Tower on its heels for a while, while it licks its wounds."

"You can't play at being soldiers and spies when your main enterprise is under assault, in other words," said David.

"Absolutely. Of course, this might mean some disruption in the Zone farming and manufacturing enterprises, which would reverberate in Anacosta. What better way to show that the Economic Tower has been neglecting its main responsibility while killing young Social Crediteers for the personal gain of its senior officials?"

"I guess we don't want to engage in another Knowledge Tower-type roundup," said David. "Not so quickly after the last one."

"No, that would definitely be seen as overreach. Here we have a purpose," said Steve. "One that almost everyone in the City would agree was legitimate."

"You realize, of course, that without Malia, we wouldn't have learned any of this," said David. "We would be virtually asleep at the wheel." Steve would have smiled at the quaint Plore-ism, when few people handled a car wheel anymore, but he was tired of Malia this and Malia that.

"I'm sure we would have found out some way," said Steve. "Nothing gets past us for very long. Enough, Harris." His normally benign brown eyes flashed irritation.

"You gave her a to-do list when she went out to the Zone today," David reminded him.

"Well, of course," said Steve. They had asked Malia to report on security installations and any developments on the truth serum front. "And then, I'm giving you a friendly warning, Harris, you'd better watch out. I don't want to see anything bad happen to either of you."

The car deposited Adam and Malia at the main house at the Zone camp, just as it had in July. And, as had happened in July, Mattison came out to meet them, looking less ruddy than he had in the summer. Adam had already talked with Mattison about his concerns that Malia might have been spying for the Antifans, although it was hard to admit that Malia had been seeing an Antifan boyfriend even as she dated him.

"Well," said Mattison, "I guess we shouldn't have allowed her to see that lab show back in July, then." He promised to cooperate with Adam's plan to try the truth serum on Malia. "It's much more effective than it was then. The casualty rate dropped significantly last month, and the results are much more reliable. Our Chinese friends are very pleased."

"I just want to know the truth," said Adam. "I'd keep her if she wasn't spying on us."

"And what do you want us to do if the truth serum shows she was spying all along?" Mattison asked. "We have an execution ground for a reason. I just want to be sure that the ADF wouldn't come out after her, but from what you told me, it seems they'd be just as pleased."

Adam shrugged. "Let's see what we find out first."

This time Adam and Malia were the only guests at the lunch table. No sign of Mrs. Mattison, who the commander eventually admitted was "visiting relatives" somewhere in North Carolina. Malia wondered whether Fern, doubtless in the kitchen downstairs, had helped prepare the meal, and whether they would see each other at all.

Mattison wanted to hear more about the Antifan raids on Monday morning. Malia related the raid at the Octavian, with both men scrutinizing her face for signs of satisfaction. Adam said about a third of the prisoners had already signed the Affirmation and been released. Both men wanted to talk more privately about what these developments meant for the Economic Tower, so Mattison suggested that Malia rest in the guesthouse while they had "meetings."

"I'm not tired at all," she said. "Would it be all right if I just walked around by myself?"

"No, I'm afraid not," said Mattison. "No unauthorized movement."

"Could I meet with my friend Fern? The one you moved to the kitchen? I really appreciated that, by the way."

"No meetings with prisoners, I'm afraid."

"Oh, I didn't realize she was a prisoner," said Malia cheerfully. "I thought she was a volunteer for Diversity." Mattison grimaced as he realized his mistake. Malia registered that Mattison's demeanor toward her was much cooler and less avuncular than it had been in July. *Am I imagining it?* She knew one could view another's behavior through a prism of one's own guilt. In her case Mattison could simply be less cordial because he wasn't entertaining a group, or perhaps he was worried about some ESZ issue that had nothing to do with her personally.

"Melia," said Adam reprovingly. Mattison drove them to the guesthouse. "Take a rest," said Adam, opening the door for her, "I'll be back in a few hours."

"Yes, amba-sah," she said. He closed the door behind her, and she heard a lock turn.

"Well," she thought. "That's ominous." She watched the jeep drive away, and then she tried the patio door. It was also locked. She texted David, "*Something's wrong. Locked in guesthouse.*"

Her heart raced while she waited for a response. It was another half hour before she heard the ping and saw, "*Ugh. Anything else?*"

"*X guy not nice like b4.*" X guy was code for "in charge."

David hesitated. "Locked in guesthouse" was concerning. They had not locked her in the guesthouse in July, even though she was completely unknown to them at that time. On its own, Mattison's demeanor could have been explained. Together, David thought Malia definitely had some cause for concern.

"*No can see Fern.*"

Not surprising, thought David, but an exception could have been made for Adam's girlfriend. A third factor, that combined with the others, was problematic.

"*Txt me every six hours or so, inc before bed and in AM,*" he responded. "*If u don't respond, wl know something wrong.*"

They agreed on a code that would not alert Adam, "*Sunny*" meant all was routine. "*Cloudy*" was a distress signal. If she was truly in danger, she should dial the ECU emergency number they had given her months ago. David didn't say it to Malia, but he wasn't sure that the ECU, even under Steve Rosen, would respond. Steve had lost several informants and officers to the ESZ already. He could countenance one more, especially someone causing complications for the Director, so close to cracking open the case.

"*Love u. Erase msgs,*" he cautioned her.

"*Love u 2.*"

She then sent a text to Rex, who was at school, but whom she hoped would see it. Rex had been a trouper when Malia told her she needed to go away for the weekend with Mr. Ross.

"I hope you're not seriously dating him," said Rex. "He's trouble. He scares me every time I see him." She also wondered how the mysterious new David felt about Malia dating Adam Ross. Adults got into all kinds of messes that teenagers were too smart to risk, she thought. Just because it was morally all right to date several people didn't mean you ought to.

You should be scared, thought Malia. "I'll explain another time," she promised, "but when you hear the whole story, you will realize why I did it." Rex had to be satisfied with this. Before leaving for the Zone, Malia gave her the code "vegetable."

"Whoever comes to you with this code, go with them," she instructed her daughter. "This person is completely reliable." She had been delighted when Rex shyly told her she would follow Malia to the United States. A few days together without the Andrewses had been very helpful.

"*Out here in EZ,*" she texted Rex, "*Very nice lunch. How did Div His exam go?*"

Malia hesitated over whether to raise the case of Lyffid Jernigan, family250, a New Woman-boy in Rex's school who had been pursuing her devotedly. Lyffid had taken Rex out for ice cream on various occasions and, according to Rex, made various overtures on park benches and invited her to their house, presumably with similar activity in mind. "Sure, eat the ice cream," Malia said, "but don't let them get you in private."

Not that I'm the best role model for such advice, she thought wryly to herself. Since Lyffid was in a protected category as a New Woman candidate and was the dauson of a senior Knowledge Tower apparatchik who had been hauled off to Beaufort, it was hard for Rex to rebuff Lyffid without social consequences. "After they lop off their penis," Malia thought to herself, "it might be safer to hang around with her." But saying so to Rex would only prompt shrieks of horror at the uttered knowledge crime.

When Malia had finished her texts, and erased David's, she was willing to remove the armband and take a nap. She knew she might not be allowed to keep the armband for the rest of the weekend at the rate things were going. Reassuringly, when Adam returned from his talks with Mattison, he seemed to behave as if nothing was wrong at all, if you considered handcuffing her to the night stand and matter-of-factly assaulting her from behind to be a completely normal activity. Malia wondered whether she had been exaggerating her unease.

Back at Beaufort, David hesitated, but picked up the phone and dialed Carolina. The raven-haired beauty soared onto his phone screen, as he did on hers. He hoped she took notice of the honor medals on his black jacket, which he had pulled on again for this call. He had served the ADF well and loyally, and it was going to hell because of an issue of principle that had literally nothing to do with Antifans.

"Hello, honey, how are you?" he asked.

"Hello, my David," she purred sweetly, "so long since I have heard from you. I was afraid that you did not really love Carolina."

"I am sorry," he said. "I've just been preoccupied, what with the raids and all the interrogating we've been doing since then. I really apologize, honey." He had in fact slapped around a few Knowledgeers this morning, including Elofea Antolides, which he mostly considered retaliation for their treatment of Malia. He had remembered all the names she had mentioned.

"You have been doing great work for Diversity, David, I know that. Will you be able to find the time to spend the weekend with me?"

"Yes, that's just what I was going to ask you," he said. "I want to be with you all weekend."

He hung up the phone with a sigh of relief. Malia was away in the Zone, and he could assuage Steve and Charlton's concerns by intensifying his courtship of Carolina. That might buy them the week or two needed to lay the final plans for his and Malia's escape.

He next texted his brother at Antifan Camp Number Six. *"Mom doctor appointment on 11 Jan; will pay doctor $251.26 for medication."* Properly understood, this meant "plan for 11/25-11/26." Marjory's recent surgery—doctors had removed a precancerous mole on her face—gave the text a credible gloss. He had even booked an appointment for her on 11 January that she would miss, but they would just call to reschedule.

He also texted: *"Momma is sending you a package today. Pls keep an eye out for it."* And that meant, "Malia is at the Zone, keep an eye out for her."

Chapter 69
Harvest Ceremonies
(Saturday/Sunday, 19-20 November)

In the bright light of morning, Malia's worries faded. Adam was unusually solicitous, ordering in breakfast without incident, and letting her eat as much as she wanted. After breakfast, he suggested they take a jeep ride, as she had requested yesterday. "Mattison says it's all right as long as you're with me," he said. He wore his brown uniform to blend in. Although he hadn't driven a vehicle in years, he knew enough from his youth to steer and apply the electric signals. He even coaxed Malia into the driver's seat a few times, which, once she got the hang of it, gave her genuine pleasure. "This is fun!" she said, as they rolled past the factory buildings. Adam smiled benignly.

They jolted around the main square, and into the fields, where workers were harvesting cauliflower and cabbage as the farm season began to draw to a close. During the winter, the workers would be redeployed to the factories. Malia said, "It seems really quiet. Are the farm workers given Saturday off?"

Adam laughed. "Are you kidding? It's only that more ESF personnel are on leave than usual." The Harvest Festival week was beginning, and the Zone would operate on a skeleton staffing basis. Malia marked that down.

He was driving back to the guesthouse close to noon when he swung around the evergreens shielding the execution grounds on the left. "Maybe you should see this," said Adam. "They don't do this every week."

He pulled the jeep up next to the bleachers. Mattison was waiting for them. "You're our guests of honor," he said. He escorted them about a third of the way up the bleachers to an area with an awning to protect viewers from the midday sun, which was strong even in November. Adam nudged Malia into a seat between him and Mattison. By now she realized what they were about to see, and it filled her with dread, much as Adam had intended.

Ahead of and below them were gallows. Several ESF troops were on the platform arranging wooden blocks and inspecting nooses that had been installed early that morning. To their right was the row of evergreens separating the execution grounds from their guesthouse; to the right and across the field were rows of metal fencing into which workers had been herded to watch. Around them sat the ESF military contingents, officers above, privates below. Perhaps due to the impending holiday, or staffing priorities, the ESF seats were about a third empty.

"Adam, I don't want to see this. I don't want to be here."

"Too bad," he said. "I think you need the lesson. And that's amba-sah to you." He had fully recovered from the momentary lapse of control last Monday morning. On his own territory, he waxed confident and powerful.

"Yes, amba-sah," she said meekly.

Mattison said, "We haven't had an execution in two weeks. This time we are dispatching two spies who were in the employ of the United States, and two pregnant women."

"What?" Malia said in shock, unsure she had heard correctly. "Are you executing women just because they're pregnant?"

Mattison glared at her. "To become pregnant in the Economic Zone betrays our cause. Ample contraceptives are available, so getting pregnant is a deliberate act of insubordination. Not to mention they waited beyond the two-month grace period that would have allowed them to have an abortion from one of our medics and return to work immediately. We understand that contraception can fail, which is why we offer the grace period. But neither of these women chose to take advantage of our forgiveness."

Malia said angrily, "A woman's right to reproductive freedom is guaranteed in the DJR. You are violating one of the fundamental clauses of the DJR Constitution."

"They exercised their right poorly," responded Mattison, sharply.

Malia slumped in her seat. Adam, looking at her, was somewhat reassured by the fact that she was reacting so emotionally to the pregnancy convictions rather than to the spying ones. If she were really an Antifan spy, wouldn't she be more upset about the other spies? Malia had possibly become a little unhinged by the Abortion Palace episode, in which he had taught her a lesson about the correct use of Choice. He had thought she had absorbed the lesson, but perhaps not.

"I apologize for her," said Adam. "Sometimes women take these issues too seriously."

"This is evil," Malia hissed.

Adam bruised her wrist, "Stop it now," he said. "Shut up and watch. And keep your eyes open."

Mattison looked levelly at her. "Really Adam, I don't think you have her under control at all, that collar notwithstanding." Yesterday at lunch, he had reached out and touched the silver choker. "Lovely," he said, "and what do those words say?" After Adam told him, Mattison grunted and said somewhat inscrutably, "We'll see."

One man and three women were being led onto the platform. All wore the shapeless denim overalls, so even a visible pregnancy would be hidden. Malia was grateful that Fern was not among the women. She would have put nothing past Adam.

Each prisoner stood before his or her assigned noose. The entire assembly rose for the DJR national anthem, "Bread and Roses," and then sang the ESF anthem, "Joyous Defenders of Socialist Wealth."

Deputy Commander Taryn Bulmer pulled out her workscreen, and read the names of the guilty prisoners, and the criminal laws, or, in the case of the two pregnant women, administrative regulations they had violated. "Sentenced to death by hanging by the Economic Strike Force martial court meeting on 14 November 2089," she read. "By order of the martial court, these sentences will now be carried out." Apparently, no appeals process existed.

Malia wanted to jump out of her seat and scream at her, "You're a woman! How can you do this?" She remembered that the divorced Taryn Bulmer had two children of her own. But Taryn would likely not hear her outburst, and those who would, such as Adam, would punish her later. If she caused a disruption now, she would jeopardize her mission. "Revenge is a dish best served cold," she reminded herself, but little good would it do these poor souls. She prayed for the victims below, around whose necks the nooses were now fastened. The most sophisticated capital punishment, reserved for the few high Social Credit murderers—or, more precisely, unauthorized murderers—was a clear eggshell device in which the offender would be instantly incinerated. But it was extremely expensive, and sometimes known to malfunction, brutally.

The Mother Earth chaplain, a stout African-American woman in green robes, was helped up onto the platform. She carried the Big Green Screen, the portable MED Bible.

She asked each victim if they wished to pray with her. Each of the first three accepted her offer, if only to prolong their moments on earth, and she uttered a mostly inaudible prayer for each. Then a mask was placed over their mouths and a cloth hood over their eyes and noses. They had breathed in their final breaths of cold fall air. None of the condemned were to be offered an opportunity to speak, even to repent publicly of their alleged crimes.

Then the chaplain came to the man. Instead of accepting her offer, he shouted, "This is abomination. I will live eternally with Christ Jesus, the Only Son of the Only Go—" Taryn nodded, and the ESF soldier behind him sprang the trap door before the man could finish his sentence. His body, lifeless, dangled from the gallows. Malia finished his prayer for him, silently. A martyr, she thought, I will tell David about him, and others when I can.

The ESF executioner then sprang each of the remaining trap doors in sequence. Within half a minute all four bodies were swinging.

Taryn concluded, "Let these deaths be a lesson that no sabotage, no spying, no unauthorized reproductive activity, and no lawbreaking will be permitted in the Economic Zone. Work diligently, serve Diversity, and you will increase your chances of enjoying the fruits of socialist labor someday. This assembly is now dismissed."

They waited to exit the bleachers until most had emptied, and then returned to the jeep. "Let's go to lunch," said Mattison, taking the driver's wheel. Adam sat next to him and Malia bounced in the back seat. "Taryn will meet us at the main house."

The meal was over. Malia asked to be excused and was directed toward the washroom. The others probably were relieved to have a moment to talk freely without her, she guessed.

But instead of going into the rest room, she followed a waitron holding a tray full of dirty dishes down the stairs into the kitchen. At the foot of the stairs, her eyes took a moment to adjust to the fluorescent lighting and the large room. "Can I help you, ma'am?" asked an ESF corporal who seemed to be in charge.

"Yes, thank you. I'm looking for Fern," said Malia.

The corporal seemed disapproving, but before he could say anything, Malia heard a shriek ring out "Malia!" and then Fern enveloped her in a giant warm hug. After her initial shock, Malia hugged her too. "Oh Malia! How I've missed you!" The corporal disappeared up the stairs.

"Fern, how are you? I've been thinking of you a lot," Malia lied, although it was not completely untrue, and she had thought of Fern when Fern most needed help. They looked at each other. Fern thought Malia was more beautiful than ever, and her hair had grown long. Malia thought that Fern's face was drawn and her brown eyes seemed overlarge, even bulging. Was she sick? The denim overalls over the long-sleeved grayish white T-shirt could not have flattered anyone.

Fern saw the corporal was gone, but of course spies were all around her in the kitchen, and any of them would receive a reward for reporting any dissatisfaction she confessed. "Oh, it's all right Malia. Thank you for arranging to have me work in the kitchen. It's much better here." In Malia's ear, she whispered, "I'm just hungry all the time." Malia knew what that was like, but no doubt it was much worse here than in the City. "Why are you here, Malia?"

"Melia," said Adam, who had come downstairs with the corporal behind him. "Come here."

Fern recognized the boyfriend who had reacted with distaste to being mistaken for the Plore Dave, but she couldn't quite remember his name. She dared not greet him.

Malia looked at Adam, then back at Fern. All the workers stared at them. "Mind your own business!" said the corporal, "back to work!" and then they returned to preparing the dinner for the awards banquet that evening.

"Every second you delay will cost you," said Adam coldly.

"Goodbye, Fern! Be well! I hope we'll see you soon!" she said, and ran over to Adam, who pushed her upstairs, but not before he'd told the corporal, indicating Fern, "I authorize you to put her in the punishment stockade for encouraging this misbehavior."

"Yes sir," said the corporal, recognizing the ESF insignia of a colonel.

"Amba-sah, it wasn't her fault!" Malia cried. But Adam said to her, "Fault isn't always the reason for punishment. Sometimes it's to teach the real culprit a lesson." As Malia ascended back into the dining room, she heard Fern's cries. Malia was overwhelmed with guilt, an added layer to her despair over the executions.

"You would have done better to have left her alone," observed Adam.

Back in the dining room, Mattison informed her, "Very bad form to interact with the staff. Didn't I tell you we don't allow interaction?"

"Maybe we should stick her among them permanently," Adam said.

"Yes, I am beginning to wonder," said Mattison. "Who would miss her? I'll drop you off at the guesthouse and we'll see you at 7 pm back here for the awards dinner." His cold stare raked over Malia. "Adam, I'll leave it up to you as to whether Melia can be trusted to attend without causing another scene. Two in one day is quite enough." Adam wondered whether sharing Malia with him tonight might appease his bad humor, some of which was now slopping over on him, Adam Ross, who needed to maintain Mattison's goodwill. The experiments were not yet over. Adam calculated that perhaps another thousand casualties might be tolerated and paid for by the ever-bountiful Chinese Communists.

Adam wanted to bring Malia to the dinner, if only because her beauty and relative youth made him look good. But he wasn't going to divulge his preference, and he planned to make her earn her dinner. Back in the guesthouse, she hurriedly texted David from the bathroom, "*sunny.*" Once it was safely sent, she deleted it.

Meanwhile, Adam mulled over how to spend the afternoon. He drew the curtains, and found the handcuffs, whips, and second set of clamps he'd ordered from the Diversity Warehouse; it was a pain with everything stored in Rehoba. "Well, bitch," he said when she reentered the room, "you've certainly caused me a lot of trouble today. What do you have to say for yourself?"

She tried to explain how awful the execution was, and how unfair, and why shouldn't she see the only real friend she had in the world, but none of these limpid complaints impressed Adam. It was just the kind of prattle you'd expect from an undeserving weakling, and not worth his taking seriously. Three punishing hours later, he grudgingly agreed she could attend the dinner after all.

They returned around 10 pm, both convinced it had been worthwhile. Adam graciously accepted his Lifetime Socialist Achievement award. Malia had sat so demurely that even Mattison could find no fault with her behavior. But she marked every time Mattison or Bulmer joked about the low staffing this week, especially at the back gate. The overall atmosphere was one of back-patting and self-congratulation. Malia's only worry was that Adam had peeled off toward the end of the evening to talk privately with Mattison, and both men jointly cast a look in her direction that did not seem innocuous. Malia hoped that the commander would not be showing up at the guesthouse later for some hospitality at her expense.

"Congratulations on your award, amba-sah," she said as they entered the guesthouse again.

"Thank you, Melia," he said. "Of course you do whatever you're asked and make all these sacrifices for Diversity, but I don't mind getting some recognition." He was in a sufficiently expansive mood that they could lie together in bed and watch a documentary about Antarctica. "We could go there, you know," he said as she rested her head against the flat surface of his front shoulder, and he fondled a breast. "Maybe for our honeymoon."

Malia's horizons were so narrow that it was hard for her to imagine going anywhere, except possibly New York. She had to keep up the pretense of being an eager bride. "Should we start planning the wedding?" They had gotten the authorization from the Marriage Office two weeks ago, Adam emphasizing that he had used his influence to secure an affirmative answer.

"Why, is your aunt nagging you?" he asked. "It shouldn't take much planning. Pick a restaurant where you can get in—it would be unfortunate if the bride couldn't attend her own wedding—and we'll just invite a few friends. I've been married before and you're not exactly a kid."

I have no friends, she thought. Except my husband and my daughter, neither of whom I can honestly and openly declare. And Fern, of course.

"Which god should we pick as our protector?" she asked.

"I'm already your god," he said flippantly, or not.

"Yes, of course, but the priestess will ask. And then they'll give you a little statue of the god or goddess for your kitchen or your home altar."

"Caishen, the Chinese God of Wealth, then," said Adam. "Because if you have wealth, you can buy anything else you want or need."

"And a white dress?" she asked piteously. "A real white bridal dress?"

"It doesn't have to be white, does it? Isn't that a little sexist? You're not going to fool anyone. I think you ought to wear bright red, after what we've done together." Adam paused. "It would look good with a gold collar."

Malia allowed herself a giggle. Adam rolled over on top of her as her hands ran through his chest hair and then around his torso. It didn't seem that Mattison would show up at this point and she was confident that Adam's sunny mood would last until bedtime.

She awoke in the half-light before dawn choking and gasping. Adam's hairy hands were gripping her neck above the choker. She gasped for breath, squirming beneath him. In another minute she would lose consciousness.

"You Antifan bitch," said Adam. "Today you're going to pay."

He inexplicably pulled away from her, and lay on his side watching her grimly as she fought her way back to breathing normally. She gagged and spat up saliva. Her heart pounded.

"What was that about?" she cried. "And you want to MARRY me? Are you a maniac?" She had decided months ago that Adam Ross was indeed a maniac of some kind, but unlikely to actually kill her. This was definitely an escalation.

"I know about your Antifan boyfriend," he told her, "And I have no idea what you've been telling him all these months. While you've been listening to me talk with Will and coming here to the Zone as our guest. Today's project will be finding out exactly what you've told him."

"What boyfriend?" she asked lamely, caught by surprise.

He gave her a withering look. "You think I'm a fool? You think that you can deceive me? You stupid—" He used a foul word that Malia had never heard spoken aloud. "I saw photographs of you together on Wisconsin Avenue in the rain." The fearful look of recognition in Malia's eyes told Adam all he needed to know.

She took the tack of offended pride. "I can't believe you don't trust me after all these months. Why did you even propose to me then? Why would I put up with all your abuse if I didn't care?"

He seized on that question, "Maybe because you're spying for the Antifans? That explains a lot.

"Anyway, we'll get to the bottom of it today. You realize we have a truth serum here, don't you? When we're done, you'll either continue to be my beloved low-credit fiancée, or, I am afraid more likely, convicted of spying on Economic Zone territory. We have capital punishment here, as you may have realized by now."

He confiscated her armband, placing it on top of the armoire that she would not be able to reach. Then he let her use the bathroom before he took a length of chain and attached one end to her collar and the other end to the night table. As he looked at her, he thought, she really looks a bit chubby. I'm going to check with the Abortion Palace and make sure they didn't screw up, he thought, the effing incompetents. Anyway, an execution would take care of that problem if they had.

"All right," he said. "Let's go back to sleep for an hour or two. I'm more tired than I thought." Within a few minutes he was snoring softly again. Malia was too outraged, and yes, afraid, to sleep. She waited until she was certain Adam was actually sleeping, and then reached inside herself to find the little metal plate, encased in paper, that Cheysa had given her. She extracted the tiny piece of metal; remembering the instructions, she placed it against the very top of the thin chain Adam had attached to the choker. She felt the heat rising under her finger, not quite hot enough to burn her. A minute later, the chain fell off onto the bed, and she quickly grasped it and laid it gently on the floor before it could jangle and wake Adam. It was providential he had not handcuffed her.

She then reached into her bosom, and pulled out one of the two small cotton pads and removed the foil backing. Just as Cheysa had taught her, she pressed the pad discreetly against Adam's leg. And then she did the same with the second pad. If these worked, he would be immobile for at least an hour, even if he woke up and saw her free and moving around. She quickly, quietly dressed, including her warm jacket, and then saw the handcuffs sitting on the desk, with the key in the lock. The cuff just fit around Adam's wrist, and she attached the other cuff to a bedpost.

The armband! She pulled the desk chair over to the armoire and retrieved hers, not without some trepidation, because the chair was unsteady. But then she could flee, with his armband as well, which she shoved into a dead rosebush at some distance from the guesthouse with the key to the handcuffs. All this would keep him from pursuing her for well over an hour, she hoped, enough time to make her getaway from the evil Economic Zone.

A hundred feet ahead, she saw one of the jeeps sitting unattended. No one was in sight. The few troops awake at this hour on a Sunday after last night's festivities were at the gates or eating in the mess hall. She quickly texted David, "*cloudy.*" But he was no doubt asleep, perhaps alongside Carolina. She hesitated to call the emergency number. Not yet.

Yesterday Malia had learned to start the jeep, and after pressing the blue button on the dashboard, off she went toward the back gate. It was less risky, she calculated, than the better tended front gate, and anyone seeing her careen through the fields would simply think she was the visiting colonel's headstrong girlfriend having a morning joy ride. Perhaps no one would challenge her.

She knew that if she could escape via the back gate, the Antifan camp was three miles further down the road. The jeep hurtled toward the rear of the camp, past tired cauliflower and broccoli fields mostly harvested.

David woke up at the sound of the arriving text with the special ring tone that meant Malia, and called her back from Carolina's luxurious bathroom. The magnificent Carolina barely noticed his departure from the platform bed, turning onto her right side. The skimpy nightgown edged over her sculpted derriere. Meanwhile, Malia was able to answer her phone, the armband next to her head, while holding onto the wheel and steering with her right hand. A few hundred yards ahead was the back gate. With any luck, the one or two troops on duty would be half asleep or paying attention to anything but the nonexistent traffic.

She quickly told him what had happened, and what she had done to Adam.

"Way to go," he said.

"I'm heading toward the Antifan camp. Once I'm out of the gate, which is just ahead. Could you let them know?"

"Yes," he said. "I'm going to make the calls right now. Good luck."

David called Beaufort's operations center and hoped the Sunday morning watch officers would quickly alert their Camp Six counterparts, who could meet Malia on the road before the ESF troops caught up with her. He also called Daniel, just in case. Daniel said he would grab his fishing gear and head that way with his truck. If the Antifans didn't meet her, he would rescue Malia. David uttered a heartfelt prayer. Surely either Lefever's troops or Daniel would reach Malia first.

The back gate was just ahead. To her alarm, the gate doors were closed. She had to get out of the jeep and investigate. No one came out of the gatehouse. Fortunately, the gate was closed but not locked. She opened it just wide enough for the jeep, got back into the vehicle, and had driven past the gate within half a minute. However, the squeaking of the slightly rusty gate had awakened or alerted the guard; as she barreled down the road, she ignored the rapidly fading shouts of "Stop! Come back here!"

Perhaps the guard would not even come after her, or alert his comrades, for fear that he would get into trouble for his lapse. If he recognized her as Ross's girlfriend, he might, just might, think she was a wild sort having a good time, but certainly not escaping from the Zone after having left the distinguished officer paralyzed and handcuffed in the guesthouse. She thought the uncertainty was mostly favoring her cause, but of course she couldn't be complacent.

Yet, as she sped down the road, she felt a great sense of triumph and confidence like never before. A year ago, no, eight months ago, who would have ever dreamed that humble Malia Jenness would have succeeded in wresting the deepest, darkest secrets from the most sinister force in the DJR—which was saying something—turning the tables on its dissolute intelligence director, and stealing a jeep in which to escape the Economic Zone? Just a few more minutes, dear God, she thought, and I will be safe among the Antifans.

But, as Malia approached the dirt road's intersection with the main road that would lead to the Antifan camp, she turned around a bend and failed to see the chain strung across the dirt road. The jeep spun off the road and landed on its side, its wheels spinning, with her crumpled in the crawl space of the front seat under the dashboard. For all of Mattison's pride in the Zone-made jeeps, they were mostly plastic and not particularly solid works of manufacture.

Chapter 70
Truth and Consequences
(Sunday, 20 November)

Daniel was first to reach Malia. She had crawled out of the vehicle but lay alongside it, half-conscious, unable to move any farther. The morning sun dappled across her face. He knelt beside her and said, "Hi Malia, I'm Daniel." She gasped, groggily, "Hi."

"Let's get you out of here. Can you walk if I pull you to your feet?"

She nodded, "I think so." She had just taken the first tentative step toward his white pickup truck when the sound of sirens grew in the distance. They were coming from the direction of the Economic Zone, not the ADF camp. Where were the Antifans? Daniel wondered. When he had passed by the camp, it was as still as at midnight. He knew David had tried to alert them as to Malia's escape. "If it's ESF, we don't know each other. I'm just a good Samaritan."

He lifted her into the passenger seat of the truck and was about to leap into his when three squad cars, not flimsy jeeps, surrounded the truck.

"Halt!" the brown-uniformed captain shouted. "Stand over there," he indicated the side of the road.

"What are you doing here?" he asked Daniel.

Daniel said, "I was on my way to the creek when I saw this accident happen." He pointed to the vantage point on the hill to the east, where the road curved toward Bullfeather Creek. The commander could see the fishing equipment in the truck bed. "I thought I had better investigate, it being so early in the morning and all."

"Do you know this woman?"

Daniel shook his head. "Never seen her before. Just trying to help. I'm the electrician over at the ADF camp there," he said, pointing now in the direction of the missing Antifans.

The captain relaxed. "Oh, yeah, I think I've seen you before. Well, she stole one of our jeeps and broke through the gate, so we're going to need to take her back to the camp."

Daniel sized up the situation. His truck was facing in the direction of the Zone camp. One car was between him and the main road, and drivers were at the ready in the other two vehicles. No way could he outrace them all back to the Antifan camp. "She may have a concussion. Do you want to me to drive her there, since she's already in my truck? I don't mind."

The captain hesitated. Normally he wouldn't encourage letting an Antifan enter the camp, but this electrician was just a Plore worker.

"Okay, but no funny business."

"No, sir," Daniel said to the much younger man.

The procession headed back toward the camp. As Daniel drove, he told Malia, "I'll let David know what's happened as soon as I can. I don't know what he'll want to do, but we were thinking of making the break next Friday night."

Through waves of pain, Malia said, fearfully, "They are going to try the truth serum machine on me today. They've killed thousands of people with it. I don't know whether I will survive it.

"And then Adam said if the machine showed I was an Antifan spy, they could execute me. I saw an execution yesterday—they killed two so-called spies and two women. The only thing the women did wrong was get pregnant." They both knew she was pregnant. Of course, she was not one of the slave laborers, but would it matter to them?

Who's Adam? thought Daniel. Obviously not one of the good guys.

"You know my brother as well as I do," said Daniel, as the back gate neared again. "He won't let you die here if he can help it. He may bring the Antifans or he may do it all himself. If the Antifans get you out of here, I will stop cursing them, for at least a few days." He smiled wryly. "But I have a lot of faith in David. His heart is in the right place. Also have faith in God."

She stared ahead bitterly. "I was so close. I thought God was with me."

"He still is," said Daniel confidently. They passed through the back gate, the sentry now joined by another two, all looking far more attentive than half an hour earlier.

"One more thing," said Malia as they headed for the main house. "The staffing situation here is lower because of the Harvest Holiday. A lot of the troops here are already on leave. This would be a good week to rescue me. And I may not have another week anyway." A grisly image of the gallows on the execution ground flashed before her eyes. No appeals process.

At the house, Daniel helped Malia out of the passenger seat. The ESF troops took charge at this point, surrounding her. "You can leave now," the captain told Daniel. "Thanks for your help."

"No problem," said Daniel, "Just being neighborly." He turned to Malia, "Good luck with your injury, ma'am." And then he was gone, an ordinary middle-aged blond Plore with a pickup truck moving as fast as possible. The ESF soldiers assumed he was eager to resume his delayed day of fishing. Daniel thought that David would be very unhappy that the Antifans, who could have reached Malia before the ESF troops, had seemingly made no effort to rescue her.

The soldiers escorted Malia up the stairs, briskly but not roughly. She was relieved they were not heading directly to the jail cells. The captain was uncertain as to whether they were dealing with a reckless guest or a criminal; he knew this was the girlfriend of Colonel Ross, which called for some delicacy. Commander Mattison came downstairs to greet her. His evident hostility gave the captain a clue that a show of sternness would be appropriate.

"You're in a lot of trouble now," said Mattison. "I thought it couldn't be worse than yesterday, but apparently it can."

After Malia had raced through the back gate, the guard had reported to the operations center that a non-ESF woman in a jeep had blown through the gate and was heading down the road. One of the guys in the ops center recognized her as Colonel Ross's girlfriend, but no one answered the door at the guesthouse. The private called for backup and they opened the door to find Ross lying handcuffed in bed, just starting to move his limbs again and grunt angrily. Wild, thought the private. The big guys have a lot of fun. The privates snapped the handcuffs and called for the doctor. Meanwhile, the squad cars were heading down the road after Malia.

By the time Malia was back at the main house, Adam was pulling on his clothes, none the worse for wear, but livid at his embarrassment in front of the doctor and the troops.

The doctor found the cotton pads in the bed and said, "looks like you were administered some kind of super muscle relaxant. Your girlfriend isn't a doctor, by any chance?"

"No," snarled Adam, "she's an Antifan spy and she's going to be permanently relaxed herself." The doctor, studiously avoiding comment, drove Adam to the main house, where they found Malia sitting on the sofa in Mattison's office. She avoided meeting Adam's eyes. Mattison sat behind his desk, chilled beyond anger. Adam took Malia's armband and handed it to Mattison. Malia felt a twinge of panic. As much as your armband was your minder, and a constraint on your mobility, it was also your connection to society, and proof of your DJR citizenship. When it disappeared, so did your status in society. Even a Plore owned his own cell phone.

"So you were halfway to the Antifan camp when you had your accident?" Mattison said.

"I wasn't going to the Antifan camp necessarily," said Malia. "I was just going anywhere away from this place." She pointed to Adam. "He tried to strangle me and he chained me to the night table, so I did the same to him and then I realized I needed to leave."

"How did you break the chain? How did you have those pads?" Mattison asked. "Who gave them to you?" Malia looked away from them.

"Well, Adam, what do you want to do with her?" asked Mattison. He wasn't sure whether this was a personal issue to be resolved between the couple or if he really needed to oversee another trial and execution, during Harvest Holiday week at that. On the other hand, it was galling that a likely Antifan spy had been traipsing around Economic Zone Camp Four and could waltz home, when they had just executed two probably innocent workers for the same crime. One of them, however, had professed an exclusivist Christianity at the last moment, justifying his execution, at least in retrospect.

"Could we have some breakfast first?" asked Malia hopefully. They looked at her with exasperation but then both remembered they hadn't eaten either.

After breakfast, Mattison called for an armed escort for Malia to take her to the chemical factory. He and Adam had agreed that the existence of the truth serum experimentation was a perfect opportunity to test Malia's Antifan ties, and a good demonstration of progress in the undertaking. "I'm not guilty of anything," Malia said sullenly.

"Good, then prove it," said Adam.

The four soldiers arrived, and taking their cues from Mattison's scowl, frog-marched her out and shoved her in the van. Mattison and Adam followed in a jeep. Mattison had called ahead and ensured that Dr. Ling would be available to administer the serum personally.

"You know, Adam," said Mattison. "This wasn't how I expected to spend my Sunday. I'd been thinking of golf."

"We can golf after this," said Adam. "I brought my clubs."

Adam insisted on sitting in the examining room while Malia was strapped into the chair. "I know what questions I want to ask," he said as Dr. Ling supervised the attendants. One injected her in the right arm with the serum. Malia felt faint just looking at the giant needle.

"Fine," said Dr. Ling, "but you need to give the questions to me to ask. Otherwise we do not have perfect controls in the experiment. Myself or a staff member always ask the questions. Even your tone can alter the response by the subject." She went into the conference room with Adam and Mattison to discuss the questions.

While they were gone, Malia recalled what David had suggested in what was then the unlikely event she would be subjected to this truth serum. "Try to convince yourself that whatever you are guilty of, you are not guilty. Just say to yourself, 'I've done nothing wrong, I've done nothing wrong.'"

"Will that really fool the testers?" Malia had asked.

"Who knows?" said David, "but it might mitigate your reaction. I think you're actually fooling yourself, or trying to. I read it in one of our Antifan medical journals."

"How much will Colonel Ross be paid by your government if I die here today?" Malia asked the white-coated physician.

"I know nothing about financial arrangements," said Dr. Ling.

"Shut up, Melia," said Adam from the conference room. "Commander Mattison already knows about our arrangements, so it does you no good to repeat this kind of slander."

Dr. Ling explained to Malia that the truth serum, like any other, would encourage her to speak the truth, but, unlike others, it would cause her extreme pain if she chose to tell an untruth. Efforts at crafting a lie would also be visible in her physiological distress signs, which one of the attendants would monitor. I don't believe you, thought Malia. You are telling me this so I will believe you and I will be open to greater pain. This is nonsense, she thought to herself.

"What is your name?" asked Dr. Ling.

"Amelia Jenness," she answered. She felt a sharp jolt of pain through her head. It was not quite her name.

"Try Malia," suggested Adam.

This time, she felt nothing. "I have done nothing wrong, nothing wrong, I am not a spy, I am not a spy," she told herself silently.

Dr. Ling asked Malia a few obvious questions to calibrate the test. "My eyes are brown," "I live in Anacosta," "I am wearing a blue blouse," "I ate toast for breakfast." Malia felt calm.

"We are ready," Dr. Ling announced. She pulled out a list of questions from Adam.

"Do you work for the Antifan Defense Forces?"

"No," said Malia, steeling herself for the pain. She was surprised it was more like a ripple through her head than another jolt. Well, technically, she didn't work for the ADF, did she?

"Did you tell anyone about your visit to this lab last time?"

"Yes," said Malia.

"Who did you tell?"

"I told my boyfriend David." Adam recalled, well, he was just a Plore. He had briefly forgotten the name of the blond man on Wisconsin Avenue, but then he remembered.

"Do you have an Antifan boyfriend?"

"No," said Malia, thinking he was her Antifan husband, not boyfriend. Adam frowned. Who was that Antifan on Wisconsin Avenue if not her boyfriend? Could he just have been her ADF handler, and there was no romantic relationship, despite the photos? So far she had shown few indications of discomfort, let alone pain.

"Who gave you the object that helped you cut the chain this morning?"

"I bought it through the Warehouse." A giant wave of pain swept through her and she cried out. Adam looked at her with some grim satisfaction.

"Who gave you the pads with the muscle relaxant drug?"

"Just a friend," she gambled. No reaction.

"What is the name of your friend?"

"Cheysa." So far so good. They didn't know Cheysa from a rock. She was buying time.

"Who does Cheysa work for?"

"She works for the Diversity Warehouse." Another scream. She felt her body rippling with a strange weakness.

"Try again. Who does Cheysa work for?"

"She told me she worked for the Diversity Warehouse." Another scream.

"Try again. Who does Cheysa work for?"

I can't keep fighting this off, Malia said to herself. Let me just say the truth, I want to tell the truth. "She works for the Antifan Defense Forces." Ah, calm again.

"Did you tell the Antifan Defense Forces about this base?"

"No. Aaagh." She struggled.

"What did you tell the Antifan Defense Forces about this base?"

"I told them nothing," she cried, the pain racking through her head. "I told them that they did experiments here. I told them that they were killing young Social Crediteers here." Ah, very good. That felt good.

"Do you love Adam Ross?"

"He tried to kill me," she cried out, which was true. That felt fine.

"Do you love Adam Ross?"

"No!" she cried, but the pain darted through her, not as sharply as the others.

"This is a hard question, as I told you," Dr. Ling addressed the window. "It is very subjective. The subject herself does not know the answer." Adam's voice crackled over the intercom. "Ask if she loves another man more than she loves Adam Ross."

"No," she answered when that question was posed, and then she crumpled in her seat, having fainted from the overwhelming agony that followed.

They revived her and resumed the questioning. Even though she had faced the initial battery of questions with fortitude and slyness, her resistance was worn down. It felt so good, really almost pleasurable, when you told the truth, even as you knew you were condemning yourself, perhaps to death, by uttering those words. Pain was to be avoided. Powerful jolts flooded her whole body when she spoke untruths. Her mouth was parched, and the nausea rose. At some point, she vomited her breakfast on herself.

Dr. Ling kept asking the same questions relentlessly, like a pounding wave, until Malia finally and mercifully collapsed into unconsciousness.

When she awoke, she was in a cell with cement walls and a steel toilet in the corner. Most of the day had passed, since the small square that passed for a window showed fading light. It was too high for her to see outside. She lay on a thin mattress with a coil poking out on one side.

I am still alive, was her first joyful thought. She moved her limbs, one by one, grateful that they all seemed to be working normally. I survived! She could not remember what she had said, but she knew that she had not outmaneuvered the truth serum. If this is how effectively it works, she thought, the Economic Tower had a powerful weapon in its ambition to thrust aside the ADF. No wonder the Economic Tower refused to share its experiments with Beaufort. The Tower's victory was nearer than they had realized.

Looking down at her chest, she saw the mottled vomit from the truth serum session, and was disgusted. There was no water for washing, and the toilet was air-powered. At least they won't shove your head in it to drown you, she thought. The silence began to unnerve her. Was anyone around? Would there be dinner?

A very young ESF soldier then appeared with a change of clothing and wet towels. "To clean yourself," he said. She thanked him, and looked at the white long-sleeved T-shirt and the denim overalls. "It's standard," he explained. It seemed that he would watch her as she undressed, washed, and dressed.

Malia was outraged. "Don't you have any women guards?"

"No," he said. "Not this week. Don't be such an individualist." He was looking forward to the diversion. It was a small reward for being the most junior member of the jail squad and left to tend the prisoner while the others headed out for their holiday festivities. "Don't forget the underwear. You need to change into that too."

Malia remembered that modesty was a false virtue. "I'll give him a show," she decided, and was rewarded when he brought her back a halfway decent—under the circumstances—pasta dinner with salad and rolls. The silverware was eco-cardboard, but it was no different in the Knowledge Tower cafeteria. Then she wondered where Adam was, especially as night fell. They were supposed to return to the City tonight, and Adam would need to show up for work at the Tower on Monday morning. She was relieved that Daniel at least would have notified David that she was in the hands of the ESF.

She was afraid that she would see mice in the cell, but it was very tidy and she saw neither vermin nor insects. At some point in the night, well after he had turned off the light and she was lying there, staring at the ceiling, the young guard was relieved by a middle-aged one. She heard the young man say, "A-class prisoner." This seemed to be promising, Malia thought, if it meant no one would bother her. Or did it mean she was particularly dangerous? She was confident that, in the morning, it would all be explained. Adam Ross might even show up to rescue her, and say that he had decided to spare her this time despite her perfidy. Was her calm indicative of her faith in God that everything would turn out all right, or faith in David and the ADF, or was she just too exhausted to worry? Strangely, she felt safe with the two ESF troops guarding her, and after pulling up the scratchy wool blankets, she soon fell asleep.

Near midnight, David went into Beaufort and authorized the chip check on Malia. He saw she was still in the Zone camp, and zooming in on the map, determined she was in the jail cells that adjoined the execution ground. It was only due to her efforts that the ADF even knew they were jail cells, since the existing drone footage had just shown a series of cement sheds. He knew they wouldn't execute her that night, and probably would go through the pretense of a trial before sentencing her. But, since they really didn't have the facilities for jailing her indefinitely, and couldn't hand her over to the ADF, it was either acquittal or death, wasn't it?

Tomorrow the commanders would meet to determine the next stage in the Economic Tower campaign and it would be his chance to have Malia rescued, whatever else happened. They owed her that much. Didn't they? He leaned forward on his desk, his head resting in his hands. He would contact Rex tomorrow—they hadn't even met, so this was a bit awkward.

Chapter 71
Hawaii
(Monday, 21 November)

The door of the Director's conference room slid shut once again as the C-Level sign flashed. Above the sign were displayed the current times for Anacosta, Beijing, London, St. Louis, and Hawaii, where the joint DJR-Chinese naval bases were located. The Antifan Navy maintained about one hundred ships in the cruiser and destroyer classes at Pearl Harbor and Kona, under the strategic command of the People's Liberation Army Navy.

"Here we are again," said Ferraro. David—serving as Charlton's plus one—tensed behind the senior commander's chair. Turning to Steve Rosen, Ferraro asked for an update.

"Sir, the main development is Malia Jenness's discovery of documents in Ross's apartment of lists of numbers and amounts of money. You've all seen these by now. At first we couldn't figure out whether this was a simple list of purchases or something more important. After running the numbers through an algorithm that corresponded to observed increases in the Mexican bank accounts, we determined that these are casualties of the experiments taking place in the Zone camp, divided into three categories, all reimbursed by presumably the Chinese Government at differential rates. We don't know how the categories differ from each other, although it may reflect the educational level or the productivity of one group of victims versus another."

"Now," said Ferraro, "We have plenty to go and arrest Adam Ross and his confederates now on corruption and murder charges. But the rest of the Economic Tower could continue with its truth serum plans, and military build-up. Young people continue to be murdered in the Economic Zone camp, helping the Tower perfect a truth serum invention that would destroy our monopoly on power. I don't think we can tolerate that any longer."

"If we destroyed that operation, it would lead to a lot of goodwill for us, especially among the low Social Credit population," said Montoya, "and the truth serum is the key to the Econ Tower grab for power. That would break the Tower's back."

The commanders looked at the current placement and strength levels of the ESF units in the Anacosta area and elsewhere. Illegal arms were beginning to reach these units, but all agreed that training in their use was sorely inadequate. Some Chinese trainers had been glimpsed at Camp 23 near Laurel, training ESF. "Basically, they're operating mess halls and marching around parade grounds at this point," said Montoya.

"We shouldn't tolerate this either," said Ferraro, "but I'd make it priority number two."

All agreed that the arrests of the corrupt Econocrats, the exposure of their evil, and the destruction of the laboratory, all well publicized, would be a boon.

"How soon can we carry this out?" asked Ferraro. "It looks like they're killing dozens of young Social Crediteers each week."

Steve Rosen spoke up at this point, much to David's relief, "Sir, I need to point out as well that as a matter of urgency, our informant was detained in the Zone camp on Saturday. Our chip search shows that she is in the prison cells there adjoining the execution grounds. We are afraid that she might herself have been subjected to the truth serum, but the chip is still working, so either they refrained from doing so or she survived it."

"Is she in any immediate danger?" asked Ferraro, flashing an involuntary glance at David along the wall.

Lefever, visiting Beaufort this week, said, "They generally have their trials on Tuesday and their executions on Saturday. We can hear the loudspeakers from the execution ground, which is the part of the Zone camp closest to ours."

"So we probably have a few days at least," said Ferraro. David was relieved that Ferraro's vindictiveness would not cause him to delay or refuse a rescue. Thank goodness the ADF—including Ferraro—at least recognized the principle that those who helped it were owed support when the time came, if possible.

"A few," said Steve, "but no guarantees, given that she is not an ordinary victim of their sham trials. They generally pick out troublesome workers for execution and accuse them of spying or unauthorized pregnancy. In this case, she is genuinely guilty on our behalf and they might want to dispatch her sooner rather than later."

Thank you, Steve, thought David. He knew Steve would defend Malia's cause to the extent he safely could, framing it in terms of Antifan values and interests. He had far more credibility than David did at this point.

Ferraro then asked how easy it would be to locate and either confiscate, or if that failed, destroy the truth serum itself. "Destroying would be easy," said Steve. "We would just destroy the whole building and hope that they hadn't moved serum vials elsewhere for safekeeping.

"If we could take Adam Ross into custody, I think we would know whether we had all the serum or where other batches of it might be," said Steve. "I would make his capture a high priority."

"Lefever, what do you think the Zone camp's state of preparedness would be if we showed up on Friday night, Saturday morning with advance paratroops followed by ground vehicles?" asked Ferraro. This operation would be a paramilitary one, compared with the police action that had detained the Knowledgeers. In this case the targets would be far more capable of firing back, although the ADF didn't think much of their skills.

"Sir, I think we would catch them entirely by surprise. They would be expecting a police operation as we did with the Knowledge Tower, focused on the urban areas such as Anacosta City. It would not occur to them that the ADF would dare to invade the camp so far from the City, let alone seize the serum."

"Our informant told us before she was captured," said Steve, "that, due to the Harvest Holiday, the camp personnel were probably at half strength, at best."

"That settles it," said Ferraro, "Early Saturday. Otherwise their personnel will start to return from the holiday. Dontellan, will you spearhead this operation with Rosen as your deputy?"

"My loyalty and my honor, sir," said ADF Total Commander Dontellan, giving Ferraro a quick Antifan salute. Dontellan was a spare, cadaverous-faced man in his mid-fifties who had risen through the Antifan army in various border posts before finding himself at Beaufort just a year ago. Ten years ago, he had commanded Lefever's own outpost.

"My loyalty and my honor, sir," echoed Steve.

Ferraro asked Steve, Walters, Lefever, and Dontellan to stay behind, and, to David's surprise, invited him and Gemma as well to the post-table. "Charlton, you too."

When the others had filtered out, and the group had reassembled around the table closer to Ferraro and Montoya, the Director turned to David.

"Harris, you see that we are going to rescue your girlfriend. I hope you realize that shows we harbor no malice at all toward her. In fact, we are grateful for the services she has rendered to the Antifan Defense Forces."

"Thank you, sir," said David deferentially. For a moment, he wondered, did this mean Ferraro was about to concede that an Antifan commander could in fact marry a low-credit woman if that woman had shown courage and valor and delivered results for the ADF?

"That said," Ferraro continued blandly, "there are some principles that are strongly cherished among our Antifans. One of the chiefest is that we are an elite force, forged in the service of the Diversity Revolution, not easily permeable by outside values. We are a wall, a WALL, against the weakness, the self-indulgence of the ordinary DJR citizens who do not see their actions as having consequences for the Diversity Revolution." He slammed his fist on the table at the second 'wall,' causing several of the attendees to jerk in their seats.

"We sometimes have made exceptions to this principle. As you know, Harris, we invite respectable and fit Plores to join our ranks, of course when they are young enough to have avoided the moral tarnishing that eventually afflicts all Plores when left to their own devices. This exception is because as a military organization, we cannot afford to overlook relevant talent. I regret to say, as much as I cherish the spirit of Diversity, it does not always produce young people with the requisite morality and physical strength we need for the ADF.

"One rule we abide by, as you have learned, is that we propagate among our own. Our ranks are mostly men, but we know that morality and values are imparted by women, especially mothers." Ferraro's mouth twisted a bit, as if the word 'mother' was somehow distasteful. But you could not argue with the fact they existed. "What would happen to our Antifan spirit if we were to entrust the raising of Antifan youth to those steeped in outside culture?"

"But," David could not help himself, "we are not talking about Plore mothers, but of legitimate Social Crediteers."

"Low Social Crediteers," emphasized Ferraro, "with the self-centered and dissolute tastes of that population. I don't mind defending them, because they carry out the daily work of the revolution, but I don't want to infect our future with that virus."

"Malia Jenness," said David, "has shown a genuine Antifan spirit in her work on behalf of the ADF. Unlike ourselves, she was under no oath, no obligation to do so. Now she is in danger of losing her life because she worked for us. I feel as though we take no risk by bringing her behind our wall and we would all the more honor our principles."

"And then everyone would look to me to make exceptions for the Plore waitress, the 70-pointer clerk at the self-driving car service, the 100-pointer airline steward they met while jetting to Say Francisco for the weekend. Harris, you have no idea of the rush of requests I would get, because they would all say, 'Commander Harris was able to do it.'"

Ferraro continued, "And it is not an easy undertaking even were I to agree with you, Harris. The Archbishop of Anacosta AND the President of the DJR must sign off on the petition. The Archbishop might realize that your 70-pointer escaped her roundup at the Earth Weekend, showing an individualistic and selfish streak, and the president is under the sway of Peace-Williams, who will do no favors for me this year, and certainly not without a deal that would strike at ADF core interests. After Saturday, he will do nothing for us. Marriage policy is jointly under the control of the White Black House and the Knowledge and Social Towers, not ourselves. We set one rule, for ourselves, and we handed it over to them, in perpetuity.

"But we can save her life. Are you trying to jeopardize even that by continuing to argue with me on this ridiculous marriage issue?"

"No, sir," said David, but his resentment was clear. He thought to himself, we know we are married. I do not need your permission. This was the last effort to make it possible to stay in the DJR, near his mother and his sisters, and to avoid risking their own lives. As he listened to Ferraro, he realized that their escape attempt would come this very weekend. If they did not try to escape, he and Malia would live together at the Avalon, checking out restaurant admission policies before going to dinner, making leisurely love on a Sunday morning as the apartment turned on its axis, playing with Frida and Ansel, or their eventual successors. They would age gently together.

"We are going to do both of you a favor, Harris. You are going to continue to rise in our ranks. Until this year, you were one of our finest officers. This woman has addled your mind. Perhaps you can marry Carolina, or someone like her, who is a true bearer of Antifan principles and can maintain the spirit in your children. But you are going to marry, and marry someone we approve of.

"As for your girlfriend, she will be going to Hawaii, permanently. We will give her a house, maybe even near a beach. I understand she likes beaches. We will give her a job on the base at Pearl Harbor, or at Kona, and she can perhaps find a fisheries official to marry. Or an Antifan sailor. Hell, she can marry a Chinese for all I care. But not an Antifan commander."

David was aghast. "Hawaii?" The Kingdom of Hawaii was a protectorate of the DJR, with a restored queen out of respect for native tradition. Even high-level Social Crediteers could not travel to Hawaii without legitimate business reasons and an application to travel beyond North America. Approval required even more stringent review than a trip to the West Coast. The cost of Malia's rescue was to never see her again.

Don't argue with him, David told himself, it's futile. We are leaving, and Ferraro can curse me out at the next commanders' meeting. Revenge is a dish best served cold.

"Yes, sir, I understand your point," he said. "My main concern is her safety."

"That's the spirit, Harris," Ferraro said, jovial in victory. "Hawaii is delightful, I am told.

"And just to avoid any confusion during the operation," said Ferraro, "You will stay here in the City and not be involved in the operation at all. Do you understand? Will you comply?"

"My loyalty and my honor, sir," said David.

"Can you say it more loudly, Harris? I don't think I quite heard the Antifan spirit in that response. Seemed a little forced."

"My loyalty and my honor, sir!"

"That's better, Harris. You're now excused." Steve thought with some relief that Harris finally seemed to be understanding the broader issues at stake. Walters determined that Carolina would be his, taking some hope in the phrase "or someone like her," which suggested that another Antifan-approved woman could be palmed off onto Harris.

After the door had closed behind David and Charlton, the Director turned to the others. "After that heterosexist comment Harris made got back to me, there was no way I was going to let him have his way here. He blew it with that Plore remark." Steve felt ashamed of his role in relaying Harris' comment about Ferraro's predilection for boys to Montoya. David was lucky he was not stewing in a cell at this moment, thought Steve. He wondered whether they should place David under house arrest until the operation was over, but he knew it would tarnish the commander's reputation before the entire ADF. This time, Steve vowed, he would not interfere.

Adam Ross was back at the Economic Tower on Monday morning, relieved to devote himself to mundane matters after that nightmarish weekend. Mattison was irritated with him for insisting on putting Malia on trial, even though the commander said, "You know, we're going to have to convict her, right? You know what that means?" Nor had Adam learned much more about Malia's spying from the truth serum session than he had already surmised. She had obviously told the Antifans about the experiments and the bank accounts, but he was well aware the ADF might well have known this already through other sources and had simply sent her after him to verify the information. Perhaps she didn't have an Antifan boyfriend, but she had Antifan helpers, including possibly that infuriating blond man, who had provided her with those drugs and steel melters that had resulted in his profound humiliation on Sunday morning in front of those mere privates. That was well worth her destruction, he told himself. He would not live this down quickly, as the story spread through the base and the troops told their comrades returning from vacation and repeated the story over and over again.

Having heard the story from Mattison, Pernella was tempted to laugh at Adam on Monday morning when they saw each other at the 9:30 am meeting, except she was clearly worried that his consorting with an Antifan spy had revealed Economic Tower secrets. Afterward, Adam had reassured her that no new secrets had been lost and the girl would be neutralized by the weekend.

He acknowledged it was not going to be easy finding another low-credit female to serve him, though, he realized. Even when you were the 250-point Intelligence Director of the Economic Tower, you couldn't simply kidnap an armband-wearing woman. There were laws. Even worse, you might inadvertently choose someone who held to feminist principles rather than abandon them at the prospect of marrying a high-level Econocrat. He sighed. Maybe he should have just taken Malia home but now it was too late.

He managed to forget Malia for most of the day, given the flurry of signatures and decisions that required his attention. Yet when he entered the Octavian at the end of the day, and saw the concierge desk with the usual Monday night attendants, he was reminded of her again. In his capacity as a Board member, he had notified the cooperative that it would have to find a replacement for Melia Jenness, who had been arrested by the Economic Strike Force.

By coincidence he rode up in the elevator with one of the retired Knowledge Tower lesbians who lived next door to him. Normally the couple avoided him, but when trapped in the elevator tonight, this neighbor noticed that Mr. Ross seemed a little more human than usual, so she tried to make small talk.

"We were afraid that the ADF had taken you away too," she said brightly, "when we saw all the painters going into your apartment the next day."

"Painters?" Adam's head swiveled.

"Yes," the lady said, puzzled by his lack of awareness. "But perhaps it was not connected at all to the raid. You were just lucky that the building was repainting."

What painters, he thought wildly. When he curtly wished the neighbor a good evening, he dashed into his apartment, unsure of where to look next. True, there was a spot on the bathroom ceiling for which he had requested repainting, and someone had touched it up, although not to his satisfaction. It was a shame that under socialism workers no longer took pride in their craft. But would this have required a crew of the size his neighbor said had entered the apartment, and the morning after the ADF raid to boot?

He had not smelled any fresh paint the next day other than in the bathroom, or seen any disturbance. Had this crew been genuine painters, wouldn't there have been evidence left behind of, well, actual painting?

If an Antifan crew had rummaged through his belongings, it was surprising that the firearm was still concealed in the shirtbox in the lower drawer. But perhaps they weren't looking for weapons, as illegal as this one was. He checked the cabinet in the breakfront where he had inserted some of the experimentation accounting under stacks of innocuous co-op mailings that he had printed off entirely to conceal more important information. It was safer not to keep these records on his computer given the ADF's far reach into everyone's cyber business. Unless they ransacked your home, they wouldn't find these.

At first glance, the papers looked undisturbed. But Adam had stacked the dozen or so sheets in a pattern in which the middle sheet was face up, while the others were face down, and two of the face-down sheets (four and nine) were turned around from the general direction. The middle sheet was face up, but although page four was turned in the correct direction, page nine aligned with the others. Adam felt a cold sweat beading on his skin. Malia could have found these sheets, but she was probably not smart enough to figure out their importance. Nor could she have photographed them, let alone memorized them. He had checked her armband before they went to dinner, given that he had left her alone in the apartment that afternoon, and had found nothing suspicious. It must have been those painters. He would demand that the manager not permit such intrusions again without notifying him.

Did the Antifans know about his profit-making in connection with the experimentation? Had they figured out the columns and the amounts? Adam had no idea. But he no longer felt safe in the Octavian, let alone in the City. They could come for him at any time; firearm or not, they would take him to Beaufort unless he decided to kill himself first. Which he, Adam Ross, was not ready to do. He resolved to immediately return to the Zone, where he would be safe. The ADF would not dare look for him there. He could work from there, and even attend meetings remotely. If things looked really dire, the jet plane would be ready to take him to Mexico. He called Will, and, without giving details, told him to meet him out at the Zone.

Chapter 72
Mother and Daughter
(Tuesday, 22 November)

David had texted Rex on Sunday night when it became clear that Malia was not returning from the Economic Zone. David and Rex hadn't yet met, but Malia had explained that this Dave was "the real thing," and she could trust him. He hoped that Rex would understand the following:

David: Your mother says eat your vegetables. She has to stay a few more days.

Rex: OK. will eat the vegetables (this was the signal that Rex understood who he was)

David: Tuesday, third bench away from carousel toward entrance, 4:15. Is that after school?

Rex: Yes

David: Look for oldish blond guy in brown jacket. (*Really, I'm only old to her,* he thought. *Carolina Cruz thinks I'm young!*)

Rex: snap

David understood enough of youth culture from his nieces and nephews to know that "snap" meant "see you then." He had seen photographs of Rex, so he knew what to expect.

He left work early on Tuesday, pleading a doctor's appointment. He bicycled home, changed into casual clothes, and took a self-driving car down to the Octavian. Waiting on the appointed bench in the botanical garden—which Malia herself would not have been permitted to enter on a Tuesday—he did a routine search underneath the bench, but it seemed intact. Just for prudence's sake he would activate the noise cylinder anyway once Rex arrived.

Rex appeared several minutes late, which was what he had expected from a teenager.

"Hi, I'm David," he said.

"I'm Rex," she responded. They did not shake hands, which might have been conspicuous. They would have looked like an odd couple to most passersby, sitting too far apart to be father and daughter, but too far apart in age to be a couple. Perhaps an uncle and niece? But few people were walking in the gardens as the sun was fading on the horizon on this blustery November afternoon.

David's first thought was that Rex resembled her mother. Malia's hair was curly, though, and Rex's was straight. Today it was held back by a blue patterned hairband. Perhaps this was how Malia had looked, confident in her world, while she was still protected at the orphanage. Rex wore a fashionable blue cloth coat and little black faux leather booties, the perfect example of a high-Social Credit child. Rex boldly scrutinized David, wondering if she could learn more about her mother by examining the man she was dating. This man did not seem a bookish sort—like her father—but he seemed serious in a different way. He was more fit than the fathers of her girlfriends, but younger, with a mostly unlined face. Perhaps he looked younger because unlike the fathers she knew, he had no children, or so she assumed. Her mother had said that David liked cats, which reassured Rex that he had a warm and kind side.

He activated the noise cylinder on his armband, at which Rex looked curiously.

"If I talk frankly, can you promise me that you will not cry or scream or draw attention to us?" he asked her sternly.

She nodded. "Yes."

"Your mother is being held captive in an Economic Zone camp near the border with the US. We are going to rescue her." It was hard for Rex to react to this matter-of-fact statement.

"We?" Rex had known only that Malia was accompanying the sinister Adam Ross as an assistant on what she thought was a routine business trip to the camp. In her 9th grade civics class, they had learned about the Tower system, which was unique to the DJR, and a key source of the country's socialist power. They dutifully noted the important role the Economic Tower played in producing goods and food for the country and making sure it was distributed fairly. She knew that most of the country's industrial and agricultural production came from the Economic Zone camps, which she had plotted on a computerized map for a homework assignment. The teacher told the students that the workers were low-Social Credit volunteers who loved Diversity. The Zone camps were presented as bustling pioneer towns, minus gun violence.

"Yes, *we*. And then we are going to cross the border into the United States. Now that I have told you this, we are both knowledge criminals. You must say nothing, nothing whatsoever, to anyone about this, because the government will kill you too if they know." Actually, David thought that Rex would probably be spared, especially if she could claim she had been kidnapped, but he was protective of his own and Malia's lives. Rex's eyes opened fearfully, but she held her tongue.

"I've come up with a good plan that will maximize our chances of crossing safely. We have some help from other people out there. But you have to trust me."

"My mother said I could trust you."

"Yes, she was right. I am your stepfather, and I will protect you like I am protecting her life and mine." A good job I've done protecting Malia so far, he thought ruefully, knowing she was defending her life, fruitlessly, in a sham trial at the camp that very afternoon.

"How are you my stepfather?"

Too much for today, David thought. "As soon as we cross the border, your mother and I will get married, and so we are family."

He wanted to close the interference before it lasted suspiciously long. "Be ready on Friday night at 10. Wear your warmest clothing. You can bring a backpack but don't overstuff it. We may have to abandon it anyway along the way. I will text you, "check out the movie," and that's your signal to meet me at the Octavian back door five minutes later. Can you remember all that?"

"Yes," she said.

"I'm about to turn off this buzzing noise, which has made it harder for people to overhear our conversation. Is there anything else you want to say, anything that we might not want overheard, before I do so?"

"What will happen to my parents?" It took him a second before he remembered the Andrewses. They had now been languishing at Beaufort for over two weeks.

"I have signed a form that will allow them to be released on Tuesday, November 29th," he said. "If all goes well for us, you can send them a note from the United States letting them know you arrived safely."

"And if it doesn't—"

"Maybe the authorities will just send you home and you can tell your parents that Ms. Melia turned out to be a wicked kidnapper and so did her boyfriend, and you're so happy to be reunited with them. Then you can forget about us, or at least me. They are doing all right at Beaufort. I've made sure that they are being treated well, I promise you." He turned off the noise cylinder. David had personally ensured that neither would be interrogated harshly, let alone beaten or sent to a Red Room.

She stared at him. "Are you an Antifan?"

"Yes, and your mother has been working for us too." He raised his hand against the mounting questions Rex wanted to ask. "We'll have more time to talk later. Get sleep, eat well, and become as strong as you can. Don't worry about your homework, it doesn't matter anymore."

She almost laughed. This was the best advice she'd gotten in years. But this man was being deadly serious—she could tell from those steady gray eyes—and she didn't want to imply that she was taking this important mission lightly. She would be brave, she promised herself.

David confirmed that she had an invitation to Harvest Dinner with a friend's family in the Octavian. It was no time for a child, or anyone, to be alone. He himself would eat the holiday dinner in Ploreville, where they still called it Thanksgiving. It would be his last in the DJR one way or the other, and he planned to bring Frida and Ansel to Marjory's for good. He would tell Marjory that he and Malia were taking a two-week vacation to the West Coast, and he didn't want to leave the cats in the hands of the new Avalon concierge.

Malia had already been marched back to her jail cell by lunchtime on Tuesday, her death sentence duly announced. The trial had taken place in a large room paneled cheaply in plywood. Malia sat in a plastic box on one side of the room, facing a six-person jury of ESF officers on the other side. Mattison himself was the judge, per ESF protocol, wearing his dress uniform. The prosecutor, an ESF captain, detailed Malia's alleged crimes, referring generically to the "national security" experimentation. Also, per protocol, Malia had no defense attorney but would be permitted to briefly speak in her own defense. It was considered unfair to put an ESF officer at the career disadvantage of defending an enemy of the state.

The chief witness against her was Adam himself, who appeared on a screen from the Economic Tower. He found it humiliating to admit publicly how this low-Social Crediteer had fooled him. But it would be sweet to have his revenge on her by showing who was truly in charge, not just in this trial, but in the world. And Mattison had threatened that if Adam refused to testify, he would simply release Malia, who would have to find her way back to the City, but would probably find help at the Antifan base down the road.

"Do you have anything to say in your defense, Ms. Jenness?" Mattison asked her, almost perfunctorily. Anything this Antifan bitch said would simply keep them all from lunch that much longer, he thought.

Malia had debated trying to whitewash her alleged crimes, but since she knew what the outcome would be regardless, she decided to go for broke. "Yes," she said from the confines of her box. Her microphone was enabled, conveying to her that she was on sufferance. She was told to stand.

"Thank you for giving me the opportunity to learn about what I have accomplished on behalf of the Antifan Defense Forces," she said, choosing her words carefully to postpone the moment at which Mattison would mute the microphone. "I have learned a great deal about the activities of the Economic Tower during my acquaintance with your Intelligence Director, Adam Ross. Never would I have dreamed that the Economic Tower would casually, cruelly destroy the lives of thousands of Social Crediteers in a laboratory experiment, treating them like animals—" The microphone was silenced, but she began to shout, to break out beyond the box.

"And every time a Social Credit citizen dies, strapped in the laboratory chair, thousands of dollars go into the bank accounts of Adam Ross, Will Kendall, Barry Mattison, and several other of your highest functionaries. Those bank accounts are in

Mexico, in violation of DJR law. They have become rich men from killing our Social Crediteers!"

The courtroom buzzed, and Mattison, horrified at the wanton disclosure, signaled to the courtroom bailiffs to silence Malia. But before they could grab at her in the box, and then while they dragged her from the courtroom, she continued to shout.

"The money comes from the Chinese Government, to which the sufferings of our young people are nothing. But why should the Chinese care, when our own leaders do not? When this truth serum is perfected, you will try to overcome the ADF and seize total power in the DJR, against our Basic Law." She finished with a lie as they dragged her from the courtroom. "You arrested me before I could tell the ADF your plans. Good for you. But they will find you and destroy you all, including that psychopath, Adam Ross!"

The door closed behind them, and the jury was immediately authorized to retreat to the deliberation room. After a five-minute absence, mostly to give the impression of deliberation, but during which they gossiped about their Harvest holidays, the jury members decreed her guilty of spying on behalf of the Antifan Defense Forces. The jury recommended a death sentence by hanging.

"Do you think she was right about those Mexican bank accounts?" one juror asked hesitatingly.

"Just ADF propaganda," another reassured her. But all secretly thought that, yes, it was certainly possible. "Do you think they'll have that squash soup again? I've already seen it three times this week."

The guards hauled Malia back into the courtroom to hear her sentence, a formality about which the ESF was strangely dutiful. Mattison raised his gavel. "By the power invested in me by the Economic Strike Force of the Economic Tower of the Diversity Justice Republic, I sentence you to death by hanging, to be carried out at the Economic Zone Camp Four on Saturday, November 26th, 2089. Do you have anything else to say?"

He barely paused as he spoke over Malia's "Yes."

"Very good. The prisoner has nothing to say. This courtroom is adjourned." The gavel slammed.

Adam's screen went dark as he signed off. In a few hours, a chauffeured car would bring him to the Zone for an extended stay. He had gambled that he was safer at the Economic Tower than at home, and that the ADF would not dare arrest him at work. But they would not find him at home. And now he and Will would enjoy in person Malia's execution on Saturday. Psychopath, really, that bitch, what a mouth she turned out to have, he muttered to himself.

Back in her cell, Malia found that her circumstances were already diminishing. Her jailers told her that in accordance with camp protocol, prisoners sentenced to death were served only gruel and water. In some ways for Malia, this was a more disturbing and concrete development than the actual, but abstract, death sentence.

"It'll make your hanging easier," explained the young guard, although he didn't specify for whom. Also in accordance with protocol, the stout MED chaplain made an appearance to offer her services and mediate with the Earth Mother on Malia's behalf.

"I think not," said Malia coldly. "I am a Christian, and I reject your idolatry. There is the Lord our Father, and Christ His Son, and none other." Being sentenced to death gave you remarkable freedom to speak your mind, she thought with dark humor. The chaplain scuttled away with surprising vigor for one so stout. But she left behind some paper pamphlets just in case Malia changed her mind as her execution approached. Malia looked scornfully at the paper, thinking it would make excellent toilet paper in lieu of the rough fiber sheets stacked next to her toilet.

The hours passed, stultifyingly. Malia began to absorb the unpleasant fact that the Economic Tower actually planned to execute her, after starving her. She finally reached for the pamphlets out of sheer boredom, first *Sin and Repentance in MED Religion*. The guard brought her gruel dinner as darkness fell. Her eyes struggled to read in the dim light:

"There are two main sources of sin in MED. One is the violation of protection that is owed to Mother Earth. Overuse of resources and failure to recycle and reuse are great sins.

"The second sin is privileging one's own existence over the lands and waters of the Earth. We all must recognize, and even celebrate, the moment at which our earthly existence is no longer needed by the collective. Some of us, due to high Social Credit scores and service to the DJR, may expire naturally at a great age. Some of us may suffer physical and mental deterioration that makes our continued existence too costly for the collective to bear. When authorities determine this time has come, one should joyously celebrate the opportunity to give one's body back to Mother Earth, our parent. To this end the DJR has established the Euthanasia Palace in all our Cities, so that the citizen may truly celebrate his or her or their life's end. Resistance to these determinations is individualistic, selfish, and thus sinful.

"If you are reading this pamphlet, you may be among those few who, because of your illegal activities, have been sentenced to death. Your death will necessarily be far more unpleasant than had you gone to a Euthanasia Palace. However, you are still privileged to have some time to think about your misdeeds and how you may still contribute to the DJR even after your death, as you become dust again."

Makes Lutherans seem almost lighthearted, Malia thought to herself.

"Stand up! You have a visitor," the guard announced. To her great surprise, Commander Mattison was let into her cell. Was this a good omen or not? Malia guessed the latter.

"I hear you have professed Christianity to our chaplain," Mattison said darkly.

"Yes, what other reaction could I have to the sham proceedings and evil that permeate this place?" said Malia. "Jesus died for your sins too, you'll be happy to know."

"Then I am glad you were sentenced to death," said Mattison. "Regardless of your spying for the Antifans, the profession of Christianity in the DJR is a capital crime."

"Sorry to put you to all that trouble earlier today then," said Malia. "I could have just let you know about the Christianity thing earlier."

"I came here to remove that choker," said Mattison stiffly. "Colonel Ross wants it back, and he would only entrust me with the combination."

"What, has he found another victim so quickly?" cried Malia. "He is certainly obeying the Mother Earth order to recycle." She had no idea that Adam Ross was once again settling into their guesthouse for the duration.

"Turn around and lift your hair," ordered Mattison, as he fiddled with the combination lock. She felt his fingers brushing against her neck, the one they intended to snap in a few days. Mattison deliberately took his time, his fumbling fingers caressing the soft nape of Malia's neck. As soon as the choker snapped off, he spun her around and planted his mouth on hers. She broke away, screaming, but the guards had discreetly stepped away for a break.

"Shut up," said Mattison. "Adam said that I was welcome to do this. He's through with you."

"This has nothing to do with Adam," Malia spat back. "I'm not his property, and I'm not yours."

"There you are wrong," said Mattison, pulling her toward him again. "Look around you." Malia was temporarily frozen, like a frog transfixed by a snake. His beefy hands were gripping her shoulders, and he was forcing his tongue into her mouth and had pushed her onto the cot and she felt his fingers groping for the latches to the overalls bottom. Think, she told herself, what would Kate tell you to do? She extended her arms fully so that her hands pushed back on his shoulders, taking advantage of his distraction, while underneath him she rolled over toward her left side, freeing her right leg to attach to his hip, creating more space to attach the other leg. With a violent shove of both legs, Malia threw Mattison off her onto the cement floor. Next, she jumped back onto her feet, quickly fastening the latch that Mattison had managed to pry open. One would not have thought these overalls could provoke lust.

Mattison cursed, as Malia said slyly, "An actual ESF military engagement!" Now that her tongue was loosened, after all these years, she luxuriated in her pent-up spite.

"I think you'll be a lot less impudent once several of us come back," said Mattison grimly, making a move to summon the guards.

"I wouldn't do that, if I were you," said Malia. "If the great commander of Zone Camp Number Four requires help from his subordinates to rape a prisoner, I think word would get around the camp pretty quickly. You really would lose some respect. I'd also like a chance to fend off several of you bastards at once—the Antifans trained me well."

Mattison stood still, considering this.

"Whereas if you just leave now, I'll let the guards think you had your way, and all of us will be happy," she said. Mattison left, slamming the door behind him, which clanged satisfactorily in Malia's ears.

Half an hour later, the middle-aged guard now on duty brought a second dinner of a cheese sandwich and a bowl of tomato soup. "Commander Mattison said this was in return for your cooperation with his needs," he said, almost apologetically, placing the tray on the cot.

"No hard feelings!" Malia said cheerfully. The gruel diet resumed in the morning, but the nighttime meal had bolstered her spirits. At lunchtime, she found a slice of bread under her napkin, and she instinctively knew Fern had managed to slide it onto the tray.

While Malia was fending off Mattison, David was sitting opposite Carolina Cruz in a charming bistro near Ada's. He had cultivated Carolina assiduously all evening. He greeted her in the Azteca lobby with a "you're so beautiful," complimented her outfit, asked about her new record deal with the Diversity Music Corporation, and praised her special Harvest Holiday song for the ADF workforce. "The way you looked in that video," he confided, "I know every man in the ADF envied me. And some women, of course." When he reached out and held her hands gently in his, she knew with smug assurance what was coming, because it happened every few months.

"Carolina, will you marry me?" he asked, pleadingly. Her affirmative answer, he knew, might win him the space he needed to avoid trouble with Beaufort for the next few days. And that was all he needed.

Carolina smiled down at her soft, pink-nailed hands. How often had she manipulated a man into professing his undying love for her, and making a proposal of marriage? Until now, she had not cared sufficiently for any one man to accept. The thought of committing herself solely to one of these solicitous eager-to-please suitors, even if they were handsome Antifans, had depressed her. David was no worse than any of them, and she knew they made a nice-looking couple together. She only had wondered whether as the years passed, since he was almost forty, he would be able to maintain the stamina she required in bed. And she was eager for her official release to date the truly compelling Brian Walters.

But she was under instructions to accept the proposal, at least for now. And she did, very convincingly, she thought. "Thank you for making me the happiest man in Anacosta," David said, bestowing a tender smile on her. His eyes watered in a way that Carolina dismissively viewed as a sign of weakness. Brian Walters would not melt at her affection, she was confident.

"Excellent, my precious," said Uncle Victor when she called to tell him that she had accepted David's proposal of marriage. Finally, he thought, Harris has become reasonable again. What man, he thought, would reject Carolina Cruz for a low-Social Credit nonentity? Once the operation was over and the girlfriend safely stowed in Hawaii, he expected that Harris would grudgingly accept a bait and switch with some other Antifan beauty.

When Ferraro called Montoya with the news, the deputy was relieved. The two had been discussing with Gemma Carpenter whether Harris would need to be kept under house arrest for his own good until the operation was over. Gemma in particular was dubious that David would stay quietly in Anacosta that night. Much as David had hoped, his proposal to Carolina had reassured them that he would comply with their demands and never see Malia Jenness again. As for David, he hoped that he would never see Carolina Cruz again, despite their plans to spend Saturday night at her apartment.

Chapter 73
Bye to the Chip
(Friday, 25 November)

It had turned out to be harder to sign out a vehicle at the last minute than David had expected given the night's unusual operational demands. He had not wanted to risk signing one out in advance. But it helped with the motor pool that he was a commander, and none of them knew that he had been banned from the operation or from leaving Anacosta. He was wearing the full Antifan battle gear that would help him blend in once the operation began. He had left his TV blaring in his apartment in case Beaufort authorized an appliance feed.

To David's relief, Rex came downstairs quickly once summoned. David hadn't been entirely confident that several days later, on Friday night, alone in her parents' apartment, Rex would keep her promise to escape with him and Malia. Who was he to her, after all? Yet there she was, with a cartoon character backpack, wearing a purple hoodie sweater to hide her identity from a street camera, looking at him appealingly for the next step.

"Let's go," he said. "First stop, Ploreville." He didn't explain. But about twenty minutes later they were pulling alongside a closed auto mechanic shop. They hurried into the shop—Ploreville by night was different from Ploreville by day and not to be lingered in, although a grown man and a teenage girl might not have occasioned suspicion given what did happen on the streets. The shop belonged to the son of Doc, who had treated the Harris family for earaches and strep throat for decades before retiring. Doc had a set of keys to the shop and a portable surgical kit, and had agreed to remove David's chip.

Rex looked worriedly at the shabby surroundings. On the other side of a transparent garage door were several tradesmen's vans and three motorcycles awaiting repair.

"I'm just going to have some minor surgery," he told her. But it was not so minor. The removal of a chip, once inserted, was a capital offense and would ensure his outlawry. The ADF performed an automated chip scan of all its officers once a day. It was really an electronic roll call, but David knew that happened only in the morning.

"Hello Davy." Doc was one of the few Plores who called David by his childhood nickname. They shook hands as Doc emerged from the deep recesses of the shop where he had been waiting. Wasting no time, Doc administered an anesthetic to the skin behind David's right ear, raised the scalpel, and within a minute removed the tan button that resembled a lima bean and had rested there, pulsing David's whereabouts since he was sixteen. Then he staunched the bleeding, and affixed a thick cloth pad to the wound. At first Doc had refused to perform the surgery, until David had explained that keeping the chip would almost certainly doom his escape, and thus forfeit his life.

"Then I will save your life," Doc had agreed. At his age, he was not particularly concerned about the risk to himself, as long as they took basic precautions by not meeting at his house. David insisted on paying him, saying, "what am I ever going to do with this cash again?" Rex watched, fascinated.

They dropped Doc off a few blocks from his house. "Good luck, Davy. Good luck, Miss," said Doc. He vaguely understood this was Davy's stepdaughter. But the ways of the City were still obscure to him. A few blocks away, David got out and smashed the chip under his heel, poking the debris into the gutter with the steel toe of his boot. Then they sped off toward 66 West. It was now 11:20 pm.

Rex fell asleep west of Manassas and they were heading south on 81 when David woke her up. In the middle of a near-winter night, it was a dark and lonely highway, their only company a handful of trucks ferrying goods back and forth between the Zones and ADF camps. At the deserted rest stop, David checked for cameras, and then demanded Rex's armband, which he destroyed with a knife before her horrified eyes and tossed into the woods.

"Why?" she hissed at him.

"Because we won't get through any checkpoint if they see a young girl is in the van. Even if you hide, the armband will tell them you're in the vehicle. It's as dangerous as my chip was. You won't need it anymore," he promised her. David told Rex to ride in the back of the van, under half a dozen blankets and tarps, and not to make a sound at the checkpoints. Now Rex began to understand the danger that awaited them. But she fell asleep again nonetheless, and they sailed through the first checkpoint without her ever realizing it. The militia at the gatehouse knew that an operation would be taking place at the ESF camp, and they assumed this authoritative Commander must be part of the advance team.

David drove more slowly along the winding roads that led toward the camps and the border. A full week after the full moon, it was mostly dark and in these backwoods there was no road lighting. A few hundred yards before David would have turned left onto the smooth road leading to the camps, he broke off to the right, onto a gravel road that led up into the hills slightly north of the ADF camp. About a mile later the road terminated at Daniel's small frame house. It was nestled in a bed of towering trees and dark except for a small lamp in the window. Daniel came out to meet them and ushered them inside quickly. It was 1:52 am.

David knew the first paratroops of the Loyalty and Honor Brigade were scheduled to land at 3:30 am, dropped from the ADF's Air Troop Carriers at altitudes well above what the ESF guards could detect. The greatest danger to the Brigade was not from the ESF, but from inviting a barrage of artillery fire from the US side of the border, so the paratroops would have to target their descent carefully. David knew that the paratroopers would then seize the main house and open the gates for the ground troops, who were making their way toward the camps along the same roads David and Rex had just traveled, as well as coming separately from Charlottesville.

The ADF assumed that Malia was safe in the jail cells, so although her rescue was on the task list, she would only be a tertiary Antifan objective. David hoped this would create a sufficient delay window so that he could make his way to the cells, force the ESF guards to free her if they hadn't already run in panic, and then flee the compound with her. Malia had told him that the jeeps were scattered around the compound, required no special access code, and were easy to operate.

David introduced Rex to Daniel, with whom she would be spending the next few hours. "This is my brother," David said. He added, smiling, "He is completely— vegetable." Rex smiled back, uncertainly. She then sat on the patched sofa, wondering if Daniel owned a telescreen, and watched the brothers as they huddled over some sketches on the kitchen table. Daniel pointed to the location of an abandoned barn where they would convene. If David texted "Onion," they would remain at Daniel's house. Otherwise, Daniel and Rex would proceed to the barn shortly after dawn. Daniel identified the old hayloft, the stalls, and other places where they could hide during the day tomorrow, sleeping, and readying themselves to cross the border.

"I have the items you asked for," said Daniel. "They're lying in a stack at the barn, by the cow pen. If anyone came across them, they would think they were ordinary boxes, maybe for feeding animals."

While the brothers talked, Rex looked around what was certainly the humblest dwelling she had ever entered. Whatever Daniel hadn't built himself, he had scavenged from yard sales or occasionally purchased at an ESF factory sale open to ADF personnel. The table was roughhewn wood; the chairs mismatched wood and metal. The sofa on which she was curled up was an ancient pre-war microfiber. Daniel and Marie probably could have purchased newer furniture, but they were comfortable with their home. It was bit ramshackle, but always clean.

"So this is rural Plore life," Rex marveled, as she fell asleep again. Daniel got up from the table when he noticed, and he gently placed an old throw blanket on her sleeping form.

When Rex woke up around dawn, David was long gone, and Daniel was making them breakfast.

David had been sitting in the car in a thicket near the back gate monitoring Antifan radio traffic, and was ready to crash through the underbrush after the entering forces. He followed the Antifan ground troops into the camp, and when challenged, gave the operation sign, "Blue Meal," presumably an indirect reference to the truth serum. The commander patches and his general recognition among ADF ranks alleviated any lingering concern by the new sentries at the gate. Once safely past the gate, David followed Malia's directions to the jail cells. Given the relative lack of interest in the Hawaii-bound prisoner, David had beaten the other Antifans to the sheds. He pulled the balaclava over his head, and jumped from the car. It was about three hours before dawn.

"Halt!" he yelled, confronting the middle-aged guard on duty. "Hands up!" The element of surprise worked for him, and the guard, shaking, complied.

"Antifan Defense Forces," David said, still proudly. "Where's your prisoner Jenness?"

The man stammered, "she's not here anymore."

David grabbed him by the lapels. "What the f--k do you mean?" Had they already killed her?

"No, no. Colonel Ross and Colonel Kendall came by ten minutes ago and took her away."

"Where did they go?" David demanded. But then he realized what was up. "What's the fastest way to the airfield?" The guard, as accustomed to heeding authority as water a streambed, suggested the north side of the main square, up through the fields and to the airfield at the far western end of the compound adjoining the factory area. The guard had grown to respect Malia, and he was relieved that someone seemed to ready to save her life. David steered through the Antifan troops now in control of the main square, without being challenged. He placed the small red and black Antifan battle flag on the hood to deter curiosity, as who would be driving around in a flagged van other than ADF senior leadership?

On the porch of the main house, Steve Rosen, directing his forces, wondered briefly who was in the van that left the main square and took a sharp turn northward, but then he began taking calls from the chemical factory, where the troops had reached the basement. They had detained Dr. Ling, who was taking them to the truth serum stores quite willingly, once she coolly assessed the situation. The serum was also stored in Chinese vaults, she knew, so what did it really matter if it were no longer available to these barbarians? The sappers were laying the explosives that would destroy the building. The ADF knew that if any serum was left undiscovered, the experiments would continue, somewhere, so the goal was to ensure its almost total destruction, at least in the DJR. A call came in from Beaufort that the overnight raids at the Octavian and Argonne had failed; neither Ross nor his confederate Kendall were found. Steve directed forces to the guesthouses and put out a general alert for the pair.

Just as Adam had ensured, the pilot had steered the small jetplane out of the hangar. It was fueled and ready to go. Around 3:15 am, Adam's armband had alerted him to an intrusion in his apartment, which he correctly inferred was an attempted arrest by the ADF. He alerted the pilot, called Will, and then he decided they would take Malia. "I want her," said Adam. Will shrugged, having become accustomed to Adam's mercurial moods regarding Malia. As their jeep hurtled toward the airfield, the first paratroopers began gliding over the installation.

The Antifans hadn't yet approached the airfield, the idiots. What kind of military force were they, these days? he sneered. Adam and Will waved to the pilot, who lowered the staircase. Malia looked around the darkened airfield, unsure of whether she should run at this point. She wasn't aware that the Antifans had begun landing, although Adam and Will, scanning the skies, knew what was happening. She had to assume that if she fled from Adam, the ESF would recapture and execute her on schedule. For all she knew, Adam was rescuing her, and perhaps he was leaving because any threat was directed against him and only him. She hesitated.

"Get up there," Adam grunted, pushing Malia up the staircase. He opened the jet door and shoved her into the cabin. Will followed, looking behind them as he closed the door. A black car was heading in their direction. "Black car coming," said Will. "Not ours. Let's get moving."

"Put on your goddamn seatbelt," Adam said to her, like a very rude flight steward. She started to obey, and then hearing the phrase "not ours," Malia decided to try to run. She moved quickly to the door, but Adam got there before her. "Back you go," he said, and he strapped her in himself. Adam and Will were sitting in the row in front of hers, but from what she could tell, they weren't fastening their seatbelts. That was for nonentities. The pilot pulled up the door.

This is Air Low-Credit, Malia joked blackly to herself. She suddenly realized that this was her first airplane trip ever. Maybe her last.

"Here's your toiletry case from the guesthouse," said Adam. "You might need it in Mexico. You're looking like a wreck this week." Then to the pilot, "Let's go, what's going on?"

"Doing the safety checks," the pilot said. "I'm not planning to crash in Alabama."

"For God's sake," said Adam. "We're not even going to get off the ground at this rate."

The black car pulled up alongside the jet. "Dammit," shouted Adam. "Forget the checks, get moving!" The pilot saw the car and they began taxiing forward. Malia opened the toiletry case and began inspecting the contents.

David leaped out of the black car and, almost invisible in the dark, called through his armband's loudspeaker: "This is the ADF! Halt and prepare for boarding!" Malia couldn't look out the window from her seat on the other side, behind Adam, but she recognized the voice. A great warm feeling of joy and relief swept over her. Daniel was right, David would never abandon her. Another dark-clad figure stood next to him, but the pilot couldn't tell whether others were nearby. He circled the plane around to try to reach the takeoff strip.

"He's not going to stop," David said to Dominic, whom he had picked up just north of the square and told he needed help to apprehend Adam Ross himself. "Grenade action." They each pulled out a grenade that was part of the Antifan soldier's battle inventory, and aimed them low at the jet wheels, careful to avoid the engine and its fuel tank. The plane body reared up and crashed on its right side.

Oh my Mother Earth, Malia thought to herself. She was glad to still be strapped in, but Adam and Will were flung downward toward the side of the aircraft on the ground. She unlatched herself, climbed on the seat now underneath the door, and started to open it herself.

"Here you go," said the pilot, behind her, finishing the job with his longer arms. "I'm not going to get myself killed by Antifans." He reached out the door and waved a white cloth at the Antifan officers.

Malia felt herself being pulled back by Adam, who had righted himself and was climbing back toward the door. "You're not going back to them," Adam said to her, as she fell back toward the other side of the airplane. The pilot clambered out of the door, still waving the cloth, and David and Dominic held fire.

Adam and Malia grappled on the floor as he struggled to place his hands around her neck. Taking advantage of his hands being occupied elsewhere, Malia grabbed the knife she had secreted in her overalls pocket from her toiletry case and plunged it into Adam's abdomen, under the ribs, right up to the hilt and upward. It went in smoothly, to her surprise and shock. Adam's eyes widened, his grip loosened on her neck, and he growled, "Bitch," before his head turned to the side and his eyes closed.

"I'm still pregnant," she said, just in case he could still hear her, since she had read that hearing was the last sense to go when you died. So many times, with each humiliation, she had sworn she would kill him, but she had never really expected to have to do it herself.

David looked at Malia from the opening in what was now the top of the jetplane. Even with his balaclava, she recognized him. "Is he dead?"

"I think so," she said.

He jumped down into the plane and quickly assessed the situation. Then he pushed Malia up through the door, where Dominic and the pilot were ready to help her climb out and run to the van.

Back on the ground, David asked Dominic to communicate to the ADF forces at the main house. "Proceed to airfield. Jet plane down and out. Adam Ross and Will Kendall in craft, Ross likely dead, Kendall unclear, prepare to engage."

"Roger," came the response. "Farrell, stay on site. Anyone else with you?"

"No," said Dominic, as David shook his head wildly. David had explained quickly as they sped toward the field that he wasn't supposed to be involved in the operation because he was too emotionally close to Malia. But he needed to rescue her, he explained. As a junior officer, Dominic had no idea how desperate David's situation was with the ADF leadership, and thought David's concern for Malia very commendable. As for himself, David would gladly let Dominic take all the credit for removing Ross and Kendall and preventing them from escaping to Mexico.

"If they ask, just say you took Ross's jeep here to the airfield," said David. He Antifan-saluted Dominic. "Thanks for everything, Farrell. You have a great career ahead." And then the van with David and Malia was screeching down the perimeter road that led to the back gate. Dominic turned to pat down the pilot.

"They were forcing me to fly them to Mexico," complained the pilot. "Can you put in a good word for me?"

"Sure," said Dominic. "You helped at the end." The Antifan troops approached, swarming over the craft. "One dead, one alive," called out the scout. Will was pulled out of the aircraft and marched, stumbling, to the Antifan vehicles. Troops took the pilot away. As Dominic watched David rescue Malia, he wondered to himself, where is Cheysa? He knew that Walters had brought Cheysa along, mostly to carry the Wurro statue that had become an Antifan standard, but Dominic knew she was unused to combat and he feared for her. Orange streaks began to inch over the horizon with the coming dawn.

Chapter 74
Manhunt On
(Saturday, 26 November)

As soon as the car got beyond the airfield, David said, "We're going to get out the back gate and find Daniel and Rex—they're waiting for us."

"No!" said Malia. "We have to find Fern."

"Find Fern? Are you crazy?" David was furious. "This is a close call even without going to the opposite end of the camp." Every second counted now.

"But I know which barracks is hers," said Malia, who had engaged her guards in conversation during the week. Especially late at night, and when they assumed she would be gone from the world in several days, they gladly chatted with her, even confiding their marital woes. They knew Fern by sight, and when Malia had expressed concern about the conditions under which Fern labored, they had reassured Malia about the slightly better accommodations the women kitchen workers enjoyed in #32. "It's number 32. We have to try."

David cast a frustrated look up at the heavens. Part of him wanted to throw Malia in the back of the van and "head out of Dodge," as the Plores said, but part of him recognized that they owed Fern a chance. And if he didn't try, then Malia would hold it against him. "Okay," he said. "Put on this bala, would you?" He gave her a plain black head covering, saying, "just so you don't attract attention in the van." He added, "and we're going to bail if we run into trouble." They drove around the perimeter road to the lower southeast side where the women's barracks lay, just north of the execution grounds. Along the way, they encountered a few Antifan vehicles at which David blinked twice each time to signal the Antifan "all right." No one stopped them.

The alleys in between the barracks were thronged with women who were emerging with the dawn out of curiosity, or fear, or both. The Antifans had not yet ventured into these muddy alleyways. Malia told David where #32 was, and they edged their way through the crowd, honking the horn. She ran into the barracks, and called out, "Fern Potts? Is Fern Potts here?"

"She's in the kitchen," called someone. "Breakfast duty."

David cursed under his breath, and they drove around the main square. Malia, remembering that the kitchen was in the basement of the main house, had David drop her off in the back of the building. She knew to avoid the main stairs thronged with Antifan officers that was Steve Rosen's staging ground. "Fern! Fern!" she called as she entered the kitchen area. The corporal was gone, but the workers were still proceeding with their normal routine, assuming the Antifans would demand breakfast. "Come with me!" Malia realized how incongruous she must have looked in a black Antifan balaclava and overalls splashed with rust-colored blood.

"Malia!" Fern cried joyfully, dropping her knife on the table, and then they ran out together. David, to his chagrin, was standing outside of the car and explaining to two ADF sergeants that he was Commander Harris and had secured the jailhouse area. They saluted and marched off. He opened the back of the van and the two women jumped in the back, and they were off toward the front gate, which was thick with Antifan troops. David slowed, stuck his head out, and said, "Make way, returning to headquarters with the action report." The troops all parted for the authoritative voice whose balaclava bore the insignia of a commander, and then the van was barreling down the road.

Meanwhile, Steve Rosen had relayed the death of Adam Ross and capture of Will Kendall to headquarters. Kendall was currently under sedation in the ESF infirmary. That reminded Steve of Malia Jenness, and he finally sent a detachment over to the jail cells to release her and bring her to the main building. The men returned ten minutes later to report that the jail cells were empty, the guards were gone, and no Antifans were on the premises.

"What?" Steve cried. "Where is she? Put out an alert, immediately!" Two sergeants arrived to report that Commander Harris had told them he had secured the jailhouse area, although they admitted they had taken his assurances at face value. Steve called headquarters.

"Hold for the Director," the operations center attendant instructed Steve, to his surprise. He had been dealing with Montoya until now, but the deputy must have gone home.

"Rosen? Is that you?" He heard the familiar rumble of Ferraro's voice. "Congratulations on the operation. I hear all is going well."

"Yes, sir. We are ten minutes from destroying the factory with the lab. We have almost 200 serum samples and whatever Dr. Ling didn't tell us about will blow with the building. Dr. Ling is in custody and we will bring her back to Beaufort—unless you don't want an international incident, since she's threatening one. We also released three subjects who were imprisoned in the basement, presumably for today's testing."

"Great job. Just bring Ling back, and we'll figure it out then. But you have a new problem."

Steve knew this would involve Harris. It always seemed to these days.

"We did our routine chip roll call, and Harris is missing."

"But he's running around here somewhere, sir. I was just told he secured the jailhouse...Yes, sir, I know he's not supposed to be here...no, we haven't found the girlfriend either."

Steve sighed. At this point, he was sure Harris had simply disobeyed the command to stay away from the exercise, but you had to give him credit for showing the Antifan spirit, even if motivated by protecting his girlfriend. Hadn't Harris just proposed to Carolina Cruz, though? The news had penetrated even the dustiest corners of Beaufort, more out of interest in the Latina siren than in the name of the commander who had won her heart.

Steve couldn't bring himself to believe that Harris had removed his chip. Why would he remove his chip and then show up at a major Antifan operation? It was probably a malfunction. David Harris had a lot running through his brain these days, which could certainly set off an electrical spark that would frizz the chip. The alternative was too dire to contemplate.

"Find the girlfriend," Ferraro said ominously. "Where is Walters? I need to speak with him."

"He's at the factory, sir. I'll patch you through to him."

Walters was playing adjutant to Dontellan, who was giving the final instructions to the sappers. They had just reported the building was entirely clear of personnel. The chemical engineers had confirmed that the chemicals in the building would make an impressive fire but one that could be contained in the immediate vicinity. The furniture factory might be consumed if stray sparks landed on it, but it too had been evacuated. Others had brought up whatever paper files could be located, including some old-fashioned file cabinets. Along with Dr. Ling, Retsinger and four laboratory assistants were in custody. They were being interrogated while the shock of detention was fresh, with the interrogators falsely holding out the promise of avoiding transfer to Beaufort.

"Sir?" asked Walters. Cheysa sat nearby on a bench holding Wurro on her lap. She felt like a piece of furniture, possibly a cabinet for holding demon statues.

"Good morning, Walters," said Ferraro. "We have a problem on our hands that I think only you can fix. And it will be a great opportunity for you to show you deserve to move up in the ADF."

Oh wow, thought Walters, it's already been a good year.

"Commander Harris failed his chip call this morning. He is supposedly on the premises of the Zone camp right now, having sprung his girlfriend from the jail. Now mind you, I wasn't looking for her to be executed. She was supposed to be in Hawaii by tonight. But when I put together a no-chip Harris and a girlfriend who can't be located, what do I get?"

"Are we absolutely sure it isn't a computer malfunction, sir?" Walters said hesitantly. Even for him, the thought of David Harris going outlaw was shocking.

"Let me help you here, Walters. When we have a no-chip Antifan officer and that no-good girlfriend absconding from an Economic Zone camp on the border with the United States, what do you think is going to happen?"

"Yes, sir."

"Here's what I want from you. Once that factory is blown up, tell Rosen and Dontellan you're on a mission from me, and they can call me directly if they want to confirm it. I want you to go track down Harris and kill him, and bring his body back to Beaufort. And I don't want him looking like a precious blond knight, you know, like Lancelot or something...."

Walters frowned. Who's this Lancelot? Do I know him?

"I want him to look like that other guy who tried to escape, you know the one we put on display in the lobby for weeks. I forgot, you're a little too young to have seen that. It made an impression, that's for sure. So if you have to shoot, go and kill that way, fish in the barrel and all that. But I'd rather see something more—dramatic, more manly. The kind of story that would make it easier to nominate you for Antifan Hero First Class at the end of the year. Just shooting an escapee, I don't know."

Walters swallowed. Antifan Hero, First, Second and Third class were the highest awards the ADF could bestow. Even if Ferraro partly reneged on the promise, he would almost certainly win Third Class. The rewards included a generous Social Credit boost, a prominent role in a ceremony aired across the country, and in this case, Carolina. But he might never get a chance to win such an award again, since they were so rare. Go for the gusto, he told himself. He wanted an opportunity to become a legend among Antifans, and to be a hero like his father.

"Yes, sir, my loyalty and honor. What about the girlfriend?"

Ferraro said, "If you can recover her safely, fine. If he's dead, she doesn't have to go to Hawaii, but she can if she wants. If she gives you trouble, you can finish her off. Neatly, humanely. We won't be displaying her corpse. She probably still has her chip, so track that. You have my instructions."

"My loyalty and honor, sir!" Walters felt grateful he had brought Wurro along. Wurro was even better than a loyal sidekick, and he wouldn't demand to share the Social Credits or Carolina.

David had once said that Walters had his good and bad traits, and that he was dogged in the direction of either once pointed that way. Walters had now sniffed the scent and would track the prey unrelentingly, with Wurro, with his constant and powerful mana, along for the ride. Walters hoped that Cheysa was up to the job of carrying Wurro on the manhunt.

From the hill above the Antifan camp, driving furiously, David saw the fireball rise over the ESF camp on his left. A giant spurt of fire bore into the sky above before opening and blossoming into an orange mushroom cloud. "Holy God," he said, and then into the back of the van, "The chemical factory just blew." Those on the ground in the camp, and even at the ADF camp down the road, felt the ground tremble beneath their feet.

"Good," Malia and Fern chorused.

David took a long look at the double row of fences that stretched along the border beyond the camps. No matter how challenging the last nine hours—only nine hours? had been, the real daunting, life-and-death confrontation lay along those steel lines on the ground, daring them. Another mile down the road, David parked the car in a clearing not visible from the road. "Malia, we've got to take out your chip," he said, reaching for the first-aid surgical kit.

"What?" she said, horror-stricken. "But that's a capital offense."

"Mine's already gone," he said. "Unless you want them to track you all the way here and kill us outright, I'd suggest we get rid of yours too. It's a risk now. Sorry."

"What about mine?" asked Fern.

"You can keep yours," said David. "They need to know they're looking for you before they can do a chip search." Fern looked relieved.

David drew on a pair of latex gloves, used several of the anesthetic pads, and tried to be as delicate as possible, but Malia wept profusely. He wanted to cry, too. Malia reminded herself that if she could tolerate Adam Ross's assaults, this minor operation, which would do her no lasting harm, and maybe even save her life, could be endured. Once the chip was extracted, David gave Malia cloths to hold against her ear while he tossed the chip far over an adjoining cliff, and threw his own armband after it. Let the pursuers be momentarily distracted. However, he knew that they were vulnerable to a heat-seeking drone if the ADF chose to fly one over these areas in search of him. How badly would the ADF want to find him?

Surely by now Beaufort knew his chip had gone missing, and also that Malia Jenness had disappeared from her jail cell. David now second-guessed his decision to remove the chip, which gave the ADF no reason to believe he and Malia might show up in Anacosta. On the bright side, it would not be easy for the ADF to find them in this overgrown forest with its not-very-accessible byways. The forest canopy would also thwart the heat-seeking drones, or at least result in a lot of false positives, he knew.

The three walked a mile until they reached the deserted barn. It was a sad gray, the paint having worn off long ago. Boards hung limply from the roof and windows. The border crossing they had picked was about a mile and a half farther west. Daniel waved to them from the barn door, Fern squealed to see Daniel, and Malia and Rex hugged. They all breakfasted in a corner of the barn on turkey and cheese sandwiches and fruit. "I raised the turkey myself," said Daniel, at which Fern squealed again. David found Fern's noisemaking annoying, but as long as it seemed to please Daniel, he would not complain. He briefly worried about whether Fern could be trusted to undertake the escape without losing her nerve and jeopardizing them all.

They set watch shifts among themselves to allow others to sleep; the sentinel stayed in the loft overlooking the road. Malia took the first shift. She would not die today, she resolved.

Chapter 75
Waiting for Walters
(Saturday, 26 November)

The detachment of Antifans from the base broke down the door of Daniel's house on the remote surmise that Commander Harris could be hiding here waiting for pursuers. Walters had not found it worth his while to come here, given the likelier trail up Purcell Road. "Where's the brother?" the squad captain asked. It was a Saturday, so Daniel would not have appeared at the base, absent an emergency. The white pickup truck they knew he drove was gone, but he could be shopping in Harrisonburg for all they knew. It was a shame the Plores had gotten away without being chipped, that's for sure, the captain thought.

They searched the house thoroughly, and the surrounding grounds, but found nothing of interest. On the kitchen table was a floor plan labeled "Upstairs remod, Jan 2090," which led the Antifans to infer that Daniel at least had no intention of crossing the border. Daniel had plunged the more incriminating drawings into the septic tank before leaving the house that morning. Even Antifans would not look in the septic tank.

The captain reported to Beaufort that they had found no one, let alone Commander Harris, at the house. "But we left a memento," he smirked, glancing behind him at the door hanging off its hinges.

Toward evening, the group convened on the floor of the barn, minus Fern, who was on watch in the hayloft. Daniel distributed the remaining sandwiches. David sat leaning against the wall of one of the horse stalls, his left arm around Malia's shoulders. Rex snuggled up against Malia's left side. Daniel sat cross-legged across from them. Thanks to Daniel, they were well draped with blankets on what was becoming a cold, cloudy night. He had also brought dark-colored warm jackets and black knit hats for Malia, Fern, and Rex; the women had arrived at the barn only with shirts and overalls, and Rex's idea of warm clothes was suited to the City, not a desolate mountaintop. "Our quartermaster," David called him, not really joking.

Malia thought that time was passing very slowly. It had been like this last night, as she counted the minutes of what she expected would be her last night on earth. And now this would be her last night in the DJR, one way or another. Her thoughts turned to Adam Ross, already cold, gone these twelve hours, never to return.

Conversation dwindled and David sensed the apprehension was rising. By this hour they were sitting in the dark of the winter barn. There was a working light bulb adjoining the horse stalls but they dared not use it. "Let's tell a story," said David. He started to tell one about a heroic Antifan before realizing this was not the time or place for that story. Even though she was a librarian, Malia hesitated; she only knew DJR propaganda. Rex was too shy to try.

"Here's a story," said Daniel. "It's about David, who became a great king in Jerusalem." His brother David smiled, knowing what was coming, but neither Malia or Rex recognized it. "It's from the Bible." Rex's eyes opened wide with fear, since this was the dark Book against which she and her peers were constantly warned. But looking at her mother's shining countenance, she relaxed. Surely this could not be wrong.

"The Hebrews under King Saul faced the Philistines on the battlefield," Daniel began, "when a giant emerged from the Philistine ranks, covered in armor. Day in and day out the giant, whose name was Goliath, taunted King Saul's army, demanding they send him a challenger, but no one dared volunteer. Then one day, a shepherd boy named David, who had been serving King Saul as a musician, was bringing food to his brothers in the army. David volunteered to fight the giant. At first Saul refused to send this youth against the giant. Then David said as a shepherd he had killed lions and bears that attacked his sheep, and would do the same to Goliath. At last Saul yielded, saying, 'Go, and may the Lord be with you.'

"When Goliath saw this young shepherd boy, who had armed himself only with five smooth stones and his sling, he mocked David. 'Come to me.' Goliath said, 'and I will give your flesh to the fowls of the air and to the beasts of the field.' But David replied, 'You come against me with a sword and with a spear, and with a shield, but I come to you in the name of the Lord of hosts, the God of the armies of Israel, whom you have defied. This very day the Lord will deliver you into my hands.' The giant Philistine advanced but David killed him with a stone flung from his slingshot that hit Goliath's forehead. Then David cut off Goliath's head with the giant's own sword, and the Israelites chased the Philistines and defeated them.

"Saul became increasingly jealous of David's military success and popularity and sought to kill him. David had to flee Saul, even though he had married Saul's daughter Michal. David hid in his own house, where the king's men were ordered to prevent him from leaving. But Michal helped him to flee through a window and escape his pursuers."

Daniel related how Jonathan—Saul's son and David's great friend—warned David of an ambush by going out into a field where he knew David was hidden. "David came out from his hiding place and the two friends met. They promised friendship forever, and then parted. After that, David wandered around Judea with his forces. He met Jonathan one last time in the wilderness of Ziph before Jonathan died in battle. Jonathan came full of caring, and strengthened David's courage in God. He told

David that David was destined to be King of Israel, and that Saul knew this. And after many years of wanderings with his followers and evading Saul's armies, David finally succeeded Saul, who had died by his own hand, after losing a battle."

Daniel was concluding, "And David was anointed King of Israel," as Fern scrambled down from the hayloft, calling softly, but panicked, "A car's coming!"

They all jumped up and scattered like field mice into the hiding places they had chosen around the barn. Daniel headed out into the woods, where he had concealed the truck. It was the time he had planned for some mischief anyway. He knew a backwoods route to the substation.

Walters and Cheysa pulled up in their jeep at the darkened barn a few minutes before 7 pm. The base had advised them that a concentration of heat had been detected here, and Walters' own readings suggested this was correct. But false positives were common, especially when a barn or other building had been occupied in the recent past. They had gone down numerous gravel roads and investigated a dozen fruitless leads. "I've seen more damn barns today than in my whole life," grumbled Walters. Cheysa was cross. Couldn't Brian simply have driven around with Wurro himself while she returned to Beaufort and her own bed? She felt like a statue herself, only less revered than Wurro.

Cheysa was in an especially grim mood because in an exuberant moment, as they jolted down yet another gravel road, Brian had confessed that the Director had promised him Carolina Cruz should their mission succeed. Initially, Cheysa had been gratified by the news that the demon was planning to leave her, but on the other hand, she, not Carolina Cruz, was babysitting a pagan statue while roaming the frightening dark byways of western Virginia in the wake of this murderous Antifan, and she was becoming increasingly cold and hungry. Then Walters said, "I know you're probably worried what this means for you, but I think we can arrange one of those three-way marriages, so you two can share me. I've been thinking that it would be a shame to lose each other after all we've been through together, right?"

"I don't want to share you with anyone," Cheysa said, which Walters promptly misinterpreted.

"Well, that's too bad," said Walters, his large, wiry hands turning the wheel as the road curved and narrowed. "You'll just have to put up with it. Maybe you can learn something from Carolina—she's incredibly hot. And don't think you're going to walk out on me, since I'm becoming an Antifan Hero after tonight. You'd only be hurting your own interests."

They finally pulled up in front of the dark barn in which David and the others were hidden. The sound detector registered a leap. "Maybe just foxes," said Walters, "but let's see. If it's nothing, we'll camp out here for the night. I can build us a fire."

They entered the barn. Walters and Cheysa switched on their flashlights, trailing them around the edges of the barn.

"I smell ham," said Walters. "Some kind of meat."

They walked past the horse stalls. Cheysa switched on the light bulb, which to their surprise, was still operating. Walters suddenly swiveled, his heat detector beeping gently as it sensed a nearby source. He reached into a pile of straw and pulled out Rex, who stumbled to her feet. "Well, look what we have here," said Walters. "Don't you look cute!" In the twilight of the barn, he did not recognize her resemblance to Malia, although Cheysa did.

Rex wanted to scream, but she knew it was futile. She stared at them sullenly.

"Who else is with you?" Walters demanded. "This isn't some high school overnight trip. Got a boyfriend around?

"You have ten seconds, or I'll make you regret this," Walters said. He counted ten seconds, more or less, while Rex glowered at him. "Very well, Cheysa, slap her around until we get some cooperation."

"No," said Cheysa.

Walters turned on her, incredulous. "What did you say to me?"

"I'm holding your Wurro," she said disdainfully.

Rex took advantage of the distraction to run, but Walters caught up easily, and dealt her a stinging slap to her face. The sound of her cry brought Malia out of the cow shed. "Stop abusing my daughter," she said firmly. "If you have to hit women, you coward, at least avoid children." Rex ran out of the barn, but Walters had lost interest in her. She'd return eventually, he figured, for lack of anywhere to go. And if she wanted to fall off a cliff in the dark, that was fine with him. He hadn't realized the librarian had a daughter, but they certainly resembled each other.

"Oh ho," Walters laughed triumphantly. "Now we're getting somewhere. Hello, Ms. Librarian, we meet again." If she's here, Harris is here, he thought. "Where's your boyfriend? I'm going to kill him." He turned and yelled into the loft, "Harris! Dammit, Harris!"

"He's not here," she lied. "He's gone to get us something to eat." Even as she said these words, she was conscious of how pathetic her lie was. It didn't even anger Walters.

"Really?" asked Walters. "Is there a takeout place nearby? Cheysa and I were getting hungry as well. Maybe he'll bring an extra Enviro-pod or two." He contemplated Malia in her dirty overalls and fleece sweater. "That isn't a particularly attractive outfit you've got on, sweetheart. You're no Carolina Cruz, but I'm prepared to overlook it." He advanced toward her, knowing full well that if David Harris, that woman-coddling Plore, were in the vicinity, he would emerge now, just as Malia had protected Rex.

Walters laid his hand on her shoulder, ripped the sweater in two, and then trailed his hand over her chest under the rough overalls fabric. Raising his voice so that Plore Harris would hear him if he were anywhere in the barn, he shouted, "I guess we can do it like animals, since we're in this barn, right? I'll let you take off those damned overalls unless you don't want to keep them afterwards because they'll be ripped to shreds.

If you behave, maybe I'll let you live." His arms encircled Malia as she struggled to break free. It was one thing to fend off Mattison, but here was possibly the most lethal Antifan alive, an apex predator, pushing her to the ground. His hands hovered over her, readying to rip the overall front in half.

Aghast, Cheysa thought of the green paper pajamas at Beaufort. She shifted her arms uncomfortably with her burden of Wurro. Would she stand by and watch Walters rape Malia? But knowing Walters, she was sure all Brian wanted to do was lure Harris out into the open.

"Walters, lay off," said David, coming out from behind a horse stall. "I'm here." His hand was on his electronic gun. Although David knew it had been disconnected, Walters might not realize that. He figured Walters would not reach for his weapon as he disengaged from Malia and scrambled to his feet.

He and Walters faced each other. Walters still wanted to kill David the old-fashioned way, in the manner beloved by the Antifans of the civil war era, hand-to-hand combat. The way that men should kill each other, Walters thought. But if David pulled that gun out, he, Walters, would finish the job quickly and just smash up Harris's corpse. The story wouldn't be quite as good that way, though, and it might yield Antifan Hero third class instead of first or second.

"Harris, I'll give you a chance to go out like a man," Walters said, "even though we know how this is going to end, don't we?

"Director Ferraro says he's looking forward to putting your corpse on display in the lobby of the building. He sends his regards."

His eyes on David, Walters said, "Let's drop the guns. Chains, knives, hands, feet. How does that sound?"

"All right, it's a deal," said David. He had no alternative but abject surrender. They eyed each other carefully as they unholstered their weapons and placed them on the respective sides of the barn. David knew that Walters was a good four inches taller than him, and maybe about 20 pounds heavier, but size could be a disadvantage if you were less nimble than your opponent.

"Cheysa, count down from ten, would you? And put my Lord Wurro in a place where he can watch the action. I want that mana flowing my way." Cheysa obeyed, positioning the statue between the two men and facing them. In the half-dark of the barn, lit only by the one bulb and the flashlights, Wurro looked like a brooding judge or possibly a sour tennis referee.

Cheysa counted down. As soon as she said "zero!" Walters sprang at David, who jumped aside. With Walters off balance, David kicked him to the ground and then prepared to deal a blow to the side of the neck. Before David could lay the blow, Walters shoved him aside, rolling over onto him and trying to smash him in the face with his fist. The two grappled, with David rolling over onto Walters. David reached for his knife left-handed, but Walters grabbed his left wrist with his right hand. David would not drop the knife, but could not maneuver it, and Walters jumped to his feet. The knife went back in its sheath, temporarily, but now Walters would remember that David had taken the knife class at Beaufort. In turn, Walters was reminded of the loops of chain at his left side, since he had excelled in that class, and began to loosen them.

As David saw Walters reach for the chain, he knew that if Walters succeeded in opening up the lengths of chain as a lasso, the knife would be useless because he would mostly be kept at bay, whereas Walters could kill him at a distance. He leapt at Walters' feet, bringing him down to the ground again, and stabbed at his midsection with the knife, but it was a glancing blow. The first blood flowed. Walters bellowed angrily, jumped to his feet again, and loosened the chains, which he began to whip around his head steadily. David watched for a moment when the chains smashed against the ground, which gave him a few seconds to dart past the landed chain and attack Walters with the knife, righthanded now. But Walters deflected David's arm with his free left arm, causing the knife to spin in the air and out of David's reach. Walters grinned as he smashed his fist into David's face, watched him fall to the ground, and then whipped the chains above David's prone body. Malia hid her eyes. It was all over, she thought.

For effect, Walters let the chain smash to one side of David's body and then to the other as David tried to roll out of the way. Antifan Hero time, Walters thought gleefully. Make it look good. He edged closer and gave David a solid kick to the solar plexus. David gasped, looking upward, knowing the final slash of the chain would be across his face and then Walters would finish beating him to death. For a brief moment, he regretted ever having gone outlaw, ruining Malia's life and bringing himself to this degraded end in a barn in the middle of nowhere.

And then, through his bloodied face, he saw the chains fly into the air toward the ceiling, and heard a huge, unearthly rasp as Walters fell toward him. He scrambled to his left as Walters' heavy body crashed down next to him. The chains landed farther back in the barn toward the feed room and the calf pen.

David stumbled to his feet, looking down at the dead man, and then into Cheysa's frightened eyes. She was still gripping her electronic gun, which she had fired at Walters' head as he was poised to bring the chains down onto David once more. She almost expected Walters to pick himself up and tackle her. Was he really gone?

"Thank you," David managed to say. His limbs were now shaking with deferred fear. Malia ran to him and held him close.

"I couldn't let the demon win," Cheysa said. For Cheysa, the final straw had been Walters' declaration he had no plans of releasing her even as he pursued Carolina Cruz. Wurro looked on impassively. The fickle mana had flowed elsewhere tonight.

Suddenly, Cheysa saw another Antifan framed in the barn door, clad in battle dress and balaclava. To Malia's alarm, Cheysa reholstered her gun, and ran to him. David braced himself, recovering his knife with his right hand while wiping blood off his face with the other.

Chapter 76
Cheysa and Dominic
(Saturday, 26 November)

As the Antifan pulled off his balaclava, David recognized, with palpable relief, Dominic Farrell. Dominic had arrived at the barn just as he'd heard Cheysa's voice counting down, and he had seen the entire fight from the shadows, where he had rooted quietly but fervently for Commander Harris. Dominic embraced Cheysa, which surprised Malia but not David, who in this case had not been quite as obtuse as Walters.

"Hello, Farrell," said David. "Friend or foe tonight?"

"Friend, sir," said Dominic. "At least I won't attack you if you don't attack me."

"Deal," said David. "I've had enough for one day."

The young couple came back into the center of the barn and sat on an overturned manger holding hands while Malia washed David's face and gave him a cloth to hold against his still-bleeding face. Rex crept back into the barn, shocked but relieved at the sight of the dead Walters facing into the dirt. Fern surveyed the scene from the hayloft where she had hidden, then climbed awkwardly down the ladder to the main floor.

"How many are you here, sir?" asked Dominic.

"That's it," said David. Strictly speaking, he did not need to refer to Daniel, who at this moment was arranging for the electric grid of the border fences and the Antifan camp to fail at midnight. Introductions were made all around. Dominic finished his rations and Cheysa ate the last sandwich in the cooler. Dominic told them that perhaps a third of the ESZ inmates had broken out of the camp and headed back toward the City or elsewhere. The ESF was scattered all over the countryside trying to round them up, like wayward cattle. Some workers had even tried to cross the border, and US artillery had obligingly pounded the border fence to open a gap for them. The group in the barn had in fact heard some heavy mid-afternoon rumbling. A few hours ago, this might have expedited their own escape, but by now the area was teeming with ESF and Antifans.

"Our base hadn't planned to do this kind of work for the ESF," said Dominic, "but headquarters told us later in the day to at least help guard the fences."

Then it was time for a serious talk. Dominic knew that David—and he guessed

Malia—no longer had their chips and must be intending to cross the border. David knew better than to try to convince him and Cheysa otherwise. "All I can ask is that you let us go and not alert the ADF to our location," said David. "Let us have a good try, since we've come so close."

Cheysa nodded, and Dominic said, "Yes."

"But now Conroy has a problem," said David. "Private, I am thrilled and grateful that you saved my life tonight. But how can you go back to Anacosta after having killed Walters? Frankly, I think the City should give you a parade and a promotion for having wiped him off the face of the earth, but the ADF might feel differently.

"We call this lethal insubordination, or what the US military informally called 'fragging.' You could be executed for having done this, as justified as it was."

Cheysa and Dominic looked at each other with alarm.

"My first thought was you could tell them that I stole your firearm and killed Walters, but obviously your gun can only be fired by yourself. We could concoct an elaborate story about your aiming at me, and missing, but a gunshot wound in Walters' head would still be difficult to explain. The story would not hold up very long. He's a favorite of the Director's and the Director would seek vengeance.

"Or you could try to just finish Walters' job and kill me now. I'm sure they'd call you Antifan Heroes and promote you both."

"What would you suggest, sir?" asked Dominic.

"Come to the United States with us. Live as free people. Read like free people. Worship God like free people."

"My mother. My sister," said Cheysa faintly.

"My mother," said Dominic, more firmly.

David said, "Conroy, you probably won't get to see your mother and sister again if you go back to the City. But if you were in the US, you might have the hope again, especially if relations start improving." He had read in the weekly ADF digest that the DJR and the US were contemplating the facilitation of cross-border family visits.

Dominic said sternly, "Commander, it's easy for you to say. The United States is a nest of white supremacists. They'd treat you fine, but Cheysa and I would be at the mercy of the racist police there. People wouldn't treat us like equals. They send your children to inferior schools and force you to live in segregated neighborhoods. Police shoot black men at will. I've read all about it in our media."

"Farrell, you read all this in *our* media, and you believe it?"

Dominic frowned.

"Has it ever occurred to you that you think you're treated equally here, but a lot of that is your being an Antifan? Antifans get treated better than any ordinary Social Crediteers, and I don't have to tell you that most Social Crediteers get treated better than Plores. If you saw the same statistics I do, you would realize that African-Americans have the same graduation rates from high school and college in the DJR that they did a hundred years ago in the US. After thirty-five years of the DJR, the average white Social Crediteer has a Social Credit score on average twenty points higher than the average black Social Crediteer, even with the race bump. How many black people are you seeing at the fancier restaurants you go to? Who makes up a disproportionate share of the Street People and the TerraCity pens? Black Social Crediteers are still clustered in the Social Tower and in eastern Anacosta neighborhoods, and you know it. Go to the Knowledge Tower," —the beating heart of the revolution— "and see how many black people you can count in an hour. You won't need both hands."

Dominic couldn't argue with Commander Harris, partly because he was still shy in front of the man who had helped him so much.

"And I will tell you from reading the US press—because I see the DJR digest of the US and foreign press—that the economic statistics for all groups are far better these days in the US and better than ours. Their Supreme Court—a real court, not an advisor to the president—has two black women and a black man, all dedicated to defending their Constitution."

"But why should we believe their statistics any more than ours?" broke in Cheysa.

"Because the US press isn't controlled by the government," said David. "Different media outlets exist across the political spectrum and they are free to report and argue and have different opinions. There are papers that cater to people of different ethnic backgrounds, too. A paper that is writing for an African-American readership won't survive if it peddles lies about what's happening to black people. I see articles from the black press in my digest, too."

Dominic still looked troubled. DJR media was quick to seize upon any incident involving minorities in the US and paint it as bleakly as possible. A Latino man beaten by "redneck" whites in the street. A black family perishing in a fire in a tenement in a poor neighborhood. But he had to admit that there must be positive stories too, though the DJR never told him those.

"A country where the people can elect their representatives and where the laws and the Constitution protect their freedom to debate, to assemble peacefully, to bear arms in self-defense, and to read and worship freely cannot be worse for anyone than a country that forbids all these human rights," David finished severely. "I'm sorry, I don't mean to lecture you. I don't want to claim the US is perfect, but white supremacists are not running the US, and the rule of law protects you. We have no rule of law here, which is what you'll realize if you stay."

Dominic thought briefly, this is a dilemma. We could kill Commander Harris and report it to Beaufort, but Cheysa will face a court-martial and execution for killing Walters. And I would never be able to forgive myself for killing Commander Harris. Or we can risk our lives and take our chances in the US. If we didn't like it there, at least we could move to Mexico or Canada.

Meanwhile, Cheysa thought, my mother and sister could deal better with me in the United States than in jail at Beaufort. And they would be in agony if I were executed. Both thought, with Walters gone, we can be together at last. That was a definite advantage. Better together in the US than separated by prison walls in the DJR.

"How are we going to get past two electrified fences and the minefield?" asked Dominic. "And on the base, they will be monitoring movement along the fences, I know."

"We have a plan," said David. "Can I trust you with details? Are you coming with us?"

The couple nodded. "Yes," said Dominic. "We don't have a choice now." David made them swear on a hastily contrived cross made out of two short sticks he found in the barn, and then they talked about the plans.

During the afternoon, Daniel had shown David the wooden platforms he had built to help them cross the minefield. In his research at Beaufort, David had learned that the mines in this area were not pressure-triggered mines, but rather heat-seeking ones. So the mines would not detonate when a person or animal stepped onto the ground and then lifted a leg, but rather when the mine detected a live creature less than nine inches away. The minefield was littered with dead squirrels and foxes for this reason. Daniel had experimented with various methods of conveying their party across the twenty yards between the two electric fences, but once David confirmed the issue was simply staying above the minefield, Daniel had decided that a series of small wooden platforms like stepping stones would enable them to cross safely. He had built thirty of these, each a foot high when unfolded. They nestled into each other so that several adults could carry about six platforms each and more in their backpacks.

"Brilliant," said David, clapping his brother on the back. "Simple but brilliant."

"Brilliant because simple," Daniel replied, smiling.

It was almost time to head out. David hadn't expected their party would number seven. Beaufort had certainly put out an alert to the base for greater attentiveness to border security tonight, and everyone knew Commander Harris was on the loose. That said, all tacitly assumed the esteemed Commander Walters would take care of Harris, so the distracted ADF base might be forgiven for erring on the side of laxity, or at least following the somewhat contradictory orders to tend to the border at the Zone camp. More hands meant it would be easier to carry the boxes. Dominic and Cheysa were still armed with their electronic firearms. All in all, David was optimistic, or at least as optimistic as one could be.

One item of business remained before they left the barn, which had seen more action in the last twelve hours than in the last twelve years.

David pointed to Wurro and said to Dominic and Cheysa, "Have a go at that hideous thing?"

Dominic and Cheysa grinned at the prospect, and each took a few shots at Wurro that blasted the idol into a dozen pieces. The electronic weapons were silent and they wasted no ammunition, given that the weapons did not use bullets but electronic signals. The electronic signals could be traced to this barn, so the Antifans probably would come by later regardless, but it was worth it. And that was the end of Wurro and his mysterious mana.

Chapter 77
Border Crossing
(Sunday, 27 November)

The group of six plodded quietly through the underbrush toward the meeting point. In the preceding weeks, Daniel had laboriously cleared a very narrow path through the forest. During the day it would barely be noticeable, and only adventurous boys would have tried it; at night, in the dark, it was invisible from the road. Daniel had painted white blazes on the stumps and trees for them to stay true. Several times, David thanked God for his serious and capable brother.

They heard only the occasional owl, and once they disturbed a thicket where deer were grazing. The deer moved a short distance away, but sensed that they had nothing to fear from these interlopers, who filed by discreetly. Trees at this elevation were mostly bare at this time of the season, but Rex felt the branches of bushes and low-lying vegetation brush against her cheeks. They all wore Antifan balaclavas, turned inside out to hide the insignia, or the black knit caps, which provided additional camouflage. Above them was the mercifully cloudy sky; it was a week after the full moon, whose illumination would not endanger them tonight.

At one point they were within a hundred yards of the road to the Antifan base that a week ago Malia had been racing to reach. They heard a distant rumble of a vehicle, but then the sound evaporated. Because of the ESF support activity tonight, David knew, there would be more vehicles moving around than usual. But he counted on Antifans dismissing stray noises, if they heard them, as escaped ESF inmates rather than a band led by David Harris. It would depend on how enterprising the Antifans were versus how much they wanted to return to the base and go to bed. Most of them had been awake for nearly twenty-four hours, so David expected them to opt for the latter if not forced to confront the group.

The woods came to an abrupt end, and they saw the two lines of ten-foot high fences ahead of them on the other side of the clearing, about a hundred feet, or thirty meters away. The top of the nearer fence was curled toward them to deter trespassers.

"They are dead," whispered Daniel, referring to the fences, as he approached them in the thicket. "You can't tell from looking, but they are safe." He brandished wire cutters. He had created a partial outage at the ADF base, which would cripple the sensors monitored in the operations center. Nor would the emergency generators operate. Unfortunately, the lights placed along that section of fence still worked. Daniel hadn't been able to identify that circuit confidently.

"I saw a patrol go by about ten minutes ago," said Daniel.

"Then we have twenty minutes, but I wouldn't assume it," said David. "Let's roll."

He and Daniel ran to the fence, leaving the others in the thicket. Dominic and Cheysa covered them with their firearms. Daniel cut a gash and then a hole in the fence. He stuck his hands through with one of the wooden platforms they had opened in the underbrush, placed it down, and then could just reach to place a second. He climbed onto that second platform, while David handed him two more. Then David signaled Malia, and then Rex after her, in the order they had established back at the barn. So far so good. Malia pushed through the gash and followed Daniel, handing him several more boxes that he steadily opened and placed before him as he proceeded through the mine field. Rex followed carrying several more, which were passed to Daniel at the front.

Each box was placed about two feet apart, and David had warned everyone to be careful and deliberate in placing their feet securely, lest they fall off and trigger the mines.

Fern went next, visibly nervous. About halfway down the line, she slipped and fell onto the ground. A blast left her stunned, holding her left arm with her right. I knew it would be her, David thought bitterly. White faced, she clambered back on the box, with Cheysa behind her bending over and extending a steadying hand. Fern made it to the end, her left arm dripping blood. By now Daniel had reached the second fence and cut a similar hole in it.

Dominic and David were next, but at the last second, Dominic told David to precede him. "I'm covering," he said. "Go!" David wanted to argue, but it made sense. He was unarmed. He followed Cheysa down the wooden stepping stones, lightly but adeptly.

Then they heard a rumble down the road. The patrol was returning fifteen minutes earlier than expected, having heard the blast. It wasn't unusual for foxes and other wildlife to trigger the mines, but the patrols were expected to inspect each blast. The base, for all its distractions, had doubled its night patrols given the alert about Commander Harris, and when the cameras failed to operate, the patrols knew they had to cover more ground, faster than usual. Per usual procedure, the patrol had dimmed the lights of the vehicle, although they still didn't expect to encounter actual escaping human beings until they neared that section of fence and saw the moving shadows across the minefield. There had never been a successful escape attempt from this base's territory before, and no reason to think Harris would fare better. Closer to the ESZ camp, the patrol would have been better prepared for escapees.

Both the patrol troops and the group were caught by surprise. Daniel was through the second fence, along with Malia, and Rex, and he had dispatched them to run down an escarpment on the right side where they could seek cover. Fern and Cheysa pushed their way through the second hole, assisted by Daniel.

Dominic had gotten through the first fence, just barely, placing the last box next to him, and seeing the two men emerging from the jeep, he crouched down, one foot on each box. There was no bulb above him, and he was clad from head to shoes in Antifan black, so he wasn't immediately visible to the patrol, which first looked ahead to the movement glimpsed, where David was running, halfway between the fences. David looked behind, saw the patrol, but couldn't help Dominic, so he kept moving, fast. An electronic bullet whizzed by him. Dominic had been correct to insist on being the sweep, but David hoped it wouldn't cost him his life.

Aiming his gun sights between the wires, Dominic raked fire across the three men in the patrol. The men fell, whether because they were injured or killed, or just for self-protection. Dominic took advantage of the several seconds afforded by his initiative to run down eight boxes, with another twenty to go. Then he fired back in that direction again, to keep the patrol at bay. As Dominic ran, he threw each box behind him some distance, which would prevent the patrol from following. He heard the patrol climbing through the fence, but because Dominic had tossed the boxes, the troops could not pursue him beyond the sixth box.

He turned around and fired again, but the patrol fired too. Suddenly, Dominic felt himself get hit in the right leg. Damn, he thought, keep going. It just felt like a pinprick. He could do it, he vowed. It wasn't serious. The hole in the second fence was ahead, and he stopped tossing boxes because every second was precious and he had created enough of a gap that the patrol troops could no longer follow without themselves triggering the mines. Their remaining shots missed, some closer than others. Dominic was pleased he had won the marksmanship prize in his class at the Antifan training academy; clearly these guys hadn't.

Dominic hurtled through the second hole, and beyond. He knew he had succeeded when he heard disgusted curses rather than angry shouts. From his days on the Pennsylvania-Ohio border, Dominic knew the protocol was not to pursue escapees past that second fence, at which point US artillery enjoyed picking off Antifans at will. He just hoped that the US forces would be able to distinguish between bad Antifan patrols and good Antifans and civilians escaping together.

Now behind the ridge just underneath and beyond the second fence, Dominic felt his leg buckle. He realized that he had been injured more seriously than he had thought when under the influence of the adrenalin, and he dropped to the ground. David, who had gotten the others to safety in a cave entrance in the cliff, returned. He offered his arm to the younger man, and Dominic limped along with him to where the others were gathered. As soon as Daniel saw Dominic, he reached into his pocket and retrieved the remote-control activation device that would allow him to restart the electrification for the fences. A few seconds later, they heard screams from the Antifans still engaging with the fences.

"I think we're safe now," said Daniel.

David grimaced, "Still too close for comfort. This is still DJR territory, technically."

"Let me look at your leg, Farrell," said David. Dominic rolled up his right pants leg, and David staunched the flowing blood with a tourniquet from the first aid kit Malia was carrying for the group. She had already bandaged Fern's arm, which would also need real medical attention as soon as they reached the US lines.

"I don't want to stay here," said David. "We need to move toward the US lines. Take off the balas. If they see those, they'll think we're Antifan scouts and fire first and ask questions later."

He reached for several white cloths he had stuffed into a jacket pocket and handed them around. "We're going to head down into the valley," he said, "Keep waving them, whether or not you see anyone. Eventually we will. I know there's a road about half a mile ahead. But don't get overconfident yet." Taking their cue from David, the other six kept quiet.

They breathed the crisp air, if not quite free, then promising freedom. So clean it hurts to breathe it, thought Rex. A narrow dirt path led to the right and down the outcrop. Before them stretched a valley with a distant flurry of lights concentrated straight ahead. "That must be the militia base," said Dominic, gritting his teeth through the pain as he continued to hop, leaning on David's arm for support. Cheysa wanted to help him too, but the path was only wide enough for two. Fern's arm throbbed, but she didn't want to complain, not now.

As they descended into the valley, through the woods, light snow began to fall, the first of the season. Trudging behind her mother, Rex stuck out her tongue to taste the gentle flakes. They formed a veil-like pattern against the dark cloudy sky.

About forty minutes later, slowed down by Dominic's injury, the group reached a paved road. "Look!" said Rex, pointing to an approaching armed detachment, about several hundred feet away.

"Halt!" the militiamen shouted, at which the group waved their white cloths frantically. About 20 years ago, a squad of Antifans had ventured a raid into this territory using the same dirt road, which the militiamen remembered well. "Hands over your heads!" The ten or so militiamen were not in uniform, but wore similar trousers and jackets in a camouflage or dark spotted pattern. All bore semi-automatic rifles. Two were women.

The escapees must have seemed a motley group to them. A teenage girl; two women in overalls who clearly had escaped the Economic Zone concentration camp that morning; a middle-aged blond man in jeans and a cloth jacket, and three Antifans, one clearly injured. The men separated the Antifans from the others, and patted them down, removing the firearms, knives, grenades, chains, and other weaponry left over from the morning's operation. Once the Antifans were disarmed, the militiamen patted down Daniel, Rex, Malia, and Fern, and found nothing worrisome. The mood lightened.

"Welcome to the United States!" the militiamen called out. "Congratulations on making it across!" Their scattered applause came as a huge relief to the group, which was still cautious in claiming victory. Someone called the base requesting vehicles for transport. "Seven deejers," said the caller, "including three Antis, all disarmed." David guessed that "deejers" was the local term for DJR persons.

"We haven't seen a real border escape in decades," said a militiaman with a bushy beard. "We hear a lot of minefield blasts, though."

"Speaking of which," said one of the two women in the group, indicating Fern, "the cloth is bleeding through. Let's take care of it now." Fern was grateful, because she felt dizzy. They sat her down, and the woman who seemed to be their medic reached for a first-aid kit. As militiamen trained their flashlights on Fern's arm, the medic unwrapped the bandages, cleaned the wound, applied a disinfectant, and rebandaged it. "It's broken," she said, "from when you fell. But we'll take care of that back at the base."

The medic then turned to Dominic, and inspected his leg. "From the way you're walking, it might have chipped the bone. We can take you to the hospital in Charleston for imaging—that's more than our base can handle." She gave him some pain relievers, which he swallowed gratefully. Then she handed water and energy drinks around to all.

Dominic was cautiously relieved. The militiamen had treated him well so far, at least no worse than anyone else. He had heard and believed all the DJR stories—each more lurid than the last—about the white supremacist militiamen guarding the US border against Diversity. He wanted to hug Cheysa, but also didn't want to give the militiamen any reason to suspect he was dangerous. He had read about the US police being trigger happy when it came to black men. But he noticed that David was also keeping his distance from Malia. It was best for the Antifans to avoid provoking concern, he realized.

Four vans showed up, silhouetted against the snowfall, which had become heavier. Daniel and David went in the first van; Cheysa and Dominic in the next; Malia, Fern and Rex in the third; and the militiamen piled in the fourth, with escorts scattered among the other vans.

As they drove to the US base, Dominic asked their guard, "Any objection if I kiss my fiancée? We're glad we're safe."

"No, don't blame you," said the militiaman, "Go for it."

In their van, David and Daniel high-fived, and Daniel said fervently, "Thanks be to God."

"I thought you deejers didn't believe in God," said their militiaman.

"These two do," said David. "We're Plores."

"We hear about how they persecute you," said the militiaman. "But you're an Antifan?"

"I am," said David, "because they took me away when I was a teenager and made me become an Antifan. My family didn't quite forgive me."

"That's not exactly true," said Daniel. "We know he had no choice. But his heart is Plore." David felt a great warmth toward his brother at the tribute.

Malia, Rex and Fern were escorted by a militiaman and the medic. Malia said, "Twenty-four hours ago, I was waiting to be hanged at the Zone camp. They accused me of being an Antifan spy. But tonight I made it to the United States. How's that for excitement?" The Americans whistled at that. Rex stared at her mother with wonder.

Back on the other side of the border, Antifan forces had reached the barn. They placed Walters' body on a stretcher, and bore it reverently to the troop carrier. It would arrive in Anacosta by early Sunday morning. They searched for the Wurro statue, which they wanted to bring back to Anacosta to inspire new generations of Antifans, but left the shattered pieces in the pigsty when they finally found them. Ferraro was finishing another late-night *Risk* game with his bodyguards when the news came from the Beaufort operations center that Walters was dead, and Harris, his infuriating girlfriend, two other Antifans, and several others had safely crossed into the United States. Ferraro slumped in his chair, for once defeated.

The call from Beaufort woke up Steve Rosen from a sound slumber shortly before 2 am. He had relished turning in that night after nearly twenty-four hours awake in the most morally justified operation he had ever undertaken. It had reinforced his pride in being an Antifan. It was a resounding success, except for the loss of about a hundred ESZ inmates who had crossed into the US, which wasn't his problem. The events of the day would help make Steve Rosen the ADF Deputy Director in several years, but the disappearance of Harris and his likely murder by Walters had been the remaining sore point. He expected to hear the bad news in the morning and to have to deal with a triumphant Walters and his Wurro on Monday. He had not allowed himself to visualize David's corpse lying in the Beaufort lobby, not yet.

He took the call with a studied reserve that the Beaufort operator attributed to sleepiness. When he hung up the phone, he balled his fists, saying to himself, "Harris, good for you! Good for you and Malia!" He was not particularly discomfited at having lost Walters, and was glad to hear the ugly statue had been destroyed. Looking at his wife's soft sleeping form, he decided she would not welcome being awakened, so he lay awake, smiling at the ceiling, before he finally fell asleep again.

Chapter 78
Into Freedom
(Sunday-Thursday, 27 November to 1 December)

The vans headed toward Charleston, West Virginia with the seven deejers early Sunday afternoon. The base had gotten stray reports that the ADF might be preparing to launch a strike to recover the group, and even though the base commander thought it highly improbable, she wouldn't take a chance. David agreed with her that Ferraro would be so enraged that he might futilely risk ADF lives to try to wreak revenge if not actually recapture the seven. So the group was moving farther into the Interior. One van took Dominic, Cheysa—who refused to be separated from him—and Fern to the hospital. A second van took Malia, Rex, and Daniel to the hotel where they would stay for the next week or so before arrangements could be made to send them to St. Louis. Later in the day they would shop for new clothes and other basics.

The third van took David, the most senior and immediately valuable escapee, to the FBI office. "We apologize for the hurry," said the base commander, "but we don't want to lose any time, and we want to start debriefing as soon as possible. Please don't think of this as an interrogation."

"I understand," said David. "If the situation were reversed, I would do the same."

After a three-hour trip, David stared out the window as they approached Charleston, which would put them out of reach of the ADF forever. He knew Charleston had been one of the most infamous battlefields of the civil war, which meant rioting had destroyed much of the downtown as the Antifan gangs had slugged it out with the local residents and the US military over decades. The DJR had proclaimed it "a physical and cultural wasteland." But here he saw tidy brick buildings, a few glass towers, cinemas, a concert hall, and even on a chilly November day after the Thanksgiving holiday, pedestrians strolling on a promenade along the waterfront. He thought that once again, at least some Harrises had returned to their home region, the western side of the Allegheny Mountains where their ancestors had settled 300 years ago and from which his family had been dragged in the civil war. The Ohio border was not far away.

The FBI field office in Columbus had dispatched agents to interview the group. US military and intelligence representatives would show up tomorrow. Two agents in coats and suit jackets—one a middle-aged black man and the other a younger white fellow with floppy dark hair—bounded down the stairs of the office building to meet them. "I'm Special Agent Keith Williams. How do you do?" said the older man. "And this is Special Agent Fred Cabelli."

"Pleased to meet you, sir," said Cabelli. David relaxed at the reassuringly respectful salutation. They ate sandwiches in the conference room while David related the story of the escape. He mentioned that he had helped Malia find her child who had been kidnapped by the DJR authorities for having committed cultural appropriation, and that child was now the teenager in their group.

"Amazing," said Williams. "I'm looking forward to meeting that brother of yours, too."

"He'll be able to tell you a lot about that ADF base as well," said David. "He's been the electrician there for decades. He's seen more there than I did."

"Your wife sounds like she knows a lot, too," said Cabelli, "especially about the Economic and Knowledge Tower types."

"Yes," said David. "She was an informant for us in this high-end apartment building where a lot of them lived. Before that, she was the final librarian for the Depository where the government kept the last paper copies of banned books. They blew it up a few months ago."

"Banned books," Williams shook his head. "You'll be pleased to know you can read whatever you want in the United States, in paper or on your workscreen. Whether some of those books will do you any good is your problem." They all laughed. David thought, I feel comfortable here, I could work with these guys.

The formal questioning began. David gave his name, age, and history. He explained how the Antifans had recruited him. In response to the agents' questions, he discussed the border security, his Antifan training, and his various assignments.

"Have you ever committed what we in the United States would consider a war crime or human rights crime?" Williams eventually asked.

David became guarded at the language. "How would you define that? As you know, the ADF does a lot of things that violate human rights from the US perspective. I recognize that. But you don't get to be a commander by saying no to operational requirements."

"Fair enough," said Williams. "What makes you valuable to us probably also means you've done things we wouldn't countenance here." He realized that David had stiffened. "Don't worry, we're not putting you on trial. It might be relevant for your onward assignments, though." There was no protocol for dealing with escaped Antifan commanders, since none had yet made it to the US before, but Williams knew that St. Louis would likely not regard David's career with equanimity. So he equivocated, but gently, and pressed for more details. He asked David to tell him about the various insignia on the leather jacket, which David had so far kept. "This yellow lightning bolt was for my role in stopping a train of refugees from crossing the US border," he admitted, "and the red x was for eliminating a fascist cell."

"How do you define a fascist cell?" Cabelli asked, which reminded David how effortlessly he had internalized the language of the DJR. David struggled to remember the incident.

"I think they were a pro-democracy club that opposed many of the policies of the DJR, such as the Social Credit system," said David, uncomfortably.

"So fascism simply meant they were opposed to the government."

"Yes."

"What about the Red Rooms?" Williams asked. David was surprised that the FBI knew about the torture chambers. He blamed most of the torture on his subordinates, particularly on the bloodthirsty Walters, but he knew this reflected poorly on him.

"But you authorized it?" Williams asked sharply. David admitted that he had done so, and had participated himself, albeit reluctantly. He had not dared refuse.

After an hour of such examination, David was impatient. "Look, I'm not proud of any of these activities. I consider them to have distracted me from my legitimate law enforcement duties. They were not the bulk of my ADF employment. But there is no way I could have stayed in the ADF without doing them. Refusing to do these things would have put me in jail."

"I hear you, Mr. Harris," said Williams. "But without knowing the whole story, we cannot move forward. I told you that I do not think you would be legally responsible here for actions that technically took place against the citizens of another country, absent an extradition agreement with that country. And even if such an agreement existed, we would not return someone who had fled to face retribution at the hands of a dictatorship."

'But without acknowledging the whole story, we cannot move forward,' David thought ruefully. That was true enough. The light was beginning to fade outside, and the agents suggested they resume the debriefing in the morning. They asked for his jacket, handing him a good quality leather jacket in exchange. "You can't wear that Antifan jacket on the streets of Charleston," they said. David regretfully complied.

After the agents sent him off in the van, Cabelli said, "I get the impression that Mr. Harris thinks he would have a seamless transition into the Bureau or local law enforcement here."

Williams replied, "He's slightly over our age limit, even with a waiver. And I'm sorry, but what he did for the Antifans isn't going to pass muster on this side of the border, even though I understand why he did it. We probably would have done the same in his situation." He paused, "Now I can see hiring his wife, though. That's some story from what he told us."

Cabelli agreed. "Very brave lady, boss. And without all the human rights baggage. Looking forward to meeting her tomorrow."

Malia and Isabelle returned to the hotel suite around that time, carrying large shopping bags bearing the name of Charleston's finest department store. A nice young lady who introduced herself as "from the government," accompanied them and paid for everything. The one department store in Anacosta was a stylish boutique that had been off limits to Malia. But anyone could enter the Charleston store, she marveled. And no one used carbon offsets, although customers were welcome to donate to a charity featured at the cash register.

They left the bags upstairs and began exploring the hotel. Malia gasped with pleasure at the banquet rooms, with their velvet curtains, embroidered chairs and thick Oriental-style carpets (or "Asian," as the deejers would say). By local standards, it was fussy and old-fashioned, but deejers would have reverently called it "pre-war."

"We could have a wedding here," she said somewhat wistfully. David had promised they would be married as soon as they crossed the border, and why not here?

Isabelle said, "I guess you deserve to be married. David's okay."

"Thank you," Malia said archly.

David found them in the lobby, ordering frilly drinks in various colors and staring at the cupola above. Isabelle was used to luxurious surroundings, but here Malia was the excited child.

"I like your new jacket!" said Malia. "We got new clothes too."

"They took the old one from me," said David. "I guess it was unavoidable." The deputy commander from the Border Patrol, who would hand them over to the Bureau officially tomorrow, asked whether there was anything else he could do for them tonight. Dinner had been arranged for them at a restaurant down the street at 7 pm.

"Can I go in...?" Malia stopped herself. "Oh, of course I can now."

David explained to the deputy commander, who shook his head with disbelief. "You're in a free country now, ma'am."

David anticipated Malia's next question. "Would it be possible to arrange for a Lutheran pastor and a wedding ceremony? When we were in the DJR, I promised that as soon as we got to the United States, we would be married properly."

"Yes, I'm sure, but aren't you already married?" David and Malia had introduced themselves as husband and wife.

"Well, it wasn't legal in the DJR. My mother's pastor married us in his living room last month with the curtains drawn." David explained that Christian pastors could only minister to Plores and it was illegal to baptize or perform a marriage involving a Social Crediteer. The commander rolled his eyes and asked, "Did you consider it a legitimate wedding?"

"Yes," said Malia. "In the eyes of God, we are married."

"In that case, the United States also considers you married. We don't care about the crazy laws you lived under there. But if you want to do it again, why not? Just give us a few days. You guys deserve a celebration."

"I would like a wedding ceremony in which we were not fearful for our lives," Malia said.

David nodded appreciatively. She had a talent for pinpointing the crux of an issue, he thought.

At that point, Cheysa and Dominic, the latter on crutches, entered the lobby. Cheysa had ordered new clothes online with their government escort. With Cheysa's help, Dominic—whose Antifan jacket had also been replaced—eased himself into an armchair. He explained the hospital had diagnosed a hairline fracture in his leg and showed them the cloth casing now around it.

"Here's another couple that might want to get married this week," said David.

"Not if I can't dance with my bride," protested Dominic. But once they told him about the planned celebration, Cheysa begged Dominic to reconsider. "We'll dance for the rest of our lives," she said. "Can you find a Methodist minister?"

The escort headed over to the front desk to confer with the staff. More drinks were ordered. It was about 6:30 pm when Daniel and Fern joined the party. The hospital had set Fern's broken arm, and she and Daniel had strolled on the promenade as the sun descended glowingly over the river. Malia and Cheysa told them about the wedding while David and Dominic smiled at each other at the women's excitement.

"Well, brother, what about you?" David teased Daniel.

Daniel and Fern looked at each other hesitantly. "Not yet," said Daniel, "but maybe not too far off."

"Good," said Isabelle piteously. "I was going to be the only one of you all alone."

"You're never going to be alone again, honey," said Malia.

"But don't count on getting a boyfriend anytime soon," said David from his armchair. "I plan to be a very strict stepfather." The adults laughed as Isabelle half-smiled over a pout. The deputy commander returned to say that the hotel would be pleased to host the double ceremony on Thursday night and would invite the ministers.

On Thursday night, the banquet room awaited the newly married couples and their well-wishers. The candelabras glowed over round tables clad in spotless white linen with gold-edged napkins. Soft dinner music played in the background, and dancing would follow dinner. David and Malia sat with the Lutheran pastor and Isabelle, and Cheysa and Dominic with the African Methodist Episcopal minister and his wife. Daniel and Fern sat at another table to maximize the opportunities for the prominent Charlestonians to meet the daring deejers who had crossed the border. Among the guests were many of the FBI and other US government officials who had spent the week debriefing the brave group and acclimating them to life in the US.

Reporters from the local media and TV stations were present to cover the wedding, the latest episode in the constant media coverage of the escapees. As if the escape itself were not enough, the roles that David, Dominic, and Malia had played in the raid on the Economic Zone camp had excited the whole nation. All seven were due in St. Louis on Monday to meet with President Thomason and members of the US Congress.

As a result of the media coverage, Dominic's widowed aunt from Cleveland had been located. She had flown with three of Dominic's cousins and their spouses to attend the wedding. They sat solemnly at their own table. His aunt was still absorbing the news, with an occasional shake of her head, that her brother's lost child was not only alive, but a grown-up hero. Dominic had already been offered a position on the Cleveland police force, but although tempted by these newfound family ties, was also weighing a commission with the United States Army. As for Cheysa, she had determined that wherever they lived, she would go back to school and become a social worker at last. When she had tentatively asked the FBI agents if it would be permitted, the agents, looking bemusedly at each other, replied, "Why wouldn't it be?"

Both Cheysa and Malia wore wedding gowns donated from local stores that recognized a good publicity opportunity. Cheysa's white gown was traditionally full and long, with a romantic scalloped neckline. The older Malia wore a more streamlined off-white dress suited to her retiring personality. David and Dominic joked that their dinner jackets and pants were not too different from Antifan uniforms.

Toasts were made to the couples, who thanked the kind people of Charleston and the US government who were introducing them to their new lives in the United States. Malia felt that something more than mere thanks was required, so she whispered in David's ear.

Then David raised his hand to call the room to attention, and said, with heartfelt gratitude, "As much as we appreciate your generosity and kindness, we need to say more than just thank you. In the last week, the people of the United States have not only just bestowed on us new clothes and new prospects, but also a new way of life. Speaking for Malia and myself, it will be wonderful to walk into any restaurant we want without having to call first to make sure that someone with her Social Credit score would be welcome. You might not realize that in the DJR, we were forbidden to legally marry because of Malia's low credit score. You may not have read that when she was just five years old, Malia's daughter was stolen from her by the government. We only recovered her through sheer luck and again by breaking the law. There she is," he pointed, "and that's a story in itself." He looked at Malia, who rose beside him.

Malia said, "We look forward to reading and watching whatever books and movies we want, traveling wherever we want, and worshiping God, not an Earth Mother. I want to learn to exercise my Second Amendment right to defend myself. I want to decide what to put in my own grocery bag."

She concluded, "A year ago I never dreamed all this would ever be possible for me. The gift you are giving us is the gift of the United States to all its people, and we truly cherish the opportunity to share it with you." Applause shook the room.

Next, David motioned to Dominic and Cheysa. The young couple hesitated, and then Dominic struggled to his feet.

"Thank you, Comman—" Dominic saw David shake his head almost imperceptibly and mouth "David."

"Thank you, David. Without you, neither Cheysa nor I would be here today. We hadn't intended to leave the DJR until the last minute, and we had no choice. Cheysa had killed her tormentor, who was about to kill David, and that made her an outlaw. Since I would never want to be without her, we came here together.

"I had always thought the United States was a frightening place, especially for black people. I believed everything the DJR told me about the US. I wanted to defend the DJR, because they told me they were defending the rights of people who were poor and who weren't white. David told me what he had been able to read about the United States, and he promised me that the US would treat me fairly. On his promise, Cheysa and I are here. So far I think we'll be fine. We've met so many good people."

Cheysa rose next to him. "We are so happy to have family waiting here for us," she said, gesturing to the Cleveland table. "We know we'll be okay. Thank you all, and God bless you."

Several hours later, David and Malia sat together comfortably on the sofa in the hotel suite, somewhat *dishabille*, with his necktie lying on the coffee table near his legs and her having removed the high heeled shoes and stockings. Isabelle was playing a video game in her bedroom. In the morning she would write to the Andrewses to let them know she was alive and well in West Virginia, with Malia, (not Melia), her mother. "Be kind to them," Malia had instructed her, secure in victory.

David's arm encircled Malia's shoulders and he pulled her toward him for a kiss. Malia ran her hand tenderly through David's hair, then rested it on his shoulder.

"Are we happy now?" David asked his bride.

"I couldn't be happier," Malia said simply. "I have you, I have Isabelle back, and we have our freedom. Our baby is safe and will never know poverty or oppression. Without you, none of this could have happened. What else is there?"

David thought briefly about his mother and sisters. "Not much," he replied, hoping the regime had abided by the Treaty of the Red and Blue and not punished them for his crime. It would be difficult to communicate with his family, at least for a while, since the DJR censors would be unusually vengeful with the incoming mail.

"Eventually you'll see them again," said Malia, now realizing what caused his brow to furrow. "I saw on the news here that there are discussions about allowing family reunions, at least on the DJR side of the border."

"Not going there, and neither are you."

"Eventually," she stated calmly, "if we have faith, it can happen. Think of all the amazing things that happened to us this year. Who would have ever guessed it was possible?"

Epilogue
August 11, 2090

I n her row house in Ploreville, Marjory Harris ran her hand over an envelope
that had just arrived from the US. She knew who the senders must be. It had
been a painful nine months since David, Malia, and even her stolid Daniel had
disappeared. Even though Marjory missed them, she privately rejoiced that they were
safe and free. Hostile ADF officers had interrogated and berated Marjory and her
daughters, until the officers realized that nothing could be gained from it. Further
punishment would violate the Treaty, and even Plores could hire lawyers.

Marjory was proud of her sons' initiative and bravery. She told herself that Elijah,
their father, would have been proud of them too. Yet she was afraid that she would
never see her sons again.

Marjory sat down on the sofa with Frida and two other cats nestling alongside
her, with their feline sixth sense about when she needed comfort. Ansel sat in the
windowsill, watching the street. As expected, the censors had sliced open the envelope
along the top and then resealed it in a deliberately clumsy manner. It had originally
contained a handwritten letter, discarded by the censors, who had also destroyed the
previous five letters sent by Daniel or David. The envelope bore a return address in
Oklahoma City. Marjory could now try writing them letters herself.

Two color photographs fluttered out of the envelope. One showed an infant,
perhaps only several weeks old, with ruddy cheeks and a smattering of brown hair
across his pate. Depending on how much you liked babies, he was smiling or needed
burping. When she turned over the photograph, she recognized David's handwriting:

Emmett Elijah Harris,
Born Wed. June 28, 2090, 5:28 pm
Oklahoma City, OK, USA
7 lbs, 4 oz, 21 inches

The second photo showed David, Malia, and the baby on her lap. The censor
had drawn a spiteful black X over David and Malia's faces, but the baby beamed
unmolested, too innocent for even the DJR to erase. Marjory held the photos to her
heart and thanked God. Then she called her daughters, and they hurried to the house

to see the snapshots for themselves. It was such a small thing, but they were grateful, and it gave them faith that better days would come.

THE END